THE LEGEND OF ADAM CAINE

John Charles Scott

authorHOUSE®

AuthorHouse™ UK Ltd.
500 Avebury Boulevard
Central Milton Keynes, MK9 2BE
www.authorhouse.co.uk
Phone: 08001974150

First published by AuthorHouse   8/26/2010

ISBN: 978-1-4520-6387-4 (sc)

This book is printed on acid-free paper.

To Charlie Lavelle, I wish you could've seen this. Wherever you ended up, you're probably running the show by now.

Acknowledgements

Thank you to all those who in my family have been so supportive of my insanity, and general weirdness (AKA, this book): Dad (my official beta reader), Mum (who wouldn't shut up about getting it published), Mary, my siblings and semi-siblings (Iain, James, Lucy, and Daniel in case you were wondering), and also my Granddad Roland Westwood (RIP), for providing me with the two words that are now tattooed on my arm.

To Rowland, my best friend, co-worker, and former housemate. FACE! Definitely the inspiration behind the Rowlandos character, and every daft moment and conversation in this book.

And thank you most of all to my sexy goddess, Julz, who has helped me no end; not just with this book, but life in general. I love you.

Prologue

4010ad.

Adam Logan Caine was encompassed in grief and pain.

It surrounded him as surely as did the darkness of the room around him, like a mist hanging round a solitary solemn mountain. Tears streamed down his cheeks, and his shoulders shook as he tried desperately to control the sobs that came hand-in-hand with the tears. His head was hung low, chin against chest, his arms draped pathetically over the arms of his high-backed chair.

Dim light from outside glinted off something solid and metal in one of his limp hands.

It was a gun, a firearm in fact; a solid-round weapon in an age of lasers and force fields, it was a rare and antiquated thing to see, but a dangerous thing nonetheless —more so in Caine's hands.

The Walther P99 —the same weapon he had recovered from a trophy cabinet on the Core Lord's flagship- was fully loaded, the action cocked, and its safety flicked to the off position.

Someone was screaming his name in the distance, but he ignored it, the noises around him sounding as if he was underwater, muffled, distant, and ultimately unimportant. His mind replayed his worst nightmare over and over, and all it did was add to his utter misery. His worst nightmare had indeed happened: she had been taken from him.

She had been taken from him.

The streams of tears became rivers, and he held the gun up higher, looking at the straight lines of the barrel and the serial number scratched off.

Then he pointed the barrel at himself, and stared into its darkness.

Her little green face kept coming unbidden to his mind, and the shouting and screaming continued in the background.

He didn't care anymore.

Why should he?

His finger tightened on the trigger.

Goodbye, Adam Caine.

He squeezed the trigger. The hammer slammed forward. There was a loud crack and a boom, and the action slammed backwards. The casing ejected sideways, and the bullet jumped out of the barrel.

And then the darkness took him.

One:
Terror

Anonymous Message

SENDER: [Unknown "ERROR: possible message tampering"]
RECIPIENT: 5-Star General Lenson Gardner -Delta-Tango System
MESSAGE ORIGIN: Uncharted System, Designated Zeta-Bravo-3-9-X-Ray-4-9; Y-40 Galaxy
MESSAGE RELAYED VIA: 52 Unmarked Civilian Relay Buoys; HMS Fortitude; Navy Intelligence Headquarters (Delta-Tango star system)
TRANSMISSION SENT: 19/01/3899AD "ERROR: possible message tampering"
TRANSMISSION RECEIVED: 31/12/3999AD

Greetings, General Gardner,
You may call me Mr. Gold.
I bring you a warning of dire events soon to come to fruition.
Are you aware of a human named Adam Caine?
I fear not.
He is the catalyst of a many great things; good or bad, who is to say? My... organisation would dearly like to see Caine's destiny come to fruition to benefit our side. I believe that you too, General, would benefit from this outcome.
Perhaps we should become, as you say, allies?
Or perhaps not -it does not matter to me, but it should matter to you.
Caine has the touch of great destiny about him; beware of him, and do nothing more than watch until you hear from me again.
Yours gratefully.
"A storm is approaching."
"A storm is always *approaching when grandfather is involved."*
-A seer and Roath Caine, speaking of his maternal grandfather.

2006.
London: the bustling, monolithic capital city of Great Britain, and once the centre of the largest, most powerful empire on Earth. Home to the most diverse group of the planet, with whites, blacks, Orientals, Africans, Indians, Americans, Russians, Europeans, Christians, Catholics, Muslims, Hindus, Buddhists, Mormons, and Jews, all living around the long, winding River Thames. History, mystery, and legend hung over the city like a cloud, permeating the streets with tales of old markets, infamous murderers, and great destruction as no other city in the world could.
Summer had only just passed, and the school term had begun in earnest, however hesitantly on the part of the local children. The sun glared down as

only it could at four minutes past one in the afternoon. Light glinted off the many marvels of the city: the sky scraping London Eye, the defunct Millennium Dome, the ancient and history-bound Houses of Parliament, and the great Thames herself.

A man, twenty-six years of age, six foot two, and reluctant employee at the Islington Cinema, strode through the turnstiles of the Uxbridge Underground station, pushing his ticket into the slot, and retrieving it the other side without losing pace.

Dozens of others entered and exited the station, hurrying to lunch dates or even work. He had to take the Underground on the Piccadilly Line across the city centre to get to work. The afternoon showing of *Pirates of the Caribbean: Dead Man's Chest* was in thirty minutes; the journey usually took him twenty, or so he hoped.

It was, by all accounts, a normal, mundane day for him; then again, mundane had become a way of life for him, with his troubled days behind him... far behind him.

Oddly enough, despite the bustle, toil and trouble of his surroundings, he quietly enjoyed the Underground. There was something soothing about the place, the people, even the warm clinging air. It cheered him up before the insanity that came with working at a multiplex cinema; his previous career had not involved interacting with the British public, and was a completely different experience from being a cinema usher, at the beck-and-call of the visiting public.

He sorely needed another career change.

For now, he needed to take the Piccadilly Line as far as Green Park station, then hop onto the Victoria Line, until Highbury & Islington, with a two minute hop on the bus to work.

Armed with a chicken sandwich, his oh-so-snazzy blue-and-black uniform, and a copy of the latest *Gaunt's Ghosts* novel, the young man stepped onto the steel carriage, and stumbled to the nearest moulded plastic-and-cushion fold-down seat that he had grown so accustomed to.

The carriage was surprisingly quiet, with only a dozen or so sat around him. A teenage couple were canoodling in a corner, whilst a dirty old man in a tweed jacket and beige breeches practically drooled from afar, though whether it was because he was a dirty old man, or just old, he couldn't tell, or couldn't care.

At the far end of the carriage sat a middle-aged couple, long past passion, trying to read a copy of yesterday's Daily Telegraph -a crumpled and discarded relic of previous travellers. They weren't having much success, their tired old eyes straining to read the tiny print, or the unreadable text on the British Army recruitment ads on the curved ceiling above.

He sighed; Islington was a long way. He opened the book, and began reading.

* * *

"Mummy," little Sasha said, tugging on her mother's dress, "can we go on the train?"

"Yes, when it gets here, honey," her mother reassured her.

They were stood in the front of the crowd at the Hammersmith station, waiting patiently for the underground train. Each of her children, Sasha and Sapphire, had one of her hands in theirs. The mother was portly, yet attractive in the way housewives had a way of being in modern Britain, with her long brown hair tied back in a ponytail, and her keen pale green eyes watching over her daughters.

Hannah, the girls' thirty-something mother, was taking them to see their father, her husband, at work. It was a day trip, something to do during the summer months when the kids were no longer at school.

In all honesty, she was going to confront her husband, having found some rather damning evidence on his affair with his secretary. She couldn't find anyone to look after the kids, so she was using the day-out excuse for her daughters' sake, whilst she fumed over Daniel's actions.

Hot air blasted through the station, and over the waiting passengers, as the train approached, everyone impatiently waiting for it to stop. The doors opened with a long low hiss, a few passengers stepped off, and the rest bundled on, with Hannah and the girls vying for the most comfortable seats.

Hannah managed to find a seat near to a handsome young man with jaw-length unkempt hair, reading a hardback novel, the title of which seemed to read: *His Last Command*. The man looked up from his novel, and threw her a genuinely warm smile. She couldn't help but blush heavily, and look away.

She held her two girls' hands tight to her, not wanting anyone to get near them; this was their first time on public transport, and they seemed a little skittish with all the big people around.

Hannah squeezed their hands as the train thumped on down the track from the station to the next.

* * *

At Baron's Court only three people stood on the platform: one a young girl dressed in rather provocative clothes that only stayed on the train until the next stop; an older woman got on the train, dressed in what could only be described as hippie clothes, all loose, no underwear, and all home-made, even the mono-strap despatch bag over one shoulder; the other person wore a thick hooded trench coat, his hands shifting in his pockets, as if with a nervous twitch.

The man, assuming it was a man under the hood, was shifty, in a dangerous, druggie sort of way. He smelled bad, like a miniature sewer in fact, and his head kept turning inside the hood, left to right, as if scoping the station out.

* * *

The Operative looked around, making sure there were plenty of humans on the metal carriages. He felt the device in his fingers; to prevent him accidentally losing the small handheld machine, his claws were plunged into his pockets. He detested the human clothes; too varied, too uncontrolled, and sometimes too bright. His legs no longer the right way, and his neck had to be shortened painfully to stay in the hood; his claws had to be retracted to avoid detection, and he wasn't even going to think about his skull-crest. He had a cloaking field to prevent anyone from actually seeing into his hood; his cover would be blown well and truly if that happened.

But his people needed the specimens; the humans of this era were more varied than his own time, and less numerous; there was a greater gene pool to select from. Against his race, the humans of this time were defenceless, despite the future humans' near-ignorance of the Operative's own race. That would change in the coming years.

If he was successful.

He stepped onto the train, unable to avoid the stench of the humans as they barged their way around the carriage, as if their lives depended on them getting a seat before anyone else.

He stood to one side, in a corner away from the rest of the passengers, trying to avoid physical contact with these disgusting animals. Not for the first time, he could not help but wonder why his race couldn't just send an armada back in time, and destroy Earth before it reached the stars. He knew the answer, and did not like it.

* * *

Fifteen more got onto the train at Baron's Court: a hobbling old Chelsea Veteran, still wearing his red jacket, gold Sergeant stripes, and tri-corner hat, his medals dangling and jangling as he hobbled onto the train, clutching his pensioner's travel card like it was his last remaining possession. It probably was, but he wasn't one to make a fuss; he hadn't for decades. Who could possibly care about a crippled old soldier?

Nobody noticed as he took one of the disabled seats, and hummed to himself.

Four got off the train, before it clattered and rumbled down the dark tracks.

* * *

Sasha began to jump around the carriage, calling Sapphire names, apparently picking up an argument from earlier. As she danced around, Hannah tried to get her to stop and be quiet so as not to disturb the rest of the passengers. Which was when Sasha accidentally bumped into the handsome young man Hannah had been trying to avoid eye contact with.

Sasha managed to stumble into him, knocking the book from his hands, and earning a quiet grumble from him. He looked annoyed, though that dissipated when he saw the pained look on Hannah's face. He could only shrug, and smile sheepishly from behind his messy brown hair.

"I'm really sorry," Hannah said, just as sheepish. She had to raise her voice for him to be heard over the clattering of the train's wheels as the carriage passed over the joins in the tracks.

"That's okay, I know what kids are like when they're bored," he replied. Sasha, cheeks a crimson red, handed him his book.

"That's a scary book," Sasha commented, eyeing the violent nature of the cover. She seemed wary of the book, as if it could reach out and hurt her at any second.

"I don't know," the big man admitted, "I haven't finished reading it yet." He smiled at her, and then turned his attention back to her mother. "I'm guessing this one belongs to you?"

"Unfortunately," she said apologetically, beckoning her youngest daughter to her. Sasha hesitated, clearly curious about the stranger.

Sasha just stood there, and stared at him as only an innocent child could. "What's your name?" she asked unabashedly.

"Adam," he smiled.

"I'm Sasha," she giggled before running away back to her mother.

"Hey Sasha, you dropped this," Adam said, holding out a well-loved stuffed bear, dressed in stripy blue pyjamas. He stood up, and strode over. Hannah was amazed at how tall and big he was, for such a young man, and his hair dangled from his head in matted locks, walking a fine line between unwashed and purposely styled, as it almost touched his shoulders.

He was wearing a hooded black duffel coat that was opened to reveal the VUE Cinemas tight uniform underneath, and his name badge: ADAM (Usher). His eyes practically twinkled with a well-earned intellect, though there was something about his strongly made face that was at odds with his stance and his eyes. Hannah was trying to put a name to it. What was it? Of course, she thought, he had a haunted look about him, with a stance that gave him the appearance of carrying the weight of the world on his shoulders. She wondered what could cause such pain in a handsome young man like him.

"Thankyou," Hannah said with a smile. Sasha accepted the bear without a word, and ran to her mother, hugging Hannah's leg tightly, and partially hiding behind it at the same time.

"That's okay," Adam shrugged. He smiled, turned, and went back to reading his book. Hannah was sure she caught him sneaking glances over her way every now again. Despite the nature of her journey on the train, she couldn't help but be flattered by his attentions. He couldn't be more than twenty-five, and she was on the wrong side of thirty; why would he be interested in her?

If Adam were a poetic man, he would have described Hannah as an angel in human form, with sharp features and an inner beauty he had not seen in years.

She tried not to talk to the young man, her anger was still bubbling under the surface, and she didn't want it to go away, not until she had resolved her 'issues' with her scumbag husband. So she tried to put Adam out of her mind, and held her daughters' hands.

* * *

There were enough specimens on the train, but there was another station around the corner, and he had no desire to attract more attention than would already be directed at this incident. If there was ever a connection made by the future humans, they could possibly be warned about what was happening before his race were even aware they had the technology to do what he was about to do.

The Device wasn't quite ready; it needed a little more manipulation to get the correct position in the space/time continuum.

Just a few more minutes.

* * *

Ninety more got onto the train at Earl's Court, Gloucester Road, South Kensington, Knightsbridge, and Hyde Park Corner. Two-thirds of *those* got off at the next station or the one after that. Three soldiers, in olive-green number-ones, and two RAF officers in their own blue-grey dress uniforms, stepped onto the train at Gloucester Road, swapping bawls of laughter after a particularly embarrassing promotion ceremony.

Two policemen, in duty uniform, boarded at South Kensington, radios bleeping and spitting static and occasional voices from the dispatch centre. Nobody questioned their presence, not after the attacks on London last year. The Prime Minister had upped the security in the capital city, putting more Police on the streets, in an attempt to make the people feel safer. It was a con, in most people's minds, but it was happening, and there wasn't a whole lot people could do, so they carried on like it was a normal day.

The passengers all avoided eye contact with the Police Constables, avoiding ever thinking why they were there.

* * *

Adam continued to read, as people dressed in suits, overalls, hoodies, jeans and funny hats boarded and exited the train. All walks of life were on the train, though Adam wasn't aware of it, his head in the book as it was.

Adam read quickly, more to get away from the crowded train than because it was an exceptionally good book, though it really was a good book.

He was just at the part where Colonel-Commissar Gaunt finally appeared when the call for the Green Park station was announced over the train's automatic PA system.

"Next stop in four minutes, will be Green Park; next stop is Green Park."

The same words flashed across a fading LED strip above the doors to the next carriage and above the exits.

* * *

The Device was ready; it had almost shorted out at one point when a stupid young male had knocked it from his claws; it felt the overwhelming urge to slice the human apart with its talons, though fought the urge in order to complete the mission. There were enough specimens in range to be transported.

It was time.

He stood up and yanked on the emergency stop cord.

Brakes screeched and the lights flickered. The passengers stumbled against the support poles and each other, panicking that something had happened on the Underground yet again, just like 7-7 last year. Someone screamed in fear, a child cried for its mummy to stop what was happening. The mother reassured the child that there was nothing wrong, just a quick stop to pick up a special passenger, but the girl did not believe her, all too aware of those around her.

The Operative couldn't help but smile at that: humans used lies and deception too much for their own good. He chuckled at the irony of that thought, but realised that this was necessary. *It was necessary for him to use deception so that his race could finally dominate all life in the nineteen galaxies.*

The Operative entered the correct coordinates, entered the activation code. He wondered how such a small object could affect the history of two great civilisations.

The code was accepted and the display on the device showed the Device was powering up to full capacity, and would release a full burst in twenty seconds.

Nineteen.

Eighteen.

Sasha and Sapphire continued to argue.

Hannah worried about her daughters, and seethed with anger over her husband.

Seventeen.

Sixteen.

The soldiers and Air Force officers continued to laugh and cheer, and swap silly stories about their units, despite the obvious rank difference. None seemed to be worried that the train had made an emergency stop —they reasoned that this was England after all, nothing really worked well so why should the Underground be any different?

Fifteen.

Fourteen.

Thirteen.

The Chelsea Veteran continued to hum to himself.

Adam continued reading, and glancing at Hannah when she wasn't looking.

Twelve.

Eleven.

Ten.

The young couple continued to kiss.

The old man opposite them continued to watch them, and drool.

Nine.
Eight.
Seven.
They were all completely unaware.
Six.
Nobody suspected anything.
Five.
They were all too worried about their selfish and insignificant problems to see the real danger.
Four.
They were doomed.
Three.
Screwed.
Two.
Fucked.
One.
Toast.

* * *

The Operative smiled as the Device blasted out a massive perfect sphere of temporal energy that encompassed the packed carriage around him. Blue-white light filled the train like a supernova, bright enough to temporarily blind every single passenger.

Screams of panic, fear and anger reverberated around the carriages, causing yet more and more panic.

The Operative enjoyed the experience, more than he'd ever admit. He enjoyed seeing the humans in a literal blind panic, could almost feel the fear around him.

The sphere of energy reached a crescendo, and emitted a squealing noise that continued to gather momentum until it reached fever pitch, and crossed into subsonic.

There was an almighty thunderclap and a perfect sphere of train, tracks, tunnel bricks, rock, and electrics disappeared, the smooth sides of the gap blistering under the intense energy.

Within five minutes of activating the Device, the Operative and the passengers were gone.

* * *

"This is the Ten O'clock News; I'm Huw Edwards. Early reports have come in of an explosion in the London Underground. Though nothing is clear yet, one report stated that forty-three people are believed dead, or possibly missing.

We will keep you updated as the reports come in..."

* * *

Footsteps echoed loudly around the corridor, as the Lord's Second strode quickly toward his destination. The lighting, as always, was dim enough to mask someone's features; it was an impressively usable fear tool.

His avian-like head bobbed as he walked, his skull-crest shook slightly, and light glinted from the overhead lamps, reflecting off well-groomed skin. His rubbery skin, black as night, was mostly hidden from sight under his red chitinous armour. The armour itself had markings etched over the shoulder plates, the left side of the chest, and down his right leg. All who saw the markings instantly knew who he was and the respect he deserved.

His slitted yellow eyes shifted from side-to-side, ever vigilant of enemies, even eyeing the dark, almost dank, ribbed corridors. Some had compared the innards of this place to the insides of a living creature, with the corridors and accessways like veins, and the rooms like organs. The Second had heard of a story among the younger warriors that there were ghosts of old warriors still wondering the corridors, lost in the maze of passageways, trying to find their way.

He had never put the stories down; he had gotten lost himself as a young warrior, and was fully aware of how confusing the facility could be. The stories were, in fact, a nice trick to getting the new recruits in line. If he didn't kill them, he would tell them to get their act together or be dragged into the corridors for the ghosts to take them to the underworld.

It was a ridiculous superstitious notion, but it spooked the new recruits, and made them that much more susceptible to intimidation from their superiors, namely him.

All thoughts of recruits and ghosts left his mind unquestioned, though, as he approached his destination.

Two massive guards were stood, as they always were when the Lord was inside, at either side of the massive gold-gilded doors, black and gold armour polished and shining, with a red reptile-skin cloak draped around their neck and one shoulder. They were part of the Lord's cadre of personal guard, chosen from among the fleets' greatest warriors. They stared straight ahead, and parted to let the Second through, their eyes remaining in one direction the whole time. It was disrespectful for common warriors to make eye contact with their superiors.

The doors cranked open, and the Second continued his stride without stopping, moving through the cavernous throne room. The room was heavily laden with trophies of slain enemies, weapons new and old, and suits of armour that didn't belong in any of the Lord's fleets. Elaborate banners hung from the bulkheads, some represented the Lord and his fleets, whilst others had been captured from conquered homeworlds, bases, and ruined warships.

He passed the head of the leader of an Okarnagan war fleet, and a spear from ancient Mertik, taken by the Lord's father centuries ago; there were weapons from old human starships from when they first reached the stars; the heads of those that had defied the Lord in past campaigns, even the stuffed corpses of animals taken on private hunts. It was an impressive array. The trophies were arranged so that they made a lengthy alleyway leading up to the Lord's high throne. The Second glanced at some of the trophies, and revelled in the glory they represented; he had been present when they were taken, even taken a few himself.

The Lord was flirting with several females, as he was wont to do, touching their chins, smiling and laughing like an amorous young hatchling. Then again, the Lord *had* done that as an amorous young hatchling, as he had done throughout his life, with the Second by his side all the way through, however much the Second was ashamed to be seen with the fool.

The females noticed the Second approach, their skull-crests quivering with feigned excitement. He knew they were ambitious creatures, desperate to be seen with the higher echelons of the fleets to move up in status. They were prostitutes, of a sort, or working females, as they were referred to in the politer parts of society. Usually they were not permitted to step foot into the Lord's presence, but the Lord was the Lord, and if he wanted something, he would get it.

The Second came to a halt, slamming the heel of his claw against the deck, standing to attention and simultaneously grabbing the *Lord's* attention. His beak opened, and his fleshy inner lips began to move.

"[My Lord,]" the Second said sternly. The Lord saw his Second's mute disapproval, and ignored it.

"[Yes, what is it, Second?]" the Lord sighed impatiently, his beak clacking quickly with irritation.

The Second glanced suspiciously at the two females.

"[Perhaps we could have some privacy, my Lord?]"

"[I'm sure they won't tell,]" the Lord replied dismissively. The Second settled the argument by unholstering his sidearm, and shooting the two females between the eyes, the energy rounds splattering blood, feathers and brain matter over the throne dais. The Lord harrumphed, and let out a big sigh.

"[And I was having such a good time,]" he said in feigned reflection. He stepped down from the throne, and moved to the Second's side, his black armour squealing in protest at being so abused. The Lord was a huge figure: two heads taller than the Second, who was himself no midget; he had a large vicious beak that could snap an arm in two; his blazing orange eyes spoke of a lifetime of war; but the Lord's rotund belly showed that he had not seen that war for several years.

"[I assume you have a reason for such an annoyance,]" the Lord stated nonchalantly.

"[Yes, sir; our *special* operative has returned with samples,]" the Second answered proudly. The Lord's inner lips creased into a semblance of a smile.

"[Good; lead the way, Second.]"

The Second nodded, span on his clawed heel and stalked toward the doors he had entered through. The Lord strode behind him, taloned hands clasped behind his back in a ridiculous posh posture.

The two stepped through the doors, whereupon four of the Lord's personal guards fell into a square formation around the Lord, carrying their trademark long staff weapons. They ignored the Second ahead of them, and kept a suspicious eye on the occasional worker passing by, and even the walls themselves, looking for potential threats to the Lord's safety. The Second thought it overly paranoid given that this was the safest, most secure place for the Lord to be.

The corridors they stepped through were, like the rest of the ship, the colour of human blood, such as it was. It was a strange thing to think, since the Lord's race had never encountered humans from their own time.

The guards' perfect marching was accompanied by the *click-click-click* of their talons on the deck. The Second found it mesmerising, like listening to the rhythmic thump of distant machinery, or staring at the red-yellow solar flares of an active star. It was comforting to have something like that sound, before entering the presence of the scum specimens that had surely been brought by the Operative. Humans were despicable creatures, with no feathers, and legs that bent the wrong way.

The party came to a stop in front of a massive set of armoured double doors, High-Core and Low Speak written in parallel lines across the joins declaring 'NO UNAUTHORISED ENTRY, UPON PAIN OF DEATH!'

The Second placed his left claw on the bio-reader, a blue light strip moved from side-to-side under his palm; he felt an odd tickling sensation move through his limb as the machine scanned his bio-signature, accepted it with a loud ping, and opened the doors for him and his party.

Screams flooded through the opening. This section of the facility had been given over to the prison bays and experiment laboratories, and the soundproofing of the armoured security doors was now no longer hiding the tortured squeals of pain from the labs and cells.

The Second wasn't perturbed by the noises, in fact he found it somewhat comforting, knowing that their enemies could be hurt so easily. He defied anyone that could withstand the torturers' horrific art, and still fight afterwards. Then again, he couldn't see into the future, and had no idea what was in store for him.

* * *

"Wake up," a voice whispered.

The man did as the voice told him, and his eyes snapped open. The voice had been unmistakably a woman's, though he couldn't possibly recognise it, and there was nobody around that could account for the voice. In fact, there was *nothing* around. A bright white light surrounded him that had no source -it just seemed to be everywhere at once, surrounding him.

He hadn't even been aware he was lying down, until he began to sit up. He then stood, and realised that there were no walls; he wasn't sure how he knew that, but he did, and it bothered him because he was sure he was in an enclosed space.

What the hell was going on? What was this place? What was that insanely bright flash earlier on the train? And what the hell was that buzzing noise? The noise got louder, and kept getting louder until the man couldn't take it anymore, piercing his ears, and reverberating around his brain. He clapped his hands over his ears.

Then suddenly it stopped, as if it had never occurred, and the man was sure he could almost feel a pair of eyes watching him from behind. He whipped round and stared into the eyes of a fetching older woman. She was petite, only high enough to have her forehead level with his sternum, if he were so inclined to that way of thinking.

She had greying blonde hair that was tied up in a bun at the back of her head; her hair framed a tiny handsome face that had once been supermodel-grade beautiful, though had sagged a little with age. Bright turquoise eyes flashed from between makeup-heavy eyelids. He could have sworn she looked as though she had had cosmetic surgery to accentuate her angular features, though wouldn't put money on that bet.

He blinked, and realised he had been staring. Which was when he noticed the squirming behind her. It wasn't a specific thing, it just seemed as though the very air around the woman was squirming. The man had seen the worst his world could offer, but looking at the area around the woman made his stomach tie itself into a bundle of knots, the nausea was so bad.

"Who are you?" he demanded, taking his mind off the squirming light.

"I am nobody, and everybody," her almost-husky voice declared as if it was the obvious answer. The man just rolled his eyes.

"That's real helpful, thanks," he grumbled, though the sarcasm seemed to be lost on the woman.

"You're welcome," she smiled sweetly. He stared at her incredulously.

"If this is a subconscious hallucination, I need a new subconscious," he complained out loud. He gestured to the whiteness around them. "What is this place?" He pointed accusingly at the woman. "Who are you? And what the *fuck* is going on?"

"There's no need to swear," she cooed smoothly. "Everything will be explained, or better yet, you can find out for yourself. You're a soldier, aren't you?"

"I was, but that's my past now," he replied suspiciously. How the hell did she know about his past?

"Is it? You really think you can leave your time in Three Commando Brigade behind? It is in your very essence, your very soul. Your time as an SB must have shown you that?"

"I left for a good reason," the man complained.

"Yes," she snorted, "and look where it's got you." She began to pace around him, brushing her hand against his muscled arms. He didn't shy away from her touch. The touch was, literally, electric, and he received a tiny static shock wherever she touched him. He could practically feel the power and energy rolling off her, as if her tiny frame couldn't possibly contain it for much longer.

"What do you want from me? Who are you?"

"For now, I'm here just to warn you. And call me Silver," she replied softly.

"Warn me about what?" he inquired, impatience getting the better of him.

"Soon you will face a choice: the lives of those closest to you will be weighed against your own soul, and your own sanity."

"That's a rather easy choice; besides, I don't have anyone close to me," the man protested.

"You will soon," the woman smiled cryptically. There was that buzzing again, and again the light around the woman began to squirm. The man was mentally prepared for it this time. "I almost forgot," she said softly. "Say argh."

"Argh?" he said incredulously. "Why the hell would I say-AAAAAARRRGGGHHHH!!"

The pain struck him like a tidal wave, coursed over his entire body, and dropped him to the floor. He could feel incredible energy arcing through his body, as he squirmed and spasmed on the floor, which remarkably had turned into a blood red colour, and become very much more real and metal, like the decking of one of the Royal Navy's warships. The room -if it could be called that- was large, not posh-hotel-bedroom-large, but empty-warehouse-large, with roof support beams that looked uncomfortably like human ribs.

The pain subsided, though the nightmare began as he looked up into the face of a beast.

It looked like a bird, but it walked like a man, covered head-to-claw in black tough rubbery skin, with a large chitinous black beak that looked like it could bite through steel. Cat-like yellow eyes glared out from under hooded eyelids, and a fleshy ridge that bisected the top of its head topped with raven-dark feathers. It was taller than a man, with limbs in proportion to their height; though hideously, its legs were bent the wrong way like a horse's rear appendages.

The man recoiled in horror despite his specialised training. It was almost as if the creature's appearance tapped into the human psyche's primordial fears, something that overrode the human ability to mask or control their emotions by taking something innocent-looking and warping it into a frightening freak of nature.

The man looked about him, and saw other humans in a similar state of panic and fear. The three nearest were, oddly enough, Hannah, Sasha, and Sapphire.

The creature moved away from the man, and growled something in its alien language to its nine companions. They all turned toward a large set of doors, the other side of the large room, and began to make their exit.

Forget your fears, the man suddenly heard in his head. The voice had sounded too much like Silver to be a coincidence. So he did as he was instructed. His military training kicked in, and he overrode the pain still lingering in his body.

Adam Caine jumped up, and launched himself at the nearest creature -probably the same one that had hit him with whatever energy had knocked him over. A shrill warning cry came from the throats of half of the exiting creatures, and Adam's target span just in time to receive a punishing precise kick to the head. Something cracked in its skull -it squealed and tumbled to the ground, clutching its head.

The other creatures began to glare hatefully at Adam as they moved cautiously toward the human. Adam didn't give them a chance to attack, lunging at the nearest and chopping the side of his fist into the creature's neck, tearing vital muscles and arteries. He followed up with a swift kick to its midriff that doubled it over and added insult to injury as he slammed the heel of his shoe into its long neck, snapping it loudly.

Adam ducked an incoming slow punch meant to knock his head off from the next creature, and snaked his arms around the other's appendages. Muscles strained as the two struggled to gain the advantage over the other. Adam did the only thing he could think of.

He snapped his knee into the creature's groin. The alien dropped to the floor like a sack of spuds, rolling around and groaning.

"That's good to know," he snorted, before the remaining creatures dove on him, dragging him to the ground. He snarled oaths at them as they in turn kicked and punched him.

Just as the hauntingly familiar black of unconsciousness took him, he saw two other creatures in more regal armour enter the room, nodding and talking to each other.

That can't be good...

* * *

"[This one shows much defiance and strength, Second,]" the Lord said excitedly, staring at the unconscious human on the cell floor.

"[Indeed, Lord. Do you want him to undergo the special experiments?]"

"[Of course, but this time leave the subject with his people in between experiments; perhaps he will show even more interesting behaviour. Fear, after all, is a great motivator for those in captivity.]"

"[As you wish, my Lord,]" the Second conceded, though he was sure that the human would become an annoyance if he was left to recover among those of his own race. Humans were reportedly extremely stubborn creatures, and their military doubly so. He had witnessed the defiant human's movements and deduced that the male had military training, even though he was wearing an oddly bright and decidedly non-military uniform.

The Lord and his bodyguard moved away, back to the throne room, and the Second gestured to the soldiers.

"[Take him to the laboratories,]" he ordered. He took one last look at the sobbing mass of humans and then followed the soldiers as they lifted the fighting human away.

* * *

Darkness began to lift from Adam's vision, and pain forked across his head. He was waking from his unconscious state, however groggily. Feeling returned to his body, and he regretted it instantly as three cracked ribs and dozens of bruises made themselves known. The sharp pain fully opened his eyes.

He was lying down on a cold hard surface, probably metal; it was unyielding when he tried to move. The movement was constrained, simply because he was restrained. Metal bonds were strapped around his wrists, ankles, and his chest to stop him from moving too much. They were tight; he couldn't budge a millimetre. Above a set of large surgical lights yet to be turned on, was a high arched ceiling with an identical human-rib-like structure as the previous room. It stretched away for twenty metres before disappearing behind active computer banks and terminals that bleeped and blurted out the same alien language the creatures had spoken before.

He found that he could move his head around, though he wasn't entirely sure that that was a good thing. There were other tables, all empty, but each were built as a stainless steel crucifix, with empty metal restraints that had stained strange colours that Adam could only surmise was blood, maybe from an alien, if that were possible.

Crap, this is going to be bad, he thought, still taking in his surroundings.

There were more of the creatures, though only the two by the large door beyond his feet were wearing the solid red body-armour. The creatures that busied around him, setting up vicious-looking surgical equipment, were of a smaller build than the presumed warriors, with smaller head-crests, and dark grey striping along their arms and the sides of their legs, like some insane Adidas tracksuit. *They must be scientists*, he thought, *or whatever equivalent they have.*

Whatever they were, they kept glancing nervously at Adam, as if he was about to jump up at any minute and snap their necks. So they weren't the threat. No, it was the two big guards glaring at him from the doorway -they were the threat. They were both carrying long staffs with wicked spiked blades bolted to the ends. So even if he could get out of his restraints, they would spear him before he made it one metre.

Then immense pain slammed into his upturned forearm. He let out a small grunt. There was a needle in his arm, tapped into one of the visible veins. The creature holding the needle pumped something clear and transparent into his bloodstream.

He could immediately feel the effects, and realised that it was familiar.

Oh bollocks, he panicked, feeling the familiar drowsiness coming on, *it's sodium pentethol. Not again.* He had been trained to resist torture and subversion techniques, but he was out of shape after a while since leaving the service, and his body wasn't as conditioned as it used to be; so he could very well be susceptible to the drug's true effects.

Everything was slightly blurred as the opiate-like effect continued. The doors beyond his feet opened with a grinding of metal, and the regal creatures from before entered, the four black-armoured warriors hanging by the door, whilst the two others moved to Adam's side. He thought he should be frightened of them, but the strangeness of their appearance had worn off quickly, and he was more worried about what they were going to do to him.

The creature with the cloak, apparently their leader if the others' deference was anything to judge, stepped closer to Adam, as if seeing a human at the zoo. That thought troubled Adam greatly: what if they viewed humanity like cattle, to be herded and prodded around to their own ends? They'd have no compunction about killing the others in the group they had captured.

Silver's words of warning came back to haunt him.

"What do you want from me?" he demanded, his voice only slightly slurred.

The leader recoiled ever-so-slightly at the sudden unfamiliar noise. It clacked and jabbered something in its native language to the creature standing next to him. Despite the incomprehensible nature of the language, Adam was sure he heard the word *English* in there about halfway. A look of revolted understanding passed over the leader's face.

"You are human," the alien said, turning back to Adam.

"Yes," Adam blurted. He cursed himself for not even *trying* to resist. The drug was more effective than he had given it credit.

"What is your designation?" it said in a strange accent bordering on a lisp that was punctuated here and there with clacks of its beak. Adam could actually see a pair of thin black lips inside the beak, presumably to communicate in spoken languages.

"My what?"

"Your name," the second-in-command explained. There was a look of brief irritation on the leader's hideously dark face, though there was nothing more.

"Yes, your name," the leader hissed impatiently.

"Adam Caine," Caine answered honestly.

"You are interestingly defiant, Adam Caine," the leader chuckled. "Let's see how defiant you are after today."

"Hunh?"

He felt yet another jab, though this time the pain was so insurmountable he nearly blacked out. When the pain subsided enough for him to focus, he looked down to see four needles sticking out of each of his limbs, with pulsing transparent tubes extending from each that reached up into what looked like a crane above Adam.

Something blue began pumping into his arms and legs through the tubes and needles; Adam could feel it moving through his bloodstream despite the residue of pain that hung about him like a hideous cloud. At first, it made his skin crawl, being able to feel it moving through him, then the feeling became an itch, and the itch soon became seriously irritating.

"What the hell have you done to me?" he growled.

Nobody answered, but the irritation quickly became a mild pain, followed by a pain no human should feel.

He screamed so loud, it could be heard even by the other kidnapped humans in their cell, three hundred metres away. The pain became so intense, he could feel every single nerve ending, every single cell, every single artery, vein, and organ in his body screaming out in pain.

Light filled his vision, blue terrible light that seared his retinas.

He felt like his entire body was being turned inside out, a piece at a time. Not just his body, but the pain was intense enough that it felt like his very soul was being torn apart.

Somewhere along the line, he lost consciousness, though he was never sure how long into the suffering it had occurred. He was sure, however, of the volume of the curse he had used to describe his predicament: "HOLY-CHRIST-ON-A-BIKE!"

* * *

The Lord and the Second watched from behind a forcefield, as the specialised chemicals were pumped into the human male's body. The change was noticeable almost immediately as the human began squirming more and more on the table, writhing in pain as the chemical reaction began in earnest.

The veins in the human's seemingly fragile skin bulged, and began to glow.

"[To think, we stole this technique from an inferior race,]" the Lord mused out loud.

"[Indeed Lord, but other races have different evolutionary paths,]" one scientist answered. "[Our race hasn't reached that stage of development yet.]"

Despite their usefulness, the Core's scientists were much more open-minded than other Core. They studied other races and cultures, even came to respect them, thus insulting their own race as a whole. The Lord only nodded once, before the Second stepped forward and sliced the scientist's head clean off with one quick stroke of the long warrior's knife sheathed on his hip. The Second stepped back beside the Lord.

Nobody moved to clean up the mess, knowing full well that the Lord would want it left there as a demonstration of his cruelty and power. Nobody uttered a sound, though the scientists pointedly stayed clear of their colleague's headless corpse; its eyes stared out of its dismembered head in a hideously grotesque look of surprise. The Second took a perverse pleasure at the scientists' fear.

On the table the human began feeling the pain of the reaction.

Taken from a long dead dead race on the edge of the High Family's territories, the chemical being pumped into the defiant human's body was designed specifically to react with the temporal energy leftover from the human's violent time travel. The reaction caused a localised temporal distortion that could be manipulated and focused by the controller.

A brilliant bright blue light encompassed the human.

His heart rate and pulse flatlined, but brain activity was through the roof, his mind clearly still working. The High Family's scientists had still to develop an effective anaesthetising compound, but they had found by accident, that stopping the heart and keeping the brain alive with certain dangerous drugs had a similar effect.

The human's near-dead form began convulsing, and suddenly light began streaming away from him, underneath him, in long lines that seemed to pass through the deck.

The Lord thought for sure that he could see a duplicate of the human forming in the streams of blue effervescent light. But then the duplicate, along with much of the light, dissipated and was gone. Only a faint glow remained around the human, as the scientists busied themselves around the table.

"[Status?]" the Second demanded of them.

"[By our readings, sire, everything is going according to plan.]"

"[Excellent,]" the Lord proclaimed, clapping his palms together. "[Proceed with the experiments.]"

As the experiments began, nobody paid attention to one of the regular red-armoured guards turning away in a very human look of utter revulsion before quietly leaving his post, and slipping out of the room.

* * *

Hannah and the others had heard Adam's bloodcurdling scream, though didn't realise who it was at the time. She clutched her two children to her, keeping her arms tight against them. They were both shaking with fear, though truth be told she was terrified out of her mind. They all were, even the ones who were undoubtedly trained for dealing with stress.

Around her she could see small groups huddled together in the arched room. There had to be forty odd humans, all from the underground train: two Police officers trying to desperately make their radios work, despite their hands shaking fiercely; three Army soldiers in their green dress uniforms, with two RAF officers in their own blue-greys, were attempting to calm the others; there was even an old man in the red jacket and tri-corn hat of a Chelsea Veteran. A couple of teenagers sat cuddling each other, perhaps hoping that this nightmare would go away if they thought about going home hard enough.

One man, with cold dead eyes, sat in the far corner, calmly eyeing up everyone like potential prey, with another two men and a woman subtly watching him from afar. A man in his mid-fifties was comforting his teenage son not far from Hannah, whilst a bigger family -two parents, five kids- tried desperately to play infantile word games to take their minds off the horror of their situation.

By the door, a young man in his twenties almost seemed to be enjoying the drama of their predicament, whilst four teenage girls hugged each other, and a young mother tried to calm her screaming baby. Glaring at the mother, an older man in an expensive suit, holding a leather briefcase, rocked backwards and forwards, trying with some futility to get a signal on his mobile phone, whilst a gay couple stood against the wall, talking about whatever came into their heads.

An older woman, probably close to retirement and wearing the uniform of an Underground train driver, was practically catatonic. Two old men were watching the others though: one was salivating, watching the young couple together, and the four teenagers, whilst the other seemed to be both watching and staring off into the distance, the same haunted look in his eyes that young Adam had.

Where had those frightening creatures taken Adam?

What were they?

What did they want?

What was this place?

Where was this place?

"Mummy," Sasha cried, her voice muffled by Hannah's body. "What are they going to do to Adam?"

"I don't know honey," she whispered.

The doors opened, and suddenly a horde of the creatures surged through the doorway, rifle-like weapons at the ready. They shouted in their native language to each other, and to the prisoners, gesturing with their weapons.

The creatures dragged the prisoners to their feet, ignoring their protests and cries of fear. The prisoners were dragged from the cell, in single-file. One creature pulled Sasha and Sapphire away from Hannah in each of its strong arms. The girls sobbed and Sasha screamed for her mummy, kicking against the immovable creature's arm.

Hannah reached out to hold their hands, but the creature holding hers yanked on her arm, twisting a muscle in her shoulder.

"Where are you taking us?" she cried, gnashing her teeth against the jab of pain in her shoulder.

The creature didn't look at her, but cackled incessantly.

* * *

The Operative stood in an immense hangar that was devoid of any small craft. Massive black hexagonal panels sat on the floor in a large grouping of twelve, vestiges of a forgotten and dead race. Wired to the edges of the formation of panels were dozens of computer consoles, some from his race, the rest from the race the technology was liberated from nearly a decade ago.

He still marveled at the insane brilliance of the technology, though was reluctant to try it again. And naturally, he believed like all others that served the Lord, that other races were inferior, and rightly so.

With a smug smile he looked upon his achievement: a huge perfectly shaped sphere. The sphere was made up of the remnants of the human Underground train, and the tunnel around it. The technology that transported it was still being tweaked; so far it couldn't transport a specific person or object, it had to transport everything in a specific circumference from the tip of the transport device. It looked bizarre, but the Operative saw it as his crowning achievement.

It had been he who had discovered the device on a conquered world, and thus had had the honour of using it for the Lord's purposes, despite his substantial physical changes.

He held the remote transport device in his claw, preparing to hand it over to the scientists in the laboratories.

He felt a presence beside him, and realised that he had been lost in thought.

He turned, and saw one of the warriors that had been guarding the human experiment. He was wearing the standard red chitinous body armour, with an energy rifle that looked brand new, straight out of the weapons factories.

"[It is a great day, is it not?]" the Operative asked.

"[I suppose,]" the warrior replied with a very human-like sigh.

"[You do not agree, warrior?]"

"[I've no doubt that you believe it's a great day, Operative,]" the warrior snorted, again another human trait. This warrior's behaviour was beginning to disturb him.

"[Are you not supposed to be guarding the experiments?]"

"[Yes, but I thought I'd come *here*, and put a spanner in the works,]" the warrior answered a bit too cheerily for the Operative's liking.

The Operative stared wide-eyed at the warrior. Having moved among the humans of London for several weeks, he had heard the expression, and understood exactly what it meant. The warrior flickered, literally, not figuratively. It was almost as if he were just an illusion or an image that was degrading, then realised the truth of it: it really was just an image.

The image kept flickering, revealing a human underneath, though the Operative never got a good look. He was frozen to the spot, unwilling to believe that a human was free in this facility, under the nose of the Lord himself. They had underestimated the humans.

The human reached over -still in his disguise- and snatched the transport control device from the Operative's claw.

"[You won't escape,]" the Operative growled. He felt something jab into the exposed flesh between his shoulder guard and torso armour. He looked down, and saw a wicked looking knife, straight, with serrated edges. A human weapon?

"Don't be so sure," the disguised human said in English. He leant forward, and his weight pushed the knife into the creature's lungs. The human pulled the knife out, the serrated edge inflicting more damage on its way out. Then he slashed the knife across the thing's throat, glad that the creatures were biologically similar to humans as the Operative's arterial blood sprayed over the deck.

The creature's last reflective thought was, *the humans will beat us.*

The Operative was dead before he hit the deck, leaving the hangar silently like a graveyard.

The Intelligence Agent pulled the corpse onto the transport panels, putting it near the sphere of the train carriage and tunnel. He slipped a pack of explosives from a pouch in his modified flak armour under his disguise armour, and attached it to the sphere. There were enough explosives in the pack to destroy the entire hangar. He inserted the detonator, and activated the remote control, giving him remote access from anywhere in the facility.

His holographic disguise was beginning to fail after two years of constant use. His unorthodox undercover work as a warrior among this group of creatures was at an end. It was time to return home to his superiors, and report the existence of this race. He supposed they thought he was dead, having not actually informed his superiors that he was *accidentally* undercover in this facility.

But the humans that had been transported here would need to be freed, or at the very least their suffering would need to be ended quickly.

He disengaged his holo-disguise, and his red armour fell away -the only part of his disguise that had been real. He located a grating that led to the vent system, hoping that nobody came across the dead body in his absence, at least until he could detonate the explosives from a safe enough distance.

* * *

Light streamed around him, and pain stabbed through his body as he picked himself off the wet wooden floor.

Wait...

Wooden floor?

The pain subsided and his vision began to focus, and now that he thought about it, it was a bit chilly as well. He looked around, and realised that he was standing on a wooden deck; a wooden *creaking* deck; a wooden creaking deck that was swaying. The scent of salt, and extremely fresh air filled Adam's nostrils, nearly stinging his sinuses with its intensity.

He was at sea, on a wooden sailing ship, and surrounded by growling sailors and soldiers. They weren't growling at anything in particular, that was just the way they talked -in growls and scowls.

The soldiers were dressed in starched red tunics and stiff black trousers, all holding muskets like they were on guard duty. Adam didn't see any cameras around so he hadn't found himself in a television show or a movie set, and he didn't see any celebrities, or in fact anyone with any decent personal hygiene, besides the men in officers' uniforms, and then just barely.

The ship looked brand new, as did the uniforms on the soldiers and Navy officers.

What the hell was going on?

First, bird-like aliens were incarcerating him, and now he was on the deck of a sailing ship in the middle of an ocean, and still wearing his shredded cinema uniform.

"What the f-"

"OI! YOU!" a commanding voice bellowed out. Adam snapped his head round, and realised that the soldiers were looking straight at him, with no less hostility than hungry Rottweilers given free reign in a butcher's shop.

"Uh-oh," Adam whispered, before being surrounded by a ring of red-jacketed soldiers, each with their sharp bayonets pointed at his upper torso.

"This is going to sound like a stupid question, and granted I feel an utter idiot for saying it, but... what year is it?"

The soldiers shot each other confused nervous glances.

One looked back at Adam, "It's the year of our Lord, sixteen-sixty-four."

It all clicked into place for Adam: the year, the uniforms, and the sailing ship.

"Jesus, you're the first Royal Marines, aren't you? Why the hell am I here? Forget that, HOW the hell am I here?"

"Are you alright mate?" one of the Marines asked. Clearly they thought he was mad, and Adam was inclined to agree with them.

Before Adam could answer, pain slammed into his chest, like someone had stuck a knife in him. He cried out, and looked down, but there was no blood, just his torn shirt. The Marines suddenly backed away from him, as blue light once again streamed away behind him, and he disappeared, vanishing into the thick salty sea air.

* * *

"[We have made the first incision,]" the lead scientist dictated for his recorder device.

The Second stood by the Lord, unmoved by the sight before him.

The subject -the human named Caine- was dead, or at least under the scientists' stasis-like procedure. His chest was being opened first with a scalpel to cut through the tissue and muscle, then with a powered saw to cut through the bone, and lastly a rib-spreading device was used to keep his bones from closing during the experiment.

The Second was still amazed that the human's insides looked so much like the colours of the Patriarch's great fleets of starships; or was it the other way around? No, that was blasphemous thinking, and thus forbidden.

Out the corner of his eye, he noticed that one of the regular red-armoured guards was missing. He cursed silently; this wasn't the kind of thing the experiments needed now. But the Lord would not allow him to leave his side to investigate.

The scientists began prodding and poking the human's organs with their indescribable instruments.

Silently, the Second fumed.

* * *

The light once again faded away, and Adam found himself not on a wooden deck, but *floating*. He was in what had to be the International Space Station; that much was obvious from the breathtaking view of Earth in the window in front of him.

"What the hell are you doing here?" an American voice demanded from behind Adam. The zero gravity was seriously limiting, and seriously disorienting, considering he had never experienced it before. He tried to turn, but found that all he did was flail a little. A soft hand touched his shoulder, and gently turned him round. The owner of the hand was a handsome, hard-set young woman, with cropped black hair, and no small amount of confusion on her incredibly beautiful face.

"I'm...not actually sure," Adam admitted. "Is this the ISS?"

The woman nodded, glancing at his torn cinema uniform, wondering how he could possibly get on the station without the use of... well, anything.

"This is going to sound like a stupid question, but what year is it?"

"2009," said the woman, a little wary. Adam was slightly shocked at the admission of the date. What was going on? Was it possible? Was he moving through time? There was a time when he believed that science fiction was exactly that: fiction. But then bird-like aliens kidnapped him, and all his beliefs went out the window: he was willing to believe anything at this point.

Eat your heart out Sam Beckett.

There was a camera flash off to Adam's right, and he blinked away the retinal afterimage the light left behind.

"What the f-"

"For the record," the photographer smiled, then looked at Adam's clothes, and turned away obviously about to call for someone to come down to investigate.

"For the record?" Adam asked.

"Don't you know?" the young woman looked at him sceptically. "We're testing the first faster-than-light drive on the new space shuttle *Freedom*."

"*Liftoff*!" someone shouted from another part of the space station.

"Dammit, I should be in the control room."

"Why?"

"I'm the engine's inventor," she replied, as if it were the most obvious thing in the universe. She didn't seem particularly perturbed by the appearance of Adam, nor his state of dress. Given the event in question he suspected that her mind was too filled with excitement and nerves to fully understand or fully comprehend.

Adam managed to grab a handhold on the bulkhead, and drag himself to the window. There was a long curving line of smoke streaking from the peninsular shape of Florida, up toward the high atmosphere, and then past the ozone layer. The launch vehicle, a massive deuterium-fuelled rocket system, disconnected from the space shuttle and fell back to Earth.

The space shuttle's own engines ignited, and blasted it out into space, speeding past the ISS.

"*The* Freedom *is leaving Earth's gravity well, Doctor Jenkins*," the disembodied voice called out over the station's intercom. "*The crew is powering up the FTL engine*."

The young woman -Doctor Jenkins- floated over to the wall, and activated the intercom panel.

"Tell them to go ahead, and activate the engine."

"*Acknowledged, Doctor*."

Adam watched with breathless anticipation, as the shuttle seemed to stretch, and then leap away from the planet, gone in an instant. It was a pivotal moment in human history -mankind's first real attempt at travelling the speed of light, and Adam had witnessed it.

Which, of course, was the perfect moment for the pain to slam into his chest. It was the same knife-in-the-chest pain as before, and it doubled Adam up even in zero gee. Dr. Jenkins floated toward him, just as the bright blue light streaked away from Adam. Within seconds, he was gone, leaving a very confused, and very scared Polly Jenkins.

* * *

Hannah, meanwhile, was stood at the front doorstep to *her* house; she didn't remember how she got there, nor why she was just standing in front of the door, staring at the varnished wood. There was a scent of something sweet in the air, like pollen. She looked down beside the concrete step, and saw her beloved flowers, planted in their spot under the entrance hall window.

She looked around, at the front lawn that stretched for twenty metres, at the hedge surrounding the large property, at the gravel drive, and the three BMWs parked in a line in front of the double garage. Her husband had come into money from both their firm, and an inheritance from his now-dead parents. It was a big place -not a mansion, but with five bedrooms, as many bathrooms, and several other rooms that served several communal purposes, the house was as close to a mansion as you could get in suburban London. The bricks were a terracotta colour mottled occasionally with light coloured moss, with a pillared porch over the front door, and large white-framed windows for all four floors.

Stood at the door, she was tempted to knock on the door; hadn't she just been in some kind of place that had aliens running it? And where were Sasha and Sapphire? Were they inside? Why weren't they with her?

The door was locked when she tried to open it. Fishing around in her pockets, she discovered her keys. Why was the sky darkening so quickly?

She hastily unlocked the door, and then stepped in. She was assaulted by more familiar smells: the leather of the upholstery, the cleaning chemicals from the new carpets, even the barely noticeable canine odour from the corner of the entrance hall where he slept.

She could hear heavy breathing from somewhere, but couldn't work out where it was coming from. She headed toward the kitchen, but found nothing, not even a steaming pan of hot food, or a pot of tea. There was no activity in the house, though she knew there should be at this time of the day. The clock said otherwise: it was spinning like a carousel out of control, adding to Hannah's growing unease.

The heavy breathing was getting incrementally louder, though it was still barely a whisper, like something intangible just behind her head, out of reach and out of sight.

She moved from the kitchen into the lounge, only to find nothing again. The family photos were all askew above the fireplace, like a strong wind had blown through here. She shook her head, and decided to check upstairs. The stairs creaked quietly, showing their age, as she ascended. The breathing noise was definitely getting louder the closer she got to the bedroom she shared with her husband.

Her own breath caught in her throat from the anticipation. She could barely move her feet; she was sure she knew what would be on the other side of that door, but she couldn't bring herself to fully think about it.

Hand out, palm forward, she pushed the door open, and stepped through into her room.

"No," she whispered, as her fears came to fruition.

Her husband was in bed with another woman -his secretary, as she had always suspected.

"Nononononono," she kept saying. Her knees buckled, and she crumpled to the floor, tears streaming down her face. Her heart broke, shattered into tiny pieces as her world came tumbling down.

Her husband, naked as the day he was born, jumped off the secretary and onto the floor, brash as ever. The secretary gathered the bed covers around her like a sarong, and stood next to her boss. Hannah's hopelessness increased as the sobs wracked her body.

And they laughed at her.

"Nononononononono," she repeated hysterically, crawling backwards, away from the two laughing idiots that had torn her life apart.

There was a light suddenly, so bright it almost blinded Hannah. The sensation of the floor disappeared beneath her, and then she felt something under her feet, something solid. She looked down at her feet, and saw concrete, the same damn concrete as her doorstep.

Hannah was stood at the front doorstep to *her* house; she didn't remember how she got there, nor why she was just standing in front of the door, staring at the varnished wooden door. There was a scent of something sweet in the air, like pollen. She looked down beside the concrete step, and saw her beloved flowers, planted in their spot under the entrance hall window.

Oh God, please no...

* * *

"LISTEN UP, PRIVATE PARTS!" Sergeant Bishop bellowed. He was *normally* a loud man, though he had to be doubly louder today as the noise from the unit's amphibious lander was insane, occasionally missing a beat when the boat hit a tall wave. Salty seawater splashed violently over the edges of the open-topped vehicle. Three soldiers, green in more ways than one, vomited as the English Channel threw them about.

Corporal Jack Digby stared in frightened contemplation at the large ramp at the front of the vehicle. It was raised to protect the craft's occupants from harm. He knew what was coming, knew how important this operation was. Holding his plastic-bagged rifle, and checking his fatigues and combat webbing.

The door obscured the view of the objective ahead, but the sides were low enough to see to either side of the transport, and behind.

Five thousand ships were anchored just off the Normandy coast, anchored against the tides of the English Channel, whilst thousands of amphibious landing vehicles raced for the beaches, bucking and jumping over the waves.

The warships behind pummelled the coast from afar, massive artillery rounds pounding the German defences, their firepower joined by a mass of RAF and USAF fighters and bombers flying above the action, keeping the Allied air forces in a superior position.

Digby looked at his watch, and then remembered that he'd already been through this, sixty-two years ago. He should have been on his way to collect his military pension, wearing his red jacket, and tricorn hat, along with his precious medals. Then he had been kidnapped by...inhuman creatures, and then dragged from the cell.

What was he doing back on the day of Operation Overlord?

Why was he once again heading for Gold Beach?

Where were the rest of the kidnappees?

As confusing as his situation was, it felt overwhelmingly good to be young again. Was he young though? Was this an illusion? He reached out, and touched the nearest soldier, a young man named Wilkins. Wilkins flinched, and nervously turned round, his shock and fright plainly evident on his face. The kid didn't say anything, but threw up the contents of his stomach onto Digby's boots.

The smell was nauseating, especially mixed with the sea air and the smoke drifting back from the beach emplacements.

The touch, the smell, the sights, and sounds, all confirmed to Digby that this was indeed real. Unless, of course, that it was a very convincing illusion. He was willing to believe that it could very well be.

"Zero-six-twenty-nine, ladies!" Sarge bellowed.

Weapons were readied, straps were tightened, and packs were straightened as the soldiers steeled themselves for the horrors ahead.

But however much they thought they were ready, they weren't.

The engines growled louder and louder as they fought the riptide onto the beach.

One soldier sobbed his heart out, praying to God to get him out of this.

The amphibious transport thumped to a halt, and the ramp dropped down into the shallow water. Five men died instantly as fire from the German machine gun positions ripped through the boat. Blood splattered everywhere, someone screamed, and then Sergeant Bishop was shouting for the advance.

Digby and Bishop bounded out of the transport, and splashed through the water, running like their lives depended on it, which just so happened to be the case. Three other soldiers made it out of the transport, the others were all dead before they could exit; Wilkins, terrified as he was, was one of the living.

The five waded through the water to the nearest spiked tank traps, then moved on again to one of the steel death-sculptures in the sand.

Bullets mashed the beach around them, kicking up dust and sand, and tearing men to pieces as they struggled to reach the objective.

"Unpack your rifles," Bishop ordered, doing the same with his.

Weapons at the ready, the small unit gathered the courage to run out into the gunfire. Bishop, being the Sarge, led the way, bellowing an incomprehensible war cry. Not nearly as loud, but just as ferocious, Digby shouted and charged at his fastest pace, right behind his sergeant. Wilkins and the others followed, rifles vibrating as their hands shook worse than Alzheimer's disease on steroids.

Bullets whickered through the air, whining as they passed the soldiers' heads within millimetres. All around them, thousands of soldiers screamed and fought and died, running up the beach, using what precious cover they could. The man beside Wilkins was dumped on his back as three machine gun rounds tore his upper torso into chunks. Bishop, Digby, and Wilkins didn't stop, but kept running. The other soldier, however, *did* stop, and moved to see to the downed soldier.

His head evaporated in a cloud of red mist and pieces of meat.

Wilkins screamed as he heard the wet squelch behind him. Bishop and Digby reached the embankment at the top of the beach, and dove to the floor, using the small hillock as cover against the German positions.

Wilkins flopped in beside the others, his face ashen with mind-numbing horror, whispering "ohmygodohmygodohmygod." He just kept repeating it, like it would save his life somehow.

"We have to get that machine gun position," Digby stated. Bishop nodded. The young Corporal took a moment to look around. Men by the hundreds were charging up the beach, some dying, some wounded, others scared out of their minds, and the rest fighting for their lives.

Men drowned, and died, and fought, and Digby was still worried that this wasn't real. He wasn't scared; he'd already experienced this moment in his mind thousands of times, but the sheer ferocity and violence of the event was making him nauseous like never before.

Someone somewhere had lugged a bazooka from the boats, and was aiming at the German position when an enemy flamethrower licked red-hot death at him. The flames encompassed him, and burnt him alive. In his death throes, the soldier spasmed and accidentally tapped the trigger spoon. The small rocket whinnied away into the sky, leaving a zigzag smoke trail. Bishop and Digby were hypnotised by the rocket that seemed to be snaking back towards them.

"Oh, no," Jack Digby cried. Bishop grabbed him by the collar, and the two, followed by the white-faced Wilkins, jumped clear of the embankment. The rocket slammed into the ground, and detonated. The sand muffled the blast, but the shockwave knocked the soldiers onto the ground, shrapnel flying in all directions. Sarge was hit in the leg by debris; Digby was hit in the ribs, though it didn't penetrate beyond the bone.

There was another wet squelch and splatter, and Digby turned to see a large hole where the Sergeant's left eye should have been. Digby turned to run back to the cover of the embankment, and could swear he saw the bullet coming straight at him. He knew it was impossible, since bullets travelled faster than the eye could see.

And yet, he saw it head-on, coming at him.

This never happened; I wasn't shot at Normandy, Wilkins was.

Just before the bullet should have hit, Digby saw a great white light. He felt something shift beneath him, and then the sand was replaced by metal underneath him.

"LISTEN UP, PRIVATE PARTS!" Sergeant Bishop bellowed. He was *normally* a loud man, though he had to be doubly louder today as the noise from the unit's amphibious lander was insane, occasionally missing a beat when the boat hit a tall wave. Salty seawater splashed violently over the edges of the open-topped vehicle. Three soldiers, green in more ways than one, vomited as the sea threw them about.

Oh God, please no...

* * *

Scientists stood around the subjects -the prisoners from the large cell. They were hooked up to the machines like lab animals, which to the scientists they were.

"[The eldest is aware of the illusion,]" one scientist stated matter-of-factly to his colleagues.

"[His illusion seems to be a memory rather than a fabrication; perhaps it was a mistake to use that mind-simulation. We should switch to an alternate program for him.]"

"[No, he is still experiencing the same responses as the other subjects,]" another replied.

"[Leave him then.]"

The scientists moved on to the next group, linked together because of their uniforms, and obvious status as soldiers.

* * *

The three bound forward, hopping over the ruined wall in front of them. Their target was ahead, as big as their mission briefing had stated. The other teams, all making up 1 Platoon of A Company of the 25th Royal Engineers, were running through the ruins on all four sides. Their target was a large palace in the centre of the ruined town, bold and brash in the arid Iraqi heat.

Their superiors were adamant that the palace was to be stormed, but the outer defences needed to be demolished, so Command had brought a rapid response unit of the Royal Engineers in to blow the walls up.

Teams of three combat engineers each were sent with explosives to deal with each of the four walls. One such team was made up of James Matthews,

Eric West, and David Whittard, friends and colleagues, and dressed in full desert warfare combat gear. Though they carried the standard SA80 L95s, they were not experienced fighters, only demolition experts.

Matthews led the way across another fallen pile of masonry, and then stopped suddenly, looking around at his surroundings.

Hadn't the three of them just been in an alien cell with a couple of dozen others?

He turned to his compatriots and saw that they were just as confused.

"What the hell is going on?" asked Matthews

West shrugged, and Whittard stared at the action around them. He could see the other teams struggling in the heat, bounding over fallen columns and wrecked walls in their heavy gear. A pair of sand-painted RAF Tornadoes roared overhead, unleashing a volley of bombs on the fortified palace. Behind them, Challengers of an armoured regiment thundered through brick and mortar.

"This mission never happened," said Whittard.

"I know; the Sheikh surrendered, and we were recalled before we got more than three feet from base," replied Matthews.

"So what the bloody hell are we doing here?" West cried.

Matthews shrugged. "Simulation maybe?" He tapped the nearest piece of debris, shaking loose some dust that tickled his throat and stung his sinuses. "Seems real enough, though." They could all feel the chill in the night air, see the stars, hear the gunfire from the other walls of the fortress.

"What shall we do then?" asked Whittard.

"May as well see the mission through," West answered for him, "I don't see a way out."

It was decided for them as louder inaccurate gunfire erupted from the fortress walls, and descended around the three friends. They all dived for cover, what little of it there was. Matthews and Whittard managed to scramble behind what looked like an upturned Land Rover, whilst West barely scraped into cover behind a tall stone column.

"What's that noise?" West had to shout to be heard, the firestorm of bullets was so loud.

Whittard and Matthews shook their heads, and then realised they could hear it too. A whistling sound, like something aerodynamic falling from a great height.

The three friends looked at each other in horror as they recognised the sound: it was indeed something aerodynamic falling from a great height: artillery fire! They couldn't see it, but were more than sure that it was coming from the direction of the British positions.

The whistling became louder, and more shrill as the shell neared the ground at an incredible pace.

The soldiers jumped up, and ran, braving the whickering machine gun fire. West went down, his leg clipped by a stray round. Whittard and Matthews stopped and turned to pick up their friend.

The shell landed and vaporised the three.

The world went white.

The three bounded forward, hopping over the ruined wall in front of them. Their target was ahead, as big as their mission briefing had stated.

Oh no....

* * *

"[These three also seem to be aware of the simulation,]" the first scientist announced.

"[What about this one?]" The second scientist pointed to an extremely shifty human on one of the simulation beds. "[The devices will not interface with his cranium. The scans show that the parts of his brain controlling his personality are badly damaged.]"

"[What could that mean?]" the third scientist asked.

"[The parts of his brain seem to be the self-control centres.]"

The third scientist wasn't an expert in human physiology; who would want to be? "[Explain,]" he demanded.

"[According to the medical data brought back by the Lord's special Operative, this human has all the signs of a compulsive killer.]"

"[Interesting,]" the first scientist nodded. "[We should inform the Lord about this one; he may have a use for him.]"

* * *

The blue light dissipated, and Adam once again found himself in a space-like structure, though this one had gravity. He looked around; the technology wasn't that much beyond what he had just seen on the ISS, probably a few years on.

He looked down at his clothes, and decided to change into something more comfortable, and less conspicuous. He found a locker with a set of blue military overalls, underneath which he wore a clean pair of underwear and a tee-shirt. He kept his work shoes on, and then went for a walk. He had started in a corridor, with white metal bulkheads and grey floors. It looked a bit too sterile for Adam, but then he was used to the grey and tiny corridors of ocean-going warships, where space was at a premium.

The floors seemed to vibrate ever so slightly, and the lights occasionally flickered. He wondered if this was some kind of advancement on what he had seen previously. A giant leap forward for mankind? He was paying so much attention to the technology and walls around him, that he didn't see the woman coming around the first corner, and barrelled straight into her.

They tumbled to the deck in a tangle of limbs. He managed to smack his head on the metal floor, and let out a "Jesus Christ!" before picking himself up. The woman, dressed in the same blue military overalls, had also retrieved herself from the floor, and stared straight into his eyes.

"Oh my god," she whispered. "It's you."

At first, Adam didn't recognise her. She had longer hair, and it was tied back in a ponytail, but it was definitely the same Doctor Jenkins from the ISS. She was as beautiful as before, and had lost a little weight, her perfect porcelain face framing her bright, curious green eyes.

"Doctor Jenkins," Adam grimaced. He was pleased to see her, but the situation he was in didn't allow for any real pleasantries.

"You're not wearing your cinema uniform," Jenkins noted.

Adam only just managed to suppress the smile trying to force its way onto his face.

"I borrowed some clothes from a locker," he shrugged, gesturing to the overalls and tee-shirt underneath. "I hope that's alright?" She didn't answer, too intent on Adam's re-appearance.

"How did you get on the *Mayflower*?" she wondered. She wasn't afraid, she seemed almost glad to see him.

"*Mayflower*? Like the forefathers?"

"She's our first colony ship," she nodded. "Equipped with everything we need to begin a colony on another world: food, plants, seeds, prefab shelters, the works. We're colonising Proxima Centauri." Adam was about to retort that that sounded very sci-fi, and then remembered where he had been previously and bit back the reply.

"But it can't have been too long since I was on the ISS."

She gestured for him to follow her; they walked through dozens of corridors, passing others in the same blue overalls as they strode. She didn't say a word, but nodded and smiled at those they met along the way. Adam felt kind of strange, walking through something that looked like the set of *Enterprise*; this had to be a spaceship: he hadn't heard of anything like this in the pipeline before he left the service. She led him through a set of sliding double doors, and onto what had to be the control centre.

There were flat screen monitors situated all around the square room. There was a central console, with a pair of chairs raised up behind it on a knee-high stepped dais. The chairs afforded a view of the entire room, and more importantly the long wide windows that stretched almost all the way around the room. There was a starfield painted on the ceiling, with the major constellations mapped out like something out of a child's bedroom. On the back wall, where the door he had entered was located, was painted several badges: those of the Royal and United States Navies, British and US Armies, RAF and USAF, and of course the flags of both countries: the Union Jack and the Stars and Stripes.

Adam watched one of the displays, and saw the shape and size of what he was standing in. He really was in a starship, a huge one by all accounts, with a bulbous long central hull, and two modules either end. The smaller module, sat at the front of the ship, was the command module, with the rear one being the engines.

"How the hell did you do all this?" breathed Adam.

"Lots of cooperation between Britain and the US, as well as some other countries. We began the initial construction on the surface, and then put it together up here in orbit. The other stuff like support and computers was installed after the main hull and decks had been put in place."

"What year is it?" Adam asked.

"2013," she replied nonchalantly.

"So you've built this thing in the four years since I last saw you."

"It's amazing what we can achieve when we cooperate fully," she smiled. She saw his amazed look as he was still taking in the scale of the project and the sheer audacity of the operation. "We launch in two weeks, though Admiral DaSilva believes it'll be more like three. Will you be staying this time?"

Adam shook his head; he could already feel the pains beginning to burn through his body.

"I honestly wish I could," he grunted, with genuine feeling behind it. He desperately wanted to see this major event in humanity's history. He desperately needed not to be back in that chamber of horrors.

But he couldn't. He could see the blue light begin to seep into the corners of his vision. Doctor Jenkins jumped back at the sight of the familiar blue light, as it streaked away behind her mysterious visitor. He cried out in pain, and then he and the light were both gone.

* * *

The Lord took a step back when he saw the clothes on the human Caine change from the simple blue and white to the rather military-like one-piece jumpsuit, similar to those his people had discovered floating in space nearby, remnants of a lost planet.

"[He seems to be manipulating the experiment from within his experiences,]" one scientist noted dispassionately. Their earlier fear of failure had dissipated, replaced with a smugness the Lord had come to expect of their profession -it was a smugness he thought was deserved, and approved highly of.

"[Perhaps you should continue the experiments instead of stating the obvious,]" the Second observed angrily. The Lord didn't say anything, just nodded thoughtfully.

The scientists continued the temporal experiments, just as another of their colleagues entered the laboratory. He approached the Lord, lowered himself to a kneeling position, and paid homage to the Lord.

"[Report,]" the Lord grumbled, annoyed that he was being interrupted.

"[The simulations on the other prisoners are going well, my Lord. Some of them have become aware that they are in a simulation, though they are still trapped by their own fears. However, there are two who the machines will not interface with.]"

"[Truly?]" said the Lord.

"[Yes, Lord. One shows signs of psychotic tendencies, the other appears to be the human equivalent of an arbiter.]"

The Lord shivered; one of his pet hates were the arbiters of his people's legal courts. Having researched the human culture, the Lord had discovered the human equivalent was even worse: lawyers were snidey, under-handed, scheming backstabbers, and the Lord wanted nothing to do with them. Though, of course, they had their uses at certain times.

The Second leaned forward to whisper in his Lord's ear.

"[I could use pieces of scum like them, my Lord.]"

"[I do not doubt it, Second,]" the Lord replied without turning round. "[A bit of betrayal?]" The Second nodded. "[Then see to it personally, Second.]"

The Second nodded again, and stepped out of the laboratory, with the recently arrived scientist at his heels.

* * *

Dark grey clouds rose up above them like a massive cliff, with the open blue sky behind and above them. The sky, and indeed the ground, didn't move past the windows particularly fast, then again, things always seemed slow from the cockpit of a Sea King helicopter. The quick, loud *thud-thud-thud* of the main rotor blades were deafening, and wind blasted past the bubble cockpit canopy.

In the pilot's seat, Flight Lieutenant Rhys Dick, glanced down at the coast rolling past below. According to the maps, it was called the Bay of Harbours, on the East Falkland Island. The clock on the readout panels read 12.30, May 21 1982.

Rhys frowned, and looked over at his co-pilot, Flight Lieutenant Rudolph Kendal. Rudi was also frowning at the clock.

Neither of them had been in the RAF in 1982, nor had they flown outside the British Isles at any time in their careers. They were search-and-rescue pilots, not combat pilots -flying in enemy territory was not in their squadron's operations, instead flying from bases in Britain to rescue those in need across the country's territory.

"What the hell is going on?" Dick cried.

"I haven't the foggiest," Kendal replied.

The winch operator, hearing their short exchange, asked what was wrong. Dick shook his head, and told him everything was fine, though he had no idea what the Flight Sergeant's name was; in fact, he had never seen the man's face before now.

Rhys switched the mike booms on their helmets to exclude the winch operator from the conversation.

"Weren't we in an alien prison cell a minute ago?" Kendall asked, gesturing to the ground that appeared to be passing by at a steady height and rate.

"We were," answered Dick, "but how did we end up in a Sea King during the Falklands War? For starters, neither of us were here, and there were no Sea Kings in service at the time. Maybe this is a simulation? They were working on virtual reality simulators at the MOD when we were in London; imagine what *aliens* can do."

The console bleated repeatedly, and the winch operator dashed across from the sliding door to the radar. Dick switched the mike booms back to the default settings.

"Picking up two contacts on the hill ahead, sirs," the Flight Sergeant reported. "Profile suggests some kind of gun battery." He craned his neck to look out the small window bubble next to the small radar alcove, and found what he was looking for. "Camouflaged gun nests on the hillocks to either side of us up ahead."

"I see them," Dick announced. Which was the exact moment the nests opened fire, spraying machine gun fire into the air around the yellow Sea King. "Call it in to the carrier, Rudi," he ordered. "We're making evasive manoeuvres." He was sure they had come from a carrier, but who knew in their situation?

The winch operator was about to shout something when a loud banging, and a wet gurgle cut off his voice over the headsets. Kendall turned to see what had happened, and almost vomited.

The machine guns had shredded the large rear compartment to pieces, and pulped the Flight Sergeant into chunks of meat and blood. The chopper began trembling, then rocking. The engine status lights were flashing a frightening red, and the Sea King began to descend toward the ground despite Dick's best efforts.

Sinus-searing smoke filled the cabin, and suddenly the rotors crumpled and flung themselves to pieces. The chopper span sideways, then over onto its side as it tumbled, uncontrolled, out of the air.

The two pilots couldn't do *anything*; they were helpless.

The ground reached up to smash them to pieces, and the world went white.

Dark grey clouds rose up above them like a massive cliff, with the open blue sky behind and above them. The sky, and indeed the ground, didn't move past the windows particularly fast, then again, things always seemed slow from the cockpit of a Sea King helicopter.

Oh fucking hell, please no...

* * *

The Agent crawled on his hands and knees through the facility's air filtration system, hoping there was some kind of shielding protecting him from the alien sensors. He'd lived among them, trying to find a way out for two years, but hadn't found one yet.

This air duct system was the same red colour as the rest of the facility, with the same curved rib-like supports every other metre, making for a cramped space around him.

Could these human newcomers help him? He had seen some military uniforms among the prisoners, and even a pair of Police uniforms. The one taken for the special experiments was muscled and tattooed enough for the Agent to believe he might be military as well.

He came to another T-junction, and turned left. He was no longer encumbered by the experimental interactive hologram that had served as his disguise for two years so he could move as a normal human moved, or as much as one could in a dark air vent.

He placed another explosive on the next junction, hoping to use the energy blasts as distractions when, or if, he made his escape.

A plan was forming...

* * *

Once again, and Adam was getting sick of the bloody sight of it, the blue light faded away. For a second, he thought that the light had had no effect; the lights were dimmed, and there were more personnel crowded into the room than there had been before, but it was definitely the bridge of the *Mayflower*.

"Oh my god, it's you," the voice of Doctor Jenkins cried. There was something not right in her voice as she bounded over to Adam. Despite the near lack of light, he could see she had been crying, and her manner indicated that she was close to tears, once again.

"This must be our favourite ghost," a stern voice called out from the area of the two command chairs that had been there during his previous visit. It was Admiral DaSilva; Adam had once met the older man when DaSilva was still the captain of the *USS Reuben James*, though he doubted the Admiral would recognise him.

The appearance of Adam's 'ghost' was being all but ignored, and Adam was curious to know what was more interesting than a time-traveller.

"You're on the bridge of the *Icarus*," Dr. Jenkins stated. Adam frowned, slightly confused. He was sure that he was on the colony ship *Mayflower*. "When the *Mayflower*'s colony module was removed and placed on Proxima Centauri's surface, we cobbled together the remains of the engines and command module, and created a starship to defend the colony and act as a shuttle between the two planets. We called her *Icarus*."

"So what the fuck is *that*?" Adam cursed, pointing out of the forward window. Earth filled much of the forward windows: the *Icarus* was clearly in orbit of the planet. Earth's atmosphere was alight with oranges and reds, and country-sized islands of smoke and clouds that stretched for hundreds of miles.

Adam knew what it was, but didn't want to even contemplate it.

"After the *Mayflower*'s launch," began Jenkins, "China and her closest allies demanded that Britain and the USA hand over the faster-than-light drive. When our governments refused, China began arming for war. Downing Street and the White House recalled *Icarus* three weeks ago; we entered orbit when Chinese nuclear weapons obliterated Los Angeles, and Southern California. Naturally, NATO fought back. And now we have this," she added, pointing to the devastation below. "We can't contact the surface, there's too much electromagnetic interference, and any attempt to land would probably be met with retaliatory strikes from Chinese forces."

"I never thought I'd live to see a Third World War," Adam breathed. And then his travelling through time began to make sense: key events in humanity's first steps into the wider universe. Could it be the start of something magnificent, or something hideous, and dangerous?

Pain spread through his veins as he watched the devastation of Earth.

Dr. Jenkins placed a comforting hand on his shoulder. She knew what was coming, knew that he would disappear once again.

The blue light began to appear, and she whispered something in his ear. He heard it, though it didn't register in his brain until the light took him away from the bridge of the *Icarus/Mayflower*.

"Will I ever see you again?"

* * *

The Agent crawled up to the air vent grill in front of him. Unlike human air vents, where there was a sophisticated filter to prevent gases and such from circulating through the facility, this vent was more of a collection of spikes to prevent *beings* from circulating stealthily, looking like a fanged mouth rather than an inanimate object. Stealthily, however, was not what the Agent was doing. As quiet as he was trying to be, the materials the air ducts were made out of seemed incapable of being quiet, making it the loudest sneaking the Agent had ever heard of.

All of his charges were set, now he had to see what he could do about setting those prisoners free.

* * *

"[The temporal energy infusing his body is starting to become too unstable for the experiment,]" said the first scientist. "[If we don't bring him back, the energies might seep into the rest of the facility, Lord.]"

The Lord nodded in reluctant agreement.

"[You've learned everything you can from his biology?]" asked the Lord.

The scientist nodded, sparing a quick glance at the monitors to check the human's vitals.

"[Patch him up, return him to the cell, and then set up the torture chamber. This one is most definitely special and shall be treated as such.]"

The scientists, and indeed the rest of the guards, snapped to follow the Lord's orders.

The Lord nodded to himself, satisfied with the experiment's progress.

He gestured to his personal guards, and the four warriors crashed to attention, spinning on their heels, and surrounding their Lord. The Lord exited, and returned to his throne room.

He was going over his strategy in his head as he walked, excited by the prospect that everything was falling into place, just as had been promised to him. The throne room doors opened, and he took a seat on his dais.

One of the regular red-armoured guards came bounding up the aisle of trophies, and practically dove to the floor to bow in front of the Lord.

"[What is it?]" the Lord said impatiently.

"[My Lord, the device in hangar three-nine has been destroyed, and your special Operative is missing.]"

"[MISSING?!]" bellowed the Lord. "[HOW CAN HE BE MISSING?!]"

"[The analysts are still scanning the debris, Lord, but they think they have found organic material among the debris.]"

"[Is the device salvageable?]"

"[They are unsure yet, Lord,]" the crouching warrior answered.

"[Unsure?]" the Lord said calmly. He stepped over to the nearest of his personal guards, pulled the warrior's sidearm out of its holster, charged the weapon, and then shot the messenger in the top of his bowed head. He turned to the guard, returning the weapon. The guard nodded, realising the honour of having the Lord use *his* sidearm.

"[Go down to the hangar, and make sure the scientists understand that they *will* repair the device. Without it, our plans cannot go ahead, and I will be *severely* displeased.]"

"[Understood, my Lord.]"

The guard hefted his staff, and bounded out of the throne room at an admirable pace.

The Lord would have to reward him...

* * *

The blue light receded, the pain returned full force, and Adam's sanity took its first tumble toward madness.

He woke up screaming, still restrained to the table, with his chest still open to the elements.

"JESUS FUCKING CHRIST!" he bellowed. He could see into his own chest, and he was still alive. The pain was so intense that his nerves shut down, and his stomach tried to retch, but couldn't without shaking and making Adam even more aware of his bloodied innards. All thoughts of his experiences left his mind as the thought of seeing his own internal organs whilst still conscious slammed him almost too close to the edge of sanity.

How could it happen?

Was that the chest pains he had felt during his transporting?

The aliens were looking at him curiously, wielding strange wicked-looking implements. They came at him with the devices, some of which spat bright sparks at him.

"Fuck off." Adam tried to breathe through the pain and insanity of it all.

He was still awake when they pulled his ribs together, fused them, and then glued the muscles and skin over the ribs.

All the while, his mind was reeling, *Oh-god-oh-god-oh-god-oh-god*.

* * *

37

Reverend Gerald Bishop found himself on a desert plain. There was barely any colour to the mass of sand, though the sun beat down mercilessly; perspiration began to pour off his middle-aged body. He looked around him, and saw only sand; just miles and miles of sand in every direction.

And then two figures appeared: one was a bearded man in loose pale robes, and sandals on his feet. The other was the opposite: he wore a black suit, somewhat out of place in this desert hellhole; then again, Bishop wasn't exactly conspicuous -he was still wearing his priestly black robes and dog collar.

He walked toward the figures, hiking up the bottom edge of his robes, preventing the material from dragging in the sand.

"You will not tempt me," the bearded man said serenely.

"Of course I will," said the black-clad man beside him, "You know it, and I know it, all that's left is the foreplay."

Bishop wasn't sure how he was hearing the two conversing, given his age, and the distance from the pair. He had a sinking feeling he knew what it was he was seeing. But hadn't he just been in a blood-coloured room with other equally frightened people? There had been creatures there; nothing like the devil in the Bible, but just as terrifying.

Was this a test from God?

If so, what was to be gained from it?

Was this even real?

Bishop didn't know, but he was willing to find out.

He quickened his pace.

The conversation wasn't going well.

"Temptation is a part of life," the black-clad figure said nonchalantly. "Men and women everywhere give into it every day; there's no shame in it."

"Giving in to *your* temptations would be immoral," replied the bearded man. Neither of them noticed the Priest nearby, watching them.

"Immorality is defined by lesser beings." Bishop could see the two small horns on the black-clad man's forehead.

The devil.

And Jesus.

Bishop realised he was seeing the temptation of Christ, one of the most critical lessons taught by the Bible.

Why was he seeing it?

Did those creatures induce this situation?

Virtual reality?

Was that even possible?

"All I'm asking is that you take this bread and water," the devil snorted.

"And then after that?" Jesus asked.

The two stopped walking only metres from Bishop.

And then a Christian's worst nightmare: Jesus took the bread offered, and bit a chunk from it.

Bishop's heart sunk; his religious beliefs came crumbling down, even as Jesus swigged the bread down with a glass of water.

The devil laughed.

This can't be happening; it can't be happening -it's not possible. And then Jesus started choking -the bread was poisoned.

Bishop ran to his Lord's aid, and caught him in his arms as he collapsed.

"NO!" the priest bellowed as his Lord's life drained away before his very eyes.

This can't be happening...

There was a white light that blinded Bishop momentarily. When the light faded there was no weight in his arms, no Jesus.

Reverend Gerald Bishop found himself on a desert plain. There was barely any colour to the mass of sand, though the sun beat down mercilessly; perspiration began to pour off his middle-aged body. He looked around him, and saw only sand; just miles and miles of sand in every direction.

My Lord, please no, not again....

* * *

And so it went on for all those taken from the London Underground.

Miriam Cornwell, an off-duty train driver for the Underground, experienced the nightmare of a train derailment over and over again.

PCs Whimble and Norman witnessed a murderous mass riot gone mad.

Aaron Mitchell and Trevor Smith were attacked and murdered again and again simply for being gay.

Kevin and Mouse Gilpin were repeatedly forced to watch the kidnapping of their five children, as single mum Jamie did with her tiny baby Sarah.

Single American father Buck and his teenage son Gary were forced into an endless hedged maze from which there was seemingly no escape.

Young writer Kenneth McDonald saw a world ruled by a big brother state where the press had no freedom and human rights were ignored.

Jenny and Rowland, an engaged couple, were continuously raped and murdered, and forced to watch each other's pain.

Old Man Reginald, the dirty old man on the train, was arrested, and put in prison for paedophilia, where he was brutally beaten and maimed.

MI5 agents Rosie Bond and Mickey Graham, tasked with tailing both Block and Bradley Stanford, were shot and tortured by a simulated Block.

All of these simulations were designed to place hopelessness in the prisoners, for the Core to see their reactions to such harsh conditions in preparation for the inevitable conflict ahead.

* * *

Hannah was the first to be led back into the cell; or rather, she was *shoved* into the cell by the alien guards. Her nerves were frayed -the whole thing with her husband in their bedroom with the secretary had to have been a simulation of some kind. It just had to be.

She was sure, of course, that they really *had* had sex in the bedroom, just never in her presence or even in the same postcode.

The incident kept playing through her mind again and again. If it was a simulation, what was the point of it? All it did was promote hopelessness using her worst fear: betrayal. Was that where the others had been taken? To experience the same complete hopelessness of a never-ending simulation that delved into their worst fears?

The doors swished open, and Sasha and Sapphire were tossed through the gap between the doors, and hit the floor, crying their eyes out. Hannah dashed to wrap her arms around her daughters, tears flowing freely from her own eyes as the two girls sobbed and cried.

She shushed and shushed, and stroked their heads gently to calm them down. She didn't want to think about what they had seen in the simulators, and she was glad they were okay, at least physically.

The doors opened again and again, each time letting in a group or individual prisoner. Everyone had the same ashen look to their faces; Hannah realised that her summation had been correct and they had endured something similar to her own nightmare.

Then the doors opened for a final time, and four of the alien guards literally threw Adam into the cell, the poor man crashing into the deck and crying out in pain.

Hannah, Sasha and Sapphire were the first to reach him. Everybody stopped in their tracks; Adam was covered in massive scars; the largest was on his chest, a Y-shape almost like an autopsy incision on one of those CSI shows, whilst others were round and about the size of a bullet, or thin and oval like a knife blade.

The big scar was recent, fresh, still healing, whilst the others were old and pale. A tattoo was sat on his shoulder: a dagger lined in red ink. But Hannah wasn't looking at the tattoo; she was watching his lips. He was saying something, gibbering, and his body shaking like he was cold.

She leaned closer, and heard his words:

"Time travel," he gibbered to himself. "T-Time travel... Jenkins... Faster-than-light... World War... Time travel... " He kept repeating it over and over. He was traumatised in the worst way -he was losing his mind; a place where nobody could help him but himself. His eyes alternated between staring off into the distance, and squeezing shut from the pain of his injuries.

"What did he say?" the old Chelsea Veteran inquired.

"Something about time travel," answered Hannah.

"What the hell did they do to him?" a member of one of the families blurted when he finally got a good look at Adam's wounds.

"He looks like he's just had an autopsy," one of the uniformed Police Constables added. Though the equipment vests and caps had been taken away from him, he still looked very much the part of a London Bobbie, as his partner did beside him.

His partner, PC Whimble, crouched down beside Hannah, and looked Adam over.

"He's had serious trauma, but it looks like it's healing," Whimble announced. "There's no bleeding, no bruising; unless he's got *internal* bleeding, he should be alright." Hannah looked at him incredulously, and Whimble explained that all policemen and women were trained in first aid.

Whimble, and his partner, PC Norman, helped carry Adam to a corner, where he could rest. Despite all that they were feeling from the simulations, some of them overcame their pain in the face of such horrific treatment.

Sasha and Sapphire sat next to their mother, leaning against her shoulders whilst she cradled Adam's head and torso in her arms. He was unconscious before she fell asleep, though in her fall toward the land of nod, she heard some of the others moving around and swearing several times.

"Anything?" Private Matthews asked. He was tapping the walls with his fist, only to find the walls were a metal alloy of some sort, despite the fact that it looked for all the world like human flesh. His knuckles produced a loud *tap-tap*, as did several other knuckles belonging to those wearing uniforms. There was no smell to the room, though he was sure that after a while the combined stink of forty-plus men, women, and children would begin to fill the room quickly.

"Besides this seemingly impenetrable door, there's no other way out," Private West replied.

"Seemingly impenetrable?" Private Whittard retorted, a mocking tone to his Geordie accent.

West made a running kick at the door, and bounced painfully off it, much to the amusement of his fellow Engineers.

"Oh. Well," Whittard looked away, mumbling, "guess that *is* impenetrable."

West, having heard his mumbling, let out a frustrated sigh and shook his head at his Geordie friend, though he now had a bit of a limp to his walk.

Flight Lieutenants Dick and Kendall were currently staring at a grouping of small air vents in the arched blood-red ceiling, discussing possible ways of breaking them open. The damn things were too high up though; even if someone stood on another's shoulders, they couldn't reach them.

"So what now?" Matthews exasperated.

"We wait," Dick decided.

* * *

The Agent watched the imprisoned humans through the air vents; they were seemingly unaware that someone was up here watching them, so close to them.

The alarm had been raised minutes ago, though they didn't seem to be actively searching for an intruder. He wondered if that was because they had discovered the remains of the warrior, and had decided his living among the humans for too long had corrupted him. He was hopeful, but this situation was deteriorating, and there was an army of alien warriors between him and his eventual escape.

His eyes drifted to the scarred man cradled in the older woman's arms. The Agent found he couldn't look at the scars for too long, his brain imagining the kind of suffering he had been through to attain those marks. That man could eventually be very useful when the Agent escaped.

Suddenly, he heard a clang off to his right; when he looked he saw nothing. Must have been some of the old machinery up here, he told himself. According to some of the other warriors -he had had no contact with any of the high-ranking officials, wasn't even sure who they were, except for the more extravagant way they dressed- there were creatures in the vents, creatures that had escaped from their home planet and hid among the underworld of these tunnels. He didn't believe there was anything here; he hadn't found any creatures so far.

He looked down, and saw the doors open in the massive cell below.

Four warriors barged their way into the cell, and slapped some of their race's hideous food in bowls on the floor before leaving the prisoners to their so-called meal. It was, at a pinch, gruel, though even that was giving it too much credit.

Bang!

That noise was louder, and definitely closer now.

Time to go. He crawled away, and found another junction, taking the upward route, scrambling up the ladder.

* * *

"[Report,]" the Second ordered. The two warriors stood in front of him didn't look him in the eye, though they could tell he was angry.

The Second already knew they had nothing to report beyond the standard searches finishing, and new ones starting.

"[We have found no trace of an intruder, Second,]" the taller warrior replied.

"[NONE?!]" the Second bellowed in their faces.

"[No *physical* evidence,]" the other warrior replied poignantly.

The bigger warrior was instantly calm; this had the Second's attention, and all thoughts of ripping the two warriors limb from black limb exited his mind in a hurry.

"[Explain.]"

The warriors shifted nervously, and exchanged glances that the Second saw as encouragement. His reputation for killing the bringers of bad news was well known throughout the warrior cadre, a reputation he fully deserved, and had worked hard to attain.

"[Many warriors have reported hearing tiny noises in the air vents.]"

"[Tiny?]" the Second queried, curious at the description.

"[The noises were so quiet that the warriors believed they were... imagining it, sir,]" the other warrior added.

The Second nodded.

"[What are your names?]"

"[Kh'har'vesh,]" the first warrior answered in a hurry.

"[Kh'har'vash,]" the second added.

It was not unheard of for the Lord's warriors to be family members, and serve in the same units, as their names suggested: "Kh" identified them as warriors, whilst the "har" was their family name, and the final prefix identified their personal names. These two -Vesh and Vash- were warrior brothers from the family of Har.

"[Vesh, and Vash, I want the two of you to lead search teams into the air vents, and discover the source of these so-called noises. It may be the intruder, it may be nothing more than a faulty air vent.]"

"[Understood, Second Yh'par'ban,]" Vesh replied, snapping his foot-talons together in a salute. The two warriors span on the balls of their avian feet, and marched out of the Second's sight.

When this was over, Second Yh'par'ban thought, he would have to kill those two brothers for using his name so frivolously, and with so much disrespect in their voices.

He would also have to report to Lord Yh'reth'gar about the investigation into the intruder.

* * *

"[The Second is not to be trusted,]" Vesh said to his older brother.

"[Agreed, little brother,]" Vash replied. "[I believe he intends to kill us.]"

"[We should consider a plan to stop him.]"

"[Or to escape.]"

As they walked, they whispered in hushed tones, creating a backup plan for themselves.

* * *

Hannah had Adam's head in her arms. The rest of his body was shaking. Every now and then, he mumbled the same things he had repeated before about time travel, something silver, and a woman named Polly Jenkins.

Most of the others were now asleep.

The cell lights were dimmed, though there was still a confused sense of time: even with the lights, there was no real night and day, though Hannah was sure they had only been there a day, maybe two. She couldn't honestly tell. Sasha and Sapphire were blissfully asleep; Sasha leaning on her big sister, whilst Sapphire had her arms wrapped defensively around her little sister. Hannah couldn't help but smile: only days ago, the girls were at each other's throats, arguing about everything under the sun, like all young sisters did.

She didn't want to think about the mess in the corner -there were no bathroom facilities so they had designated the far corner as the toilet where they could squat and do their business. There was a pile of excrement there already, as the older and younger members of the group couldn't hold it in. The smell was nauseating, and more than one person had thrown up on the floor.

"Silver," Adam whispered, and suddenly bolted upright, eyes wide open, alert like a jungle cat.

The sudden movement, rather than the brief noise, woke the others up. Bleary-eyed, they all turned to the source of the disturbance.

"You're awake," Jack Digby croaked wearily. Besides Adam, he seemed to be the one suffering the most from the ordeal. He was old, and frail, and previous injuries sustained in his long-ago military service had hampered and dogged him his entire life.

"What do you remember?" Hannah asked. "You kept mumbling something about time travel, and a woman named Polly Jenkins."

"I-" he paused, wondering if they would think him mad. "I can't be sure, but I think I was travelling through time."

The others stared at one another, the same thought on their mind: *he's bloody mad.*

But Digby, bless his old heart, wasn't so quick to judge.

"How?" the old Chelsea Veteran asked, throwing scowls at the disbelievers. Adam could see he was as open-minded as he had become in the last few days.

"I don't know; they talked about it in an alien language. I kept flashing to other places: places I've never been before. I saw the future: man's first faster-than-light engine; the first mission to colonise another planet; the beginning of World War Three." He closed his eyes, the haunting vision of seeing Earth's atmosphere ablaze with massive detonations. "At first, I was sure I was imagining it, but I could touch things, smell things, even talk to the people." He gestured to the torn overalls that had magically appeared on his body. "I got this from the colony ship, *Mayflower.*" He paused. "And there was a woman."

"Polly Jenkins?" one of the gay couple suggested.

Adam nodded. He stood up, and wobbled a bit before gaining his balance.

"Given the state you were in when they brought you back," Hannah began, "I really suggest you don't walk around."

"I doubt that'll matter to *them*," Adam snorted, nodding at the door.

"What do they want?" Digby asked, trying to get to his feet. The father of the large Gilpin family, Kevin, helped him up, though the Chelsea Veteran shrugged off the help as soon as he was standing. Kevin paid no heed to the veteran's attitude, after all, Digby was once a soldier; he didn't *want* the help -he didn't want to be seen to be helpless and weak.

"I honestly don't know," Adam answered truthfully, "but something tells me they're not here to fix the Chelsea-Arsenal game."

Kevin's wife, Mouse, demanded, "Who are they?"

"I. Don't. Know," Adam answered forcefully. "Aliens would be my guess."

"*Guess*?" someone else asked in a rather snooty voice. The owner stood up and stamped into Adam's view. Why were they asking *him* all these questions?

"They didn't exactly give me a brochure," Adam retorted angrily. "Who are you anyway?"

"Kenneth McDonald," the man answered. He was about the same age as Adam, in his mid-twenties, though his long hair was straightened and jet-black. "I'm a writer."

"That's helpful," Adam grumbled.

"I beg your pardon?" Kenneth the writer said, stepping in front of Adam. Despite the situation, McDonald was full of swaggering arrogance that came from someone who always got their way. "As a reporter and writer, I have certain rights that deserve some respect, and you will tell me what is going on!"

There was a tear on the left shoulder of Adam's overalls. The military personnel saw it, and were somewhat shocked. The tattoo was a red combat knife surrounded by a black shield and a depiction of the sea with the words 'By Strength And Guile' underneath.

"Shit," exclaimed Matthews.

"Yeah," Lieutenant Dick nodded.

Whittard finally explained for the benefit of the civilians, "He's Special Boat Service."

* * *

2006.

A man named Block hurried through the streets of London; he knew he was being followed, he knew they were MI5 brought in because of the severity and scope of his crimes.

He made it to the nearest Underground station when he caught sight of his tail: a man and a woman, eyeing him suspiciously from the wrong side of the turnstiles. He hurried toward the escalators that would take him deeper into the station, and closer toward freedom.

He had murdered a slew of girls, tortured them in more and more sickening ways, and then left clues for the Police to follow ineptly. It had been all over the news, as had the information that MI5 had taken an interest in the case. He had been taken to trial, but his slippery lawyer had made some kind of deal behind closed doors, and Block was free.

He made it to the escalators, and bound down them two steps at a time. The MI5 agents quickened their pace, trying to keep him in view.

The throng of people made it hard to see the agents behind him, which meant that they could barely see him either.

He chuckled as the pair of agents bundled into an old couple on the escalators.

Hot air blasted through the lobby between the platforms, denoting the arrival of a train. Block bolted for the platform the train was arriving at, just in time for the doors of the carriage to open.

Block stepped onto the train, only moments before the agents did.

Block stumbled into a young man with a briefcase. Block realised with no small horror that it was his slippery lawyer on his way to late day at work.

* * *

Bradley Stanford, Junior Partner at his father's firm, Stanford Brothers, stood gawping at the screen. The revelation of Caine's previous career was a stunner. His firm had dealt with a case representing a murdered Marine Colonel, and Bradley was very aware of the Royal Marines' well-earned reputation as being the hardiest and most dangerous of the world's military.

Bradley Stanford was, in fact, the same age as Adam, only older by a month, with an expensive shoes and suit -now soiled- dark scared eyes, and clutching his leather briefcase to his chest, like a precious lifeline.

The man stood by his side was unhealthily thin, with severely cut blonde hair, sunken eyes, and a blade-thin face, with a permanent scowl that could scare the stripes off a zebra. The man had called himself Block. Bradley knew him from a case he had been working on before getting on the fateful underground journey. Block had been accused of murdering twelve young women. The case had been strong but Bradley had got him off on a technicality and a bribe, thus attracting the attention of MI5.

He had been dragged from the strange dentist's chair along with Block. The creatures were hideous, and frightening. Bradley was scared out of his mind.

The creatures' leader turned to Bradley, its inner lips trying to form words in English.

"What is Special Boat Service?" the creature asked.

Bradley stammered, but couldn't form any words other than complete gibberish.

Block answered, in that low, sadistic growl that was permanently a part of his scary repertoire.

"They are an elite strike force that specialise in water-based, and small-unit combat."

The creature seemed to take this in.

"They are dangerous," the creature nodded.

"They are nothing," Block growled.

"Indeed? Then perhaps we should send you back in there?"

"Gladly," the pale man sneered.

"I think not," the creature said with disdain. "My Lord and I have plans for the two of you."

"Why us?" Bradley finally spoke.

Second Yh'par'ban's inner lips receded into an evil grin. "Because you both have no love for your fellow humans, or are at least biologically willing to betray them. But not now: later."

"How can you possibly know that?" Bradley queried nervously. The creature didn't say anything, but simply nodded to the guards.

"Where are you taking me?" Block demanded. Bradley didn't complain that Block didn't include him in that statement: he was more than willing to be removed from Block's disturbing presence. The guards manhandled them out of the room, of which Bradley had blissfully seen precious little on account of the bad lighting.

"You'll see," the creature cackled.

* * *

Bradley and Block were taken to another large room, one with several of the dentist chairs they had inhabited before. The creatures escorting them gestured to the tables. Bradley didn't understand, and Block was just being difficult for the sake of being difficult.

The nearest creature to Bradley picked him up with rough calloused hands and threw him onto the table. Block, seeing the potential for a fight, turned and made to strike the nearest alien, but was backhanded, and then manhandled onto the table, before solid manacles snapped over his wrists and ankles.

Weedier creatures stepped into the room, bringing equipment and several small vials of a blue glowing liquid that they kept eyeing warily.

Before they knew it, they had IV drips in their arms, and were screaming in pain.

* * *

"[Inject the supplement,]" the Second ordered.

Another pair of small vials appeared from the trolley; this time they were a bright green, although they were in fact a similar chemical to the blue version. The Second didn't know the technical term given to it by the scientists, nor cared.

The green liquid pumped through the small transparent tubes, and the two subjects began jerking and spasming as if having an epileptic fit.

A sickly pale green light began to emanate from the two humans.

In an uncharacteristically philosophical moment, the Second -still staring at the green light- thought that perhaps Time itself was rebelling against the unorthodox method in which the scientists were showing the two humans the possible future.

The moment passed in a flash.

* * *

The green light, and the mind-numbing pain that went with it, dissipated to reveal something that was definitely not the room they had been in before. They were stood in front of a massive viewport, standing on a metal deck, not unlike the flooring they had encountered so far in the alien facility.

On the other side of the window was an insane display of destruction.

It was Earth, far below them, the crest of the Arctic spinning terribly slowly into view.

The Earth was on fire.

Missiles launched from the surface, striking starships in orbit, trailed lines of smoke, whilst powerful energy weapons fired down on the planet, scorching the ground, and boiling any of the oceans they touched. Filthy brown clouds hung in the atmosphere, like flies over a corpse.

Bright red starships descended through the planet's atmosphere, weapons blazing, swatting human aircraft out of the air with hideously advanced technology. Transports landed in every major city, troops pouring out onto the streets.

Elite troops stormed 10 Downing Street, the White House, and every other building that housed the leaders of the world. The troops dragged presidents, prime ministers, premieres, emperors, kings and queens from their residences and brutally executed them in front of the public.

Humans were tortured in their thousands, others were killed, the rest were forced into slavery, lines of them walking the streets under the guard of the aliens, whilst their cities burned around them.

It was a nightmare.

Block revelled in the fear he imagined was rolling off the planet below.

Bradley soiled himself, shaking violently enough to almost vibrate. Tears rolled down his cheeks; they were not, however, tears of sadness and anguish at his planet's plight, but tears of fear -fear for his own life. Upon seeing the destruction of his homeworld, he was more worried about his own sad pathetic life, than his people.

"Glorious, is it not?" a deep voice said loudly. The two humans turned to see an overweight version of the creatures, with a more intricate set of armour.

The creature stepped down off of a throne-like dais, and two more creatures, both with red cloaks over one shoulder, and carrying some kind of pike, stepped down with him, their yellow eyes never looking anywhere but straight forward.

Bradley was terrified out of his mind, and managed to soil himself again.

The big creature's inner lips crudely copied a human smile.

"This is what your world *should* be."

"What is this?" Block asked calm-as-you-like.

"This is what your world will be if you help us. This event takes place a year after you were taken from your people. Help us, and there will be much reward."

"How is this possible?" The Lord knew he was referring to the time travel.

"We acquired certain technologies and chemicals that allow us to experience many possible futures, mister Block."

Block didn't know how the Lord could know who they were, or how he was here as if he had stepped through from the past -he simply didn't want the headache that would surely come with the answer.

Too terrified for words, Bradley said nothing except whimper incoherently.

Block sneered at the young lawyer, then turned to the creature.

"What would you have me do?"

* * *

Adam woke from an indistinct nightmare. What had it been about? He shook it off, realising it didn't matter compared to the nightmare he was currently still stuck in. Little Sasha had her head resting on his chest, Sapphire's on his stomach. Hannah was sleeping beside him, her arm entwined with his. When the hell had *that* happened? He hadn't even remembered falling asleep, let alone with three women of varying ages resting on him.

The others began waking up slowly, some from nightmares, some from blank nothingness.

They had all slept, but none of them looked it. There were no beds, no blankets; they all had to make do with the hard metal floor. Adam didn't mind so much -he'd slept on far rougher floors. But the others were revolted by the lack of facilities, as if being clean was something to worry about.

The revelation of his former career hadn't gone over well with the non-military members of the survivors, though he suspected that those *in* the military were slightly in awe of him. They didn't say anything, though he saw the looks in their eyes, as if seeing some war hero or something.

Adam didn't like the attention.

The doors to the cell opened suddenly, and several of the aliens bounded through, snapping orders in their clacking language, and aiming weapons in Adam's direction. They were taking no chances -taking him whilst he was barely awake, and not giving him time to react and fight back. The leading warrior fired his rifle, the stun bolt hitting Adam squarely in the chest.

He spasmed and yelped in pain before succumbing to the darkness of unconsciousness.

Hannah, Sasha, Sapphire and the soldiers and RAF officers shouted and swore at the aliens to let him go as they dragged him away; none of them actually tried to hit the aliens, since the barrels of more rifles were suddenly pointed in their direction threateningly.

* * *

"Getting really tired of being chained up," Adam called out when he finally opened his eyes. His head was pounding, threatening to detonate his head if it carried on.

"Something tells me you wouldn't lie still if we didn't," the Second smiled evilly.

"Could always try and find out," Adam snorted, tugging at the solid manacles tying him to yet another steel table, probably even the same one.

The Second simply looked over at a table nearby.

Inwardly, Adam screamed for help, though he didn't show it on his face. These creatures were insane, and this one in particular seemed to be in love with inflicting pain.

The table the creature looked at was covered with instruments that could only be used for torture. There were wicked serrated blades, electronic prongs attached to energy sources, and what could only be an alien blowtorch.

"I am going to enjoy this," the Second cackled.

He reached for the serrated blade at the nearest end of the collection.

Adam silently prayed to whomever was listening to hurry up and rescue him. He was certainly trained to resist torture and interrogation, but there was a point that training and willpower simply wouldn't be enough to hold off the pain. And he was still weak from the time travel and being stunned.

The Second rose the knife precisely, and then plunged the implement into Adam's leg.

Adam didn't cry out, didn't make a sound.

The Second missed all the main arteries, so that Adam wouldn't bleed to death right there on the table, thus spoiling his pleasure. The pain was bad, though Adam had had worse.

"Pussy," he breathed.

The Second twisted the knife, and a hundred searing pokers suddenly flared up in his leg. Adam still did not cry out in pain, though there were no more insults.

A second knife was jammed into his other leg.

And a fist slammed into his cheek, snapping his head round. He bit the inside of his mouth, and crimson blood welled up, spilling from between his lips.

A pair of alien warriors stood to either side of the table, glaring at Adam hatefully.

The fist punched him again and again. His cheek was swelling up, bruises forming quickly. Another fist slammed into his midsection, driving the wind from his lungs. He coughed up blood from the cuts in his mouth, and spat it out on his chest. Another clawed fist crunched into his soft side, right into his kidneys.

"What the fuck do you want from me?" he finally blurted.

A cackling laughter passed between the aliens.

"Nothing," the Second replied. "This is just an... examination into the human tolerance for pain."

The knife twisted again, and Adam finally cried out in pain.

* * *

The Agent watched from above, lying face down in the air vents, peering through the grill, as the human was tortured. He felt nauseous just watching.

* * *

The Second cackled as he sliced the human's leg meat with varying blades. The man's blood was beginning to drain.

He continued to slice, opening small shallow cuts all over to maximise the pain without too much mess. Still the human didn't admit defeat by crying out.

In a moment of rash anger, the Second plunged the straight dagger into Adam's belly. He was pleased to hear the human finally give in. Adam had let out a bloodcurdling roar of pain. The man was shaking, and pale.

His blood lust sated for now, the Second pulled the dagger out.

"[Patch him up, throw him back to his friends.]"

* * *

The Agent, still watching, vomited in the vent. He did it as quietly as he could, though knew someone had heard him. He moved on, crawling through yet more vents. He wondered if he should free the human being tortured below.

No, he thought, *I haven't finished in here yet.*

The decision would haunt him for years to come.

* * *

Adam was dumped unceremoniously into the cell, his limp form slapping painfully against the unyielding metal floor.

The guards retreated, and the doors were locked once again.

Hannah rushed to Adam's side.

"Oh my God, what did they do to you?" she cried.

"They..." he gasped for breath. "Tortured me." Another long pause as he struggled for breath. "They wanted to know human pain tolerances."

"Jesus Christ, they really did a number on him," Lieutenant Dick exclaimed.

"What purpose does this serve?" Hannah whispered, as Adam lay on his back, his hands resting limply on his chest. His own blood was soaked into the overalls he wore, blurring the difference between clothes and skin.

PC Whimble crouched down, and checked him over. He went pale at the sight of the new wounds Adam had received.

"Jesus, this guy's soaked up enough injuries to sink a battleship," Whimble exclaimed. "He's been stabbed in both upper legs, and there are dozens of minor lacerations over his body. But it's all been healed."

"Everything life-threatening anyway," PC Norman said from beside him, pointing at a small bruised bulge in the side of Adam's ribcage. "Looks like they didn't bother to heal his broken ribs."

Hannah, in a tender moment, kissed Adam on the forehead. But he was gone, unconscious from the pain of his injuries.

The group all watched as Hannah and the two Constables tended to the wounded Marine. They were all dirty, exhausted, and their nerves were fraying to the point of obliteration, but for the most part, they were all concerned for Adam's well-being. For some the concern was genuine, seeing another in pain, for others it was relief that it wasn't them in that position.

They came for him again after another sleep cycle, barging in to the cell, weapons pointing into the other prisoners' faces, warning them away. The fleshy nostrils on their beaks contracted when they were assaulted by the smell of the human faeces and the unclean state of the prisoners.

West, his nerves frayed, made an attempt to stop them from taking the downed Marine. As punishment, he was smashed in the face with the butt of one of the rifles. His friends instantly formed a cordon around him, to prevent the guards from laying into him fully.

The creatures backed off cautiously, cackling in laughter at the forced bravery of their charges.

They dragged Adam out of the cell -he was still unconscious.

The Agent, in a bold move, activated his holo-disguise, and jumped down into an empty corridor. He needed to get past a broken air vent that had buckled inward years ago. There hadn't been enough space for a human of any size to get past. So he had backtracked, exited the vent into the corridor, and gone searching for the nearest vent access hatch.

He wasn't planning on staying out of the vents for long: the creatures were by now aware that his disguise's appearance was a traitor. He sneaked as quietly as he could down the corridor, and through into another hangar, much like the one that had contained the strange device until he blew it to fernikking hell.

He turned a corner, and slammed awkwardly into a warrior.

The two tumbled to the floor in a clatter of long limbs, blades skittering away across the deck. The warrior let out a gurgled cry of disbelief.

Something smashed, and the holo-disguise flickered, and disappeared.

"Nark!" the Agent swore.

The two, human and alien both, jumped to their feet, scrambling for their fallen weapons. The Agent's combat knife was too far away to be useful, so they both went for the serrated blade dropped by the alien. The Agent got to it first, snapping it up, spinning round, and backhanding the alien across the face.

It stumbled back for a brief second.

The Agent plunged the knife at the creature's heart.

The tip of the blade stopped barely a millimetre from its chest. The creature had its taloned hands wrapped around the Agent's wrist, squeezing harshly, and without remorse.

They grunted with the effort of struggling against each other's strength; they were evenly matched, and the Agent had spent two years fighting alongside these creatures to know their physical strength. So the Agent dropped the knife; as he thought, the creature let go of his wrists in an attempt to retrieve the blade.

The Agent drove his knee into the thing's face. It flew backwards, blood spurting from its tiny beak-nostrils.

The Agent snatched the blade up, and dove at the creature's chest, blade point-first.

* * *

This time, Adam wasn't manacled to a metal table.

Instead, his hands were bound behind him with a rope, and he was placed face-down on the floor of yet another large room.

He was sure he could hear water splashing somewhere, but didn't know where it was coming from, or what it could mean. His chest was throbbing, and he found that the metal flooring was pressing his broken ribs into his lungs, labouring his breathing severely.

The Second stepped into his view, without saying a word. The creature nodded to someone outside Adam's view, and suddenly a massive metal claw picked up Adam.

Adam tried to struggle, but the claw squeezed until it cut the circulation off to his extremities.

Adam quickly found out what the water noise was: it was a tank, a huge water tank, and he had a sudden vision of him being eaten alive by something large and shark-like with pointed teeth.

Before he had a chance to take a deep breath, the water rushed up to meet him, and suddenly he was underwater. The water itself was startlingly crystal clear, with glass sides surrounded by dozens of glaring warriors. There was no shark, and Adam thanked whatever lord was looking over him for that. Of course, the claw didn't release him, instead it held him there, dangling, unable to move, or breath without a lungful of water.

He struggled to get himself free, and found he could kick with his legs, but it did sod all for his predicament, as he was still in the sodding crane.

The tiny amount of air in his lungs began to burn in his chest, his body struggling to hold onto precious life.

All those times Adam had heard other soldiers talk of how their lives flashed before their eyes when they thought they were going to die, he had never believed it. He had been shot, stabbed, beaten, even crushed by a falling building, but had never come truly close to death. Until now.

Visions of growing up in father's Cambridgeshire home flashed through his mind, followed by his harsh childhood with his sisters, leaving private school, joining the Royal Marines, the multitudes of missions he was sent on -they all flashed by horribly quickly. One stuck in his mind: the passing out parade after finishing basic training, where Mother and his youngest sisters had watched, waving and giggling as the recruits marched around the square in full dress uniform. Mother had been immensely proud of him, Father had disowned him.

Red began to creep into his vision as he began the irrevocable descent into death.

The air was gone now, and he panicked. His legs became heavy, even with the massive crane around him. His body began to shut down, betraying him to the warm water.

His vision blacked out, and he stopped struggling.

Soon, his heart stopped, his lungs shut down, and his body was still.

Adam Caine was dead.

* * *

The Agent stood up from the corpse of the warrior, leaving the knife in its chest.

He was breathing heavily, not from the effort of killing, but the sheer shock he had received at being rumbled in such a stupid way.

Of course, fate and irony go hand-in-hand in the big wide universe.

He heard footsteps from around the corner he had turned seconds ago. The corridors were horrible conductors of noise, bouncing echoes upon echoes around the walls until the original sound was no longer discernable from the echoes. The footsteps could actually be coming from any direction.

"Nark," he whispered, knowing he was only seconds away from discovery yet again. He hooked his hands under the armpits of the dead creature. He had to hide the body sharpish. He hauled with all his strength, the armour scraping against the deck. The noise was tremendous as sparks even lifted from underneath the body. Whoever was coming must have heard him, because the approaching footsteps quickened their pace, and became louder and louder, accompanied by the *click-click-click* of sharp talons on metal.

The Agent found an access panel close by. It was marked as tool storage, though he doubted it had been used in years. Opening it, he found there was indeed no tools, but enough space for himself and the corpse.

* * *

Vesh and Vash span round the corner almost the instant the Agent closed the tool storage locker. They didn't see the scrape marks, though they were sure there had been something here.

The two brothers looked at each other warily, then back to the gloomy corridor.

They walked on, dismissing the noise as nothing more than the ghosts that haunted the corridors.

Second Yh'par'ban would understand.

* * *

The Agent understood.

The two warriors had been spooked by the noise, and he watched them through the tiny slitted grill in the locker door. The smell from the corpse was hideous. It was bad enough when they were alive, but their blood seemed to be designed to smell almost toxic enough to gag a maggot.

The footsteps of the two warriors disappeared, and the Agent opened the locker door, breathing a sigh of relief as he stepped out. He cursed himself for his stupidity; now he would have to dispose of the body, and quickly before yet another patrol came along.

Once again, he grabbed the armpits of the creature, and began to drag it. He could see the hatch he was looking for, circular and smack in the middle of the ceiling, away from any method of accessing it from below.

This was going to be difficult.

* * *

Adam didn't understand.

He was alive.

Well, he wasn't too sure of that.

Could this be the afterlife?

Stuck in a permanent blackness?

Then he realised his eyes were still closed.

He felt so bad he just couldn't believe it. His body felt like it had been pushed through a mincer and then put back together in the wrong order. Pain emanated from every part of him. He tried to move, but his muscles protested, stiff as they were. He was in that much pain he could clearly feel his bones beneath his muscles.

He was groggy, and his vision was blurred.

All he could see was a rocky floor, cracked and dented by some unknown force.

Where the hell was he?

And what was that horrible smell?

Of course he knew what it was: decay, decomposition, death. How could he have possibly forgotten? It was a smell he had been intimately familiar with for many years.

It was strong, not just coming from one direction, but every direction.

Stale sweat lingered in the air as well, not to mention the metallic tang of pints and pints of blood yet to dry.

There was a raucous cheering sound as his hearing began to return as well. The noise shrieked from all around, like agitated birds in an aviary.

His vision snapped fully into focus, and he wished he was still blind.

He was lying in a purpose-built wide pit, about the size of a football field. Alien skeletons littered the floor, which was marred by splashes of brain matter, blood, and the occasional rotted internal organ. The stone sides rose up three stories high, topped off with metal fencing woven around metal spikes, some of which had already been used as kebab sticks, bits of body parts still hanging on the pointed ends.

This was like nothing he had ever seen before.

There was even an ominous black steel gate on the opposite side of the arena, just like in those movies that included a giant frightening creature that tried to eat the hero or heroine. Only this wasn't a movie, nor did he think there was going to be anything approaching a happy ending.

Despite the bad lighting, he could see the same armoured bird-like creatures pounding fists into the air, chanting and jeering. The big regale creature he had seen before his time travelling appeared beside a tall throne sunk into a pulpit above the arena.

The creature raised its arms for silence, and received it instantly.

The creature clacked on for some time in its native language, gaining some murmured assents among the crowd, before he turned to Adam.

"I am Lord Yh'reth'gar, you, human, are Adam Caine, and you are about to die."

I thought I was already dead, Adam's mind complained.

There was an evil glint in the creature's equally evil eyes.

A murderous roar of jeering launched itself into the air as the crowd went berserk, screaming insults in broken and stilted English at the bewildered Adam. He managed to pick himself up off the floor, with the help of the slick walls. He didn't want to think about the *reason* the walls were slippery

The doors cranked open, rising up like a portcullis on an old English castle. The metal squealed in protest. It really was like something out of a '70s swords-and-sandals film; a perversion of Roman arenas of old.

Just how barbaric are these people? Adam wondered.

The door fully opened, and something stamped out, the floor vibrating with every footstep. The beast had to duck through the door it was so big, and stepped out into the arena, staring at Adam with a primal hate.

The beast reared up, and roared so loud Adam had to cover his ears.

It was a Tyrannosaurus Rex.

"Oh shit."

* * *

This has to be a nightmare, Adam thought. *There's no possible way this is real.*

Fifteen metres long, five-and-a-half high, and weighing in at an insane eight tonnes, it was definitely a T-Rex. Its tough mottled green skin covered massive rippling muscles powerful enough to crush a tank. Its tail flicked slowly behind it, counterbalancing its front-heavy body, whilst its metre-and-a-half head pointed directly at Adam, carrying dozens of razor-sharp flesh-tearing teeth longer than a bread knife, in a permanent, vicious, grinning mouth.

Sixty-five million years and nineteen metres separated the two.

Adam couldn't move, he was frightened stiff.

The massive carnivorous dinosaur had evoked a primordial fear in him, a fear that dated back to the first mammals millions of years ago.

There was a single collective pause of silence in the crowd.

The metal gates closed behind the beast.

The T-Rex roared again, ducked its head down, and charged.

Adam was still rooted to the spot, unable to accept that this was a dinosaur.

Each footstep created a stomping bang as its weight landed on the floor via its muscled legs.

Stomp.

Adam stood stock-still.

Stomp.

He couldn't move.

Stomp.

Inches away from him, the Rex lunged with its massive mouth open, revealing the glinting knife-teeth within. Adam's survival instinct kicked in, and he dived out of the beast's reach, passing inches in front of the thing's jaw line. He rolled, and came to his feet, the exhaustion and pain forgotten as surges of adrenaline filled his body with new strength.

The beast, too big to turn as quickly, slammed headfirst into the stone wall, cracking the structure, and roaring in frustration.

The crowd booed and hissed their displeasure, but Lord Yh'reth'gar smiled. This was going to be interesting.

Using its tiny forearms to balance itself, the Rex picked itself up, and turned, causing yet more vibrations through the floor. It flicked its tail, clipping Adam, who had been concentrating on the thing's mouth.

He flew backwards through the air, and crashed into the wall. Yet another rib fractured, adding to his injuries.

The dinosaur charged him again, swaying its head from to side-to-side, not falling for the same thing again.

"So, you can learn," Adam breathed.

Dreading the decision, he charged forward himself, bellowing an incomprehensible war cry to release the intense fright in his body. Centimetres from the dinosaur's massive head, Adam dove, and rolled under the beast's snapping jaws, passing between its huge legs. He rolled lengthways out of the way of the tail. The Rex wasn't the only one who could learn.

The Rex had reached too far down, and its attempt at snapping up Adam overbalanced it.

It tipped over onto its front, cracking its lower jaw on the floor.

It let out a great big huff of stale breath.

It squealed.

Adam was suddenly on its head, pounding with his fists into its skull. It was too tough, and the beast began to rock its head, trying to shake Adam into a position whereupon it could eat him with its monstrous mouth. He punched again and again, using his legs to clamp onto its neck.

The creature roared in pain as Adam switched tactics and punched with both fists into both of its football-sized obsidian eyes.

It was blind.

Adam lost his grip, and tumbled backwards, bouncing off its bulging flank, gasping as the breath left his damaged lungs. The Rex's flailing legs nearly squashed him as it tried to blindly right itself. It roared and howled, smashing its head against the walls, as if that would stop the pain.

The crowd were not pleased, seeing their favourite sport ruined by a dirty human. More boos and hisses spat down at Adam.

He desperately looked around for some kind of weapon, and saw, to his surprise, a spear dropped by a previous victim. It was two metres long, with a dark metal shaft, and a blood-encrusted blade that curved into a wicked point.

With a weak roar, the dinosaur jumped to its feet.

It sniffed the air; Adam realised he hadn't thought about that possibility.

It found his scent, let out an ear-splitting roar, and lunged at Adam.

It wouldn't matter where he went, it would know where he was all the time, no matter what speed he could run.

"Bollocks," he cursed.

He jumped backwards, the spear in both hands, holding the weapon steady, pointing the tip toward the T-Rex. He shut his eyes; there were just some deaths he did not need to witness, and being eaten by a sixty-five-million-year old killing machine was one of them, especially when *he* was the intended victim.

Adam could smell the hot rank breath he was so close. He felt immense pressure on the end of the spear, and it slammed into his stomach, squashing his innards horrendously painfully.

He waited for the inevitable munching and death to ensue.

Nothing.

The dinosaur let out a huge stuttered stale breath, and then silence.

Adam dared open his eyes, and looked straight into the teeth of the Tyrannosaurus. The huge rending teeth were only an inch from his nose, and the huge head was resting on his legs. The beast wasn't breathing. He could see the tip of the spear protruding from the top of the beast's head, covered in fresh brain matter. Considering how small the brain of a dinosaur was in proportion to the rest of the body, it was a million-to-one shot.

The crowd was silent, almost in fearful awe as Adam levered the massive head away from him, and extracted himself from the floor.

He limped to the centre of the arena, and glared at the surrounding crowd.

"SCREW YOU!!!" he bellowed in his loudest drill sergeant voice.

"Indeed," the enthroned alien chuckled.

Adam hadn't been expecting an answer to the rhetorical movie quote.

"You are interestingly defiant, Adam Caine," Lord Yh'reth'gar clacked. "You have defeated your past."

The phrase struck a chord in Adam's exhausted mind. *Of course*, he thought, *the dinosaur was taken from its* own *time, just like they put me through that time travel experiment, seeing Earth's future. And here I was, thinking it was a genetic experiment of some sort. Silly me.*

"Now you must defeat your present," the Lord ordered, gesturing to the gates once again.

The gates opened, and out stepped a figure in the same red armour and garb as the other warrior aliens.

Except the wearer wasn't one of the aliens.

It was a human. Not just any human, it was one of the prisoners from Adam's cell; one of the two he had noticed hadn't been returned to the cell with the others.

The man was unhealthily thin, though he must have been strong enough to wear the thick chitinous armour. Beady, hooded grey eyes stared out from an angular, skinny face, with almost-white blonde hair. Adam's mind compared him to Hannibal Lecter, though he was sure the man standing before him was worse somehow. Just looking into those dead eyes sent unconscious shivers down his spine.

"Block," Lord Yh'reth'gar called, looking at the armoured human. "Kill him... if you can."

Block sneered at the Lord, then cackled evilly at Adam, flexing his fists.

Christ, Adam thought, *the psycho's enjoying this.*

Block charged, growling and snarling his contentment.

Adam, bone-weary and riddled with immense pain, didn't move. He couldn't move. His body just would not let him. Block laid in with his shoulder, tackling the bigger man to the ground.

The psycho didn't let up, punching and kicking Adam, venting fury he'd kept in check for days, screaming nonsensically, almost as though he were possessed by a demon.

He wore out quickly, breathing heavily as he spat insult after hideous insult at the downed man.

Adam, unwilling to endure any more pain, lashed out with his foot, catching Block on the chin. It snapped his head back, and blood spurted from his mouth.

Adam's strength was waning, his vision was blurring again, and his heart and lungs were nearly at the point of shutting down. He needed to end this quickly, before he could no longer fight, or even breathe. He wouldn't kill the man, no matter how much he may deserve it.

The crowd were jeering again, their blood sport renewed once more. Adam was more than happy to spoil their fun.

Block looked up in time to see Adam bearing down on him, rage in his eyes. Pissing off a policeman was one thing, as he had done a month ago, but angering a trained professional soldier was something completely different, and altogether more frightening.

It took one punch, only one, to smash Block's jaw, and knock him out cold.

Both men collapsed.

Adam blacked out.

His heart stopped... again.

* * *

When he returned to the cell, Adam slumped against the wall.

He was beaten.

His will was weakening.

The others around him, specifically the soldiers, Hannah, and her two girls, grew more and more worried about him. Although the aliens had healed his most grievous wounds, they left the smaller ones untouched, weakening him bit by bit. Yet it wasn't the injuries that were the main concern: his mental state was fraying. Being beaten again and again was taking its toll on Adam's psyche.

Having been dumped in the cell after his post-fight healing, Adam had sought comfort in the nearest empty corner, pulled his knees to his chest, and sobbed.

He couldn't take anymore.
He just couldn't.

* * *

A day and a night went by.

Blissfully, the creatures didn't come for Adam for a while, giving Adam some much needed rest.

When he woke, he found the three combat engineers discussing with Jack Digby, the differences between the modern and wartime Army.

"Good evening," Hannah said softly. She had a worried look on her face, though Adam wasn't sure it was unwarranted. His vision still swam, and his limbs were still in agony. But he could move, which was decidedly more important than the pain. Unsteadily, he managed to brace himself against the wall, and stand up.

"Adam, what are you doing?" Hannah demanded, in a very motherly voice.

"I've got to get out of here," Adam said weakly. He took one step back from the doors, and hoofed a massive kick. The impact shuddered down his leg, adding to the damage he had already sustained. "Y'hear me?" he shouted to the ceiling. "I want out!" He kicked the door again, and again, shouting out to whoever was listening.

A voice called out over some kind of hidden tannoy system. "*Enough!*" Adam thought it sounded like Yh'reth'gar's voice. "*You will not be able to break out of that room, Adam Caine; I suggest you stop before you injure yourself permanently.*"

Adam didn't heed the warning, and didn't notice the alarmed looks on many of the faces of the other prisoners at the mention of his name.

"Jesus Christ, you're Adam Caine," exclaimed Private West.

Adam stopped when he finally realised they were all staring at him.
"So?"

"You're a bloody war hero," Whittard said, slightly in awe. "The youngest soldier to become a Warrant Officer, and earned the Victoria Cross in Bosnia." Hannah's eyes opened so wide they almost popped out of her head. The prisoners were mostly British, and knew what the VC was, and what it meant to be awarded one.

Adam sighed. He didn't need this now. So he kept kicking, harder and harder each time.

The others were shocked to see that he was actually denting the door.

Suddenly, the doors opened, and Adam's hideously strong kick planted itself on the chest of the warrior coming through to beat him unconscious, launching the alien back to smash into the opposite wall.

Adam was hit multiple times by the energy weapons they used, and was thrown to the floor, landing at Hannah's feet. The children in the group cried in anguish and fear at seeing such treatment, whilst the adults looked at Adam with a mixture of pity and horror, seeing the punishment the man was taking.

The aliens left almost immediately, leaving the humans to once again tend to Adam.

* * *

When he came round again, Hannah cradled Adam in her arms, using strips of her skirt to dab his sweating forehead. She looked down into his pained face. Why were they doing this solely to him? What purpose did it serve? Was it because of his status as a soldier? Or simply because he had been the most defiant? She had been shocked to hear who he was: like many in Britain, she was aware of the SBS' reputation, and she had heard that one of their number had recently earned the Victoria Cross, though not who it had been.

Hadn't she represented a Nathaniel Caine some years ago? A man with more money than God, and who claimed that his son had deserted him to serve in the armed services, thus disowned? Could it be the same son, currently lying in her arms?

She was sure he wouldn't appreciate her asking.

His wounds were healing, though they were extensive. She worried that they may get infected in the poor conditions of the cell -several days without a flushing toilet made for a hideous smell that almost choked everyone in their sleep. They were ignoring it now, trying not to look at the pile of human excretion in the corner they had designated as the latrine area.

She looked back at his face, and saw him looking right back. She could see what the creatures saw in him: defiance, stubbornness that bordered on psychotic, courage, even nobility. Beneath all that was a longing; a longing that was mirrored in her own.

God help us, she thought, *are we falling in love?*

Then suddenly, Adam shoved her backwards and over onto her arse. She was about to shout at Adam when he was hit by stun blasts. Lost in her thoughts, she hadn't heard the door open, nor seen the creatures creep up behind them.

Adam had, and saved her from the agony and unconsciousness.

He cried out in immense pain, blue lightning arcing over his body as he arched his back, and went into convulsions.

"Why are you doing this?" Hannah spat at the creatures.

In reply, they clacked their insidious laughter at her, their obsidian beaks moving in an oddly human fashion.

They dragged Adam away.

When they were gone, she guiltily hoped they would kill him, so that his pain would finally be over.

But she didn't think it would ever be that easy.

* * *

This is way too easy, the Agent said to himself. He was still in the damn air vents, crawling around on his hands and knees. He'd finally set the last charge, having almost been caught several times by increasingly frequent patrols.

Now, he had to set the human prisoners free.

He was once again above their cell, avoiding looking at the pile in the corner.

The prisoners were bedraggled, their clothes dirty, their hair greasy and messy, and the smell was bloody awful.

He'd seen the one called Adam Caine dragged out.

Caine was the key: he was strong enough to free himself, if given an ample opportunity. The Agent grinned: he would *give* Caine the opportunity.

* * *

Adam was taken to a massive hangar, his limp feet dragging on the deck.

He was awake enough to see the strange massive device in the centre of the hangar, with lots of octagonal black disks arranged in a pattern, and the same strange blue light as he had seen before hung over the whole thing. This couldn't be good, even though it looked like someone had taken a grenade to it.

He was being taken to yet another table with manacles. How many of these things were there?

Like before, he was clamped to the table. But unlike before, several wire connections were being clipped to his skin, which could mean only one thing: electrocution.

He was too weak from the stun blasts to fight back, or even make a marginally witty comment.

He knew what was coming, and wasn't prepared in the least, despite all his training.

With a nod from one of the warriors, the scientists that seemed to be as numerous as the table-restraints threw a switch, and electricity, or something like it, poured through Adam's weakened body.

White-hot pain stabbed through the connections to his skin, burning him, and spreading through the rest of him.

He jerked and convulsed on the table, bruising himself.

Unable to control himself, he bit his tongue, and spat blood out over his chest.

* * *

The Agent watched from an air vent grill in the wall of the hangar, hoping this round of torture would end quicker for Caine. The Agent could see it in his face: Caine was losing the battle to keep a hold on his fragile soul and even more fragile sanity. He could smell the burning flesh, which stung his sinuses, and made his stomach retch in protest.

Then the unthinkable happened.

The duct plating around him began to buckle.

Damn this old place, the Agent had barely time to think before he, and a good portion of the metal wall crashed to the hangar floor. The Agent finally picked himself up off the floor, only to find fifteen stun weapons pointed at his face.

"Um... Ah," he said before being knocked out.

* * *

Vesh and Vash stepped up to the Second, who was stood in the massive command centre.

"[Report,]" Yh'par'ban ordered.

"[Second, whilst we were electrocuting the human Caine, another human interrupted us.]"

The Second turned to look at the two brothers.

"[What?!]"

Vesh nodded

"[He was hiding in the air vents; one of the bulkheads collapsed and he was revealed to us -we believe this is the one that killed your special operative.]"

The Second nodded thoughtfully, stroking his chin.

"[Have them taken to the throne room -Lord Yh'reth'gar will want to see them both. Continue your search; there may be more humans sneaking around.]"

The two warriors bowed, and then left the Second's presence.

* * *

Adam was released from the table, and the two humans were dragged from the hangar to the throne room on their backs, feet scraping the deck. Adam was barely aware of the mounted trophies that lined their reversing entry into the cavernous room, though his brain unconsciously registered a horrifyingly familiar grouping of matt-black rifles and pistols, uniforms, and attire all mounted in a glass case.

The two humans were released by their captors, then manacled, and forcefully turned toward the throne dais. The Agent was groggy, though awake. Adam was barely breathing; his eyes were squeezed shut, trying to shut out the pain. The creatures hadn't healed him this time, and he was barely alive.

"Adam Caine, and our annoying intruder," Lord Yh'reth'gar announced, as if welcoming old friends into his home. He stepped down off of his throne. At the base of the stepped dais stood the usual cadre of armed personal guards, as well as Second Yh'par'ban, who was not armed, though the Agent suspected that there was some kind of weapon hidden on the Second's person, as there always had been.

"You are the one who destroyed our device in the hangar they found you in?" the Lord asked the Agent. He looked at the Agent like a man would look at a piece of turd he had just stepped on.

The Agent flashed the Lord a predatory grin, and earned a smack across the chops from the nearest warrior.

"My superiors know you are here," the Agent lied. In all likelihood, they thought he was dead, his body somewhere in another galaxy. "If I miss my check-in point, the Terran Navy will come here, and crush you like bugs."

The Lord and the Second both let out barking laughs.

"You are alone; your Navy has no idea we are here," the Lord said smugly. "The two of you are going to die," he added.

Adam was stirring beside the Agent.

"Just get it over with," Adam whispered. "Please." Tears were rolling down his cheeks. Inside, the Agent's heart broke for the man beside him: the Lord's people had broken him. *Damn them*, he cursed. Seeing such a strong man succumbing to the ministrations of these animals was disheartening. The Agent sagged, hunching over, his weight on his knees.

"No, first you will listen to how your planet will die, so that you can go to your graves, knowing you have failed to protect your people." The Lord seemed to delight in saying this, though as an Intelligence agent, the Agent knew he should be listening. "We will travel back in time, as we brought you and your friends forward in time, Adam Caine." This woke Adam up, his eyes, red and raw, staring directly into the alien's.

"What?"

The Agent swore; he had assumed Caine and the others were simply Terrans in the wrong place at the wrong time. But time-travellers? The Lord found Caine's ignorance all the more delicious.

"Yes, by the human calendar, you are in the fortieth-century, some two thousand years after you were born. In fact, you are standing in the exact spot on Earth where your country was governed from."

"What the *fuck* are you talking about?"

"Earth is gone, some one hundred years ago, destroyed, obliterated," the Lord answered with a chuckle. The warriors around chuckled with him, as if their entire race seemed to be in on some big cosmic joke.

"You're lying," Adam protested weakly. He looked to his fellow human for comfort, but found none. The Agent shook his head; his father had once told him how painful it had been to see Earth tear itself apart hours after the asteroid strike.

"I'm sorry," said the Agent, hoping Caine saw the sincerity in his face.

Fresh tears ran down Caine's cheeks at the realisation that everything had gone: his home, his estranged family, his whole planet, gone, and he had never known it; not only that, but now an alien was telling him he was in the future, brought here by some technological marvel. *The machine in the hangar where I was electrocuted*, he realised.

The Lord let out a massive bellow of laughter, right from his belly. The laughter made something snap in Adam's mind, the pain of his tortures gone, the sadness becoming something else.

The Agent saw this and noted the change; all he saw now was anger -the kind of anger that came from a man with nothing to lose.

The Lord's insane laughter subsided, and he leaned down to whisper in Adam's ear.

"The human race will be destroyed; by me," the Lord sneered.

Adam looked up slowly, a feral growl escaping from his lips. His training began to kick in, and he could feel fresh adrenaline rushing through his veins as his insane anger took over relentlessly.

"Bollocks will it."

The growl became a full roar as he strained against the manacles.

At first, nothing happened, and then the impossible happened as the Agent gawped in stunned silence.

The manacles snapped, pieces flying in all directions. The Lord backed away in a hurry, suddenly aware of just how precarious his survival had suddenly become.

Adam turned on the nearest warrior, grabbed its stun weapon, and smashed his fist hard into its forehead, slamming the warrior into a glass display. The glass shattered, and the Lord let out a protesting yelp. Adam picked the corpse up, and, incredibly, flung it at the throne, smashing against the heavy gold chair, and spilling foul-smelling blood over the dais.

Adam turned the curved energy weapon on the other aliens and began firing, before the black-armoured guards pounced on him, fists raised to strike, their weapons forgotten in the heat of their vengeance. Adam blasted the first guard with the gun, before slamming the barrel into the next, snapping its neck and sending it crashing to the ground. A fist connected with his hand, and he let go of the gun, before lashing out with his foot, side-kicking the third guard in the leg before elbowing it in the face. The last guard, filled with rage at seeing his fellows being so easily beaten, flew at Adam, talons, and claws poised.

It slashed Adam's chest before he could raise his arm. More crimson flowed down his front.

"Shit," he cursed, and then proceeded to batter the alien to death, pounding with his fists, and screaming with rage as he did so. Adam hadn't noticed that the creature had died upon the fourth hard punch; he just kept punching and punching until its hideous black blood covered his hammering arms.

He looked down at his arms, breathing hard, and then turned toward the Agent.

The Agent, seeing the inconsolable fury in Adam's eyes and his posture, backed away, not wanting to become another bloody mess on the floor.

"Adam, my name is Major Raymond Sansky," the Agent stated, hoping that that would bring the other man out of his murderous rage. It did. Adam stopped short, his eyes wide. He looked over to the throne, and found that the Lord and his second-in-command were gone.

"Is it true what he said?" Adam asked, still looking past the throne.

Sansky nodded sadly.

"As far as I know, since I've been out of contact with my superiors, it's the end of the year thirty-nine-ninety-nine. We haven't got time for a history lesson; we need to get off this ship," Sansky said forcefully.

"I've got a debt to settle," Adam pointed out with a growl, stepping toward the throne again.

Sansky stepped in his way. "We've got to free your friends, get off this ship, and escape to Terran territory. *Then* we can come back, and blow this place to hell."

"*Terran?*" Adam questioned.

"It's a long story." Sansky half-turned and gestured for Adam to undo his restraints. Adam looked toward the throne, then back at Sansky, and then slowly nodded and found the unconscious body of one of the warriors he had blasted blindly without thinking. The warrior had a key for the manacles tucked into its belt. Adam retrieved it, and set Sansky free.

"The warriors will storm this place any minute," Sansky pointed out.

Adam nodded.

He finally remembered the case he had seen but not concentrated on. Jogging over to it, he realised they were twenty-first century weapons: a British SA80-L95, just like he had used in the Marines, along with a Glock 9mm, with enough ammunition to bring down a city. There was even a special forces-black military uniform, complete with equipment vest, boots, and unit patch. Harrowingly, the patch was identical to the one on Adam's stolen *Mayflower* overalls, and Adam worried what fate had become of the *Mayflower* and *Icarus* to earn a place in the Lord's throne room displays.

"We don't have time for this," Sansky protested, retrieving one of the stun weapons. He picked up another, and placed the sling over his shoulders, hoping to give it to one of the soldiers in the cell, or at least use it in an emergency.

"I need a change of clothes."

* * *

Five minutes later, Adam felt at home. Dressed in the uniform, carrying the familiar weapon again, it was almost as if he had never left the Service. They could hear the repeated attempts by the warriors outside to get through the suddenly locked doors. Adam wrapped the overalls around his waist.

The two soldiers, both from different eras, stood to either side of the doors.

Sansky held up a detonator device, and Adam, despite not recognising it, understood what he wanted to do.

Silently, Sansky held up three fingers, and counted down, before slapping the big red button on top of the detonator stick. Major Sansky's explosives -placed all around the ship as distractions- detonated. The ship vibrated, then shook violently. Sparks flew from ruptured conduits in the walls. The glass cases smashed. The displays clattered to the floor. There was rampant alien cursing from behind the buckling door.

"Shit," Adam snorted.

"I've been waiting to do that for two years," Sansky said humourlessly. Wordlessly, the two opened the doors.

Adam fired short controlled bursts from his solid-round automatic rifle, aiming for heads and necks. Blood and brains splattered everywhere, the aliens unprepared for such a ferocious weapon to be unleashed in such close quarters.

Sansky, blasting at anything that moved, had to squint his eyes due to the muzzle flash from Caine's weapon. The noise in the confined corridor was deafening. But Caine didn't flinch once; standing there, sighting down the gun, with a determined look on his face, he was the epitome of a professional soldier.

It took a minute of straight-out firing to take down the twenty warriors -including the two door guards on duty as always- crowding round the doors. Neither men had sustained injuries, which they thanked their lucky stars for.

Adam looked to Sansky for direction, who led the time-traveller down the left corridor.

Smoke was pouring out of the air vents, settling on the ceiling as the two soldiers made their way through the chaos.

"I work for Terran Naval Intelligence," Sansky suddenly explained, after reaching a deserted elevator, and stepping in. "I was sent to a planet called Rel Major to investigate the First Minister of Mertik for possible charges of corruption. When I got there, Lord Yh'reth'gar's fleet was in orbit pounding the place. When I landed, they discovered me, and I had to think quickly; so I disguised myself as one of the creatures, and joined the ranks, hoping to get some information from them, then jump ship."

"I take it, it didn't work out that way," Adam said weakly. The adrenaline was wearing off, and he was sagging against the elevator wall, trying to catch his breath. He shook off Major Sansky's attempts to help him stay upright.

"No, it didn't," Sansky replied, returning to his story. "The fleet positioned itself straight into the debris field that used to be Terra. I still haven't figured out how they got into the system without Pluto Station detecting it."

"Pluto Station?" Adam queried.

Sansky had to keep reminding himself that Caine had missed out on two thousand years of human history.

"It's a listening post; used to be a massive docking facility until Terra's destruction. Now it's tiny, and the only real Navy presence in the Sol system, other than the occasional smuggler, and what's left of Titan Colony of course."

"Of course," said Adam, the sarcasm liberally dripping off the word.

The elevator came to a halt, and the doors opened.

Adam was immediately hit by a throwing knife, or something similar, that pierced his left shoulder. He cried out, and squeezed off three rounds, tearing the attacker's head apart in a bloody gory splatter.

Ahead, there were half a dozen aliens guarding the cell entrance.

* * *

Hannah could hear gunfire. Not the energy blasts of the aliens' weapons, but real, solid, thumping gunfire from a machine gun.

There was an audible crack from outside the cell as something loud fired. There was rampant swearing and cursing in English, and a messy squelch, though she couldn't make out the voice's owner. Something whumped again and again on the door, until they yielded under the attack, and shrieked open.

The prisoners stood up, preparing for the inevitable energy blasts that would claim them all. Except there were no aliens behind the door –well, there were dead ones- but none alive. Between the doors stood Adam Caine, holding a rifle, wearing a black military uniform, and accompanied by another human man who gently threw the downed stun weapons to the three soldiers, and the two RAF officers.

The newcomer, who identified himself as Major Sansky, was not particularly tall, nor anything approaching short, with a slim frame, sandy-white hair, and a small unassuming face. His face was the kind you saw in the street, but forgot seconds later -the perfect Intelligence agent. He was wearing grey military combat fatigues, though there were no rank tapes, or unit patches, nothing to identify him.

They looked the weapons over, not entirely knowing what to do with them, other than pull the trigger. They shrugged, and then filed out of the cell, sweeping the guns around for targets, the combat engineers taking one side of the door, the pilots taking the other.

Sasha and Sapphire bolted toward Adam, and wrapped themselves around his legs. He grimaced as they held on too tightly to the area damaged by the Second's earlier ministrations. He returned the hug, a bit clumsily, Hannah noticed. She hugged him as well, and the others even tried to hug him, seeing him as their saviour. He clearly didn't enjoy the attention.

She looked into his big eyes, and something passed between them, something she had only heard of in cheesy romance films and Mills & Boon novels. She couldn't explain it, but it was definitely there: powerful, passionate, and delicate at the same time.

He looked away, prying the two young girls' arms off his wounded legs.

He was looking exhausted beyond comprehension, pale, unhealthy, his eyes sunken into the sockets, with the skin around his eyes so dark they looked bruised. He was dying, she could see it, though was sure he would never say so.

"Let's go," he said to everyone.

Scared, ill, filthy, and bedraggled, the prisoners followed the soldiers out of the cell, clinging to each other, helping each other walk after days without much movement at all.

Adam and Sansky took the lead, with the three engineers falling back to act as a rearguard.

Scientists suddenly came running out of a side door, and stopped dead when they saw Adam standing there, armed, uniformed, and looking extremely frightening.

Adam put a round through the head of the first one, whilst the others ran.

Adam switched to automatic, and gunned them down as well, brutally, and mercilessly.

Sansky didn't once complain: he'd *witnessed* what those scientists had done to Adam.

But Hannah and the others looked at him, with a sick feeling in their stomachs. He stalked off down the corridor, silently and swiftly. The others had to jog to keep up with the big man, despite his injuries.

"Does anyone else think this is too easy?" Hannah whispered to no-one in particular. She realised that the others around her were nodding. She wondered if Adam and the mysterious man with him had thought of that. They had, though Hannah didn't know that at the time.

"Mummy," Sasha cried, hugging her mother's leg.

She was scared. Then again, everybody was scared, though only a few didn't show it.

Up ahead, there was a t-junction, and Adam and the stranger were discussing which way to go.

"That way will take us to the hangars," Sansky was saying, pointing to the left. "We could grab a small ship, and get off this thing. The other way leads to the elevators to the command centre." Adam nodded, though it was clear he wasn't ready to leave yet. Hannah, and indeed Sansky, could see in his eyes, the silent need, longing even, for revenge and retribution against his former captors.

"Please, Adam," she whispered, "let's go home."

Adam span at the mention of home, and there was something sad about his face, like he was carrying an awful burdening secret. The sadness was covered up with the stoicism she expected of a professional soldier.

Without another word, he turned back, and marched off down the corridor, toward the *hangars*, Sansky right behind him. Once again, the others struggled to keep up. The long corridors seemed to go on for miles as the minutes ticked by. The doomy gloom of the corridors seemed to sap the strength of any meaningful conversation from the escapees, none willing to talk in case it gave them away. The corridor ahead curved sharply off to the right, and suddenly warriors, screaming obscenities, and firing pulse pistols charged from the corner.

The pulses of energy sent the prisoners scattering to the floor.

One unlucky man, Aaron Mitchell, took an energy pulse to his face before he could duck. His entire face disappeared in the energy, and his lifeless body slumped to the deck. His partner, Trevor Smith, screamed, sobbed, and threw up on the floor at the mess of his dead lover. He had to be pried away by Kevin and Mouse Gilpin to leave the body behind. Another prisoner, one of the group of four young girls, was slammed backwards, smoke pouring from the ruin of her stomach. She didn't scream, or cry; she couldn't -she was dead before she hit the ground. Her three friends crowded round her, crying their eyes out.

Adam returned fire.

On full automatic.

The loud noise was frightening, and briefly stopped the charging warriors in their tracks, wondering what could make such a hideous sound. The SA80's muzzle flared, and bullets tore the warriors apart, piercing the crab-esque armour, and thrashing through skin.

When Adam stopped firing, the warriors were dead, and on the ground, a bloody mess of gore and alien ichor.

He turned to check on the others.

One of the downed warriors, having not actually died, suddenly reached up with his pulse pistol, and fired two shots, exacting a small revenge before haemorrhaging out and dying.

Adam was hit in the leg, and then in the chest after the first spun him round. He fell backwards, onto the pile of corpses, and grunted in pain. Hannah rushed to him. The wound was cauterised, the heat from the energy pulse searing the wound shut, preventing him from bleeding out. But there was damage to his chest that couldn't be so readily ignored. He was breathing erratically, and he was shaking, the after-effects of the adrenaline rush setting in. His eyes were squeezed shut; he was in terrible pain. The shot had penetrated the armoured equipment vest, stripped away his skin, and partially seared through his ribs. He coughed up blood every few seconds.

"We have to get him to a doctor," Hannah said, looking at Sansky. He nodded, unwilling to leave his new comrade-in-arms to die. It was the priest that stepped forward, volunteering to half-carry Adam as far as was needed. Adam was heavy, weighed down by the rifle and ammunition, which he was unwilling to give up.

Adam ordered the others to move on ahead without him; he told them to find whatever transport was there, and start it up, ready to go when he arrived.

The others moved off at a brisk pace, leaving the two corpses behind.

It was slow going for Adam and the priest, who mentioned his name as Father Bishop. Adam didn't make a joke about his surname, but limped along, clamping a hand to his chest, and leaning on the priest's shoulders.

* * *

They stepped through into the hangar, and found it practically devoid of anything, except for two craft picked up on Rel Major. One was a famously generic starfighter, available just about everywhere. The other was a swan-like Craj transport -one of those converted from old mining ships years ago, no doubt captured from the home planet of the Craj Territory. The ship was long, four hundred metres in fact, with four engine nacelles arranged at the rear in a straight up-down-left-right cross with tubular cargo bays bulging out of its skinny midsection. The bridge/command centre was at the tip of the swan neck at the front of the ship, with a ramp-like defunct mining laser sloping down from the base of the neck. There were no running lights on, or any other signs of power, but Sansky had expected that.

Sansky and the others raced to the transport, some limping, and forgetting their ill health in the haste to escape. None of them made a comment on how unbelievable it was they were about to fly in a starship.

Sansky opened the control panel for the pedestrian door on the port side of the ship, opened it, and jumped inside, leaving the soldiers to help the others. He ignored the hideous mess left behind by the Core's boarding party, avoiding the beaten, mangled, and burned bodies of the transport's rightful owners.

Without power, the small elevator to the command centre was unmoving, so Sansky bound up the ladder as fast as he could.

In the large command centre, Sansky powered up the controls, praying there was some power left to escape. The ship was old, beaten and battered to hell, but durable. The controls lit up, and the displays read all the power supplies were at nominal levels.

"Yes," he shouted, punching the air.

The two RAF officers appeared behind him.

"What can we do?" they asked.

"Help me fly this thing," Sansky ordered. The two officers looked at each other incredulously. They were twenty-first-century chopper pilots, not *spaceship* pilots. The Major saw their dilemma, and pointed to the seats either side of him. "Just follow my orders, and you'll be fine."

"Yes, sir," they immediately replied, sitting in their assigned seats.

The ship was almost ready when Hannah came up to the bridge, ashen and white-faced, her hands trembling, and raised in surrender. Sansky was about to ask her what was going on when behind her came an alien warrior, holding a pulse pistol to Hannah's head.

He gestured for Sansky and the others to move away from the controls. The creature's finger began to tighten on his pistol's trigger.

In an orgy of gore, the creature's face suddenly exploded, and the body toppled over. Behind the creature stood Adam, supported by Father Bishop, his rifle in one hand, trained at where the creature's head had once been, the barrel smoking.

It was the priest who spoke.

"Can we please get the *hell* out of this place?"

* * *

With some coaxing, and constant orders from Sansky to the RAF officers, the Craj transport lifted off the deck of the hangar. Unfortunately, the doors to space outside were shut.

"Now what?" cried Lieutenant Dick.

Sansky looked around for the mining laser control, and found it. There was barely any power, but maybe enough for his purpose. He cycled the laser up to full power, watching as the blue-lit counter scrawled slowly upwards.

The sensors began to bleat loudly at Dick's console.

"Dammit," said Sansky, "they're waiting for us out there."

* * *

The Second, commanding a full cadre of warriors, was trying to gain entry to the hangar in which the prisoners had escaped through. They had passed the bodies of the fallen warriors, and the corpses of the two humans left behind. He had no doubt that Adam Caine had been responsible for the deaths of those warriors.

The doors to the hangar had been automatically sealed because a ship was powering up inside. Even if they somehow managed to escape from the hangar, there was still several squadrons of starfighters waiting for them beyond the doors.

"[GET IT OPEN!]" he bellowed to the warriors around him.

At first, they tried to force the doors with their claws and hands

That didn't work, so they resorted to grouping in a line, and firing their pistols. The door buckled, melted, then opened.

* * *

"This is going to be bright," Sansky announced.

Everybody squinted and shut their eyes, although Adam was already unconscious on the deck, at the rear of the small bridge, with Hannah and Bishop tending to him.

Sansky slapped the fire control for the laser.

* * *

The Second stepped between the molten metal of the doors, avoiding the hissing material, and ignoring the sharp tang of the steam and smoke. He heard the noise building from the front of the stolen ship. Some kind of energy build-up was coming from the rear of the ship -which was, distressingly, now pointed at the doors the Second and his men had come through.

Horrified by what he knew was coming next, he sneakily backed away, out into the corridor, leaving his warriors to face the wrath of the escaping ship's engines as they tried, in vain, to stop the ship with their pulse pistols.

* * *

The mining laser -designed to drill deeply into dense asteroids- had no trouble getting through the hangar doors. There was no forcefield to keep the atmosphere in though, and suddenly air rushed toward the new opening, dragging equipment, warriors, and weapons out into space, screaming wordlessly as they gulped for non-existent air.

The backwash of the transport's engines incinerated those warriors not dragged out into space. The intense heat seared through the back wall as Sansky slammed the ship into full throttle.

The Second, already several yards down the corridor, away from the destruction, hung onto a railing for dear life as the atmosphere hurtled past him, soundlessly cursing the name of Caine the entire time.

* * *

Space met them beyond the doors.

"Mary mother of God," Reverend Bishop exclaimed. "We were in space the whole time?"

Sansky nodded sadly. The worst was yet to come for them.

"We're in the exact spot where Terra once stood," Sansky stated. They all looked at him as if he was mad. "Earth. It was destroyed a century ago by an asteroid. These creatures have been hiding here in Earth's remains for the last two years."

They all stared at the starfield beyond the dust and rock, dumbfounded. Sansky kicked the ship into high gear, and the transport rushed through the opening, scraping the sides of the lasered doors, and escaping into space.

Spike starfighters chased after them, first one or two, then three or four squadrons worth. Laser fire jumped out at the Craj transport, smacking its rear-end violently. There were no shields so the energy pummelled the hull relentlessly, scorching, searing, and then buckling the hull plating.

Sansky slid the ship from side-to-side as best he could, but the thing had the manoeuvrability of a brick. He wasn't a top-notch pilot, and only had basic piloting skills, but he was doing his best to keep the fighters away from the ship. They kept on him as far as the edge of the debris field, who were then forced to turn back before exiting the field; they didn't want to be detected by Pluto Station's powerful sensors, and thus rumble the secret operation.

The escapees were home free.

Then the ship rocked again, under the impact of bigger lasers.

"Dammit," Sansky cursed. There was a group of Core cruisers hiding among the remains of Mars and Venus. And they were firing on the transport from a massive distance.

The run to the Linkway was bumpy, the cruisers' huge weapons batteries firing even when the transport was out of range, the lethal rounds exploding nearby, bouncing the fragile ship around like an avalanche.

"This is going to be scary," Sansky warned. The heavens opened, a swirl of blues that opened up like a flower's petals into space, and continued to swirl like a toilet being flushed. A darker blue hole, almost purple, appeared at the centre of the swirl, and then swallowed the transport whole.

Sansky enjoyed the uneventful transition to the Linkways, though the looks on the faces of the others on the bridge said otherwise. Dick was looking at *him* for an explanation.

"Don't worry, it's harmless," he reassured them. "The Linkways are everywhere, linking every star system in the nineteen galaxies, like tunnels under the fabric of space. Blue ones indicate Linkways between star systems, red ones between galaxies, and green ones for ones that are unusable. Don't ask me why. Scientists have been trying to figure that out for centuries. It's just the way it is."

The tunnel of blue light rushed past around the ship, swirling, mixing with other hues of blues.

It was beautiful, even more so after several days in torturous captivity.

* * *

HMS Polly Jenkins.

Thirteen-hundred metres of Terran warship, the *Polly Jenkins* was two months into its last six-month tour, before its decommissioning. The ship was old, the second of its class, built six hundred years ago. The *Spearhead*-class ship had lasted past many of its sister ships, despite the fact that all Terran vessels now followed a similar structural design, save for its size.

The long, armoured doorstopper-shaped bow, making up a third of the Heavy Cruiser's length, was attached to a long main hull that looked like a flattened cube; two chunky engine nacelles spread out from the main hull's stern, with a long, low command spine down the ventral length of the ship. The whole ship was made from a strange blue-tinted metal, giving it the appearance of a cartoon whale in space.

She was big, powerful, and the flagship for Taskforce Delta-9-4.

The taskforce was made up of eight ships: *Polly Jenkins* herself, and a smaller Cruiser, *Falklands*, with three Destroyers -*New South Wales*, *Devonshire*, and *Kansas*- as well as three two-hundred-metre-long gunships -*Pearl Harbour*, *Templar*, and the *Swindon*. The group was currently hanging in space, situated around the entrance to Proxima Centauri's Linkway exit, subbing for the system's customs station whilst it was taken offline for repairs and refitting.

On the house-sized two-storey bridge of the *Polly Jenkins*, sat in the central command chair, Captain Virgil Barkley could see the *Falklands* and *Swindon* in formation off the port-bow, beyond the massive viewports and the bulk of his own ship. Like so many of his ilk, he was tall, thin, and pale; a lifelong spacer, his long white hair was tied back in a regulation braiding under his peaked cap. The bridge was filled with the green-tinted holographic computer displays and consoles common to modern Terran warships, enlightening the whole room with shades of turquoise.

Uniformed enlisted men, women, and officers all worked to keep the ship running in tip-top shape at various stations around the bridge; some of them chatted to each other about families, or sports back home. Barkley did not chastise them for it, as he knew some captains did. When the ship was in combat, *then* it would be inappropriate, but not when the ship was in such a relaxed assignment.

Barkley was lazily reading through a main systems diagnostic on the chair's holographic display when his Executive Officer, Commander Janis Mkdorn, stepped up to the command chair.

"Janis," Barkley faux smiled. "I'm glad to see that football injury has healed."

In all honesty, he wasn't; Mkdorn had been lumped on him by the Admiralty as a favour to a member of the Parliament. The woman didn't crack a smile, a joke, or even an informal greeting. She was stiff, too formal, and the crew did not like her, though she played a mean ninety minutes of football on the hangar decks. This was when one of the junior officers had tackled her too hard, and broken her fibia.

"Captain," Mkdorn sighed, no longer arguing with him about his informal use of her name, "we just received a communiqué from Pluto Station; apparently, they've picked up some kind of energy disturbance from just outside the Earth debris field."

"And they want us to check it out?" Barkley snorted.

"Commander Chase said that none of their shuttles are currently operational, and that there was a bottle of Port in it if we did."

Barkley snorted again.

"Alright," he sighed, "Contact the *Swindon*, get them round there, and tell her commander she can have a glass of Port herself if she finds anything interesting."

Humourlessly, she nodded and moved away to the communications station.

"Captain!" the sensors operator cried out. "There's a Craj transport coming through the Linkway."

"I thought the Craj were wiped out two years ago," Mkdorn said, suddenly at his side.

"So did I," admitted Barkley. He remembered the day the news had been released; the Craj had been an ally of the Terrans since before the destruction of the homeworld. No clue had been left behind as to the identity of the attackers, not even survivors of the devastation on Rel Major.

"Captain, she's sending out a Navy Intelligence identity code," the comms officer added.

Barkley frowned. "Use the tractor beam to bring her alongside; Mkdorn, identify the code."

"The code belongs to a Major Raymond Sansky," the young woman replied some minutes later, "he's listed as missing in action, and the code has been flagged by NI."

"Send on the details to Navy Intelligence, and the Admiralty, please, Commander."

"Aye, Captain."

Two:
Rel Major

"Life would be so much simpler if I never volunteered for anything."
-Raymond Sansky, shortly before the Rel Major mission.

3997ad.
(Two years ago.)
Rel star system; Craj Territory.

Stars twinkled incessantly, some disappearing forever, others only just being born. Still others moved in the distance, comets, rogue stars, even distant nebulae caught in the stellar drift of the universe.

But the closest were starships, freighters, and hundreds of other assorted vessels coming and going from the capital planet of the Craj race. Rel Major was a city-world, a planet covered pole-to-pole by apartment buildings, stadiums, offices, spaceports, hangars, bars, clubs, stores, and other less reputable establishments. It was renowned for its immense opportunities for trade among many races.

The planet was a hive of activity.

It was under attack.

Spiked, red warships escorting a massive titan of similar design pounded the planet below, with massive bombardments from their laser batteries. They were coloured the same crimson as human blood, with spikes of weapons jutting out at random intervals. The ships had more in common with sea anemone than starships. They weren't just bombarding the planet: they had already destroyed the orbiting space stations, and had pummelled Craj warships to pieces.

From under the shadow of a dying twin-hulled private starjammer emerged a small black stealth vessel, hidden even from the private ship. It was small, wedge-shaped, a modified Terran Rhino starfighter, re-designed to fool the sensors of other ships. It prowled between the warships in orbit, passing traders, and freight-haulers. Raymond Sansky sat in the cramped one-man cockpit. He had been ordered to Rel, to follow the First Minister of Mertik, trying to uncover possible corruption. He had found this nightmare waiting for him upon leaving the Linkway.

He had to get out of the confusion of ships.

He almost had to abort his approach to the surface twice, after nearly colliding with other vessels skimming across the higher reaches of the planet's atmosphere. If he'd thought the amount of ships in orbit was horrendous, he was shocked to see Rel Major's *sky* full of ships, skimmers, hovercars, airships, blimps, and dozens of ground rescue vehicles.

Not all of the ships were whole, or even recognisable. One freighter, out of fuel, almost all of its cargo midsection missing and its engines spewing black smoke, came down on an executive shuttle. The shuttles occupants

-coincidentally the First Minister of Mertik, and his family and entourage- were instantly liquefied by a ruptured fuel line. The freighter's engines -a dangerous mix of alien and human technology- detonated seconds after crashing, obliterating ten square miles of buildings.

Sansky saw it all, the mayhem of wounded vessels attempting to land, and failing. He saw two ships, both on a corrupted landing trajectory, slam into the side of a large Craj troop transport. Yellow-skinned, grey-uniformed soldiers tumbled into the abyss of the city below, burning and screaming.

A fireball descended from the heavens -a dying Craj warship pulled into the planet's gravity well. Its path took it almost horizontally, ploughing through skyscrapers, collapsing whole city blocks, before it came to a flaming stop in the ruins of a sports stadium.

A mass conveyance vessel, laden with refugees from nearby planets, spouted fire from its cargo holds, twitching figures wreathed in bright fire. Coolants spilled from rents in its rear hull, splashing over a public park, searing away all life inside its small walls, a hideous sinus-melting smell lingering for decades afterward. The ship began to list as it hovered, waiting for landing permission. Panicking, the captain turned the ship, manoeuvring into a hail of incoming patrol fighters.

Unable to evade quick enough, the fighters slammed nose first into the front end of the massive transport. Half the ship disappeared in a blaze of fire, a shower of hull plating raining down below. The rear half, still with the majority of its sentient cargo, dropped from the sky, and fell on the central government building. In the blink of an eye, the Craj government was annihilated.

Things were getting worse though, the planet's government was effectively gone, and the planet's atmosphere was awash with accidental mayhem.

But now there was something deliberate about the destruction.

Ahead of the Terran starfighter, pulses of destructive energy slapped a disused laser silo, destroying its armour, and then detonating the power core, fire boiling out of the popped shell like gas ignited in a balloon.

Anti-aircraft rounds leapt into the air in long trails. The gunners were panicking, randomly firing into the sky, as energy weapons fire pummelled the planet from orbit.

Tracer rounds stitched into dozens of helpless civilian craft, ripping hulls apart like paper. Gunners were simply unaware of what they were hitting, firing blindly into the air, hoping to hit something, anything.

Beams of bright white light flashed down into the atmosphere, destroying power plants, power distribution centres, power lines, buffers, and finally the defence silos themselves, touching off their magazines, and causing yet more incredible destruction among the surrounding buildings.

From Sansky's viewpoint, the planet was ablaze, screams of anguish and pain resonating across the communications channels like something out of a nightmare. Pleas for help or mercy killings cried out equally loudly, shaking Raymond to his very soul.

He frowned; the weapons fire coming from above wasn't only directed at military assets. This was a random act of brutality on a scale Sansky had never seen before. Already, he could see the red warships descending slowly into the planet's atmosphere.

Ahead of the speeding starfighter, a flock of fluffy long-necked birds erupted from a high-rise building's roof, fluttering their wings, and rising into the sky ahead of the fighter. He swerved the craft to avoid the flock, and wandered straight into AA fire. The starboard wing was sheared off, sparks spraying from the flight console.

He cried out in pain, as some of the sparks scorched his skin. Desperately, he tried to control the fighter's descent, but he knew he was fighting a losing battle.

The metal and concrete ground began to look closer and bigger in the canopy.

The ship bobbed and jerked as he steered the craft with only one engine.

A ruined defence tower loomed up ahead, like a giant cliff.

The fighter, bleeding power, dove straight for the armoured walls, hurtling through the air at great speeds.

Sansky screamed.

* * *

Hours later, the cities were in ruins; fire spread through Rel's mass of buildings, killing hundreds; buildings collapsed by the dozen. There were ships in the sky. The invading fleet were still there, sending down troops and shuttles to 'occupy' the planet.

Sansky's view was partially obscured, from his position at the bottom of the ruined defence tower. It was odd, he thought, that the 'occupying force' weren't behaving like an occupying force: they weren't staying in buildings to occupy them, merely moving through them as though they were searching for something, though who or what there was no telling. The troops -red-armoured troops with oily black skin, chitinous beaks, moving in a very bird-like way, and had a disposition towards criminally insane- were moving from building-to-building, killing anything that moved, even the wildlife floating around.

The starfighter was still hanging above, its nose jammed into the tower. Sansky was crouching in its shadow, at the base of the abandoned tower.

His black Special Forces fatigues were tattered and dirty. It had been only hours since crashing, but he had already had trouble surviving, almost running into several search parties, and having to stun a native who tried to give his position away.

He desperately needed a way off the planet; the starfighter was unusable as an option, though he could remotely detonate the ship's power core, thus denying it to these creatures, and covering his presence on Rel

Hiding behind a crumbling wall, he watched as a fire-team of six soldiers searched along a street littered with downed vehicles, and burning corpses.

Each soldier carried a chunky long rifle in two clawed hands, pocket- covered bandoliers over their armour, with holsters on each hip. They were intimidating in all the right ways, and Sansky had no problem admitting it to himself.

As he hid, watching the soldiers, and taking in the devastated surroundings, it hit him just how alone he currently was: the Craj, a great friend to the Terran Consortium, were gone, their government and military obliterated in one fell swoop. There was no back-up for this mission, and there were no Terran vessels in nearby star systems to come to his rescue. He was stuck here without help.

He was so caught up in his own thoughts that he didn't notice the second half of the alien squad approach him from behind.

There was a clacking and chattering behind him. He turned to see the six-man fire-team coming up.

They had their rifles pointed at him, except for the leader, who was gesturing threateningly at him, whilst clearly bellowing challenges.

Fear gripped his short frame.

He did the only thing he could think of in the situation.

He ran.

The alien soldiers bellowed harsh curses as he bolted through an open doorway to his left, stomping up a steep set of steps, and past a floor full of empty glass offices.

The soldiers were only a few steps behind, shouting in their native language, presumably to get him to stop running, as if he was *that* stupid. One of them loosed a few energy rounds at him. The rounds missed, smashing ceiling-to-floor windows all around him as he ran.

He took a right, and almost had his head blown off as an energy round impacted on the wall's corner, showering him with debris and dust.

Coughing and spluttering, he kept going, trying to lose his chasers in the miasmic maze-like habitat building. It wasn't working because he could hear their boots pounding against the floor only metres behind him.

There was an emergency exit at the end of the corridor, one that looked very inviting.

One of the soldiers suddenly appeared ahead of him, and he barrelled straight into it. The two tumbled to the floor, the alien going headfirst. Its neck snapped as its head hit the floor, a sickening crack that reverberated trough its body so much, even Sansky could feel it. There was a short gurgle from its beak, and then it was gone, the neck at a horrible angle, its eyes wide open in pained shock.

There were more footsteps behind him, almost near the corner.

There was only one option: he would have to pretend to be one of them, until such time as he could return home. He snatched his holo-disguise from his equipment vest, and scanned the dead body, saving the creature's characteristics in its memory. He slapped the vocal translator strip onto his throat, above his Adam's apple. He had a backup holographic disguise unit, and slapped that on the corpse. The alien's appearance was replaced with his own, though still quite dead. He clicked the remote control on the small panel that controlled the starfighter's power core, detonating the fighter.

His own disguise snapped over him like a cloud in a hurricane, just as the other creatures rounded the corner.

"[I see you actually managed to kill something,]" the unit leader growled in its clacking language. Sansky found he could understand it, thanks to the small translator stuck to his throat.

"[Finally,]" Sansky agreed.

The unit leader gestured for him to follow, and they all filed out of the corridor, and out of the building.

There was a crump of detonation, and all the aliens suddenly looked at Sansky.

He shrugged, hoping the holo-disguise would translate it.

"[Shoved a grenade in his mouth,]" he explained.

The aliens all started bellowing with laughter, and Sansky hated this idea already. It made him sick to his stomach.

Three:
Recovery & Revenge

"They say revenge is a dish best served cold. I reckon that's bullshit; revenge is like a fire that burns and consumes you until there is nothing left but death and ash."

-From *The Book of Caine*, by Roath Caine.

3999ad.

Great beams of shimmering green light latched onto the Craj transport, and dragged the thing alongside the *Polly Jenkins*. Barkley stood on the bridge, watching the holographic vid-feed from the airlock cameras.

Several crewmen opened the airlock, and were met by a man in nondescript military grey fatigues, and a group of bedraggled men, women, and children, all human. They were dressed in odd clothes, though Barkley couldn't place what part of the universe they had been made. Not that he was a fashion expert, but latest trends were usually evident even on a starship.

Several medical technicians moved through the airlock and returned with an anti-grav stretcher carrying a bloody, unconscious soldier, who was still cradling his rifle. The uniform was outdated, as was the rifle, though the man had a wild look about him, even in sleep.

In the display, Commander Mkdorn greeted the man in grey fatigues.

"*I am Commander Mkdorn, executive officer of the* HMS Polly Jenkins," Mkdorn nodded to the stranger.

"*Major Raymond Sansky, Navy Intelligence*," the stranger replied, throwing off a quick salute. Mkdorn returned the salute.

"*Who are all these people?*" Barkley cringed at Mkdorn's arrogant tone, as if those poor people were beneath her.

"*Survivors*," Sansky said wearily. "*We just escaped from... a pretty hideous prison. Most of them are only mentally harmed, but that one on the gurney was tortured like I've never heard of before.*" To Barkley, the Major looked beyond tired, the same haunted visage as those 'survivors' he had arrived with.

Barkley brought up a holographic display and scanned Sansky's DNA. Everything checked out; he was who he said he was. The others didn't come up in the system; every citizen in the Terran Consortium was required to provide a sample of their DNA to prevent identity theft. These survivors didn't register in any known database.

He turned to the commander of the ship's Army security contingent.

"Escort them all to the medical section," Barkley ordered. "Put guards on every entrance and exit. Tell the med staff they're under quarantine, until we can determine who they are, and where they're from."

The Army Captain nodded, and left the bridge.

Barkley stroked his chin in contemplation. He would have to contact the Admiralty.

* * *

The medical ward was clean, and sterile, more so than the hospitals they had left behind in... in nowhere.

Hannah sat on the edge of her medical cot, pulling on her medical slippers as the stunning revelation hit her. Earth was gone, wiped out by an asteroid a century ago. Even in the fortieth-century, they couldn't go home -it was gone forever; it no longer existed.

She jumped off the bed.

The contemporary military were still having trouble believing their story of being from the past, though Major Sansky had been adamantly trying to convince the ship's crew and captain that this was indeed the truth.

They had been quarantined to the *HMS Polly Jenkins'* medical ward for a full week, though the medical staff had been an absolute godsend. Thanks to Adam's fevered ranting about time travel, and the woman Polly Jenkins, the Underground survivors had been shocked beyond comprehension upon hearing the name of the great ship. According to the ship's medical staff, Polly Jenkins was the woman who invented the faster-than-light drive only a few years after Hannah and the others had been kidnapped. Adam's story about being thrown through time by the creatures had apparently been confirmed -how else could he have known those things.

Some of the survivors were here in this room: twelve beds, placed with the headboards against the walls, their feet pointing inward to the centre aisle, all arranged in two rows. The rest were in other parts of the medical facilities.

It was night-cycle on the ship, minimal staff on the ward. The ship's chief medical officer was still in his office; Hannah didn't want to bother him again. Despite the filthy state they had been in, the oxygen depravation, and the obvious beginnings of malnutrition, the survivors were fine, except Trevor Smith, who was almost catatonic. The young girl who had been killed had left behind three young friends, who still cried, and hugged each other when they weren't asleep.

Sasha and Sapphire were asleep in the beds next to hers, and she gave each a kiss on the forehead, before heading for the intensive care unit, with its sole occupant.

Adam was there, lying in a bed, his eyes closed, breathing for himself. He hadn't needed any machines to breath for him, though he had lost a lot of blood. The doctor had practically had a heart attack when he had seen the extent of Adam's injuries; he had no explanation for why Adam wasn't waking up, though said it might have to do with contact with a dangerous energy source. He'd declined to respond to Hannah's suggestion that Adam might be too far gone mentally.

Adam was restrained; even unconscious his body had fought against the treatment by the *Polly Jenkins'* medical staff, so they had placed leather restraints on his wrists and ankles.

Hannah looked down into his face; he was peaceful, completely opposite to how she had perceived him the last fortnight. He was handsome, even in a coma, and she once again found herself drawn to him. She kissed his lips, and quickly pulled back, hoping nobody had seen. His eyes were twitching under the lids; he was dreaming.

* * *

Adam wasn't dreaming, unfortunately for him.

He found himself in an all-too-familiar place.

He was surrounded by the same white nothingness as before. He looked down, and found that he was topless, wearing only a pair of medical scrub bottoms. He was clean, and dry, no blood anywhere except where it should be: in his body. His limbs weren't hurting, though he felt really weak. Oddly enough, his hair hadn't changed; it was still long, unkempt, unbrushed.

The buzzing came, and the whiteness ahead of him squirmed, like a mass of maggots.

Like clouds coming together, Silver appeared.

"You again," Adam sighed.

She nodded.

"It was you all along wasn't it?"

"What was?" she asked, false innocence on her face.

"Keeping me alive," he answered sternly. He wasn't in the mood for this enigmatic crap. "No matter how much training and conditioning I have, I could never have survived those torture sessions. You were helping somehow."

She sighed, heavily, and looked into his eyes.

"I... assisted you when you needed it," she admitted, somewhat reluctantly. "Though you really didn't need it as much as you think."

"How?"

Again, she sighed, as if she was revealing the universe's biggest secret to him. In fact, from the way she was casting nervous glances around her, he wondered if she really was.

"My... people... they have a way with time and temporal energy." Adam noted the hesitation, but said nothing. "We can view the past, present, and future; we can manipulate temporal energy."

"Basically, you screw with time," said Adam.

She looked at him, hurt in her eyes.

"It's far more complicated than that, *Warrant Officer* Caine," Silver retorted. The use of his former honorary rank was a nasty sting.

"You came to *me*," Adam said, jabbing an angry finger at her. "And I am getting tired of this mysterious bullshit. What do you want with me? How do you know who I am?"

* * *

Hannah laid her head on Adam's chest, and listened to his heartbeat; first it was steady and slow, just like anyone deep in sleep; then it changed, and became heavier, angrier, more erratic as it got faster and faster. His eyes were still closed when she looked up, but they were flickering back and forth under his eyelids like they were racing a Formula One car.

Christ, what is he dreaming about?

* * *

"There is a darkness growing in this universe," Silver explained, sitting on an armchair that magically appeared behind her. Adam turned, and found an identical chair, with the same hideous beige flower pattern, and thick padding. He sat down, his seething anger calming to the point where he was only *mildly* angry.

"We don't know what this darkness is," continued Silver. "It could be these creatures that held you captive; then again, it could be something bigger and far worse. We only became aware of them when they took you and your friends."

"The device is in their hangar; the time machine."

Silver nodded at Adam's statement.

"But that thing was huge, how is it you've only just become aware of them?"

Silver harrumphed, her mature features scrunched in irritation. "Someone must have been hiding them. Before, they could have only sent one or two through unnoticed. The temporal energy involved in bringing so many humans through would have been impossible to hide from us."

"So whoever was hiding the creatures' activities would have known they couldn't hide bigger activities," Adam pointed out. "If they could hide it from *you*, it probably means it's one of your own people doing the hiding."

Silver became silent, obviously worried about the prospect of one of her own people working against her.

"My people... are not as powerful as you think, Adam," she admitted. "We are a fractured race; in fact, there are only a few hundred of us left."

"I'm sorry," Adam said sincerely. "What happened?"

"Same as most civilisations; we went to war, and lost." She shook the thought off, and returned to her original conversation. Adam didn't say anything: if she didn't want to say anything, he wasn't going to push it. "Time is made up of strands," she suddenly said. She steepled the tips of her fingers, and looked down at the white below them in contemplation. "There are an infinite number, each following the life of every single individual in the universe." Adam was slightly put out by the sudden randomness of her statement. "Most strands are small and insignificant, some are larger, more influential, but every few millennia, there is a massive strand, bigger then the rest, one that changes events on a universal scale, attracting all the others to it. The last individual to do that was Polly Jenkins. She introduced humanity to the big wide universe."

Adam, whose attention had began to wane when the conversation had turned Matrix-like, locked eyes with her.

"What happened to the *Icarus*?" he asked. "I took a uniform and weapons from Yh'reth'gar's throne room that belonged to the *Icarus* and *Mayflower* crew."

"They accidentally stumbled close to Core space," she replied. "I... I don't think you want to know what happened to them there. You've already experienced their brand of hospitality. Although some of them disappeared from our view; where or when they went we don't know."

Adam paled.

The time travelling visions he had seen of Polly Jenkins' life and accomplishments; Silver had manipulated those visions for him to see. He *had* wondered why Yh'reth'gar's people would purposely, or accidentally, show him incredible things like humanity achieving the speed of light, or colonising another planet, or even World War Three.

Again, she changed the subject once again away from a difficult topic.

"There is another of those large strands, one that appeared only two weeks ago," Silver added. "It's already attracting others, building momentum. That strand is *you*. Whether you believe it or not, you are-"

"What? The new chosen one?" Adam exclaimed. "I am not Neo, or Anakin Skywalker. Do me a favour, that messiah crap isn't going to work on me."

The armchair he was sitting on began to recline back, laying him out. Curiously, he didn't fight it.

"You will come to see it," Silver stated matter-of-factly. "Not soon, but eventually, you will."

"A prophecy?" Adam snorted.

Silver's last words haunted him from the moment she spoke them.

She whispered, "Just a simple hope."

* * *

Adam suddenly sat up, eyes open.

"SILVER!!" he bellowed.

His muscled arms strained against the straps.

Hannah instinctively jumped back, knocking a chair over.

He looked around, confusion at the change in surroundings. He saw Hannah, and relaxed. She called a nurse to remove his restraints, and the doctor entered, a grudging smile on his face.

"I see you are awake," the gruff old man acknowledged.

"Where are we?" Adam asked, looking at the futuristic surroundings. It was a white room, uncomfortably like the whiteness of Silver's room. Eerie ghost-like green transparent holograms floated in the air around him, beeping and whistling gently, displaying his own vitals.

"Adam," Hannah replied soothingly. "We're in the medical bay of a starship."

"The *HMS Polly Jenkins*," the doctor nodded.

Adam burst out laughing, tears rolling down his cheeks at the sheer hilarity of the coincidence.

The doctor looked at him with pity, and thought that Adam was losing his mind.

* * *

Adam put the digipad down.

It was, apparently, a brief history of important human events since the time he had disappeared from. He hadn't wanted to read the *full* history, which the nurses had claimed had several volumes on humanity alone.

The device itself was about the size of a hardback novel, made of an extremely light white metal with rounded corners, and a completely interactive touch-screen that filled almost one entire side. Adam had expected technology like this, though was surprised that it was similar in appearance to tech in his own century.

The history had been unexpected. He had hoped that the future would be a Star Trek-like utopia -what else had he fought for? And the mention of a 'mysterious man' appearing around Dr. Jenkins had been surprising -after all, he never thought *he* would be mentioned alongside such incredible events in history. There was even a blurry picture of a man and a woman resembling him and Jenkins; a picture by the man that had indeed flashed a camera in his face.

Space travel was achieved through an ancient network of subspace tunnels colloquially named the Linkway, with different variations of it depending on the distance travelled, and what part of the universe you were in.

Incredibly, Earth —or rather Terra- was gone, obliterated a hundred years ago by a rogue asteroid that destabilised the bizarrely named Terran Consortium for some years.

Hannah entered the small room, standing beside his medical bed.

"Checking up on what we missed?" she asked with a knowing smile. She'd done the same thing upon waking after the oxygen depravation had knocked her out half way to the medical bay.

"Some wars, some peace treaties; not all that different from our own time," he quipped, though it fell on deaf ears. She could see in his face he was disappointed.

"You're worried you fought for nothing when you were in the armed forces," answered Hannah.

"Is everyone I meet in this century a mind reader?" Adam snapped. He immediately regretted saying it, seeing Hannah's gorgeous face crestfallen. He apologised profusely.

"I read a history file on you," she admitted. "Staff Sergeant (Warrant Officer Honorary) Adam Logan Caine, Royal Marines Commando; awarded the Victoria Cross for saving the lives of three thousand soldiers and civilians in Kosovo. The file says your reason for leaving is classified, even after two thousand years, and that you were attached to the Special Boat Service for several years: the youngest soldier in the SBS' history."

It also says that if you hadn't disappeared you would have been the seventeenth Earl of Cambridge, and you were the only son of the third richest man in the world, Nathaniel Caine."

Adam suddenly became very interested in the quality of the stitching on his bed sheets.

"I'm sorry; I didn't mean to make you uncomfortable. I'm guessing family is a sore subject for you as well."

"Tyrant for a father, parents divorced, siblings that hate you?" he snorted.

She nodded, another knowing smile on her lips.

"My husband cheated on me," she replied.

"Oh. I think that trumps my disgusting, posh, uptight family card."

She chortled with laughter at his crude attempt at humour.

"I'll see your uptight family card with a pair of daughter cards," she grinned.

"I fold."

Adam couldn't help but beam an ear-to-ear smile.

Hannah wrapped her hand around his. Before, or even during, their internment, he would have removed his hand. Now, it felt good, comforting at a time when he *needed* comforting. He smiled even more, all thoughts of Silver, and strands of time dissipated from his mind, and his whole world seemed to centre on Hannah.

She leaned down, and kissed him on the lips; at first it was tentative, and soft, but as the moment took them over, and neither wanted it to end, it became fiercer, hungrier. In minutes, they were all over each other, stripping clothes off, hoping the nurse wouldn't interrupt.

* * *

"What do you think, Commander?" Barkley probed. "Are they time-travellers?"

Mkdorn sighed.

The two were stood next to his command chair, reviewing the relevant data on their new passengers.

"All the data seems to indicate they are," Mkdorn allowed. "But the idea of time travel is too far-fetched to be believable."

"Agreed, but we can't just dismiss their claims out of hand; there are all sorts of weird things going on these days -open-mindedness is wise in this situation."

"Captain I do not believe you should trust them," Mkdorn said forcefully.

"Why? Because they say they're time travellers?"

"Yes. You are being reckless with these people, and I don't think-"

"I am the captain of this vessel," Barkley interrupted, his voice low so as not to attract the attention of the bridge's officers and crew. "I do not trust *you,*

Commander, because you were placed here simply as a favour for a Member of Parliament, against my express wishes. Do not presume to give *me* orders."

Mkdorn was about to make an arrogant retort when a young ensign approached and cleared her throat.

"Major Sansky is demanding to see you, Captain."

* * *

Major Raymond Sansky of Terran Navy Intelligence stood in Captain Barkley's private office. He had almost shouted at the doctor, and threatened his commission, to let him out of quarantine to talk to the ship's commanding officer. A Private Van Hoon had then escorted him to the captain's office.

Van Hoon was a member of the Terran Army's 3rd Fleet Protection Group -a collection of Army regiments dedicated to the security of the Terran Navy's ships, and tasked with boarding other ships, among other things. Van Hoon, typical of Terran Army, was tall, muscled, with bland features, and wore the dark green fatigues, and grey carapace armour of his Brigade.

"I have to take a shuttle to Delta-Tango, Captain," Sansky demanded.

"The taskforce will stay on-station at Proxima Centauri's Linkway entrance," Barkley returned, angry at yet another Intelligence spook, "and you are not authorised to take a shuttle off the ship, *Major*."

Sansky, angry at the ignorant ship captain, turned away from the captain's desk, and paced around the office. It was a spacious office, set just off the huge bridge, with a big white desk facing away from the large viewports that gave the captain a breathtaking view of the ship's prow. There were no pictures of family, or friends, no mementos of previous assignments, just holographic systems displays of the ship, hanging in mid-air before the white bulkheads. Digipads of personnel assignments, duty rosters, and Navy communiqués littered the smooth white desk.

"Then let me use the ship's communications grid," said Sansky, "and I can contact Intelligence Headquarters by hologram."

Barkley sighed, and then nodded.

"Alright, Major."

He contacted the bridge, and asked them to allow Sansky to contact Delta-Tango.

The holo-projectors in the office flickered, and the transparent floating displays disappeared, replaced by an emerald-green hovering control panel in front of Sansky. He tapped in the communications channel, and then selected the destination, before typing in his own authorization and clearance codes. The transparent holographic control panel moved to Sansky's right.

Another hologram flickered to life in front of him, in the shape of a human male; instead of a green-tinged hologram like the control panels all over the ship, this one was fully coloured and no longer transparent, as if the man was standing right there in front of him.

Sansky, wearing standard Navy overalls from the ship's stores, stood to attention, and snapped off a salute. He noted that Captain Barkley was stood to attention, without saluting, behind his desk.

"General," Sansky said, a nervous twinge in his voice. 5-Star General Lenson Gardner, the head of Navy Intelligence, was white-haired, short-tempered, a sly, crafty bugger, and a barrel-chested brute of a man. At one-hundred-and-twenty, the man was still very much alive, big, and strong.

"*Major Sansky,*" the old General growled. "*You were officially declared dead eighteen months ago.*"

"I almost *was* dead, sir," replied Sansky.

"*We received a brief status report from you two years ago, though it was only a positional marker. When we sent a ship to investigate, all they found was Rel Major in ruins, and no sign of you or your starfighter. We were... annoyed, to say the least. At first, it was assumed you had gone deep undercover.*"

"I never achieved my mission objective, General. The whole planet went to hell, I had to ditch my fighter, and then infiltrate the attacking force just to survive."

"*Who are they?*" Gardner demanded. Suddenly, his eye line changed to his right, and another holographic figure appeared. Gardner snapped to attention.

It was High Admiral Jessica Scarlett, First Star Lady, and supreme commander of all Terran military forces. She was stately, shorthaired, medium-height with a medium build; her soft features hid a harsh, uncompromising personality that brooked no fools. Gardner had obviously informed her of Sansky's timely resurrection.

"*At ease,*" she beckoned, waiting for the others to stand easy. "*You didn't answer the General's question, Major.*"

"Sorry, ma'am." He cleared his throat, preparing to brief the most famous, and most celebrated officer in the history of the Navy, on a race he himself had discovered and infiltrated. "They call themselves the Core; a race of avian-like creatures. They're ill tempered, vicious to the point of psychopathic, and all bred for a life of war. They invade planets, destroy the military and governments, murder the populous, and then steal whatever technology they can find."

"*Scavengers,*" Scarlett said, disgust in her voice. "*Hardly worth bothering with.*"

"It's not *them* that I'm worried about, Admiral, though they are dangerous," said Sansky. "It's what they've scavenged." The two senior officers looked at him expectantly. "A month after the destruction of Rel Major," Sansky continued, "they came across a barren planet, and found a device beneath the surface. According to the artificial intelligence *protecting* the device, it could control incredible amounts of temporal energy. Thing of it is, ma'am... they weren't lying."

"*Temporal energy?*" Gardner scoffed. "*You mean time travel?*"

"Exactly, sir; except on a massive scale. The device recovered was the size of a large hangar; but the field it could produce may ultimately encompass starships. Their Lord and commander indicated an invasion of some sort."

"*Where are they?*" Scarlett asked. She didn't seem to find the idea of time travel quite as ridiculous as Sansky had thought. It was a testament to his abilities that the Admiral and General took his word at face value.

"Terra."

Scarlett looked crestfallen at this knowledge; the Terran system was essentially abandoned, but it was still a holy place for Terrans and humans all over the universe; to think these Core would violate the graveyard of the homeworld itself was unconscionable. Both she and Gardner had been born on Terra, and it was rumoured they had watched the homeworld die.

They exchanged long, angered looks.

"*Captain Barkley,*" she snapped, looking back at the two younger officers, "*what is the status of this man Adam Caine?*" Sansky noted Gardner's flicker of recognition at the mention of Adam's name. What was that all about? Sansky hadn't mentioned Caine's name once, not even in his brief report to Scarlett herself. How could both her and Gardner possibly know who the escapee was?

"Physically, he's recovering, ma'am. Mentally, he's traumatised. Whatever they did to him, they spared no expense."

"*Captain, Major, I want the two of you to propose an attack plan to prevent this time device from reaching its potential. You have nine hours, and then I want a full holo-conference with the two of you, these people you freed, and the commander of every Naval vessel and fighter squadron within the sector. Even if there is no time travelling machine, the presence of alien intruders in the ruins of our homeworld is beyond intolerable. Do I make myself perfectly crystal clear, gentlemen?*"

"Yes, ma'am," the two officers replied simultaneously. Gardner nodded to someone not visible in the holographic images. The General and Admiral disappeared, and the floating control panels returned to the walls around them.

"I suppose we'd better get started," sighed Sansky.

"This isn't going to be easy," Barkley sighed in sympathy. All animosity had, for now, been forgotten, and the two officers set to work.

* * *

The message came down from the Captain, so the doctor sent a nurse into the private recovery room.

The nurse knocked on the door, but didn't wait for an answer.

She stepped into the room, and to her embarrassment found Adam Caine and Hannah Spears naked on his medical bed, sweating, and peacefully asleep. She contemplated not waking them, but the Captain had made it an order. She cleared her throat, loudly.

Adam jerked awake, instantly alert. The movement shocked Hannah out of her sleep, and the two of them suddenly went completely red, moving away from each other. The nurse turned away, and let them dress in private.

"Captain Barkley has requested your presence in the main briefing bay in eight hours and forty-three minutes, sir," the nurse reported without turning round.

"If we don't know where that is?" Hannah ventured, getting her clothes back on in record time.

"Ask someone, or ask the computer."

"That simple is it?" Adam snorted.

The nurse simply nodded, and then left, leaving the two behind to look at each other.

"Hungry?" Hannah asked. She'd had time to review at least some of the ship's plans.

* * *

They found a small mess hall not far from the medical ward. The doctor had insisted they stay in quarantine, but had then waved them away, muttering about ungrateful patients breaking quarantine on a whim.

They found some food that looked vaguely like chicken, yet tasted more like freeze-dried rice. It wasn't the worst thing in the world, though Adam had tasted better from a ration pack. The chef had told them it was a nutritional supplement designed specifically for the military.

"Christ, even in Kosovo we got to eat sausage and chips, or a curry once in a while," Adam snorted. "Now they've got food engineered for them." He shook his head. For the first time, he wondered if he really was out of his element in this futuristic place, with spaceships, holographic computers, and powerful beings who could appear in your mind at a moment's notice. He mentally shrugged the thought off, easily concentrating on Hannah, who sat the other side of a small circular table, wolfing down the chicken-rice.

"What did you do in the Boat Service?" she asked once they'd finished their meal.

"Officially I was just an SB operator in one of the main squadrons."

"And unofficially?" she ventured.

He looked away, shame so readily readable on his face.

"I was a killer."

"All soldiers are trained to kill, especially those in the SBS," Hannah said reassuringly, placing a soft hand over his.

Adam shook his head. "I was one of those ordered behind enemy lines, to scout out and then eliminate a target, whether it was a building... or a person, using whatever means necessary: demolitions, sniper rifles, knives, poisons, you name it, I did it. All in the name of Queen and country. They chose me above all others because I was more savage and stealthier than the rest."

"Is that why you left?"

He nodded, "I was ordered to take out a civilian target to draw out some tyrant MI6 wanted taken down. I refused. The Ministry of Defence gave me an option: complete the mission, or take an honourable discharge. I took the latter." He looked off into the distance, past Hannah, past the future. "I wish I had stayed in the regular Marine units, as a grunt. Life would have been so much easier, and so much less dangerous."

Hannah smiled, and it warmed Adam more than he could say.

"If you had," she said softly so only he could hear, "you would never have been here to save us."

Adam returned the smile, and placed his other hand on top of hers.

They talked for two hours, about their families, their lives before that fateful train journey, their favourite foods, films, even colours, until they reached relationships.

"I never actually caught him," said Hannah, referring to her husband and his secretary. "The simulations the Core showed me were of me walking in and finding them in bed together, and them laughing at how stupid I was." She smiled sadly. "I was on my way to confront him when we were kidnapped."

"I'm sorry. I've never been in a serious relationship. Dated an Army supplies officer back when I first returned from the Congo, but she left me for someone who wasn't off being shot at as a daily routine. My father would never have approved anyhow."

Hannah leaned over the table, and kissed him softly on the lips.

"Perhaps this future is a way for us all to start over."

"Once this mission is over, then yes."

"Mission?" she asked suddenly, withdrawing her hand. "You're not seriously thinking about going along with Sansky, and going back to that ship? That's suicide; besides, you're not a serving soldier anymore. You're not Warrant Officer Caine -you're just Adam. *My* Adam."

"I *have* to go back; I *need* to make sure Yh'reth'gar and his second die so that they can never hurt you, Sasha, Sapphire, or anyone else ever again."

"No," Hannah simply said.

"No?"

"This isn't about saving the world from tyranny like when you were a Marine -this is about you wanting revenge," Hannah retorted angrily. "That's what you want. You want to make them pay for what they did to you. Vengeance is an ugly thing, a nasty thing, you should never give into it; especially since you were a professional soldier, and you have people who care about you." Now she was upset. "What about Sasha? I've seen how she looks up to you, and Sapphire as well. If you give in to that petty vengeance, you'll be no better than those bastards that you want to kill. You'll be nothing, just another murderer with a lust for violence that you're so worried of becoming."

"Petty vengeance?" he cried. Heads around the mess hall were turning at the rising noise. "There's nothing petty about this; billions of lives are at stake."

"The soldiers of this century are perfectly capable of handling it; they're trained for combat in this environment. What could you possibly do that they can't?" Even as she said it, she was sure she didn't want to hear the answer to it; she'd witnessed what he could do. Adam didn't reply to the comment though.

He didn't have to.

"I- I have to go; I'm sorry Hannah, but I have to."

"What if we ran away?" Her keen mind already cycling through the possibility as she blurted it out. "What if we got on some kind of transport to the other side of the universe? One of the nurses told me there are nineteen galaxies to get lost in -that's a lot of places to go to. We could run away with Sasha and Sapphire, and never look back."

Adam squeezed his eyes shut, fighting back an invisible rising pain. He so desperately wanted to do exactly that: forget the last few weeks, forget his previous life, and search this incredible new frontier.

Sansky had mentioned there were nineteen whole habitable galaxies explored or catalogued. That was a big place to disappear into.

"Please Adam," she pleaded, "don't go on this mission." She could see in his eyes that she was losing this fight to keep him with her, his struggle to decide what was right. And she was so desperate to keep him with her; strong and handsome, Adam had shown her a kindness and love she hadn't felt since the days when her husband and she had still been passionate.

"I have to," decided Adam, with a finality that broke Hannah's heart.

She stood up, her chair slamming back loudly, finally drawing the attention of *all* the personnel sitting at the other tables.

"So that's it?" said Hannah, her voice soft, almost a whisper. "Love-me-and-leave-me? If you had one iota of humanity left you would take up my offer, and disappear with me, and my daughters, to live a quiet life."

She made to leave, avoiding eye contact with any of the spectators. She turned back to Adam before leaving.

"Maybe all that killing, all that death and destruction, all that torture has robbed you of the one thing that could have made you human: your soul. I thought you had one, but maybe it was just an echo of who you used to be –that gorgeous young man on the train. You are not that man anymore. You're cold, heartless."

She ran off, covering her mouth so that he wouldn't see her bottom lip trembling.

When she was gone, he slammed his fist into the table so hard, the furniture cracked.

* * *

Jack Digby and the balding old priest had discovered an observation room not far from the medical ward. It wasn't a room so much as a corridor with massive windows that looked out over the ship's port engine nacelle. The realisation of this future wasn't sitting well with them, and they were having a hard time coping with it.

The holograms, and the ship itself had particularly unnerved Jack, who was used to his tiny flat in an apartment block in London, where the television was his only concession to the computer-dependant culture that had developed in modern Britain.

"This place is frightening," Jack admitted, albeit reluctantly.

The priest nodded. "The nurses told me that the belief in God has shrunk to a handful of people out on the frontier of *another galaxy*." Jack, a some-time churchgoer, shook his head almost in unison with the priest.

"We don't belong here," Jack croaked, his voice breaking slightly as he thought of just how useless he was in this era. "I almost miss the War; at least there I had a purpose."

"You served?" the priest asked, looking at his newfound friend.

Jack nodded, grimacing at the experience of reliving it back in that simulated hell. "Dunkirk was my first action, though Normandy was the worst of it. Served in the Army until 1958, took my pension and said goodbye. And yourself?"

The priest shook his head. "I was only six when the War ended. My father served as a Sergeant in the Rifle Brigade- although I think they call them the Royal Green Jackets now. I didn't really know him, but the history books say he died at Normandy after a rocket launcher misfired."

Now Jack Digby had never been a superstitious man, nor was he a true believer in Christianity -it was something his late wife had been a fanatic about- but right then and there he believed there really was some greater being watching over them. "Your father was Sergeant Bishop? Sergeant Terence Bishop?"

The priest just stared at him, eyes wide, and jaw almost hitting his chest.

"I was Bishop's Corporal during the landings. It's where I got my Sergeant's stripes."

The two old men just stared at each other in silent amazement.

A snort escaped from Digby's aging lips, which expanded into a chuckle, and soon enough, the two of them were laughing. In fact, they were laughing so hard and loud, one of the nurses came to see what the noise was about.

"Sorry," apologised Bishop between guffaws and spluttered giggles, "we were just laughing at the hopelessness of our situation." This caused more laughter to spill out of them. The young nurse beamed a big smile at the two old men laughing like they were teenagers again.

"If you're really feeling so hopeless and helpless," she started, "there's a *Nightingale*-class medical ship -the *HMS Klinsmann* I think- leaving Proxima Centauri for the outer rim of the Milky Way. I'm told there's a big plague breaking out on some of the smaller backwater planets. They may need someone to steel their faith, and to give sermons and the like."

Bishop looked at her incredulously.

"My great-grandfather was a Catholic," she explained. "I can talk to my CO if you like, arrange transport for you and anyone else who would like to go. You can requisition clothing from the ship's stores before you go."

"The *Klinsmann* you say?" Digby smiled.

The nurse nodded, and left them.

Bishop leaned in closer, "Didn't Jurgen Klinsmann used to play for Tottenham Hotspur?"

* * *

One of the off-duty Army personnel reluctantly directed Adam to a gymnasium on the deck below the mess hall. The gymnasium itself was pretty standard, though the equipment was as futuristic as the rest of the ship, completely made up of glowing green holograms. There was a selection of rowing machines, cycles, and weight-lifting devices, the designs almost unchanged in two thousand years, all rendered in emerald-green holographic projections.

Some of the soldiers who used the gym must have had an interest in the twenty-first century, because hanging from the ceiling, at the back of the spacious room, there was a leathery punch bag, well-used. With all the futuristic crap around him, Adam found it to be a strange comfort.

There was nobody around, so he punched the bag once, then twice, and then growled a nonsensical cry of anguish as he laid more punches on faster and harder with each hit.

He wasn't even aware there was someone else in the room until after he had stopped.

When he turned, Sasha was standing in the doorway, holding her beloved stuffed toy, eyes wide at his insane rage.

"Sasha?"

"Why did you make my mummy cry?" she asked, innocently, fiddling with the fluffy ear of the toy.

"I didn't mean to, Sasha," Adam replied, the anger draining out of him. He sat down on the floor next to her, though she kept her distance; even a child knew not to get too close to a large man who was clearly so angry, and so dangerous.

"But why did you? Mummy said you haven't got a soul, that you're a bad man."

"She's right," he realised, looking into the tiny girl's big eyes. "I'm a killer; that's all I'll ever be."

"But you saved us," Sasha insisted.

"But not myself." When Sasha looked at him blankly, he added, "when you're older you'll understand that."

"You still saved us," she persisted. Her fears forgotten, she walked up to him, and hugged him, throwing her tiny fragile arms around his neck, and then gave him a peck on the cheek, before her older sister finally found her, and took her away from the "bad man."

He didn't feel any sadness; perhaps he wouldn't ever. All he could feel was an empty anger, at himself, at the Core, at those responsible for recruiting him to the Boat Service back home. Could he have refused those assignments? Joined a regular unit? No, he was too good at what he did for his superiors to let him waste away in a squad.

He stood back up, spun, and laid a heavy, lazy roundhouse kick on the punch bag, disintegrating it, and showering the gym with harmless white powder.

* * *

Sansky and Barkley had finally come up with a plan, but it would take a week to get the necessary equipment, ships, and personnel into place. After finishing up with Barkley, he had headed down to the medical bay, and found a rather miserable atmosphere. Word travelled fast on a starship, even one as big as the *Polly Jenkins*. The nurses were all talking about Adam's huge rippling muscles when he had entered the medical bay. Hannah Spears was crying her eyes out, the others were silent, and Caine was nowhere to be seen, though an FPB trooper had reported the vandalism of a punch bag in the gymnasium on the deck below.

With only a few words, he asked those that could walk to join him, including the children.

They followed him to the double doors of a room labelled, "Briefing Bay."

Sansky swiped his newly printed ID card across the reader, and the double doors opened, followed by two sets of armoured blast doors beyond that.

The group stepped through a short corridor and into a large room that was big enough to comfortably hold the forward half of a Boeing 747. The doors shut behind them with a clank, locking into place. There were no lights except at the centre, where a massive round holographic chart table resided -the lighting gave the impression that the walls were not there, all but invisible in the shadows. Captain Barkley was already there, along with the commander of the *Polly Jenkins'* starfighter wing, Wing Commander Farnham.

"Where's Caine?" demanded Barkley, having noticed his absence in the group.

Sansky shrugged.

The doors opened once again, and in stepped Caine, escorted by an armoured FPG trooper. The trooper pointed him to the table, and then retreated to the corridor outside.

"Now that we're all here," Sansky said archly, stepping up to the raised table. Caine stood beside him, though the other survivors stayed away from the table, preferring not to be a part of the meeting, just observing. Sansky saw the glares thrown in Adam's direction from his fellow escapees. All he could see in Adam's eyes was a cold emptiness. Clearly something had snapped in his newfound friend.

"Computer," said Barkley, "activate encrypted holographic communications."

There was a beep, and suddenly the table was surrounded by flickering holographic images of other Terran Navy officers. Two of these were Admiral Scarlett, and General Gardner. When Adam saw Scarlett, he couldn't believe his eyes.

He whispered, "It's Mary Poppins." Indeed, Admiral Jessica Scarlett was the spitting image of none other than an older Julie Andrews, though he was sure none of the contemporary military types would understand the reference, nor would they find it amusing.

"*This must be Caine,*" Scarlett stated.

Adam nodded but kept his trap shut.

"*You have your proposal, gentlemen?*" she asked.

Sansky and Barkley nodded.

Sansky activated the holographic chart table, and then the two laid down their plan for the senior officers.

Every now and then, throughout the briefing, Adam could feel General Gardner's eyes on him, watching him, sizing him up. *What the hell was that about?* he wondered.

When Sansky and Barkley had finished their extensive plan, Scarlett's eyes were open wide with surprise, and not a little shock. And there was something else in her expression: pride. Adam put it down to Sansky proving himself to his superiors, after a two-year absence from Navy Intelligence. He figured that Sansky was probably a favoured agent of the higher-ups.

"That's insane, Raymond," Adam finally spoke.

The Naval officers looked at him incredulously, but said nothing, waiting for one of the *senior* officers to rebuke him. They didn't.

"*The time-traveller's right,*" Gardner growled. Adam noted that the General had already labelled him a time-traveller, despite the fact that he was convinced nobody believed the story of how Adam and co came to be in the fortieth-century.

"Possibly, sir," Raymond nodded with a chuckle. "But we think it will work."

Scarlett nodded, and looked around her at the other officers.

"*Not very many resources in your sector,*" she noted.

"No, Admiral, the other capital ships in the sector are in the Proxima Shipyards, undergoing refitting. But we have the *Polly Jenkins* and her group, as well as three other cruisers, nine frigates, six destroyers, and fourteen gunships, all on their way here. We have eight *Rhino* squadrons, and two *Stickleback* squadrons between the cruisers. It may be enough, it may not. There's no way to tell how many ships the Core have in the area besides the three cruisers and the flagship in the Terran dust cloud itself."

"*The flagship itself?*" Gardner questioned.

"She's a Titan, sir. It would be wise for our capital ships to try and stay clear of her except when we land the boarding parties."

"*I'm sending the* HMS Cerberus *and her carrier group to you,*" Scarlett reported, "*but they may get there too late. You'll be on your own. Captain Barkley, you'll be in command of the fleet action, Major Sansky you'll take control of the ground action, and for that you'll need a promotion to Colonel; an overdue promotion wouldn't you agree?*"

Sansky was dumbfounded. He nodded enthusiastically.

"*Well then, Colonel,*" Gardner grinned. "*Good luck, and god speed.*"

"*To all of you,*" Scarlett added, though she was looking directly at Adam.

The holograms of the two senior officers disappeared.

"*Is this for real, Virgil?*" the captain of the cruiser *HMS Exeter* blurted, his holographic hands leaning on the edge of the map table.

Barkley nodded. "I'm afraid so." He sighed, and looked round at all of the other ship and unit commanders. "Look, I know that the Navy hasn't seen this kind of large-scale action since the last Interior War at the beginning of the thirty-first century. But there is more at stake here than booting squatters out of the remains of the homeworld. You don't have high enough classification to know what is truly at stake, but believe me, if we pull this off, we may well save all of humanity."

"*You must be joking,*" retorted the captain of the gunship *HMS Genevieve*.

"No," Sansky replied. "And there is no question of doing this. It has to be done; no matter how ugly it gets, remember Captain Barkley's words: *everything is at stake here.*"

"We do this for Terra," Barkley announced.

"*For Terra,*" the *Exeter's* captain murmured.

"For Britain," Hannah exclaimed.

"For home," said someone from behind her.

"For some bangers and mash," Adam grumbled. The 41st-century humans looked at him blankly, whilst the humans from his own time just snorted with amusement.

Nobody had a suitable reply to that, and signed off, their holograms disappearing. The briefing was essentially over, with Captain Barkley and Wing Commander Farnham filing out of the Briefing Bay, talking about personnel re-assignments, and promotions as they left.

Sansky turned to Adam, "Are you still coming with us?"

Adam glanced at Hannah, who avoided eye contact, and then nodded. "Let's get this over with."

* * *

Yh'reth'gar seethed.

The scientists were making promise after promise, still repairing the time machine.

They were a day away, according to their last update.

Lord Yh'reth'gar was pacing in his throne room, in front of the throne itself. Second Yh'par'ban was nearby, away from the Lord, watching his friend becoming more and more agitated.

"[The Terrans know we are here,]" Yh'reth'gar growled.

"[They don't know our strength,]" Yh'par'ban returned. "[I doubt they will have enough time to gather sufficient force to destroy us.]"

"[Our benefactor has assured us victory,]" Yh'reth'gar pointed out.

"[I do not trust him, Lord,]" the Second grumbled.

"[Neither do I. The spy, and Caine will be a problem,]" Yh'reth'gar complained. It was true; those two humans could be a serious pain if they ever got aboard the flagship. Caine especially would be out for blood, if Yh'par'ban had judged correctly. The spy would be a minor nuisance, but his experience among the Core could prove annoying.

"[Alert the other ships,]" Yh'reth'gar ordered. "[Tell them to prepare for anything, and report anything out of the ordinary.]"

Second Yh'par'ban nodded silently, not bothering to insult the Lord by telling him he had already done just that the moment he had escaped from the disintegrating corridor, cycles ago. The Lord was a buffoon, but a dangerous, powerful, and highly influential buffoon.

The Terrans were indeed coming, and Second Yh'par'ban would be prepared, whatever the outcome.

* * *

Just as the two Core nobles plotted the destruction of the Terran forces, four stealth-model Rhino starfighters darted out of the Linkway and spilled into the Terran star system. Currently, the Mars debris field obscured the Linkway from any sensors within Terra's own debris field. Essentially a reverse delta wing, the cockpit was centred at the midsection, with pairs of laser cannons along the front of the wings. The Rhino was the most common type of starfighter in the Terran Consortium, and the most reliable. These four were matt-black, their engine emissions designed to be low; they were all from Starfighter Command's reconnaissance squadrons, designated as Echo Flight. None of the craft had markings, or running lights, and the cockpit canopies were dulled so as not to let any errant light out.

Echo One, the flight's leader, skimmed across a large chunk of rock, a rock that had once been a part of Mount Olympus on Mars.

The upcoming operation depended upon Echo Flight's reconnaissance of the star system.

Stealth was vital.

The flight passed over another Mars-born rock in a loose diamond formation, and almost slammed into the massive red hull of an enemy cruiser; a cruiser that had been hiding behind the rock. Echo One yanked on the control stick as hard as he could, sending his craft into a climb, over the spiked cruiser. He ran the scans, and cursed at the magnitude of his mistake.

The enemy were now aware the Terrans had detected them; the surprise was no longer necessarily viable. He needed to warn the fleet at Proxima Centauri.

Two's sudden scream was cut short as a man-sized chunk of rock appeared ahead of him, and speedily punched through the Rhino's cockpit, pulverising the pilot, and turning the craft into a steaming wreck of twisted metal. Echo Two's Rhino began to drift away. In a somewhat pyrrhic victory, the wreck slammed into the bridge of the cruiser's unshielded mass.

Echo Three's engines were shredded by anti-starfighter laser fire, detonating the fuel cells.

Echo Four was hit by a rock that destroyed his nose cone, crushing the cockpit module so that the flight stick impaled the pilot through the chest. He was still screaming when his fighter slammed into a spiked enemy fighter.

Echo One began firing into the confusion in desperation, spraying laser fire in front of his fighter, jinking and juking around small chunks of planet. Rocks careened past his cockpit, narrowly missing by a hand span. Dust clogged up the engines, shorting out everything but the life support. The craft drifted away from the sudden and brutal massacre, the enemy gunners leaving it alone, knowing that it was no longer a threat to the big ship.

Echo One died of asphyxiation nine hours later. But by then, no one knew nor cared.

The message was out, and away.

* * *

"You alright?" Sansky asked.

The two new friends were in the *Polly Jenkins'* armoury, gearing up. Adam opened a locker mysteriously labelled with his name. He opened it, and was shocked to discover the uniform he had arrived in, and his SA80 rifle along with all the remaining ammunition. He shook his head and retrieved his equipment.

"Sure, why not?" Adam replied.

"Come off it, Adam, the entire ship is talking about you and your friend Hannah."

"She... We.... I..."

"You're in love with her," Sansky smiled. It wasn't a question, it was a statement, and Adam wasn't sure he could argue against it. The two soldiers changed into their gear. Adam refused to put on the armour Raymond was dressing in, on the simple fact that he was used to flak armour and fatigues.

"You going to do anything about it?" Raymond asked.

"That's not the life I can live right now," Adam admitted.

"Maybe you should think about making a life with her."

Adam nodded, "Maybe, but I'm not the settling type. Besides.... after what's happened... I don't think I could live a quiet life."

"A warrior through and through."

* * *

Virgil Barkley stood on the bridge of his ship, away from his comfortable command chair: he had no wish to be comfortable during this operation. He was very much aware of the fact that the Terran military were not directly experienced when it came to outright combat on the scale they would about to be thrown in to. The Navy hadn't come up against an enemy that matched their own size and force in centuries. This was indeed going to be a serious test of the Navy's abilities.

The fleet hung, motionless, beyond the *Polly Jenkins'* bow and sides, awaiting the order to go.

Two chunky troop transports were already shuttling across their payload of Army regiments; the ships' presence would be a hindrance to the operation, and they would never get close enough to the enemy to deliver its troops. So the *Polly Jenkins*, and the other cruisers in the hastily gathered battlegroup were setting aside vital hangar bay space for the Army's dropships.

"Captain!" the communications officer called out, running across the bridge.

"This is not a cattle market, Lieutenant; this is a starship -unless we're in combat, keep your voice down." Barkley prided himself on having a quiet ship, and many of the crew were comfortable with it, though there were always a few who disagreed.

"Of course, sir; my apologies. We just received a communiqué from Echo Flight; it appears they were destroyed. Echo One sent the message just before we permanently lost contact with him. He sends a text message, only a few words." The junior Lieutenant held up a digipad for Barkley's viewing.

The message was indeed short and to the point:

THEY KNOW YOU ARE COMING.

"Damn," the old captain cursed softly. "Get Colonel Sansky and that fellow Caine up here on the double."

Sansky appeared minutes later, quicker than Barkley had given him credit. The newly-promoted Colonel was dressed in the black fatigues and grey carapace armour of the frontline Terran Army, a plasma rifle slung over one shoulder, a plasma pistol holstered on his hip, and his featureless helmet clipped to the back of his armoured belt.

Barkley didn't even realise Caine was there until the so-called time-traveller nodded to the Navy captain. It was deeply unsettling, not hearing the man sneak up on him, though it answered the question as to whether Caine was necessary in the upcoming fight. The man was almost invisible on the darkened bridge, barely discernable from the shadows nearby.

Fernikking man's probably better than the entire Terran Army with that kind of supernatural silence, thought Barkley.

Caine had his long unkempt hair tied back, with several braids among the fair locks -the kind that warriors of ancient Terra once wore. He too seemed to be wearing the black fatigues, though not the carapace armour. Barkley wondered about this choice, though it seemed to make sense given the man's background.

A speck of light glinted off of something dark and metallic cradled in Caine's hands. Barkley could just make out the dark outline of the automatic rifle Caine had been rescued with. He threw a quick glare at Sansky, reasoning that the Intelligence agent had probably fished the weapon and its ammunition from the locked storage bay it had been placed in.

"You requested us, Captain?" Sansky said, still adjusting his carapace armour.

"Yes, Colonel. Your Echo Flight reported in."

"Oh?"

"I'm afraid they were destroyed," Barkley reported, his voice containing more sympathy than Sansky had given him credit for. "I'm sorry. I understand their commander was a friend of yours."

Sansky nodded; Squadron Leader Griscombe was an old friend from the beginning of Sansky's Intelligence career. Sansky had been the one to recommend Griscombe for the position of leading Starfighter Command's premier reconnaissance squadron. Suddenly, he found himself staring off into the distance, and a comforting hand on his shoulder. When he turned to look, he was slightly surprised to find Adam's hand on his shoulder. Sansky smiled his gratitude.

"Was there a message?" Sansky asked.

"It was short, and to the point," Barkley replied. He quoted the message, "They know you are coming."

"Damn, so much for the element of surprise." Sansky gave a heavy sigh. "What's our status?"

"*Exeter* and *Carthage* are here, as well as all the promised frigates and gunships. We are still waiting on the *Heracles*; the *Iron Duke*, *Albion*, and *Endurance* are still on their way from an escort duty in the Alpha Centauri system. The Light Brigade is settling in here on the *Polly Jenkins*, and on the *Carthage* and *Falklands*."

"Any word from the *Cerberus*?"

"None," Barkley replied. "But we weren't expecting to for another day. I'm going to send a destroyer and two gunships to watch over the Linkway exit to the Sol system."

"Sounds good," Sansky agreed, "But you didn't need to tell me that; fleet is your expertise and purview, not mine."

"Call it professional courtesy," Barkley shrugged nonchalantly. "I'll send the *Kansas*, with the *McCampbell* and *Gascoigne*."

Sansky nodded, and the two soldiers left the bridge, though Barkley never heard Caine make a single audible sound, which sent a shiver up his spine. The man worried him deeply. *And to think*, he thought, *there were dozens like him in his century.*

Barkley turned to his XO, "Commander, order the *Kansas*, *McCampbell*, and *Gascoigne* to move out to the Linkway exit to Sol. They're to report anything and everything no matter how small or petty it might be."

Mkdorn nodded, and moved off to carry out her orders.

* * *

"Understood, Commander Mkdorn," the commander of the *Kansas* replied.

"*Sorry Captain Barkley couldn't pass the order on himself, Commander,*" Mkdorn's hologram apologised. "*He's a busy man at the moment.*"

"Of course, Commander," the man said.

Mkdorn's hologram nodded, and then dissipated.

"Let's get going shall we?" the *Kansas'* commander said jovially. "Half sublight ahead, take us to the Linkway, and set a course for the Sol exit." The bridge crew got to work instantly, and the destroyer's engines switched from idle station keeping to half speed, the two gunships moving to flanking positions.

The tiny patrol unit set sail, and left the growing fleet behind, plunging into the surreal blue softness of the Linkway.

* * *

Second Yh'par'ban watched the floating debris of the four human starfighters from the massive bridge of the Lord's flagship. The pompous idiot was in his throne room -thankfully.

Those sensors that had penetrated the dust cloud -once the human homeworld- had detected heightened activity from the Linkway entrance to the system. Yh'par'ban had surmised that the four black destroyed fighters had managed to transmit some kind of message out before their demise. It was a fair bet the Terrans would be here soon. The fleet had been at full alert since Caine and the others had escaped their prison, two weeks prior.

Yh'par'ban could feel it in his bones: the humans were definitely coming.

"[Order the *Enduring Pain* to take a squadron of fighters, and investigate the entrance to the Linkway. If it's Terran warships spying on us, tell them to destroy the humans with all necessary force.]"

The warriors manning the bridge nodded, and set to work.

* * *

The medical ship *HMS Klinsmann* hung at the mouth to the Linkway, awaiting its final volunteers to board. Long, wide and low, it followed the same architecture as the massing warships around it, with a command spine, engine nacelles, and a straight-lined overall blocky design. A small shuttle darted across space, leaving the *Polly Jenkins'* hangar bays and racing toward the medical ship. The pilot swung the craft in through the big ship's largest hangar and settled the extended landing gear onto the blast-proof deck. He was in a hurry: the fleet was leaving soon, and he had to fly three more supply runs to Proxima Centauri before that happened.

His six passengers stepped off the shuttle, carrying what little possessions they had in standard military kit bags. The three teenage girls, all attractive, and none older than fifteen, were the first off the shuttle, all with red-rimmed eyes, and sad expressions on their faces. The pilot wasn't entirely sure that young girls belonged on a medical transport, especially as volunteers heading for a plague-infested sector.

The other three passengers stepped off cautiously, two old men carefully guiding a younger man between them. The older men had the weary look of those who had seen it all, whilst the younger man was wild-eyed, his eyes permanently staring off into the distance, unaware of his surroundings; the pilot had seen it before, in the faces of those who had lost loved ones in combat zones.

Once the shuttle had left, *HMS Klinsmann* quietly left the Proxima Centauri system, with the six time-travellers on board.

* * *

Kansas, McCampbell and *Gascoigne* had been on-station for two hours, awaiting instructions, and passing any and all sensor data to the fleet flagship. There was nothing substantial there, as far as the sensors could determine.

There was the usual hodgepodge of interference from the planets' twisted remains, and the Linkway's entrance/exit made the available search area narrow, but there were some strange faint energy readings from the direction of Terra. Nothing could be pinned down as to what it could be, but the readings were definitely getting stronger.

On the *Kansas'* small bridge, the sensors officer called out to her commander.

"Sir, we just picked up an energy spike in the vicinity of Old Earth," she reported. "Could be starship engines powering up." The commander frowned at the use of the name of the homeworld; Terra was Terra -there hadn't been an Earth for a hundred years.

"Show me," he said, leaning forward in his command chair at the centre of the bridge. A three-dimensional holographic image of the dust clouds blinked into existence in front of the young commander.

Through the forward window, there was an unusual red patch getting more and more distinct at the very edge of Terra's remains like a cloud stained with blood, before forming into a blood-red starship, covered in vicious mismatched spikes. Judging by the size, it was bigger than the *Kansas*, equivalent to a frigate or even a light cruiser.

"Heading?" he asked.

"They're coming straight at us, Commander," the sensors officer answered.

"Us, or the Linkway?"

"No way to tell if they've actually detected us, sir, or whether they're planning on moving on."

"Get Captain Barkley on the line," he ordered to nobody in particular.

Seconds later, with the alien vessel closing slowly and cautiously, Captain Barkley's holographic image replaced the commander's tactical schematic.

"Commander; news?"

"Alien ships are approaching our position, Captain."

"Do they match Colonel Sansky's description of the enemy's technology?" Barkley inquired.

"The technology is the same, but the size puts it at frigate or light cruiser size."

"Are they arming weapons, and locking on?"

The *Kansas'* commander glanced at his executive officer, who answered for him. "Their weapons were armed as soon as they exited the debris field."

Barkley sighed. *"All our promised forces from Command are here. It's now or never. We'll move now, and be at your position within twenty minutes. Fire on them only if they make an aggressive move on you. Destroy them if you can, but not at the expense of you and your ships."*

"Understood, Captain."

Suddenly the deck tipped, and the commander had to hold on to the arms of his command chair, the inertial dampers strained to compensate for the sudden movement. Captain Barkley's hologram flickered, and stayed disturbingly upright, the holographic projection unaffected by the shift in gravity.

"What the hell was that!?"

"We're being fired upon, Commander!" his XO shouted.

"By what?"

"Some kind of anti-shield missile, sir. Shields are down to eighty-three point nine percent."

The commander turned to the hologram before him. "You'd better hurry, they're weapons are already on us, Captain."

Barkley nodded, reached out to an invisible control panel, and his hologram disappeared, replaced by the tactical schematics.

"There's a squadron of starfighters moving ahead of the enemy vessel, Commander," the sensors operator announced. On the tactical display, the commander could see the small shapes darting ahead of the big ship.

"Task *McCampbell* and *Gascoigne* to take care of the fighters, we'll have to handle the light cruiser ourselves."

"Commander, we have multiple weapon locks from *multiple* directions," the XO announced.

"Source?"

"They're coming from within the Terra, Mars, and Venus debris fields."

"This is going to be interesting," the commander exasperated sarcastically.

* * *

"All ships," Barkley announced, using audio comms only. "This is Captain Barkley; proceed with the mission. You know your places and assignments. Move out." He nodded to Commander Mkdorn, who proceeded to get the *Polly Jenkins* on its way.

Barkley felt the deck vibrations grow stronger under his feet: the ship's massive engines were powering up. Despite the seriousness of the situation, it felt good to be on the move again, instead of hanging in front of a Linkway exit, acting as a customs outpost. His ship, however, was old, older than most, and with its decommissioning only months away, Barkley was very aware of how dangerous this would be.

* * *

Sansky led Adam to the embarkation point, which turned out to be a teleportation device. It was massive, big enough even to fit a two-bedroom house on the circular foot-high disc. There were no markings; it was just a big matt-grey disk in the middle of the circular room.

There was a pair of consoles on either side of the disk, only one currently manned, with a pair of technicians, racing through the final diagnostics.

"So, what does this thing do?" Adam asked. Nobody had yet seen fit to explain to him precisely what happened to the human body in the teleportation process. Sansky had deliberately avoided telling Adam in case he backed out of the operation.

Sansky shrugged, and nodded to the technicians. One of them stepped forward from their diagnostics, and explained. All of it was scientific and way above Adam's head.

"In English please," Adam groaned.

"English?" the technician sputtered. He looked at Adam as if he were mad.

"The English language is now called Standard, since humanity is no longer limited to one planet," Sansky explained. He turned to the technician, "He means he wants it explained in simple terms."

"Ah," the technician said in recognition, "You're one of the time-travellers from the twenty-first century."

Adam shook his head -apparently there were no secrets on board the *Polly Jenkins*.

"Yes," he said simply.

"Well essentially, the device converts you into a form of sub-atomic energy, and then reconstitutes your molecules in the target area."

"So it tears me apart, and then puts me back together somewhere else," Adam worried.

"It's better you don't think about it, Adam," Sansky said encouragingly, clapping a hand on the other's shoulder.

Adam nodded, and gave an acknowledging smile, but was not in the least bit encouraged.

The main doors to the teleport bay -one of nine such bays according to Sansky- parted with a swish and a sigh, and through it stepped a platoon of Terran Army soldiers. Unlike Sansky, and the others in the attack force, these soldiers were dressed in black carapace armour, rather than grey, and they had images of swords painted in white onto the solid plates of their armour. These were apparently the special ops force Sansky had been waiting for.

"I'm Major Slayd," the leader of the soldiers announced, his helmet tucked under his arm, rifle slung over one shoulder. Slayd was a bullish man, with a shaven, square-ish head. The soldiers that followed him spread out around the room, thirty in all, all facing toward the middle, all as silent as wraiths. Adam found the almost-featureless helmets of the soldiers disturbing, making them no better than robots in his eyes.

"Colonel Sansky," the Intelligence agent smiled. "Glad you could make it, Major." The two soldiers shook hands, armoured gauntlets scraping as they did so. Sansky had already explained the existence of the 'Hunters', the Terran Army's 21st Infantry Regiment; they were the only Army Regiment to be permanently attached to Navy Intelligence, after a heroic special operations action decades ago led by a man named Vassily. It was a tale of heroism that Adam heard many times growing up: Rourke's Drift, D-Day, and the like.

The main doors slashed open once again, and Hannah Spears stepped through, wearing combat fatigues, light body armour, and a holstered plasma pistol on her hip. The uniform looked slightly too big for her, though to Adam's eyes, it seemed to suit her slightly podgy frame. Her hair was tied back, which gave her an air of sophistication, and Adam could see the lawyer she had once been: strong, capable, and willing to win.

There was, however, a severe look of determination on her face.

"Hannah," Adam said, stepping forward, "What are you doing?"

"The same as you, Adam," she answered. He could see she was still angry at him.

"You're not a soldier," he insisted. "You're not trained for this."

"You're no longer a soldier, either," she argued.

"You know why I'm here."

"I'm not letting you go into this by yourself," she rebutted.

Adam looked at Sansky for some kind of help. Sansky shrugged, "She's got as much right to fight as you have, Adam. She has got two daughters to defend after all."

Adam let out a heavy sigh, then span on his heel, and stepped onto the circular platform. He gripped his antiquated rifle like the trained professional he was, keeping the butt of the gun tight against his shoulder, and the barrel pointed down at the deck at a standby stance.

He was angry, angry that Hannah had turned up like this. He was angry that she would probably witness the atrocities he would have to commit to exact the vengeance he was after. He loved Hannah; he didn't want her around when the shit hit the fan -he wasn't sure he could protect her.

"Let's get this over with," Adam growled.

* * *

The enemy fighters, essentially five-metre-long red flying spikes with wings, swarmed over the *McCampbell*, unleashing small fighter-based missiles. Four of them struck the gunship's shields, white-blue blossoms of energy waving across the shields. Despite the bombardment, the shields held. The fighters flashed past the *McCampbell* and *Gascoigne*, aiming for the *Kansas*, the obvious bigger threat. The gunships' guns tracked the fighters, throwing anti-starfighter rounds into the space around them.

Two fighters were obliterated in balls of fire.

McCampbell and *Gascoigne* peeled back, turning to take the fighters from behind. Half of the fighters turned back to meet the threat, firing yet more missiles.

Terran Navy gunships were designed specifically to combat starfighters, and had more manoeuvrability than larger ships. The two gunships twisted suddenly, out of the way of the missiles, and let the fighters pass between them, slashing destructive energy in an inescapable crossfire at the fighters. They took down all but three of the attacking starfighters with that tactic.

Kansas, meanwhile, was fending off a new group of fighters, and exchanging long-range fire with the approaching light cruiser. The fighters were using their missiles to wear down the *Kansas'* shields. Despite the strange tactic involved -starfighters weren't designed for fighting capital ships- it worked. The shields of the *Kansas* suddenly failed catastrophically, pummelled by both the fighters and the enemy warship. Shield projectors exploded under the weight of fire, explosions rippling along its hull.

The ship began to list, even as the *McCampbell* and *Gascoigne* rushed to save her. *McCampbell* was hit amidships by a stray pulse of energy from the light cruiser, her damaged shields unable to stop it. *McCampbell* became a rolling fireball, her fiery death taking out several of the starfighters.

Kansas tried in vain to return fire, but the other ship was too big, and the starfighters were still swarming her.

The enemy guns raked the hull of the *Kansas,* obliterating it one piece at a time. The destroyer's hull caved and snapped in half under the sheer amount of fire it was sustaining. Flames licked from the ship's interior, briefly filling the Linkway entrance. The remains of the *Kansas* floated apart, and the *Gascoigne* darted through the gap, retreating from the enemy. It didn't get far before the enemy guns found it, and pounded it into tiny pieces.

The Core light cruiser *Enduring Pain* took up station at the very edge of the Linkway exit, its guns training on the wreckages of the Terran warships. The remaining fighters circled around once, and then sped back to the flagship.

The *Enduring Pain,* intent on searching for killable survivors, never saw the other ships approaching from within the Linkway, her sensors were directed so intently on the wreckages.

Enduring Pain's shields dropped under a hideous punishment, before her hull began to twist and buckle. It detonated in a fiery explosion, her wreckage spreading away from the Linkway.

The heavy cruiser *Polly Jenkins,* and its companion, the *Falklands,* powered through the debris brushing *Enduring Pain*'s pathetic ruins out of the way, weapons flashing as the gunners swept the wreckage away from the ships. Behind the two massive ships came the rest of Taskforce Delta-Nine-Four. The small fleet moved out of the Linkway at flanking speed, booming through space toward the Mars debris field.

* * *

Virgil Barkley, sat in his large command chair, watched the corpse of the *Kansas* flash past the bridge as his beloved ship moved at top speed. He mourned the loss of the destroyer, as he surely would mourn the loss of many more this day.

* * *

Falklands and the *Polly Jenkins* stormed towards the Mars debris field, as planned, with the smaller destroyers and gunships racing behind and between them, like pets scrambling for food from their masters. The taskforce's fighter squadrons, led by Wing Commander Farnham, formed a screen to the sides of the capital ships.

The Mars debris field began to twitch, the clouds of dust and rock expanding, and bulging until finally the Core vessels hiding beneath burst forth, picking up speed. There were three cruiser-sized warships, with only a small escort of starfighters. *Polly Jenkins* didn't slow for the enemy fighters, instead she ploughed right through them, crushing several against her formidable shields. *Falklands* avoided the tiny craft by putting a bit more distance between it and its bigger cousin.

The three Core cruisers spread out as well, weapons locking on their distant and rapidly closing targets.

* * *

Wing Commander Farnham, sat in the cockpit of his Rhino, watched nervously as the enemy approached. Captain Barkley had already tasked his Fighter Wing to take care of the enemy fighters. 12th Fighter Wing, three squadrons in total, was evenly matched with the enemy wing, though one of Farnham's squadrons was made up of Stickleback bombers.

"All squadrons," he called, activating his fighter's multi-squadron comms channel. "This is Wing Lead, Rhinos stay ahead of the Sticklebacks, make a pass-through on the targets, then break by squadrons. And for nark's sake, stay out of the cruisers' firing solutions."

A chorus of acknowledgements replied over the channel.

"Twelve-fifty-first 'Arrows'," he said, changing the comms to his own squadron's channel. "Follow me in. Once we take care of the fighters, you have permission to use remaining ordnance on the big ships."

Another chorus of enthusiastic acknowledgements sounded from his squadron's pilots.

He flipped the lasers housed in the nose and wingtips of his craft to rapid fire. His engines were still all in the green. Shields were holding against the minute dust particles leaking from the debris field ahead. For now, the dust was a minor nuisance, but if the fighters' shields dropped, the dust could interfere with the engines, with horrific consequences.

The Heads-Up-Display, built into the transparent cockpit canopy, bleated a warning signal, announcing that an enemy fighter had a missile lock on him.

His own missile targeting system gave a lock tone.

The leading fighter was targeted, a red box and crosshair flashing over the target on the HUD. The distance between the two lines of starfighters scrolled down insanely fast on Farnham's displays.

He found he was sweating in his flightsuit, the nervousness of the prospect of such a hair-raising combat striking him to the core. He was determined not to let it get to him; his squadrons only ever dealt with fugitives and smugglers, not combat-ready troops gunning straight for them. But his pilots would not see him panic or worry; he would not allow it.

This fight truly would be a test of their skills.

The distance counter reached optimum missile range, and Farnham reflexively tapped the missile launch control on the control stick between his knees. The missile whooshed away silently through space, covering the distance to the target in no time at all. It struck the enemy craft dead on, detonating on its shields, stripping the target of any protection.

More missiles slashed away from his squadron-mates, leaving smoke trails behind.

Having learned the futility of depending on their shields to protect them, the red spiked fighters dodged and weaved, the missiles passing by them harmlessly.

Farnham cursed, and prepared himself for the inevitable dogfight.

The red fighters flashed past his cockpit.

The two forces exchanged laser fire, but because the craft were moving too fast, there was no chance of hitting anything, except on a fluke. Unfortunately, Arrow Three was hit in the tail by a laser shot that deflected off one of its companion's shields; his shields were fully forward, unprepared for the lucky shot; the back end was shredded as the laser pierced the fuel tank.

Farnham saw Arrow Three's indicator light blink and then disappear on his monitors.

He pulled on the control stick, and rolled at the same time, bringing his fighter in behind the trailing edge of the enemy fighter units. His wingman, Arrow Two, was right beside him the whole time. The enemy, however, was having none of it, and suddenly darted off in all directions.

"Break by wing-pairs," he ordered into his comms mike.

The entire situation descended into sudden chaos as pairs of Rhinos and Sticklebacks mixed it up with the red spikes, dancing, swirling, and manoeuvring around each other to get a clear shot on a target... any target. Small flashes of lasers flitted in the empty space between them, and the occasional wild missile curved out of the engagement zone to never be seen again. Bright balls of fire and debris marked where a starfighter had died violently.

Farnham aimed the nose of his ship for the centre of the conflagration, and pushed his fighter to full throttle for a brief second. A warning tone beeped at him.

"*Arrow Lead, you have a spike on your tail,*" Arrow Two called out over the comm.

"Got it, Two," he replied. He pulled the craft into a long climb, rolled twice, then dove back down on his port wing, bringing the ship around to tuck in behind the flying spike. He opened up with his lasers, and stitched the energy all over the back-end of the spike, chewing up the shields, then eating through the fighter-craft itself. The spike's front suddenly dipped, and its tail flipped over.

At first, Farnham worried that the spike was pulling a stunt to get a bead on him, but the red craft kept flipping, its canopy and engines darkened. Farnham pulled away, and searched for another target.

He glanced over at where the *Polly Jenkins* was powering through, and saw something equivalent to a battle of the gods.

* * *

"Port shields down to eighty-seven percent, Captain," Mkdorn reported calmly.

Barkley was standing up now, away from his command chair so that he could properly see what was happening. Holographic displays hung around him at waist height, feeding him information on the starfighter brawl to port, the fight between the *Falklands* and one of the enemy cruisers, and data regarding the rest of his taskforce.

New South Wales was a burning wreck, tumbling away from the fight, and the *Devonshire* was being pounded on mercilessly, her shields near breaking point as it skimmed across the dorsal side of the nearest cruiser. *Pearl Harbour*, *Templar*, and the *Swindon* were hanging back away from the capital ships, waiting to step in to assist the starfighters if they broke.

But despite all that, *Polly Jenkins* was holding her own, against two of the enemy cruisers no less.

Massive pulses of energy the size of houses thundered between the *Polly Jenkins* and her attackers. One unlucky sod in a starfighter got too close to the slugfest, and was vaporised by an energy pulse bigger than the craft itself.

The deck vibrated and shook ever-so-slightly as the opposing bombardment weakened the shields, a little bit more.

"Captain," Mkdorn announced, her voice showing a little strain of worry, "port shields are now down to fifty-one percent, starboard and dorsal shields down to sixty-eight. Shield generators are experiencing serious feedback; if we're not careful, we could lose the shields altogether."

Damn this old ship, Barkley cursed inwardly, just as the *Devonshire* took an over-sized torpedo to her exposed engine nacelle. *Devonshire*'s stern exploded in a wash of blue fire, her potentially unstable fuel igniting in space. The remains of the destroyer tumbled, and slammed into the shields of the cruiser it had been attacking.

Barkley saw the opportunity, and though he mourned the loss of a fine crew and ship, celebrated the opening *Devonshire* had provided.

"All port batteries, target the shields where the *Devonshire* just hit," he ordered out loud. The big laser batteries answered by thumping out a wave of laser that struck the exact spot the *Devonshire* had impacted on. The shields were stripped away, and the gunners greedily took advantage, pouring everything they could into the enemy ship's hull.

Hull plating boiled and bent under the onslaught, and then burst. Fire leapt into space, along with screaming Core crewmen who were unlucky enough to be in that area when it was exposed to the vacuum.

The Core cruiser began to roll slowly to one side, unwittingly presenting its command centre to the *Polly Jenkins'* gunners. The gunners hammered the cruiser, until the ship's atmosphere could be seen to be exiting the ship through hundreds of holes. The cruiser fell away from the engagement, eventually colliding with a large asteroid.

Barkley was suddenly thrown to the deck, passing through the floating holograms on his way down. He smacked his head painfully on the deck, his forehead bleeding just above his left eye.

"What the fernikking hell was that?!" he cried in an uncharacteristic outburst.

"Torpedo, Captain," Mkdorn reported, who was also picking herself off the deck.

"From the cruiser?"

"Yes, sir, at close range. But that's insane, there's just as much chance they'll be damaged as us."

"Damage report," he ordered, returning to his floating holograms.

"Starboard shields are down, engineers are already working on shunting emergency power to those shield generators. Massive hull breaches on decks fifteen, sixteen, and seventeen. One of the Army transports was destroyed in the blast, sir." Barkley glanced solemnly at Mkdorn, and nodded. With one of the transports gone, that meant that a third of one of the Army regiments was also gone, killed before they could get into action.

"Tell group two to get here *now*," he ordered.

"Aye, sir," the XO answered crisply.

* * *

No matter how good the Core's intelligence was on the twenty-first century humans, they had little to nothing on the fortieth-century humans, and were thus unaware that human warships, and indeed their civilian ships, were equipped with faster-than-light drives, though were rarely used.

So, the *HMS Exeter*, a *Brightsword*-class cruiser, appeared behind the two remaining Core cruisers, along with five frigates, two destroyers, and six gunships.

The newcomers to the fight quickly overwhelmed the Core cruisers. *Falklands* was trailing fire, and hull plating, and moved away from the suddenly one-sided fight to make hasty repairs.

At a signal from the *Polly Jenkins*, the 12th Fighter Wing, and the remains of 200 Squadron off the *Falklands*, made a dash for the enemy capital ships, leaving the Core spikes suddenly very exposed, which was when *Pearl Harbour*, *Templar* and *Swindon* opened fire, decimating the fighter squadrons into puffs of dust in the solar winds.

* * *

Second Yh'par'ban was seething with rage. The battlegroup in the Mars field had been destroyed, despite heavy losses for the humans, and now, according to the messages sent back to the flagship from the dying cruisers, there were more humans to reinforce them.

"[Contact our ships in the Venus field, tell them to move to intercept the humans,]" he ordered to nobody in particular. It would be done, no matter who he said it to.

* * *

"Captain, we're receiving telemetry from Pluto Station," Mkdorn reported. "Commander Chase is reporting movement in the Venus debris field. Possible engine signatures are also being detected."

"Tell group three they're free to join the party," Barkley smiled, nursing his head.

* * *

Like group two, group three had been waiting outside the star system, their FTL drives ready to go at a moment's notice. When red ships began pouring from what was once Venus, group three jumped into the system, directly above the emerging ships.

The cruisers *Heracles* and *Carthage*, along with four frigates, four destroyers, and six gunships, rained a hail of energy down onto the ships. With their sensors almost blinded until they exited the debris, the Core cruisers, all four of them, were unable to know what was waiting for them, and thus caught unprepared with their shields down.

It was a massacre, torpedoes and lasers obliterating everything until there was nothing left.

* * *

"Now the pincer closes," Barkley murmured to himself.

The losses had been expected, but the plan was going according to... well, plan. The fleet had attacked when the three debris fields were aligned to the system's star, Sol, so that the enemy ships in either the Mars field or Venus field would be unaware of what was going on in the other, and the fields themselves would protect them from line-of sight of anything watching from the Terra field.

Now the Terran Navy forces moved toward Terra itself, the two large groups moving from different directions to prevent anything escaping.

"Captain, we're picking up some seriously massive energy distortions coming from the Terran debris field."

"Sansky's time machine?" he pondered out loud.

"Could be," Mkdorn acknowledged.

Barkley realised he had been wrong about Mkdorn: in the face of danger, her attitude had been the right one, and once this was over, he would see that he no longer felt any ill will toward his XO.

"Full speed ahead," he ordered. "Bring *Falklands* and *Exeter* in on our flanks. This is going to get messy."

* * *

Lord Yh'reth'gar looked with wide eyes at the pictures from the scouts at the edge of the debris field.

"[DAMN!]" he bellowed. The device was nearly ready, only hours away from completion. He had hoped the humans wouldn't arrive until then. To arrive just as he was leaving for their past would have been a sweet victory indeed.

"[Calm yourself, Yh'reth'gar,]" a soothing voice said from beside him.

"[Do not tell me to be calm, Mysterious One,]" the Lord said to his benefactor. The benefactor had apparently chosen to take on the appearance of a small human this time, though he/she/it usually looked like a warrior of the Core. He didn't know who this being was, or what it truly wanted, but it had helped more times than he could count. The being was immortal, of that he was sure, and it could move in and out of the Lord's ship like a wraith, unseen and unheard.

"[The humans *will* witness your glory and majesty,]" the benefactor cooed.

"[They had better,]" Yh'reth'gar growled. "[Much is at stake here.]"

"[More than you could possibly know. All I ask is that you give me the human, Adam Caine, and our deal will be done.]" With that, the benefactor disappeared in a haze of squirming white, accompanied by an awful buzzing noise.

Yh'reth'gar would have to see that the repair process was sped up. With almost his entire cadre of fifty bodyguards, he marched down to the hangar in which the time machine was situated, and bellowed, cursed, threatened, and threw things at the scientists to get them going faster.

* * *

"Two minutes to entry into the debris field," Mkdorn reported. She had chosen to literally be by his side for the final phase of the operation. The man would surely get a promotion for the successful outcome of this mission, she thought, and being close to him would guarantee her own promotion.

Like Barkley, she was staring intently at the view beyond the *Polly Jenkins'* armoured prow. She had never once set foot in the Sol system, let alone fought a vicious space battle among the remains of holy ancient Terra itself.

The light brown dust surrounded darker shadows of asteroids and chunks of lava, cooled by the desolate cold of the vacuum. She swore she could see a faint outline of something massive at the heart of the field, or maybe it was just her imagination.

* * *

Yh'par'ban was getting nervous.

There were too many variables at play here. The human fleet was stronger than he had anticipated, and far more canny than he had given them credit for. They had obliterated the two defence fleets in the other debris fields, and were making their way here, to destroy the time travelling device presumably.

He turned to the royal bodyguard Yh'reth'gar had sent down to keep an eye on Yh'par'ban. "[Get the two humans, and the genetic samples we took, and be ready to leave in case this turns sour.]"

The guard hesitated for just a second, but then bowed, and carried out the order. After all, Yh'par'ban was a member of the High Family, tasked with the protection of the family's interests, and the Family itself; defying him meant defying the High Family.

"[Status of the human fleets?]" he demanded of the command crew.

"[The fleet from the Mars field is closest, only a tenth of a demi-cycle away,]" one crewman answered quickly. "[The other will be on us moments after that.]"

"[Take the fleet out of the field,]" he ordered. The command crew stared at him like he was mad. "[I WILL NOT CONTINUE TO SKULK IN THIS DEBRIS FIELD!]" he screamed. He drew his sidearm, and shot the nearest two crewmen through the head, prompting the rest to suddenly carry out his orders.

The flagship was more than just a ship: it was a weapon, and it was a symbol of terror. Yh'par'ban cackled in glee at the thought of the humans running from the flagship in fright, his confidence in the situation restored.

* * *

Wing Commander Farnham was racing toward the debris field, along with the survivors of his Wing, bolstered by the squadrons from the *Exeter*. The fleet was right behind them, racing to take out whatever was hiding ahead of them.

Farnham could make a faint outline of something vast, but it was indistinct, barely noticeable.

And then it moved.

And then it appeared.

It was incomprehensibly massive, about the same length as the diameter of a small moon. It was red, like the smaller ships, with spikes all across its deformed hull. It seemed as though it hadn't been built, rather than thrown together from an amalgam of parts. It bulged in the middle, with long spikes for wings, and a spiked collection of towers at the top of the bulge, with the bow a vertical curved hammerhead, and the stern a long tapered motley collection of engines.

It was a titan, a metal planet unto itself, and it dwarfed the entire attacking human fleet.

The starfighter's computer told him it was 300 miles long, and it had friends.

A battleship-sized warship escorted it, along with a cloud of starfighters, and a dozen pairs of frigates and light cruisers ran alongside. All of them were specks next to the sheer magnitude of the titan.

Fear gripped Farnham's heart.

How could they possibly fight this thing?

* * *

Barkley saw the titan, and managed to fight off the shake that gripped his hands upon seeing it.

Several of the bridge crew swore loudly.

Barkley didn't reprimand them: he found he couldn't say the words and mean them.

He hoped all this fighting and dying was worth it, because his fleet were about to sell their lives on the word of a declared-dead Intelligence officer, and a madman from the past.

"What's the status of the *Cerberus*?" he asked Mkdorn quietly.

Taking the hint, she whispered the reply so as not to alarm the crew. "Two days in the Linkway, at last contact, sir."

Barkley squeezed his eyes shut.

"Contact them again, and tell them to stop messing about in the Linkway, and get here *now*. And send them the sensor data of this monster to convince them."

"Sir," Mkdorn nodded.

"FULL SPEED AHEAD!" he bellowed to the bridge crew. He turned to his communications officer. "*Exeter, Falklands* and all starfighters are to take care of the battleship, and the escorts, whilst we and the others will deal with the titan." He turned to the weapons officer, "Go for its engines, its power plant, anything you can target to slow it down."

"We're well within teleport range, Captain," Mkdorn reported.

"Let's see if we can make a hole for the Hunters, shall we? Launch the Army transports as soon as we're within five kilometres of that thing."

* * *

Normally, a ship the size of the *Polly Jenkins* was no match for a titan, even with an attending fleet. But, the Terrans weren't targeting at random, they were targeting a specific part of the titan: the line of division between the thing's port and bow shields, a weak spot on most starships.

The battleship and its smaller brethren were not in weapons range yet.

The remainder of the fleet pounded and pounded the spot, opening a small gap the size of a house. The titan did not fight back, as if it did not deem the humans worthy of its god-like notice.

The gap was big enough.

Now the fleet had to wait, and pray.

* * *

The teleporter had found the gap in the flagship's shields, and dematerialised Adam, Hannah, Sansky, Slayd, and eight platoons, fully one whole company, of 21st Hunters.

Only Adam didn't feel the materialisation at the other end.

Once again, he found himself in the stark white surroundings of Silver's construct. The buzzing returned, and the squirming whiteness, and Silver appeared.

"Adam," she smiled.

"What is this?" a voice cried, and Adam turned in horror to see Hannah, gawping in fright at the surroundings. He looked suspiciously at Silver.

"Where the hell are we?" Hannah demanded. "This isn't the flagship."

"I apologise for this, Mrs. Spears, but I only intended to bring Adam here."

"I'll explain later, Hannah," Adam said as calm as he could in a tone that indicted he would do no such thing. Hannah took this into consideration, and nodded, leaving the situation in Adam's capable hands.

"I thought I was the only one who could see you; something to do with the temporal energy," the former soldier exclaimed.

"Hannah Spears has the same temporal energy in her as you do, though she's here by accident; my apologies, but I wanted to tell you about what will happen after you defeat the Core." She stepped forward. "Once you leave here, find the ship *Gold Royale* on the planet Fayde, there the beginning of the journey towards your destiny."

"What did I say about all that destiny crap? I'm not interested."

"It is there nonetheless, whether you believe in your eventual destiny or not," Silver said earnestly. "Be careful though, there are others about, manipulating events."

"Screwing with time, you mean," Adam spat, repeating his earlier statement. Beside him, Hannah was shaking at the oddness of the white, and the appearance of the woman, Silver, the one Adam had shouted in his sleep.

"I don't have time to explain everything," Silver said hurriedly, looking around her. The whiteness was blotching, grey and black patches growing across it like a plague, or a fire. "The temporal energy in your bodies is fading, and you'll soon be back in the real world."

"You can't do this to us. You can't just say *Gold Royale*, and expect me to do as you order."

"Goodbye, Adam Caine; hopefully I'll see you soon, but then again, who knows?" Silver smiled, and then she was gone, as was the whiteness.

The two humans materialised on the flagship.

* * *

Sansky, Slayd, and 1 Platoon also materialised.
Sansky looked around him.

"Where the hell are Adam and Hannah?"

* * *

"[Caine is coming, Lord Yh'reth'gar,]" the now-indistinct benefactor whispered at the Lord's side.

* * *

Adam and Hannah were deposited on a grated balcony, not where they were supposed to be. There was no sign of Raymond, or the Hunters. There was, however, a massive canyon below them.

It was metal, with hordes of Core crewmen and warriors running around in a mass bustle.

Something large sat at the centre of the insanity, pulsing strobes of red energy away along massive conduits, presumably going to the rest of the ship.

"Must be the engine room," Adam breathed. It was hot, and humid, with steam rising from the main floor far below. Orange glows spread from all directions, sometimes in river-like wavy lines, other times as just spots, like lava sitting in a crater. If Adam were in a poetic mood he would have compared it to the very pits of hell itself.

He would have, had the warriors stalking toward him not distracted him.

He brought his rifle up in an instant, and blew the first warrior's head off in a gory mess. The bullets continued on, and slammed into the cackling face of the warrior behind. The alien toppled over the railings, and fell screaming to the canyon floor below.

Hannah removed her own plasma pistol from its sidearm, and started blasting at the warriors coming from the other direction. She took out two more of the aliens without even aiming properly. She had never fired a gun in her life, let alone been in a full-on combat situation.

"We're not going to get out of here, Adam," she shouted over the gunfire. So far, the warriors hadn't returned fire, but it was only a matter of time. Adam wondered if they were worried about hitting the engines, or whatever machinery was down in that hell-pit.

"Yes we are," he replied, gritting his teeth, and switching to automatic. He loosed off dozens of rounds, killing as many warriors. He grabbed Hannah's hand, and they ran, stepping over the bodies. She stared in horror at the carnage he had wrought -carnage he hadn't even thought twice about.

"We've got to find an exit," he shouted.

There was a roar below them. At first, he thought it was another blasted Tyrannosaur, but when he looked down, he found four thousand Core staring back.

"Shit."

Energy pulses leaped up at them, splashing the balcony around them as they ran. The balcony shook violently under the waves of enemy fire, and something came loose, ricocheting off the grating with a distinctly loud ping.

Still holding Hannah's hand, Adam dove for the nearest wall, grabbing a handle just as the walkway gave way underneath them. The grated walkway fell into the fiery depths of the engine room. Hannah screamed, and Adam grunted as his one hand took the weight of him in full battle gear, but also Hannah in her own gear.

His muscles strained under the effort, even as she kept screeching for him to pull her up.

He growled for her to be quiet, but she kept shrieking, putting him off his concentration as his fingers began to slip from the railing.

He roared, and pulled with all of his considerable might. Hannah flew upwards, screaming as she went. She crashed into the wall, cracking something in her arm as she tried to break her fall. Adam was right behind her, pulling himself up, now he had both hands free.

He let out an anguished sigh as he flopped onto the grating next to Hannah.

She was regretting joining the mission to this ship as they ran, hoping that she hadn't made the wrong decision in leaving Sasha and Sapphire alone on the *Polly Jenkins*. They were probably scared out of their minds, sat in the armoured heart of that warship, unable to do anything as the starship was torn apart during the battle. How could she leave them like that? She was their mother for Christ's sake! But Adam needed her just as badly –he needed someone to help ground him so he didn't destroy himself on some insane suicide mission.

More warriors charged down the walkway toward them, dragging her thoughts away from her precious children.

They were trapped.

Screwed.

"I love you," Hannah shouted in desperation, thinking this was the last moment they would have alive.

"I know," Adam replied in a very Han Solo way.

A bright white light filled the insanely massive engine room.

* * *

There was a long, low flash of light, and two figures were deposited from the Core teleportation beam.

"Welcome Adam Caine," the Lord boomed, with an evil grin on his inner lips.

Adam looked up, confused and dazed by the effects of the teleport, and was horrified to find that he was once again in the same hangar as the time machine. Scientists buzzed and clacked worriedly over the great device, more frightened of their Lord, than the sudden appearance of the man they tortured.

"I am glad you could be here, to see my most glorious victory."

Hannah whimpered out loud, and huddled against Adam.

The Lord's black-armoured guards surrounded Adam and Hannah, and drove them to their knees, the energised tips of their staffs hovering inches away from their unprotected faces. Adam cursed the name of Silver for not putting them back with Sansky and the others. Obviously though, it wasn't Silver's fault.

As if by the very mention of Silver, the squirming background he had seen in her white 'room' appeared, and a loud buzzing pierced the very air, as a shape formed beside Yh'reth'gar. None of the guards, not even Yh'reth'gar, seemed worried by it. Adam wondered if this was what Silver had warned him about: someone of her race helping Yh'reth'gar and the Core conquer Earth. And then it struck him that she could have been lying the whole time: the squirming background, and buzzing seemed to be Silver's trademarks, and she had said that the construct was *hers*, not someone else's.

What if she had made the whole thing about destiny and strands in time up?

What if she were really in league with the Core?

After all, he and Hannah had been talking to *her* when they were whisked away to the engine deck.

"Please, don't let it be her," he whispered.

The buzzing and squirming stopped, and the figure finally stepped through.

"Hello, Adam."

* * *

"Hang on," Adam said, with no small amount of confused relief, "who the fuck are *you*?"

The figure that had stepped through from the buzzing and squirming was a tall, elderly gent, dressed in a dinner jacket and bowtie. He was human, or at least looked it.

"You may call me Mister Gold," the gent smiled, and made a theatrical bow.

"You're one of Silver's race," Adam said. "The one who was hiding Yh'reth'gar's time travel activities?"

"At the behest of his father, actually," Gold chuckled.

Adam looked at him incredulously. "Father?" he and Hannah said simultaneously.

"Funny isn't it?" Gold joked. Adam found the man, or being, or whatever he was, to be deeply disturbing; his smile was cold, evil, with an ancient malevolence behind it that chilled Adam to the bone; the way he moved was more like a predator stalking its prey, lithely, efficiently, and yet still hiding behind that butler-esque visage.

"Why do you want to invade Earth?" Adam asked directly, shaking off the cobwebs of tiredness that had suddenly crept into his mind. Was this thing inducing that? Was it poking around his head? He didn't know, and didn't want to find out.

"Because his -"

"-- his father requested it," Adam finished. "Party line is it?"

Yh'reth'gar slapped Adam round the face, hard. Blood welled up in his mouth; he'd bitten his tongue.

One of the scientists approached Lord Yh'reth'gar, bowed, and then whispered into what passed for his ear.

"Good," the Lord's inner lips declared. "The device is ready."

Adam looked over to the device and saw a blue orb, the same colour as the time travel energy he had encountered before, hanging in mid-air at the centre of the polygonal disks. It was growing, from the size of a hand, to the size of a man in the space of seconds. And it was still growing. Rows of Core warriors waited by the device, waiting for the chance to invade Earth in the past.

"Where and when shall we set it for?" the Lord said, theatrically pondering the question. He snapped his fingers and let out an, "Ah-ha! I know where and when." He strode over to the scientists and began talking enthusiastically. They replied just as enthusiastically, though whether out of sycophantic pleasure, or simple pride, Adam wasn't sure.

The guards placed restraints on his wrists, as well as Hannah's.

He turned to Gold, whilst the Lord was out of earshot.

"Why are you really doing this? Sansky told me the Core had never encountered humans before, let alone want to hold some insane grudge against us." The idea hit him like a bolt of lightning. Everything was falling into place: Silver's inability to previously detect the Core's machinations, why the Core were even interested in Earth in the first place. "*You* persuaded them to go through all this. Because you've seen something in the future that destroys you, or embarrasses you badly enough to want humanity destroyed."

"You would love to know wouldn't you?" Gold sneered.

The Lord returned to them, a childish smile on his fleshy black inner lips.

"I have a special surprise for you, Adam Caine, for all the trouble you've caused." Yh'reth'gar seemed to take great pleasure in telling Adam this. He gestured to the guards to pick the prisoners up off the floor, and then walked slowly back to the device. The guards pushed Adam and Hannah along with the butts of their staffs.

Adam could see distinct shapes in the orb, colours even. He could see green in the lower half of the orb, and figures, all gathered around something, all looking down at the ground. It was a funeral, and not just any. Adam could just make out the name on the headstone. He was horrified, shocked beyond belief.

The gravestone read: "Adam L. Caine; beloved son, brother, and soldier."

Adam dropped to his knees at the sight of his own grave. His sanity, where it had started to heal, was blasted to pieces. He crawled into a ball, and his eyes went blank, no longer seeing anything, just the horrors that had been unleashed on him these past few weeks. He was gone.

The Lord and Gold laughed, as Hannah tried to comfort Adam, soothing him with words she hoped he could hear.

* * *

The ship was disintegrating around him, Barkley realised, as the bulkheads behind him buckled. Arrogantly, the titan was still taking no notice of the *Polly Jenkins'* attack, or of the *Heracles* or the *Carthage* arriving from the Venus field.

The titan filled the large panoramic viewports, blotting out Sol system's sun.

The battleship, and its escorts were pounding the human fleet. The remaining Army transports hadn't left the hangar bays: the first one to leave the hangars had been destroyed in a firestorm, its occupants screaming in a fiery death. The Colonels of the three surviving regiments were refusing to take their men out into the engagement zone where their unarmed transports would be horrendously vulnerable, despite Barkley's threats of punishment.

Falklands was down, drifting with no lights or any activity, whilst any communications to the cruiser were met with ear-splitting static. Fire spewed from her engines, what was once her command deck, her hangar bays, even the windows along one side of its hull.

The frigates *Ranger*, *Nova Scotia* and *Vivid* were gone, pieces of them scattered out in front of the indomitable Core battleship. Even now, Barkley watched as the frigate *Flying Fox*, and the destroyer *Gold Rover* were torn apart by the merciless enemy.

Exeter was trying to move across and above *Polly Jenkins*, exchanging crippling blows with the battleship. The fight had come to a standstill: the *Polly Jenkins* and *Exeter* facing the battleship at full stop, whilst *Carthage* and *Heracles* chewed ineffectually at the titan's rear shields. The previous gap in the monster's bow had been closed by horrendous amounts of energy pumped from its engines.

His head swam, as he realised for the first time that they may not pull this mission off. His bridge was in tatters: conduits were hanging open across the way, whilst several of the serving officers lay dead, killed by flying shrapnel. Smoke was pouring in from somewhere, obscuring part of the viewports. A falling pylon had crushed the command chair when some of the upper floor of the bridge collapsed. Barkley had thanked his lucky stars that he had been standing away from it at the time.

The *Polly Jenkins* was dying around him, of that he was sure.

Then something caught his eye: a blue light, growing from the tip of the largest of the spikes on the front of the titan. Barkley watched, transfixed, almost screamed in horror as a beam of blue energy leapt out from the titan, and brutally swatted the *Exeter* from existence.

* * *

"[Success, sir,]" the warrior manning the beam weapon controls announced.

Yh'par'ban could see it for himself: the annoying human cruiser had been vaporised with one shot. Now they had to wait for what felt like an age for the weapon to recharge.

"[Well done, warrior,]" the Second grinned. The warrior was pleased with himself, and rightfully so; after all, he had been the one to capture the technology in the first place, it was only right for him to be the one to test it in combat.

"[Sir,]" the warrior at the sensors station called out. "[I'm picking up other human life-signs.]"

"[Where?]" the Second asked, with a sense of dread.

"[Here, on the flagship.]"

"[Can you pinpoint?]"

"[Negative, sir. They must be using some kind of jamming signal.]" The warrior didn't apologise, and the Second didn't blame him: it wasn't the warrior's fault the humans were using dirty tricks to hide their efforts.

* * *

"The jamming device is working," Sansky announced.

The platoon had stopped at a cross-junction. Their target was the hangar with the time machine, whilst the other platoons had been ordered to assist the Navy's efforts in destroying the titan itself. 2 and 3 Platoons were off to capture any of the ship's external weapons they could get their hands on; 4 and 5 Platoons were headed for the engineering deck to shut the engines down if possible or at least throw a spanner in the works; 6 and 7 Platoons were scouring the area around 1 Platoon for any Core warriors, to delay them getting to Major Slayd and the Colonel. Nobody had heard from 8 Platoon.

* * *

Lieutenant Marlotte, commander of 8 Platoon, awoke with a headache. He couldn't feel his legs, and his suit's power had somehow been drained, because the targeting displays in the eyepieces of the helmet were gone.

Marlotte wrenched the helmet off; his vision was clearing. He looked about, and couldn't see his men, though he could see shadowy bumps all around him.

Where the hell were they?

He tried to move, but found his legs were stuck. His vision clear again, he looked down, and cried out in sheer terror. The teleporter must have scattered his platoon off the assigned point because his legs and groin had disappeared into the bulkhead.

"Oh Mary mother of God," he whimpered. He had heard gruesome stories of teleporter accidents materialising travellers into bulkheads or the power core of a starship. He had passed them off as fanciful ghost stories. He had never thought them to be true.

He looked around at the shadowy bumps, and found to his insane horror that the bumps were his men. He couldn't see all of them, but they were there: none of them were alive. Marlotte had been the lucky one: frozen armoured hands and legs stuck out of the red bulkheads of an empty cargo bay. One soldier had been deposited horizontally, the back of him embedded in the floor, his face a grotesque caricature of fear and pain. Of the intact heads he could see, he realised that many of the soldiers must have been briefly aware of what had happened to them, as they all had shocked or confused, or even frightened looks on their faces.

Marlotte vomited, tried to move, and then vomited again.

He scrambled to find his sidearm -but that was with his legs in the wall. His plasma rifle had apparently skittered away whilst he was unconscious because it was lying out of his reach.

He vomited again.

Then he found the grenade belt still strapped around his shoulder.

There were footsteps approaching: was it the enemy? Or one of the other platoons?

The clacking of beaks, and scraping of chitinous armour told him it was the enemy. He looked down at the grenade belt, screamed, pulled the pin on one, and bit down on it.

Lieutenant Marlotte was vaporised by the blast, along with the entombed corpses of his platoon, and the battalion of Core warriors approaching down the corridor.

* * *

Sansky felt the vibration through the deck.

"What the hell was that?"

"One of the other platoons perhaps?" Slayd suggested.

Sansky shook his head, and focused on the task at hand. The platoon was moving, jogging through the empty, dingy, misty corridors. They had found only a few warriors, each of which had been dispatched quickly and quietly.

For Sansky it felt strange to be fighting alongside the Hunters; he had spent two years living among the Core, who believed that armour was for decoration, not protection, now he was running into battle alongside heavily-armoured humans, with cold, featureless helmets, and chunky body plates.

At the head of the platoon, with Slayd by his side, Sansky led the Hunters to the arena: the same arena Adam had fought in. Going through the arena was the only way to get to the time machine without being spotted.

The doors opened, and the Hunters moved silently into the seating area, high above the fighting circle, rifles training around them as they moved. They were the best of the best, and it showed. They made no sound, not even in the big bulky armour that was a standard chunky design throughout the Army.

The lighting had been dimmed in the stadium seats. It was murky, like the rest of the ship. Sansky could see the corpse of something monstrous in the arena. Was that what Adam had been forced to fight? Had he really killed that thing?

Sansky pointed to the doors at the other side of the stadium seats, and the Hunters followed his gesture. Something moved in the corner of Sansky's vision.

He turned, and saw yet another of the monstrous creatures in the circle below. It was sniffing the corpse. *Is that a Tyrannosaurus?* he worried, thinking back to his history lessons in primary school of how the dinosaurs had been the dominant species millions of years ago on ancient Terra.

The dinosaur didn't seem to notice the silent soldiers at first, but then it sniffed the air, growled, and then roared mightily.

Caine had taken down one of the creatures with his bare hands and a spear. 1 Platoon took no such chances, and unleashed volleys of plasma fire into the dinosaur, tearing the creature to ribbons.

They moved on, warier than ever.

* * *

2 and 3 Platoon came upon one of the battleship-sized weapon batteries, mostly by accident, and a little luck. Lieutenant Leanders led the charge through the doors, his rifle sweeping side-to-side as he ran. Two armoured crewmen, caught completely unawares, were expertly gunned down in seconds, their heads gone in a mess of gore.

2 Platoon led the way into the control room, all five squads fanning out in a textbook pattern. The warriors manning the control room were gunned down mercilessly with short bursts from the Terrans' plasma rifles. The Hunters moved like shadows, silent and deadly in the gloom. Their eyes glowed green in the dark -targeting data flashing up on the inside of their specialised eyepieces.

3 Platoon split from the other unit, and filed in pairs through a side door. They bound down a flight of long wide stairs, boots clattering on the grated stairway.

Armed enemy warriors appeared at the base of the stairs, shouting curses, and blindly shooting pulses of lethal energy up at the descending soldiers. The three Hunters beside Lieutenant Mkmillun took hits to various body parts, and flew backwards into the men behind them.

Mkmillun slammed into the first warrior, using his shoulder guard to lever the alien up and over him. The Hunter behind him planted a plasma-round through the warrior's neck.

Two more warriors were cut down before a stray shot took Mkmillun's entire head off, leaving little more than a charred stump. As if using this as a cue, dozens more warriors poured through another door, their strange spiked energy weapons trained forward.

A wave of lethal laser energy splashed across the Hunters, bringing down half of their numbers in an instant. The screams of the dying, and the clattering of armoured bodies falling on metal decking could be heard even up in the control room.

Bottled up in the stairway as they were, there was no room to dive for cover, in fact there was no *cover*.

The remains of 3 Platoon were slaughtered to a man, before the wave of aliens washed up the stairs, and charged at the control room.

Leanders saw them coming, detailing two squads to hold the main doorway, whilst he and a fire-team could work on using the battery's controls. A strangled yelp came over the comms, and Leanders looked up to see two Hunters dragging another away from the doors, the armour on his chest completely gone, replaced by a smoking hole, with the man's cauterised lungs showing underneath.

Two more Hunters, one missing an arm, another missing his throat, fell to the floor, whilst the others laid it on.

The aliens charged en masse, their numbers so thick that the dead were simply carried along with the charge, unable to fall to the ground.

Spikes pierced black armour, and plasma rifles were used to club beaked faces as the fight got dirty, essentially a vicious brawl. This was no longer a covert op, but a sheer unadulterated fight for survival.

Someone fired their plasma rifle at close range, annihilating the torso of one unlucky alien, and the warrior behind him. Another shot, fired from a distance, took the head off of one of the taller aliens, followed by two more squads laying in to the fight. If they broke, Leanders would be unable to complete the mission.

If they could use the turrets to their advantage, the Terran Navy group would have a fighting chance at pulling this off.

* * *

"[Sir, we've lost contact with one of the main batteries, and yet the battery is actively targeting.]"

Yh'par'ban thought about this for a second.

"[It is likely one of the human units that confound our internal sensors. Destroy the battery with a feedback pulse,]" Yh'par'ban finally answered. It was a strange order, but Yh'par'ban was not willing to let a laser battery of that size fall into the humans' hands just so they could turn the weapons on the other Core ships protecting the flagship.

The warrior in question nodded, and turned to his task.

* * *

Leanders had the controls ready, now all he had to do was find a target. He aimed the majority of the battery targeting the battleship, and raised his armoured hand to slap the fire control.

2 Platoon, the bodies of their comrades, and the multitude of Core warriors were incinerated, as the induced feedback cooked off the battery's fuel stores. The fireball took the weapons battery with it, and tore a chunk out of the side of the titan.

Steam poured from the hole, the oxygen evaporated by the explosion; the fires blasted themselves out, with hull plating and screaming crewmembers sucked out into the void. Amazingly, the titan's major systems were unaffected, and the ship as a whole carried on as if nothing had happened.

* * *

The deck shook harder this time, and Sansky had to steady himself against the bulkhead.

"That was definitely an internal explosion," he exclaimed.

Slayd frantically tried to contact 2 and 3 Platoons, but was having no luck getting a response. Sansky was sure the combination of the explosion and the lack of contact with the two missing platoons could only mean they were dead.

* * *

6 and 7 Platoon unwittingly stepped into one of the massive barracks sections of the flagship, waking two thousand pissed off Core warriors. The humans were cut down in minutes, barely able to give a proper defence, and never heard from again.

* * *

Barkley saw the titan's battery explode, and hope filled his heart: Sansky and Caine were still fighting for them, somehow, somewhere.

The *Heracles* turned to avoid the recharged beam weapon, and for its trouble had its stern sliced clean off. With no engines to power, it hung in space, a sitting target. The Core battleship took no time at all, and turned its considerable guns on the dying cruiser.

Carthage was running for the dorsal section of the titan, away from the guns of the destructive battleship. Two pairs of Core light cruiser chased after it, hounding it with laser and missiles.

The *Polly Jenkins*, built during harsher, more conflicted times with thicker and more robust armour plating, was holding up against the battleship, though it wouldn't last long.

"Hurry up, Sansky."

* * *

As if hearing the Captain's call, Sansky and 1 Platoon hurried their step. They had received the commander of 7 Platoon's gurgled warning, before the channel had been cut off. The Core were aware of the Terran soldiers' presence.

It wasn't far, only another mile through the twisting corridors.

* * *

There was no order anymore. The corpses of the other ships filled the space between the *Polly Jenkins* and the Core battleship. The Terran heavy cruiser's guns were gone, obliterated. She was falling apart; after six hundred years of service, she was going out in combat.

Barkley lay on the deck of his bridge, a ceiling support lying on top of his legs, pinning him to the floor; he was completely numb, which was certainly not good for his future health. Mkdorn was unconscious, slumped over a console, where she had been stunned by a power surge in that same console.

They were the only two left alive on the bridge -the others had either evacuated or been killed by falling bulkhead panels or exploding consoles. He had ordered the crew to leave him there in case more fell on them. Acrid smoke filled the bridge, searing Barkley's lungs as he tried to breathe. His long white hair had been singed, leaving crispy stalks.

He looked up and saw through the viewports the final death throes of the cruiser *Carthage* as it spiralled toward the titan's engine section. Barkley kept expecting it to smash against the titan's shields, but it didn't, it kept going, and going, and then suddenly slammed nose first into the engines of the monster vessel. There was a brilliant white flash of light from the titan's stern, and Barkley cheered as much as the smoke would let him without coughing and spluttering.

* * *

The hangar shook violently, and Hannah was knocked so that she lay over Adam's side. He was whispering to himself, though Hannah couldn't understand a word of it, as though he were speaking in some ancient language.

The Lord screamed something nonsensical, and turned to Mister Gold.

"[You promised us no interference,]" the Lord said, pointing an accusing talon at the powerful being.

"[I held up my end of the bargain,]" Gold smiled. He reached for Adam, intending to take him away. Hannah saw him, and moved to cover Adam from the vile touch of the malevolent being.

Pulses of laser fire erupted from the entrance to the hangar, slicing through the ranks of the warriors and royal guards alike.

Hannah saw Colonel Sansky and the Hunters, firing at the Core warriors, slaughtering the aliens. She leaned down to Adam's face, and above the tumult of the weapons fire, and the haunting voices of his nightmares, he heard five little words that meant the world to him.

"I love you, Adam Caine."

Adam's eyes snapped into focus, and he looked at Hannah suddenly.

He smiled.

* * *

The Core warriors had been taken by surprise by 1 Platoon's attack, but now they were firing back, and taking cover. This was going to be reduced to a slugging match, Sansky realised. He exchanged knowing glances with Major Slayd, just before a Core energy round blew the major's face off.

Seeing their leader down made the Hunters pause for a brief second, and three more were taken down, each hit multiple times. They all found cover, behind crates, by the doors to the hangar itself, even behind the corpses of their friends. The room was filled with laser fire, each side slowly taking their toll on the other side, whittling away their numbers.

The Lord was leading, firing pot shots with an ornate sidearm.

Gold was gone, nowhere to be seen, probably skulking back to whatever dimension he had come from. Yh'par'ban was still commanding the flagship from the command centre. These human intruders would be beaten back, and then the invasion would begin in earnest.

* * *

Yh'par'ban was savouring the victory; there was no need to destroy the enemy heavy cruiser just yet. There were still some of the smaller ships dancing around the battle, with the battered remnants of the Terran starfighter squadrons.

The universe, as always, had a sense of humour.

Warning flashes and alarms blared out as the ship rocked under the impact of the *Carthage*'s death. Yh'par'ban was on the deck, knocked by a collapsing conduit, though he was up again in an instant. He saw the sight through the windows, and cried out to the heavens.

* * *

Cerberus had arrived.

Barkley was cackling with laughter as the super-heavy carrier roared through space, unleashing hell on the Core battleship and its smaller brethren, leaving smoking metallic corpses behind them. The remains of Barkley's assault fleet turned, like dogs under threat, and snapped their jaws at their pursuers, blasting them with everything they had.

Cerberus, only half the size of the titan, was still big enough to take it on, and pounded the titan's shields mercilessly. Her attending fleet was like a wave, pouring fire on the flagship as they blew past. *Cerberus* raked the titan from bow to stern, obliterating everything it touched. Her two accompanying battleships joined the slaughter, punching missiles and torpedoes into the titan's flank.

The *Cerberus*' attack was so fierce, that it snapped the rear engine section of the titan completely off. Fire gouted from the torn sections, crew, and warriors disappearing into space, sparks of energy flashed from the wrecked power conduits. The ship groaned, power feedbacks phenomenal.

* * *

Sansky and the others heard the hail from the *Cerberus*, and prepared themselves to be retrieved via teleport. But the deck suddenly heaved to the right, and threw everybody around, Core and human alike.

The Lord was scrambling to get to the time machine, to escape to who knew where.

Except someone stood in his way.

Incredibly, Adam Caine was stood erect, a staff weapon from one of the Lord's guards in his hands. He was standing perfectly still, despite the deck heaving every which way as the artificial gravity fluctuated again.

The Lord saw the wicked intent in Caine's eyes, and screamed for the human to stop.

Adam threw the spear, and the energised tip of the staff smashed into the power core of the time machine, destroying it forever in a blaze of sparks and blinding white light. Several of the guards found a way to stand by bracing themselves against the surrounding equipment. Caine snatched one of their weapons away, and then killed both of them.

There was a murderous glint in the human's eyes, and it frightened Yh'reth'gar.

More guards approached Adam with the same technique.

They died too, their blood spraying over the Lord as Adam used his captured spear to slice their throats. He revelled in it, roaring in manic defiance, giving in to the bloodlust within. He killed, and killed, and killed, until he found that there were no more of the royal guard, only corpses. Those red-armoured warriors that remained did not attack, choosing their own lives over their Lord.

Adam stepped towards the Lord as the gravity righted itself again. The tip of the spear was suddenly centimetres away from the Lord's beak. Hannah was right there beside Adam.

"Please don't do this, Adam; he's defeated, his ship is falling apart, and his people are being beaten. You don't need to kill anymore." She pleaded and pleaded, but he didn't listen; he couldn't now his blood was up. He turned for a second, only for a second to tell her to leave, when the Lord charged and barrelled into them. The two humans went over onto their backs, but the Lord didn't stop, he kept running for another door.

"I have to finish this," Adam insisted. "Go with Sansky and the others."

"Not without you," she complained. He nodded, and suddenly her plasma pistol was in his hand, set to a stun setting.

"I'm sorry," he whispered, and shot her. She fell to the floor, not a mark on her.

Adam turned and bolted in the direction of the Lord's escape.

* * *

Sansky recovered the unconscious Hannah, and slapped the communications control on his wrist. He bellowed for Caine to come back, but to no avail as the big man disappeared behind a massive deluge of falling debris. He couldn't see the wayward soldier. He was torn between finding his friend and rescuing the others; he squeezed his eyes shut.

"Sansky to *Cerberus*, if you're going to teleport us back, you better do it now."

Sparks and masonry fell from the ceiling as he said it, and crushed the time machine.

"Mission accomplished," he added with a tinge of sadness.

Sansky, Hannah, and the surviving Hunters were engulfed by the white light of the *Cerberus'* teleporter just as the wall behind them collapsed in an orgy of self-destruction. It fell and crushed the spot they had occupied moments before.

* * *

Cerberus' gunners hammered the titan, tearing its hull to shreds.

A communication from 4 and 5 Platoons of the Hunters alerted the *Cerberus'* commander to the fact that they had set the massive titan for a self-destruct, having found a disrupted and chaotic engineering room easily. They too were teleported away. The *Cerberus* moved to flanking speed, along with the rest of the moving ships, including the brutally damaged *Polly Jenkins*, controlled from its engineering deck by the ship's chief engineer.

* * *

Instead of blowing up in an orgy of fire and destruction, the titan's mass of scavenged anti-matter and artificial singularity drive technology worked against it, as the ship imploded, leaving a hole in the space-time continuum, and sucking the outside and insides of the ship separately into the small spatial fracture, gone forever. The *Cerberus* and the two Terran battleships, the *White Knight*, and the *Valhalla* pounded those escorts not taken with the titan to little pieces, leaving nothing to chance.

* * *

Colonel Sansky and Hannah Spears watched from one of the *Cerberus'* insanely huge observation decks as the clean-up operation began almost the instant the titan was gone. The ship's mass of starfighters was tasked with searching for any and all survivors. The ships would be here for months, running salvage missions and the like.

But neither of them cared.

Hannah was sobbing her heart out, leaning her head on Sansky's armoured shoulder. Sansky had to keep his own tears from spilling out uncontrollably, for fear of upsetting the poor woman even more. He knew Hannah and Adam had been close, that much was obvious. The poor woman had been put through hell these last few weeks. Now she was showing it.

Adam Caine was dead.

No matter how troubled or violent he had been, he was a hero, and a friend.

Fresh off the ruin of the *Polly Jenkins*, the remaining time-travellers howled and wailed in sadness and anguish as they came and hugged and huddled with Hannah and the armoured Sansky.

"Why did he have to die?" cried Hannah.

"Because he's a hero," Sansky replied, his voice nearly a whisper. "Heroes always die. He affected all of our lives; we would all be dead if it were not for him. God be with you, Adam Caine, in all the dark places that you must tread," Sansky whispered before giving in to his own sobs.

* * *

Vesh and Vash sat in an escape ship.

The body of the royal guard, its head twisted too far to be alive, was on the deck. Vesh was at the controls, and Vash was locking the humans Block and Bradley Stanford up in the rear compartment. The DNA taken from Caine during the temporal experiments was sealed in a forcefield-protected vial.

Vesh set a course for the Linkway, and eventually Core territory.

The Patriarch would need to know that had happened here.

* * *

The deck heaved, and twisted, and buckled, and eventually tore, but he made it to the escape craft, hidden in his private hangar.

The Lord ducked into the craft, calling the computer to activate engines, and get him out of there. The craft was small, thirty metres long, with enough space to sleep two comfortably. It had been a prize taken from the Gorri in his home galaxy. Like the Gorri, it was soft and fluffy, with delicate wings, no weapons, but an engine that could tear the ship out of hell if it needed to.

He found Second Yh'par'ban sitting in the co-pilot seat, as if awaiting the Lord's orders.

"[Why are you not in the command centre?]" the Lord asked.

"[The same reason you are, Lord; to escape.]"

"[Then let us escape, and return to our people,]" the Lord said, slumping into the pilot's chair.

Neither of them noticed something silently sneak into the ship behind them, and hide in an open closet.

The ship raced out of the tiny hangar, fire and death following it as it escaped the flagship's hideous demise. The Lord piloted the ship steadily through the nearby dust clouds, and between the asteroids that had once been Earth. At first, the Lord believed he had evaded the Terran ships, but there was something shadowing the escape craft.

* * *

Wing Commander Farnham, still in his battered starfighter, saw the shiny metal craft escape from the titan, and gave chase, weaving between the asteroids just as the escape craft did, trying to match the other move-for-move.

He had somehow survived the final massacre, along with two of his squadron, and a further five from the other squadrons of the entirety of the assault force. Those fighters had already limped to the *Cerberus'* welcoming hangar bays; he ignored their pleas for him to return with them. He *had* to know what the escaping ship was, and why it was hightailing it away from the combat zone, and away from the Terran Navy ships. If it was one of the Core, they had to be stopped.

Incredibly, the craft he was pursuing had escaped the notice of the other Navy assets, passing through the Mars debris field, and heading straight for the Linkway entrance.

Farnham was having none of it.

His fuel levels were practically at zero, his ordnance had been spent, the lasers on his ship damaged by the dogfight, except for one on the nose.

He sighted the crosshairs on his HUD onto the silvery craft.

He didn't wait for a tone, but simply fired on rapid fire until the laser spat nothing but tiny sparks, indicating the lasers' energy cells had run dry.

The lasers hit the wing of the escaping craft, bouncing it so that it clipped the asteroid it was passing at that time. The wing broke off in a spasm of sparks, and it went flying backwards, twirling like an out-of-control ballerina. Farnham stared in morbid fascination as the twisting tumbling wing came straight for him.

The decorated Wing Commander didn't utter a sound as the wing slammed into his cockpit, and detonated what little was left of the fighter's fuel.

* * *

The craft bounced as the wing tore free, and the Lord watched it with horrid fascination as it collided with the trailing Terran starfighter, the one he had not even been aware was there until its death. Something bounced free behind the two Core royalty, and Second Yh'par'ban muttered a curse as he saw the cause.

A pulse of energy slapped into the control console of the ship, giving Yh'reth'gar a shocking surge of electricity.

He turned to see what his Second was cursing at, and saw Adam Caine standing there, like some avenging angel, his energy pistol pointed at them both. He was already squeezing the trigger when the ship bounced again.

The shot went wild, and Adam stumbled to one side.

Yh'par'ban charged him, taking Adam in his mid-section, and tackling him to the deck. The Lord ignored the fight, and tried desperately to get the ship under control, even as it headed straight for one of the biggest asteroids, the same one where the human recon patrol had been killed earlier.

Adam kicked out, his knee connecting with the Second's shoulder. The two combatants jumped away from each other, circling each other, gauging the other's reactions. Adam was first to strike, a heavy kick that missed Yh'par'ban's head by millimetres, a kick that might well have taken his head clean off if he hadn't ducked.

The Second retaliated, slashing out with the claws on his fingers. The sharp claws bit deep into Adam's chest, down to the bone. Adam cried out, and lashed out with his foot again, this time connecting with his opponent's chest.

The Second let out a distinct "Whoof!" as the air rushed out of his lungs, and he was thrown backwards into the rear of the ship. Adam turned his attention to the Lord, who had managed to retain control of the ship, and thus not noticed that his Second had been beaten quite so easily.

Adam's punch came from nowhere, and snapped the Lord's bulbous head round, his fin quivering under the impact. The creature was dazed and confused, the concussion evident in his slow moves.

Adam turned back to the closet he had been hiding in, and found the object that had been pressing on his legs. It looked like an alien space suit, designed to protect against the vacuum. He quickly removed his faithful weapons and webbing, and put the suit on. It seemed to fit easily enough, and wasn't too hard to figure out to control.

He turned his attention back to the concussed Lord.

The ship went dark as something huge appeared ahead of them -an asteroid, bigger than the entirety of Great Britain.

"Crap," he cursed. He didn't know how to fly the thing, nor cared as a matter of fact. The Second was still out of sight in the back of the ship. So Adam made his decision.

He grabbed the Lord, and slapped what appeared to be the door control, and kept slapping it until the override kicked in, and the airlock opened completely, exposing the inside of the ship to the vacuum of space.

The Lord died slowly and silently, gasping for oxygen that had violently disappeared. The two figures were dragged out into space.

* * *

"Any news on Caine?" Barkley asked his XO.

Lying in bed, he was grateful for the rest. They were on the medical deck of the incredibly massive *HMS Cerberus*, surrounded by wounded soldiers and Navy crews.

Mkdorn shook her head; like him, she had bandages around her head, though she was fortunate to have not sustained more than a concussion, and any movement caused pain that rivalled the original wound.

"Admiral Scarlett herself is coming out here to see what happened. Not surprising really."

"How'd we do?" he asked, concerned as always.

"The *Polly Jenkins* is nothing but scrap -she's too old to be repaired so extensively, but we got out with three frigates: the *Fort Austin*, *Sir Galahad*, and the *King Arthur*, plus two destroyers, the *Tracker* and *Albion*, and two gunships, the *Archer* and *Billingsley*. Farnham's dead, and we lost almost all the starfighters, not to mention we came through with only twenty-five percent of our crew. On the bright side, all of the time-travellers survived." They sat in uncomfortable silence as the news sunk in. She spoke up suddenly. "There's a rumour going round you'll be promoted to Commodore, and put in charge of a fleet."

"And you want a promotion to Captain?" Barkley chuckled.

"It's only fair," Mkdorn shrugged casually.

His raucous laughter could be heard down the hallways.

* * *

In the exact centre of what a century ago had been the moon Phobos, floated a figure in a red armoured EVA suit.

The figure wasn't moving, just floating there, drifting among the debris of the once-famous Martian satellite, staring out at the stars, waiting for someone, or some*thing* to rescue him.

Injured from the fight with Second Yh'par'ban, Adam Caine was breathing shallow, taking solace in the fact that the Core had been prevented from invading Earth of the past, and Lord Yh'reth'gar was dead. He was sure Yh'reth'gar was dead, he had seen the creature experience the horror of explosive decompression, an ugly sight to be sure, but a cruel, necessary one in Adam's opinion.

The Lord's second-in-command had escaped; the alien escape craft had veered away from the asteroid at the last second. Adam suspected that *that* pathetic creature wouldn't show his face again, lest the Lord's family decided to exact their own vengeance upon him.

Despite the seriousness of his situation though, Adam couldn't help but sigh heavily, and talk to the empty space outside of the suit.

"Bloody hell; I wish I'd brought a book to read."

Four:
Gold Royale

"Say what you will about luxury cruise liners: they're fat, with no weapons, and full of preening, over-spoilt fernikking arseholes. But they are sure as hell stylish, and I would love to spend my last days living aboard one."

-Attributed to Captain Jared MkFay, *H.M.S. Forge of Command.*

4000ad.

An object floated in space, shrouded in shadow, and eclipsed by dozens of asteroids and chunks of hewn metal from the fall of Terra.

It was red and armoured, with two arms, two legs, and an armoured helmet. The armour was chitinous, like a crab's, and was segmented and sealed to protect against the lethal elements of space. Harsh, jagged black lettering was scorched into the chest, arm, and leg plating, detailing the original owner's dubious accomplishments.

Inside, the near-unconscious Adam Caine hallucinated. He swore that he was in space, surrounded by the asteroids of the Mars-Jupiter Field, sat in an alien space suit. He felt a sense of elation that he had gained his revenge on Lord Yh'reth'gar and Mr. Gold, and yet sadness that he was going to die out here in the cold of space, alone. Perhaps this was his punishment for all the death and destruction he had wrought in the recent weeks, or punishment for his deeds as an SB operator.

He could see the Terran Navy's rescue and salvage operations millions of miles away, though he could no longer see anything approaching the shape of a ship. He knew that somewhere down there, near the debris of ancient Earth, were the remains of the *HMS Polly Jenkins* hanging like a skeleton in water, along with the rest of Captain Barkley's devastated attack force.

He felt himself drifting toward sleep, his eyelids getting heavier and heavier.

Crap, the air's run out, he panicked, just as his vision began to black out.

* * *

Space around Adam waved and shimmered, and something large and covered in spikes decloaked above him. It was as black as the space around it, though there were no running lights or engine glows like Adam had seen on other ships previously; nor were there any lights to suggest windows of any sort.

A piercing white light struck out from the midsection of the ship, and surrounded Adam. He felt a warm tingling throughout his body, and wondered once again if he was imagining what was happening.

His eyes finally closed, though he could feel himself being drawn toward the source of the tingling heat.

There was a clanking noise, and then he felt nothing at all.

* * *

When his eyes opened, he couldn't see much of anything -a side-effect of the oxygen depravation he presumed. The smells, however, were incredibly nauseating. It was like the massive cell on Yh'reth'gar's flagship, only worse, like it had been used again and again over many decades.

There was even the tang of aged blood mixed in with the excrement, vomit and death -all the signs of a prison cell with no toilet, or access to medical facilities.

His eyes began to come into focus, details becoming more apparent, though his head was pounding, and his body felt like several trains had hit it at once. His limbs were sluggish -another after-effect of the oxygen starvation.

He was indeed in some kind of cell, with dark metal bars, and stone-like walls and floor. Surely a spaceship would have metal floors, and forcefields? More than likely it was a style choice, or a psychological choice to add to the fears of their prisoners.

"You look confused," a soft voice chuckled from within the cell.

Adam's senses snapped fully on, and he was up on his feet, in a ready stance. There was a figure sat in the corner of the cell, tall, skinny, its skin a pale green, its head longer and higher than a humans. In fact, he was like that all over: his limbs longer than a humans could possibly be, his torso unnaturally thin, and ribs visible under the skin. All of its bones, in fact, were visible; clearly the alien had been here for more than a few days, his ragged, soiled clothes notwithstanding.

"Who are you?" asked Adam. He stood by the bars, craning his neck to see outside. But all he saw within the narrow view were more cell doors.

"My name is M'Der Tr'n," the alien replied. Adam looked at him blankly. Tr'n chuckled. "You don't recognise the name?" Adam shook his head nonchalantly, returning his attention to the corridor outside. Tr'n snorted with amusement. "I am an historian; pretty famous until I was stuck in here."

"I'm not exactly from around here," Adam retorted, finally turning back to the alien.

"Where are you from? You're human, so I assume you're from one of the Terran colonies in the Consortium," the alien pondered, looking Adam up and down. Whoever had thrown him in the prison cell had stripped the Core EVA suit off him, so he was still wearing the black combat fatigues he had worn during the assault on the Core flagship; they were a little worn with a few scrapes and tears from the fighting, but were mostly in one piece.

"You wouldn't believe me if I told you," grimaced Adam, not too keen on going into any detail.

"I wouldn't do that if I were you," the alien pointed out; Adam was about an inch from touching the metal bars of the door to test its strength. Adam touched it anyway, and jerked back from the door, shocked by the small energy current flowing through the metal.

"Told you." Adam ignored the alien's sarcasm. "Maybe you should sit down before you fall down."

"Thanks, I'll stand," growled Adam.

"Suit yourself."

"I usually do."

The alien grunted in amusement.

"Who the hell are these people, anyway?" Adam demanded, looking accusingly at his cellmate. The alien flinched and looked away from Adam's withering gaze.

"The Saajil are a race of slavers from the outskirts of the Large Magellanic Cloud; they're scavengers, and murderers, with nothing more in mind than the exploitation and then extinction of anything not of their race."

"Sounds familiar," Adam muttered under his breath.

"I heard rumours and stories of isolated independent colonies being kidnapped by them. I was following one such rumour on Ursa Minor: a miner who claimed to be the only survivor of one of their attacks. They were supposed to be just a legend until they picked me up from the mine I was investigating; one of those stories to scare children into doing what they're told; like the human bogeyman, or the Abominable Sandman on Mertik. All cultures have something similar, even the Saajil I dare say."

Adam swore under his breath, not wanting to hear many more lectures by an alien who resembled his mono-toned history teacher back in Cambridge. Besides, it almost seemed as though the alien was lying, covering up something else, but Adam couldn't put his finger on it.

There was, however, a definite vibrancy to this alien, almost as if he had a relentless, optimistic curiosity about him that he never tried to suppress.

Adam had seen that kind of optimism in raw recruits fresh out of commando training; those who didn't quash that optimism usually ended up being seriously injured or worse. Clearly though, it worked for this M'Der Tr'n.

"You're military, aren't you?" the alien asked, breaking Adam from his reverie. "Though the long hair suggests either you're Special Forces, or you've been out of the service for a while." Adam glared at him, not wanting to have to explain his career to this stranger. "What Terran unit were you in? The Hunters? Pathfinders? Parachute Brigade?"

Adam grumbled something incoherent about minding people's own business. He was about to repeat himself louder for the benefit of his new cellmate, when he decided against it. There was no telling how long he would be in this cell, or what might happen –there was no point being annoyed or abusive with the one person that was friendly to him.

"Special Boat Service," he admitted, before finally sitting down on the uncomfortable uneven floor.

M'Der Tr'n's face went blank for a few seconds as he dredged up the memory of the unit in question.

"Special Boat Service; created during you World War Two. Established as a top secret black ops unit specialising in water-borne attacks, though they were technically a part of the Royal Marines Commando Brigade. They were disbanded in 2789 when the Terran Navy's Fleet Protection Group was created. Only one 'operator' held out, a Colour Sergeant Kara Marazov from the New Terra barracks." The alien looked at Adam, having recited the information like one of those cheesy introductions to an action movie. "So either you're lying, or you're thousands of years old."

"Neither."

"The only alternative is-"

"Time travel," Adam interrupted. His eyes stared off into the distance for a second. "Adam Logan Caine; Staff Sergeant, 2nd Squadron, Special Boat Service; before that I was in 40 Commando, 3 Cdo. Brigade. I was born in Cambridgeshire, England, May 1980. I suspect the Terran Navy classified the specifics of how I got here top secret. If you want answers, I suggest you contact Colonel Raymond Sansky of Navy Intelligence."

"Time travel is impossible." The alien let out a snort of laughter at Adam's apparent dry humour, ignorant of the fact that he was being absolutely serious.

There were screams and shouts of fear among the other prisoners as heavy footsteps sounded down the corridor. Despite having only just sat down, Adam stood up, and faced the door, steeling himself for what was to come.

The alien historian saw in Adam's face what the human had in mind.

"You can't escape."

"Don't bet on it mate," the other growled.

The footsteps stopped outside their cell, and there was a muffled shout, followed by the clanking of gears.

The door opened with a screech of old, tortured metal, and there stood the strangest sight Adam had seen: it was a humanoid dressed in matt-black solid armour plating, with pointed boots, all very much like a knight of Camelot, except for one thing: it was only three feet tall.

"You're the terrifying Saajil?" he said, right before he put his boot in the thing's armoured face.

* * *

The woman ran.

She had been running for days, never stopping, not even to eat or drink. Her pursuers were tireless, never letting up, never stopping. She was so scared, her flight had been automatic, and dropping everything she was doing in order to escape.

This wasn't your average fugitive hunt either. She'd been standing on Mount Vesuvius, watching Pompeii be buried under an avalanche of molten rock when they had turned up to capture her.

So she ran, right through Earth's dark ages, through Rigel's religious crusades, even through the unbelievably peaceful exploration phase of the Saajil's first steps into space, until she landed in the human Second World War, during Dunkirk.

As the Luftwaffe strafed the British troops, they caught up with her, two faceless underlings each grabbing her arm, before stepping through a portal with her in tow.

The woman whimpered as she realized where she had been taken, and who was orchestrating her capture. Even as she was strapped to the torture chair, the disturbingly soothing voice she so feared spoke.

"Hello, Silver."

* * *

The spire-like Fayde Police cruiser *AR-558* found a black warship hanging lifelessly above Fayde's fourth moon. Any challenges were met with static, and there was no engine activity, though life-support was active. Two lifesigns were detected in one specific area of the ship, on the bridge, and neither were moving.

Four teams were sent to board it, fully armed, and fully armoured, running through a quick sweep of every level. They found hundreds of cells, filled with dead inmates and slaves. The crew was dead, slaughtered by some unknown force. There was blood everywhere. None of the teams openly mentioned their fears of the infamous Saajil, though some were amused to find that the Saajil themselves were basically midgets in armour.

The largest team broke into the ship's command centre, only to find a human in combat fatigues lying there, blood plastered all over him, his breathing heavy and shallow, his eyes closed.

He didn't complain or struggle when the Police officers snapped restraints on him, and guided him to one of their own holding cells. The second lifesign had disappeared somewhere, though an escape pod had been detected punching out before the Fayde Police could dock.

* * *

Fayde City.

If ever a city fell into the categorical euphemism of skyscraper, it was Fayde City, the capital of the planet Fayde -an independent star system on the edge of the Andromeda galaxy.

Sat in the middle of a continent of farmland, it covered a similar square distance as old Great Britain, with concentric circles of skyscraper buildings, one within another, each inner circle taller than its outer neighbour, but shorter than the next inner circle. In all, two hundred circles of buildings reached up into the sky, with the final massive central spire reaching past the atmosphere and into space, like an insect hive gone mad. This was tipped with a tall space dock that spread out in the vacuum, like an insect spreading out across a glass window.

This central construct was the location of the city and planet's government, and its Police Force.

Adam was dumped in an interrogation room on the four-hundred-and-ninetieth floor, with a table and four chairs for company. Like all good interrogation rooms throughout the universe, it was blank, with low lighting, a bland paintjob, and a one-way glass window filling the wall opposite the suspect.

None of the local Police wanted anything to do with the case: some were too scared of the stories of the Saajil to want to interrogate their *killer*, whilst others had seen Adam's bloody visage, and were horrified by his cold, blank stare when he had awoken. He never threatened anyone, though the Fayde military were called when his military uniform was brought up.

Four officers, fully two-thirds of Fayde's tiny military intelligence division, filed into the interrogation room, all wearing purple dress uniforms, with their gold braiding and epaulettes, soft caps tucked neatly and precisely under one arm. From what Adam had seen, it seemed as though the local Police were more of an effective fighting force than the military, which made this interrogation that much more confusing.

None of the intelligence officers looked barely a day out of primary school. All wet behind the ears with no experience, and probably paid-for commissions. His violence-induced haze was fading, his eyes becoming more active, more aware of what was going on.

"Well, mister. You're in a lot of trouble," one of the whelps began, sitting in one of the chairs opposite him. Another sat next to him, whilst the others stood to attention either side of him. They were trying to intimidate him.

It would never work, not after all that had happened to him in recent weeks. Their natural appearance was also not that frightening, quite the opposite in fact, as their furry walrus-like faces were strangely cute, like cartoon characters, complete with long upper tusks in their mouths, and long wiry whiskers from their cheeks. *First, scary hobbits,* he thought, *now half-witted walking walruses.*

"Mister?" snorted Adam. He was still handcuffed, though his hands were in front of him, instead of behind him, like they should be. "I'm not a mister."

"So who, or what, are you?" the second whelp demanded.

Adam smiled.

"Caine, Adam L. Staff Sergeant."

The first whelp blinked. "I beg your pardon?"

"I don't have time to muck about with a bunch of children who want to play Gestapo; I have to get to the *Gold Royale*. Where am I?"

"You're on Fayde; in the capital no less. You're going to be spending a very long time here in our prisons."

"I'm on Fayde?" blurted Adam, wondering what the hell kind of coincidence it was to be stuck on this planet having told Silver he didn't want to go on her 'journey'. "Damn that crazy old woman." The whelps looked at him like he was mad. He probably was mad, though that wasn't actually the point.

"You murdered three hundred beings," said the first whelp.

"They were holding me prisoner," Adam replied, putting enough menace into his voice to make them understand his implication. In all fairness, his last real memory before waking here was meeting the Saajil face-to-face as he was escaping from the prison cell. He didn't tell them that –they wouldn't believe him.

"You don't deny it?" the second whelp asked with some surprise in his own voice, as if this were easier than expected. He was obviously too stupid to have paid attention to Adam's implication.

"No, they were slavers, they deserved far worse."

"So you're confessing to murdering to all those people?" The first whelp's eyes widened with an incredulous look, even as he asked the question.

"I didn't murder them; they would have killed me the first chance they got. They were slavers." He said this last sentence slowly, to draw their attention to the fact of the matter. "I only did it because they had me held captive, and I'm getting tired of being cuffed, imprisoned, and tortured."

"We have your recorded confession, so no need for a trial; you'll be sent to our maximum security prison in the Wildlands."

Adam blinked. It was as if they refused to see anything other than the deaths themselves, completely ignoring the fact that the 'victims' were mass-murderers themselves. Or was it something else? Adam's innate paranoia went through the roof when he began to consider that perhaps these morons were fully aware of what was going on, and someone else had sicked them onto him. Or was their naivety and stupidity being manipulated?

Like the Core had been manipulated into attacking twentieth-century Earth.

Gold. Christ, even if these guys are completely ignorant, Gold could still have manipulated things to his advantage.

Was this what the future was going to be like for him? Constantly second-guessing everything to make sure unseen enemies weren't manipulating his actions from whatever high-and-mighty place they resided?

If Gold was really involved, Adam needed to get out of that place as soon as possible, preferably before they threw him in yet another cell.

Suddenly, he realised the intelligence officers were saying something.

"Are you listening to me?"

"No, sorry." Adam gave them a smile that didn't reflect in his eyes. "I was planning my escape."

The walrus-faces all began honking with laughter, finding this statement hysterically funny. When they finally managed to get themselves under control, wiping tears of laughter from their blubbery cheeks, the first whelp asked him how.

So Adam explained.

"When this officer to my right comes towards me to restrain me, I'll take his legs out with a kick, then punch him in the throat, whilst sliding my chair into his friend there." He nodded to the other officer that had been silent behind him.

"Then I'm going to overturn the table, and squash the two of you, steal your keys, and hopefully sneak out of this building."

More honking belly laughs.

The officer to Adam's right moved forward to restrain Adam, just in case.

Adam did exactly as he said he would do, and found himself staring at the unconscious forms of the four officers, shaking his head at the oxymoron of the Fayde military intelligence.

He looked around the room and, to his surprise, found an air vent just big enough for him to fit in.

There was a knock on the door —one of the Police officers wondering what all the noise was.

Adam rolled his eyes, cleared his throat, and shouted in his best approximation of the walrus-faces' gruff accent, "Just giving the prisoner a walk round the block, if you know what I mean." Adam squeezed his eyes shut, praying the peace officer fell for it. He heard a honking chuckle through the door.

"So stupidity isn't limited to their military," Adam muttered under his breath.

Astonishingly, the peace officer heard him and opened the door; his lower jaw dropped as he saw the military officers all lying on the floor, and Adam's booted feet disappearing into the air vent.

Adam got away just in time to hear the alien shout something in its native language, a series of pig-like squeals and grunts that didn't sound like anything but incoherent gibberish.

Using seams jutting out of the vent walls, Adam dragged his sorry backside up the vertical shaft, until he came to an intersecting horizontal. Praying it led somewhere he followed the straight tunnel on his hands and knees, all the while listening out for the telltale sign that someone was following him. He ignored the claustrophobia that threatened to bring too many uncomfortable memories to the fore.

All he could hear was the increasing beat of his heart, and his breathing, both sounding louder in the confines of the vent, or at least to Adam's tiring ears.

If there really is a God, he mused, *he's having a real big laugh at my expense.*

* * *

"WHERE IS ADAM CAINE?!" Silver's captor bellowed in her face. The old man was furious; she wouldn't give up the information he needed to continue his plans. She was being most stubborn.

"Don't you know where he is?" sneered Silver.

One of the old man's faceless minions punched her hard across the face, splitting her lip. She didn't bleed; she couldn't —her blood had dried out hundreds of years ago, like all of her race.

"For some reason, I can no longer detect him within the time stream. Either he is dead, or someone is protecting him *via* the time stream, though my sources tell me he is on a planet called Fayde, near to the *Gold Royale*."

"So what do you want from me?" she coughed.

"Reverse whatever it is you did to Caine, and tell me why he's so important to *you*."

She laughed, though her injuries stopped her from fully enjoying it, sending sharp pains through her semi-corporeal body.

"He is the Strand."

The butler-esque Mr. Gold flinched, and stumbled backward as if he'd been slapped.

"Adam Caine is the *Strand*?"

He laughed.

* * *

Adam whipped his head round; he was sure he just heard a familiar voice's laughs echoing through the air vents, but it just must have been his imagination. He could have sworn it sounded like Gold, but he was sure that prick was nowhere nearby, otherwise the being would have to gloat a bit more.

He was near to what he was sure was an exit: the sounds of traffic were starting to filter through a grilled section up ahead. Either it was the outside world, or the Police motor pool, which wasn't an exciting prospect.

He turned around, and moved toward the grille feet first, before putting his weight behind several heavy kicks, rattling the grille until it flew off its hinges.

Adam was suddenly assaulted by the noise and smells of the air traffic: the blast of horns in traffic jams, the smell of some kind of gases being pumped from thousands of air cars. He leaned over the edge, and saw to his dismay that he was hundreds, if not thousands, of storeys above the ground, staring down a sheer drop with no ledges or balconies. In fact, he couldn't even see the ground below. There were barely any windows that he could see, probably because the walls were armoured —more than likely since it seemed to be a headquarters of some kind.

Towering edifices of glass and metal rose up above him, across the way, obscuring the planet's white star, and throwing the streets and airways into complete darkness. Powerful lights lit the dark canyons as dozens of aircraft buzzed between the monstrous buildings.

"Holy shit," he cursed. This was a whole new experience.

So far, his only contact with the fortieth-century —or the forty-first century since New Year's Eve had come and gone during his sojourn on the *Polly Jenkins*- had been the insides of several starships, usually in mortal danger.

Fayde City was like an organized New York on steroids.

And it wasn't just the city itself: vehicles without wheels or wings flew past his position, essentially cars stuck to circular disks which he presumed were some kind of anti-gravity devices. Like his own time, the vehicles were not limited to one shape or size: some were small two-seater jobs, whilst fat, bulbous behemoths trundled along the airways, company logos emblazoned on their sides.

There were no open-topped vehicles, and Adam found it was because the air was thinner up here. He was having some trouble breathing properly, though it wasn't debilitating.

A long thin craft, with windows down its sides, slid by underneath, stopping beside a large opening a storey below him, presumably letting a bunch of cops off to start their shift.

Adam swore and cursed, and then jumped awkwardly from the air vent to land with a bang on top of the skybus. The grey-blue roof of the craft was as sturdy as it looked, and Adam's breath evacuated his lungs in a painful rush.

The bus moved on as its passengers settled, seemingly unaware of Adam's presence on the roof.

Despite the bus pilot's lack of awareness, apparently someone else was as horns blared, trying to get the driver to see the human on his roof. And, of course, there was the inevitable siren in the background, above the rushing wind that threatened to blast Adam from his perch.

He turned to see a quartet of disk-mounted cars with black hulls, and green and red flashing lights affixed to the roof and flanks.

They were headed directly toward him.

"Crap."

Ignoring the sharp pain in his chest –the telltale sign of a fractured rib- he braced his feet against a couple of small protrusions on the roof, and stood up, facing into the wind created by the passage of the unaerodynamic craft beneath and the wakes of others passing by. The towering buildings rushed past, curving away in the distance.

Adam looked around him for some way of getting off the slow-moving bus, and found to his surprise one of the whale-like cargo craft passing in the airlane just beneath and to the right of the bus.

Adam cursed his innate recklessness again, and then jumped. He crashed into the roof of the cargo compartment, and rolled, managing to avoid hurting himself this time.

The Police vehicles came in fast, two speeding ahead to bracket the cargo craft. The other two closed on Adam himself, black-tinted windows hiding the officers inside. The vehicles were sleeker than the others around them –clearly the police received more advanced vehicles than the civilians.

The cargo craft was heading for a yawning opening in the side of a building ahead, crossing the airlanes slowly, and the pilot still unaware of the police vehicles around them.

The police officers in the approaching vehicles were shocked to see Adam jump again, diving onto another cargo craft as it passed its identical twin, heading out for a run to another of the buildings.

And then he jumped again, this time onto the back of a speeding Sports Utility Vehicle that was overtaking. It dove for the city floor, panicking that the police were after them, though they could have no idea that this was only partially true.

Adam hung on for dear life, as the flying SUV hurtled downward, before levelling out and heading for a gap in the buildings. There were distant shouts of dismay from the driver as the police ordered them to slow down and pull over on the comms channels. The driver seemed to be ignoring the orders as they continued to swerve dangerously around the local traffic.

The buildings below grew increasingly further and further away beneath the SUV, giving way to the grassy farmlands surrounding the capital city. Naturally, the police had clearly been waiting for the craft to leave the city before doing anything potentially lethal, because they suddenly opened fire.

A laser pulse slapped the side of the SUV, tumbling Adam off the roof. He was barely able to grab onto the anti-gravity disk before he could be thrown off completely. Something rattled within the craft, then cracked and banged several times, before the back end tore off completely, flames pouring violently into the whipping wind around it.

Suddenly, the door handle Adam had been holding onto fell to pieces in his hand.

"SHIT!"

His stomach lurched badly, as gravity reached up, and yanked him from the vehicle. Panic gripped him as he plummeted toward an old roadway far below. The wind whipped him partially round to face the sky, and then he smashed into something solid.

Pain cascaded up his left side as bones snapped, and muscles tore themselves to pieces. He coughed up blood as something pierced one of his organs. He bellowed curses to the sky, even as the thing beneath him rushed toward another city with the same circular patterning as Fayde City far behind him.

The police weren't following him, figuring he had died in the fall. He lay still to keep up the illusion, though in all honesty he couldn't move without debilitating pains racking him, so it was best all round just to stay still.

The journey was uneventful, passing into the new city without any fuss, though Adam suspected there were a few odd looks from the locals when they saw him on the roof of whatever it was he was on.

Oddly enough, the vehicle was heading toward a collection of dark skeletal constructs that looked suspiciously like a shipyard of some sort. He could see the massive double-clamshell of some uber-ship far away, eclipsing everything, even the towering buildings around it. There were several other ships around it, though nothing anywhere near the same size, even a Terran Navy warship, slightly smaller than the *HMS Polly Jenkins*, if he was any judge.

A Terran Navy presence here on this planet could give him some difficulties; General Gardner's reaction to his presence alone was enough to send him halfway across the universe, assuming he actually wasn't already halfway across the universe. Christ, for all he knew, Navy Headquarters was in the next star system over, and he could be only moments away from being right in the thick of it once again.

The vehicle beneath him –a freezer lorry as it turned out- headed directly for the chunky spire that protruded from the centre of the shipyard, presumably the control section, or whatever passed for air traffic control on this planet.

He needed to find the *Gold Royale*.

Even though he didn't believe in Silver's 'journey', getting aboard was still an opportunity for free passage away from this planet; assuming he could find it in time before it moved on from Fayde.

He found it increasingly harder and harder to keep his eyes open as the pain began to overwhelm him.

Just as the vehicle slowed to a halt inside the control tower's cargo bay, Adam blacked out. He neither heard nor saw anything after that.

* * *

"What does he intend to do?" Gold demanded of his prisoner.

Silver said nothing, just staring at the blank ceiling.

"DAMMIT, SILVER, TELL ME WHAT CAINE INTENDS TO DO NEXT!"

Silver just smiled.

She may have been chased, captured, and interrogated, but she had won. Gold was desperate to know about Caine, to the point that he seemed almost afraid of what Caine might be capable of, especially after the revelation of the human's eventual position in the grand scheme of things.

"He's going to kill you," was all Silver said before Gold lashed out with a tendril of energy and struck her as hard as he could.

Silver screamed.

* * *

Adam woke with a start, cold sweat beaded on his skin. He'd been having an indistinct nightmare about Silver and Mr. Gold, from what he could remember.

"Where am I?"

"You're on the *Gold Royale*," a voice said. Adam turned in the medical bed he was lying in, and looked into the eyes of a remarkable woman. She wore a uniform not unlike the Terran Navy's, though it was more ostentatious with extra braiding, and a gaudier ship-patch, which indeed identified it as the *Gold Royale*.

She was human, with fair hair, a gaunt, stern face, and rich blue eyes that held an innocence that Adam hadn't seen in the mirror since he was a child. She was also reasonably short, especially considering Adam's own size, and stick-thin, as if a strong breeze would snap her in half.

"And you are?"

"I'm Commander Gorman, *Gold Royale*'s Executive Officer. The Captain wanted to come down in person, but he has more important duties to attend to." Adam ignored the thinly veiled insult, and her obvious annoyance that she was here attending to him.

"I'm-"

"Commander Caine, I know," she interrupted, her irritation showing even more, almost as if she were in the midst of deciding whether or not to leave the peach-walled medical bay. Adam's mind was panicking –what had Silver dumped him in now, giving him a Navy cover? Why did he need a cover story anyway? To protect him from Gold with a uniform the arsehole couldn't touch? "The CMO believes that, in a matter of hours, you will have a near-clean bill of health. He mentioned your scars. Actually his exact words were, 'What did he do, fall into a grinder?'"

"Something like that," Adam murmured.

Gorman looked at him curiously, though said nothing more on the subject. "Your uniforms have been forwarded to your suite, as has your money." Adam tried not to show the shock he felt show on his face, though it looked more like he was wincing in pain.

"How long have I been out?"

"Seven Terran days," she replied. She seemed to enjoy twisting the proverbial knife, and Adam realised he wasn't ever going to get on with this woman.

Seven days, though, was long enough for Gold to find him, or whatever allies the bastard had in place nearby. Adam pulled back the covers of his medical bed, and found he was utterly naked. Unabashedly, he stood on the cold, hard floor, and stared at Gorman, silently daring her to stare back. Something akin to shame or embarrassment flashed through her face and she looked away before pointing to a set of pale medical overalls on the next bed over, all neatly folded and emblazoned with the double-clamshell symbol of the enormous ship he had seen from afar as he had passed into the new city.

He dressed himself in the overalls; Gorman didn't make the usual protests he always had from the doctors who told him he had to rest a little while longer to heal properly. She seemed to understand he had ignored that advice before –Adam figured she had probably done the same thing more than once, in whatever career she had had thus far.

"The ship launches tomorrow morning at 0800." Gorman started to leave. "If you have any unfinished business here on Fayde, I suggest you get it done before our repairs are done." Adam just nodded. Gorman walked out of the medical bay, leaving him alone.

Like the *Polly Jenkins*, this medical bay had holographic interfaces and displays hovering in the air, though only the ones above Adam's bed were actually active, showing his vital functions and medical status. There were no right angles in the room, with the walls a peach colour, presumably as a subtle method to calm patients. The room itself was large enough to hold an RAF Tornado comfortably enough; there were thirteen beds in all, and Adam wondered just how many more rooms there were like this one.

He limped out of the room, and discovered a large lobby not unlike a grand hotel's. It had the same peach walls as the previous room, though it was high enough to fit two Sea Kings on top of one another, and four times as wide. Like the smaller medical bay, there were no right angles, though there was a set of wide, plush carpeted stairs leading to an equally wide landing above, with more oval doors leading to other equally peach rooms.

There was a very feminine feline alien sat behind what he assumed was the nurse's station. She wore a pale blue uniform with the *Gold Royale* patch on her arm, though the uniform was much skimpier than the one worn by Commander Gorman. Whiskers shivered from her cheeks, uncomfortably reminiscent of the intelligence officers he had beaten before escaping Fayde City, stoking a rising panic in him.

She noticed him standing in the doorway to his ward, and smiled, which quieted his rising paranoia. She was just a nurse, or something similar; her appearance shouldn't be raising his paranoia levels just because she had whiskers.

So he smiled, and walked over to her large, smooth, rounded desk. She smiled again.

"You should still be in bed, Commander Caine." Her purring voice seemed to relax him even more.

"Sorry," he smiled. "I was just getting restless."

"I do not doubt it. Just be sure that the doctor sees you in the next day to give you a final check-up."

"Sure." He couldn't help but inwardly chuckle at how nice this woman was, especially compared to how he had been treated in the last few weeks by various people.

"There was a message left for you, Commander." She handed him a small slip of paper, making him wonder why a futuristic alien ship such as this would have things on plain old paper. He read the message, and swore loudly. The cat-nurse blanched, and he apologised profusely.

"Where is the departures terminal for the outside control tower?" he asked as gently as possible.

"Out through the medical bay main entrance, then turn left, and follow the signs." She pointed to a large set of oval doors opposite her station.

"Thankyou."

After three wrong turns, and more swearing, he finally found what he was looking for, and stepped through into a large wide room that contained a multitude of sofas, almost all different sizes, and styles. It was like a branch of MFI, except put together by someone with varying tastes to accommodate all sorts of bizarre alien species with varying views on comfort.

In the far corner, Adam caught sight of a walking jellyfish wearing a tuxedo, trailing slimy tendrils along the floor. Every time one of its servants tried to pick up a tendril to keep it off the floor, they got an electric shock. Adam found it amusing that the servants kept trying despite the pain, almost as if they weren't intelligent enough to understand what was happening, or simply sycophantic enough to warrant it.

Close by, a gaggle of young cats –the same humanoid race as the nurse– kept jumping up and down excitedly, all wearing some kind of royal blue school uniform, whilst an older, grey-furred cat tried desperately to keep them calm: a schoolteacher and his excited pupils.

An unusually tall man with green skin walked past towards the spaceport proper, and nodded to him. He seemed familiar. Was that the 'historian' he had shared a cell with in the Saajil ship?

Caine grumbled when he caught sight of another familiar face waving him over.

"Raymond."

"Adam," Sansky replied. He wore the olive-green dress uniform of his calling, his officer's peaked cap tucked under one arm, a dark green kit bag by his feet. Caine noted with some pride the Colonel's rank pips on his shoulders, and the various medals. "Why didn't you tell anyone where you were?"

"I've been busy," replied Adam, wondering how much his friend knew. "Slavers, police chase, that sort of thing."

"Business as usual then," Sansky grimaced.

Adam shrugged. He gestured for the colonel to have a seat on an obnoxiously pink leather lounger. Or at least, he hoped it was leather, because if it wasn't he didn't want to think about the other possibilities.

"What are you doing here, Raymond?" Adam realised how callous that sounded, and tried to explain. "It's just, people have been trying to kill me, even the ones who *don't* know me. And how did you know where I was?"

Sansky suddenly looked ill.

"What? What is it, Raymond?"

Sansky looked around the room suspiciously, reigniting Adam's paranoia once again. The Intelligence agent lowered his voice to a near-whisper.

"There are rumours about you. Not just in Navy Intelligence, but other organizations. And not just the military, either." He paused, and took another look around to make sure nobody was listening too closely. "For years, I have been hearing stories about a secret organization. Several of us, including several of the Admiralty, have been trying to find information on them. So far, we've found nothing but their name: Kombat 3899."

"That's the year Earth was destroyed," Adam nodded.

"Which is why we think that it's Terran. However, there is a possibility that there is an outside influence." Again, another pause, and a look around. "We found evidence of corruption among several of the independent governments bordering our territories. One of their agents that was interrogated refused to say anything except this, 'Gold wants Caine dead.'"

"That's a pretty strange thing to say for counter-intelligence, especially if he didn't say anything else. A bit too specific as well."

"He's not the only one. This Gold wants you dead like nothing I've ever heard of. The Fayde authorities are looking into what happened to you, though obviously they're not going to look too closely. The Admiralty, however, are extremely concerned over a human that could slaughter a ship's crew single-handedly."

Adam harrumphed. He had some working knowledge of secret organizations within governments, though it only extended to being their unwitting pawn. It was standard for those kinds of investigations to be swept under the rug by those in power. Adam had thought that backstabbing, greed, and the cloak-and-dagger stuff was limited to humans in his own century; he had hoped that the forty-first century would have brought some kind of enlightenment, but apparently things hadn't changed in two thousand years. Non-human cultures seemed to be even worse, or at least those he had had contact with.

"Have you heard anything from this Silver character Hannah was talking about?"

It was like someone had flicked a switch on in Adam's brain. He had spent days fighting to survive, and had forgotten about Hannah, about Sasha and Sapphire, and the other surviving time-travellers. He had forgotten Hannah's declaration of love for him, his own Han Solo-esque acknowledgement; he had forgotten how Sasha had looked up to him, had depended on him for safety.

"No, not yet. Gold escaped from the titan; maybe he's after her as well."

Had he forgotten on purpose? Intentionally forced it out of his mind so that he could survive the last few weeks without distraction?

Survival: was that all he was good at these days -surviving one crisis long enough to be thrown headfirst into the next one? That was what he had been trained to do –to kill, and survive. But he wasn't in the military anymore, surely there was more to life?

Raymond looked as though he had read Adam's mind.

"Hannah doesn't know that you're alive."

"I wouldn't bet on it," Adam groaned. He was looking past his friend's shoulder.

Hannah stood there, fury in her delicate features, her arms crossed, and one foot tapping the floor impatiently like a schoolteacher of old. Sasha and Sapphire hid behind her, unwilling to risk the wrath of their mother by bounding enthusiastically over to Adam.

"Some intelligence agent you are," Adam whispered.

Sansky coughed, trying to hide his snorts of amusement.

Hannah was wearing a set of nondescript grey overalls that clung to her attractive figure like butter on bread. Her hair was tied back in a severe ponytail that just added to her severe appearance.

She strode over to the two men, drew her arm back, and slapped Adam round the face. There was a loud crack as she hit as hard as she could with the palm of her hand; a crack heard across the room, though nobody seemed to pay attention. She then proceeded to slap Raymond just as hard.

Both men looked flabbergasted.

"What was that for?" cried Adam.

"Why didn't you tell me you were still alive?!" she screamed. Her face was wrinkled and red with anger, almost a deep crimson in fact, and she kept glaring at Raymond every seconds.

"I've only just come out of a week-long coma," Adam protested. Hannah's fury dissipated, and changed to the concern that he had seen on her face during their internment together.

"I didn't know," she whispered, looking deep into his tortured eyes. Before anyone could say anything more, she jumped into his arms, and hugged him tight enough that even *he* struggled to breathe properly. She was nearly hyperventilating, her face buried in his muscled neck, her shoulders shaking. When she pulled her face away, tears were streaming down her face, and her lip was trembling, sobs escaping from her.

Adam held her tight –as tight as he could without actually hurting her.

"I missed you," she sobbed.

"I know."

"I missed you."

"I'm so sorry," he whispered. "I was captured by some slavers. I..." He paused, the words escaping him for a few seconds. "I had to do some horrible things to escape." He put her back down on the carpet, refusing to make eye contact with her.

"It's okay. I understand." She put her hand against the cheek she had slapped, stroking his bearding jaw line. He hadn't even realised he was growing a beard.

"I..." Again he paused and looked away. "I never gave them a chance to do anything bad. I just slaughtered them." She could see in his eyes that he was telling the truth, and that he was tortured by what he had done, no matter who they had been.

Her last words before the assault on the titan came back to haunt her. She had called him a cold-blooded bastard, and essentially disowned him, despite negating that in the titan's massive engine room.

Suddenly, he backed away, looking at her mournfully.

"What you said on the *Polly Jenkins* was true. I am a killer. It's what I'm trained for. It's what I'm good at. I can't... I can't stay around you and the others."

"Don't... you can't mean that. Not ever." She looked at him with shock and horror as she realised what he was implying. "The Core are gone; you had your revenge on them. What can you possibly need out there that requires you to go alone?" Her voice was starting to rise in volume and pitch again, her anger returning.

Adam looked pleadingly at Hannah.

Why couldn't she understand?

The bag Sansky had been looking after suddenly appeared in the Colonel's hand in front of Adam. The big man took it, noticing it was reasonably heavy, though no heavier than the equipment and weapons he once wore as a Royal Marine. He nodded his thanks to Sansky. He didn't say anything, but just looked at Hannah.

She finally, irrevocably, realised she couldn't do anything for him, not until he had faced whatever horrendous demons were bottled up in his mind and heart. She knew he loved her. She knew that he would eventually come back to her. But she also knew that at heart he was still the Royal Marine, still the warrior.

She refused to accept any of it, however.

"You can't leave me!" she screamed. "I need you!"

Tears were finally forming in his eyes, and his bottom lip was having trouble staying still. He tried to say something, tried to explain, but his voice choked in his throat.

"I'll send you a postcard." Even as it left his mouth, he knew what he had said was utter nonsense and was an utterly stupid thing to say given the circumstances. It was an incredibly snide remark, and he was sure it had irreparably damaged his tenuous relationship with Hannah.

He nodded to them, gave a bittersweet smile to Sasha.

He turned, and left.

"Don't forget what I told you," shouted Sansky. Adam waved over his shoulder, stepped through onto the *Gold Royale*, and was gone.

"Mummy," Sasha cried. "Will we ever see him again?"

Hannah hugged her youngest daughter.

"I hope so."

* * *

"Welcome back aboard, Commander Caine," Gorman sighed, as Adam strode past her without a word. A pair of women in olive green uniforms barged past her, with the insignia of Navy Intelligence on their arms. Neither paid attention to the cruise liner's XO, though Gorman frowned at their suspicious behaviour.

Their attention seemed to be entirely on Caine.

She tapped her comms-unit.

"Bridge, this is Commander Gorman."

"*Bridge here,*" came the reply.

"Two Navy Intelligence officers just walked onto the ship. I want them monitored constantly; they may be here to harass Commander Caine."

"*Understood, Commander.*"

"And you better tell the Captain," she added.

"*I'm sure he'll be thrilled,*" the officer on the other end of the channel commented.

"If you can, try and use the arrivals area surveillance to get an ID on them."

"*Will do, Commander.*"

Gorman watched the back of the two officers disappear round a far corner.

* * *

Majors Drummond and Dunn strode purposefully through the corridors, their strides matched perfectly as they followed their target.

Both had the short, cropped hair common among the regular military units, and the straight, stiff-backed gait of those that had spent too much time on the parade ground, and not enough in actual, bowel-clenching combat

They kept their distance from Caine, just enough so that he wasn't aware of them, but close enough so that they could react to anything he might do.

"Identification please," a deep, commanding voice demanded. They spun to see who it was. Both were shocked that it was the Captain of the *Gold Royale* himself: Brag Franks.

Tall, wiry, with a bushy brown beard, and a kind but stern human face topped by the peaked cap of his esteemed office, Franks was an imposing figure in his gaudy dress uniform.

"This is an NI operation, do not interfere," Drummond growled.

"The *Gold Royale*, and in fact, the Fayde star system are not under Terran rule or even allied with Terra. You have no authority whatsoever over me, my ship, or my crew." Franks gave them a toothy grin that shone from behind his beard. "I, however, have ultimate authority on board this ship. Identification please." He held out his hand expectantly, palm facing up.

Anger thundered across Drummond's face.

"You will comply, Captain. Things can be unpleasant if you do not."

Franks' eye-line suddenly switched to something just behind the two officers, just off their shoulder. They turned to see what he was looking at. Both gasped when they realised their target was standing there, a grim smile on his face, looking incredibly menacing.

"Looking for me?" He seemed ready to rip them limb-from-limb, and neither was sure he wouldn't actually do it.

"General Gardner simply wanted to make sure you were properly looked after," replied Dunn, jutting her chin out, as if to dare Caine to do something. "And we have his *full* authority." She glared at Franks as she said this.

"Not. On. This. Ship." Franks glared right back at Dunn, having to tilt his head down to look her directly in the eye. Caine wasn't exactly unimposing either, fully a head higher even than Franks.

"Leave me alone," Caine growled.

"We're under orders," the two intelligence officers said in unison. Adam dropped his kit bag. Before anyone knew what was happening, Dunn was on the floor, holding her stinging face, and Drummond was leaning against the wall, holding her arm, both grunting in pain. Franks had barely seen Caine move, though he was now standing over the floored Dunn, ready to throw another lightning-fast punch.

"Get them off my ship," demanded Franks. Four security guards, all of different species, appeared from another corridor, and took positions around Dunn and Drummond, two for each officer, each holding a short, cylindrical baton of black metal the tips of which sparked with a bright luminescent dome of contained energy.

The security guards escorted Dunn and Drummond off the ship, and shoved them into the arms of a squad of waiting of Fayde police officers.

Franks accompanied Adam to his suite.

Neither said much besides introducing themselves. To Adam, Brag Franks was just like his favourite uncle David that handed out gifts, hugs, and gave easy smiles and jokes at family gatherings. The beard helped.

"Have you ever been on one of these luxury liners?" Franks suddenly asked, after the pleasantries were out the way. He had noticed how Adam was gawping at the ship's luxurious corridors. Franks obviously assumed that he had spent all his life on starships.

Adam shook his head. "Spent my career on the *Heracles* ever since leaving the Academy." It wasn't a complete lie, since the *Heracles* had been part of Sansky and Barkley's operation in the Sol system.

"*Heracles*? She's a *Longbow*-class isn't she?"

"She *was*."

"*Was*?" Franks looked at him suspiciously.

"She was destroyed during a classified operation a week ago. Lost with almost all hands, except for a few of us. I was lucky enough to be overseeing damage control in one of the lower decks when we were hit badly. Managed to get an EVA suit on before three decks' worth of hull plating gave way, and dragged me and twenty others into space."

"Why didn't you report in with your superiors?"

"The official term is AWOL."

Franks didn't seem to be surprised—there were simply too many coincidences for it to be anything else. Caine's flimsy cover had more holes than a cheese grater.

"You don't seem surprised," Adam commented, stating the bloody obvious.

Franks gave a sad smile. "The only thing I'm surprised about is that you could afford a suite here for the duration of stay you requested."

"A friend paid for it."

"This friend have anything to do with your going AWOL?" Franks looked at Adam, wondering if Adam was actually defecting, or something similar.

"Something like that."

Franks nodded as if this confirmed his suspicions. Clearly he thought Adam's benefactor –Silver- was a spy luring the big human away from a respectable career.

"Here are your quarters." Franks gestured with his chin toward double doors coloured a pale sky blue mottled with white patterns that reminded Adam of clouds. When they stepped closer, he realised that they actually were clouds, floating across the doors like a projection. He glanced around the plush peach corridor, but there were no marks, divots, dips, or holes in the walls or ceiling. Franks noticed Adam's glances, and smiled to himself.

"There are no projectors. The doors are made of a metal that absorbs complicated patterns and images. All entrances to the hotel suites are made from the same material. The doors on your floor all have the clouds and blue-sky images, though you can change it if you so wish. Just make a call to the floor manager if you need anything."

He pointed to a glowing purple globe hanging above the door. "That will register your DNA within a two-metre radius. There are manual overrides here and on the other side if the globe isn't working or loses power." He gestured to the small code pad next to the door. "The holographic attendant inside will answer any more of your questions."

"Thankyou, Captain," smiled Adam.

"My pleasure, Commander Caine." They shook hands amicably, and Adam stepped through the opening doors to his suite.

* * *

Franks waited until the doors had closed before breathing a sigh of relief. He felt uncomfortable around the big man; maybe it was his imagination, but it was like the man radiated a presence of power, of destiny.

Franks shook his head.

He was getting too old to be thinking melodramatically about destiny and power.

However, Caine was indeed lying about being an officer in the Terran Navy. He was probably military –he certainly had the build, and the movements of someone who had seen plenty of combat: the long, easy, loping strides that conserved his energy, and could keep him going for miles and miles. And then there was his speed, strength, and obvious training.

But the long hair was a giveaway that Caine had been out of the military for a while. Not to mention the faded scars that he had seen in the medical bay, whilst Caine was unconscious.

Besides, no Terran cruiser XO could afford the exorbitant fees of the *Gold Royale*, or would reasonably know someone who could.

He headed for his office for his daily meeting with Commander Gorman, his own XO.

She was already waiting for him in the plush office, sipping at a hot, steaming mug of caffeine extract, reviewing a digipad in one hand. She sat in one of two high-backed black leather chairs that sat on one side of the semi-circular white desk, a desk that curved around Franks' own swivelling chair. The office itself was modest, with no real decorations other than a few awards, promotions, and medals he had earned during his career in the Terran and Merchant navies. There was a family holograph that sat hovering in three-dimensional above one corner of his desk: himself with his brother, father, and seven cousins during a big family reunion on their home planet of Karmana four years ago.

"You're early, Commander," Franks stated, moving round the end of his desk to sit in his comfortable chair. There was still paperwork scattered across his desk from the previous night.

"I just came from engineering."

"What's our status?"

"We're still on schedule for launch tomorrow morning. That ion storm around the Jacer Expanse fused all the energy conduits on Decks 119 through 121, so the engineers re-routed power from those decks, and locked all entrances in and out of there, so only the engineering teams can enter."

"Any other good news?"

"Some of the shuttle bay staff are complaining about the ship that was placed there in Commander Caine's name. They say that it's making some creepy noises."

"Probably just the hull plating adjusting to the ship's gravity." He didn't sound convinced either, though he never said it. "Any other business?"

Gorman fidgeted in her seat for a few seconds.

"I am not comfortable with Commander Caine being on this ship."

"You're not the only one."

"You think he's a defector."

"Wouldn't be the first time we've had one of those on board." He leaned toward the holographic computer terminal, and accessed the Navy's public interface network. He skimmed through the Navy's public records, hoping to confirm Caine's story. The name 'Caine, Adam Logan' popped up on the holographic display with a picture of a shorthaired Caine. Everything else was blank, with big red letters splashed across the file marking out TOP SECRET. With a harrumph, he pulled out of the file, and searched for the name using a connection to the Public Interface Network. The search came up with several hits.

One in particular was a history file.

Franks read it, then read it again, and re-read once more to be sure.

"This can't be right."

"What is it, Captain?"

"According to this, there's only one recorded Adam Caine in the last two thousand years, and he disappeared from London with forty-odd others in 2006 AD."

"He's two thousand years old?"

Franks nodded.

"According to this. That's not all. He was a Commando and a member of some secret military unit, awarded the highest honours possible, and the son of the sixteenth Earl of Cambridge, whatever that means."

Both sat in stupefied silence, neither knowing what to say in the face of such data.

"This can't be true. It has to be a joke." Again, Franks didn't sound entirely convinced.

"You could always ask him," Gorman shrugged. "Aren't you hosting a dinner for some of our guests? You could invite him to that, ask him questions, try and catch him in a lie."

Franks nodded, not seeing much of a choice.

Usually, he didn't interfere or stick his nose into the affairs of his passengers and guests, but this was different, as Navy Intelligence was after Caine for some reason, despite apparently not being a Navy officer. Interfering with NI's business was bad news as the *Gold Royale* passed through Terran space on a regular basis, and came into contact with many of their warships along the way.

Intelligence could make things very difficult for the star liner if they decided it was in their interest.

He sent the message to Caine's suite, and prayed that things would all work out.

* * *

Adam slapped his new bag onto the carpeted floor, gawping at the luxurious suite he had been given. It wasn't as big as he had expected, but it was still bigger than his apartment had been in Uxbridge. He could fit four Ford Transits side-by-side in the sleeping area, with a no-frills king-size bed, a walk-in closet, and double doors leading to the spacious bathroom.

The room, like much of what he had seen of the ship was decorated a soothing pastel peach colour.

Something flickered in the corner of his eye, and he turned to see a faceless female hologram flickering in the middle of the room, thin shafts of green light trickling between her and a bead of light in the far corner. The woman had no distinct features other than her uniform, which looked like a simplified version of Franks and Gorman's uniforms –representing a lower rank.

"*Welcome to your suite on board the* Gold Royale, *the most luxurious starliner in the nineteen galaxies.*" The faceless hologram droned on about the history of the ship, what deck his suite was on, and the location of the major facilities on board the ship, including casinos, restaurants, swimming pools, spas, and dozens of others usually included in a hotel. According to the hologram, Captain Franks had left a message for him to attend a dinner function that night, in dress uniform if possible.

The hologram flickered away, leaving Adam in peace.

He opened the bag, and found to his amazement that it contained three sets of camouflage combat fatigues in different colours, with a combat equipment vest, an L95 SA80, a Walther P99, a Navy-issue plasma pistol, and plenty of ammunition for each. He guffawed, wondering just how the hell Raymond had got a hold of twenty-first century equipment like this, then thought better of it, knowing the answer would give him a headache.

He looked in the closet, and was surprised to find full uniforms for a Terran Navy Commander hanging from a metal rung to one side. The uniforms were all neatly pressed, complete with peaked caps, shoes, and medals and rank tapes.

"Silver's thought of everything," he breathed.

"*Thankyou*," answered Silver's voice.

Adam spun.

In the exact spot where the faceless hologram had been, stood Silver, bold-as-you-like. She was smiling, and looked exactly the same as the first time he had met her four or so weeks before.

Then suddenly she flickered.

"You're just another hologram."

"Perhaps; perhaps not."

"I'm really too tired for this cryptic shit, Silver. What is going on? How are you now a hologram? How did you afford this suite? And why the fuck did you book me in as a Terran Navy officer?"

The hologram didn't express any emotion other than continue to smile, which made it all the more disconcerting for Adam to deal with. Even the smile didn't seem to extend to the hologram's eyes.

"As you have probably already deduced, Gold has other allies besides the Core. Some have already moved against you?" Adam answered with a nod. *"Then things are cascading quicker than I had predicted. I programmed this interactive hologram to answer any of your questions in case I can't see you in person."*

"Why can't you come yourself?"

"Either I'm dead, or I've been captured. Either way, that means you're on your own, unless you recruit others to help you. The cover story is for you to use in case you are detained or captured by local authorities loyal to Terra. My race is extremely wealthy, hence why I could afford the suite." There was a pause; an ever-so-slight pause that Adam was sure was not part of the hologram's programming. *"There are few of us left. Which is why we use others to fight our battles. We travel through time starting wars we cannot hope to stop."*

"Why start them then?"

"Some of us start them to prevent greater evils. The rest, like the one you call Gold, do it to further their goals, or simply to create chaos."

"What greater evils?" asked Adam, stepping up to within a few inches of the hologram.

"Adolf Hitler. Hitler was one of the greatest evils your world had seen for hundreds of years before or since; there were only a few like him in all of your planet's history, despite the violent, turbulent nature of your people. He was the culmination of six millennia of violence, ignorance, and darkness. Your Second World War brought about an end to that, and paved the way for a prolonged period of peace."

"Some peace," he retorted.

"Quite."

"So what now? And please don't give me that bollocks about timelines, strands, or my destiny. I just want to start a new life."

The hologram smiled again, but again, there was no true emotion in its face.

"Do you really think you could ever forget the life you left behind on Earth? Or what has transpired since you came to this century?" The hologram placed its hands behind its back, clasped together like an old-fashioned teacher. *"If you wanted to start a new life away from death and destruction, you would not have come aboard the* Gold Royale. *You would have disappeared with Hannah Spears and her daughters where nobody could find you, not even me."*

Adam sighed, knowing she was right.

"*Instead,*" she continued, "*you boarded the ship, accepted this suite, the cover, and the uniforms. You're preparing yourself for what's to come.*"

"I just have to accept my destiny," snorted Adam.

"*Exactly.*" The hologram smiled again. "*It's a long road ahead, but you're strong; you're a survivor. There's also a nice surprise I left for you in the main shuttle bay.*"

Adam looked at the hologram questioningly, but it flickered and disappeared.

"Dammit."

* * *

Two hours later, he was climbing into the dress uniform left for him in the walk-in closet. It was all black; almost identical to those worn by the Royal Navy in his own time, with gold braiding looped around one shoulder, small campaign markers on one side of his chest, even a Victoria Cross underneath, with a nametag on the other side. The peaked cap was the last to go on, peak first. A ship's patch sat on his arm, and rank stripes on the ends of his sleeves. The only difference between the Terran uniform and the Royal Navy uniform was the jacket and shoes. The styles were different, the Terran being more futuristic and simplistic than its double-breasted ancestor. The shoes were just as black, and just as mirror-shined as ever, though they had no laces, being simple slip-ons, with comfortable soles.

The doorbell chimed.

That would be the floor manager, here to escort him to the Captain's dining room.

Adam stepped out into the bedroom, and looked at himself in the full-length mirror.

"Mum would have loved this," he grumbled to himself.

The doorbell chimed again.

"Open sesame?" he ventured a guess. It seemed to work, as the doors slid apart, revealing a young human woman in a revealing dress. He barely gave her a glance.

"Commander Caine?" the woman asked.

"That's me."

"Good."

He turned to look down the barrel of an exotic pistol. It was purple, with a glowing blue globe flashing randomly, mixing blues with whites that made it look like a ball of bright water; it hummed gently, confirming to Adam that it was an energy weapon rather than solid-round. There were few straight lines on it, not like the Walther stuck in his kit bag, which was inconveniently sitting on his bed, ten metres away, where he couldn't get to it.

She wasn't unattractive, but it seemed as though her make-up had been slapped on in a hurry and left there for days on end. Her hair was fraying and greying at the very edges, offsetting the youthfulness of her chubby face.

The pistol was actually shaking in her hand. She was a novice, or she had abused too many substances to physically keep her hand steady.

"You're not the floor manager," he said dryly. "I didn't let a Tyrannosaurus intimidate me; a hooker with a fancy gun isn't going to do squat."

Truthfully, the Tyrannosaur had scared him shitless, and had nearly killed him, but she couldn't know that. Then again, he didn't care if she did pull the trigger; it wasn't a death wish, just acceptance –if this was his time, then it was his time, simple as that.

"Who told you to shoot me?" he asked gently.

"They said they could wipe my record clean," she answered in a shaky voice. She had a slightly Russian accent, though for all he knew, it could be an accent native to another planet completely. "They can give me back my old life on Tyvas VII."

"Who?"

"Two women in uniforms."

Adam frowned. Why would those two Intelligence officers be so open about this? To scare him? To make him figuratively flinch? There was no sense to it, unless they wanted to make it look like a deserting officer had been executed. There would be fewer questions asked openly that way.

The painted woman moved into the suite, letting the doors close behind her so that nobody could see what was happening. Adam wondered how she had gotten on the ship, and surmised that she was probably here with another of the guests.

She was too green to know what she was doing.

She stepped forward, placing the gun against his forehead, her eyes looking directly at his own. That was her mistake.

She didn't notice his hands suddenly whip up, and snare hers in a vice-grip, clamping down on her wrists and twisting them fast enough so that there was an audible crack as something in her arm gave. She screamed so loudly, he was sure she would wake the neighbours.

He kicked her in the chest for good measure, sending her flying backwards against the wall. He didn't see her touch a gold bracelet on her damaged wrist. It didn't take long for the backup to arrive.

She had been a diversion –to keep him occupied, and keep him in the room whilst the real shooters moved into position outside the suite, waiting for him to inevitably take down the girl. She had been cannon fodder –expendable.

The doors slid open, and in came ten armed men, all pointing pistols of the same design as the girl's. They wore the black carapace armour, and black fatigues he had seen the 21st 'Hunters' wear during the assault on Yh'reth'gar's flagship. They were special ops, or at least they were in *this* century. He hadn't seen them fight except in a straight firefight through a narrow doorway, and so had no way to properly judge their skills.

They moved like they knew what they were doing, pistol arm ramrod straight, the other bent to accommodate any recoil.

They spread out, preparing to encircle him, ignoring the prostitute's cries of pain, and the mass bruising along her wrists.

Adam never gave them the chance to surround him, charging the nearest Hunter before the soldier had time to realise what was going on. Adam jumped within arm's reach, and slammed an uppercut into the chin of the man's helmet, sending him tumbling to the floor. Adam ignored the pain in his knuckles where it connected with the solid helmet.

The next Hunter shoved his pistol into the side of Adam's head. He half-spun, wrapped a meaty arm around the other's then spun and drove his elbow into the Hunter's visor, smashing it and the face beneath, leaving him screaming on the floor.

Two more tried to club him with the butts of their pistols, but instead found his foot in their chests. They fell to the floor, clamping hands over their breastplates and grunting in agony.

Three others managed to get a few kicks and punches in against Adam's side before they too went down, clutching broken limbs.

The doors swished opened again, and in stepped the two Intelligence officers. One held another of the glowing pistols. She shot him with it, not taking any chances, a bright beam of light leaping from the gun. The blue energy drained from the globe on the back of the gun, and engulfed Adam, blacking him out.

* * *

They limped down the corridor, away from Caine's suite, two of the uninjured carrying him each with an arm over their shoulders. The others groaned and wheezed, trying to keep up as Majors Dunn and Drummond led the way.

They entered the arrivals lobby, with Adam still unconscious, to find Captain Franks, and Commander Gorman waiting impatiently for them, surrounded by a contingent of the ship's armed guards.

"Stand aside, Captain, this is Navy business," Drummond called forcefully.

"You and I both know Adam Caine is not, nor has ever been, a member of the Terran Navy," Franks growled. "So you have no right to detain him."

"We have *every* right," Dunn complained. She was gripping her pistol tightly, expecting the worse. The *Gold Royale* guards were not armed with guns but energy batons, originally designed for crowd control or riot duty. They sent a shock of electricity into the target, with the intention of forcing them away from the user.

Franks was about to argue more, when he stopped, and his eyes widened with shock.

There was a flurry of cracks, and muffled cries and curses, and then silence. Dunn and Drummond turned slowly, horror on their faces, and found Adam Caine standing in the midst of the downed squad of Hunters, a stun pistol pointed at Drummond's head.

"You're Kombat 3899, aren't you?" His voice was growling and menacingly low, like an agitated lion. "Don't deny it. I know enough about secret organisations to recognize the signs, not to mention you actually tried to violate this ship's treaties with the Terran authorities. Units like yours don't care about treaties, or the laws of others; they believe themselves so righteous that they're above the law. Don't you?" The two officers didn't reply, though Adam could see that the shock in their eyes: they really thought they were being so secretive.

So he shot them.

"I'm glad that thing was on stun," Franks commented as his guards dragged the Hunters and their superiors off the ship.

"It's on stun?" Adam complained, staring at the pistol in his hand. "Damn, I thought it was set to kill."

Franks' eyebrows shot up, though he said nothing.

"So you know who I am," Adam stated when the guards returned several minutes later. They filed out of the lobby, away to whatever part of the ship they were responsible for. The two men stood alone in the spacious lobby.

"I know that the history file says you were born in the Terran year 1980, on Earth itself. It also says you were a decorated soldier."

Adam gave the captain a sad smile.

"Both are true."

Franks didn't seem surprised, or put out by the information. Then again, cruise liners in Adam's time were known for the anonymity and well being of passengers.

"Come on," Franks smiled, clapping a hand on Adam's shoulder. "You can tell me everything on the way to dinner."

Adam grinned.

* * *

SENDER: [Unknown]
RECIPIENT: [Unknown]
MESSAGE ORIGIN: Roosh City, Fayde star-system
MESSAGE RELAYED VIA: 52 Unmarked Civilian Relay Buoys; HMS Fortitude; Navy Intelligence Headquarters (Delta-Tango star system)
TRANSMISSION SENT: 13/01/4000AD
TRANSMISSION RECEIVED: 13/01/4000AD

Alpha-8 reporting to Alpha-1
Caine has arrived on luxury liner *Gold Royale*. He resisted our attempt to extract him, and disabled the Hunters we sent in. He has befriended the ship's captain.

Franks may be an intelligence asset; will proceed with bringing him in to the fold. If not, he is aware of our presence, and may have to be dealt with.

Caine is also aware of the organisation, possibly through Colonel Sansky of NI. Sansky and the time-travellers may also intervene in our plans for Caine, though they have thus far done no such thing.

Will follow *Gold Royale* at a distance.

Alpha-8 out.

Five:
Odyssey Station

"The perfect killer is an elusive thing, seldom sought after, and never wished upon anyone, not even your worst enemy."

-From the memoirs of Prof. Zagrabbanalam Lar, former Head of Biology, New Amsterdam University.

There was a bloodcurdling scream of fear and intense pain, followed by a hideous sound of rending flesh and a wet squelch and thump of a dismembered body hitting the deck. Air gurgled from the lungs of Doctor Zh'V's ruined body, though there was no-one else to hear it.

Zh'V's colleagues had bolted at the first sign of the intruders, crying out in terror and soiling themselves as they went. Zh'V had simply stood there, his long purple face wide with scientific curiosity and complete unadulterated fear.

He had been the first to die, but he was not the last.

The intruder stalked the surviving scientists through the station's darkened corridors, hunting each down as they fled n panic in separate directions.

Doctor Kareff backed herself into a dark room, breathing a sigh of relief as she heard the intruder bound past. She heard something shift almost silently behind her, and could smell something rotten and decayed. The smell was overpowering, and she gagged. She looked round to locate the source, and found eyes staring back at her -dozens of them.

She screamed as she realised the intruder was not alone.

The scream was cut off as she was torn apart by slicing bony blades.

A shivering green form watched the feeding frenzy from above in the air vents. She couldn't stop shaking from the sheer mind-numbing ferocious terror.

She whimpered.

One of the intruders snapped its head round to look up at the ceiling; it looked straight at *her*.

It knew she was there.

She screamed.

* * *

4000ad.

The blue tunnel of light rushed around the behemoth form of the star liner *Gold Royale* as it cruised lazily through the Linkway like a whale. One or two other, smaller ships passed it by every few minutes, traversing the busy Linkway between Fayde and Romgen on the spiral-edge of the Milky Way.

A column of ore haulers overtook the lumbering giant three hours out from the transition to the Romgen star system. Each was a long cigar of dirty grey metal, stained in parts by spillages of the materials they carried, flying bow-to-stern with only a shuttle-length between each ship. They passed with a few sarcastic waves from their pilots.

A wing-pair of Terran Rhino interceptors flashed past the *Gold Royale* chasing a twin-hulled stock freighter intent on getting its illegal supplies to its distant destination. To the dismay of the liner's crew, the freighter skimmed over the massive unshielded hull, and used the ship's engine wake to shake off its pursuers.

The Terran starfighters were shaken about so badly by the wake that their engines stalled momentarily, leaving the freighter to make a free run for the Milky Way's outer rim star systems.

The Fregati flagship *Foetar* rumbled past, its five angular hulls reflecting the brilliant swirl of blue light from the energy tunnel around.

It was an amazing sight, Adam decided.

He was stood on the balcony of the curving observation deck at the very top of the *Gold Royale*. There were comfortable benches and cushioned seats for viewing all around; Adam preferred to stand at the railings, and watch the traffic wander past outside under the massive observation dome that stretched above him as far as he could see in either direction within the ship. The view was breathtaking.

He had been on the *Gold Royale* for ten days, and not a lot had happened; nothing spectacular anyway. He had spent most of the time listening to reams of history files and lectures via the holographic interface in his suite. So far, he had caught up on only one thousand years of history, and that was only the *Terran* history. There were nineteen galaxies in all, with thousands of cultures in each; some, like the Terran Consortium, was made up of several cultures, and still others were spread over a wide area, like the tribesmen of Mongolia back home.

There was no mention of the Core, just as he had expected.

The history file on himself was limited to the public facts of his military career, and a few brief comments on his familial background.

Even as he stared out at the vast expanse of the Linkway, he thought on how insignificant his life had been compared to what was out here in space, in the greater universe. His mother had always said that mankind refused to believe that other intelligent life existed beyond its tiny little world because they believed racially to be superior beings.

Were they wrong, or what?

In retrospect, he didn't much care for that sort of thinking. Philosophy had never been his strong suit, even with father breathing down his neck every five minutes, testing him despite constant protests and hate-filled remarks. Philosophy was for those who got paid for it.

Adam had steadfastly tried to ignore his family's upper-class way of thinking, and become one of the 'common people' as one of his older sisters had described him. He had spent weeks during the school holidays learning tracking and fieldcraft skills with father's under-paid grounds keepers in the manor's grounds and the countryside around it. Joining the Royal Marines had simply been a step up from that, and had been an easy decision to make, given that he was so unwelcome in his father's home.

There were no longer any ships in view of the balcony so Adam turned to lean on the railing. The floor itself was made from some transparent metal so that you had a view of what was beneath. He had hardly believed it when he saw the name of the establishment below.

CASINO ROYALE was written in mauve above a set of double doors that opened onto a hall of speedy elevators, one of which led to the casino below.

Adam wondered if the name was intentional, or whether it had simply been naming it after the ship itself with no knowledge of the James Bond novel.

Below, it was like Las Vegas, with roulette wheels, card tables, futuristic slot machines, plus a host of other games that he didn't recognise. Apparently, the casino was open twenty-nine hours a day.

He was still getting used to the idea of more than twenty-four hours in a day. Apparently, twenty-nine hours was the universal standard, whatever the hell that meant.

It was the night cycle on the ship, so there were hardly any other stargazers sat under the observation dome with him. There was a pair of off-duty crew still in uniform giggling and cuddling, apparently enjoying a romantic night away from their jobs. Images of kissing Hannah came unbidden to his thoughts.

Adam sighed; that wasn't the reminder he needed right now.

He turned back to the sight of the Linkway when a rumbling charged through the flooring beneath him. The two crewmembers sat nearby jumped out of their voluminous settee, worried looks on their faces.

If they were worried, it meant that wasn't a normal occurrence. Outside the dome, the Linkway turned a sickly green, and suddenly ripped apart. The ship jumped, throwing Adam onto his arse. There were screams from below, confirming that he wasn't the only one knocked over. Shouts of anguish and fear filtered up through the grated floor.

There was a loud tearing sound, like rocks breaking against one another.

Adam looked round in horror to see a white zigzagging line crawling across the transparent material of the dome.

"Oh, shit."

He sprinted toward the elevator lobby, the two crewmembers right behind him. Then it went deathly quiet, as if there were no sound at all. It didn't last long, however, as a roaring sound battered Adam's eardrums, and a fierce wind slammed against him. He dove for the floor, clutching the seams of the floor plating with his fingers.

He barely heard the muffled shout from behind him.

He turned to see a steward being dragged along the floor by an invisible force towards the crack in the dome.

There was a tortured scream of immense amounts of shattered glass, and the dome finally gave way. The steward, unlucky enough not to be hanging on to anything, was ripped from the floor, and sent tumbling into space.

Adam belatedly realised they were no longer in the Linkway, but in the black of regular space.

The steward, screaming soundlessly without air, disappeared quickly from Adam's view. Luckily, the two canoodling crewmembers had managed to copy Adam, and were hanging on to the near-invisible seams in the floor with their fingers. He pointed toward the elevator lobby for their benefit, making big gestures to make sure he was understood. They nodded, not questioning him.

Hand-over-hand, wind buffeting him, Adam crawled toward the elevators.

He didn't want to think what was happening to the unsuspecting patrons of the casino below. He shut everything else, and put all his strength into pulling himself toward the open doors. He frowned –shouldn't the doors have closed to prevent this sort of thing? His question was answered when sparks erupted briefly from inside the door control panel.

"Crap," he tried to say. No sound actually left his lips –in fact, there was no sound at all. The wind had dissipated too. At first, he thought that meant there was no longer any air escaping through the hole above.

He was half right; there was no air at all to escape through the hole. It had all gone.

"Shit," he mouthed.

The effort of crawling was beginning to hurt his muscles, pain imbuing his arms and chest. With no air, his body wasn't getting the oxygen it needed. The oxygen he held in his lungs was burning away fast, and he was still metres from the doors.

Finally, the doors fizzed and bucked, and slammed shut.

Except Adam was on the wrong side still.

He mouthed curses that were anatomically impossible, though the vacuum swallowed them whole.

He was just giving up the ghost when he felt a familiar tingling sensation spread over his body. The soundless, airless vacuum was replaced with a strange sigh before he was once again back in the medical bay he had started off in ten days ago.

He took a grateful deep breath before coughing through a dry throat.

He wasn't alone.

The two crewmembers were similarly coughing and heaving beside him, whilst a collection of assorted beings lay lifeless in other corners of the room. *Gold Royale*'s medical staff moved among them, checking for life.

Adam was sickened to realise he and the other two were the only ones left alive.

The casino had been a major design flaw, and dozens had suffered the fatal consequences.

The doctor that treated him days before approached him and the others, and waved a strange wand device in front of them, which Adam took to be a medical scanner of some sort. It beeped, and several lights blinked rapidly. The doctor grunted, and looked up from his scanner.

"Aside from a touch of oxygen depravation, you're fine, Commander Caine." Adam nodded, and moved towards the door, ignoring the mass of finely dressed corpses. Even out the corner of his eye, he could see some were still stuck in the positions they had died in. Some were caught in vacuum-forced rigour, their faces still screaming soundlessly, eyes still open. Adam shuddered and strode out of the medical bay.

He asked the nurse at the duty station the directions to the bridge.

The nurse was glad to help, giving him a series of long and complicated directions that eventually led to the command centre of the flying city.

Like the bridge of the *Polly Jenkins*, the bridge of the *Gold Royale* was plastered with holographic displays, monitors, workstations, and computer consoles, though they were coloured a soft blue rather than the bright green the Terran Navy habitually used.

The bridge was a mess: crewmen were screaming at each other for data, whilst alert panels blared loudly for attention. The command centre was made up of three levels; the lowest was further out than the one above, and so on. Adam had stepped out onto the central level.

At the fore of the bridge, an island of calm among the chaos, stood Captain Franks, arms folded, playing with the beard hair on his chin. Commander Gorman stood several metres to his left, barking orders to the crew around them.

Adam hurried up beside Franks, totally ignored by the crew.

Franks didn't flinch when he suddenly found Adam Caine stood by his side, though he was somewhat alarmed the fake Terran officer had managed to get onto the bridge unchallenged. He was still unsure as to what to make of the younger man, and had thus avoided being near him until he could decide whether to befriend him properly. They had had a few dinners with Commander Gorman and some of the other guests, but always formal and always impersonal.

Caine was a picture of calm, staring out of the massive forward viewing windows with no emotion on his face.

Franks had been informed that Caine had almost fallen victim to the failure of the observation dome's structure at the top of the ship, and his subsequent via the ship's teleporters.

"What happened?" Caine asked.

"The Linkway collapsed for some reason," Gorman answered for her captain. Despite her initial brusqueness with Caine during their first few interactions, she had had an amicable relationship with him, even smiling once or twice —something she rarely did around the crew. "We think it was because of its proximity to an unusual gravitic anomaly."

Caine looked at her like she was mad.

She smiled, clearly enjoying the superiority of knowing he was a fake, and thus didn't have the knowledge of the real thing.

"There's a black hole out there somewhere."

"If it's that powerful, why haven't you found it already?" asked Caine.

Gorman was about to make a retort when the senior sensor officer spoke up from nearby.

"Captain, I'm detecting the black hole, but..."

"But what?" demanded Franks.

"It's coming from *within* a man-made structure three hundred thousand kilometres off our port." The officer's fingers flew over his holographic console, and a holographic image leaped into existence in front of Franks. His eyes opened wide. The structure was sat above the small black hole, with two giant struts either side of the anomaly, connecting underneath like a hanging basket. A forcefield was flickering around the anomaly, losing integrity. However, the design of the facility was clear. Incredibly, though, it was neither Gorman nor Franks who made the obvious leap.

"It's Terran," said Caine. Despite his lack of knowledge of contemporary technology, it seemed he was at least partially aware of what Terran space stations looked like, or at least the construction technology.

"What station is that?" Gorman queried.

"The computer lists it as a research facility called 'Odyssey Station'," replied the sensor officer.

"Researching what exactly?" This from Franks himself. The sensor officer shook his head in frustration, announcing the station's purpose as top secret, classified by Navy Intelligence. Franks and Caine shared a mutual grimace at the mention of Terran Navy Intelligence.

"Captain," the communications officer announced, "the station is sending out an automated distress signal."

"Details?"

"Nothing specific, sir, but it was cut short. It just keeps repeating the same letters over and over again. 'SOS.'"

Caine let out a colourful curse.

Franks wasn't aware of what the phrase meant. He looked at Caine questioningly.

"It's an old maritime tradition. SOS stands for Save Our Souls. It's a cry for help."

Franks swore.

"Any life signs?" he asked out loud.

"They are intermittent, Captain, and keep changing from human to something else the computer cannot identify." Franks wondered why. "I honestly could not tell you why, sir. Their bio-readings are fluctuating, as if they are in a constant state of flux."

Caine's face went blank.

Franks shook his head dismissively, not wanting to have to explain. He tapped the comms activation control floating in front of him. "Engineering, what is your status?"

"*Captain, main engines are down,*" a disembodied voice answered. "*We are flying on the back-ups, though I would not recommend using main engines just yet* as that emergency transition to realspace blew out power conduits throughout the drive section. I can give you thrusters, but that is about it, sir."

"Understood; do your best."

"*As always, Captain,*" the voice said with a little smile. "*Engineering out.*"

"Security," Franks stated, changing to a different channel on the intercom. "Assemble a search-and-rescue team in the main shuttlebay, armed with stun pistols. I will meet you down there."

"Captain," Gorman warned, "it is strictly against regulations in *any* navy for you to go over there, especially with a possibly unstable black hole directly beneath the facility."

"I'll go," Caine suddenly said. "I'll lead your security team."

Franks opened his mouth and closed it several times like a fish, contemplating the possibility. He sighed, and then slowly nodded. "You'll need a weapon and something other than those Navy uniforms you have to keep wearing."

"That's okay, I've got some kit in my suite."

Franks snorted at the revelation, shook his head in amusement, and returned to the diagnostic display of the space station, leaving Gorman to escort Caine back to his suite.

Gorman waited for Caine outside his suite, tapping her foot impatiently.

His doors slid open, and he stepped out, dressed in full black combat fatigues and equipment vest, and carrying an ancient solid-round rifle. The uniform, and the weapon, were in perfect condition considering that nobody had probably used one in thousands of years.

The uniform actually seemed to suit him perfectly, even with his long hair.

"It suits you," she commented as they strode back down the corridor.

"Thanks," he replied warily.

"The rifle is not necessary; it is only a search-and-rescue, and you will be with our best guards."

"Several years on the frontlines and behind enemy lines have taught me to be prepared for anything. I'm not taking any chances, especially after the last few weeks I've had."

She showed him to the shuttlebay, pointing to a small craft that had a similar thin clamshell design as the *Gold Royale*. A team of security guards, dressed in their best uniforms, so it seemed, and armed with energy pistols, waited for Adam and Gorman at the entry ramp of the small ship. None of them were human, and none were much taller than Gorman.

They all seemed somewhat in awe of him as he approached, dressed in combat gear as he was, and armed with a nasty-looking weapon.

"This is Commander Caine," Gorman announced, gesturing to Adam for the benefit of the guards, and not letting up that he was anything but a Terran Navy officer. "He will be taking command of the mission on behalf of the Captain. You follow his orders like you would the Captain's, or mine." She handed Caine a personal comms device that he pocketed straight away.

The guards nodded a welcome, though none spoke other than to acknowledge the order. They filed up the short ramp into the sleek shuttle, clambering in and taking their seats in the rear of the vessel. Adam sighed, smiled sadly at Gorman, and jumped in the shuttle.

Gorman wondered why he had been so reluctant to enter the shuttle after having volunteered for the mission in the first place. Was he that scarred by combat he no longer had any optimism for it? Or was it a death wish? She realised that both options scared her.

* * *

The door cycled shut behind Adam as he stepped across the cramped passenger compartment, and stepped up behind the human pilot.

"Soon as you're ready, pilot," Adam ordered.

"Pilot Feyton, sir. First Class." The young woman seemed inordinately pleased with her title. *She probably earned it flying cargo runs,* Adam mused.

"First Class Pilot then. Let's get this thing moving as quick as possible, shall we?" He had meant it to sound sarcastic, but she apparently took it as a compliment, and was now under the impression he gave a monkeys about her flying skills beyond getting to the objective in one piece.

Feyton nodded enthusiastically, her braided bangles bouncing as she did so. Adam steadied himself against the bulkhead as Feyton powered up the shuttle's anti-gravs, lifting it off and hovering above the deck.

Outside, a forcefield flashed into existence across the inside of the giant shuttlebay doors, presumably to keep the ship's atmosphere in, and keep anything unwanted outside.

On the other side of the bay, something winked at him. It was a ship, covered in a blue marbled hull, the shape of a crescent moon, with stubby, crescent-shaped wings midway up, and a triangular cockpit window just above them on the outside of the crescent. To Adam's untrained eyes, it was beautiful; briefly, he wondered which guest it belonged to –he hadn't had the time to come down to the shuttlebay to check on whatever it was Silver had left him.

The great doors grumbled open, each sliding away to reveal the vacuum beyond, uncomfortably reminding Adam of his close encounter with it less than an hour before.

"Hold on tight, Commander," Feyton announced, even though he was already holding on to a support beam with one hand. The shuttle suddenly shot forward, through the forcefield, and out into space. Adam nearly lost his footing, though was lucky enough to find another support beam behind him so he could comfortably wedge himself in.

Feyton swung the craft out and around the hull of the *Gold Royale* to face the ominously dark Odyssey Station. There were no running or navigation lights on the outer station, nor could Adam see any *internal* lighting currently active.

"You all have torches?" he said, turning to the guards. They nodded. "You're going to need them." He fished out the lamp-pack from his kit, and snapped it to the underside of his rifle's barrel.

The shuttle began to vibrate, and before long it was shaking violently. Adam presumed it was something to do with the black hole that was visibly outgrowing the station above and around it.

"Feyton, can you take us up and over the station, close enough to inspect the hull."

"What for, sir?"

"I want to see if there's any outside damage before we start bumbling around in there." It had been standard procedure during operations into enemy-held buildings: scope the building for any possible threats from the crumbling structure itself before determining entry points. He suddenly had a thought. "Can your sensors do a visual sweep of the station?"

"Of course," she answered nonchalantly, slowing the shuttle, and turning to a smaller console on her left, spinning her chair as she did so, leaving the craft on autopilot. Her eyes scanned over the sensor data. "I am not reading any hull fractures or breaches. In fact, the station's outer hull is hole-free, though there are stresses along the ventral supports for that black hole."

"Life support?"

She nodded. "Some sections have been sealed and depressurised, but life support is still working in the others. The shuttlebay doors have been fused shut."

"Any airlocks?" he queried. He was faking the knowledge, but it seemed to him that a space station as big as Odyssey would have airlocks either in case of emergencies, or for ships that were too big to land in the shuttlebay. Although, if this really was a top-secret facility, then anything was possible.

"There is an airlock on the command deck that this shuttle can dock with."

"Sounds good. Gently does it, please; I'd rather not end up a stain on the side of that thing." She didn't take the comment as being malicious, just him being nervous —which was exactly what he was. In this small ship he felt slightly claustrophobic; more so, with a dozen armed guards sat in the back, who were more nervous than him. They were 'combat virgins' as Sergeant Graham used to say.

Hopefully, this really would be as easy as everybody else made it out to be, though his personal experiences told him otherwise. In fact, his experience was telling him to run like the wind, to get the hell away from this universe and not look back.

But that wasn't an option anymore.

The shuttle cruised toward the ominous grey structure, and docked with the small airlock. The seals hissed as the two atmospheres hit each other.

The shuttle door opened, and a rank, stale smell suddenly filled the passenger compartment. One of the guards —a green-skinned, fin-headed fellow- vomited up his dinner. The others retched and dry-heaved, though thankfully nothing exited *their* bodies.

Adam led the way, the butt of his rifle dug into his shoulder so that any direction the rifle was pointing, he was looking. The corridor they exited onto was pitch black, their torches necessary from the get-go.

He pointed to the nearest three guards, and gestured one way down the corridor. "You three check the main command centre; search through the station's computer to see what happened here, and try and get something online other than emergency power."

The three guards nodded, and jogged off down the corridor, the shafts of light from their torches flailing around as they went; in the military, that was usually a sign they were unfit, trying to use all their strength to pump their arms to keep up with the others.

He pointed to the next three. "You three with me; the rest split into two groups and search the lower- and mid-levels for survivors. We're going to find out what those intermittent life readings are."

Despite being scared out of their minds, the guards all nodded resolutely before splitting into their assigned groups, their lamps wobbling a little as their hands –or paws- began to quake slightly.

"What are your names?" he asked of the three that remained with him.

The first, a silver-furred cat-like humanoid, pronounced its name as a long purring noise. Caine tried to recreate the noise, but gave up and labelled him Purr.

The other two, both of the same pointy-eared grey-skinned race, declared themselves as Triona and Melona. None of them smiled, and Adam couldn't really blame them. The darkness of the facility, and the creaking and groaning of the metal around them, was giving him the heebie-jeebies too. Triona was carrying the portable sensor in one hand.

"Can you get a more specific location from that?" asked Adam, nodding to the device.

Triona activated the sensor, and panned it around, finally settling on a direction, which led away down another dark corridor.

"That way, Commander, though it's still pretty vague."

"Let's go then," Adam said, making it an order rather than a suggestion.

Adam led the way, rifle pointed ahead of him as they stepped cautiously through the broken blackness.

The sensor in Triona's hand suddenly beeped for attention.

"Humanoid up ahead, in one of the storage rooms."

Caine moved quicker, pulling further ahead from the others, his pulse racing as he once again stepped toward danger. The four came to a generic grey door with no markings on, and a small control pad to one side. The pad was unlit, receiving no power.

Purr and Triona moved to one side of the door, whilst Melona stood the other. Adam stood in front, weapon raised. He could see the others were terrified, and flinched every time they heard a scratching or shuffling noise from the other side of the door.

Caine forced his own rising panic down into the depths, and took a step back, leaning on his back foot. With no power, the door would have to be forced manually. They tried to *pull* the door open with their hands. He rocked backwards, then forwards, then back again until he had gained sufficient momentum. He put all that momentum and strength into one massive kick that caved the door in.

But the door held.

Purr disappeared for a minute, and then reappeared with a metal pole from one of the other storage rooms. The four of them levered the door open with a grunt of effort and a squeal of metal grinding on metal. Caine was first through.

He charged into the room.

"Shit."

* * *

"Captain," Gorman called, recently returned from belowdecks. "We're detecting several other vessels nearby. They were all dragged into realspace at the same time as us." She looked down at the console she was stood at. "The freighters *E11g*, *Arktown*, and *441-F* as well as a fuel tanker, two Terran starfighters, and a Fregati warship."

"I'm assuming the Fregati are refusing any help?" asked Franks.

Gorman nodded in response.

"Alright, begin rescue operations for the freighters and tanker. Give them what they need, within reason. The starfighters can come into one of our secondary shuttlebays if they so wish."

"Yes, sir." Gorman turned to issue the necessary orders to the crew, directing them personally. Franks returned his attention to the grey mass of Odyssey Station in the distance.

"Status on the boarding party?" he asked.

"Pilot Feyton reports she has docked and Commander Caine's team have boarded the structure." It had been a junior officer that had answered, always eager to please.

"Understood, keep constant communication with the shuttle, if you can."

* * *

T'Yop, and his old drinking buddies Lash-Gev and Arg-891a, were one of the teams searching the lower levels. So far, they had found nothing but empty storage rooms and living quarters, even the odd cold meal or bit of paperwork left unfinished. But there was no sign of a crew, nor any sign that there had been one for a long time.

They were already searching the next floor down, chatting whilst they were doing so. They had all decided that they would meet up after the next duty shift, and decide on doing something big for their vacations over a few drinks.

They started bawling with laughter when T'Yop mentioned that that's what they did after *every* duty shift.

It was only when T'Yop couldn't hear Arg-891a laughing that he realised something was wrong. He turned to his friend.

"Arg? Where are you?"

He was gone.
He turned round.
Lash-Gev was gone too.
"Gods preserve me."

* * *

Lash-Gev, an old Tricelera, could barely feel whatever it was that had stuck him in the chest. All he could feel was something wet across his chest. When he looked down he could see the glinting wetness of his own blood plastered all over his upper torso.

It was dark, and he could hear several somethings moving around him, away from his active torchlight. There were quiet growls of pleasure, accompanied by the snapping of jaws and tearing of something he dearly hoped wasn't flesh.

There was a squeal of animal anger, an answering growl, followed by something that sounded like a pained yelp. Something wet bounced near to Lash-Gev. He looked round from his lying position on the floor, reached over, and found something fleshy and round. He held it up, and threw it back down.

It was Arg's head, no longer attached to his body.

Lash-Gev screamed.

Something moved up beside him, something with rows of razor-sharp teeth.

He screamed again.

More of them appeared, all around him, saliva, and something worse, drooling from their lipless mouths. They were hungry. They had already eaten Arg-891a, and now they were expecting dessert.

He screamed and howled at the top of his lungs, even as they began eating his internal organs. Nobody heard him.

* * *

"Dammit, tell that fuel tanker to pull away from the others. If she goes, it's going to take the freighters with it!" Franks' face was red with anger. None of the captains of the other ships were paying any attention to his suggestions. Each one constantly demanded the complete attention of the *Gold Royale*'s engineers to repair their ships, not the others. Each thought themselves more important.

The fuel tanker seemed to be flown by a moron.

Or a blind man.

Their course corrections made no sense, and they kept coming dangerously close to colliding with the smaller freighters, not to mention the *Gold Royale* herself. Her captain claimed that their engines were malfunctioning, though Franks could tell from the man's voice that he was lying.

The *Foetar* still hung at a distance from both Odyssey Station and the starliner, not deigning to help out.

They're probably the smart ones, thought Franks.

He didn't want to even think about the multitudes of complaints from his own stuffy passengers at the rough ride. They would have to lump it. His comm unit was constantly beeping, almost always a passenger wanting to tell him how shoddy the piloting was.

"Watch out!" He heard the voice of the *E11g*'s captain scream through the local comm network.

The fuel tanker was veering to one side at a great speed, too fast for the smaller freighter to avoid. The tanker smashed the *E11g*'s port side into pieces, crushing its entire engine block, and ripping away the dorsal hull plating entirely. The freighter, completely crippled, went spinning away from the force of the hit and collided with the bigger *441-F*. Both exploded on impact, taking both crews with it.

The *Arktown*, now repaired by *Gold Royale*'s engineers, moved away from the black hole, on a course out of the system.

Franks was about to shout down the comms at the tanker's crew, when the *Foetar* disabled its engines with a pinpoint-accurate barrage. The voice of its captain came over the speakers.

"Civilian ships, cease your squabbling. We will rectify the situation momentarily." The link clicked as the Fregati cut the channel from his end.

"What does that mean?" someone asked.

Warning lights flashed on.

"They're locking onto us, the fuel tanker, and the *Arktown*," the sensors operator called out. "They're trying to lock their missiles onto the station, but they're having trouble locking on because of the gravitic mass of the black hole."

The *Gold Royale* and its new charges had no weapons to speak of, certainly not enough to defend itself from the *Foetar*.

Franks couldn't do anything but get the engineers motivated and hope that Caine could get out sooner rather than later.

* * *

"So what's your name then?"

The small girl could not have been more than six years old. She was shaking, terrified out of her mind, her eyes filled with fear as they darted from Adam to Purr, and back to Adam. Triona and Melona had been tasked with watching the door, jumping at every creak and groan. She didn't seem to pay the two much attention.

Her skin was a deep emerald green, even in the limited light of the search team's lamps. Her eyes were a deeper blue, though her whites were bloodshot from fatigue, and her dark blue hair was messy, unwashed, and matted with something Adam didn't want to think about in too much detail.

She shook her head, hugging her knees so they were pulled up tight to her chest. She wasn't just shaking; she was quaking now, so badly Adam thought she was having a seizure. He put his big arm around her tiny shoulders. She stopped shaking, and leaned into him. Before long, she was clinging to him.

"Don't you have a name?" he asked. She shook her head.

"Are you my daddy?" she whispered in a soft innocent voice.

Adam was about to open his mouth to answer when the lights flickered on, and a humming noise built up in the floors and walls. The station began to vibrate all over, juddering Adam and the others. Adam exchanged a worried glance with Purr, who had become his second by default.

"That can't be good," he grunted.

The comms device in his pocket began to beep and vibrate. He fished it out, and pressed the flashing blue button.

"Caine here."

"*Commander, you better get up here on the double. You are going to want to see this.*" He recognised the voice of one of the team he had sent to the command centre. He gestured to his own team, before shouldering his rifle and picking up the alien girl in his powerful arms, though to be honest, she would have clung on anyway.

Now that power had been restored, there was no need for the torches. The corridors of the station were almost identical to the ones he had encountered on the *HMS Polly Jenkins*. The walls and floor were once a clinically stark white, though they were now dirtied as if nobody had bothered to clean the place in a long time.

Adam couldn't actually see any source for the bright lighting, and wondered if it was holographic like the rest of Terran technology.

They entered the command centre after two quick elevator rides, and a short flight of stairs, the young girl still clinging to Adam as if she might die if she touched the floor. He didn't mind; she wasn't heavy at all.

The team he had sent up here were frantically trying to get in touch with the *Gold Royale*.

"Report," he ordered, stepping up beside the nearest of the three –a nearly-human being with four small eyes in place of a human's two, each of which rotated individually within its socket, giving him a complete 180-degree vision.

"The black hole below us is destabilising."

"Surely the station is equipped to handle that?"

"It probably was, sir," Four-Eyes replied succinctly. "But with the station's power down, the containment fields were down too, and for a while as well."

"How long was the containment down?"

"From the records, it seems they were down for approximately thirty-nine days, Commander."

"How long before things inevitably go wrong for us?" asked Adam. Four-Eyes tapped a variety of seemingly random buttons, gave out a grunt, and then turned back to Caine.

"In three hours, the black hole's accretion disk will eclipse the station, and the hole itself will start to fully pull us in. We've got the containment fields back up on automatic, but they're failing even now, so they'll only slow our descent.

After that, the station will be torn to pieces. Eventually, the *Gold Royale* too if she is still here."

"Do they know what's going on?"

"*Royale*'s sensors are state-of-the-art," Purr answered. "But she's a cruise liner, not a Terran warship." Purr had obviously intended this as a dig at Adam, or at least the fake Adam that was the XO of a Terran Navy starship, not the time-traveller Adam that few people knew.

He had no real idea why Purr was angry; maybe the feline had been discharged from the Navy? Or maybe the Navy had done something to Purr personally. Adam didn't care at this juncture.

"Any luck contacting the ship?" he asked to nobody in particular. There was a definite round of negative head shaking in response. Adam cursed under his breath. This, of course, was the moment four of the six guards he had sent to the lower levels suddenly burst into the command centre. Two were carrying another, each with one of his arms over their shoulders. He was pale, despite his silvery scaly skin, and shaking more than the little girl had.

Clearly, the guard had seen whatever it was the girl was terrified of.

"What happened?" he demanded. "Where are the other two?"

"We don't know, sir," an octopus in a uniform answered. Eight tentacles, all with sleeves on, vibrated worriedly at even intervals around its chest.

The girl was suddenly gripping tighter and tighter onto Adam, and he could see out the corner of his eye that she was seeing something over his shoulder; something that everybody else was apparently oblivious to, concentrating as they were on their friends. Calmly, Adam peeled the girl's curling fingers off of him, and placed her feet on the ground as softly as he could. He straightened up, stared at the pale, shaking guard, whose eyes were widening as he caught sight of whatever it was. Adam reached behind him, spun, and brought his rifle up.

The SA80 roared as he squeezed the trigger, and let loose a burst on full auto.

The creature, caught mid-leap, was torn in half, spraying black ichor across the holographic consoles. The creature let out a piercing scream as it died, before its lifeless head and upper torso collided with Four-Eyes, and the rest of it landed next to the traumatised young girl. Four-Eyes let out a yelp of disgust and fear, and jumped backwards.

"What is that?" Four-Eyes cried.

"I don't know," Adam admitted. "But it's not alone."

Three more of the creatures had dropped down, and were stood at the other side of the command centre. They weren't moving, just watching them, though Adam could see no eyes; it stood like a hunched man, back legs bent, though it had five upper arms, each ending in three long, bone blades. Their skin was patched, different shades of reds and pink flesh that glistened like a wet corpse. Rows of needle-like teeth filled each creature's mouth, dull and rotten like the rest of their bodies.

The smell was hideous. It was the same decayed flesh smell as they had detected when they first boarded the station. Except this smell was so bad,

Adam felt like he had been punched in the nose. His freshly shaved upper lip suddenly felt wet. He put his fingers up to feel what it was, and found it was his own blood. The guards were all suffering spontaneous nosebleeds –although in the case of Octopus, ink dribbled out of several unnameable orifices.

Adam brought his rifle up again, and squeezed the trigger.

"Everybody get back to the shuttle!" he bellowed as he loosed another dozen rounds. The first creature's head came apart in a bloody mess, whilst the second creature's legs were blown off. The third creature bound across the room, using the consoles as stepping-stones, moving quicker than Adam could see. It charged, jumped, and dove at Four-Eyes.

Four-Eyes tried to whip his stun pistol out of its holster, but he wasn't quick enough. The creature tore into him in an instant, shredding him into bloody ribbons before Adam's eyes. Four-Eyes never let out so much as a scream.

The others were getting over their stupefied horror, backing away toward the entrance, their pistols unholstered, and pointing at the remaining creature.

Adam fired again, but all that happened was the dull clack of an empty magazine.

He swore.

It saw him.

He was the closest to it, and thus its closest target.

It jumped.

He dove to his left, out of its reach, before it was engulfed by a wave of stun energy that threw it backwards into another console. Adam heard its spine snap. He rolled back up to stand beside the little girl, scooped her up, and sprinted to the door. After slipping the rifle's strap over his shoulder, he reached down and plucked out the Walther and checked its readings in one swift movement.

There was a continuous sound of thudding behind him. Adam turned, and saw ten of the creatures dropping down from an air vent in the high ceiling. More continued to drop down even as Adam shouted for the others to run. The girl in one hand, the Walther in the other, Adam charged down the corridor after the others, letting off a shot or two blindly behind him as he went.

The young girl was crying her eyes out.

A lucky bullet took one of the creatures above its mouth, blowing its brains out the back of its low head. The corpse hit the floor with a wet thud, and tripped up the two behind it.

Suddenly the lights went out.

"Oh Gods!" somebody screamed further on. Adam holstered his pistol, and retrieved the lamp-pack from his rifle.

Why weren't the creatures all over them? They moved fast as lightning. *We should already be dead*, Adam worried.

Up ahead, somebody died messily. Adam could hear the flesh tearing even from his position at the rear, and the screams of the dying and the frightened.

They set a bloody trap.

With his torch lit, he slipped off down a side-corridor, hoping to find a way round without the creatures getting in the way. At least three of the others had

had the same idea; that, or they had simply seen his light veer off, and followed its source.

Adam tried to quiet the girl, who was hysterical with fear, bawling and crying so much Adam had to place his lamp-holding hand across her mouth. They slipped into a room, doused the torches they were holding, and crouched by the door frame. They all held their breath, stilling the revulsion in them as they heard the bloodcurdling screams of their comrades. Someone whimpered beside Adam. He recognised the voice as belonging to Purr. His own hand was still clamped over the girl's tiny mouth.

Then he heard something sniffing, and the tapping of claws on metal. The sound was barely two feet away. The sniffing continued; with a thrill of horror, Adam realised that without eyes, they relied on their other senses, like a blind person adjusting to losing his sight.

He switched his lamp on, and flinched badly as he came face-to-face with one of the creatures. It growled, drew its head back to snap *his* head off, and squealed as Adam slammed his torch into its head. There was a wet squelch as the torch connected, and Adam wondered just how well armoured they were. He jumped up, and kicked the creature in the head.

They started running again, continuing down the corridor, away from where the main group of creatures had converged to trap them seconds ago.

Adam couldn't hear any of the telltale signs of being followed, but didn't slow down, despite carrying full combat gear, a heavy rifle, and a young girl.

They were all breathing heavily, either unfit, or like Adam, carrying a great deal of extra weight. Purr pointed ahead, and they all saw the staircase leading down. They bound down the steps two, three, even four at a time. Adam kept urging them to move faster, even though he still couldn't hear the creatures anywhere in earshot.

They flew down thirteen flights of stairs before they came to the right floor. Purr seemed to have a flawless sense of direction, unerringly leading them exactly where they needed to go.

Adam kicked in the half-open door with brute strength, barely stopping as he charged down the stairs, getting a run-up. Just before he connected however, there was a great rumble, and the station shook violently, energy conduits spewing sparks as they snapped under the sudden strain. The jolt threw Adam against the nearest wall. Recovering quickly, he launched his foot at the door, just above the handle. Despite the metal material, the door lurched open, the lock smashing under Adam's powerful kick.

He entered the corridor beyond, and found, to his amazement and everybody else's, that it was no longer there.

"Shit."

* * *

Franks couldn't believe what he was seeing.

The Foetar, having locked onto the surviving ships, was now manoeuvring above the fuel tanker. Light green beams of energy flashed from the Foetar and splayed across the length of the tanker's hull. It was a tractor beam.

"What the hell are they doing?" wandered Franks.

The comms speakers crackled to life.

"*Civilian ships, this is the* Foetar. *Stand to, and prepare to receive engineering assistance.* Do not *move unless told to do so, or you will be fired upon.* Arktown, *you may leave, please call for help as soon as you leave the singularity's gravitic interference. Fuel tanker: your captain and senior officers will be taken into custody to answer for the deaths of the crews of the* E11g *and* 441-F. *That will be all.*"

Franks stared at the holographic visage of the *Foetar*, dumbfounded.

Gorman was next to him all of a sudden.

"The *Foetar*'s still trying to target the station," she whispered. "And they're ignoring our hails. Do you think they'll really destroy the station? Surely it won't get rid of the singularity."

Franks shook his head.

"Communications, anything from Caine's team?" he demanded.

"Nothing on the comms channels, Captain. Not even from the shuttle, though it's still docked there."

"What could have happened?" pondered Gorman by his side. She was being infuriatingly calm about the situation, completely anathema to Franks' visibly agitated anger. "Captain," she suddenly snapped, "could you please stop pacing up and down?" Franks stopped in his tracks; he hadn't even noticed that he was indeed pacing up and down the small command area at the centre of the massive bridge.

"What about teleporters? Can we use them to rescue the security team?"

"We cannot even detect them on sensors; we could never get a lock on them. We would end up teleporting half the station up with no guarantee we would get the team back in one piece."

"I know, I'm just venting," Franks growled.

"You are worried about Caine." It was a statement not a question. He looked at her questioningly. "You are starting to use those old word contractions like Caine does." Franks was about to make a witty retort when a shout could be heard over the bridge.

"CAPTAIN! LOOK!" The sensors officer was pointing towards the forward windows, and the holographic display of the station hovering near to franks and Gorman.

In both the hologram and the real thing out in space, the black hole's accretion disk suddenly grew beyond the confines of the containment struts hanging in a rhomboid shape below the station proper. The struts were actually bending, then suddenly tearing off the station, and disappearing down into the pitch black of the quantum singularity. Then the lower half of the station was violently ripped off, massive shards disappearing forever into the blackness. Hull plating was torn off in individual pieces, furniture and personal belongings were pulled into space, even the massive space frame crumbled to shreds.

"Oh Gods," Gorman whispered. "It's being pulled in."

* * *

"That's-"

"Weird," Purr finished for Adam. Something of an understatement, actually, but he didn't make *that* comment out loud. They were staring into the very blackness of the black hole beneath the station, the floor, ceiling, and walls simply no longer there, exposing the corridor to space.

"Emergency forcefields must be holding," Purr commented, his voice somewhat shaky. He was terrified by the raw power of the thing beneath them, more so than the creatures that had been trying to murder them.

Just to emphasise Purr's point, the blue energy field flickered across the entire width of the corridor.

"That field isn't going to hold against the black hole," Adam guessed. "We need to find another way round."

"You're the Navy officer, you tell us," Triona snarled.

"This is a highly classified facility. Do you really think I'd be aware of how this place was laid out?" Adam said as an answer. That shut him up.

Caine pointed in the opposite direction from the forcefield, and started walking. Purr followed without question, though the others were somewhat hesitant to trust the human; they trailed in Purr's wake quickly enough when the forcefield flickered again.

Adam led them round a corner, only to find a similar opening in the midst of the station.

"Dammit."

The only other way out was the stairs. They would have to go up, over, and find another way down. Unless...

"Can you get a hold of Feyton on one of those personal comms device? Maybe patch into whatever's left of the station's systems?"

Purr nodded, and set to work, shutting everything out so he could work. He guessed what Commander Caine had planned, and was nervous at the prospect.

"Work quickly," Adam said through gritted teeth. Purr looked up to see Caine had put the girl down again, and was already swapping his rifle's magazine for a fresh one, slapping in the metal sickle-shaped clip without even looking. His eyes were locked on to something behind Purr, and the feline knew exactly what it was without turning round. He moved closer to the forcefield, concentrating on his work.

"Hurry," Adam added unnecessarily.

Three of the nightmarish creatures stalked down the corridor towards them, metres away.

The other guards stunned one with combined fire, before Adam fired his rifle on full auto again, taking the head clean off of one, and the legs off the other. The legless creature scrabbled around on the floor, blood leaking everywhere, squealing in pain as it tried to rise on the stubs of its destroyed legs. Adam put it out of its misery with one high-powered shot through its brain.

The guards were shaking with terror.

They were backed into a corner with no obvious means of escape.

"Got it!" Purr exclaimed excitedly, just as six of the creatures appeared from around the corner. He let out a lion growl that Adam was sure was a colourful native curse.

"Get Feyton over here, now! And see if you can't download the station's logs. I'd like to get out of this with at least the knowledge of what happened here."

The girl wrapped her arms around his leg, hugging him in what she believed to be the final few moments of her life.

The creatures charged, and one was on a fur-ball of a security guard in the blink of an eye, who screamed and screamed and screamed as he died horribly. In his death throes, Furball's spasming hand squeezed the trigger on his stun pistol. The energy slapped the guard next to him. The guard fell to the ground, and was dragged unconscious into the group of creatures and fed upon in a flurry of blades and teeth.

Adam continued to blast at the creatures with his rifle, having to change magazines twice. One creature leaped into the air, and misjudged the jump, crashing sideways into the big human, and bowling the girl over onto the floor. It righted itself and snapped its jaws at the girl.

"You aren't going to touch her, you ugly motherfucker," he growled, before plunging his combat knife into the top of its head. He twisted the knife for good measure, not having to wait long until it stopped spasming and struggling against its own death.

He whipped his Walther out, and shot two more creatures sneaking up behind him, blowing out the backs of their skulls. The remaining two guards —which included Purr- fired on the other creatures, bringing them down before Adam shot them point blank, ending their potential as a threat.

No more of the creatures came, despite the minutes that dragged on.

"I have the logs," Purr announced.

"Good," Adam said through gritted teeth, his Walther pointed down the corridor unflinching, waiting for the inevitable.

Of course, as Adam had always believed, the universe had a wicked sense of humour, and never let up when the opportunity to do so was there. The station suddenly shook more violently than ever, and the survivors were thrown to the floor. Adam looked out through the forcefield, and saw other parts of the station collapsing into the black hole. A hideous rumbling came from somewhere towards the centre of the station.

Outside the forcefield, the shuttle came into view, and all of Adam's doubts about Feyton's piloting abilities were quashed as she jinked and juked around debris bigger than her craft.

* * *

Feyton gritted her teeth.

Commander Caine had demanded too much from her.

She flew cargo or passengers; she wasn't an ex-combat pilot like the *Gold Royale*'s senior helmsman. But she was doing her best, swerving round an awfully big chunk of the station being pulled into the singularity. The thrusters were screaming, fighting against the insane gravitic effects, whilst trying to manoeuvre around the remains of the station.

The shuttle's computer locked onto the signal one of the guards had activated via the crumbling station's computer.

"Hah!" she cried, slapping her knee in exhausted joy. She could see the opening where Commander Caine and the others were waiting for her. Something smacked the shuttle's rear-end and dragged it round ninety-degrees from the opening. The metal hull squealed and pitched backwards as the chunk of station stuck to the shuttle like a Denebian slug.

She cried out for deliverance when the chunk was suddenly ripped off by the gravity, and thrown into the maelstrom below. The craft's sublight engines kicked in, and pushed it forward, toward the shielded opening.

The forcefield was flickering badly now, and she was barely able to discern the figures on the other side, though she could see arms waving at her.

The comms unit on her console fizzed to life.

"*Feyton, hurry up, this place is falling apart around us.*" It was Commander Caine, and his voice was filled with anger. Clearly things were going worse than even she knew.

"I am moving as fast as is safely possible, Commander."

"*Does your shuttle have teleporters?*"

"Yes, sir. But I can only take two at a time."

"*There's a little girl right next to me; take her and Purr first.*"

"Acknowledged, Commander." She shuffled the shuttle in sideways on, to give herself enough time and space to speed off if needed. She activated station-keeping mode, and turned to the teleporter control console to her right.

She found four life-signs just beyond the forcefield.

She locked on to the two nearest to the field, and slapped the teleport activation control. Light filled the shuttle, and in the passenger compartment behind her, the young green-skinned girl and the feline security guard flashed into existence. She was clearly disoriented by the teleport.

"Where's my daddy?" the little girl asked, looking around. Feyton looked at the feline security guard, a question on her lips.

"She's already grown quite an attachment to Commander Caine," Purr answered.

Feyton shook her head, and turned back to the teleport controls. Interference from the singularity was playing merry hell with shuttle's systems already. She could still detect Caine and the other guard, though she could only beam over one at a time.

She locked onto the remaining guard, and teleported him over.

"Wait."

"What is it?" Purr asked.

"I am detecting another life-form over there, though it is like nothing in the computer's records."

"Where?"

"Next to Commander Caine."

* * *

Adam heard the clapping, even over the grinding and squealing of the dying station around him. The floor shook beneath him, constantly rumbling and quaking. Sparks flew from dormant power lines, and dead computer consoles. Beyond the field, he could see the shuttle's manoeuvring thrusters flaring constantly to keep the craft stabilised and hanging in space parallel to the opening.

The clapping, naturally, wasn't imagined.

It came from the figure stood four metres away from Adam, dressed in the same black tuxedo and bowtie, he always seemed to appear in.

"Gold," Adam growled. "Why am I not surprised? Was this your doing?"

Gold smiled. It was the smile he had given Adam in that hangar weeks ago on Yh'reth'gar's titan, the one that had nearly spelled the doom of everyone he held dear. It was unsettling, but Adam had gotten used to the horrifying so if something was unsettling, he could live with it.

Gold took a step toward him.

The big human's hand instinctively brought up his Walther to point the barrel at Gold's head.

He could feel a tingling sensation come and go several times throughout, and wondered whether it was Gold's doing, or side-effects of being too close to the black hole.

* * *

"Something is blocking the signal!" Feyton cried.

"What!?"

"Something is preventing me from teleporting Commander Caine out of the station."

Purr craned his neck to see into the opening. He saw two figures, presumably Caine, and the extra life form that had appeared at the very last second.

"What is going on over there?" he wondered.

* * *

"Actually, I found you by accident," Gold admitted.

"Those creatures. What were they?"

Gold smiled again, and Adam could practically feel the malevolence rolling over him. He shuddered involuntarily.

"Those creatures are an experiment of mine. They were designed to be the ultimate security guards. They have performed perfectly, do you not think?"

"I think you're a sick, twisted old man," Adam replied, the 9mm still pointed between Gold's eyes.

"Quite probably," Gold chuckled. "But you cannot do anything about it, can you?" Adam's hand didn't shake, didn't flinch, it stayed perfectly calm and still. Gold noted this with some amusement. "You will not kill me in cold blood. It is not in your nature as a... hero." Now it was Adam's turn to be amused, though not at the hero comment.

"You really don't know me at all, do you?" he snorted.

"The vagaries of your sordid little life do not concern me in the least bit, Adam Caine."

"Then you don't know what I used to be good at. What I still am good at."

"It does not matter. You will not kill me."

Adam smiled and squeezed the trigger. The shot rang out and reverberated down the corridor. The bullet passed through Gold's shocked incorporeal face, and slammed into the killer creature that had been standing behind, waiting to strike at Adam. It slumped to the ground in a heap of dead limbs.

"Well I never," Gold exclaimed, as if insulted.

However, his concentration had been diverted to let the bullet pass through him.

Adam Caine disappeared in a flash of the shuttle's teleporter, whisked away just as the corridor completely disintegrated.

* * *

"Got him!" Feyton whooped.

"Then get us out of here *now*!" Purr shouted back.

Caine slumped against the bulkhead, letting out a heavy sigh of relief. The girl jumped into his arms, and snuggled in for a hug. Caine didn't seem to fight it, and just wrapped his big arms around the girl, holding her tight to him.

"Are you my daddy?" she kept asking. Caine didn't reply, but calmly shushed her to sleep. Purr suspected the child was traumatised, as were himself and the other surviving guard, Simili. Caine didn't seem traumatised, in fact it seemed as though he had been in this situation before, and had accepted the situation without much comment.

Purr refused to sit and rest until they were back aboard the *Gold Royale*. Feyton asked about the other guards, but he didn't answer, didn't tell her about the dozens of killer creatures that had ripped his friends and colleagues apart like human butter. He just wanted to get back to his quarters on the ship, and stay under the shower for hours upon end.

He wasn't sure he would ever sleep again.

*　*　*

"Captain, the station is fully collapsing into the singularity," the sensors officer reported unnecessarily. Franks could see for himself. The station was crumpling in on itself; its skeletal spaceframe could no longer hold its shape. The hull was stripped from the frame, and sucked into the hole, whilst the frame itself came apart piece-by-piece, spinning and pin wheeling into the maelstrom to disappear forever, taking the shuttle, the security guards, and Adam Caine with it.

He offered up a silent prayer to whatever gods were watching over those pour souls.

"Wait, what's that?" Gorman was pointing to a sensor contact on the holographic display in front of them. It was small, and kept flickering like a light being turned on and off quickly. Whatever it was, it was fighting against the extreme gravitic currents, barely moving. The computer couldn't get a sensor lock for long enough to determines what it was, but it was definitely moving under its own power.

*　*　*

"Can this thing not go any faster?" demanded Purr. He was gripping the back of Feyton's chair so tightly that his blunt claws were digging into the cushioning. The shuttle was shaking so badly, he was feeling nauseous, and not a little too worried about their predicament.

The shuttle was barely moving, and any extra power to the engines would severely overload them and either shut down or explode.

"Pardon?" Purr said suddenly. Commander Caine had muttered something that Purr could not hear over the noise of the shaking shuttle.

"Slingshot!" Caine shouted.

"I could kick myself," Feyton shouted without turning round. "Why the fernikking hell did I not think of that?" Her fingers flew over her console, as she worked out the calculations. "Everybody hang on. This is going to be rougher. If it does not work, it has been nice knowing you."

*　*　*

"They are being pulled in," Gorman breathed.

Franks frowned. Whatever it was —he hadn't been optimistic enough to think of it as the shuttle- it had been making progress in escaping, but had crested only halfway from the edge of the accretion disk. Now it was slipping back, tumbling around with the currents towards the centre.

Except, it was picking up speed, and it wasn't tumbling, it was manoeuvring.

*　*　*

"Sublight engines are at maximum," Feyton called out. The shuttle was bouncing now rather than shaking, and the pilot swore something had come loose in the back of the ship, and was rattling around somewhere.

The engines were overheating; they weren't designed with these extreme speeds in mind, and were struggling to keep up with the gravity's effects.

"Here we go," Feyton shouted.

The ship suddenly lurched, and Purr was thrown to the deck. He looked up to see Caine still holding the girl to him, as if nothing else were going on.

There was a loud creaking sound from all around, and a bang from the rear of the shuttle. Purr panicked. *This is the end; we are all going to die in this coffin.*

But death didn't come. Regular, black space loomed over the shuttle, the *Gold Royale* sitting proudly ahead like a beacon in the night.

Feyton was laughing hysterically, letting all that building tension go in one big lump.

"*Shuttle One,*" a familiar voice announced from the comms speakers, "*glad to see you made it in one piece.*"

"Thankyou, Captain. Glad to be seen."

Sitting up against the side of the compartment, Purr finally relaxed.

* * *

Adam was barely aware of the doctors and nurses examining him and the young girl for injuries. The girl was suffering from malnutrition and dehydration. When she finally fell asleep again, after the doctor had given her the nutrients she needed via IV drip, Adam made his way to Franks' office just off the bridge.

Franks was sat behind his desk, writing something on the portable computer pads the Terran Navy guys had called digipads, though it was a bit more rounded and futuristic than the ones on the *Polly Jenkins*. Franks was deep in thought when Adam stepped up to the desk.

"Any news?" Adam asked.

Franks flinched and looked up from the digipad. He gave Adam a sad smile.

"Working on a cruise liner, I never thought I would have to write letters to the families of crew who had died in the line of duty."

Adam gave his own sad smile. "Benefit of being an NCO was that I never had to either. Can't say I would want to in fact."

Franks gestured to one of the seats on the opposite side of his sweeping desk.

"Gorman is looking through the data you extracted from the station computer. Should be done by now."

Eerily, Gorman chose that moment to step into the office from the bridge, another digipad in her hands. She didn't look happy, and Adam was sure he didn't want to know what it was she had found. In all fairness, he didn't want to know how and when Gold had put those creatures on Odyssey Station, he only cared about what the girl's identity was and where she had come from.

"No luck on your little girl, I am afraid, Caine," she apologised. She sat in the other seat beside Adam. "Odyssey Station received its scheduled freight supply run two weeks ago. There is no record of the ship's crew bringing a young girl with them, or even a report of a stowaway; the same goes for the station. Whoever this little girl is, nobody was aware of her until you found her."

"Your doctor's already calling her Eve," Adam sighed, "though it sounds a bit risqué given the reference. She seemed to like it."

"What about the creatures?" Franks wasn't expecting anything other than in the negative; neither was Adam.

Gorman shook her head. "The things caught them by surprise; there was never any time to make any logs. I suppose it is possible one of them was complicit with this Mister Gold you mentioned, but if they were, they ended up as food same as the rest of the station's inhabitants, with no mention of it in the data you brought back. We have dropped warning buoys around the black hole, but this place is a bit far out of the way so I do not think we have to worry about it just yet."

"So unless we encounter these things, we'll never know what they are beyond being a genetic experiment." Adam nodded at Franks' statement; if he ever came across Gold again he'd use a bigger gun, and *force* the information out of the fucker. Franks sighed. "We'll have to put out a missing persons report, see if anyone answers it. For now, though, I suspect putting her anywhere but your quarters would upset her, Mister Caine."

Adam nodded. Given the girl's predilection for being undetected, she'd end up sneaking into his quarters no matter where her own quarters were meant to be.

"I'll have your floor manager arrange for another bed to be put into your suite," Gorman suggested. Adam nodded his thanks, and stood up.

"Thankyou for volunteering for the mission," Franks called before Adam reached the exit. "I know you never had to, considering you were not being paid." Adam shrugged, unsure what to say. To be honest, he didn't know why he had volunteered; possibly because he was getting restless just sitting around reading history files.

He stopped before the doors.

"I noticed that there are a couple of dozen holographic environment suites. Both of you meet me at the main entrance in two hours in civvies, no uniforms. We're going to be doing something to take our minds off today for a couple of hours. I'll bring some appropriate attire."

Franks and Gorman exchanged worried glances.

* * *

They complied, however, and found themselves standing at the large entrance to the holographic environment deck. Both looked slightly uncomfortable wearing civilian clothes, neither really knowing what to wear beyond generic trousers and shirts, though not before getting the ship under way to its next stop using the ship's rarely-used FTL drive. There was no way to get back into the Linkway at that point in space, so FTL was the only alternative.

The Foetar had disappeared with the fuel tanker's captain and officers, heading in the direction of Romgen.

They turned to see Adam and Eve holding hands. Eve was still silent, though she seemed a bit more at ease than the doctor had informed him. They both wore the same white long-sleeved top, each with a big thick red cross plastered over the front, running up-down and left-right, with a red rose stitched onto the left breast. Eve's was a bit big for her, almost like she had borrowed it off a big brother.

Adam was smiling, which threw Franks off somewhat. Caine seemed like such a serious person he was sure the man never really smiled. But there he was, beaming like a proud father.

He was carrying a throwaway bag in one hand.

"You made it," he grinned. "Follow us." The two strode between the two officers and approached the clerk at the doors. "Suite twelve, please, under the name Caine."

The clerk nodded, and gestured for the four to follow him with a wave of one tentacle. They strode down a long corridor, passing several sets of double doors before arriving at the semi-circular entrance to Suite Twelve. The display above the doors showed a roaring crowd, half wearing similar colours to Adam and Eve, the rest wearing black in various forms.

Adam handed the contents of the bag to Franks and Gorman. It was more of the white and red shirts, though Franks' had a slogan on the front, declaring that he loved England.

The doors to the suite opened, and the sounds of a hundred thousand sports fans cheering blasted past them.

Adam turned to the others.

"Welcome to the Stade De France in Paris; this is the Rugby World Cup final, England versus New Zealand." He grinned, and lifted Eve onto his shoulders, who giggled profusely at being lifted off the ground by her new best friend.

Franks and Gorman threw each other a shrug, donned the England Rugby shirts, and followed Adam and Eve. Adam was singing something with 'Rule Britannia' in some of the lines, and Eve was clapping along to it, giggling constantly.

Six:
The Accidental Enema

"Happiness is a relative thing, in more ways than one."
-Ancient Rijiin proverb.

March 4000ad.

Eve giggled.

She'd been doing that a lot in the month since Adam had found her on Odyssey Station. He hadn't had the courage or the will to ask her about her experiences on the station; his own were traumatic enough to know what she must have been through.

The past month had been spent relaxing, playing games, and generally just enjoying the facilities available on the *Gold Royale*. Eve seemed to share his love for Rugby, though she was too young to understand the specifics of the rules, or indeed who the teams were, she just continued to giggle and cheer whenever one of the players went diving to the floor, or there was a scrum, ruck or maul.

Today, they were visiting the biggest of the swimming facilities. It wasn't a pool per se, although there was a *generic* pool in one small corner. The rest, however, was something else entirely: massive water slides taller than houses ran in spirals and wiggles over everything else, water splashing over the edges where a rider came perilously close to the edge.

Adam was currently holding Eve on the surface of the water, making sure her head didn't dip under. She was wearing a one-piece swimming costume with inflatable water wings, looking like every other six-year-old in the universe learning how to swim. Adam had thought she looked cute, and when he told her so she had told him to shut up. To his face.

Captain Franks –Brag- had said she had already picked up some of his other bad habits, though Adam had never actually heard her swearing.

Just recently, his dreams, and his waking thoughts had continued to turn to his family. Not the family he had gained here on the *Gold Royale*, but the one he had left behind on Earth, in the twenty-first century. He didn't miss his family specifically, just the idea of family, which was becoming a stronger need now he had time to stop and think about it.

Eve brought his attention back to the here and now by splashing him with water and giggling out loud.

He chuckled, and splashed her back.

* * *

"Entering the nebula now, Captain," the helmsman announced.

"Thankyou, helm," Franks answered.

The journey since Odyssey Station had been uneventful. Franks had asked the operating company to let the ship dock for a few weeks so the crew could take some R&R. They had denied the request and demanded the ship be at the next stop early, just to show how much they cared.

This nebula was a part of the cruise. It was a chance for the passengers to view some of the natural beauty of the universe. The ship came through here twice a standard Terran year, and stayed for several day-cycles at a time.

"Ready to purge waste elements, Captain," the bridge's engineering officer announced from a nearby holographic console. As always, he himself was stood in his little command area at the fore of the central open command deck, watching over his own holographic displays that hung around him in a circle like a mini amphitheatre.

"Purge when ready," Franks ordered nonchalantly.

"Purging," the officer said in reply. Franks watched the stream of chemical waste float off into the nebula, and then thought nothing of it as he checked on the schedules. He was supposed to have met Adam and Eve down in the biggest of the ship's luxury water parks an hour ago.

Something beeped loudly on the sensors station, and then beeped even louder.

"Captain, I am detecting a massive build-up of some kind of energy out in the nebula." The sensor officer's fingers were flying over his console, a furrowed brow marking his frustrated concentration.

"Well?"

"Sir, the computer does not recognise the energy pattern. It... It is heading this way, Captain."

"Directly for us?"

The officer nodded warily.

Franks saw it coming, arcing through the murky clouds of the nebula. It seemed as though it was coming straight towards *him*. It struck the ship's shields, and spread across the energy field put up by the ship like a plasma ball.

"Shields are failing!" somebody cried.

The shields collapsed, and the energy kept coming. It passed through the bridge's massive forward window without cracking or harming it, and lanced across the bridge. It struck Franks square in the chest, and threw him twenty feet backwards to skid to a halt at the feet of Commander Gorman.

Gorman leant down and checked his pulse. It was weak, and his breathing was shallow.

"He is alive! Teleport him to the medical bay now!"

Franks' unconscious form disappeared in a flash of white light, leaving Gorman staring at the window the energy had come through.

"Commander," the comms officer called out, "there is a report of someone in the water park being struck by the same energy blast." Before the officer reported the name, Gorman knew who it was going to be, simply because the fates always seemed to conspire against them. "They say it was Commander Caine."

* * *

Eve was screaming, tears rolling down her eyes.

Smoke was wafting from the charred burn on his chest, and he was lying face up in the water, bobbing up and down in time with the generated waves. Eve was trying to wake him up by shaking him, but the waves kept dragging him out of reach, and she had to keep paddling to keep up, making big splashes with every struggling stroke.

The muscled lifeguard on duty splashed into the shallow end of the pool and pulled Adam out of the water onto the rough edge. Eve clung to him, shaking him, whilst the lifeguard tried to check his vitals. She kept getting in the way, screaming for the lifeguard to help him.

"Medical Bay," the lifeguard called over Eve's shouts, automatically activating the audio channel. "Emergency teleport one, make that two, to you."

"*Acknowledged*," a deep male voice replied over the channel.

Adam and Eve disappeared in a flash of light.

* * *

Commander Gorman walked into the medical bay some minutes later, having caught three different elevators to get there.

She found the duty nurse, who showed her to a medical ward on the upper level. There, the ship's doctor was scanning the two inert forms: Caine and Captain Franks. Young Eve was sat on a chair by Caine's side, her head buried in her hands, and her shoulders shaking.

Gorman called the doctor over so she could have a private word with him out of Eve's earshot.

"What is their condition?" she asked.

"They are both in comas, though for the life of me I do not know how or why. Their brain patterns read as though they are awake, and yet they are definitely unconscious. To be honest, this is beyond my expertise. This is a cruise liner, not a warship or an explorer vessel. We are equipped for slips and trips, not energy burns or comas."

Gorman sighed.

"There is one thing though," the doctor whispered, pointing to the holographic displays hanging over the two medical beds. One part of it was marked 'brain activity'. Gorman was shocked to see that the squiggly lines denoting each of their brain waves were identical.

"Is that normal?"

The doctor shook his head.

* * *

There was something sharp in the air, like the smell of old wood.

Brag turned to see if he could find the source of the smell, and found himself looking at a parade ground. It was a wide cement concourse laid out in front of a massive building that stretched away behind for further than he could see. Trees were lined up beyond an expanse of green grass, sentinels watching over the building.

A parade ground, he realised.

It was not empty, with a horde of onlookers clapping from the very edges of the big square.

A military band played out marching tunes, whilst everybody's attention was fixed on the parading soldiers, all dressed in olive-green dress uniforms and green berets, carrying empty rifles of the kind that he had seen Adam carrying.

They were marching in perfect formation around the parade ground, each step or manoeuvre taken with as much gusto and confidence as the bombastic brass section of the marching band they were keeping time with. There were four troop sections, each led by a soldier with big white stripes on their arms who saluted to the officer on the podium as they passed, and bawled to the men to turn their eyes right.

Brag had been in the Terran Navy, but never had he been subjected to this, save for a brief salute to his training officer, and to accept his Ensign's rank tapes.

With the civilian crowd, the officer on the podium, and the sparkling uniforms, it had to be a passing out parade —soldiers that had finished their training and were ready to be fully accepted into the military proper.

He wondered where he was. He didn't recognise the unit patches, nor did he recognise the styling of the civilian clothes. Could this be the past? Caine's past? *Terra*'s past? Gods, was he standing on the lost homeworld itself? His grandfather had droned on about how beautiful it was, but Brag hadn't found the stories particularly entertaining when he was younger. Now though, the thought of standing on the hallowed ground of Terra made him giddy with wonder.

As the parade came to a halt, and the officer handed out a pair of awards, Brag pondered on how he had got here. The last thing he could remember was standing on the bridge of the *Gold Royale*, the blast of energy coming straight for him, then a searing white-hot pain in his chest, and then this.

Some part of him, registering a presence out the corner of his eye, made him turn to his right. There stood Adam Caine, wearing an old, fading set of green-and-brown camouflage fatigues, the jacket of which hung open, as if he were only being casual. Brag looked down, and found that he too was wearing the same, only his didn't quite sit right on his body, the fatigues not designed with tall, thin spacers in mind.

"What is this place?" Brag demanded, not a little freaked out by this. Adam, however, was nothing if not calm.

"Lympstone, where *all* Royal Marines are trained to get their green commando berets. This is my passing out parade." Ignoring the confused look on Brag's face, he continued. "I don't think this is time travel, since nobody seems aware of us. Must be linked to whatever it was that hit us." Brag's eyebrows shot up in surprise. "Simple deduction," Adam explained. "I got hit by that beam; I'm here, you're here, so that means you were probably hit by it as well."

Brag shook his head and let out a snort of amusement.

The parade had come to a close; the soldiers were dispersing to be with their loved ones, whilst the band was sauntering off towards the big building.

Something caught Adam's eye in the civilian crowd, and he hurried towards an older woman surrounded by women and girls, all with the same facial structure as Adam. *His sisters*, Brag realised, seeing how the younger ones flocked to the younger Adam.

This was Adam's memory, Brag concluded, looking at the older Adam striding towards his family. He rushed to join his new friend, and fell into step beside him. Nobody noticed the two men in camouflage, leading Brag to the conclusion that the two of them were not a part of the memory, just observers.

The older Adam confirmed this when he tried to hug his mother, and simply blundered through her and fell to the floor, without anybody noticing, least of all her. It wasn't that he went under her arm or anything; he simply passed through her as if she didn't exist. *Or he didn't exist.*

With a touch of sadness, preceded by some colourful swearing and cursing, the older Adam stood and moved back towards Brag.

"I'm so proud of you," Adam's mother cried. She was a tall woman, though she didn't have her son's frame. She did, however, have the same light brown hair that hung just above her near-exposed shoulders. She had the same sculpted cheekbones and chin that he did, only her skin was starting to sag, and an army of freckles marched down her neck and collarbone. She was beaming with happiness. "A Royal Marine," she breathed, her voice filled with obvious pride.

Younger Adam was fresh-faced, something Brag never thought possible, his hair shorn close to his scalp like all good infantrymen. His cheeks flushed red with embarrassment, and he looked down at the ground, squirming under the attention his mother was giving him.

"Thanks, Mum," he said sheepishly.

The girls around her all glared at the young Adam.

"Father was right," the eldest of them harrumphed. "You shouldn't lower yourself to a common trooper. You'll never become something important."

"Why don't you go fuck yourself, Amanda?" young Adam snarled. They all looked at him with shock, the younger ones wailing at the use of foul language. The swearing was something Brag had noticed was a big part of Adam's combative personality. "In fact, why don't you go back to that drunken husband you keep bragging about, you spoilt little shit?" Amanda was about to make an angry retort when she belatedly became aware that her younger brother was holding a rifle. Brag wondered if it had been loaded, and then presumed it hadn't for the parade, though Amanda didn't look so convinced.

Her face flushed redder with embarrassment than Adam had, and then led her sisters off in a huff.

Adam's mother frowned, and placed a comforting hand on his shoulder.

"You didn't have to do that," she said softly.

"Someone had to," young Adam grimaced. "Besides, I've been wanting to do that for years. And now I don't have to put up with it anymore." His mother shot an alarmed look at him. "I'll write and phone you Mum, even see you, but I don't want to go back to Father's estate. They're all so pompous and spoiled it just pisses me off."

Tears streamed down his mother's cheeks as she realised she would, likely as not, never see her son again. She pulled him into a big hug, and buried her head in his chest, sobbing.

"Where are they sending you?" she asked in between sobs.

"Northern Ireland," young Adam whispered.

A big bear of a man approached mother and son wearing the same green beret as the younger Adam; he was wearing similarly patterned camouflage to Brag and the older Adam, though his was neat and tidy, with the jacket zipped up and his sleeves rolled up. He had a great bushy beard, with a large frame that appeared both overweight and heavily muscled at the same time. His rank tapes had three downward-sloping chevrons.

Young Adam snapped to attention, letting go of his mother.

"Private Caine?"

"Yes, Sergeant?"

The huge sergeant waved him to ease.

"I'm Sergeant Graham. Are you ready to join your new unit, Private?" Brag noticed that the big sergeant wasn't being sarcastic; he seemed genuinely pleased to see the younger man. Brag looked over to the older version of his friend, and saw he was smiling at the sergeant.

"Graham pretty much became my surrogate father after I joined his unit," the older Adam explained. "I owe him a great deal. Just wish I could've changed things." Brag was about to ask what Adam meant when Lympstone, young Adam, his mother and the big sergeant disappeared in a rush of light and indistinct movement.

Brag didn't see his friend's brief look of despair as the vision went away.

* * *

An LCAC hovercraft skimmed across the waves almost silently, leaving an invisible wake behind it. There were no lights, the sky was pitch black, and the river itself was an oily black colour in the dark. The hovercraft, painted a dark green though nobody could see it, bounced over the waves and launched itself onto the hard sand of the embankment.

The pilot stopped the craft, slewing it sideways to a halt.

Four figures jumped down from the sides, armed and uniformed as only Royal Marine Commandos could. Brag and the older Adam were stood on the tree line, flanked by a veritable army of palm trees and thick underbrush. They were looking down the beach, watching as the four soldiers stalked up towards them, low and silent.

Brag looked to his friend questioningly.

Adam actually whimpered, making Brag wonder what was coming next.

"This is the Congo Republic, about eighteen months after what you just saw at Lympstone. I'd only just been promoted to Lance Corporal —the youngest NCO in two hundred years." Adam gave a little smile at this tidbit, which quickly disappeared. "The Congo was hit by a massive civil war that involved several other surrounding countries fighting for both sides. The Royal Marines were tasked with extracting all British citizens from the country. This was my team's third trip. Sergeant Graham and I were recommended to Lieutenant Hodgson by our company captain to extract a group of my father's business partners that were trapped here."

There was a *poomf* noise behind them, and Brag turned to see a puff of smoke among the trees. The puff turned into a trail of smoke, and an object launched over Brag's head, and dipped down.

The four Marines dove to the ground.

The missile missed the Marines, and slammed into the hovercraft. It exploded with a bright flash, sending spiralling bits of debris in all directions. Two of the Marines were shredded where they lay.

Another cried out in pain, and Brag could just make out the beard of Sergeant Graham under the heavy ghillie suit. The other could only be Adam Caine. The young Adam crawled over to Graham, studiously avoiding the bloody remains of the other two Marines, and checked his sergeant's carotid pulse. He frowned, and the Sergeant suddenly coughed. Brag could see a glinting wet patch up one of the big man's leg.

"Sarge?"

"Leave me, Adam. I'm screwed."

"Yeah right I'm leaving you here." Adam leaned down, and was about to help his sergeant up onto his feet when a bang sounded out. Young Adam dropped to one knee, and without thinking fired his rifle into the tree line. There was a wet squelch and a scream of sudden pain. The firing from the trees stopped straight away.

There had only been one enemy nearby.

Young Adam slung his rifle-strap over one shoulder, and then suddenly pulled off Graham's trouser belt and tied it tightly around the bigger man's wounded leg. Graham howled in pain. Adam tried to shush him quiet. It was too late though, as he could hear voices raised in alarm in the distance, flashing spotlights, and the random noises of machine guns being fired into the air to scare their attackers' enemies.

Adam dragged the other man to his feet, and then the two walked as fast as they feasibly could in the opposite direction from the voices.

"Dammit, Lance Corporal, I order you to leave me here," Graham growled through the pain.

"With respect, Sarge, shut the fuck up. It's only three miles to the Angola border, and then we'll be home free so your wife can cook us that Sunday roast you keep bragging about."

"Only if you promise to get a girlfriend," Graham snorted.

"Deal."

The older Adam didn't follow them, but just plunged his hands into his trouser pockets and watched the two disappear from view around the curve of the river embankment.

"We never made it to the Angola border," he suddenly said.

Brag looked at him with no small alarm, his mind spinning as he tried to imagine what the locals had done to him and the sergeant. Adam smiled.

"A U.S. Army Ranger patrol found us about an hour later, and shipped us back to the *HMS Ocean*." The beach and the dark night vanished as if in response to Adam's statement.

* * *

The doctor had tried to explain to Eve what was wrong with Caine, but she refused to believe he was sick, as if she thought him immortal. He was just sleeping, she told the doctor.

Honestly, he had no idea what had happened to his captain and the one passenger who seemed to be a regular customer of the medical bay. They were both in comas; their brainwave patterns had not changed, though their eyes kept flitting around like mad behind their eyelids. They were dreaming, though they weren't asleep in the conventional sense.

Eve had refused to leave Caine's bedside, curling up beside him on the bed, and falling asleep herself. The doctor had been about to remove her when Commander Gorman had prevented him, and told him to leave her there.

The doctor sighed.

Whatever was happening, it was out of his hands.

* * *

Brag and Adam appeared outside a stately mansion.

They both could see a younger Adam stood in the middle of the driveway as a wheeled taxi drove off. Brag had seen pictures of the twentieth-century ground vehicles, and was still amazed that it could actually go anywhere they were so primitive.

Younger Adam was wearing his camo fatigues, carrying a large kit bag. Brag could just about see the rank tape on young Adam's chest epaulette. It had Sergeant's stripes, with a small representation of a crown above the top chevron; a Staff Sergeant.

The older Adam was grimacing.

"This is my father's estate," he sighed. "I'd just got back from being captured in Afghanistan." Brag could see the results of that, watching as younger Adam hobbled up the driveway. The younger version of Adam passed the two older men without a blink, and Brag could see the extensive scarring on Adam's exposed forearms, and even a pinched line across his neck that older Adam also possessed.

Younger Adam seemed apprehensive as he stopped and stared at the front door.

"This was the first time I'd been home since before I signed up to the Marines," older Adam whispered, as if worried he would be heard. "I'd already joined the Special Boat Service after that incident in the Congo. My superiors had to order me to go home and recuperate from being tortured by the Taliban."

"What happened to Sergeant Graham?" Brag asked.

"He disagreed with my decision to join the SBS, and what we did there. He quit frontline duties, and went back to the training barracks. I never spoke to him again. One of the few regrets I have about not wanting to go back to the twenty-first century."

"Did you ever get a girlfriend like you promised Graham?"

Older Adam nodded.

"I dated an officer from RMB Chivenor's Logistics Regiment, but she broke it off because she thought I couldn't commit to marriage or a long-term relationship."

"Married to the job," Brag stated with a knowing smile.

Older Adam just snorted, never taking his eyes off the young Staff Sergeant approaching the doorbell. Younger Adam was about to ring the bell when the big oak door opened seemingly by its own volition. A greying woman bounced out of the house, and wrapped her arms around Adam. Brag realised it was his mother, and was surprised by how much she had aged since the last time he had seen her, presumably only a small number of years.

Adam's mother saw the scars on his exposed flesh and gasped.

"Graham told us you had been captured," she whispered. Young Adam winced, obviously not wanting to be reminded about his recent internment. "He wasn't very specific though."

"It was classified, Mum. He shouldn't even have told you that much."

She noticed the rank tapes, and a smile touched the corners of her lips.

"You've been promoted?"

"Staff Sergeant," young Adam replied, squirming in place like he had next to the parade ground under his mother's embarrassing pride. Ignoring his scarring, both physically and emotionally, she produced a massive, beaming grin, and hugged him again.

"Congratulations," a deep voice grumbled from the open door. Brag turned to see a large, overweight man who barely resembled a much older, much less fit Adam Caine.

"Thankyou," young Adam sneered with no small amount of sarcasm.

"Welcome back to Cambridge. Your mother has been talking about nothing else." Brag noticed that younger Adam's face was now contorted with anger, balling his fists.

"I came back to see Mum, not anybody else. I was actually *ordered* to come home by my superiors."

"And if you had bothered with using my contacts, you could have been the superior officer instead of a lowly Sergeant." Caine senior leaned against the stone walling of the steps leading to the door.

"I'm a Staff Sergeant in the Special Boat Service," younger Adam said through gritted teeth. "And I did it without *your* help."

Several people came out through the doorway, trying to see what the commotion was about. Among them were many of Adam's sisters, including the oldest young Adam had shouted at before. From behind her came the drunk husband Adam had mentioned, cheeks rosy red from the alcohol, along with several of his friends, presumably husbands or boyfriends of the other sisters. Young Adam groaned, and sent a pleading look to his mother, clearly having intended the reunion to only be between the two of them.

"You know what father? I've spent my whole military career trying to prove to my family that I have made something of myself without riches or contacts. Now I realise that was a waste of time. So I'll tell you what; FUCK OFF!!"

The fat father seemed to recoil at Adam's ferocity. Then again, Brag had heard explosions that were quieter than that.

Unfortunately, the husbands and boyfriends of the sisters, all six of them, seemed to take this personally, whether because they were too smashed to understand, or recklessly trying to defend the honour of the man who was bankrolling whatever lives they were living. They advanced on Adam, all hurling abuse at the soldier son.

Brag could see what was coming a mile off.

Drunken men, no matter how many of them there were, were never any competition for a trained killer like Caine.

Brag barely saw Adam move, but within seconds, all six were on their backsides, and unconscious, livid bruises already appearing on them.

Adam's father's eyes were wide with shock, whilst the sisters were staring at Adam as if he were an alien. His mother, however, was smiling, enjoying seeing those spoilt bastards being knocked down several hundred pegs. Young Adam's face was serene, nonchalantly accepting the violence as something minor.

"Mum, you want to get something to eat, in Cambridge?"

His mother smiled, and slipped her hand under Adam's hooked arm.

"Where the hell do you think you're going?" his father shouted.

"I'm taking my mother out to lunch," Adam growled. "We're going somewhere where the average IQ is more than eight." Adam gave his hated father a false smile, and then the two were off down the drive, hand-in-hand, mother and son.

And then the mansion vanished.

* * *

Brag was breathing heavily, panting from the shock of the rapidly changing scenery. This time, younger Adam was hobbling yet again, coming out of a plain green building on crutches.

"Where are we now?" Brag wondered.

Adam sighed, weary from revisiting painful memories. He span on the spot, taking a look at their surroundings. There were trees behind some of the closer buildings, obscuring what Brag thought looked like a large collection of hangars, along with several other buildings around them.

"Looks like RMB Chivenor, where the Brigade's logistics regiment were based. I was sent here to recover from injuries I sustained during some pretty intense operations in Kosovo. Got the Victoria Cross here as well."

He was struggling a little, trying to get down the short stone steps, his crutches catching in the small nooks and crannies in the old building's entrance. He was muttering to himself each time he tried to get out.

"Dammit; defeated by a bloody step."

"Next time ask for help," a woman's voice said from behind Brag and older Adam. "I know you SB guys have a lot of pride in being self-reliant and all that, but even *you* have to admit you need help on this assignment."

"Getting myself out of the infirmary you mean?" younger Adam smiled crookedly. The woman passed Brag and his friend, arms folded in front of her. She was gorgeous, and the uniform seemed to fit her quite comfortably. Her strawberry-blonde hair was tied back in a bun, her black beret tucked into her trouser pocket. She cleared her throat. Adam's face fell. "Ma'am."

She snorted briefly before helping him off the stair.

"I thought I wasn't going to see you until tonight, Leftenant," younger Adam smiled.

The woman suddenly looked uncomfortable, avoiding eye contact with the soldier.

"I don't think that we should continue this... relationship, or whatever it is we have."

"I come back from an horrendous mission, and you dump me? Why, if you don't mind my asking, *Leftenant*?" Brag had already had the unfortunate experience of witnessing Adam's anger, and was sure he could see the woman –the officer- wilting under that angry gaze.

"Adam, I'm a commando supplies officer. I have no combat experience, and I don't want it. When I met you, it was exciting, thrilling even; I ignored the scars, the long stares whenever someone mentioned combat or some military operation they saw on the ten o'clock news. Being with you, however, has been a hard experience of not knowing where you are, and whether you're coming back in one piece. I need to be with someone who'll be there when it counts."

Young Adam looked at her incredulously.

"I was there for you when your father died, wasn't I? I was there for your sister's divorce, wasn't I?"

She nodded, but gave no other answer.

Brag could see the anguish on the woman's face –he had seen it once before as well, when his own wife had left him because of his own career choices- she was making a hard decision, and one she was sure was the right one.

"Please, Adam, don't make this any harder. I need to be with a man who I know will be alright, who will be safe, and I won't have to worry about him for weeks on end. I'm so tired of worrying about you." She straightened herself, and dropped her arms by her side. "Goodbye, Warrant Officer Caine. I doubt we'll meet again."

"Of course, ma'am." Young Adam tried to salute, but the crutches prevented him, making it look like a spasm.

The Lieutenant strode stiffly away, leaving the younger Adam glaring at her back. Chivenor disappeared in another haze of changing scenery.

* * *

Brag was getting travelsick now, and was about to make a comment to his friend, when the big soldier tensed up. The two were standing in a dark room; a long wooden table sat in the centre, reflecting what little light there was visible. At the opposite end of the room was a big screen, blank at the moment, though someone was setting up a slide show to one side of the room.

There was another figure stood on the opposite side of the room to the projector, stood at parade rest, wearing some kind of dress uniform that was obscured by the oppressive darkness of the room; the figure had the same build and appearance as the man stood beside Brag, but with less hair.

A set of doors opened, and in stepped three older men, light spilling in from the hallway outside. One wore a similar uniform to Adam's, whilst the others wore tailored suits.

Younger Adam snapped to attention.

"At ease, Staff Sergeant," the uniformed man ordered. Caine nodded, and returned to parade rest. "This is Defence Minister Hoon MP, and Agent MacDuff from MI6."

"If I may ask, sir..."

The officer nodded, and gestured for all to take seats. Young Adam was alone on his side of the table, as if the others were too stuffy to sit with a common NCO.

"We brought you here, Staff Sergeant," the Defence Minister began, "because we are in need of your talents."

"Sir?"

"Downing Street has been made aware of your missions, Staff," the man with a Brigadier-General's rank tapes told the NCO. Young Adam just nodded along to what he was hearing.

"And the mission?"

The older men traded glances with each other, and then laid out what they had in mind for Caine's mission. It took two hours, and he was completely silent throughout the entirety of the briefing, but Brag could see the rage boiling up inside the younger version of his friend.

When the intelligence agent finished the briefing on the new Mogadishu operation and the current political climate in Somalia, and what targets he was expected to take out, one of which even Brag found hard to believe, they all looked at Adam expectantly.

"Your thoughts, Caine?" Hoon demanded impatiently.

"So, this entire operation depends on me killing a child to bring out his father, this chairman of the ICU who may be linked to al-Qaeda." He glared at them angrily. "And you were expecting me to kill this child in cold blood?"

"Essentially, yes," MacDuff answered nonchalantly. "It wouldn't be the first time."

"That was different. Collateral damage is one thing, but what you're talking about is murder, straight and simple."

"I've read your file, Staff Sergeant Caine," Hoon said calmly from the end of the table. "You come from a privileged background, yet you chose to enter commando training as a grunt instead of an officer. You've had something to prove from day one, and you never returned home except once when you were ordered to by your regiment XO. You've been promoted again and again purely on your actions, you have been given an honorary senior rank when dealing with foreign forces. You were sponsored for duty within the Special Boat Service, and excelled at lone missions. But you alienated your mentor and best friend, and your girlfriend. According to your psychiatric file you're borderline psychotic —your life *is* the Commando Brigade. You've got a Victoria Cross to prove it."

Adam stood from his seat suddenly, knocking his chair over.

"I am not going to commit murder just to bait someone; get someone else to do it!" Adam was almost shouting now.

"You are a Marine," the General barked, "and you will do as you are ordered!"

"Anyone who orders me to commit cold-blooded murder on an innocent does not deserve respect from anyone under their command. If you try and force me, I will walk out!" He belatedly added, "Sir!"

"Then get the hell back to Poole," bellowed the General, "and await more orders!"

"Yes sir!" Adam shouted back before storming out of the room.

* * *

"I am getting tired of this crap," Adam growled as the briefing room disappeared from sight to be replaced by a rocking floor, and plastic moulded seats. When Brag looked at his friend, he was surprised to see that his friend's face was filled with anguish and not anger.

Adam was looking at himself, an almost exact copy, which meant that the memory was within the last few months or so. Younger Adam was wearing civilian clothes, with a multi-coloured uniform underneath a thick coat, and holding a hardback book with a sandwich poking out of his coat pocket.

A handsome woman with her two young daughters was seated opposite him, the mother sneaking glances at him as he read his novel.

Older Adam shut his eyes, and turned around.

"I don't want to watch this."
You don't have to, a voice said in the two men's minds.

* * *

"Doctor!" the nurse cried.
The doctor ran to Franks' and Caine's bedsides to see what she was pointing at. She was gesturing nervously at the holographic displays.
"What in all the gods' names is that?"
Their brainwave patterns had not changed, but now on the display there was a separate brainwave intertwining with theirs, something completely alien to the two humans lying on the beds.

* * *

They didn't reappear anywhere on Earth this time; in fact, they found themselves surrounded by a red and blue mist, floating far above the *Gold Royale*.
Brag panicked, kicking and flailing his arms before realising he was breathing. In fact, there was a sweet smell to the air around him. Beside him, Adam was looking somewhat bemused.
"What the hell is this?" Brag shouted.
Adam shook his head, though he seemed to be finding the situation amusing. Then again, if what Adam had told Brag about his first month in this century was true, this was probably just another eventful day in the life of Adam Caine.
A shape fizzled before them, resolving into a human being. Not just any human being, oh no, it was Adam's mother, exactly as they had last seen her in the memory. Except she wasn't Adam's mother. She glowed, as if with an internal light, wafts of smoky tendrils dissipating from her body at random intervals.
"Who are you?" Adam asked.
The thing that looked like his mother gestured around them.
"I am all around."
"You're a nebula?" Brag chortled. He could hardly believe it. "Nebulae are inanimate clouds of dust and energy. How can one possibly be alive?"
Adam was chuckling.
"It never said it was a nebula," he explained. "I think the term is non-corporeal, though I can't imagine what you'd want with my memories, especially the ones about my family. That was you, wasn't it? Inducing memories?" He eyed the thing pretending to be his mother. It smiled back at him.
"You are very perceptive and open for one who has experienced so much violence in such a short span of time. I was once like you, trying to find my place in the universe. But unlike me, you have the touch of great destiny. You have something far more important than simple existence in your future. The solar winds speak of a Great Strand in time, the likes of which has never been seen.

A hero, if you will. And no matter how far you go, you will never escape your destiny. Accept it, and move on."

Adam muttered something under his breath about destiny shoving its head up its arse, which both the cloud-thing and Brag chose to ignore.

"Darkness is coming, Adam Caine, and you need to be ready; even I am not sure of what that darkness is, and I cannot help you. But know that there are many that are counting on you to succeed."

"Why did you make us relive Adam's memories?" Brag demanded.

"To get the measure of his character, as you might call it. And to show *you* that he is not just a soldier on the run, but something far nobler, no matter how much blood he covers himself in. But more importantly, to show him that he is something far more than just another soldier. He is a warrior —one of great heart and courage."

Brag looked at his newfound friend, and saw that Adam was accepting this as if it were nothing special. The cloud-thing was right, however. Brag had just assumed Adam was trying to escape his bloody past, and thought nothing of the acts of bravery Adam had struggled through simply to be alive.

He was sure this would take some time to work out in his head.

"Also, stop polluting me with your waste," the cloud-thing smiled, though there was no humour in those human eyes. It pointed to the *Gold Royale* beneath them, and Brag saw the waste being pumped out into what the crew thought was a simple nebula.

He swore under his breath.

"Promise you won't do *that* again, or drive your starship through here, and I will leave the two of you alone."

"Of course," Brag nodded.

* * *

With a giant gasp of air, the two men woke from their comas simultaneously.

The nurse jumped back in fright, and the doctor gawped at the two humans. Their brainwaves had returned to normal the instant before waking, the mysterious other signature vanishing in the blink of an eye.

The two men exchanged exhausted smiles before swinging round to dangle their feet from the edge of their beds.

Adam noticed the depression in the bed beside where he had been laying.

"Where's Eve?"

"Commander Gorman took her back to your suite," the doctor answered. He wasn't looking at Adam though; he was staring at the displays above Adam and Brag's heads. According to the readings, both men were fine, as if they had never been struck by the energy and put into comas.

The burns on their chests had miraculously healed without his help. He scratched his balding head, and harrumphed, no longer wanting to know how or why because he didn't want the headache.

"I better go and try to explain this to Gorman," Franks sighed.

Adam nodded.

The induced memories of his past had brought up some strange feelings about his relationship with little Eve. He needed time to sort them out. He needed to go somewhere quiet...

When Adam finally returned to his suite, he found Eve asleep in *his* bed. He could see her chest rise and fall as she breathed in and out shallowly, dreaming restfully, peacefully.

He'd been up all night thinking; mostly about his own past and the memories the cloud life form had induced, but also his future. The cloud had mentioned that he had a great destiny ahead of him, as had Silver over two months ago. He wasn't ready to embrace that, though more and more he found himself being dragged into the affairs of others when he didn't want to be. Is this what Silver had foreseen when she booked him on the *Gold Royale*?

Adam shook the thought off; he wasn't going to start second-guessing everything he did because it might be part of some big plan to save the universe or destroy it. And then there was the fact that Gold was after him, not to mention that nobody had responded to Adam's missing persons report on Eve being found. He had to wonder if anybody cared that she was missing from wherever she had once called home.

Not wanting to wake Eve from her slumber, he leant against the far wall and watched her, contemplating whether he should go through with what he had in mind.

He was so lost in thought that he didn't notice that Eve was waking up.

"What's wrong?" she asked groggily, rubbing her eyes clumsily like all children seemed to do when they were tired. He sighed and moved over to sit on the edge of the bed.

"I've been thinking," he said carefully. She rested her head on him, leaving him to stroke her silky smooth blue hair.

"About what?"

"About what you first said to me on Odyssey Station," he replied. She frowned, clearly trying to recall the specifics of something so minor to her during those terror-filled days. "Do you remember?" he asked. She shook her head. "You asked me if I was your daddy."

She shrugged; Adam wondered –not for the first time- if her young fragile mind had purposely blanked those memories of Odyssey Station. He had seen and heard of war vets who had used it temporarily as a coping strategy, though he doubted Eve was aware of what had happened to her memories.

"Would you want me to be your daddy?" he asked, looking at her face to gauge her reaction. Her eyes widened as it began to dawn on her what he could possibly mean. Her tiny jaw dropped.

"You want to be my daddy?" she asked, her voice rising in pitch as the excitement got the better of her.

Adam grinned.

"Yes."

The word was barely out of his mouth when she bound out from under her bed sheets, across the bed, and wrapped her arms around his neck. Despite her size, she was strong, and she held on to him for what seemed to Adam to be hours.

Tears rolled down his cheeks as she giggled inanely the whole time. They weren't the tears of anguish, pain or sadness that had threatened to well up for months, but tears of utter joy.

"I love you, daddy," she whispered.

He smiled, beamed even.

"I love you too," he whispered back, meaning every word. "I promise I'll never leave you."

"You promise?" she said, a hopeful note in her voice.

"Yeah," he smiled.

He would have to deal with the paperwork and the inevitable lectures from Franks and Gorman in the morning, but for now he just wanted to enjoy the peaceful bliss of being with his daughter.

His daughter.

A human woman sighed with visible relief as she stepped out of the offices of *Grace, Find & Lerp*. The alien senior partner had been incredibly excited about having her become a member of his law staff. He seemed extremely confident that she would be able to start working on cases within the week.

She wondered if her friend in the Navy had had some words with the senior partner, though she brushed the paranoia away, instead revelling in the incredibly generous offer.

She had accepted of course, and the Navy had provided her and her family with an apartment in New Amsterdam itself, not far from the firm's offices. Her children were set to start new schools in the city as well, though she suspected they would not do as well as they would have done in their old schools.

They were all happy, finally moving on with their lives.

Hannah Spears smiled.

She hadn't done that a lot since coming to this century, but it was becoming more and more common, and she liked it a great deal.

Her benefactor came strolling down the street, not bothered by the hundreds of air-trams, and anti-grav vehicles buzzing between the buildings around her, high above street level. He was wearing a casual form of his Navy uniform.

"Colonel Sansky," she smiled.

He snorted.

"How many times do I have to tell you? You are not in the military, so you can call me Raymond."

"Sorry...*Raymond*. Thankyou for putting in a good word for me."

Sansky shrugged. "They are a prestigious law firm; they are pretty famous, and they actually asked for you. Apparently they were excited to have someone on their team who had a working knowledge of twentieth-century Terran law."

"They want me to start in a couple of days," she sighed.

"You sound disappointed." He gestured her towards a nearby café; Sasha and Sapphire were with family Hannah had discovered here on New Terra, though technically they were direct descendants of her estranged sister Rebecca.

"I guess I'd always hoped the future would be less like my own time where everything was free, and you didn't have to fight to keep your family fed and clothed." She looked around at the unfamiliar landscape of New Amsterdam's utopian visage. "Probably watched too many episodes of *Star Trek* when I was young."

Sansky raised a confused eyebrow at the reference, though she didn't explain.

"Do humans still drink coffee in this century?"

He smiled.

"Something like coffee."

"Then you can buy me one, *Colonel*."

Seven:
Weirdness

"If nothing else, my grandfather was regularly thrown into the most insane situations anyone in the universe could ever dream of. I've never understood how or why, but he seems to just attract these events like a magnet."
-Roath Caine

Soon She will see.
Soon they will all see.
The barriers will break, and reality will come apart.

* * *

April 4000ad.

Adam frowned at the hologram standing at the centre of the suite he shared with Eve. It was male, and wearing the uniform and insignia of a Navy Intelligence Colonel, with a peaked officer's cap jammed onto his head.

"Raymond," sighed Adam.

Raymond Sansky's hologram was currently frozen, letters hanging in mid-air in front of him denoting the origin of the message, the sender, and where it was relayed. According to the lettering, the message originated from the planet of New Terra in the Milky Way galaxy, relayed via the city of Blue Falls. The *Gold Royale*'s computer identified Blue Falls as being the capital of New Terra, and the seat of the Terran Parliament.

The message had arrived only an hour before, eliciting no small amount of surprise from Adam at the user's sender. He had not heard from Raymond since the day *Gold Royale* left Fayde behind. He worried that something horrible had happened to Hannah and the girls.

He was about to find out.

"Computer, play message."

The lettering disappeared, and then Raymond's visage shifted slightly, the subject suddenly coming alive as if he had been stuck on pause. Despite wearing a formal dress uniform, Raymond had an easy smile plastered to his face.

"Hello Adam. Unfortunately, I have no new information on 3899 besides what I already told you although I have included a data packet indicating all my personal intelligence on 3899, including a list of those I suspect are allied with them. Politically, the Terran military has been unusually quiet, as have the other empires and allies, so I am afraid there is no news there."

Raymond gave an apologetic shrug.

"As for your fellow time-travellers? Well, Hannah has been offered a job at the Grace, Find & Lerp Solicitors in New Amsterdam. For now, she and the girls are staying with relatives, or I should say, descendants." Raymond's hologram

reached over to something off-camera, his hand bringing back a small digi-pad. *"Privates West, Matthews, and Whittard have enlisted and joined the 1201st Army Regiment, a combat engineer unit. Flight Lieutenants Dick and Kendal have been recruited by Starfighter Command's Search-and-Rescue Division, and I believe are currently flying rescue operations in the Savage Halo off the* HMS Queen Charlotte Bay. *Uh, let's see."*

He seemed to scroll down the list, and snorted with amusement.

"Ironically, the Navy got Kevin and Mouse Gilpin jobs as dry-dock supervisors in the Fayde City docks, and a very large apartment in the city. Constables Whimble and Norman have been recruited by the NTPD into the Riot Response Unit. Miriam Cornwell is working as an air-tram driver; that young couple Jenny and Rowland have been accepted into the University of New Amsterdam." He sighed, not quite used to these long speeches. *"Those two MI5 agents, Rose Bond and Michael Graham, are currently going through extra training so they can serve the Navy Intelligence in the field."*

He then put the digi-pad down, and started searching around, as if he had lost something.

"Ah-ha," he declared, bringing another pad into view. Adam wondered briefly if the office Raymond was in was anywhere close to being slightly tidy. *Probably not,* he mused.

"Kenneth MacDonald is writing a novel on his experiences with the Core; we're trying to block it, but the Admiralty wants it published. I know what you're thinking Adam," the colonel said with a grin, *"it is probably not going to be a long novel considering how little he contributed to our escape. Apparently, though, it is six-hundred pages long."* Sansky's hologram shook his head, then looked back to his digi-pad. *"That old man, Reginald, has been given a small pension and retired to the outer-rim of Andromeda, where Whimble and Norman are keeping an eye on him. They tell me he was under investigation for paedophilia in your century, though there's currently no evidence. Young Jamie and her baby, Sarah, have been given to a set of relatives on Proxima Centauri, and that Buck and his teenage son Gary are both working in New Amsterdam for local merchants."*

The hologram looked up, directly at Adam, though he hoped Raymond was just guessing where he would be in the room upon hearing this.

"There's no sign of Block and Bradley Stanford, though one of our relays in the Dark Galaxy briefly picked up signs of a Core escape craft heading for the Y-40 galaxy; my guess is we will not see them for a long time, if at all."

Raymond reached for the end message control when he suddenly said, *"Oh! I nearly forgot. Your friends the priest and the war veteran have taken the three girls and the partner of the man killed in our escape aboard the* HMS Klinsmann. *She is a medical transport, headed for the Rewq Sector where there are some plagues wiping out planets. I do not know why they went, only that they did. Currently, the Klinsmann is out of contact with their headquarters, so we cannot determine if they stayed onboard."*

Raymond put the digi-pad down, and smiled.

"*Good luck, my friend. I hope that the* Gold Royale *has brought you the answers you needed. I am sure I will see you soon, or at least hear from you soon.*"

"See you Raymond," Adam smiled wistfully.

The hologram froze, and then disappeared from view, leaving a few brief words about the type of file in the message and its size, time and date of creation.

Eve was waking from her snooze.

"Daddy?" she queried. He was just stood there, arms folded across his big chest, in the middle of the room; he found he was staring at the empty space where the hologram had been standing.

He couldn't help but smile; being called daddy by the little bundle of joy was still a heart-warming, yet wholly new, experience. It brought a knot to his throat, and a deep red to his cheeks.

"I thought you were asleep." He stepped across the spacious room to her single bed —one the *Gold Royale*'s crew had installed after he had made it known he was sleeping on the floor in favour of letting Eve have his bed.

"I was, daddy, but it's breakfast time." She pointed to the digital clock beside his own bed, which was set at a right angle from the bottom of her bed; Adam noticed that it was now eight in the ship's morning.

"Oh yeah," he chuckled, "so it is."

Eve giggled at her adopted father's seeming absentmindedness.

"Have a shower, get dressed, and then we'll go to breakfast with Captain Franks and Commander Gorman."

"Okay," replied Eve as she bounced out of bed and into the bathroom.

* * *

"Captain," the communications officer called out across the *Gold Royale*'s massive bridge, "we are receiving a transmission hail from a Terran Navy starship approaching us from aft."

Franks spun on the spot from his holographic command post.

"Hostile?"

The officer shook his head.

"It's the *HMS St. George*, sir," the officer replied, the surprise in the man's voice evident. The *St. George* was a titan —a floating palace built for the Terran royal family nine centuries ago. She was old, but big enough to still be menacing. The *St. George* dwarfed *Gold Royale*, more than thirty times the size of the liner.

"What could they possibly want with *us*?"

"Her captain is saying the Queen is demanding to see Commander Caine."

Franks frowned; he was about to correct the officer for calling Adam that but stopped himself —only himself and his XO knew the truth about the time-traveller. Perhaps the Queen had been made aware of whom he truly was.

"I suppose *Gold Royale* is at her disposal."

"Yes, sir," the officer nodded.

Franks turned back to his command interface, watching as the titan pulled closer to the *Gold Royale*, both ships gliding effortlessly through the Linkway. A large shuttle darted between the two giants, sliding into *Gold Royale*'s main shuttlebay; it was a modified Navy cargo shuttle, and Franks was sure that it was armed and armoured to the teeth to have to carry the royal figurehead of all Terran territory.

"Roll out the red carpet," he murmured. "Communications; have the XO, and Commander Caine, meet me in the main shuttlebay in uniform immediately." He strode off the bridge before anybody could reply.

* * *

Eve wouldn't leave his side, no matter how much he threatened to ground her. She was too excited about meeting a real queen, and was quite happy about Adam wearing the Terran Navy uniform Silver had left him. It fit perfectly, which he found disconcerting.

He placed the peaked cap on top of his head, and then led Eve out of their quarters by the hand. The two strode down the corridor, and then into the nearest elevator; or rather, Adam strode, and Eve skipped along in her frilly blue dress that he had bought her the other day.

Franks and Gorman were waiting for them, neither particularly surprised to see Eve almost dragging her father along with barely restrained excitement. Neither looked particularly happy; of course, neither had explained to Adam what was going on, only that he had to report to the main shuttlebay immediately.

The main cargo ramp of the chunky modified shuttle opened up, quietly touching down on the shuttlebay floor.

Harmless steam was still squirting from the engine exhausts, dissipating as it hit the cool metal floor. Out of the corner of his eye, Adam noticed the crescent-shaped ship in the shadows of the cavernous bay, though it towered over the generic sea-shell-like shuttles belonging to the *Gold Royale*'s auxiliary complement.

Two figures clunked down the ramp, dressed in a gold-plated version of the Terran Army's carapace armour, armed with the chunky standard issue plasma rifles. With the gold plating, their helmets had more shadows to their angles, making them seem more sinister, and more like golden skulls, though they were still just as featureless as the regular troops.

The two guards took positions at the base of the ramp, standing on either side of the metal, weapons against their chest plates.

Several other figures, wearing various modern military uniforms, descended the ramp, all with severe looks of worry on their faces, scanning the shuttlebay around them, as if worried someone might pop out and shoot at them.

Then somebody else descended, and Adam found he could only gawp as Franks and Gorman snapped to attention, and saluted.

She wore a high-cut sleeveless dress that breezed just above the floor, all made out of what Adam assumed was some kind of reptile skin that shimmered different colours in the bay's lighting. The dress was tight fitting, and pale, a contrast to the wearer's ebony skin.

The dress wasn't, however, what Adam was gawping at: she was beautiful.

Not just the standard of beauty though; she was the perfect specimen a human woman could possibly be, with sculpted facial features, and bright blue eyes that shone like spotlights and contained a youthful exuberant strength in them. Her raven-black straight hair was tied back in a long single braid, with a large diamond-encrusted crown on top.

She was truly a princess, and she looked barely old enough to legally drink alcohol.

Adam was still gawping when he realised everybody was glaring at *him*.

Before anybody could dress him down for not showing the proper protocol of respect, the woman —who Adam still did not know who she was- jumped down from the ramp, circumventing the officers and guards, and stepped in front of Brag Franks.

"Permission to come on board, Captain," she smiled.

Franks hesitated, unsure of what to do.

"Uh, permission granted, your majesty," he replied with a bit of a stammer. If Adam's eyebrows were not attached to his face, they would have come off, and hit the ceiling of the bay. As it was, they seemed to reach up almost to his hairline, his eyes so wide he was worried they would pop out of their sockets.

"Majesty?" he blurted.

The woman grinned, something he was sure she was not used to.

One of the officers stepped forward, dressed in the same uniform as Adam, though the officer was not even human, nor even male. She was a wolf-like Rijiin, thin and tall, towering above even Adam's great stature, and had several big fat stripes on the cuffs of her sleeves. She was a Vice-Admiral if he was any judge. He didn't have any experience with the Rijiins and so couldn't tell if she was angry, or if that was just how she normally looked.

"She is the Queen of Terra, and as such, deserves the proper respect owed to her position."

Out the corner of his eye, he could see Brag becoming agitated with seeming worry. Brag was probably worried that Adam was close to adding a Terran Vice-Admiral to his list of kills.

"What the hell do you think you are doing," the alien admiral barked, "wearing the uniform of a Naval officer?"

"It's simply a cover to prevent certain... agencies from attacking me openly. My benefactor's idea, I can assure you. I've never been a big fan of any navy anyway." That wasn't entirely true, Adam admitted to himself, but it was just to get a rise out of the admiral.

"You would be wise to take that uniform off before it plunges you into more trouble than you can handle," the admiral sneered, her lips pulling back to reveal sharp white canines. Her ears flickered angrily, her nostrils flaring madly as she stepped closer to Adam. Little Evie stepped behind him, trying to hide from the nasty officer.

"I believe *mister* Caine is more than capable of handling anything thrown at him," the Queen said, her voice incredibly soothing in a way that reminded him of his mother when he was still a toddler. The Queen placed a soft hand on the admiral's shoulder. "Admiral, I think it would be wise not to antagonise the man we came so far to see, would you not agree."

The admiral bowed her head apologetically.

"Of course your majesty." The Rijiin stepped away from Adam obediently, but continued to eye him suspiciously.

"You *are* Staff Sergeant Adam Caine, of Three Commando Brigade, and the Special Boat Service?"

Adam was slightly taken aback by her knowledge of his past.

"I used to be."

"Then who are you now?"

"For now, I'm just a passenger on this cruise liner. After that, who knows?"

"Then could I interest you in a job?" she smiled.

Adam snorted, "I just want to pass my time on the *Gold Royale* as quietly as possible with my daughter."

"Dau-" the young Queen started, then saw a little green face pop out from behind Adam's leg. That soft smile came again, after the confusion had subsided. "Hello there, little one. And who might you be?"

"I'm Evelyn Cassandra Caine," the reply came as Eve stepped out beside her father, unsuccessfully trying to put her hands on her hips. She was attempting to be defiant like her dad, though it just came off as looking silly for someone her age.

The Queen looked at Eve, then at Adam, then back at Eve, trying to determine if there was any resemblance at all, of which there was none.

"Will your majesty be staying on the *Gold Royale* for long?" Brag queried.

"If you have any room, Captain Franks. The *St. George* has to stop at Fort Zeus for a day for re-fuelling and some minor repairs. I already have my luggage, and I ask you to billet those with me."

"Of course," Franks smiled, "we have plenty of room for you, and your people."

"With your permission then, majesty," the Rijiin admiral added, "I shall return to the *St. George* and take her to Fort Zeus."

"Take your time, Admiral," the Queen nodded. The admiral bowed, and then strode back up the cargo ramp. Everybody cleared a space for the shuttle as it took off on its anti-gravs so as not to fry the Queen and the others.

Holding his breath so as not to cough, Adam watched the shuttle rocket away, his eyes once again sliding over to the shadows, where that pale blue ship stood, almost begging him to have a look inside. He shook the thought off as he realised Brag was smiling at him.

"What?"

215

Brag stood aside as the Queen softly strode out of the bay, led by Gorman, surrounded by her royal gold guards, and followed by her entourage of uniformed officers, and civilian assistants. Eve slipped out of Adam's grasp, and bolted after the Queen without a word. He didn't stop her; she seemed to be curious about her majesty, and she would be safe with those gold-plated guards.

"That's *your* ship."

"Pardon?" exclaimed Adam.

His friend chuckled.

"That is the ship under your name," Franks nodded, gesturing to the blue crescent. "It was brought in here when you were dragged aboard unconscious. Do you want to go and see it?"

Adam hesitated as he thought about the answer; yes, he did want to see it, but with the Queen interested in his presence aboard the *Royale*, more than likely he wouldn't get to enjoy it for long.

"No," he said with a long sigh. "Maybe tomorrow."

Brag nodded, and the two wordlessly strode out the double-doors into the corridor, where they could both hear Eve's excited jabbering from a distance. She was talking the Queen's ear off by the sound of it.

"How did I get on board?" Adam finally asked. It hadn't bothered him before, but now that Brag had reminded him, he was curious to know how he got to his intended destination when he was unconscious, and unable to speak.

"He said he was a friend of yours; an historian, though he would not give us his name."

Adam chuckled, which grew into belly laugh as he realised what had happened.

"His name was M'Der Tr'n; said he was famous, though I never bothered to find out. Figured he was just embellishing the truth."

Brag suddenly placed a hand on his arm, a shocked look on his face.

"You met *the* M'Der Tr'n?"

Adam nodded.

"He really *is* the most famous -oof!" Somebody barged between them, shoving both men aside. Whoever it was, they were in a hurry, charging down the corridor like a lunatic, and yet at the same time, the impatient being said nothing to apologise, or to chide them for being in the way, which made Adam somewhat suspicious.

"Hey, you!" he called out. The being –a human male- didn't even turn around, but just kept going, straight towards the Queen, which was when Adam noticed the device in the man's hand. It was long, almost like a Policeman's telescopic baton, though thicker, like a bicycle handle. The telescopic front seemed to be glowing, and Adam immediately assumed it was a weapon. Without looking to Brag for confirmation, he charged after the assailant.

He didn't warn the man, but as the attacker came within spitting distance of the Queen's guards, Adam roared, and dove for him.

Just as the Queen and her entourage turned to see the commotion, and just as the attacker began pressing down on a large flat button on the light-stick,

Adam rugby-tackled him to the floor. He heard bones snap in the man's hand as his hand hit the deck, squashing it around the hard metal.

The man shrieked, and let go of the device, depressing the button. A ball of energy appeared at the tip of the device, but it dissipated as quickly as it appeared. The assailant frowned, turning his bushy eyebrows into a v-shape. He pointed the device at himself, trying to see if there was a blockage down the barrel.

There was nothing.

He screamed, though, as another ball of energy encompassed him.

Adam rolled away from him.

"SOON YOU SHALL SEE!" the man cried. "SOON THE BARRIERS OF REALITY WILL BE BROUGHT DOWN AROUND YOU!! ALL OF YOU! SOON THE ARCBANE WILL BE UNLEASHED AND YOU WILL ALL DIE!!"

Then the ball of energy disappeared, taking the man screaming in pain with it.

Brag finally caught up, huffing and puffing.

"I am getting too old for this," he announced, still eyeing the scorched carpet where the assailant had previously been occupying. "What was he talking about? What is the Arcbane?"

Adam shook his head.

"Bad grammar?"

Brag snorted, and then turned to make sure the Queen and her people were okay. Eve came running out from behind the crowd, and wrapped her arms around Adam's neck, who was still sat on the floor, staring at the scorch-mark.

"Daddy? Are you okay?"

Adam smiled; he was going to have to get used to being called that —Eve sure had made the transition better than he expected. It had only been seven days since he had adopted her, and they had spent much of that time playing with the liner's recreational facilities —just last night, he had taken her to see the original animated film *The Jungle Book*, and both of them had loved every minute of it.

"I'm okay, Evie," he replied, lightly patting her shoulder.

"Who was that?"

Adam sighed.

"I don't know, but I'm sure we can find out."

He stood up, using the wall for leverage, and turned to the Queen, who was somewhat flustered, and was fending off questions from the surrounding entourage. She motioned them to be silent, and strode over to the two Caine's.

"Already, I owe you my life," she said.

Adam looked at her suspiciously.

"Already?" he echoed. He sighed. "You want me to your bodyguard." It wasn't a question, just a statement.

She nodded eagerly.

"I suppose next you'll want me to call you Al."

"Who is Al?"

"Never mind."

* * *

Adam refused.

He did it politely, took Eve's hand, and the two walked down the corridor, leaving the Terran monarch watching his back. Which, of course, was when a herd of African elephants stampeded down the corridor, the lead animal shoving Adam and Eve aside with its trunk as the thundering family barrelled down a cross-junction and disappeared from view.

Adam's face was a study in shocked expressions: his eyes were wide open, and his jaw hanging open.

There was a thump behind him, and as he turned around, found that one of the royal guards had slipped in a large pile of elephant dung. Adam had to struggle to keep a straight face at the armoured soldier writhing around, trying unsuccessfully to stand up in the shit.

Adam could see Brag talking into a personal comms device. He seemed pretty shocked at what had happened –the stampede more than the botched attack. The captain was being pretty emphatic about whatever he was talking about, and kept pointing to the scorch-mark on the carpet, and the piles of elephant dung that had appeared so quickly. *Had the elephants been holding it in for months or something?*

Brag approached Adam, sidestepping the dung, and the stricken guard.

"What the hell was that?"

Franks shrugged, shaking his head.

"Engineering says the holographic systems in this area are fully functional, with no malfunctions, so they were not holo images. They were real. Readings from the internal sensors indicate that they just appeared in the corridor; at the moment, they seem to be heading directly for the nearest of the *Royale*'s water parks."

"A watering hole; though I can't imagine that the processed water in that place is going to do them any good."

"We could stun them, keep them contained somewhere like a shuttlebay."

"It would only upset them to be in a confined space, and make things worse."

Franks gave his friend a sidelong glance, wondering how the man could possibly know the behaviour of elephants. He didn't question it though; Adam seemed to have a knack for knowing the right obscure thing at the right time.

"What about blocking off a section of corridors, letting them run free in a controlled area?"

"Not a bad idea," Franks nodded, before implementing the plan with his officers. Then his comm unit bleeped for attention. He pressed the activation stud, "Franks here." It was the ship's third-in-command, Lieutenant Commander o'Shov.

"Captain, I have just received fourteen separate reports of bizarre incidents across the ship. So far, several of the crew claim to have seen a variety of mythical creatures; the Lady M'a'll'ei claims to have had her royal suite trampled to pieces by a parade of toy soldiers. A Vilani flea circus is causing havoc in the main crew mess hall. A human male named Abraham Lincoln was just shot dead in Theatre Six, and the Messiah of Severa III is currently giving his most infamous speech during the early days of the Severan Regime."

"Any casualties?" asked Franks. Adam saw the look on Franks' face: the captain clearly didn't want a repeat of the Odyssey Station crisis –this was a cruise liner, not a warship, and its crew and staff were not soldiers.

"A few bumps and bruises, and a lot of loud mouths," came the chuckled reply.

"What's the overall situation?"

"We are on schedule for our next port of call. The St. George *just passed out of sensor range, and we are getting some very strange readings across the ship, though we cannot identify what the sensors are showing us."*

Franks sighed, gave one look at the Queen and her entourage, and spoke into the comm unit. "I will be on the bridge in a few minutes, commander."

"Understood, Captain."

Franks clapped a hand on Adam's shoulder, and then strode off down the corridor, narrowly avoiding a particularly large pile of elephant dung.

"This journey just gets weirder and weirder," Adam muttered to himself, before walking off himself, Eve up in his powerful arms.

* * *

On the main engineering deck, the chief engineer and several of his subordinates were gathered around a flat central control console. Above the console hung a three-dimensional holographic representation of the *Gold Royale*. They were pointing at parts of the ship that had experienced the weird events, and theorising, trying desperately to figure out what was going on.

It had been two hours since the events had plagued the ship, and then they had stopped without warning.

There were no answers, however, and there were no commonalities between the events; some seemed to involve time travel, whilst others included mythical creatures or things that only existed in the imagination.

It was as if reality was breaking down in spurts.

Somebody on the engineering deck cried in dismay, and everybody turned to see what he or she was looking at. They were looking up, and found themselves staring out into an unfamiliar night sky. Menacing triangular starships pounded a motley assortment of vessels, next to a giant unfinished metal sphere, above a moon covered with forests. Starfighters danced around each other, dying in droves in the desperate fight for survival. One starfighter was torn apart by laser fire, and pieces of it came crashing down onto the engineering deck.

The sky disappeared, replaced by the familiar ceiling of main engineering. The chief engineer looked around, and found that the wreckage of the starfighter was still there. Its pilot was injured, and was clambering out of the spherical cockpit. It wore a black uniform, with hoses feeding into a black glossy helmet.

The pilot pulled out a pistol.

"What is this place?" the muffled voice demanded, waving the gun at them. "Where am I? Is this a Rebel ship? Are you enemies of the Empire?"

* * *

Commander Gorman had volunteered to take Eve to see the gardens in Green Sector, giving Adam some time to himself. Except he was restless; since Odyssey Station, he had spent every hour with Eve, and now he was alone, he felt lonely without her.

So he had opted for a run.

It had been a peaceful run around the deck, nodding and greeting those he passed. It had been peaceful, until the Queen had decided to join him. She was wearing a pretty simple set of tight jogging clothes, sleeveless and a bland grey.

She had questions, and he couldn't shut her up. She wanted to know about Great Britain, about his home in Cambridge, and she wanted to know about his military career. So he had sped up.

She kept up, even when he was close to sprinting.

She was fit, but she was still young and inexperienced stamina-wise, and was starting to wear herself thin. Sweat was pouring down her face, blotching her clothes, and her breathing was getting harder and harder. He was taking a perverse pleasure in tormenting her, despite the fact that she seemed to be only around eighteen years old.

An hour in, he glanced sideways, and found she was no longer there. He stopped, and found her fifty metres back, struggling for breath. He was barely sweating.

He strolled up to her, hands on hips.

"You're pretty good," he admitted.

"And you've been trained," she smiled.

He was about to add something else when he heard a bang, followed by another, and then another, until they formed what sounded like footsteps. The Queen stood up, and then her eyes widened in horror, her face falling. She was rooted to the spot in utter fear.

Adam became aware of a heavy breathing noise that wasn't his own or the Queen's. It was a familiar breathing sound, one he had heard four months ago.

He turned slowly, and saw what he had thought was dead.

"A T-Rex," he whispered.

Not just any Tyrannosaur either: it had a large pole jutting out of the top of its skull, where Adam himself had planted it. It was the Rex from Lord Yh'reth'gar's flagship. It stood there, just watching them, its breathing ragged as if it were hurt.

"Oh my gods," the Queen whispered.

Adam was frozen with indecision. What the hell was it doing here, on the Gold Royale? He had beaten the carnivorous beast before he could do it again -even though he was sure he had actually *killed* it last time. On the other hand, if he stood and fought the thing again, the Queen could be hurt, or worse.

He span, and barrelled into the Queen, lifting her off her feet, and carrying her over one shoulder before bolting away from the Rex. His quarters were just around the corner. The *boom-boom-boom* of the dinosaur's footsteps let him know that it was chasing him, though the ceiling was too low to let it run at full pace.

"Computer, open doors to Adam Caine's suite."

The computer registered his voiceprint, and opened the doors.

He dove through the open doors, carrying the Queen with him. The Rex's jaws crashed into the doorframe millimetres from Adam's head. The dinosaur squealed as it hit the unyielding alien metal, its scaly hide bouncing off the walls, leaving it to stumble away from the doors.

Sparks flew from the doors.

"Dammit, the doors aren't going to shut." He dragged the Queen away from the doors, and into the suite proper, heaving her onto the bed. He disappeared into his walk-in closet, and came back out with his SA80 rifle. He stood before the doors, and waited for the creature to charge again. It did, though its size meant it couldn't fit through, no matter how much roaring it did.

Adam switched to full auto, and emptied his rifle's magazine into its writhing head. The bullets smacked into the thick scaly skin, tearing chunks out of the creature's head. It roared in pain, and backed away, stumbling around, banging into walls, and making more noise than an earthquake.

Adam took a few steps back.

The massive dinosaur made one last desperate attempt to hurt its enemy, but simply collapsed across the doorway.

"Uh-oh," Adam exclaimed.

He ran to the door, and found that the thing's back had completely filled the door, sealing him into his quarters with the Queen. He grumbled something unintelligible that she couldn't hear, turned, and then made his way to the bed.

He tried the suite's intercom, but whatever had brought the Rex back from the dead, and onto the *Gold Royale*, was interfering with the communications system. He sighed, exasperated at being stuck in his own quarters with a woman who had shown a strangely unhealthy interest in him.

He propped the rifle against the nearest wall, where he would be able to get to it if the Rex decided to cheat death a second time. He strode over to the bed, and checked to see if she had any injuries. She didn't, though she was still shivering with fear.

"It's dead," he said as soothingly as possible.

"Are you sure?" she said, softly enough that he could only just hear her.

"No," he admitted. "That's the second time I've had to kill it. The last time I killed it, it had a bloody great spike in its brain." She nodded, taking this in, and seeming to accept it at face value as being comforting for her. She leaned forward, and forcefully kissed him. He resisted, making her pull away.

"Why do you resist? I've seen the way you look at me."

"Because you're only twelve years older than my daughter, and you're the Queen of Terra, for crying out loud."

"You're only in your twenties," she pointed out.

"I can't."

"Your file doesn't say you're married, or that you have a long-term relationship with anybody."

He eyed her suspiciously. "You've been reading about me?" He sighed. "There was someone recently, but it didn't work out. I'm... I'm a killer. She was a good person, and I didn't want to keep dragging her into these situations where she would continually be exposed to my dark side."

"Do you love her?" she asked.

He nodded, hoping she wouldn't keep bringing up Hannah. But he could see that her face had fallen somewhat; what was she up to?

He didn't get an answer right away, instead being on the receiving end of another kiss. This time, he didn't resist, instead, he wrapped his big arms around her, and pulled her onto his lap.

Forgive me, Hannah.

* * *

"What is that you've found?" Gorman queried as she bent down next to Eve. The little girl was crouching next to one of the massive floral displays, holding something in her little green hands.

Eve turned, and held out her hand.

There was a small white creature sat in the palm of her hand. It was tiny, and spherical, except for two eyestalks sticking out the top, evenly spaced. Its eyes were round white balls that seemed to be open constantly, and it had a tiny mouth that seemed perpetually turned up into a smile. It was cute, incredibly so; it bounced up and down on Eve's hand, and made excited purring noises.

"I called him Bouncer," Eve grinned.

"Where did it come from?" Gorman worried. Just because a creature *looked* cute, did not mean that it was not dangerous. Adam Caine was proof of that; cute, handsome even, but she had never met a more dangerous individual.

"It was just lying in the flower bed; it was scared so I picked it up, and started stroking it." She held it up, and Bouncer started bouncing excitedly, making giggling sounds as it did so. Gorman reluctantly held out her hand, and started stroking it as well. It purred even louder, shivering with enjoyment.

"Shall we show your father? And perhaps the captain?"

Bouncer did not seem to like this idea, and started growling.

There was a loud honk of steam. Gorman looked up to see a steam train coming directly towards them. She grabbed Eve and Bouncer, and dove out of the way. The train roared past, battering the three with its wake, steam hissing over them.

When it finally huffed into the distance, Gorman noted.

"That's not good."

* * *

Adam woke with something sticking into his back.

He shifted position, which woke the queen from their two-hour slumber.

Which was when he realised they were lying under his duvet, in the middle of a jungle. Animals twittered and chirped in the background, whilst primates bickered and squawked nearby. The object sticking into his back was a lump of fallen leaves and twigs.

"This is really not good," Adam muttered. He looked around, still naked as the day he was born. To his dismay the Rex was still there, lying on its side against two trees that were space apart enough to be the same size as his suite's doorway.

Sunlight was beaming down through the jungle canopy overhead, whilst a decent breeze swayed the trees themselves. Each footstep he took set off a crunch from the undergrowth, dry and brittle from the heat permeating wherever they were.

Luckily, their clothes were still lying where they left them, and the two dressed as quickly as they could. The rifle, however, was nowhere to be seen, leaving him feeling as naked as he had moments ago.

"How is this possible?" asked the young Queen, who took Adam's hand in hers, and hugged his arm. She was terrified by the insane goings on around them. He, however, was getting used to it.

"I don't know, but there must be a way back."

"How can you tell?"

He looked at her, and realised what a mistake he had made in sleeping with her: before, she had been a strong young woman, but now in the face of such overwhelming insanity, she was a terrified teenage girl.

I'm so sorry for betraying you, Hannah.

"How do we get back then?" she panicked, snapping him out of his guilt-ridden reverie.

He was staring at the Rex.

"That was where the door was, so presumably, we just have to step between those two trees. As long as the Rex doesn't come back to life, we'll be fine." He stopped in his tracks. "That is, once we've moved that eighteen-foot-high, fifty-foot-long, ten-tonne dinosaur out of our bloody way."

Adam scratched his head, looking around for a tree trunk to use for leverage.

He found one, and realised that it was too long.

"Crap."

* * *

"Report," Franks ordered. Alarms were blaring left and right, all across the bridge, different noises, and different colours, all threatening to give Brag a serious headache. "Shut those alarms off," he added.

Lieutenant Commander o'Shov appeared by his side, his nostrils flaring in worry.

"The strange phenomena are appearing all across the ship. There are reports of even stranger occurrences; beings and events from childhood nightmares -even imaginary creatures from stories people have read recently. And we have also lost contact with main engineering. They reported seeing a massive space battle above them, and then the line went dead."

Brag rubbed his eyes.

"Any casualties?"

The blunt-nosed herbivore shook his head.

"Bumps and bruises, sir. Still nothing major, and no fatalities."

"You make it sound inevitable someone will be killed," snorted Brag.

"My race are herbivores, sir; we expect the worst to happen, because it usually does given the opportunity."

"Has there been any contact with the Queen, or Commander Caine?"

Again, the third-in-command shook his head, his hairless wrinkly skin a dull green under the lights of the alerts. "The Queen's military aides were insistent that she went out for a jog four hours ago, but has not returned. The same goes for Commander Caine. There was a report from one of the guests staying near the commander's quarters of a dinosaur charging after two humans."

Brag sighed.

"We can't worry about them, even if one of them is the Queen of Terra, and the other is my friend. We need to get in contact with the engineering deck."

"Yes, sir. As you humans say, we will keep on it."

Franks could only nod.

"Captain!" the sensors officer called out.

Brag turned from his holographic command post.

"Captain, the weird occurrences."

"What about them?"

"They all have a specific energy pattern about them, and I think I have found the greatest concentration of them." Brag moved over to stand behind the sensor officer's holographic station, staring at sensor displays that were more refined than his command post. The officer continued, zooming in on a specific area of the primary hull. "This spot has a three-hundred percent greater concentration than any other part of the ship. I am also detecting three specific life-forms from within that section: Commander Gorman, Evelyn Caine, and an unknown life-form."

"Grab a portable scanner, and a security team, and come with me."

"Yes, sir."

* * *

The steam train was still chuffing around somewhere nearby, though Gorman could still no longer see it. She was more concerned with the family group of Navininian Giant Slugs. They weren't carnivorous, they were simply huge, and were oblivious to Gorman's presence, or indeed the presence of little Eve, and her new friend Bouncer.

The largest slithered by, ignoring Gorman as she scrambled out of its way, still holding onto Eve, who in turn was still holding onto Bouncer. The little ball was wailing in distress, scared of the massive vomit-green slugs as they slid past.

The more that Bouncer wailed the more bizarre occurrences seemed to take place.

Horses thundered through the sky above, and fire danced around the flowers and bushes as if it were a living, breathing being. Pixies the size of Gorman's eyelashes fluttered around them, singing beautiful songs.

"How could I have been so stupid?" she cried.

It was so obvious to her now.

"Eve, you have to stroke Bouncer; you have to make him happy."

"I don't know how," complained Eve, as the *Starship Titanic* fell from the sky wreathed in flames, and dashed itself to pieces on Saturn's atmosphere. The random improbable occurrences were getting worse with every minute, and Gorman was worried that pretty soon something insane would happen to hurt them.

"Gorman?" a familiar voice shouted over the tumult of the horses, the living flames, the minute pixies, and the dying *Titanic*. It was the captain, with several others from the crew, including a security team.

"Captain?" she called back.

"Are you hurt, Kathlyyn?"

"No, sir, just a little scared."

Franks looked around, and nodded.

"There is all sorts of these events happening across the ship," he said, getting straight down to business. "The energy patterns that go with these events have been detected, and the greatest concentration seems to be right here in this area." He nodded to the young sensors officer, who whipped out a portable scanner, and started waving it around. At first, the waving seemed to be generalised, and then he seemed to home in on the target.

Everybody found that the scanner was now pointing at Bouncer, though Gorman had already concluded that the cute little being had had something to do with it.

"The energy patterns are all emanating from this creature," the sensors officer confirmed.

"How can that be?"

The officer shook his head, and shrugged. "I honestly could not tell you, sir; an alternate universe maybe? I am a sensors officer, not a scientist."

Brag suddenly thought of Adam, and how the time-travelling soldier would have come up with some daft suggestion that usually ended up close to the mark. Not that that was a precedent; Adam was just such a strange person that it seemed to make sense that he would be the one to come up with an answer.

Gorman was the one that broke the pause.

"So what do we do now, Captain?"

* * *

Adam had resorted to punching and kicking the thick hide of the Rex. There was nothing to move the thing from his side. Their only hope was if the *Gold Royale*'s crew moved the Rex, or disintegrated it by laser, or something. Anything; he just wanted to get out of here. He'd had enough of jungles in Africa.

"I am truly sorry," the young Queen suddenly said.

"What for?" Adam huffed as he gave up his attack on the dinosaur, and sat with his back against the creature.

"For trapping you here." She slumped beside him, and rested her head on his shoulder.

"You didn't, the Rex did," he countered, slapping the leathery skin behind him.

"It was my fault that man attacked me." Adam looked at her with no small confusion. She sighed. "He was... a suitor I turned down. You see, when my father –the King– died, I was given the throne, and all the responsibilities. But I have no sisters or brothers, and my mother is desperate for our family to hold onto the crown. So I have to be married soon, and have an heir. That man was creepy, and he wanted power more than he wanted love."

Adam couldn't help the surprised look on his face.

"That all sounds like something out of the Dark Ages, not the supposedly enlightened forty-first century. Even in my century, we didn't have that kind of behaviour; it's unheard of; it's barbaric, even primitive. Not only that, but for *you* to be actively doing it –you're throwing away your life as a young woman. You shouldn't have to worry about being a queen, or having a baby. If this last day has taught you anything, it's that *everything* is possible."

He paused, a frown creasing his face before anger set in.

"Is that why you came to see me? To be your Prince Regent, and to be the father of *your* heir? I can tell you now, that that *isn't* going to happen. I have a family now, and I have no desire to go back to that pompous, shitty life."

"I'm sorry. But if you were to agree to an arranged marriage, we could pay you handsomely, or even give you power, or give you a real officer's commission in the Terran Navy." They both stood, Adam pacing, and the Queen worriedly rambling on nervously. "My Uncle claimed there are other ways to make you; ways that involve your daughter being threatened."

Suddenly, there was an invisible line that had been irrevocably between them. Both knew she had crossed it, and both knew the situation had changed.

"Are you threatening me?" he shouted, his face a contortion of rage. He stepped up to her, and suddenly he looked like a giant to her, his muscles and sheer height making him all the more terrifying; it just confirmed everything she already knew about him —confirmed why the officers of the *St. George*, and the officers of her Army bodyguard, had every right not to want Her Majesty to be in the same room as him, especially not alone.

"M-my uncle said he has friends that are more powerful than anything you can imagine."

Adam snorted, the anger subsiding, replaced by what she took to be contempt.

"You mean Kombat 3899?"

Her eyes widened in surprise.

"How do you know them?"

"Because they've been chasing me for months, and I've had some experience with secretive organisations like theirs. I was in the SBS after all, assuming you truly know who they were." When she nodded, he continued. "Why are you in bed with 3899? Power? Greed?"

"My uncle wants to be the power *behind* the throne, and wants *me* to be the one on the throne. But he needs them to do it; he's one of their primary benefactors."

"I can think of another benefactor," Adam mumbled, the image of an old man in a tuxedo flashing behind his eyes. "What I don't understand is why. Even in the twentieth and twenty-first centuries, the monarch was nothing but a figurehead; I assume that's still the case two millennia on."

She nodded.

"The monarch is the monarch, and I think that 3899 have plans for my government."

"They seem to have plans for everybody," grumbled Adam. "You should tell your uncle not to be involved with them. Order him if you have to; they're worse than you can believe, and I'm pretty sure they're in bed with someone who comes pretty close to being the definition of evil." He doubted she would listen to him, or if she did, her uncle would most likely not listen to *her*, and dismiss her as being just a child. It was worth a try to at least put a small dent in 3899's plans, and by association, Gold's.

There was a sound of whirring machinery, and suddenly the dinosaur was sliding across the jungle floor, away from them, and unblocking the door.

There was a flash of light, and a puff of smoke, and Adam and the Queen were suddenly standing back in his suite, the bed sheets still ruffled, the rifle still propped against the wall.

Several crewmen popped their heads round the edge of the door.

"Sorry it took so long to rescue you, Commander, majesty. The teleporters are down, and the weird occurrences are happening more frequently, some worse than your situation, sir, ma'am."

Adam glanced at the Queen.

"I'm not so sure about that," he muttered under his breath. Apparently, her majesty heard it though, because a look of embarrassed sadness passed over her face. "What's happening?" This was said to the crewmen entering the suite.

"Captain Franks took a team into Green Sector; apparently that's where all this is coming from."

Adam reeled as if he had been hit; Green Sector had been where Gorman had taken Evelyn to view the gardens. He bolted out of the suite, leaving behind a confused group of crewmen. The Queen ran behind him, trying desperately to keep up with the big man.

Adam tried to ask the computer for directions to the gardens since he hadn't had time to memorise the ship's plans yet; all he got, however, was an ancient Rijiin love-song that sounded like Chaz & Dave -if they were howling wolves.

So Adam grabbed the nearest member of the crew, and demanded to know how to get there. The crewman, a Rijiin ironically, saw the look of serious determination on Adam's face, and wondered if the big human would actually hurt him.

The Rijiin gestured for them to follow, and the three sprinted off down the corridor.

* * *

The helmeted TIE-Fighter pilot was still pointing his blaster pistol at the *Gold Royale*'s engineering staff, wondering what the hell was going on, when one of the ship's security detail barrelled into him, bundling him to the floor in a tangle of limbs.

The TIE pilot lashed out, and clipped the guard across the side of the head with the butt of his pistol. The guard yelped, and collapsed to the deck, unconscious.

The pilot recovered enough to stand back up.

When he turned round, there were suddenly a dozen stun pistols, pointing directly at his face -the barrels of the exotic weapons mere millimetres from his nose.

"Somebody tie him up," the chief engineer ordered.

The TIE pilot harrumphed.

"Rebel scum."

* * *

Adam, the Queen, and the Rijiin crewman were about to enter Green Sector, when the ship disappeared around them, and was replaced by the M5 motorway. Except it was empty -devoid of traffic. There were no bird songs in the air, or noise of any kind, indicating nearby life.

There was, however, a motorbike sat in the middle lane of the motorway, the motor idling in neutral. Its occupants were nowhere to be seen, and Adam was sure he could see a sign far in the distance, one he didn't remember seeing on this part of the M5, at least not the last time he had been through here. To one side of the road, he could see the expanse of Taunton -a town he had visited only briefly during his stay at the Marines barracks a few miles north.

The bike itself was a Harley Davidson Road King, the same model Adam had owned before being kidnapped by the Core, probably still sitting in the apartment building's underground car park.

"Nice," Adam smiled, giving a nod of approval to whatever intelligence –or lack of- had conjured up this scenario. He swung into the seat, gripping the handles, a nostalgic smile on his lips. He turned to the Queen. "You coming then?" She eyed the primitive vehicle up suspiciously, wondering how it moved without the help of energy-based engines or anti-gravs.

"It's called a motorcycle, it runs on petroleum, with a combustion engine. It's fun." He held out a hand, though his face said it would be anything like fun to her. She took the hand, and he pulled gently onto the small back seat directly behind him. She roughly wrapped her arms around his midsection.

He keyed the ignition, and revved the engine, getting a few roars from it before tapping the kickstand into its stored position. He turned to the Rijiin crewman and told him to wait at the edge of the road until the situation was finally resolved, or until the ship's corridor returned.

The Queen squealed as the bike launched along the motorway, gaining speed as Adam continued to slowly twist the throttle, changing gears. The engine roared louder than anything she had heard before, the cushioned seat beneath her vibrating ever so slightly. The wind blasted through her hair, threatening to rip it off. When she looked in the palm-sized wing mirrors, she noticed a feral grin of glee on Adam's face.

He was enjoying it more than she could say; to be able to let rip like this was something he couldn't describe, and he had to control himself from letting out a whoop of excitement.

A large road sign came up ahead, after twenty minutes of driving at over a hundred miles per hour.

There was one long white arrow on the big green sign, with a smaller one breaking off midway. The long arrow pointed to 'Red Sector, Section 190.' The other pointed to 'Green Sector.'

Out of long habit, Adam flicked the left indicator on, and swept the roaring Harley up the sloped turn-off, and into Green Sector.

* * *

"Okay, so there is no way to stun it, or probably kill it," Franks moaned. He was lying on the floor, blackened from the blast of some energy ball that had engulfed him and his team when he ordered one of his team to stun the little Bouncer without hurting Eve.

Bouncer had growled at them, and then the ball of energy had swept Franks, Gorman, and the rest of the team away from the little green girl and her new friend. Comically, he and his team were blackened down their fronts, face and all, their hair sticking out backwards like the comedies of old.

229

Franks struggled to keep his footing; the team had probably been stunned, but there was most likely something flame-related within that energy, as the carbon scoring would not have happened otherwise.

The sensor officer was already throwing away the melted ruins of his portable scanner, a look of pained embarrassment across his features. The officer shrugged an apology to his captain, before frowning and looking around for the source of a noise that they could all now hear.

The noise got louder and louder, like a roaring engine being over-revved for the sheer joy of it, until a motorcycle carrying Adam Caine and her majesty the Queen −minus her regale attire- jumped over a grouping of shrubberies before coming crashing down on the grass behind Franks, narrowly avoiding the returning alien steam train that thundered past at a hideous rate.

Adam shut the thing's engine off before stepping off, and approaching Eve.

"What's going on, Evie?" he asked, his voice softer than Franks had heard it before.

"It's my friend, Bouncer," Eve replied, holding her hands so that they protected the cute little being. Bouncer was chirruping happily, and then growling at Adam every so often, threatened by the presence of the big man.

Adam tried to make himself seem less threatening by crouching down to lower than Eve's eye line, and placing a gentle hand on his daughter's forearm.

Bouncer growled, and the great storm of 1987 −the one Michael Fish so famously got wrong- suddenly blasted through the gardens, ripping shrubberies, trees, and grass from their planted positions, and hurled them at Adam, Franks, and the others with such force that Franks and his officers were lifted off their feet, and tossed them across the gardens, landing painfully out of Adam's view. He could barely hear their cries of pain and surprise over the roaring thunder of the wind.

His low profile was only going to keep him anchored to the ground for so long.

He jumped towards Eve, and wrapped his arms around her. She was screaming for her daddy to save her. The wind was picking up, even as Adam held her tight; he could feel his feet slipping.

Eve was screaming, the wind was howling, and little Bouncer was alternating between angry growls and scared whimpers. Just as Adam lost his footing, the wind stopped howling, Eve was still screaming, but Bouncer was nowhere to be seen.

Adam was on his back on the ruined grass.

There were cuts and abrasions all over his body, where the plants and leaves had been turned into living weapons, their thin edges slicing through his skin. They were nothing harsh, but there were dozens of wounds, and they were *all* bleeding.

"Are you okay, Evie?" he whispered, the wind knocked out of him after he'd hit the ground.

She wasn't looking up at him; she was staring at her empty hands, her face frozen in a rictus of horror, her delicate green features making him heartbroken.

"Where's Bouncer?" she cried. Tears started flowing down her cheeks, though she didn't sob. Adam held her close.

"*I am truly sorry for our son's inconvenience,*" a heavenly voice said from behind Adam. He stood up, Eve still wrapped up in his arms. The source of the voice wasn't exactly there, though there was definitely a presence floating in front of him: two golden clouds that hovered a metre above the ground. They both exhibited an inner glow that made them seem like angels; Adam wondered if they had anything to do with humans' association between golden beings and angels.

"Your son?"

"*Although his age is thousands of your years, and thus older than you, he is still a child, and our offspring. He has been... a nuisance to many, not just his own parents.*"

"No kidding," snorted Adam, gesturing to the chaos around him.

"*Again, we are truly sorry,*" said the cloud on the left. The clouds came nearer to Adam, flickering as if with excitement. "*You are the Earthman they call Caine?*"

"I am."

"*You are the Strand,*" one of them said, in imitation of a gasp, or something that sounded like it. "*You are the one she spoke of.*" Adam didn't need to be told who *she* was, nor what she had been saying. The clouds suddenly started flickering, as if angry, or afraid, he couldn't obviously tell. "*There is a great darkness coming, Adam Caine.*"

"If it comes near me, I'll kick it in the crown jewels."

"*The darkness is coming,*" the left cloud's partner insisted.

Adam sighed.

"Is it stuck in traffic or something? I just want to know why it hasn't turned up is all. And the next non-corporeal superbeing that tries to give me some overly cryptic warning about a great darkness will be shoved head-first into the nearest black hole."

It wasn't a threat Adam was really going to back up even if he wanted to, though he was definitely angry about all these ancient beings, living clouds, and nebulae never actually detailing their warnings.

The clouds backed away, unwilling to risk the possibility of disappearing down a quantum singularity.

There was a tug on Adam's trouser leg, and found it was Eve trying to get his attention, and she was still hiding behind him. Her tears were still going, but she no longer looked as forlorn as she had before. Strangely, though, he knew what she wanted, and couldn't explain how he knew, except noticing her reaction to the missing little ball of cuteness.

"Where is your son now?" he asked of the clouds.

"*He is being punished for hurting those aboard this vessel,*" the cloud on the right replied, the excitement passed over.

"Can Eve at least say goodbye?" Adam queried. "Children make friends very quickly; they aren't as jaded as their parents, or adults in general."

The clouds flickered.

"*Of course,*" they replied simultaneously.

Their tiny little son appeared in Eve's hands, and she started skipping around, giggling with utter joy at having her newfound friend back with her. Adam could hear the little being's happy chirrups as the two danced around the room. Adam turned to the cloud-beings.

"How did it happen?"

"*We use an improbability field to jump from place to place. When a similar type of energy was released from your attacker, our son was attracted to it, but the instability of the energy weapon's pattern opened up a rift that seems to have somehow latched onto our offspring's moods, creating improbable situations that create utter havoc.*" That pretty much answered Adam's questions, except for one.

"What's the Arcbane?"

The clouds flickered again, definitely angry, Adam realised.

Their son chirruped what sounded like an actual goodbye in English, before brushing himself up against Eve's face. Eve said goodbye to the little creature, before it disappeared completely –and probably forever, Adam figured.

"*Do not ask about the Arcbane. That is something that mortals, even you Earthman, are not meant to know.*"

Adam opened his mouth to repeat his question, when he suddenly realised that he and Eve were standing alone, the clouds no longer nearby.

"That was seriously weird."

They weren't entirely alone though, as Captain Jack Sparrow stood on the edge of one of the shrubbery pits, holding a taut rope that hung unattached to anything beside him.

"Gentlemen; I wash my hands of this weirdness." Then he jumped off the ledge, and was gone. There was a flash of blinding light, and Adam and Eve were standing on the grass as if nothing had happened, the trees, flowers and grass blades all back in their original places as if they hadn't been subject to hurricane-force winds.

"I stand corrected; *that* was seriously weird."

* * *

Having explained everything to Brag and Gorman, and finding out there were no serious injuries or deaths, Adam took Eve to their suite and put her to bed. He didn't say a single word to the Queen as he did so. He didn't want to talk to her, not after what she had admitted about her intentions, and who she was indirectly allied to.

A passing Terran *Longbow*-class cruiser –the *HMS Legendary*- was co-opted by the Queen's military advisors, who whisked her off the *Gold Royale* in a hurry.

She sat in the *Legendary*'s medical bay, having felt extremely faint and nauseous all of a sudden. The doctor approached her bedside, wary of the gold-armoured bodyguards, and her entourage nearby.

He spoke in hushed tones, so only the Queen could hear him.

"I have good news, your majesty."

She looked at him quizzically.

"You are pregnant."

The Queen sobbed.

* * *

Adam sat in the dark, poring over tomes of data on everything he could find about this Arcbane. There was nothing except vague legends of destruction, and half-whispered rumours of dead star systems.

Whatever this Arcbane was, and it held Adam's curiosity quite well, it was well hidden. That, or it simply didn't exist, and he was being strung along.

He tried a different tack.

He input the word into the ship's translation. The computer cycled through hundreds of variables, until it came to ancient Rijiin. It translated Arcbane into that language, which made no sense at all, because he could not read the language. So the computer spat it back out in Standard; not English, but *Standard* –apparently there were some grammatical differences, which changed some of the translations with other languages.

The words it spat out horrified Adam.

Galaxy Killer.

* * *

A week ago.

"Good luck, my friend. I hope that the *Gold Royale* has brought you the answers you needed. I am sure I will see you soon, or at least hear from you soon." Raymond Sansky signed off, removing his peaked cap as the camera switched off, and the holo-letter was saved for sending.

He was not in the Navy office in New Amsterdam, though the letter would be routed through there. He did not want his friend Adam to know where he was, because the truth would hurt him, greater than any wound he had received previously, and Adam had received a great many.

He placed his peaked cap on the nearby settee, and accessed the file's settings, adjusting it so that Adam would only see him, and not the background. He masked the file's origins, and then sent it on its merry way.

"Raymond?" a feminine voice called from the bedroom. "Have you finished your paperwork yet?"

"Yep," he called back, "just coming." He unbuttoned his uniform jacket, took it off, and threw it on top of the cap, revealing his naked torso underneath. "I never realised you could be so impatient." He grinned when the woman in question appeared in the doorway to his bedroom.

Utterly naked except for the bed sheet she had stolen from the bed they had shared, Hannah Spears smiled sweetly.

"Come to bed, honey." She held out a beckoning hand. He grinned, and took the hand. "Who were you sending a letter to anyway?"

"Nobody," Raymond replied.

Eight:
Destruction & Fortitude

"It was the best of times, it was the worst of times."
-First and last two lines of *A Tale of Two Cities*.

1996ad.

The recruits were panting hard and fast, bounding over hedges and small wooden fences. The rain hammered down on them, stinging them with cold hard water, turning the loose soil beneath their feet to horrible, sucking mud.

The Physical Training Instructor bellowed for them to move it, go faster, and pump their arms harder. But they were fast losing energy, and the will to carry on.

The rain let up, and they breathed a sigh of relief when their silhouetted destination came into view. The buildings grew larger and larger over the long minutes before resolving into their barrack building, a lengthy construction built to house fifty recruits in single comfortable rooms.

The PTI bellowed for them to sprint the last hundred metres. Someone complained loudly that it was their first day of training and that the PTI should ease up on them. The PTI bawled him out, using loud and obnoxious expletives.

Which was when they all noticed the youngest of the recruits stood at ease in the shadow of the barrack building. He was barely sweating or panting from the effort of running, but they had all seen him start the exercise at the same time as them.

The PTI ran over to the young recruit, and shouted in his face.

"You! What did you think you were doing whilst the others were running? Taking a stroll? How did you get here before *them*?" His face was red with anger, unused to new recruits beating him on their first day.

The recruit shrugged. "I ran, Corporal. Same as the rest of 'em."

"I don't believe you recruit! You cheated didn't you? Took a short cut, didn't you?"

The young recruit glared at the PTI defiantly.

"No, Corporal!" he shouted in response. "I refuse to cheat!"

"DO YOU NOW?!" the PTI bellowed, but the recruits could all see he had lost his bluster. A smile crept across the Corporal's face. "Good." He eyes the too-young young man up and down, noting the already bulging muscles under the boy's tee-shirt and shorts. "What's your name, recruit?"

"Caine, Corporal. Adam Caine."

* * *

3988ad.

The Savage Halo was, by all rights exactly as it sounded. Savage.

There were no civilisations in the small galaxy that wasn't at war with someone else. Most of the galaxy's races were too primitive to do more than fight with rocks or swords. There were a few races, however, that had reached up into space and decided to conquer those around them.

The most technologically advanced native species of the Savage Halo had seemingly decided to give up their conquering ways and attempt to bring peace to their corner of space. So they asked for assistance from the Terran Consortium, who in turn ordered the Navy to send a diplomatic envoy in the form of one of the most experienced captains and crews they had.

The *HMS Clementine Andover* slid through space like a knife, its sleek but blocky hull reflecting the light of the local star, Nimon.

Captain Franks stepped down from his command chair, tiring of his XO's complaints about the boring nature of this assignment.

"We're not a diplomatic envoy, Captain," said the balding human. He leaned in close to Franks so as to whisper conspiratorially. "We're a warship."

"We're here to prevent or stop a war, Commander," Franks reminded him. "What's more important than that?"

Suitably chastised, the XO disappeared from view, conversing quietly with one of the bridge officers. Franks stood in silence.

"Incoming vessel, Captain," called the sensors operator.

"Identification?"

"It's Nonian, sir: same race that called us in."

"Good, open a channel, and-"

"They're firing on us, Captain!"

"What?"

He had ordered the shields to be lowered and weapons to stay offline as a gesture of peace and goodwill to the Nonians. That order came back to haunt him; the unprotected bow of the *Clementine Andover* was torn apart by concentrated fire.

"Get those shields up!" he bellowed. The deck heaved, and he and his XO were tossed to the floor unceremoniously.

"Shield emitters are fried!"

"Helm, get us the hell out of here!"

The deck tipped again in the opposite direction under an almighty impact.

"More Nonian vessels, Captain! Dozens of them. Only a few are firing on us, the rest are bombarding the neutral planet below."

The regular humming of the engines faltered and changed to a whining pitch that pierced the ears of the crew.

"Engines are failing!" the XO shouted over the noise. A feedback pulse in the console he was standing at suddenly overloaded the electronics. It blew up in his face, shrapnel ripping through his skull.

Franks rushed to his XO's side, and felt for a pulse.

"Nark!" he swore.

"Captain, engines are gone, weapons are still offline and our communications are being jammed."

After six years of commanding the Clementine Andover, Franks gave the order every ship commander dreaded.

"Abandon ship! Get to the escape pods."

The bridge cleared of officers and enlisted extremely quickly, leaving Brag a few seconds to say goodbye to his beloved starship, and his trusted XO.

He had to be dragged from the bridge, and shoved into a cramped escape pod.

The pod slammed forward, and out into space, just as the starship began to break apart. The Nonians' energy weapon accidentally hit the crystalline/anti-matter engine core.

And in a flash it was gone.

* * *

July 4000ad.

"No, Luke; I am your father."

Everybody gasped at the exclamation, except one who just chuckled, even as Luke Skywalker cried out in denial, still clutching the hand his nemesis had lopped off. He looked around, searching for a way out, ignoring Vader's prattling about the dark side and the Emperor. He returned his attention to the black-clad warrior, and gave a knowing smile, before falling into the abyss below.

When the credits blasted onto the theatre's screen several scenes later, and the lights brightened, Brag was shaking his head.

"I never would have guessed it," he said in wonder.

Adam clapped a hand on his friend's shoulder.

"Neither did I, first time I saw it," he admitted.

"But it is such an amazing story."

"Do they not have stories like *The Empire Strikes Back* in this century?" asked Adam, wondering if people in this time had no love for movies as they did in his own time.

"Not really," replied Brag. "At least, not in the same way. These days, most movies are holographic –it's not interactive like that rugby match you took us to, but they're still engrossing. It is so exhilarating to be able to take a step back and watch it in one of these theatres." He looked around him, as if seeing the place for the first time. "Twelve years I have been on this ship, and I never even knew this was here."

Adam smiled.

"It's a big ship," he nodded.

They waited for everybody else to file out of the small theatre, and then strolled out themselves.

"So what now, Adam? We watch *Return of the Jedi*, or do something else?"

Adam gave him a sidelong glance.

"You really haven't had much time off the job have you?"

Brag gave a silent shrug, something he had accidentally picked up from Adam just by being around the bigger man.

"Well," Adam said slowly, "I did receive my pilot's license this morning, so I suppose we could take my ship out for a celebratory run around those asteroids I saw earlier."

Brag nodded.

"Sure."

* * *

Kathlyyn Gorman strode down the corridor followed by a contingent of security guards led by the self-named Purr. A stun pistol was holstered on one hip, and she carried a small torch in one hand, leading the way as they approached one of the larger luxury suites on the *Gold Royale*.

The doors were closed, the DNA reader dark. Even the lights in the corridor kept flickering, as if there were a power overload in that section.

They had been called to this suite because one of the maids had heard screams from inside.

Gorman looked to Purr, who was somewhat reluctant to step anywhere near the doors, and nodded to him. He was carrying a small security device that let the crew access a set of doors by bypassing and overriding the door control systems to let the user through without any physical violence. Purr snapped the flat device to the doors, and pushed the big red flashing button in the centre.

There were several clicks and whirrs, as the device bypassed the doors security systems. The flashing red button stopped flashing, indicating that it had unlocked the doors. The security guards all pulled their stun pistols from their holsters, holding them barrel forward at arm's length in two hands, just as Caine had taught them.

The doors slid open to reveal the darkened suite beyond.

Warily, they trudged through a small entrance hallway. As they came to the dining room just off the hall, one of the guards doubled over and vomited. Two more wailed in distress.

Gorman had to fight to keep her lunch down in her stomach where it belonged.

There was blood plastered over everything; and not just blood either. Entrails were thrown liberally around the room, still slick with internal fluids, whilst organs of all descriptions were stuck to bits of furniture.

Gorman was shaking with revulsion as she stepped over the bloody mess.

Purr was frozen to the spot, reliving the horror of Odyssey Station; he had only been out of therapy for a week, and was now being physically reminded of that experience.

Gorman lost her footing on something wet and fell to the floor. She found herself sitting on something soft, and her stomach rebelled by finally ejecting her lunch all over the floor.

There was a swish of movement off in the dark recesses of the bedroom, and Gorman turned in time to see Purr's fellow survivor, Simili, torn into ribbons. There was more movement, more screams, and more death.

Purr was still frozen to the spot when he died, his head swiped off his neck by something long, bony, and sharp.

Gorman, still on the floor, watched as she was surrounded by bone and muscle. She backed herself into a corner.

Blades were raised and teeth were exposed.

Commander Gorman screamed.

* * *

On the bridge, the communications officer could not get through to the XO, and the watch officer was getting worried. Gorman had taken the team down an hour ago, and now there was no reply on any channel from anywhere on that deck.

Lieutenant Commander o'Shov, the ship's herbivore third in command after Gorman and Franks, was stood in the command area of the bridge, staring at the comms officer as if that would make things all right.

His people were natural prey on his homeworld, and were subject to panic at the most extraordinary times. He had overcome this when he joined the crew of the *Gold Royale*, but now he was experiencing panic. He was practised enough that he didn't show it on his smooth, almost featureless face.

With the Captain off the ship, and the XO suddenly missing, he was in command. This wasn't how he had intended to become the ship's commander –during a crisis.

"Commander," the sensors officer shouted out, "I am picking up something dropping out of FTL speeds."

"What? Where?"

"Behind us, Commander. I cannot get a specific read on it, but it has the mass of something big."

"Bigger than us?"

"Negative, Commander; profile suggests it could be a Terran *Knight*-class battleship."

The panic in o'Shov rose to almost insurmountable levels; the uninhabited planetoid *Gold Royale* was currently orbiting was far from Terran jurisdiction. If one of their frighteningly powerful battleships were here, it was because they were after one of the questionable passengers on board.

"They are hailing us, sir," the comms officer announced.

"Let us see the ship first," o'Shov replied.

A holographic image of the battleship appeared before him. It did not look like the standard *Knight*-class he had seen in Terran space. Rather than the deep blue that all Terran starship hulls possessed, this one had a matt-black hull that the eye slid over. If he had been looking at the real thing, he was sure he would not be able to distinguish its shape in front of the starfield around it.

"They are hailing again, sir. They seem to be quite insistent this time."

Lieutenant Commander o'Shov sighed, nodded, and then steeled himself for what he was sure was going to be a disagreeable conversation.

A human female appeared in holographic form beside him. She wore an olive-green uniform instead of the expected black that the Terran Navy habitually wore. She had a severely shaven head, and an angry expression that o'Shov thought could probably curdle *thil* water.

"How can we help you?"

"*We demand you hand over Adam Caine.* Now."

* * *

"YAHOOOO!" Adam whooped as he spun his ship around another bulbous asteroid. In the seat beside him, First Class Pilot Feyton clung desperately to her chair, gritting her teeth as Adam pulled manoeuvre after insane manoeuvre in the dense asteroid belt.

Adam had felt no small surprise to find his ship was the blue beauty he had glimpsed several times upon visiting the shuttlebay. The inside was just as amazing as the outside, with two small bunkrooms, each with a tiny en suite shower, toilet, and sink, all decorated the same strange blue that shimmered in the light.

Parts of the ship looked alien, whilst others, like the insanely tiny mess and galley, were very human.

For the past two months, since leaving the Queen on the *HMS Legendary* behind, Feyton had been teaching Adam how to fly the small ship.

Today, Adam had actually managed to acquire a generic pilot's license to legally fly in most territories, and had gone on a joyride through an asteroid belt near to the ship's orbit of an uninhabited planet.

In the other two seats in the cramped cockpit sat his daughter Evelyn, and Franks, who was grumbling about the tight manoeuvres Adam was performing, making comments about wanting to keep his lunch in his stomach. Eve, however, was giggling with joy.

The cockpit's window was huge, stretching back to behind the two rear passengers, affording everybody a clear view of space around them. The view was spectacular, despite the asteroids rushing past dangerously close.

Despite Adam's zero flight experience, he had a natural talent aided by the ship's semi-sentient artificial intelligence. He was, in fact, flying at a capacity that Feyton could never match in all her wildest dreams. It was frightening how quickly he had learnt. So frightening, in fact, she had to wonder if he had taken learning drugs to help assimilate the knowledge at a much faster pace. When she asked him about it, he had flat out denied it.

He whooped again, followed by another of Eve's cute giggles, as the asteroid fell away and the strange ship shot up and above the belt. He set it in autopilot, letting it glide above the curving plane of the asteroid belt. He swivelled in his chair to look at the others, winking at Eve, who giggled again and clapped her hands together.

"Well, what do you think?" he asked with a grin.

Brag was still trying to quell his stomach, and Feyton was slightly pale.

"I'd say you missed your calling as a fighter pilot," said Brag. "Have you given it a name yet?" Brag gestured to the ship around them, though Adam knew what he had meant.

"*Kara Marazov*," he replied without hesitation. Franks and Feyton looked at him questioningly. He chuckled. "Kara Marazov was the last Royal Marine before the units were disbanded or renamed. She refused the redeployment orders where nobody else would."

"Sounds appropriate," Franks nodded.

Something beeped for attention on the sensor display. Adam turned back to it.

"If I'm reading this right, something just appeared beside the *Gold Royale*. Something big. The computer's putting an image up." Adam pointed ahead, and a holographic image of the *Gold Royale* and something else appeared above the main control console.

"The sensors are *that* powerful?" Brag exclaimed. Adam wasn't listening; he was staring at the ship hovering behind the cruise liner. It was angular, with the same architectural design as the *Polly Jenkins*, except it was matt-black, like the US Air Force's F-117 Nighthawks with their stealth hulls.

Brag leaned out of his chair so he could get a closer look at the mystery ship.

"That's a Terran *Knight*-class battleship. But we are too far out of the Navy's jurisdiction for it to be a coincidence, especially with that hull." Brag seemed worried, and Adam couldn't blame him —if that was really a stealth ship, there was an outstandingly good chance that it reported to Navy Intelligence, and if it did, they were most likely there to capture Adam.

"They are launching fighters," Feyton pointed out. "Rhinos by the looks of them, though they are black as well."

"Recon fighters," Adam grunted, remembering Echo Flight from the battle for Ancient Terra's remains. He grabbed the controls. "Everybody hold on tight." He switched over to manual control, and threw the ship forwards, towards the two big ships, ramping it up to full throttle.

* * *

"Major!" the battleship's XO shouted.

Major Dunn was on the bridge, whilst Drummond was briefing a mass boarding party made up of two entire companies of the Hunters regiment. The ship's captain was in his office just off the bridge, fuming that Dunn and Drummond had seconded the great N.I. vessel to their needs.

The cruise liner's watch officer had told Dunn that the captain and Adam Caine were not on the ship, and that the XO was missing. Dunn had told him that if neither the captain nor the XO appeared within the hour, the battleship would open fire on them.

"What is it, Commander?" she demanded impatiently.

"There is a ship approaching, ma'am."

"What kind?"

"The computer does not recognise it, Major."

Dunn frowned. Who could that be?

"Lock weapons," she ordered. She was not going to take any chances.

* * *

"They're trying to lock weapons," Feyton cried.

Adam threw the *Kara Marazov* directly towards the *Gold Royale*, not bothering with any manoeuvres, just wanting to get the others into a safe place –the small ship was exposed out in the middle of space with a battleship bringing its huge weapons to bear.

* * *

"Major, that ship is moving too fast for our weapons to track it."

Dunn raged silently, glaring at the holographic image of the strange crescent-shaped ship as it slipped into the *Gold Royale*'s main shuttlebay.

She ordered the go-ahead to Drummond.

* * *

One of the junior bridge officers met the four off the *Kara Marazov*, and filled them in on what had happened.

"Commander Gorman still hasn't reported in?" asked Adam.

The officer shook his head, leading them out of the shuttlebay. "No she has not, Commander Caine," the officer replied, reminding Adam that only Franks and Gorman knew who and what he really was, and that the rest still knew him as a Terran Navy warship XO on extended leave. "She took a security team down to Red Section to investigate screams from one of the luxury suites. We have not heard from her or the team since."

Adam pointed to a computer terminal next to the exit from the shuttlebay. "Can you access the cameras in that section?"

The officer nodded, though he seemed slightly confused.

Adam's paranoia was rising in the back of his mind.

The junior officer activated the dormant console, and accessed the visual recorders in Red Section. The young human let out a grunt of triumph, before looking utterly perplexed: the screen was dark.

No, not dark, Adam realised. The *lighting* in the corridor being viewed was dark. There was the occasional flash of light as the computer tried to push power through the conduits. The corridor was empty for a few seconds, then the next time the lights flickered Adam saw what he had hoped had gone down with Odyssey Station.

It was a gaggle of the creatures he, Eve, and three others had barely survived.

He held back the loud swearing and cursing that came unbidden to his mind.

"Can you contact anyone else in that section?" he asked.

The junior officer tried, but Adam wasn't surprised when he admitted defeat.

"Seal off that deck," Adam said, practically making it an order. Franks, to his credit, didn't hesitate in ordering the deck sealed off. Adam's reaction was enough to convince him how bad things had just turned. "I'm sorry Brag, but I'm afraid Gorman is probably already dead. Pretty soon those things are going to overrun the ship, and I'm sure that Navy ship is going to try to board."

Brag squeezed his eyes shut, knowing it was true just by the sight of the vicious creatures. If Gorman and her team had blundered into them without prior knowledge or the training Adam had had, she was indeed dead. He offered a silent prayer up to whatever gods Gorman and the team had prayed to. He had to be emotionally unattached; otherwise he would be no good to the rest of his crew -or whatever was left of them at any rate.

"The Navy will try to board through this or one of the other shuttlebays," Brag stated from what knowledge he had of Navy procedures. "Probably one of the smaller ones to avoid being noticed."

"The ship needs to be evacuated," Adam said bluntly.

Brag didn't agree; in fact he outright refused. The creatures were contained, and the Navy could be too. The liner was big enough that it could conceivably weather a sustained bombardment from the battleship.

"Lots of people *will* die, Brag," Adam said sincerely.

"This ship can withstand a lot."

Adam shook his head, disappointed that his friend couldn't see that this situation was lost. He lifted Eve up in his arms, who wrapped her own arms around his neck to steady herself. Adam stalked out of the shuttlebay, daughter in hand; Feyton followed them out, leaving Brag with his junior officer.

"How's o'Shov holding up?" he queried as the two headed for the bridge.

"He is doing well under the circumstances, sir," the young man answered stiffly. "The Navy are not giving him much of a choice but to cooperate."

"Even if Caine leaves this ship, the Navy will still want us to be interrogated," Brag added.

"Could Commander Caine be right, sir?"

Brag couldn't help but hesitate.

"No."

* * *

243

1996ad.

He couldn't breathe.

Not surprising, given that he was underwater. There was no way to escape, except go forward. Going back meant bumping into more recruits behind him.

He pulled himself along the half-wooden half-stone cramped tunnel, ignoring the burning sensation of his oxygen running out in his lungs. He could see a shifting glow up ahead: light from the end of the submerged tunnel being partially obscured by other recruits.

His arms and legs began to burn without oxygen to fuel them; his muscles became stiffer and stiffer. The bone-numbing cold didn't help either.

But he made it.

Recruit Caine burst from the water, and jumped onto the muddy ground next to it. The instructors stared wide-eyed at his sudden burst of strength. He managed to hide how he almost stumbled to the ground, his muscles refusing to work properly.

"Keep going, Caine!" boomed one of the Corporals.

Feeling the strength return to his limbs, Caine, in full battle dress fatigues bolted in the direction of the next obstacle, leaving behind the infamous underwater tunnel.

* * *

3988ad.

They had been captured.

Having survived the destruction of their ship, the Terrans had been taken onto the Nonian command vessel, handcuffed, and brought to a large cargo bay.

Brag was forced to kneel down in front of the Nonian Arbiter –the ship's captain.

"What will the Terran Navy do next?" he demanded.

"I do not know," replied Franks.

The Arbiter slapped him round the face, stinging his cheek and leaving a red handprint.

"What will they do?"

"I do not know," Franks repeated.

The Arbiter nodded to one of his men, who promptly shot Franks' communications officer.

"I will kill every member of your crew one at a time until you tell me what I want to know. If the Nonian Empire were to move on its warmongering neighbours, will the Navy interfere? Or will they see their folly and keep out, unwilling to risk precious ships and manpower?"

Franks just glared at him.

Another nod, and one of the *Andover*'s enlisted died.

"WHAT WILL THEY DO?!"

Franks, seeing how desperate the Arbiter was, just kept silent.

The Arbiter backhanded him, stinging the other cheek.

"Go to hell," spat the human.

"TELL ME!"

Franks stayed silent.

With a single nod to the men around him, the Arbiter signed the deaths of the humans. The Nonians gunned down every single member of Franks' surviving crew, but left the captain untouched.

Franks stared wide-eyed at the massacre of his own people.

Tears rolled down his cheeks.

"You're a monster," he whimpered.

The Arbiter shouted, "I am simply following my orders, Captain."

"That's what all monsters say."

"Go back to your Navy. Tell them of the horror of what you saw today. Perhaps one day we shall meet again. Perhaps not. Goodbye, Captain."

Franks never saw the rifle butt that knocked him out cold.

* * *

4000ad.

The Hunters did indeed board the ship through one of the smaller shuttlebays.

Their commander, a young lieutenant colonel, spread the two companies throughout that deck without any resistance. They were somewhat confused that the lighting was extremely bad.

The colonel and his command squad blundered into a luxury suite to find the shredded remains of Commander Gorman and her security team...

* * *

The brood was eternally hungry, and the new soldiers seemed like a dream come true, despite their hard shells. The brood hunted the Hunters, slaughtering the boarders without caring who they were or what they were doing.

They feasted.

* * *

As he was eaten alive, the lieutenant colonel accidentally activated his comms device.

On the bridge of the battleship, Dunn heard the bloodcurdling screams of the dying infantry commander. It chilled her to the bone, and several of the bridge crew vomited or wailed in horror. Gardner had warned her that Caine had successfully survived contact with the pet creatures of the Intelligence Director's mysterious ally. She had hoped she never had to be involved with them herself.

"Back the *Fortitude* away from the *Gold Royale*," she barked hurriedly to the XO. "And plot targeting solutions on them. Fire when ready." She ignored his look of alarm and disgust, but he made no comment.

"Yes, ma'am."

* * *

"They're firing!" the sensors officer shouted. The bridge shook and anybody standing was knocked to the floor. Warning klaxons blared as the massive ship quaked under the bombardment. Something crackled above Brag, but he ignored it as he strode onto the bridge.

"REPORT!" he bellowed.

"Engines failing, Captain," o'Shov shouted from the engineering console. The engineer on duty was unconscious on the floor. "Shields are gone. Manoeuvring thrusters are blown out along our port side. Our reactor is experiencing coolant failures. Whatever they hit us with, it did the job." Franks turned to his second officer when the herbivore didn't add anything more. The officer was staring at his captain. "We're losing our orbit, Captain."

Brag sighed, realising Adam had been right all along; which, of course, was when the crackling sound returned. He looked up, to see –with no small amount of horror- the bridge's massive transparent canopy cracking and fracturing all the way down to the lower level. To his eyes, it looked like a river out of control, cascading down the mountainside of his family's holdings on Karmana.

It was bad news no matter how he looked at it –it meant the ship's integrity fields were destabilizing along with everything else, and they were designed to keep going no matter what. The ship was breaking apart.

"EVERYONE OUT! RIGHT NOW!" he bellowed. Nobody argued, or even hesitated.

One officer tripped in the scramble to evacuate the massive bridge, causing a pile-up on the emergency stairs leading to the nearest exit. Brag shouted for them to pick themselves up, but apparently they had been hurt, the instigator clutching an ankle.

There was a scream of tortured glass, and then an ear-splitting roar as the vacuum of space tore the canopy away from the ship, in a cloud of shattered crystal.

Brag held onto the doorframe of the exit; he could only watch as those in the pile-up were wrenched into the black of space, kicking and screaming in sheer terror. Brag shut their screams out, wondering why the emergency forcefields were not already in place.

Because the power's been shut off to those systems, he groaned inwardly. Hands grabbed at him, and pulled him forcefully into the corridor outside. Still trying to catch his breath from the sudden explosive decompression of his bridge, he lay on the floor gasping for air. Those that had pulled him in were now using brute force to close the double doors that led to the abandoned bridge.

The force of the decompression was so strong it sucked one of the security guards trying to close the door out into space before he knew what was going on. As the door finally shut, the roaring of the ship's air supply rushing out the gap stopped, leaving the officers in silence. They all seemed to look accusingly at Franks, as if he had let this happen. He had seen that look before, after the destruction of the *Clementine Andover*. He had seen it in the mirror.

Maybe it was my fault, he worried. *Maybe I should never have let Adam Caine onto this ship, despite having had my suspicions from the very beginning. Even after I found out what and who he was, perhaps I should have refused to let him aboard. No; no matter what he did before, he was clearly being chased without provocation.*

He shook the thought off, letting himself worry about it later when they all survived.

For now, he had to get these officers off the ship, and save as many other people as possible.

"All hands," he called, after finally catching his breath. He hoped the computer had enough power to automatically transmit his order. "This is the Captain. Abandon ship. I repeat, all hands abandon ship immediately. This is not a drill." His heart sank as once again he said goodbye to his ship.

* * *

Dunn watched as the *Gold Royale* vented flames. Chunks of hull plating ripped off as it hit the atmosphere along with the front tip of the upper hull. Objects tumbled out of that section, and Dunn imagined that at least some of them must have been guests and some of the crew along with their belongings.

She sighed.

She would have to report to her superiors that Caine was dead.

There was no feasible way the man could survive a crash like that.

* * *

Adam and Eve had gathered their belongings and been barely a few seconds out of the door when they were thrown to the carpeted floor.

Adam was next to his daughter in a flash, checking her for injuries. She was crying, though she only had a couple of bruises. He was wearing his full black combat fatigues, with his rifle slung behind his back, and equipment pouches full of ammo and other combat gear. With the Odyssey creatures aboard, he was taking no chances.

The other uniforms he'd left behind in the suite, instead opting to stuff his large black Bergen with Eve's clothes, leaving enough room for his camouflage fatigues.

"Are you okay, Evie?"

She nodded through the tears. He scooped her up, and jogged down the corridor. Everybody on this floor seemed to be staying in their suites, as if that would protect them from the creatures, or whatever was happening to the ship itself. Now, it seemed, they were also hiding from the Navy battleship.

"We've got to get off this ship," he told her. "We can use the *Kara Marazov* to get as many others off as possible."

"What about Uncle Brag?"

Before he could answer, the corridor suddenly tilted to one side, and Adam found himself flying towards one of the walls. He managed to put himself between the wall and Eve. He slammed into the wall, and felt something crack in his side.

Probably yet another fractured rib. One more to add to my collection.

He winced as he picked himself off the deck, managing to prevent Eve from any harm.

"*All hands,*" Brag's voice issued from invisible speakers along the corridor and throughout the ship. "*This is the Captain. Abandon ship. I repeat, all hands abandon ship immediately. This is not a drill.*"

Brag hadn't taken a long time to come around to his way of thinking, though Adam wondered if it was too late for all of them.

The ship continued to shake around them, occasionally tipping as something else broke off. Adam eventually opted to walking with one hand against the wall to steady himself, and Eve, as they went.

Adam came to what he was sure was the main shuttlebay where the *Kara Marazov* was parked. The computer had been too busy with keeping the ship in one piece to give him directions. They stood outside the door when the deck tipped again, and the corridor suddenly swapped ceiling for floor as Adam went flying backwards, and crashed into something solid. Something else cracked in his chest.

He cried out, and realised that Eve was no longer in his arms.

She was screaming in pain, and Adam could see she had slipped out of his grip, and smacked against the wall as well. He panicked, the fathering instinct in him snapping him into action. Just as he was about to scoop her up in his big arms, she screamed even louder. He tried to find a source for the pain; she wasn't screaming in pain, she was looking over his shoulder.

The SA80 was in his hands in an instant.

It was some of the creatures, stalking almost silently down the corridor towards father and daughter, their grinning teeth glinting in the light of the overheads. Adam blew the head off the first one with a burst of three rounds, and then sprayed the rest on full auto, taking down half a dozen before the clip ran out with a dry clack.

The creatures charged, several of them dragging dead limbs from Adam's attack.

Adam didn't have time to change clips, instead choosing to place himself over Eve to protect her.

"Close your eyes, honey," he whispered before squeezing his eyes shut. He felt a tingling sensation throughout his body a moment before the creatures reached him.

* * *

The brood was hungry, and their master's prey was ahead.

Several of the brood were crippled, or outright murdered, by something white-hot that flashed and banged loudly in the target's hands, and tore the brood apart. Some of the brood turned on the injured and feasted on their flesh, whilst the rest launched themselves towards the master's prey.

Their hunger was almost unbearable.

Saliva flowed from their mouths.

Muscles pumping, they dove for the target.

And crashed into the floor.

The prey was gone.

* * *

Adam still had his eyes squeezed shut when he realised that he should have been dead. He opened one eye, then the other, and found that he and Eve were no longer in the corridor, but in the shuttlebay.

Brag Franks and Feyton stood over them at a cargo teleporter control console.

The captain had a grim look to him.

Adam couldn't blame him; he was about to leave his ship behind.

"What happened?" Adam asked.

"The Navy fired on us," Brag answered. Adam saw the sadness in his eyes, and wondered if the starship captain was feeling guilty about not being able to save everybody on board the *Gold Royale*. "The creatures are spreading like wildfire." He jerked a thumb over his shoulder. "Got as many passengers into the shuttles as possible, and your ship is filled with the remainders of the crew we could find. But there isn't much. Those things have probably got the rest. We cannot contact them anyway."

Adam picked up Eve, and they ran to the upright crescent-shaped ship.

Shuttle engines were throttling up, ready to lift off. The deck was rumbling and quaking under Adam's feet as they clambered into the *Kara Marazov*. A piece of the shuttlebay was torn out, dragging a shuttle with it to tumble into the planet's atmosphere.

"When the *Gold Royale* hits the ground, it will explode with the equivalent of several hundred megatons," Brag mentioned worriedly as they all strapped into the cockpit. Adam had left Eve in the back with the *Royale*'s doctor and head nurse. Eve had screamed for her daddy to stay, but he was needed to pilot the ship safely away from the *Gold Royale*. It was his ship after all, and he had shown he was a better flier than anybody else.

Lieutenant Commander o'Shov sat shivering in the fourth chair. He was as white as a sheet, shaking, and staring off into the distance. Adam was sure he was suffering from post-traumatic stress disorder, though didn't give it much thought until after the escape; an escape that was too far away for Adam to be able to envisage clearly.

The shuttlebay was continuing to disintegrate, equipment, bulkheads, and hull plating torn out and disappearing through the growing hole at one end of the massive shuttlebay doors. There was fire roaring across the hole, the ship's hull burning as it plummeted through the atmosphere.

"Where's the battleship?" Adam asked, looking to Feyton in the co-pilot's chair.

"She's turning away. Fighters are returning to the ship, and I am picking up an energy build-up that *has* to be their FTL drive warming up."

"Good," Adam grimaced. Brag could see in his friend's face that the former Royal Marine was setting himself to do something stupid. "Do the shuttles have FTL capability?" Brag and Feyton shook their heads. "Contact them, tell them to keep a stationary orbit on the far side of the planet, and call for help only when the coast is clear."

Feyton nodded, and did what she was told.

The shuttlebay doors were suddenly ripped to pieces and sucked out into the maelstrom created by the dying starship's surrounding wake.

Adam activated the anti-gravs and let the *Kara Marazov* hover above the deck for a few seconds. He then slammed the ship forward. It jumped out of the shuttlebay, and into the insane winds and fires of the liner's wake. The shuttles followed them out at random intervals, speeding into the turbulence that poured off the *Gold Royale*.

The last one out was too slow; it was hit multiple times by debris and hulled before tumbling away to slam against the liner's hull in a barely visible fireball.

The other shuttles were bounced about as they escaped and sped away through the atmosphere to the other side of the planet. The *Kara Marazov* didn't join them, instead hanging in mid-air, letting the *Gold Royale* drop away behind them.

Adam and the others watched the *Gold Royale* come apart bit-by-bit.

Brag held back the tears of sadness that desperately wanted to pour out. He had served as *Gold Royale*'s captain for twelve years. To see it all go up literally in flames was upsetting to say the least.

The massive remains of the *Gold Royale* plummeted toward the ground like a meteorite, leaving a trail of fire behind it that lit up the night side of the planet.

It hit the ground.

Brag only saw a flash.

A brief flash, and his beloved starship was gone forever.

Just a small flash.

And twelve years went up in smoke.

Smoke and dust spread across the planet below, turning the atmosphere a toxic grey and killing off anything it touched. The shockwave from the exploding reactor core flattened mountains and hills in every direction.

Adam was already turning the *Kara Marazov* away from the planet, framing the Terran battleship with the edges of the cockpit canopy. The engines were flaring an intense blue as the ship made the run-up to faster-than-light speeds.

Kara Marazov kept high orbit and watched the battleship disappear.

Adam turned to Brag.

"Any place you and your crew want to be dropped off?"

Brag sighed.

"I suppose I ought to get to the company's headquarters, deliver my report to the board of directors before they can hear whatever propaganda Navy Intelligence release to them and the public." Bag sighed heavily. "I have to explain my side of the story before it is twisted and corrupted by others."

"What planet?" Adam asked.

"Freya IV, on the edge of the Andromeda galaxy. Do you know where it is?"

Adam shook his head. "No, but I'm sure the computer can still set a course; if you're sure you want to go there. You could come with Eve and I. Both of you. I don't actually know where we'll go; maybe we'll just explore this universe."

Brag nodded solemnly.

There was a crackle of static from the comms unit, and the lights dimmed for a brief minute before silence descended on the cockpit. Adam was about to say something when the holographic projector on top of his control console suddenly jumped to life.

A cone of faint blue light projected onto the floor, ending in the twelve-inch image of a woman dressed in white, with her hair in two familiar buns.

It was Princess Leia.

She was looking directly at Adam.

Except, it wasn't Princess Leia. It was Silver; or at least, it looked like Silver. Adam had learned from her that appearances could be deceiving in many ways. Was this just a message implanted into the ship's computer to activate at a certain time?

The image of Silver bent down, and reached forward, as if to place a disk into something off-camera.

"Help me, Obi-Wan Kenobi. You're my only hope."

Then the image stood up, and reached out a pleading hand towards Adam before disappearing completely.

Having been subjected to Adam's *Star Wars* nights on the *Gold Royale*, Brag gawped at the fading after-image.

"That was surreal," he stated.

From the pilot's seat, Adam groaned in despair. "I'm getting used to it."

"Who is she?"

Adam sighed heavily, sagging in his chair.

"She's a friend in need." He sighed again. Something beeped on the control console. When Adam turned to check it out, he found that a set of spatial coordinates had been dumped into the computer's active memory. Was this where Silver was? Or was it something else entirely?

"You need any help?" Brag smiled.

"Possibly, but you need to get to Freya IV before N.I."

251

Adam found the location of Freya IV in the computer and set a course, before tentatively activating the ship's FTL drive. The stars outside turned into streaks of light, and then the *Kara Marazov* was gone.

* * *

Majors Dunn and Drummond stood before the holographic communications projector, waiting for their superior officer to return their hail.

The *Fortitude* was on a heading to Freya IV to the *Gold Royale*'s home base, where the two Intelligence officers would attempt to... *convince* the company's executives to be discreet about the matter at hand. With no evidence to prove anything other than whatever they told the executives, nobody would know any better.

The holo-projector flickered to life, and their aged commanding officer appeared before them, though the holo-picture kept flickering every now and then as the encrypted channel constantly kept it secure.

"Report," the grizzled human grumbled. Clearly, they had woken the old man from a decent night's sleep, though he was wearing his military uniform immaculately.

"We made contact with the *Gold Royale*, sir. They refused to hand over Caine."

"And? Do not waste my time when you could have made a full report through encrypted message."

"We sent two companies of Hunters over to board the liner. When they boarded, they were at first met with no resistance —at the time we assumed it was because the liner's crew were aware of what we were doing. We know for certain now that your ally's genetic creatures slaughtered them. We shot the cruise liner down."

The old man's face screwed in a mixture of surprise and rage.

"He promised me he would not interfere in our operations," the man grumbled. *"Damn him, and damn all of his race. Where are you now?"*

"The *Fortitude* is heading for Freya IV where we will meet with the company's chiefs. We have reviewed their files; we are certain they will bend under pressure."

The old man nodded.

"Good. What happened to Caine?"

Dunn and Drummond exchanged worried glances; Dunn let Drummond field this question.

"There was no evidence that he ever left the *Gold Royale* before it was destroyed; nor was there any evidence that any of the crew or passengers escaped either, so there are no witnesses to what happened, besides ourselves and the *Fortitude*'s crew."

Both intelligence agents could see the rage boiling up in their CO, and both worried that he may order the ship's crew to kill them both.

"If anybody finds out a Terran Navy warship was involved, there will be a universal uproar like nothing we have ever seen before. I do not want this to see the light of day, or we could all end up in prison, or worse. Do I make myself clear?"

"Yes, sir," Drummond and Dunn replied simultaneously.

Four-star General Lenson Gardner nodded, and then pressed something outside of the holo-camera's view, before the hologram disappeared completely from view. Dunn -the senior of the two- turned to her companion.

"Tell the *Fortitude*'s captain to push the FTL engines to maximum. I will try to contact Freya IV, and order their main security force there to let us through without incident."

Drummond nodded, whilst Dunn just stood there, staring at the empty space Gardner's hologram had previously occupied.

Even in death, Caine may bring us down.

* * *

The mysterious and somewhat melancholic form of the *HMS Fortitude* rumbled into orbit of Freya IV some two days later, her reactors, and FTL crystals nearing complete breakdown. The planetary security force had indeed made sure there was no interference with the battleship's entrance into the system, though only after Dunn threatened them with revealing some of their more heinous crimes against their own people to the rest of the universe.

"Prepare a landing party," Dunn ordered.

The ship's captain, still annoyed at being second fiddle on his ship, nodded reluctantly, following his orders. The ship had an Army unit on board, separate from the Hunters that hadn't been sent over to the *Gold Royale*. They would be the ones sent down with Dunn and Drummond; it was what they were trained for as part of the Fleet Protection Group, though as members of the *Fortitude*'s complement, they were made to wear black carapace in place of their greys.

One of the sensor officers called out.

"Captain! I am picking up a small ship exiting FTL speed directly below us. It looks like it came from along the same path as us."

"Could it have escaped from the *Gold Royale*?" the captain demanded.

"It is listed as being berthed on the *Gold Royale*, sir, though there is no owner listed in the inventory files we downloaded from the liner. It was the ship that escaped from our guns before we destroyed the *Royale*."

"No need to look it up," Dunn said from behind the two ship officers. Her arms were folded across her chest, and there was a massive frown on her severe face. "It can only belong to Adam Caine; he has a knack for survival. Destroy the ship before they can land on the surface."

* * *

"They're locking onto us," Adam announced.

The *Kara Marazov*'s finely-tuned sensors were aware of it instantaneously, though it wouldn't do a lick of good if the *Fortitude*'s massive weapons got a lucky hit on the smaller ship. As manoeuvrable as the *Kara* was, it was still only a small ship, and a battleship's weapons were designed to take on other battleships, and would wipe the *Kara* away without a fuss.

"I have the company's landing beacon on the sensors," Feyton reported.

"Lock onto it," Adam ordered. "See if you can get them to open up their hangars, assuming they have any down there. I really don't want to stay in orbit whilst they fuck about in their cushioned chairs."

He pushed the ship into a steep dive, directly toward the population centre that the beacon was transmitting from.

"We've broken the *Fortitude*'s weapons lock," Feyton added as the planet got bigger and bigger in the cockpit window. "But they're sending a squadron of Rhinos after us." She was pointing at the sensor readings, indicating the twelve smaller sensor reports swiftly moving directly towards the *Kara*.

"Dammit," cursed Adam.

Freya IV was a busy planet, commercially, or so Feyton had explained on the journey here. But the planet wasn't strategically important to any of the major races, nor was it on any of the major trade routes, though there was obviously some big trade here. With that in mind, Adam realised that the system was busier than it should have been.

There was a convoy of mass haulers in high orbit, along with a multitude of smaller freighters closer to the *Kara*'s size. There were the odd one or two piratical-looking starships that were leaving orbit in the opposite direction to the *Kara*.

Adam aimed for the mass haulers, hoping to lose the fighters among the press of larger ships like an asteroid field. Brag, returning from looking after his surviving crew in the rear of the ship, saw what he was doing, and groaned.

"Adam, this isn't the *Millennium Falcon*, they are not asteroids ahead, and those are not TIE-Fighters chasing us."

"Thankyou, C-3PO for pointing that out," grumbled Adam. He didn't pay attention, pumping more power into the sub-light engines. The mass haulers grew bigger impossibly quickly, looming ahead like giant asteroids, just as Brag had said.

"This is going to be rough," he added, before skimming the ship over the nearest hauler just as the Rhinos caught up to them. Adam dove the ship down the side of the hauler, twisting it onto its side as it did so. There was a thump and loud cursing from behind Adam; he didn't turn to see what it was, but realised that Brag hadn't strapped in before the manoeuvre.

"Thankyou for the warning," complained Franks.

"No problem," Adam quipped over one shoulder. He twisted the ship again, pulling it over and then under two different haulers. The majority of the Rhinos had broken off and gone wide over the entire convoy to try and cut the *Kara* off. But a flight of four of them darted in behind the *Kara*, sticking to their wing-pairs as best as they could.

They were good pilots, Adam noticed, but the *Kara*'s fine-tuned engines and manoeuvring thrusters outclassed them in a heartbeat. One tried to zip round a knot of communications masts, but the fighter was too cumbersome and slow to avoid the hidden second knot. It clipped the masts, shearing the wing off. It tumbled over, and slammed into its wingman, both disappearing in a bright orange fireball.

By this time, as Adam hurdled two more haulers, the convoy began to panic, blindly manoeuvring away from the action. One hauler tried to get out of its starboard neighbour's way, slamming into the one to its port side. The fireball chased the *Kara* and its pursuers out and into low orbit.

One of the chasing starfighters wasn't fast enough to escape the blast, and was engulfed in the flames of the dying haulers.

Flames erupted around the *Kara*'s shields as she dove through Freya IV's atmosphere. This was where Adam managed to get ahead of the remaining starfighters, his ship's streamlined hull letting it slip further ahead through the turbulent ionosphere, the fighters trailing behind.

They punched out directly above the landing beacon, staring down at the city below –a bird's-eye view. Feyton pointed to a large building at the edge of the city centre. There were ships coming and going from the roof of the structure, whilst hundreds of air-cars, trams, and vehicles weaved around the city itself.

Suddenly, the *Kara* lurched forward, the ship briefly vibrating as something hit from behind.

"What was that?" cried Adam.

"Sensors were blinded for a second," replied Feyton, her hands dancing over the console in front of her, "the lead fighter took advantage. He hit us with a pair of laser rounds. Shields are holding."

The ship shook again, and everybody was thrown forward into his or her restraints.

"Internal grav-generators are offline," Feyton announced, panic rising in her voice. Everybody was feeling the effects of having no artificial gravity, all of them being pulled toward the planet's surface within the confines of the cockpit.

Adam's stomach raged against the abuse, trying to unload its contents onto the flight controls. It didn't, thank Christ, though it came close.

"Adam, what are you doing?" asked Brag, who was becoming alarmed at the speed the ground was coming towards them.

"A little Han Solo stupidity," came the reply. He nudged the ship over to starboard, pointing the nose away from the beacon.

"Gods, you are insane," Franks exclaimed, tightening his seat's restraints, and shutting his eyes. Lieutenant Commander o'Shov was praying to his people's gentle gods, hoping that the ship would not slam nose-first into the city below. He could hear wailing from the bunkroom, and hoped Adam heard it too –maybe he would pull off if he knew Eve was crying her eyes out with fear.

"Adam, pull up," he commanded in his best captain's voice.

"I can't, not now, we're too close to getting to the hangar."

"It won't do us any good if we splatter against the ground, Adam," he pointed out.

The tallest of the city's buildings grew closer and closer, until Brag could almost reach out and touch it. He could see every detail of the roof, from the workers taking a secret puff on their bac-sticks; he could see the shining metal of the communications masts, and the individual bricks and mortar that made up the sides of the building.

The smokers looked up in sudden panic, and dove to the floor.

The building flashed past as Adam deftly slipped the *Kara* to one side to thunder down past the glass side of the skyscraper.

"GODS THAT WAS CLOSE!" he cried.

Adam slipped the ship under the air-traffic, missing family, police, and cargo vehicles by the narrowest of margins. The Rhino that had dogged the *Kara* didn't follow, instead pulling up and over the traffic, and then back towards the sky, though its sensors were still trained on the *Kara* as it raced through suddenly empty lanes of traffic.

Adam sank back into his seat, and breathed an audible sigh of relief.

* * *

1996ad.

Darkness covered Dartmoor like a blanket, the distant lights of Okehampton in the North and Exeter in the East almost impossible to see from the Tors. The moon was hidden behind dark, brooding clouds.

A squad of recruits, accompanied by an instructor acting as an observer, stepped carefully along the worn mud path under Oke Tor, moving in single file, trying not to put their heads above the hilltop to keep anyone from seeing their silhouettes.

They moved almost silently, each carrying full combat gear, an SA80 full of blanks and a large Bergen on their backs —at least for the duration for the night exercise.

They were the best of the recruits: the brightest.

They didn't stand a chance.

The rearguard disappeared without a noise, followed by the next two. The instructor hadn't seen what had taken them, but didn't tell the squad's leader that anyone was missing.

It was only until one more was taken that someone called out in alarm from the squad, and the squad leader called a halt next to a large collection of dry bushes.

A pair of hands whipped out from the bush, and pulled the squad leader into the flora.

The vanguard recruit suddenly looked alarmed as someone else from the squad disappeared, leaving him and the instructor alone. He was visibly concerned, scanning the bushes with his blank-filled rifle.

Something snapped behind him. He turned to see what it was, and instantly realised his obvious mistake. He didn't get his rifle up in time, as Recruit Caine leaped out of the bushes, grabbed the rifle barrel, and swept his fellow recruit's legs out from under him with a low spinning kick.

The instructor was dumbfounded enough that he forgot to call an end to the exercise. Caine moved towards him, prompting a shout.

"End ex!"

Caine nodded and stood at the parade easy position.

He was covered in a well-made ghillie suit covered in long grass, his exposed face plastered with black and green camo paint.

"When I started this exercise, I was expecting you to lose, Caine. Where did you learn to operate like that?"

"My father's groundskeeper was a former Commando, Corporal. He taught me everything he knew, including survival craft."

The instructor just shook his head.

"You are without doubt the stealthiest sonunvabitch I have ever seen or heard of, Caine."

"Thankyou, Corporal," replied Caine, beaming with pride.

"Now go and untie your fellow recruits."

* * *

3988ad.

Franks woke up in one of the *Clementine Andover*'s escape pods.

He didn't know how long he had been there, nor even where the pod had ended up. He presumed the Nonian Arbiter had indeed left him alone for the Navy to find him.

It didn't take long for them to arrive.

The frigate HMS Four Seasons dropped out of FTL speed and quickly brought the escape pod in.

When the door opened, and the frigate's commander peered in, he frowned.

"Captain Franks? Where's your crew?"

With bloodshot eyes, and tears streaming down his cheeks, Franks answered.

"They're all dead."

* * *

4000ad.

"*WHAT?!*"

Dunn could practically feel Gardner's rage even through the holographic communications. The man might have been old, but there was a reason he had stayed Director of Navy Intelligence for over half a century.

"We think it was Caine that escaped in that blue ship," Dunn winced.

"*CAINE? YOU ASSURED ME HE WAS DEAD!!*"

"There was no evidence to suggest he was anything but dead, sir," Drummond complained, a little too hurriedly. "It was not until we saw the little blue ship that we realised that it could only be Adam Caine."

"He is a born survivor, sir," Dunn interjected to assist her colleague.

Gardner glared daggers at her, making the senior Major stand back a little, worried that the old general might have actually found a way of strangling someone via holographic communications. He did not attempt it, though she still looked at him warily, something she was sure would please him immensely.

"*Did you at least contact the company executives? Did you at least accomplish that much? Or are you so incompetent you could not even do that simple little task?*"

"Negative, General," replied Drummond. "They were jamming us the moment the *Kara Marazov* locked onto their beacon."

"*What is the* Kara Marazov?"

"Caine's ship. We could only get a silhouette of the thing; it is made of some material we are not aware of. It is definitely something to be worried about."

"*Well, at least we gained something from this whole debacle. Caine no longer has a base of operations, and is mobile. It is a start, at least.*" He let out a massive breath, folding his arms uncomfortably across his chest. "*Make sure there are no witnesses. Caine will be a problem, though my... ally believes he can destroy him once and for all. Alpha-1 out.*" Gardner jabbed a control off-camera, and the transmission ended.

"He must be angry to use his 3899 codename," Dunn commented. "Order the captain to get moving to the outer edge of the system. Caine will be too careful to have us notice him leave. He will probably be seen whenever he wants to be seen."

* * *

The early morning wind blasted a deep chill across the landing pad.

Adam and Brag stood on the edge of the pad, the *Kara Marazov* standing behind them, the company's techs having prepped the ship for a quick takeoff. They both watched the skies, knowing that the *Fortitude* was still up there.

"What will you do now?" asked Brag. All the *Gold Royale* survivors they had brought to Freya had been interviewed, and debriefed. The company held Franks and his crew blameless -had even offered them all jobs on the new liner that was near completion. Franks had agreed to consult on how the security procedures and such, for the new ship, would be put in place.

"Go to the coordinates Silver left for me," his friend replied.

"Do you trust her?"

"It's not a matter of trust; she's helped me in the past, so I've no reason not to trust her. I just hope I can find out what's going on before anything bad happens. That's assuming something bad hasn't already happened."

The two continued to stare into the sky.

"Captain Caine," the chief technician called out. "Your ship is ready for lift-off."

"Thankyou, chief," Adam nodded. The tech strode off toward the hangar entrance, leaving the two friends alone on the rooftop. Eve was in the ship, probably in her pyjamas, getting out of bed.

"*Captain* Caine?" Brag smiled. "That's a step up from Warrant Officer or Commander."

"I'll see you soon, *Captain* Franks."

The two laughed for a good few minutes, before Adam gave his friend a great big bear hug. The two separated and gave each other a big smile, before Adam plunged his hands into his pockets, and sauntered off to his beautiful ship. The big man didn't wave, or blow a kiss, as Brag had half-expected from the strange time-traveller.

The *Kara Marazov* hummed as its anti-gravs kicked in, and the landing struts folded into the ship's lower main fin. It span on the spot, and then lifted into the sky, a lot more sedately than it had done so before, as if Adam was completely relaxed about being close to his shadowy enemies.

Brag saluted the ascending ship.

"Good luck, Captain Caine."

* * *

SENDER: [Unknown]
RECIPIENT: [Unknown]
MESSAGE ORIGIN: HMS Fortitude
MESSAGE RELAYED VIA: 40 Unmarked Civilian Relay Buoys; Navy Intelligence Headquarters (Delta-Tango system)
TRANSMISSION SENT: 20/06/4000AD
TRANSMISSION RECEIVED: 20/06/4000AD
Alpha-9 and I will continue to look out for signs of Caine's mystery ship.
Alpha-9 suggested we speak to Franks.
I am in agreement.
Alpha-8 out.

* * *

A week later.

Soft sunlight wafted over verdant jungles of lush green, equally sending shafts of light and shadow down on the undergrowth below. Animals screeched in protest at the canopy, shunning the rays, and sticking to the surrounding darkness. The jungles spread across the planet like an unstoppable plague, broken only by the peaks of mountains and the tips of ancient ruined structures, standing defiantly against nature's slow-burning wrath.

At the centre of a massive clearing, stood a mature human woman, waiting patiently and watching the clear sky for a sign of things to come.

It came in the form of a dark dot in the sky, steadily growing larger as the object came closer to her.

The dot formed into a cross, the vertical line longer than the horizontal.

It didn't take a direct route, the object gracefully sliding out to her right and then circling at a distance around behind the ancient temple. It came into full view as it swung toward her, slipping through the breeze effortlessly.

It wasn't a big starship; in fact it was pretty small: a vertical crescent coloured a brilliant pale blue with tiny horizontal crescent wings and a triangular cockpit window that was blacked out from outside viewing.

The graceful ship slowed in front of the woman, anti-gravs humming loudly, kicking up the dust of the dead underbrush. Curved landing struts folded out of the lower fin to touch down on the dusty ground. The engines cycled down to standby, followed by an eerie absence of noise.

A hatch opened above the left wing, and out stepped Adam Caine.

* * *

"Are you sure about this, daddy?" Eve worried, still holding his hand as the two stepped onto the *Kara Marazov*'s port wing.

Adam desperately wanted to lie to her, and tell her everything was all right, but the words refused to form on his lips. Even from this distance, Adam was sure the woman down below was another of Silver's race. The problem was that his experiences with their race was not entirely a good one: Silver was a mysterious personality who had so far given Adam cryptic clues to his own nature and support during his internment. But the other side of that coin was Gold, who had been consistently trying to kill him.

It was a fifty-fifty chance that this newcomer was going to be friendly.

"Stay with the ship, Evie," he commanded, ushering his adopted daughter back into the airlock. She complained, but complied with the order, huffing and sulking as she returned inside.

Adam stared at the woman, and hoped she was an ally. He wasn't up to more fighting; he was still healing from his injuries sustained during the *Gold Royale*'s destruction. But this was the coordinates Silver had left in the *Kara*'s computer, so he had come here anyway, leaving his friend Brag on Freya IV to fend for himself for a while.

It looked like it should be a scene from an Indiana Jones movie, with the ancient temples, and sinister jungle. The woman just continued to stand there, arms folded like some schoolteacher, watching him even as he climbed down the side of his ship. He hit the floor with a puff of dust, and strolled over to the woman.

"Staff Sergeant Caine," the woman nodded in greeting.

"So what do I call you?" he asked in return, stopping two paces in front of her as if he were on parade. "Platinum? Diamond? Ruby?"

The woman smiled.

"Diamond will do I suppose; as a human, I doubt that you would be capable of pronouncing my given name." It sounded to Adam like an arrogant response given the circumstance, though he was sure it had something to do with her own superiority complex simply from being a member of her time-oriented race.

"How do you know who I am?"

The woman smiled, and it didn't ease Adam's worries one bit.

"The same way your friend Silver does," she shrugged, as if that were a comforting answer for him. "As I am sure you know, my people are able to view events in time just as you would walk through a museum, viewing but not able to touch the displays."

"Where is she? She left a message in my ship's computer that she needed help, and left the coordinates of this planet."

"She left me a similar message," Diamond sighed. She gestured toward the temple, stepping to one side to indicate that he walk by her side. Adam gave one last worried look towards the cockpit, where he saw Eve waving from behind the window. He gave her a wave, and a smile, and then followed Diamond.

"Her message indicated that I should help you, because of your associations with the one you call Gold." She saw the scowl appear on his face. "My apologies; I am not as good with your language as Silver; I was referring to your conflicts with him and his agents so far." The scowl disappeared, and a look of understanding passed over him. "Outside those of my own race, you are the only being capable of hurting my kind, or have shown the willingness to do so."

"Is that why I'm here? To swap stories about past battles?"

Diamond stopped.

"No; to teach you about *future* battles." She turned to face him, and looked him straight in the eyes, the same piercing stare that Silver used when she had something terribly important to impart to him, which to be fair, was all the time. "You have a destiny, whether you chose to acknowledge it or not; and even if you do not, you need more skills than you currently have to be able to beat Gold and his agents and survive."

"I've been doing pretty well so far," he retorted.

Suddenly she grabbed his shoulder, the one he had wrenched during the frantic escape from the dying *Gold Royale*. He cried out in pain as her sudden crushing grip ripped muscles in his shoulder joint. He didn't move or collapse, didn't lash out at Diamond.

"Are you truly ready?" she smiled; and it wasn't a good smile.

Adam nodded.

"Then let us begin."

"Begin what?" he said through gritted teeth.

She didn't answer, instead just walking away, leaving him cradling his shoulder.

"Begin what?"

Again she didn't answer, still walking away towards the temple.

"BEGIN WHAT?!" he shouted.

The realisation that she wasn't going to give him a straight answer, or an answer of any kind, made him pause for a few minutes.

"Dammit."

* * *

In the jungle, a bush moved of its own accord, rustling its leaves as it shook with every movement. It occasionally passed through the shafts of light slashing down from the canopy above. The movements weren't big, in fact it barely moved in the slight warm breeze.

The daylight was fading above the trees, vines wrapping around trunks, stretching towards the sunlight as if wanting to desperately touch the sun.

From the bush protruded the very tip of a dark metal cylinder.

The cylinder let out a small spark, and a sharp whisper of noise.

Something large crashed down into the undergrowth in the distance.

"Well done," a voice said. The bush moved finally, two legs appearing underneath, a pair of arms either side holding a silenced solid-round sniper rifle.

Diamond appeared from nothingness, materialising by Adam's side before the two strode toward the source of the crashing noise.

"They really did train you well in your prior military service," Diamond allowed as they walked. She had her hands clasped behind her back like a parade ground officer. "You were also taught to shoot by your father's groundskeeper, yes?"

Adam eyed her suspiciously.

"You *have* done your homework."

"I have seen your past," Diamond reminded him. They strode through the undergrowth. Adam was dressed in jungle fatigues that Diamond had issued him, and a ghillie suit he had put together using a bundle of spare wiring from some derelict machinery, and wads of the local fauna. The rifle was another gift from Diamond, somehow having obtained an Intervention sniper rifle, complete with four magazines of solid ammo, and a customised silencer. Every now and again he unconsciously fingered the pistol grip and the forward handgrip, strangely reassured by its familiar presence.

"If you've seen my past, you know I left the service."

"As I saw it, you left for the right reasons," she replied nonchalantly. "There are few who can say that, especially in regards to your previous line of work. Granted, you are untamed, but you have the ability to endure, to move on."

"Is that a request, or an order?"

"A suggestion," she shrugged.

They rounded a particularly large tree trunk, and discovered the remains of Adam's target. It was a lizard, of a sort, though it was longer than thirty metres, with an oversized stupid-looking head, eight legs, four eyes, and scales thick enough to make super-heavy tanks hesitate.

"Godzilla's got nothing on this guy," Adam commented quietly as the two figures stood beside the head of the beast, the head itself higher than either one of them. The creature had no apparent sign of injury, except for a river of blood pouring from the eye Adam's bullet had ruined. He had half-expected its brain to be somewhere completely alien, like its belly, but it apparently conformed to most biological similarities with Earth's own lizards.

"This is a Ramnja, not a Godzilla," Diamond remarked scoldingly. "The local tribes used to use them as beasts of burden."

"They don't anymore?"

Diamond shook her head. "A lethal virus wiped out the tribes several centuries ago, leaving behind their temples, and freeing their enslaved animals. This planet has become a haven for criminals attempting to flee your friends in the Terran Navy, hence how you found that piece of machinery to hold your camouflage together." She eyed the ghillie suit as if it were about to jump up and bite her, rustling in the breeze as it was.

Adam looked at her with no small amount of alarm. Diamond saw the look, and reassured him the virus was no longer a threat.

"There's probably some form of it on this planet; there's a mercenary enclave on the opposite side of the equator —I'm sure one of them caught it at some point."

"So now that I've killed this Ramnja, what now?"

Diamond let out a sigh.

"We supplement your prior skills with better endurance and stamina."

"Are you seriously trying to say I'm unfit?" he demanded, his voice a low growl at the perceived slight against him.

"You are truly aggravating, Adam Caine. By human standards, you are truly a remarkable specimen, but the universe is a much bigger place than just the human race; you have shown resilience to pain and injury, and won against incredible odds, yet that is only the beginning, for you and for the universe."

His eyes narrowed suspiciously.

"Do you believe in destiny?"

Diamond unclasped her hands, and idly fingered the scales on the dead lizard, as if in a world of her own. She let go of a long sigh, making Adam curious to know if her race actually needed to breathe, or if it was just a reflex action.

"I believe in time," she answered finally, as if that were a real answer. "Time is everything, time is everywhere —all we have in life is time."

Adam opened his mouth to say something sarcastic, but the words caught in his throat when he saw the sad look in Diamond's eyes. It was ever so brief, but it was definitely there, a flash of real, vulnerable emotion hidden behind that ancient, mysterious face. The flash disappeared, and Diamond's defences were raised again, her stony gaze boring into him as he realised he was staring.

"Come, we must begin your training." She spun, and strode away, or marched as Adam saw it.

"I know I'm-"

* * *

"-Gonna regret this."

The jungle was gone in a flash of familiar squirming white light, replaced by a mountainside. Except it wasn't a normal mountain; there was ash clogging the air, and smoke, and the sky was dark, darker than night itself.

Angry orange colours highlighted the smoke that hung over his head, bathing Adam in the same colours. Intense heat raged at him, making him perspire instantly.

He was no longer holding his sniper rifle, though the fatigues and gillie suit were still there.

"A volcano? You're kidding me right?"

"I am afraid not," Diamond retorted. She was standing there, calm-as-you-like, completely ignoring the raging volcano around them. "This is your first true test, at least as far as I am concerned."

"What kind of test?"

"Endurance." With one finger, she pointed to something beside him, something he hadn't noticed before. He swore when he realised she was pointing at a lava flow that was emerging from the rocky ground.

And it was rolling directly toward him.

"Run," she commanded.

So he did.

He bound down that volcano as if his life depended on it; which in fact it did. The lava was increasing speed as it rolled down the mountain after him, like wrath itself bearing down upon him in the dark of the smoke cover.

This chase was worse than the escape from Yh'reth'gar's flagship, harder and faster than the chase through Fayde City, and more frightening than the battles on Odyssey Station and the dying *Gold Royale*. He was racing down a rocky mountainside, every footstep bringing the possibility of slipping and falling, or the rock underneath his feet crumbling and causing his fall.

He bound from rock to rock, the heat unbearable as the lava kept coming. He stumbled once, almost tumbling to his death, as his combat boot caught in a hidden divot, throwing him forwards onto an outcropping. The lava spat at him even as he tumbled, landing on his side, once again breaking a rib.

"Why is it always my ribs?" he wheezed to the heavens. The lava splashed over the lip of the outcropping, flinging tiny particles at him, singing his uniform, and burning the gillie suit. He shrugged the camo off, and hopped off the outcropping, just as it was overcome by the liquid hot magma.

He raced off once again, hobbling down the rock, his every breath an effort of sheer will, pain racing through his ribs, ash and smoke clogging his lungs.

There was a rumbling from underneath his feet, followed by a hissing noise. When Adam glanced to one side, he noticed steam rushing out of the ground in thin geysers, bleeding off into the atmosphere. It didn't look good, even to Adam's unscientific eyes. The rumbling grew stronger, resonating through his body as the lava built up under the ground, contained by the massive amounts of rock around it.

The ground shook.

"Crapcrapcrapcrapcrapcrapcrapcrapcrapcrap."

Arms out for balance, legs pumping, Adam forgot his own safety, and charged down the mountain, ignoring the crumbling rock, ignoring the smoke and the flow of lava behind him.

The volcano was about to experience a blow-out, followed by a pyroclastic flow. He had seen it on the news back home: Mount St. Helens in the States, and Mount Etna in Sicily. Pyroclastic flows were an incredibly destructive force for buildings and towns, let alone a single human being: a massive wave of ash and debris that wiped out all life in its path.

The world shook.

Adam fell as the ash and debris was thrown into the dark sky. He hit his head on a blunt rock. His vision threatened to black out under the pain and stars flashed in front of his eyes. He was up in an instant, tentatively aware of the danger from all around.

The ash and debris were dragged down from the sky by the planet's gravity, directly towards him.

So he ran, once more fighting through the pain, as he always did.

He didn't dare look back in case it distracted him from keeping his balance, and let the flow finish him off.

There was a small structure at the bottom of the rise, about the size of a pillbox. It was round, and grey, like many military structures, especially in the forty-first century. He hoped to God it was also as strongly built as many other contemporary Terran technologies.

It felt like hours went by as he charged down the mountainside, when in fact it had only been a minute or so. He dove through the doorway, landing on the floor in an uncomfortable heap.

Diamond stood over him, arms folded across her chest, an amused look on her face.

"I suggest you close the door before we are both vaporised by that pyroclastic flow," she said, pointing out the door in the direction Adam had just come from.

"Huh?"

He looked round just as the lava and the ash and debris were about to hit the bunker. He jumped at the door, slamming the heavy metal plating shut. The impact on the other side jerked Adam away, the wave of destruction rumbling eerily around them.

"What the hell kind of endurance test was that?" he cried, finally catching his breath, and cradling his damaged ribs.

"I never said the test had finished," Diamond replied.

Adam stared at her silence, before the bunker disappeared in a flash of the same squirming white. He was disheartened to see that he was stood back at the top of the volcano, to one side of the lava flow, and *behind* the wave of destructive ash.

"Off you go," Diamond told him, nodding down the mountain with what he thought looked like an actual smile. She turned round, and there was once again a tug of a smile on her lips. Adam didn't need to turn around to know there was another river of magma behind him; he could feel the intense heat on his back.

So Adam ran.

Diamond subjected him to this test three more times without healing his injuries.

After the fourth consecutive run, catching his breath in the bunker, Diamond gave a harrumph of annoyance.

"You truly are a remarkable specimen, Adam Caine."

Then everything turned white, and they were back on the concourse next to the *Kara Marazov*.

Adam attempted to stand, stumbling as he did so. In the distance, far away on the horizon, he could see a plume of smoke rising into the air. The volcano had to have been a few hundred miles away even though Adam was still wheezing from the smoke inhalation.

"You passed with, what you humans call, flying colours."

"I thought I was supposed to be training, not take fuckin' tests. If you've seen my past, then you know what I will pass and what I will fail!" She nodded at this. "Then why bother putting through these tests? Why not just train me?"

She leaned against the lower fin of the *Kara*, giving out a harrumph of frustration and resignation.

"For the kind of training you require, to be taught is to do."

Adam looked at her blankly.

"The only way to teach you is to put you in a dangerous situation where you have to use alternate methods to complete your objectives. Running around obstacle courses and shooting ranges is not necessary; this is not going to be anything like your Lympstone training barracks."

"Oh."

"Heal, and then you will be sent into your training situation."

She strode away, leaving Adam thoroughly confused. When he climbed onto the *Kara*'s port wing, little Eve was waiting for him, impatient as only a six-year-old girl could be.

"Daddy!" she cried, as she saw his wounds.

"I'm okay, Evie," he winced. He stumbled into the tiny med-bay, or cabinet as Adam had once called it. It was about the size of a cabinet; with the bio-bed stood several degrees diagonally back from sheer vertical, hidden straps apparent for patients not willing or physically unable to stay in the bed. He leant against the table and activated the alien medical scanner with a few terse words.

A holographic representation of his innards shimmered beside him, in front of the floor-to-ceiling consoles. According to the scan, he had two broken ribs, a fractured forearm, and a dozen burns from the spitting lava.

The medical computer automatically activated the regeneration unit, though he was sure it would only be able to heal the broken bones, and disinfect the burns. For some reason, the med-comp wasn't capable of regenerating skin, at least not anymore. According to the computer, it had been able to once, but for some unknown technical reason, it couldn't.

Tingling sensations shivered over his body, as blue rays of healing energy spread across him. He spent an hour in that bed, Eve watching nervously from the tiny corridor. When the blue light dissipated, he breathed easily, rubbing his chest where the fast healing had left him sore.

"Are you okay, Daddy?"

He smiled at his green-skinned daughter, and opened his arms. She bounced into him, wrapping her arms around his legs.

"Are we staying Daddy?"

"For a short while. But you've got to stay with the ship." He kneeled down, and gave her a big bear hug, lifting her up in the air. She giggled incessantly. "C'mon, let's have some dinner." He strode into the cockpit, put her in the rear passenger seat, and unfolded a table that was attached to the arm of the chair. It slid over Eve's lap neatly, effectively trapping her in the seat so he could get the dinner.

He stepped back into the corridor, and returned with two plates of steaming hot food from the ship's food dispenser, a device that worked much like the replicators in *Star Trek*, using the same energy as the healing device to create and cook food from nothing.

The two ate in silence, though purely because Eve was constantly stuffing her face with the alien nourishment. Adam thought the food tasted bland, but Eve's taste buds were apparently able to enjoy it more. Besides, the stuff looked like an expensive Chilli con carne and was supposed to be full of all the nutrients, vitamins, and proteins that the body needed in a day.

He had barely eaten half of his dinner when she started literally licking her plate clean.

"Evie, I know we're not in company, but licking your plate clean is kind of a no-no in most societies."

"Why?"

He shrugged, trying to think of a logical answer.

"Most people just don't think it's polite."

"Don't you like licking your plate?"

He chuckled.

"Of course, but I haven't finished my dinner yet."

She nodded as if this was an acceptable answer. She yawned, tired from her impatient wandering around the ship.

"C'mon you, off to bed," he smiled.

"M'okay, Daddy," she pouted. She pushed the swing-table away from her, and jumped off the seat. Adam followed her, making sure she got changed rather than simply jump into her bunk with her regular clothes on as he had the habit of doing.

She closed her eyes under the fluffy duvet, and before long was in the land of nod, leaving Adam to contemplate what Diamond could possibly have in mind for him.

* * *

He found out.

The hard way.

She had had no intention of putting him through any special training mission.

"I am sorry for disappointing you, Adam Caine," Diamond had announced the morning after his volcano running, "but due to unforeseen circumstances, your training mission has been postponed. For the next six weeks, you will be expected to follow a rigorous regime of exercise drills, followed by martial arts drills, and then a random exercise in the jungle each day."

"Bollocks," Adam had muttered under his breath.

So, every day for six weeks he lifted weights and performed cardio-vascular exercises, followed by martial arts training that he had never experienced before, though had heard of similar styles being created on Earth. It was similar to something called Kaysee, a mixture of different styles jumbled together to give a wider variety of ability.

The six weeks went by in a flash of sweat, pain, and profuse use of foul language on Adam's part until one day Diamond declared that he was finally ready.

He had hunted dangerous predators through the jungle, some of which had come very close to killing him; he had learned the martial arts to a high degree; he had become stronger and faster than he ever had thanks to the aerobic exercises.

He was shattered.

"You may have a day of rest," she allowed.

Of course, as soon as he sat down on the temple steps, she sat down as well, one eye constantly watching Eve as the little girl finally got out of her exile inside the ship. She was skipping around -chasing what Adam thought was probably a pet of Diamond's, or perhaps simply a very genial, curious feline.

"You were right," said Adam, as he chewed on a slice of bread from the ship.

"Regarding?"

"This really isn't like Lympstone. You're harsher than my instructors there for starters, and I haven't climbed a single piece of wooden obstacle throughout."

"The universe is a more dangerous place than twenty-first century Earth ever was. There are wholly different dangers than you've faced before, or at least before you came to this century. You need extra training to be able to deal with whatever people like Gold can throw at you."

"Why are your people so scattered?" he asked all of a sudden.

There was a hint of a sad smile tugging at the edges of her mouth.

"There are few of us, and we each have our own way of seeing the universe. Some of us, like Silver, work behind the scenes to ensure others fight the good fight, whilst several like Gold simply want power and dominion over others."

"And you? Where do you fit in to it all?" He said this through a mouthful of bread, still hungry from the day's exertions. The sun was setting over the jungle's horizon, beating down on the temple's steps like a hammer, impossibly brighter and stronger than the midday sun.

"I...I am just the instructor, nothing more."

"You haven't *wanted* more?"

Again, the tiny fragment of a sad smile.

"Like your own people, mine were once part of a great interstellar empire. But in our arrogance, we believed we could control the space-time continuum itself. We tore ourselves apart through civil war that lasted for millennia."

"The war wasn't just in space was it? You fought throughout time." He put the plate aside; he was more interested in the story of Diamond's people than the plate of old food.

"The war ended when one of our kind sacrificed their physical body to destroy our ability to move through time. Oh, we can still be there and watch the events unfold, but we can no longer interact as we used to."

Eve was screaming with laughter as the little feline pounced on her, and started licking her face. Adam smiled at the sight, glad that even in this miserable place, and after all that had happened, Eve was able to have some kind of innocent fun. He wondered how long that would last whilst being with him on his journeys.

"You are worried you may become a bad influence on her," said Diamond when she saw his look of concern on his face. He could only nod in agreement.

"What kind of a life would she have with me?"

"You are her father, biological or not. What you tell her, she will listen to."

Adam was suddenly looking at Diamond in a new light; that sounded like the kind of comment that only a parent could make.

"You had children?"

When she didn't answer, he was sure there was something she was hiding, hiding something from him specifically.

"I had a son," she finally answered. "But he was wayward, and wanted more than our people could give him."

He didn't know how, but he was sure he had already met this wayward son.

"Gold."

The shock on her face would have been priceless if the subject matter weren't so serious.

"If Gold is your son, why have you not done anything about him? Why have you not stopped him from allying with the Core, or breeding those genetically-engineered creatures?"

She stood up angrily, and Adam had the sudden urge to run to the ship and take off. It had only just occurred to him what pissing off this woman might mean for his personal well-being.

"If Evelyn turned evil, could *you* kill her to stop her?"

"If it meant saving millions of lives?" He thought about it for a second. "Yes."

She was taken aback by his severe honesty, and the anger dissipated from her face.

"Perhaps you truly are the Strand that Silver believes you to be."

With that, she walked away, climbing the steps of the stone temple until she passed through an open doorway, and disappeared from sight.

Adam wolfed down the remainder of the plate of food before walking with Eve back to the ship. The little feline ran off to be with whatever parents it had, presumably nearby. Eve waved it goodbye before it disappeared into the jungle.

Both slept soundly that night.

* * *

Diamond came the next morning, just after breakfast. She seemed warier of him than before, their previous conversation obviously unsettling her more than she had anticipated.

She was carrying a large suitcase in one hand.

"You have one hour to ready yourself," she declared before turning away.

Inside he found a black one-piece suit of some kind of armour-weave, with a masked hood. The eyepieces were green, and the suit itself was laced with electronic wiring of some kind.

A round disk about the size of Adam's palm was attached to the inside of the suitcase. It flickered to life, projecting a two-inch-high hologram of Silver into mid-air above the suitcase. Curiously, this time, she was wearing the brown and cream robes of a Jedi Knight, indicating a strange sense of humour.

"Hello again, Adam. This is not so much a gift as me issuing you your new uniform. This is a Normec nx-1 stealth suit; it's only a prototype at the moment, but I managed to get my hands on one and sent it to your instructor to give to you. The material is an armour-weave capable of deflecting energy weapons, and infused with a camouflage property that lets its wearer literally blend in with the background, though it is far from being an invisible suit. The wiring weaved through the suit is made of a specific metal that protects the wearer from electronic attack." She paused briefly, as though collecting her thoughts together.

"The helmet-mask's wiring also includes psychic inhibition circuitry, to prevent any stray thoughts from being heard by even the strongest telepath. I have also included, with the suit, a plasma carbine; essentially it is a smaller version of the Terran Navy plasma rifle.

"Good luck, Adam, and maybe I'll see you soon."

* * *

Exactly one hour later, Adam was ready, feeling like an utter pratt in the skin-tight suit. He had slung the Intervention over his shoulder, letting it rest against his back. He held the plasma carbine by the stock in one hand, with his P99 sidearm holstered on his hip. He had donned the helmet-mask, trying to get used to seeing everything in different spectrums. Although the eyepieces appeared green from the outside, he could switch to see everything in full colour, infrared, ultraviolet, and several others he did not recognise, all selected from the wafer-thin control panel on his forearm.

"You look like an assassin," Diamond commented.

Adam harrumphed, and rolled his eyes behind the blank mask.

Diamond gestured for him to come closer as she did the same.

"Did Silver know she was going to be captured?" His voice came from the mask distorted, deepened almost to a baritone growl, modified by an electronic strip that pressed on his throat and his vocal chords.

"She must have," the not-woman replied, "otherwise she would not have prepared all this for you. Perhaps after you destroyed Gold's chance to invade Earth in the past it became inevitable he would find her and capture her. I am surprised he did not kill her. Perhaps he is keeping her alive in order to draw you in and kill *you*."

Adam gave out a long sigh. "I wouldn't put it past him."

They faced each other.

"What is my training mission then?"

Once again, she took on the air of the overbearing instructor.

"You are to infiltrate the mercenary enclave on the other side of the planet. There you will find a particularly nasty character called Garvion. He is their leader, and has been threatening several of the nearby star systems. You are to take him out, and any who resist you. I do not have any details on the enclave's structure, or those within; let that be part of your self-training."

"Anything else I should know?"

Diamond shook her head, and then nodded once.

The flash of squirming white light covered his vision, and then was gone in an instant.

He was definitely no longer in the jungle. In fact, he was currently standing on the roof of a tall building that resembled an air traffic control tower in the twenty-first century, except its sides were curved rather than straight like old human architecture. Aerials and satellite dishes jutted out from the building around him. He turned round, trying to get a better look at the enclave. It wasn't as big as he thought it might be, though it was still large enough to be considered a military base. None of the architecture was the same from building-to-building, except the two hangars next to the tower he was standing on, which looked decidedly human in origin.

Other buildings were of different shapes and sizes, some domes, some inverted domes, one even being a collection of small pods connected by metal tunnels, and a central larger pod.

A ship lifted off through the roof doors of one of the hangars, blazing a contrail into the evening sky. *Another thing I must get used to*, he reminded himself, *it was morning back at the temple, but it's nearly night here on the other side of the world.*

The ship was the twin-hulled freighter he had seen rush past the *Gold Royale* on that fateful day before the nightmare of Odyssey Station. It reminded him of the ocean-going catamarans of Earth, though there were no sails, and this ship was nowhere near as sleek.

Darkness was falling over this area of the planet, and the exterior lights of the enclave were coming online. The calls of predator animals and their panicking prey could be heard in the background, out in the pervasive jungle that surrounded the enclave as much as it did Diamond's temple.

Two yards from his feet there was a round hatch with a strong latch. He bent down, twisted it, and gently lifted the hatch a crack so he could see in. It wasn't an air traffic control tower as he had initially suspected, but a security post that watched over the whole facility like some giant steel sentinel.

There were three armed figures inside.

If this was really a security post, then he would need to take out all of the guards so that none could get off a warning. He checked his inventory, and found no grenades he could use to take them all out at the same time.

So he screwed a silencer onto his P99, and aimed it into the gap between the hatch and its frame. He squeezed the trigger, blowing out the brains of the first guard, splattering the matter across the window. The other two jumped up from their seats in alarm, shocked by the suddenness of their comrade's death. Adam shot the second guard in the head, before shooting the third in two of his four legs; he would need one alive to show him how to permanently deactivate the enclave's entire security system so he could move around the base at will.

He jumped down into the room, to find every window framed with dozens of monitors and computer consoles, and he had little to no experience with forty-first century computers. He was suddenly glad that he had kept the other guard alive.

He placed the barrel/silencer of his pistol against the forehead of the three-armed, four-legged guard.

"Deactivate the enclave's security system," he growled. The guard was shivering with pain, eyes wide as the shock set in. "Do it, or I'll blow your brains out."

The guard nodded enthusiastically, dragging himself to one of the nearby consoles. He tapped in a series of commands, the gun still to his head. The consoles flashed blue, and then went completely dark.

"Deactivated it is," the guard announced in broken grammar.

"Cheers," said Adam with his modified voice, before slamming the butt of the pistol into the alien's temple. He hoped it didn't kill the guard only stunned him;

killing needlessly wasn't what he was about. The other guards were *necessary* kills, and he was sure there would be others before the end came.

The door behind him slid open, revealing another guard walking through with hot beverages. The guard stopped in his tracks, and gawped at what he perceived to be a ghost.

Adam shot him through the throat, to prevent anybody from hearing him scream, and then shot him twice more at point blank range to kill him.

A necessary kill.

He dragged the body into the security post, and then slammed his elbow into the outside control to prevent anyone from gaining easy entry. There was only a single cream four-foot corridor from the security door to a small empty personnel lift. He stepped in, taking a position to one side, so as not to be an immediate target.

So far, this had been an easy assignment.

He punched the down button on the small wall-mounted control panel, worried that this would only go to one destination, and a pretty nasty one at that.

There was no feeling of motion when the elevator did move, making it slightly eerie for Adam, despite having spent months on the *Gold Royale*, and a fortnight on the *Polly Jenkins*. There was, however, a low humming noise, like the anti-gravs on the SUV he had fallen off outside Fayde City.

That humming ceased when the doors opened onto a long corridor. The corridor was lined with single pale doors, the walls a similar cream colour to the tiny corridor upstairs. Each door was a dark blue, completely at contrast with the walls. None of the doors had writing on them, though there were barely visible marks on them. He switched his vision over to ultraviolet, and found that there were several lines in different languages, one of which happened to be Standard.

Most of these doors were barracks rooms, though the end door was the entrance to a mess hall. He holstered the pistol, and unslung the sniper rifle. He pressed the butt of the stock against his shoulder, holding it with both hands. He silently stepped to the mess hall door, though not until he'd elbowed all the controls for each of the other doors, preventing reinforcements.

He knelt beside the doorframe, rifle pointed toward the door.

Unfortunately, the door opened before he could open it.

The spider-faced mercenary on the other side instantly went for its energy sidearm. Adam never gave him the chance, putting two silenced rounds through the spider's chest. He pulled the body into the corridor, and then popped his head round the corner.

The mess hall was pretty much what he was expecting, with lines of chairs and tables. The room was darkened, except for the kitchenette in the corner. Somebody was cooking though, because there was banging and crashing and something was bubbling away.

Adam crept to the doorway of the kitchen, and found to his amazement it was an old man dressed in pyjamas.

"If you're going to come in then come in," said the old man without turning round.

Adam could see long white hair flowing from a green head; hair that had once been a brilliantly deep blue. The pyjamas were dark silk that reflected the light as a shimmer across the long two-piece. The old man turned around. The green-skinned wrinkly old man carried himself with the weight of years of command; Adam had seen it a lot in the military, and certain heads of state. He found he actually recognised the man, or at least his facial features were familiar.

Disturbingly familiar.

"Garvion, I presume."

The old man smiled, some of the wrinkles wrinkled even more, and Adam realised they were actually scars.

"You are Adam Caine," said Garvion, pointing to Adam.

Adam stopped in his tracks, caught completely off-guard by the revelation that he was expected. Was this a trap? Diamond had admitted to him that Gold was her son, and that she couldn't kill him. Was that just maternal instinct, or was it something far more sinister? Had she set him up to be killed by these mercenaries so that Silver and her allies would not implicate her?

"You do not need to agree or disagree," Garvion pointed out. "I already know who you are, and why you are here."

"Do you now?" Adam said as emotionlessly as he could, hoping the voice modifier didn't convey any of the fear he was feeling at the possibility of not knowing what was happening to little Eve.

The man standing in front of him was, after all, Evelyn's biological father.

* * *

The clues were in the face.

Eve had a perfectly sculpted face, despite her age, with her cheekbones and chin very prominent, just as this man had; both were identically structured around their brilliant blue eyes, and the old man's white hair was tinged slightly blue, the colour still hanging on for dear life.

"You are the current owner of my daughter," the old man croaked.

"You make it sound like she's just a piece of property," countered Adam. "Or is that just a ploy to make me think she means nothing to you?"

"Then you agree that she is my daughter."

"Only so far as you had conceived her. Besides that, there is no way you are her father –a father would never have abandoned a girl like Eve."

"As you have to come and get me?" smiled Garvion, revealing the pearl-white teeth behind that lipless mouth.

"She's in a safe place."

Garvion chuckled, turning back to whatever the hell he was cooking. He dipped a wooden spoon into the big pot, pulled it out, and took a sip. He gurgled with pleasure at this, all but giving himself a pat on the back for his apparently marvellous work.

"Do you really believe that she is safe?"

Adam raised the rifle to point the barrel at Garvion's back.

"What have you done?" When Garvion didn't answer, Adam stepped closer, pressing the rifle's barrel into the alien's back. The old man stiffened, lowering the spoon back into the sauce.

And then he spun, still holding the spoon. He brushed the barrel away from him, and slung the sauce at Adam's head. The sauce just splashed against his mask, steaming happily away, but not actually doing anything except just that.

Adam elbowed Garvion in the face, breaking the alien's green nose, and splattering green blood from his nostrils.

He was angry now, the thought of Eve being captured by these hired thugs enough to want to slaughter them all. *No*, he told himself, *no unnecessary killing; I'm not a monster like Garvion and Gold.*

"What have you done with my daughter?!" Adam bellowed in Garvion's face.

"She... she's not your daughter. She belongs to me," protested Garvion, a little too weakly for it to be believable.

"What have you done with her?" Adam demanded again.

Garvion squeezed his eyes shut briefly, either from the pain, or because he was about to give up the information and severely piss someone else off. Adam suspected he knew who that other person was.

"She was supposed to take her whilst you attacked this facility; I don't know if she succeeded."

"Why? What was her plan?"

"She –she said that if you were going to kill her son, she would take your daughter. She hired us." Adam wasn't sure why the old man had ventured that information so easily. He didn't think Garvion was actually showing some kind of compassion for his biological offspring; more likely it was because he did not want to be killed for his employer's vengeance.

"DADDY!" Eve's voice snapped Adam's head round instantly. Diamond was standing at the centre of the mess hall, holding Eve's hand a little too hard. She was crying from the pain of having her hand held too tightly. A knot of sympathetic pain roiled in his gut at the thought of his little girl being hurt.

"Let her go," Adam said in a threatening modified voice.

"I am truly sorry it had to be this way," Diamond apologised. "But I cannot allow you to kill my son, despite what he has done, and what he plans to do in the future."

"He's a monster," complained Adam.

Again, there was that hint of a sad smile on Diamond's lips.

"He is still my son."

Adam sighed, almost physically feeling the rising tension in the room.

"The only way this ends is with one of us dead."

She nodded in agreement, letting Eve go, before charging straight at Adam. He reacted instantly, faster than even *he* thought possible, squeezing the trigger on full automatic, and hosing Diamond with half the rifle's magazine. Each and every bullet passed straight through her non-corporeal body, without ever harming her, ricocheting harmlessly off the ceiling and embedding into the tables at the far end of the room.

Diamond's body solidified a second before they came into contact, slamming into Adam, and tumbling both to the ground. The rifle and the plasma carbine skittered away across the polished floor.

Adam lashed out with his foot, forcing Diamond to revert to her non-corporeal self. He rolled out from under her before she could strike back, jumping to his feet with no small amount of acrobatics. He threw a side-on kick at her head, which missed completely.

And then the two jumped in close, and started trading blows.

The martial arts she had taught him came in handy, allowing him to use the moves to block each solidified elbow, punch, and kick that she threw at him.

She roared in frustration, the veneer of her calmness disappearing, as she realised she had taught him too well. The kicks and punches came thick and fast, testing even Adam's blinding speed.

Adam's arms began to burn with the effort of trying to keep up with her attacks. He found himself backing towards the wall behind him. He let his concentration slip a little to see where the wall was in relation to himself, only to find Diamond exploiting that slip.

One punch got through his defences, slamming into his cheek, fracturing the cheekbone. She hit him so hard he was sure he could see stars. Blood dribbled from his mouth –he'd bitten the inside of his own cheek.

She followed that up with a punch to the stomach, which lifted him off the floor for a brief second. When his feet touched the ground once again, he found they would not stand up under his weight. His knees wobbled, and he collapsed to the floor.

He dragged the mask off to spit the blood welling up in his mouth onto the floor.

"Why train me?" he struggled to say. "Why bother if you were going to kill me and Eve?"

"I was never going to kill you; I had hoped you might join me if this mission didn't kill you first. But I underestimated just how good you were at this." As she said this, Garvion stepped into the mess hall, holding Adam's plasma carbine, and a fierce look of need for vengeance on his scarred old face. "No," Diamond commanded, pointing at the mercenary commander, "Even in his weakened state, he could still kill you."

Adam, though shocked at this revelation, gave Garvion a feral toothy grin. The old man seemed slightly unsettled by this, and took a step back, lowering the plasma carbine in front of his stomach. Adam could see the magazine clearly from here, and smiled. Both Diamond and Garvion were slightly unsettled by this, shifting uncomfortably, which meant Diamond had stayed in her solidified state.

Summoning more strength than he was sure he had, he kicked out with his feet, catching Diamond in the chest, and launching her corporeal body the five metres towards Garvion.

At the same time, Adam shouted, "Evie, get down!"

Everything seemed to happen in slow motion, except Adam's hand, which whipped out his sidearm, aimed and tightened on the trigger. The bullet jumped across the room like lightning, passing Diamond as she flew backwards, a look of shock on her face, and slammed into the non-metallic plasma magazine. It flayed the magazine cover, and sparked off the energy inside.

The resulting explosion engulfed both Diamond and Garvion, throwing both in opposite directions.

The resulting fireball passed over Adam and Evelyn harmlessly, but vaporised Garvion's hands and charred the rest of him. When the fire disappeared, consuming itself, the fire alarms blared out for attention, and the water sprinklers splashed on, spraying everything in the mess hall and kitchen with water.

Adam picked himself painfully up off the floor, ignoring the bruises from the fight. He strode over to Eve, who was cowering under a table, holstered his sidearm, and scooped her up in his big arms. She was shaking with fright and shock, her precious green face slightly paler than normal.

Adam stepped over to Garvion, whose body was burned beyond recognition, and growled at him.

"That's for abandoning your daughter."

Eve wasn't aware of what he was saying, or at least he hoped she wasn't; if Diamond hadn't told her who Garvion was, then it was possible she didn't know. He didn't want Eve to know that her biological father had abandoned her like trash, and was in fact an evil man.

Diamond was groaning on the floor, her burns already healing. She was still weakened by the blast however, and thus wasn't a threat to him or Eve. At the moment.

He lay Eve down on the wet floor, unholstered his P99 once again, and placed the barrel against the immortal woman's forehead.

"Take us back to the ship."

She nodded weakly.

The mess hall disappeared just as a large group of mercenaries forced their way through the doors at either end, demanding to know what was going on. The flash of white came and went, and they were suddenly back outside the temple, the *Kara Marazov* sitting exactly where he had left it.

He left Diamond lying on the worn grass, and carried Eve back to the ship, putting her to bed, before returning to Diamond an hour later after finding something in the ship's hold. Her burns were almost fully healed now, and pretty soon she would attack him again. She sat up, struggling to keep her arms from collapsing out from under her.

Adam, still holding the pistol in one hand, crouched down in front of her. He handed her the item he had found, slightly heavier than before. She accepted it, but didn't open it.

It was a hardback book:

His Last Command by Dan Abnett.

She was puzzled by the gift.

"What is this?"

"It's a book," replied Adam, a smile on his lips that had no humour in it whatsoever. "One I was reading when I was captured by the Core funnily enough, although it's not the same copy. It's a good book, about a man who was lost, and then finds himself again." He paused and frowned. "Well, that was the impression I got the first time I read it. Perhaps it will do you some good one day, if you ever bother to read it. Seems to me that you're lost, and need to be found."

"When did the roles become reversed between us?" She tried to smile, but it looked pathetic under her pain.

He stood back up.

"When you tried to kill me and my daughter."

Diamond snorted with amusement.

"Where is your son holding Silver?"

Diamond looked away, thinking through the endless scenarios of what she could tell him, before staring him eye-to-eye. He didn't back down under penetrating gaze, and she knew he wouldn't, not after all the training, and certainly not after having defeated her, using his wits rather than just brawn as he had done so since coming to this retched century.

"I do not know where he is holding her," she admitted. "But I know he had plans for something in the Arathea star system. I do not know the specifics, but he *will* be there I assure you."

Adam nodded.

"Goodbye, Diamond." He spun on the spot, and then strode away towards his ship. Then he stopped, as if just remembering something. Without looking, he shot her in the leg from a distance. She screamed in pain as the bullet tore her shin to pieces.

"That's for threatening my daughter!" he shouted back over his shoulder.

Diamond watched him climb into the *Kara Marazov*, and power up the ship. The ship gently lifted off the ground, letting the small claw-like landing struts fold back into the ship's lower fin. Off in the distance, ships were coming across the horizon towards her and the *Kara*, presumably mercenaries from the enclave wanting revenge on their attacker.

The *Kara* never gave them the chance to get anywhere near close. It turned slowly so that the cockpit was facing directly up to the sky. There was a pregnant pause whereupon she thought the crescent ship's engines might fail and crash back to the ground.

It did not crash.

The engines roared louder than her ancient ears could handle, and then it shot up into the sky as if flung by a catapult. Within seconds, it had disappeared from view, leaving the mercenary ships and Diamond behind in a cloud of dust.

She eyed the book next to her, and then pushed it away.

She would read it some other time, when she had healed.

* * *

When the *Kara Marazov* cleared the atmosphere of the planet, he set the autopilot to fly around in the Linkways for a while, to let both he and Eve heal a little before their next crisis.

The splash of the blue Linkway entrance reared up before them, engulfing the ship wholly. Adam sighed, and tipped his head back to rest on the headrest of the high-backed pilot's chair.

"Computer, bring up any news files relating to Captain Brag Franks or the cruise liner *Gold Royale*." There were a couple of dozen as it turned out, most relating simply to the ship going down, with nobody having any clue as to how or why it was destroyed over the planet Mirschab.

Several of the news reports had survivors of the ship's demise talking about their horrific experience at the hands of a mysterious black battleship. One of the former guests of the floating city told a tale of a mystery soldier saving everybody's lives, clad in black and carrying a young child. It was a somewhat exaggerated version of what had happened to Adam –he was pretty sure he didn't bend steel with his bare hands or pick up a shuttle to free a trapped guest.

There was, however, a follow-up report made by a young reporter that simply used her first name.

She was human, or appeared to be on the monitor in front of him –his concept of being human was somewhat outdated in this century. She was the epitome of the young stunningly attractive female reporter, with a jacket that left little to the imagination cleavage-wise. She was full of youthful enthusiasm, probably younger than Adam was by a few years. Her hair was loose around her shoulders. Clearly, she had not used qualifications or experience to get where she was.

"*Good evening, this is Klawdier reporting from Freya IV, where it is reported that the alliance of corporations responsible for building and funding the luxury cruise liner* Gold Royale *have called a planning meeting to discuss the funding of another liner. So far, the executives of two-dozen companies have been in discussions for the last twelve hours without end.*"

She was stood on the steps of a massive building that seemed to blot out the sun no matter which way the camera went. Behind her, a pair of doors opened. Through it came a pair of men carrying a small podium of some sort. They placed it down in front of the doors, set up a communications receiver on the top of the podium before retreating to a safe distance.

A tall, elderly grey-skinned gent, who was thin enough that he might break in a strong breeze, stepped onto the podium, and cleared his throat.

"Good evening, ladies, and gentlemen."

The gentleman then droned on about the technical specs of their new starship that would essentially be another floating city. When it came to questions from the press, Klawdier was the first to be allowed to ask one, though Adam suspected that was because the old man was staring at her cleavage.

"Will Captain Franks be involved with this new liner?" Klawdier queried.

The old gentleman cleared his throat again, fiddling with the knot of his suit tie.

"We have approached Captain Franks and asked him to command this new ship, but he has refused, claiming to want some vacation time to visit old and new friends. As far as we know, he is still on New Terra on vacation, and still against commanding another cruise liner. Next question?"

Adam turned off the news report, and tapped in the command to head to New Terra. The computer came up with an estimate of how long it would take: ten days, even through the Linkway –Diamond's planet had been on the other side of the Andromeda Galaxy after all.

Adam set a course, and then sat back.

"I hope this ship's got something to read."

* * *

1996ad.

Lympstone.

Having said goodbye to his mother, Caine threw his kit bags onto the back of the troop truck. He was assigned to 40 Commando outside Taunton, and would be joining the Troop in Northern Ireland. He didn't feel guilty about leaving his family behind; after all, they had been the primary reason for joining the Commandos.

Sergeant Graham, along with a dozen other newly minted Commandos, sat in the back of the big soft-top truck with him. Caine could see a beaming smile on the big man's face.

The sergeant leaned in to whisper in Adam's ear.

"I know you've only just turned seventeen, Caine. There's a reason we let you continue with the training: your abilities. We have high hopes for your career in the Royal Marines."

* * *

3988ad.

Fort Zeus.

They had cleared him of any wrongdoing.

Despite that, he had sat through the formal hearing, staring at the five flag officers with something like guilt, but worse. The faces of his crew kept coming unbidden to his mind's eyes. But the flag officers had told him that nothing more could have been done, and thus Franks was guilty of nothing more than surviving.

After exiting the hearing, he broke down in tears –right there in the corridor for all to see.

As much as he loved the Navy, he couldn't bear being in it anymore. When the officers had given their unanimous verdict, he had told them he was officially resigning his commission. Although they had protested, the three admirals and two commodores had understood.

A hand appeared in front of Franks, holding a starch-pressed handkerchief. It belonged to a human man dressed in an incredibly expensive grey suit that probably cost a year of Brag's wages.

"Let me buy you a drink," the hand's owner said. "I've come to offer you a job."

"What kind of job?"

The man smiled.

"Have you ever heard of the *Gold Royale*?"

Nine: Unbreakable

"Unbreakable."
-Evelyn Caine, on her father.
"Impossible man."
-General Lenson Gardner describing Adam Caine.

September 4000ad.

"I do not know where he is," the subject growled.

The subject had been held in the interrogation room for four hours, three of which had been on his own. They had snatched him, soldiers in black uniforms, and bundled him into a waiting grav-limo before dumping him unceremoniously in the interrogation room.

"You knew him," the harsh, shaven female interrogator said, leaning on her hands across the table so that she was almost in his face. He wasn't actually afraid of them, more frustrated that they were holding him against his will and refused to let him go until he gave them what they wanted.

"It has been two months since I last saw him."

"Indeed," the other interrogator sneered. "But you suspect where he might be."

The subject sighed, and gave a sad nod.

"I do not know its name, or the coordinates. But it was important enough to him to drop everything and head for it."

The two interrogators shared a glance and a nod.

"Okay, here's the deal. You find him, you give him to us, and we can get you your own command in the fleet."

"You cannot be serious," the subject guffawed.

"We are very serious." The two interrogators stood shoulder-to-shoulder and crossed their arms. The subject thought the two uniformed women could have been identical twins if it were not for the hairless visage of the younger woman.

The subject couldn't deny that their offer wasn't incredibly tempting. In all fairness, he had no reason not to give in to their request. One person who had caused him so much grief was not worth the chance to get back command of a starship.

Inwardly, he groaned.

"What do you want me to do?"

* * *

"HMS Icebreaker Chief Engineer's Log; twenty-second of the eighth, four-thousand A.D.

We have been experiencing major fluctuations in the power conduits connected to the primary FTL crystal. The energy output is interfering with the sublight engines, and we have had to stop for repairs more than once.

I just cannot find the cause.

The Captain, XO, and senior officers are adamant that this experimental vessel will be an overwhelming success. I am not so confident. I designed this ship, after all. I know that the Admiralty, and various corporations who sponsored this project, are pressuring the Captain, but we cannot rush this, or people will get hurt.

I just hope we can find the fault in the ship's engines before we reach the test site in two days."

* * *

"Another one, sir?"

Brag Franks looked up at the waitress, and smiled, his toothy grin almost entirely hidden by his bushy black beard. He'd been growing it longer for weeks, and was annoyed to see the flecks of grey in it, as well as the greying of his short hair. He was still as tall and thin as ever, though he liked to think he was wiry instead of unhealthily thin.

He sat on the third floor of a large café, at a circular metal table on a balcony overlooking a massive spaceport.

The waitress was human, the only one he had seen in the establishment, and wore a generic pale green dress, with a smile that had no humour in it. Clearly, she had been working there too long. The other one she was referring to was the empty caffeine mug sat on his table.

"Yes, please," he grinned. There was a glimmer of a smile, this time genuine, and her cheeks flushed red before she left to attend to his next drink.

He watched her go, and felt a flush of something he had rarely felt in twenty years: longing. He was divorced, had had only his siblings and parents to see; his life had been his career, and now he regretted it.

The spaceport below was a sprawling complex of raised landing pads, hangars, cargo cranes, control towers, and even dry-docks. Big ships sat like beached whales, whilst smaller ships hung in large frames like flies trapped in a spider's web, walkways and gantries leading away in structured patterns, connecting with elevator shafts.

Beyond the spaceport was the massive city of New Amsterdam. It wasn't the biggest of cities, not even the capital of New Terra. But it was the most beautiful. New Amsterdam was built around smooth pearl towers, supposedly the remains of an ancient race that died of disease millennia ago. Light glinted off the towering edifices, rising gracefully above the other buildings of the city.

The system's star was nearing the horizon, spreading an orange haze across the city and spaceport.

It was rather spectacular, hence the place's name: Sundown Café.

The café was quiet before the dinner rush.

Well, quiet inside.

Starships still rumbled overhead, shaking the whole building.

One in particular caught his eye, silently gliding down toward a small landing pad tucked in amongst a bundle of inactive cranes. The ship was a shimmering blue vertical half-crescent that looked like the wind had swept the tops backward along with the tiny side wings. It was the ship he had been waiting for.

The ship waggled.

It was an old tradition among fighter pilots to waggle their wings as they passed someone as a sign of respect, or playfulness depending on the pilot.

Brag grinned, downed the mug of caffeine that had appeared, and then jumped out of his chair. He left the change and a generous tip, and loped out of the café, leaving the human woman with a wink and a smile. He made his way cheerily through the thronging crowds of people rushing to the skybus terminals for the journey home from work. The crowds dissipated as he neared the private hangars.

He found the hangar he was looking for, and discovered a small girl with green skin and silky blue hair

"Uncle Brag!"

The girl's face lit up like a supernova, a grin splitting across it. She charged toward him, and leaped into his arms, giving him a vice-like hug. She had obviously been getting more than lessons on life from her father, as she had never been able to leap that high before.

"Hello, Evelyn," he beamed.

"It's been a while," a deep voice chuckled.

Brag turned to see the big soldier leaning against the doorframe. He didn't bother to correct himself; no matter how long Adam Caine had been out of the service, he was still, at heart, the Royal Marine Commando that Brag had read about in the public history files.

He was certainly still big enough, though the long unkempt hair tended to put people off that idea, especially with the week-old stubble. Unlike previous times he had seen the big man, Adam was wearing primitive hand made clothes that looked more at home on an old knight when not wearing his armour.

"I'm sorry I haven't been in contact," Adam said sheepishly. "We've been... away from civilisation." Adam shrugged helplessly. It still looked strange to Brag: the big, muscled, tortured soldier who had endured unimaginable horrors being father to a young girl full of life like little Eve. Then again, Adam had the kind of physical energy that could power an entire star, making him perhaps the only person able to keep up with the little bundle of joy.

"Oddly enough, I've just finished two months of vacation here in New Amsterdam."

"Is *that* what this city is called?" Adam said in wonder. Apparently, wherever he had been, he had obviously not bothered to look at any star charts or read any more history files.

Brag snorted.

"What are you doing on New Terra?" he asked, finally putting Eve down on her own two feet.

"Looking for you, actually."

"Oh?"

"The news was reporting how the *Gold Royale* was destroyed by a mysterious battleship, and that its captain was vacationing on New Terra. A friend of mine said you had been spotted in New Amsterdam."

"I thought you said you didn't know what this city was called," Brag asked, his eyes narrowing suspiciously at his time-travelling friend.

A mischievous look crept into Adam's facial features. "Did I say that?"

Brag shook his head with a great deal of amusement.

"To be honest, I could do with some help in my search."

Brag's eyebrows shot up in surprise. He had never heard those words from Adam before. Generally, the big man rarely needed help, and never asked for it, even if he received it from time-to-time.

"You haven't found Silver yet?"

Adam looked around suspiciously before beckoning Brag into the hangar, his daughter holding his hand.

"We've been busy," Adam stated, hugging his daughter to his leg. Brag saw a brief look of pain behind Adam's eyes, making him wonder just what he had been up to in the last two months. "I... I'm not allowed to talk about it." There was an uncomfortable silence as Brag realised Adam was never going to tell him about whatever it was, or wherever it was that the small Caine family had been.

Brag let it go, however. "How long are you here?"

Adam smiled.

"How long will it take to pack your things?"

* * *

"Engineer's Log; twenty-third of the eighth, four thousand A.D.

We have found the problem: something has been chewing on the power lines on Deck 23. They were only minor marks that were easily fixable, but they still caused some rather specific damage. Whatever made the marks it knew what to chew, and what not to chew; one of my junior engineers suggested it might be one of the lawyers representing the ship's corporate sponsors.

I'm not entirely ready to disagree, especially given that one of them looks ready to chew the bulkheads along with her Navy Intelligence partner.

The sergeant of the ship's Fleet Protection squad has reassured me that there is no evidence of rodents or other vermin on board the Icebreaker. This morning, though, our escort, the destroyer HMS Crystal Palace, reported that they too had experienced power fluctuations. They have also found chewing marks.

I have put my engineering crew on the lookout for any evidence of vermin infestation..."

* * *

A four-man repair team on the *Crystal Palace* wandered into a walk-in storage bay, one that happened to have a vital energy conduit behind it. The lighting in the bay, and the outside corridor was flickering on and off. The younger ones in the team were extremely nervous: they had heard the stories told by the Icebreaker's crew, and had heard of the markings in other parts of the Crystal Palace's engineering section.

The leader of the team was first into the bay, sweeping his torch left-to-right as he moved between the stacks of crates.

"Somebody fix those damn lights," the leader growled. He stopped in his tracks when nobody replied or made a mewling complaint. He turned, and found that there was nobody there. He was on his own.

His torchlight passed over something on the floor.

Something wet.

He was about to swear when he heard a breathing noise, oh-so-close to his head.

He turned.

He saw teeth.

He screamed.

He felt no more.

* * *

"So where are we going, Captain?" Brag asked mischievously. It felt good for the roles to be reversed: Adam the captain, Brag the visitor on his ship. He didn't miss commanding a starship —the responsibility especially. The decisions he had to make were a miserable part of his former occupation, on both of his previous ships.

So now he sat in the co-pilot's seat, looking over the part alien, part Terran control console. There were screens hanging either side of the console, showing displays of the ship's power consumption, the FTL drive's status, along with a screen by Adam that showed visual representations of all the ship's weapons, and their status.

New Amsterdam had fallen away from the ship over a day before, the ship travelling through the Linkways towards their first destination in their search for Adam's friend.

"My... contact believes that there may be clues to Silver's location in a solar system called Arathea."

"Are you kidding?" Brag exclaimed. "I thought you watched the news. Arathea is the location of an experiment by the Navy working in conjunction with some of the biggest corporations in the nineteen galaxies. It's supposed to be the first big search and rescue vessel, called the Icebreaker."

Adam gave a tiny smile. "Icebreakers were ocean-going vessels that were designed to smash their way through... well, the ice, especially in the Arctic and

Antarctic regions of Earth. The Royal Navy had at least two of them before I left."

Now it was Brag's turn to smile. It was easy to forget sometimes that Adam Caine had been born on Earth, something Brag couldn't lay claim to. It was something that made him feel a twinge of jealousy towards Caine.

"The ship is based on those early Earth designs, using a solid, hardened bow to push debris and asteroids out of its path without depending on energy shields, forcefields, or tractor beams. Basically, the Icebreaker is designed to rescue ships in distress where more conventional vessels could not reach without serious damage."

"And I bet there are one or two people outraged that it might have other applications," Adam snorted. Brag just frowned at him, uncomprehending. Adam shook his head at his friend's clear naivety. "If a ship has the capability to push asteroids and debris aside without the assistance of energy-draining systems like tractor beams, it could conceivably be used as a first strike weapon. More than likely, this experiment will bring out all sorts of groups either protesting against its possible military uses, or stolen for the very same reason."

"You really think so?" Brag queried.

"I wouldn't be surprised," shrugged Adam. "When is the experiment set to take place?"

Brag checked the chronometer on the console before him.

"In exactly one hour. How far are we out from Arathea?"

As if to answer, Adam turned the ship down another Linkway, and the ship was suddenly bursting out into realspace.

"Never mind."

They weren't alone: there were several dozen other ships as well. Adam and Brag didn't recognise all of them, although those that they didn't carried the symbols and identification codes of the biggest of the news establishments. Most of those were small, though each was bigger than the Kara Marazov, whilst the really big ships sat to one side: warships of varying races.

Brag saw a pair of Terran Longbow-class cruisers at the fore of the group, accompanied by three gunships and a squadron of Rhino starfighters flying patrol sorties across the system. A big Rijiin cruiser, recognisable by its four vertical-horizontal engine nacelle wings and its spherical forward hull, hung beside the Terrans along with a small Rathgar patrol ship as well as representatives from several other independent militaries, including a Fayde Police flag vessel, and an Alliance frigate.

"So where is this clue you're supposed to find?"

Adam shrugged. "On the Icebreaker?" he suggested.

"Even in this ship, we'd never get close enough to it before we were destroyed by those." He reinforced his point by gesturing to the Terran and Rijiin warships, which were starting to move inexplicably toward a point off to the left of all the onlookers. "They're moving to escort the Icebreaker when it comes out of FTL speeds."

* * *

"*Security Log, HMS Crystal Palace; twenty-third of the eighth, four-thousand A.D.*

A repair team went missing seven hours ago. For a while, I had sporadic reports of others going missing, and screams being heard throughout the ship. Then the Captain reported that the XO was dead, torn apart by something in his quarters.

Even after my years of service in the Fleet Protection Group, I have never seen violence like that. There was blood everywhere, and not just blood. To be honest, that was not the worst thing; the XO had been dating one of the engineering officers. We found her headless remains under his bed, missing most of her skin and internal organs.

From then on, creatures I have never seen before murdered half the crew. My squad were slaughtered when we tried to rescue the Captain and bridge crew from being under siege by the things. There has been no time to send a distress signal, so the Icebreaker is unaware of what has transpired on the Crystal Palace.

Before I managed to drag my half-dead Corporal out of there, I spotted an old man dressed in a tuxedo walking among the creatures as if he were their master. I swear he looked like one of those butlers from the cheesy horror holo-movies I used to watch as a teenager.

Now I am holed up in the armoury. Corporal Ming is dead from his injuries, and I can hear the creatures banging on the door, trying to claw their way in. I am terrified out of my mind about what I know is coming to get me. Nobody answers my hails over the intercom; I think everybody else is dead.

Gods, I hope someone here's this log, and is able to retrieve some kind of justice or revenge from it. I hope my wife does not... wait, what is that buzzing sound?

Who the hell are you?

Gold? What sort of name is that?

No wait, you can't let those creatures in here.

Because they'll kill us both that's why!

Oh Gods, what have you done?

No, please. Please have mercy.

No. No. NO! OH GOOOODS!!!

AAARRRGGGHHH!!!

[End Log]

* * *

Gold smiled down at the shredded corpses of the Terran soldiers.

He barely gave them a second of thought before turning away.

"Now, my children, we shall control this vessel, and surprise those that wait for us." He stopped, feeling a familiar sensation: there was someone on the Icebreaker he recognised, someone he had had dealings with before –someone he had tried to kill. Not only that, but he felt an intensely strong presence ahead at the *Crystal Palace*'s destination. It was a presence he had hoped would not interfere with this operation.

He growled the name like it would kill him if it escaped his lips in a hurry. "Caine."

* * *

The *Icebreaker* broke from FTL speeds four minutes early, the *Crystal Palace* by its side all the way. The size of a cruiser, it had the same design features as all Terran Navy vessels, except that it had a massive four-sided pyramid stuck to its front, the point facing forwards. If anything, it had more in common with the 19th-century railroad trains of the USA with their front-mounted cattle ploughs than the ocean-going icebreakers of the nineteenth- and twentieth-centuries.

Like other Terran vessels, Icebreaker had the same dark blue colouring to its hull, except the fore-mounted plough, which was a glittering chrome colour, presumably made of a different material to the rest of the ship.

"Something's wrong," Brag announced, his eyes glued to the Kara Marazov's sensor displays. When Adam didn't say anything, he realised the younger man was waiting for an explanation. "The *Crystal Palace* isn't responding to any hails from the other Terran ships, and she's still keeping pace with the *Icebreaker*."

"She's not supposed to?" Adam inquired.

"No, according to the reports, *Crystal Palace* was only to escort the Icebreaker between its base and the experiment location in case of pirate attack, and then break off. She's keeping perfect pace with the other ship, though."

"Evelyn strap yourself in."

* * *

One of the lawyers was panicking, threatening to sue the *Icebreaker*'s captain, XO, and the entire Navy if the ship was not immediately taken away from the possible danger zone.

"Why the hell did you come on board a rescue ship if you didn't want to be in danger?" one of the other lawyers sneered in his face. The panicking lawyer pretended not to hear the strange woman stood next to the Intelligence Colonel, instead continuing to shout threats in the captain's face.

The communications officer was having no luck contacting the *Crystal Palace*. A few minutes later, and he could not contact the other Navy vessels due to jamming from the escorting destroyer, though he could still monitor other transmissions.

The sensors officer suddenly shouted out.

"Captain, there's a civilian ship approaching us on our starboard side. They seem to be ignoring the other ships and coming straight for us."

"A coincidence, perhaps?"

"The ID code is for a private yacht called the *Kara Marazov*."

One of the lawyers −in fact, the one holding hands with the Intelligence Colonel- spluttered suddenly. The captain looked at her questioningly.

"Is there something you want to discuss?" he demanded, making it an order rather than a suggestion. The woman nodded.

"Colour Sergeant Kara Marazov was the last Royal Marine before the Fleet Protection Group was established." The Intelligence officer next to her widened his eyes in shocked recognition. The captain had never heard of Royal Marines or Kara Marazov, but they must have existed for the Intelligence agent to be surprised by the mention of the name.

"Jesus," the lawyer breathed. "I never thought he would get himself a starship." The intelligence agent was shaking his head. So was the captain, but for a whole other reason: he hadn't a clue what the two were on about.

* * *

"Someone's jamming the *Icebreaker*'s communications."

"It's the *Crystal Palace*," Adam answered. "And they're locking weapons on us. Wait, not just us; they're locking onto the other civilian ships as well."

"Damn."

Adam activated the comms. "*HMS Crystal Palace*, this is the private yacht Kara Marazov. Please desist in targeting us, or we will fire upon you." Brag looked at him like he was mad; the Kara was tough, but not enough to stand up to a Terran Navy destroyer, doubly so with three other, far larger vessels nearby.

The communications console lit up: someone on the *Crystal Palace* was returning the call, and the Terran cruiser captains were screaming for the Kara to back off or they would be destroyed.

Adam opened the incoming transmission from the *Crystal*.

"*Hello, Adam Caine,*" a male voice said. Adam froze as the old man's face appeared on one of the screens. Brag thought the voice sounded like it was full of malevolence, as did the old man's face.

"Gold," Adam growled back. "Why are you on that destroyer?"

"*I just came to see the show, Staff Sergeant,*" Gold smiled. "Or is it Commander or Captain now?" There was no humour in that smile; in fact, Eve started crying the moment she saw him. Of course, this just gave Gold more of a chance to be nasty. "*Don't tell me you've been breeding already, Caine. You humanoid races truly are disgusting.*"

Brag saw a glimmer of amusement under the anger that was clearly building in his friend. Had this Gold just revealed too much to his supposedly sworn enemy?

"What's wrong with being humanoid? Or being a parent for that matter?" asked Adam. He saw Gold falter for a brief second. Adam wasn't going to let go of that little snippet of information.

Then the moment was gone, and the malice and hate flowed off of the screen in invisible waves once again. Eve was sobbing, hugging herself as she tried to comprehend what was happening around her. Adam squirmed in his chair with each sob, and Brag could see the conflict he was having: argue with his enemy, or comfort his upset daughter.

"I don't suppose there's any point me asking how you got control of the Crystal Palace, or if the crew is still alive." Adam seemed to deflate in front of the former starship captain. Did he hold that much of a burden on his shoulders that he blamed himself for the deaths of all those Gold killed? "How did you get the creatures aboard? And why isn't the Icebreaker affected?"

"*You really believe I would tell* you?"

"You do have a tendency to brag. Where's Silver?"

"*I do not know what you mean.*" Somehow, the question had caught Gold off-guard, as if he had been concentrating all his effort on insulting and upsetting Adam and his daughter.

"Where is Silver?" This time, Adam put a great stress on the words, locking the Kara's weapons onto the destroyer's command centre. "Where. Is. Silver. I won't ask again." He tapped the images of each of the ship's weapons, activating them. He raised the shields as well, and kept the ship at station keeping above the *Icebreaker*.

Gold's eyes widened with surprise.

"*You wouldn't,*" he said.

Adam double-tapped a finger each on the missile images at the same time. Several months ago, he had promised himself that the next time he saw Gold he would use a bigger gun to shoot the monster.

"Watch me."

* * *

On the *Icebreaker*, the crew and passengers watched as a hatch slid open seamlessly in each of the Kara's small wings. Two sleek, midnight blue missiles punched out of their racks, and snaked away from the ship, leaving twin trails of drive smoke behind them.

The missiles sped out, then back, back towards the *Crystal Palace*.

Incredibly, the *Crystal* tried to manoeuvre; but a ship its size simply cannot hope to out-run a missile launched so close to it. And, of course, Gold was not a starship officer and thus had not seen fit to activate the ship's defences.

The missiles struck the destroyer's bridge dead-on. The explosion was so strong it ripped the unprotected ship almost in half, spilling the genetic killing machines out into space in a fiery bloom.

The ship listed to one side, dead in space.

Hannah Spears, representing the corporation that had hired her as a lawyer three and a half months ago, stood beside Raymond Sansky, watching the conflict with growing sadness. Adam had changed: he had found himself a ship and a willingness to use it. She glared at the screen. He hadn't contacted her, hadn't even sent word to her of what he was up to -nothing.

* * *

The last thing Adam saw of the destroyer's bridge was Gold's shocked face engulfed in flames. He had no illusions that Gold had survived; he had shot the bastard through the head, and the bullet just passed right through him, and Diamond had survived a detonating energy rifle. Something as petty as a starship being destroyed around him wasn't going to be much more than an annoyance to him.

The Terran warship captains all started screaming for him to surrender.

He sighed —he'd probably just saved their lives, or at the very least prevented those genetic killing machines from spreading again, leaving Gold to have to start all over again with those things. Now, Navy Intelligence had yet another reason to chase after him, despite the fact he hadn't seen or heard from them during his two-month... sabbatical.

He exchanged a knowing glance with Brag.

"Let's get out of here," Brag sighed, clapping a comforting hand on Adam's shoulder.

"Course?"

"There's an uninhabited star system fifteen light-years from here with a dense nebula," he answered, looking over the computer's star charts. "Just outside of the Terran Navy's jurisdiction." He plotted it into the navigational computer, and Adam slapped in the command to activate the FTL drive.

* * *

"There he goes again," Hannah sighed.

The *Kara Marazov* flitted past the bridge of the *Icebreaker*, before stretching and disappearing to faster than the speed of light.

She suddenly felt very tired, the memories of five months ago coming back to the fore of her mind and robbing her of any real control over her sadness. Raymond drew her into a hug, and kissed her on the forehead.

Without feeling any resentment or jealousy towards his friend, he said, "It'll be alright, honey. We'll find him before anyone else can."

* * *

The *Kara Marazov* slowed from FTL just outside high orbit of a long-dead planetoid. The computer listed it as uninhabited, and it had apparently been that way for millennia before even Adam was born. Like the other two in the system, this planet was just an uneven, spherical hunk of rock. The system's star was a red giant, only hundreds of years from collapsing and turning into a supernova. It shone like a lighthouse through the nebula that hung over the planetoid like an ominous rain cloud.

Adam parked the ship tentatively just inside the cloud —recent experience with living nebulae had taught both him and Brag the necessity of not being too hasty in judging its composition.

"So what now?" Brag wondered.

"We wait for someone to chase us," Adam shrugged. Brag frowned at the tactic, curious to see if Adam actually had a plan, or if he was making it up as he went along as he usually did. Then again, Adam could actually be completely insane.

The bigger man swivelled his seat around, and unstrapped himself from his high-backed chair. He the kneeled down in front of Eve's chair, and hugged her. She had cried the entire journey here, though had been fairly silent about it after leaving Arathea. Adam shushed her, unstrapping her from her chair, and picking her up in his powerful arms.

Brag watched them go, as Adam put her to bed.

* * *

Adam pulled the duvet up to Eve's chin.

Her eyes were rimmed a darker green, indicating she had indeed been crying. She had tied her long blue hair back before going to bed, and was nestled under the covers quick as a flash. She had obviously been looking forward to going to sleep.

"You okay, princess?" he asked softly. He had used some of Silver's money to decorate the small bedroom to make it more comfortable for her; she was only six after all. The small things made her happy: he wasn't the only one who found the idea of this little family more comforting than anything else.

He still had not managed to find out what had happened to her before Odyssey Station; her DNA, description, or even her picture had brought no hits anywhere. Whatever had happened, she was grateful to have a father to look after her. And he was just as grateful to have a daughter –he spoiled her rotten, though he was still stern with her on the insanely rare occasions she was out of line.

"That man was scary," she said.

"Yeah, I know," he replied, gently stroking her hair. "He's evil." He sighed. "You remember what I told you about my friend?"

"That she's a prisoner?"

"Yep," he nodded. "That scary man calls himself mister Gold, and is the one holding my friend prisoner. Me and Brag have to find her before Gold can hurt her."

"Where?"

He let out a long and heavy sigh.

"I don't know yet," he admitted. He continued to stroke her hair; it seemed to comfort her no end, and her sparkling eyes started to flutter closed.

"You'll find her daddy," she whispered.

He frowned; at six, she wasn't old enough to be insightful, so hearing those words was somewhat disconcerting to him. "Why do you say that?"

"You're my daddy; you're a hero. Heroes always beat the baddies." And like that, the insight was gone, covered with the kind of thing only young, naïve children could possibly say. He stroked her hair again, kissed her on the cheek, and made to leave her tiny room. "I love you, daddy," she whispered as he waved the room's lights off.

Adam smiled.

"I love you too, princess," he whispered back.

He stepped out into the cramped corridor, and then out into the cockpit, where Brag was fiddling with the communications console. Adam looked at him suspiciously before Brag turned around, finally noticing he was there.

"There was a glitch in the comms system. I thought it was internal, but there's a ship out there, trying to worm their way into our system."

The holographic projector above the main control consoles flashed up an image of the approaching ship. The text scrolling around the image identified it as a Terran Navy personnel shuttle.

"That isn't what I was expecting," Adam snorted.

"You were expecting something else?"

"At least one of the cruisers we saw before," shrugged Adam. He sat down in the pilot's chair, activating the ship's engines but keeping them idle, ready to go at a moment's notice. "Can they see us?"

"I don't think so." Brag shook his head, checking the sensors. "I think the worm is designed to latch on to the nearest vessel's computer, and then infiltrate the comms units before sending out its location."

"Did the worm get that far?"

Brag shook his head again.

"No, this ship's computer is too alien for the worm to be able to affect it profoundly. The computer is already deleting the worm's subroutines." He was staring at a visual representation of the inside of the Kara's computer cortex, where blots of light kept winking out, representing the subroutines being deleted.

Adam opened a channel to the shuttle, keeping the communications in stealth mode so that the shuttle's occupants couldn't trace the call, audio only.

"This is the *Kara Marazov*, calling unknown Terran Navy shuttle. Desist in your attempts to infiltrate this ship or you will be fired upon." Brag's head whipped round, his eyebrows shooting up in surprise, an alarmed look on his face.

"Is that any way to talk to a friend, Adam?" the reply came. Adam just gave a small grunt at the male voice, not allowing any surprise to creep into his own voice.

"Didn't think it would be you the Navy sent after me, Raymond."

"The Navy didn't send me —not exactly anyway; we're here to help you."

"We?" Adam rolled his eyes as he realised who else was on the shuttle. "Where is Hannah?"

"I'm here, Adam."

Brag saw Adam squirm in his chair as soon as the woman's voice came through over the comms channel.

"What are you here to help me with?"

"3899," Raymond Sansky answered.

Adam sighed, rubbing his eyes as if he were suddenly very tired. He leaned forward, and pushed the throttle up a little, gently piloting the ship out of the nebula. The shuttle had passed the Kara's position, and was slowly drifting into an orbit of the dead planetoid below. Both men heard the swearing over the comms as Sansky was shocked by the sudden appearance of the Kara directly behind him.

"Does your shuttle have a teleporter?"

"A small one, yes."

"Teleport to the rear of the cockpit. We'll see you in a moment."

There was no disembodied comment at Adam's use of 'we', instead the shuttle slowed to a halt. There was a sudden bright white light behind Adam and Brag that coalesced into the shapes of Colonel Raymond Sansky and Hannah Spears.

Sansky wore the olive-green dress uniform of Navy Intelligence, whilst Hannah looked the epitome of a working woman: she wore a chocolate dress and jacket that was cut maybe a little too tight, leaving little to the imagination in terms of her generous figure. She wore a frilly yellow blouse underneath that opened to reveal her cleavage. Her hair was tied back into a severe bun that made her look like a strict schoolteacher.

Gone was the gentle, tortured mother; stood in front of Adam was the lawyer she had been before he had met her on the train on that fateful day. She wasn't smiling, though Raymond had the traces of one itching at the corners of his mouth at seeing his friend once again.

"Welcome aboard the *Kara Marazov*," Adam nodded, without a hint of emotion. Brag could see his friend's jaw twitch. He was trying to contain whatever emotions were boiling up from within. Clearly, something big had happened between Adam and the woman.

"You've got an amazing ship here, Adam," Raymond nodded, smiling.

"A gift from Silver," Adam replied nonchalantly. Raymond's smile dropped suddenly at the mention of Silver. The intelligence operative grimaced, and he and Hannah exchanged an uncomfortable look of shared knowledge. Adam suddenly became aware of the two looking at Brag.

"Um, this is my friend Brag Franks. Brag, this is Colonel Raymond Sansky of Navy Intelligence, and Hannah Spears." Brag nodded a welcome before turning back to the control console.

"Daddy?" a small voice said from behind the two guests. "What's going on?"

Hannah's eyes widened considerably as little Evelyn trundled past her, and ran into her father's arms.

"This is my daughter, Evelyn," Adam smiled, ignoring Hannah's broken-hearted look. They weren't together, so as far as he was concerned he didn't owe her an explanation, though he was sure she would demand one eventually.

Adam sat in his pilot's chair, and Eve jumped onto his lap, wrapping her arms as far round him as possible —which wasn't much considering their respective sizes.

Brag could almost physically feel the rising tension in the cockpit.

"What is it about 3899 you wanted to warn me about?" Adam asked, wanting to get this over with as quickly as possible. "They've already tried to kill us or capture us more than once. Majors Dunn and Drummond seem to be a big part of the organisation, and they seem to have control over much of the Navy and Army. 3899 also seem to have a black stealth battleship that destroyed the *Gold Royale*."

"I heard that was an accident," Raymond complained.

Brag let out a note of derision, though didn't turn around. "The battleship opened fire on the Gold Royale's engines because I refused to hand Adam over to them."

"And they may be connected to mister Gold," added Adam. Raymond swore, Hannah paled, and Eve whimpered at the mention of the scary man. "He has Silver. She sent a distress call a couple of months ago; I was told to come to Arathea to find some clue to her where she's being held."

"And what did you find?" Hannah said, speaking for the first time since arriving.

"Nothing."

Brag sat up straight. "That's not entirely true. We missed something when we were escaping from Arathea." He paused, bringing a visual image of the attack on the Crystal Palace up on one of the larger display screens, replacing detailed scans of Sansky's shuttle. The image was of the Kara's missiles snaking through space towards the destroyer. The image froze, and then rewound to before the missile launch. Brag zoomed the image onto the destroyer itself, and Adam finally saw what his friend had found.

"They were already moving to leave when we locked onto them." He chuckled at the obviousness of the observation. "Can you tell what course they set?"

"From the speed and direction of the turn, and the strength of the thrusters' burns, I should be able to extrapolate their course." There was an uncomfortable, tension-filled pause as everybody waited for Brag's results. "Ah-ha," he exclaimed. "The course they set was directly toward the very centre of the Andromeda galaxy."

Adam sighed. "Before we go get Silver, I need to get the Navy off our backs."

Brag looked at him questioningly.

"How?"

Adam directed a feral grin at Raymond.

* * *

Delta-Tango system was essentially a *dead* system, filled with hundreds, if not thousands, of moon-sized rocks. Gravitic anomalies peppered the spaces in between like the typhoons of ancient Terra, making travelling through intensely dangerous.

Only a fool would try to pass through the rocks.

This was precisely why the Terran Navy had built their headquarters into the floating rocks. Air-tight offices, briefing rooms, wardrooms, map rooms, armouries, storage, data libraries, mess halls, bunk rooms, operation centres, hangars, dry-docks, ranges, and weapons batteries all contained within the very centre of the asteroid field. Ominous, heavily armed and armoured security stations hung at the edge of the field, overlooking the entire system, whilst a starship the size of a moon waited at an external dry-dock, and hundreds of starfighters patrolled the area. Other warships slipped in and out of the rocks, most of them cruiser-sized or below, whilst several of the Knight-class manoeuvred through, knocking some of the rocks out of the way.

High Admiral Jessica Scarlett, supreme commander of all Terran military forces, stood with her hands clasped at the small of her back, watching the busy military base outside through the two-storey, high windows. Some said she was the most powerful individual in the nineteen galaxies, though she always denied it when confronted with the opinion.

The doors to her massive office slid open, and two aging men stepped through onto the thick, soft carpet. One wore the uniform of an Army General, whilst the other wore a tweed jacket, and carried a brown leather despatch bag.

"General Gardner," she stated. "And this is?"

The aging, slightly hunched Gardner opened his mouth to reply when the man next to him prevented him.

"Admiral Scarlett," the old man beamed in a heavily accented voice. "I am Professor Hans Gruber of ze University of New Terra. It is a pleasure to finally meet somevon of such fame and power."

Scarlett turned, and was somewhat taken aback by the appearance of the professor. He was tall, taller than both her and Gardner, with a big bushy white moustache that looked like he had a furry animal stuck to his upper lip, whilst his fluffy white hair stuck up in all directions like he had been electrocuted in a comedy holo-movie. There were liver spots on his wrinkled face, and a huge grin permanently stitched onto him.

"Your accent," she began.

"German of old Terra," he interrupted.

"You are our twenty-first century expert?"

"*Ja, mein frau.* Vot is it you need of me, Admiral?"

Scarlett exchanged a brief look with Gardner.

"We need to know what a certain person will do. We have no idea what kind of a person he is, and his culture is somewhat antiquated so it is hard to predict where he will go, and what kind of attitudes."

"May I ask who is zee man in qvestion?"

"His name is Adam Caine," Gardner growled, as if saying the name made him nauseous. Scarlett was only vaguely aware that Gardner had had Caine followed, and the time-traveller had given everybody the slip time and time again.

"Ja, I haff heard of zis man. A Royal Marine of ze country of Great Britain. Zey are honourable soldiers who are stubborn, better-trained zan any other military force before or since. Zey were disbanded simply because it vas too dangerous to keep zat kind of large-scale organisation togezzer."

Scarlett was about to ask a question when the intercom on her desk chimed for her attention. She strode over to the massive piece of metal furniture, and tapped the intercom control.

"Scarlett here."

"My lady, this is Captain Gorr from the FPG. We just found five guards unconscious in Hangar 34." Scarlett groaned; Hangar 34 was under construction, awaiting use for a new class of stealth ship. If something was wrong in there, more than likely it was an espionage attempt by a rival power, though that was next to impossible.

"It's him," Gardner sneered. "It's Caine."

It made sense; an expert on Caine's century was here to advise on how to find him —she was sure Caine would try to interfere given his record for giving people the slip.

Gardner stepped over to the tall, cathedral-sized windows to see if he could find the Hangar from the High Admiral's office. Professor Gruber stood by, hands in pockets.

"We did not find anything, Admiral," Captain Gorr reported. *"It looks like they were knocked out by a remote flash-bang device. There is no evidence of anybody else in here."*

Gardner growled a curse from his vantage point.

Suddenly, there was a massive bang as several big explosives detonated at once. The office shook as one went off nearby.

"Admiral, the explosions took out several systems," Gorr reported via the intercom. *"No casualties."*

"None?"

"No, ma'am. The explosions somehow locked all the hangar doors, and took out some of the power in the docks. Whoever did it, they knew what they were doing. We're disabled until we get some additional power to us."

Gorr signed off, leaving the office in silence.

"He is playing you," Gruber announced, "showing you zat he can take out your resources vizout harming a living soul."

"He is good," Scarlett admitted with a nod. She turned back to the visage of the base outside, and then froze when she heard a hauntingly familiar voice.

"Thankyou, Admiral." It had been the unmistakable voice of Adam Caine. She span, and to her horror, Professor Gruber was gone, and no sign of the voice's source. She looked down, and saw a disgusting pile of flesh. No, not flesh, a fleshy mask and fake white hair, lying in a mess with the tweed jacket, and the case. She ran to the pile, followed quickly by Gardner who had cottoned on at the same time as her.

There was a click behind them.

They turned, and there was Caine, dressed in a one-piece black bodyglove. He was holding a twenty-first century pistol, a silencer on the barrel.

"Leave me alone."

"Or what?" Gardner growled.

"Or I show you what a Royal Marine can do when pushed into a corner. The results are quite messy I can assure you."

There was something else in his other hand.

A flash-bang grenade.

It rolled effortlessly from his fingers, and bounced across the floor towards the two senior officers. Before the grenade went off, Scarlett heard Caine speak once more, repeating his warning.

"Leave. Me. Alone."

* * *

The *Kara Marazov* raced out of the Delta-Tango system, chased by Rhino starfighters and half a dozen Navy cruisers, weapons blazing as they tried to bring the alien craft to a halt and capture it.

The ship reached the edge of the star system, and flashed to FTL speeds, leaving the disabled Navy Headquarters behind, and headed straight for the centre of the Andromeda galaxy.

* * *

Silver was trapped in a spherical jail cell.

It was hanging in nowhere, surrounded by nothing and everything. She could see the centre of her people's power, brighter than any star, far below her. She had never seen it before, and wondered if she would ever see it again.

It was so beautiful down there.

Lights jumped and twirled, as if the very stars were dancing to some inaudible tune. Clouds of dust particulates flowed between them like rivers whilst dead planets jostled each other around like a giant game of snooker.

All this passed her little bubble without comment from her.

She was tired, tortured, and without hope.

And Gold continued to rub it in.

Until one day, he materialised beside her cell.

"Your boy is causing some serious problems for myself, and my allies."

Hope rose within her.

"Adam? He's alive?" Despite the physical pain she felt, she started to chuckle, which grew into a snorting laugh, and then descended into a full belly-laugh.

"What is so damned funny?"

Through the racks of laughter, she managed to gurgle the words, "Adam's going to kill you."

Gold stormed off angrily, leaving Silver to her growing hope.

* * *

"That's..."

"Insane," Brag nodded, agreeing with Adam.

Ahead of them was the bright centre of the Andromeda galaxy. Except, it wasn't just bright light from the multitude of stars clustered so close together; there were other things moving in there. Adam compared them to coloured ink floating on top of water.

"The gravitic anomalies alone will tear us apart," Brag stated. "There are some weird temporal energy readings as well; off the charts. They don't match with anything in the other galaxy cores."

"Temporal?" Adam pondered, ignoring Hannah's look of shock at the implication of the dreaded time-travel. "It's definitely the place then." He gripped the controls, and then launched the ship into full throttle. It roared straight toward the very centre before Adam warmed up the FTL drive and slammed it through the outer edge of the galactic core.

Bright light blasted through the cockpit, overwhelming the automatic dimmers in the windows. The ship started to shake violently. If it weren't for the straps on all the chairs, all of the impromptu crew would be sprawled on the deck or the ceiling, or possibly even the walls; the ship's artificial gravity was randomly switching directions under the stress of the gravity of dozens of stars gathered together.

Hannah felt like she was about to be sick, though her lunch refused to make an appearance on the deck; which was just as well given the random directions of the ship's gravity.

She held onto little Eve as if the green-skinned girl was one of her own. As she looked after the little alien, she couldn't help but think of Sasha and Sapphire, and how they would want to be here with Adam. They were both with family she had discovered on New Terra, attending the school in the small town she and Raymond now lived in. She wondered how she was going to explain that little nugget of information. She had loved him after all -still loved him in fact; how would he take it? She had seen him in his worst possible moments: being tortured, and then exacting bloody revenge on his captors, a bloodthirsty look on his face.

And yet, Adam had found space in his previously cold heart to adopt a little girl as his own daughter, and seemed to genuinely love her as if she were his own. Despite the situation, she found herself angry with Adam for not staying with her, instead of running off around the universe. If he had stayed, he could have been Sasha and Sapphire's father, instead of some stranger who once saved their lives.

The ship continued to violently shake around them as they descended further and further into the galactic core. Black holes appeared all around them, but somehow they made it past them.

Eve was crying her eyes out at being thrown about. Every time her voice was loud enough to be heard over the screeching and creaking of the ship's hull,

Hannah could see Adam flinch as he tried to concentrate on flying the ship's accelerated tumble; from Hannah's vantage point, she was sure Adam simply wanted to take his daughter away from here. But she knew his sense of duty would override that to stop someone like Gold.

And then the ship stopped shaking, and the light outside dimmed to a bearable level. The gravity returned to normal, and Eve's sobs quietened down.

Hannah heard a gasp from Franks.

Ahead they could all see rivers of coloured clouds flowing between hundreds of stars. Above it all, there were dozens of what looked like soap bubbles floating above the stars, each with a small figure inside, like a Kinder Surprise.

"Oh-no," Adam groaned. He was pointing to something on the sensors. "They followed us in."

Franks swore, and Raymond seemed to look embarrassed. The pilot and co-pilot turned slowly toward Raymond, looking suspiciously.

"What is it?" Hannah demanded.

"There's a Knight-class battleship directly behind us," Adam growled. "I didn't see it before because all the anomalies were blinding the sensors. Except that this battleship is not like the others. It's black, has no markings, and for some reason, the last time we saw it, it was carrying two companies of Hunters, and our old friends Drummond and Dunn." Adam's eyes narrowed. "You know the ship, don't you?"

Raymond sighed.

"Construction on the HMS Fortitude was started just before my assignment to Rel Major. She was built using a stealth material that deflects sensors, and with the latest armour, shields, weapons, sensor equipment, engines, and the latest starfighter technology. She was supposed to be the first of a new fleet. On her maiden voyage, she was supposedly attacked and destroyed with all hands."

"So much for the Navy's intelligence," Adam snorted. "I'm guessing it belongs to 3899 now."

"They're not locking onto us," Brag announced. "I don't think they can see us yet."

"Daddy," Eve wailed, pointing to something over Adam's shoulder. "Scary man." Adam's eyes widened, turned, and saw Gold standing in mid-air, glaring at the Kara Marazov, arms folded across his chest.

"All of you stay in here," Adam ordered, his tone indicating he wasn't going to accept no for an answer. "I don't know how, but the sensors say that there's oxygen and some kind of solid surface out there, so I'm going out there to finish this once and for all. Brag, be ready on the cannons; if any of those creatures appear nearby, open fire on them and Gold. And if you can, get missile locks on the Fortitude's major systems. In this place, we might have an advantage over them."

Brag nodded.

Adam disappeared into a lower deck, and then reappeared ten minutes later, wearing the black skin-tight armour-weave suit, and carrying his cherished SA80 and Walther P99. He kissed Eve on the forehead and promised he would see her soon, before nodding silently to the others and leaving the ship.

* * *

He stepped off the port wing of his ship, and stepped out onto nothingness that felt like solid ground. He looked down, and was amazed that he really was standing on nothingness. It was intensely disorienting, even worse than the vertigo he had experienced when he first looked out of the back of a Hercules four-prop at thirty-thousand feet over the Atlantic.

So what the hell am I standing on? Get it together, Adam, or you're not going to be any use to anyone. Gold was smiling, apparently noticing Adam's discomfort. In fact, Adam could now hear him chuckling, which sent shivers up and down his spine so much he thought there was an underground train network in his back.

He took a tentative step forward, and found there was a flash under his foot, like a forcefield or something similar.

Christ, I feel like Indiana Jones.

He took another step, and the flash appeared again. He shook his head, gripped his rifle, and started walking.

Gold seemed to stop chuckling as he realised that Adam wasn't going to be so easily disturbed by the insane environment. A part of Adam's brain –the rational part- almost completely shut down, refusing to believe that he was hanging in mid-air without a James Bond jet pack in sight. The irrational part of his brain –the part that had brought him through all the horrors of the past ten years- simply kept him walking toward Gold.

He racked the slide on the rifle, flicked the safety off, and made sure the Walther was loaded and ready.

"Well, I have to admit I thought you would never actually make it here," Gold said, with no small amount of surprise. He clasped his hands behind his back, once again assuming the air of a clichéd butler. "That ship of yours is quite astounding."

"That sounds like surprise in your voice, Gold."

"Perhaps," the alien conceded. "Then again, perhaps I planned this."

Adam snorted. "You really do talk a lot of old bollocks, don't you?" He stopped walking only a few metres from his opponent.

Gold looked as though he had been slapped, and anger flushed his face red.

So their race aren't entirely non-corporeal, Adam mused. *If he shows physical signs of anger like Diamond, embarrassment, and such, then he probably has a weakness.*

"You are extremely crass for someone who was born and raised as a member of the British upper-class," Gold sniffed.

"A career in the Marines will do that to you, I'm afraid," Adam smiled back.

"So what now, Adam Caine? We keep bumping into each other down the years?"

"No, this is where it ends; for you."

Gold chuckled, shaking his head.

And then, suddenly, he started to fade.

"Oh no you don't," Adam growled. Without thinking, Adam charged towards the bastard. There was a bright rush of light that engulfed Gold and Adam before dissipating completely, taking the two with it.

* * *

In the cockpit of the *Kara Marazov*, Adam's friends and family watched as the two figures vanished from view. Hannah gasped, and Eve screeched for her daddy to come back to her. Sansky was literally on the edge of his seat, peering over Franks' shoulder at the main sensors display. His eyes widened at the readings, and jumped into the pilot's chair to get a better look.

"Temporal readings have risen dramatically," Raymond breathed, hoping he had the readout right.

"I thought this place was already full of temporal energy," Franks commented.

"It is, but this is concentrated beyond anything I've ever heard of."

"So?"

Raymond sighed.

"It's time travel."

* * *

Wind blasted over Adam as he fell into a bottomless pit of streaming colours. It wasn't like the rivers that he had seen in Andromeda's galactic core, but the streams of energy that had peeled off him eight months ago on Yh'reth'gar's flagship.

Great, another round of time travel, Adam grimaced, *just when I thought I would escape all that Quantum Leap crap.*

The wind continued to blast him even as he could see shapes forming around him. They were indistinct at first as the blues flashed past him in torrents. Then he could see the shapes of people, vehicles, even buildings. There was a roar, and then suddenly he was standing in the middle of a busy thoroughfare.

Hundreds of humans all looked at him as if time travelling were an everyday occurrence. Or was it? Had they thought that he had teleported in to that spot? Teleportation was common in the forty-first century... perhaps this wasn't time travel? Perhaps it had been some emergency teleporter Gold made use of in just such an event as had taken place.

Adam's questions were answered when he looked above the buildings of the street around him was a sight he never thought he would lay eyes on again: Big Ben, in all its shining glory. It stood in front of insanely tall buildings that had the same architectural design as the Terran buildings in New Amsterdam: modular-looking grey structures that reached far into the sky.

"Oh my God, this is London; this is Earth." Several passers-by looked at him like he was mad, talking to himself as he clearly was. None of them seemed to be concerned that he was carrying a large, menacing firearm.

"Well done, Caine," Gold's sarcasm growled from behind him. "Your powers of deduction are truly astounding."

"Thankyou, I'm quite proud of my detective skills," Adam sneered. He thought briefly about firing on Gold, but that would do nothing to the old man, and would probably just start a mass panic in the crowds around the two opponents. Perhaps a grenade might finally kill him... no, Adam needed to get back to the forty-first century, where his daughter awaited him. Then he would kill the bastard.

Adam tried not to let the awe of his surroundings get to him; he had spent a year without seeing Earth —the last time had been from space during his last sojourn through time, watching as the countries of his home planet attempted to annihilate each other. It wasn't a pleasant image to have rattling around in his brain, but it was there all the same.

Adam gazed around him, belatedly realising he was standing only a block away from Piccadilly Square; he could just see the big screened adverts on the sides of buildings in the square, barely any different than London in 2006.

"So what time period have you brought us to?" he asked, resting his hands on top of his rifle.

"I didn't bring you; you jumped into the vortex."

Adam shrugged, and Gold sighed.

"This is May fourteenth, of the Terran year thirty-eight-ninety-nine AD."

Adam's brain struggled to remember what significance that date had. It was right on the tip of his tongue when the ground vibrated beneath him. He would have thought that it was some big vehicle passing nearby if it were not for the fact that there weren't any vehicles passing by at that moment.

The ground continued to rumble. The frightened looks on those around him were enough to convince him this was not a normal thing.

And then several large fireballs streaked across the sky. They trailed long white tails of smoke and fire, smashing aircraft and starships out of the air like they were merely playthings.

Screams of panic and fear filled the streets, and Adam watched as the people fled from the sight of the asteroids plunging across the British sky. They didn't look big, but he knew that looks could be deceiving —the asteroids could be far away. Another asteroid roared over Adam's head, and he could even feel the heat from its burning carcass. It slammed through several buildings, and then plunged through the London Eye.

Adam's hand shook involuntarily; the sheer destruction of what he could see made 9/11 look like a small fender bender in comparison.

Something, God knew what, clicked in his head, connecting the date with the asteroids: Earth's destruction.

And he was stuck in the middle of it.

Holy crap, he worried, *I'm literally going to see the end of my own world. After all those battles, this is how it's going to end. I'll never see Eve, or Hannah, or Brag or the others.*

Beside him, Gold was laughing; he was enjoying seeing his enemy fall from grace so badly. Adam's hand instinctively went to the hilt of his combat knife. He slid it out of its small scabbard, and swung it in a tight circle to his left. The knife passed through Gold's neck just like the bullets had on the remains of Odyssey Station. Gold laughed even harder.

Meteorites hurtled through the air, blasting apart more craft and smashing through buildings.

How could this happen? How could asteroids get anywhere near the homeworld of humanity without anyone knowing? He recalled the history file had mentioned EMP, though the specifics were lost to him, as he had been drugged up in the Polly Jenkins' med-bay. Whatever, there had to be a reason. Adam wasn't sure it mattered though, as the planet was being bombarded.

Asteroids were now filling the sky, some falling nearby, others continuing on into the distance. Up in the sky, behind it all, he could see something big moving, and getting bigger and bigger with every second. There were brief flashes around the object, making him wonder if that was the Terran Navy trying to obliterate it with their ships.

Gold was still laughing. "Come, Caine, and watch the end of your world from a better vantage point." Wind slammed into Adam, and the world turned white, only to be replaced by the bland white of the interior of a Terran space station.

Adam and Gold stood in one of the station's observation domes, Earth filling half their view. Adam could now clearly see the devastation wrought on his planet: continents were ablaze, cities were darkened by power cuts, whilst even the oceans seemed to be boiling, mimicking the Bible's idea of Armageddon.

He looked up, and saw to his amazement and utter horror, an asteroid bigger than Earth's moon slowly tumbling towards Earth. The flashes he had seen before were indeed the Terran Navy attempting to physically stop the massive asteroid; but the flashes weren't their weapons, it was the ships themselves. Each time one of them got close to the rock, their power suddenly went out, and they were dragged into the asteroid's gravitic pull before exploding on the surface.

Even now, he watched, as what he assumed was a Terran titan was snapped in half in a blur of fireballs and debris.

He almost couldn't watch.

The asteroid could not be stopped, though there were thousands of craft leaving the planet in a wave, metal filling the sky like locusts.

An evacuation, he thought. *How many of them will survive though?*

The asteroid struck Earth with such force that the planet's atmosphere rippled before completely giving way. The asteroid crunched into the Earth's crust, the great speeds of the two planetary bodies crumbling each one.

Magma boiled out of the Earth's cores, cooling and steaming as it touched the vacuum of space. The crust splintered along every continent. Adam didn't want to count the amount of people who died when the atmosphere was stripped away in a puff of steam and smoke.

Then the planet collapsed in on itself, the remains of the killer asteroid shattering into millions of pieces.

Adam had expected there to be an explosion or a shockwave like in Star Wars, but there was nothing other than rock, debris, and dying starships. Adam dropped to his knees, and placed his forehead against the transparent material. He felt sick –he'd just seen his home die in front of his very eyes, and could do nothing to stop it.

Something red out the corner of his eye caught his attention. With his forehead still on the window, he turned his head to see what it was, and caught a glimpse of a red spiked starship identical to one of those that had protected Yh'reth'gar's flagship during the final assault.

It was a Core cruiser.

But what were they doing here?

And then it occurred to him that maybe this was the reason the Core had not made any open moves against the Terrans, despite their alliance to Gold: because they had destroyed Earth, and probably thought humanity were no threat.

Nah, that doesn't make any sense, Adam thought, *the Core were fanatical about killing humans or using them to their own advantages. Certainly Yh'reth'gar had been. Why destroy Earth, but not the rest of humanity? The Terran Consortium covers almost two galaxies after all.*

There was a rush of light and wind behind him. Without thinking, he stood, span, and dove at Gold, just as the creature was fading away once again.

* * *

Hannah was still trying to calm little hysterical Eve down when Adam and the creature Gold reappeared in a flash of squirming light.

Hannah handed the little green girl to Franks and made for the exit.

"Where do you think you're going?" demanded Sansky.

"Out there to help Adam."

"Then I'll go, and you stay here," he ordered, pushing past her.

"I am not one of your agents: you can't order me around."

He let out an angry sigh, and shook his head in frustration.

"Fine, but I'm coming with you."

The two bolted out of the Kara's cockpit, leaving Franks and Evie alone.

"Bye then," said Franks.

* * *

The wind disappeared, and Adam and Gold were back in Andromeda's core.

"This is the end of our sparring. Goodbye, Caine." He nodded, and suddenly a score of the Odyssey creatures surrounded Adam, teeth sharper than ever, arm-blades glinting reflections of the surrounding light. Gold walked off in the other direction; Adam knew better than to try and shoot him. So he flicked the rifle on full auto, and sprayed it in a circle, taking out six of the creatures.

They were more cautious than the previous incarnations, and Adam found he had time to take out another three before the first was on him. It was too fast for even Adam, plunging two of its blades into his shoulders, and bowling them both onto whatever they were standing on. Adam managed to barely get a hand around one of the other blades, before jamming his elbow under its chin to prevent it biting his head clean off.

It shook and shook, trying to get itself free, jiggling the blades in Adam's shoulders around, causing terrific pain to lance through him. He cried out, and his strength waned for a second, letting the snapping jaws come within a centimetre of taking his face off. He could smell its rotting breath, like a hundred corpses. He hooked his knees under its chest, and then got his feet into a good position, before sharply extending his legs, sending the creature yelping away, though not before tearing its blades out of his shoulders, trailing his blood.

It suddenly exploded in mid-air, along with the remaining creatures, all torn apart into steaming, bloody chunks. It took Adam a second to realise that the Kara Marazov had opened fire with its four plasma cannons.

Brag had been waiting for Adam to get down on the ground, to get a clear shot.

Gasping at the pain, Adam struggled to his feet, only to find Hannah and Raymond running out to him.

"I told you to stay inside," Adam gurgled. There was blood welling up in his mouth; either he had bitten his tongue, or he was bleeding internally. Again.

"You really think we'd sit there and watch you die?" Hannah exclaimed, cradling Adam's head in her hands. Raymond was holding what Adam took to be a med-pack. He opened it, and brought out a device that looked like an energy weapon. He activated it, and pointed it at Adam's wounds. A wide beam of blue energy leapt out of the end of the device, and waved across his wounds.

Searing pain radiated out from his shoulders, and he gasped again. Several long minutes later, the wounds had been shut and cauterised. The internal bleeding had been stopped, but there was still excruciating pain from the areas where the blades had pierced.

Raymond helped him to his feet, and slung the med-kit over one shoulder, before producing two Navy-issue plasma pistols. He handed one to Hannah, knowing full well that she wanted to stay to make sure Adam was alive and well. So did Raymond.

Adam knew better than to argue a second time, and gripped his rifle before taking a long stride. One of the creatures twitched all over suddenly, and Adam put a round through its head. He strode off in the direction Gold had walked off, ignoring the immense pain flaring through his body.

He started to jog, barely able to see Gold in the distance.

Then he began sprinting, leaving the other two behind him, his strength and training kicking in like never before, despite the equipment he was wearing, and the injuries he had sustained.

* * *

Gold turned to see, with no small amount of horror, Adam Caine charging towards him once again, a murderous look on his face, the rifle in his hands gripped tightly. He had been so smug minutes ago, happy and ecstatic that Caine was taken care of. He had heard the ship's weapons in the background behind him, and simply put it down to Caine's friends taking their vengeance on the creatures.

Except, Caine wasn't dead.

The inferior being had once again defied death itself to get to Gold.

"No," he breathed, "it can't be."

But Caine stopped in his tracks as something massive roared overhead: it was Gold's Terran allies, the black-hulled *HMS Fortitude*, belonging to the self-righteous Kombat 3899. It slowed, and hung above Gold and Caine like a massive thundercloud.

One of Gold's bubble-cells drifted behind him and then to his left, before stopping. Inside the cell, Silver was banging on the sides, pointing to the bubble around her. Adam seemed to understand, pulled the rifle up against his shoulder, and fired.

The bubble shattered instantly, and Silver fell weakly out and onto the invisible floor. Adam helped her up, not reacting when he saw the cuts and bruises on her face.

Of course, in Adam's world, when something good happens, invariably, something bad is just around the corner: A dozen figures teleported in a ring around Adam, Silver, and Gold, ten of which were clad in black carapace armour, and holding matt-black plasma rifles.

"Hunters," Adam growled, "led by Majors Dumb and Dumber."

Dunn scowled, and Drummond sneered.

"What the hell are you two doing here?" Adam demanded.

"We have come to lay claim to what rightfully belongs to Terra," Dunn said, with a superior air. She ignored the fact that Colonel Sansky was a superior officer, or the fact that they were stood on nothingness, or even the rifle now being pointed at her shaven head.

Gold was chuckling. Neither he nor Adam were surprised, a fact that disturbed both of them. Adam didn't flinch, not once. He ignored the Hunters pointing guns at him; in the energy-rich environment there was sod-all guarantee that their weapons would be able to fire anything other than sparks. He ignored the looks of contempt from Dunn and Drummond, and then blew Dunn's brains out. Her body collapsed, then fell down through the invisible floor, and kept falling into the rivers of energy below.

Drummond's jaw dropped, as did Hannah's and Silver's.

Gold was *still* chuckling. He had obviously been expecting the duplicity of 3899's agents.

The Hunters didn't open fire, instead their rifles lowered slightly as they all hesitated, unsure of what to do next. Even Drummond looked slightly befuddled.

"This is our people's centre of power," Silver suddenly explained in a hurry. "It's the source of our time-travelling abilities. Without it, we are simply a humanoid race with long lives. There's no time to explain, but a large energy source has to be detonated at the very centre."

"Like a ship's reactor?" Raymond asked. He wasn't looking at Silver; he was looking at the *HMS Fortitude* above them.

Adam scooped Silver up in his arms, and then bolted toward the Kara, only moments ahead of Hannah and Raymond. Drummond and the Hunters were still unsure of what to do. Sensing things had taken a turn for the worse Drummond had herself and the soldiers teleported back to the ship, leaving Gold gawping after his retreating enemies. He could feel Silver's greater power keeping him from using his own.

This isn't fair, he complained. *You can't do this.*

"YOU CAN'T!!!" he bellowed.

He stood there, impotent as the *Kara Marazov* began to move; the alien ship launched a wave of missiles on the unshielded *Fortitude*, Brag's earlier targetting doing the trick quite nicely in the energy-rich environment.

Explosions rippled across the Terran warship's black hull as Caine's ship pummelled the battleship mercilessly. Normally, a ship of that size couldn't hope to outgun a Terran battleship, but its alien systems, its overloaded warheads, and its powerful sensors outclassed the *Fortitude* in sheer style. Also, the galactic core was messing with the bigger ship's systems, randomly overloading the shields and sensors even before being attacked.

Burnt, twisted hull plating the size of houses fell all around Gold, narrowly missing him.

It seemed that the *Fortitude* had become the living embodiment of Gold's schemes and plans: falling apart around his ears. Escape pods, shuttles, and starfighters punched out of the great ship, even as the Kara flitted around its aft section, pounding it with wave after wave of lethal energy and missiles. The escaping craft didn't bother to stop to exact revenge on the Kara, instead opting to get the hell out of there, and back to civilisation.

The *Fortitude* began to list nose-down, flames pouring from her hind end. She sunk, and came within inches of hitting Gold. It crashed through several more of the bubble cells, before disappearing into the white light.

"No," he whispered. "NO!"

Fortitude's reactor, breached by the *Kara*'s powerful weapons, detonated, mixing with the masses of temporal energy that had been roiling around in the galactic core for thousands of years. The surviving bubbles, his experiments, began drifting down toward the detonation, as if being pulled. Then everything else began slowly sinking, even the invisible floor Gold now stood on.

The bubbles burst, tumbling his experiments down, screaming as they realised that this was finally the end. The floor underneath Gold began to rumble and shake, and suddenly started to crack.

He slapped the emergency teleport on his wrist, and disappeared in a flash of light, just as the floor beneath him shattered, and the shards sucked into the vortex below.

* * *

"This one's going to be close," Adam cried. Sat at the controls, he could see the stars in the galactic core being pulled toward the growing distortion far behind the *Kara*. Even the clouds of energy and dust were starting to flow downwards, like the lava flows during his 'tests' with Diamond.

Silver cried out in anguish as her powers suddenly diminished and she became permanently corporeal. It was a horrendously painful experience. Not only that, she knew the rest of her people were experiencing the same change all over the universe.

The pull on the *Kara* was getting stronger and stronger, slowing her down faster and faster as she tried to escape. Adam had the engines at 110 percent, and could already hear the groans and creaks from them, even down in the cockpit. The speed was decreasing when suddenly, like a rubber band snapping, the ship shot forward.

Except, it wasn't over.

That would be too easy, wouldn't it?

A massive shockwave knocked the ship over, tumbling it out into space. Sparks flew in the cockpit, Eve wailed, and something mechanical screamed. Adam couldn't move to see what it was, the g-forces from the tumbling nightmare pressing his entire body into the chair. He was sure the others were experiencing exactly the same.

Then the shockwave passed, and the ship's autopilot righted them.

They all breathed a huge sigh of relief.

Adam turned and was about to make a quip about being lucky when the weapons lock alarm blared for attention.

"Come on, you can't be serious."

"I'm afraid so," Brag said apologetically. There was a gasp behind Caine, and when he turned, he found the barrel of a plasma pistol inches from his nose. "I'm sorry, Adam, but could you please get out of your chair, and step away from the controls."

"What the hell is this?"

"I'm so sorry, Adam, but you cost me everything. Now you're going to repay that debt by letting me hand you over to Navy Intelligence."

"I'm a senior agent for NI," Raymond growled. "This isn't a sanctioned operation; Intelligence doesn't want Adam captured, followed, or surveilled. The people doing this work for an unauthorised, unofficial organisation called Kombat 3899."

"I am aware of who they are, Colonel." Brag's weapon didn't falter as he turned to the others. "But they have power, and they promised me they would give me a command in the Navy. I'll have a life again."

Adam growled.

Eve moved suddenly, and Brag's gun swung round to point at the movement. Big mistake, he realised, as Adam moved quickly out of his field of vision. The big man moved faster than the eye could see, and instantly had his hands snaked around Brag's wrist.

"Please, you must comply," Brag pleaded.

"You turned a gun on my daughter," roared Adam, before twisting his hands, and loudly snapping Brag's wrist. He hadn't let a non-corporeal super-being threaten little Evie, let alone someone purporting to be his friend.

The former starship captain fell to the floor in agony. Adam looked at him like he was a piece of turd on the bottom of his shoe. He had never tolerated betrayal, especially now when his daughter had been in danger.

Sadness welled up within him; Brag had been his best friend, one of the few people he could trust in this nightmarish universe, and now that very same man had betrayed him, and his daughter, to those who wanted nothing more to kill them or capture them all, within a matter of seconds. Had he planned this all along? Adam realised how the Fortitude had found them so quickly after leaving Delta-Tango and why Brag had looked so guilty when Adam had caught him messing with the comms controls.

He forced the tears back, and grabbed Brag by the wrist. He dragged the man out of the cockpit, and to the airlock on the port side.

"Put that on," he said, his voice barely above an angry whisper. He was pointing to a generic EVA suit hanging from a hook by the airlock doors. Brag complied, not wanting to argue with a demonstrably stronger, faster, bigger man. He slipped into the suit without a sound, wincing silently every time he moved his wrist, and then snapped the small helmet on. Adam slapped the airlock cycle control, opening the inner door. He pushed Brag in.

"You bastard," he sneered, before closing the small door, and slapping the outer door control.

* * *

Brag Franks was blasted into space by the sudden depressurisation of the airlock. He didn't float far though, only a few metres off the port wing of the *Kara*. The crescent-shaped ship suddenly leaped forward, and was gone before he could take more than a few long breaths.

"What have I done?"

* * *

Diamond, mother of Gold, and instructor to the unbreakable Caine, found herself suddenly mortal again. She had been watching the past history of the planet where she had trained Caine, when suddenly immense pain suffused her entire body, and she was dragged back to the present, and unceremoniously dumped onto the grass around her temple.

She had tried for hours to travel through time, or even to teleport several metres. She just couldn't.

She knew what it meant; it meant that someone had destroyed the temporal core of the Andromeda galaxy with enough force to return her –and probably all of her race- to humanoid/corporeal form.

She suspected that Adam Caine had something to do with it.

Who else?

She noticed the book he had given her just lying where she had left it two weeks ago. It was a little dusty, though since there was no rain in this area of the jungle, it hadn't degraded.

She sighed, and picked up the book.

"Perhaps you were right, Caine."

She opened the front cover, and was horrified to find that the inside had been hollowed out, and an electronic device had been put inside. There was a timer on the device, announcing that there was only five seconds left to go before it activated.

"Damn you, Caine," she said.

The explosion vaporised her, and a two-metre circle of the grass around her.

* * *

Two tense, silent days later, the *Kara* was back at the lifeless planet where they had left Sansky's shuttle hidden in the nearby nebula.

Adam and Eve were stood in the cockpit, holding hands, whilst Raymond and Hannah were gathering themselves from their own chairs. Silver was also stood with them, though she had no intention of leaving just yet.

"I'm sorry for what happened," Hannah said softly, placing a comforting hand on his shoulder.

"Thankyou," he nodded back. "You two should be happy together." Hannah looked at him with horror, and Raymond's face was somewhat blank. Hannah tried to say something, but nothing came out. He smiled, the guilt of having slept with the Terran Queen abating completely. "I can see the way you two look at each other when you think I'm not paying attention." He held out a hand to Raymond, who shook it gratefully. "Good luck. I hope you'll invite me to the wedding." He knew he wouldn't be, and knew that even if he was invited he had no intention of going. "Say hi to Sasha and Sapphire for me."

"We will," Hannah promised. She nodded wordlessly to Silver before stepping out of the cockpit, and heading for the airlock.

"I'll try to keep Intelligence off your back for as long as I can, Adam," Raymond stated, though Adam knew that Raymond would not be successful, despite his rank, and influence. He too nodded to Silver, though more of a courtesy than anything else; neither knew each other, nor were they ever likely to.

"What is the Arcbane?"

Silver paused, and waited for Sansky and Hannah to disappear in the emergency teleporter beam before replying. She had a horribly shocked look on her face, confirming Adam's suspicions that the name was important.

"It is a weapon, as I'm sure you have probably already guessed. But it is too dangerous for anyone to possess, no matter how much of a saint they may or may not be. The Arcbane is a device of utter dread from the ancient times; it was a legend among my people. A ghost story, if you will. I discovered the truth of it some centuries ago, not long after your disappearance from the London Underground, in fact." She sighed, fingering the back of the co-pilot's chair. "I had to hide it from others."

"Gold."

Silver nodded. "The Arcbane can never be used; not ever."

"I know. When I translated Arcbane into ancient Rijiin, then back into Standard, it came out as 'galaxy killer'. If it's so powerful, why not destroy it?"

"The device was built by the first race; their technology is far beyond that of even my people. I have no interest in meddling with that kind of volatility. Besides, it was lost during the Great Cataclysm that destroyed their race. Nobody knows where it went or even if it still exists."

The two allies stood side-by-side, staring out of the cockpit window.

"So. What are you going to do now then, Silver?"

"Could you drop me off at a planet called Gol Trath?"

Adam felt no small amount of sadness; he had hoped she would at least stay for a while, show him the universe, explain what the hell had just happened back in Andromeda's core.

However, she wasn't omnipotent anymore -the shockwave and the preceding destruction of the source of her people's time-travelling abilities had robbed her of everything but long life, trapping her in human form, as it would have done for all her people, Gold included.

"I need to go find whatever of my people are left. Besides, I imagine Gold is out there somewhere, causing trouble as usual, and I can't keep asking you to fight him over and over again."

"Well, it's been... interesting knowing you, Silver." Adam smiled, sat Evelyn in the co-pilot's chair, and strapped her in, before settling into the pilot's seat.

"What are you going to do after this?" Silver asked, taking her own seat.

Adam sighed, his eyes squinting through the cockpit window, as if he could see all the way to Gol Trath. Raymond's shuttle was pulling away and heading back to the Linkway, its course unknown to him.

Adam looked over at his little daughter, who was giggling at finally being allowed to sit in the co-pilot's chair.

A feral grin passed over his lips.

"I go back to doing what I do best."

"Which is?"

He kept grinning.

"Hunting."

* * *

January 4001ad.
Death.

It was on a backwater planet that he met his demise.

The society that lived there were primitive, barely intelligent enough to create much more than rudimentary spears and fur wraps, much like Earth's ice age. Unlike that long-dead planet, though, this world was covered with jungle, and was frequently wracked with continent-stomping monsoons.

As he ran, he didn't care that he was surrounded by thick jungle foliage.

He didn't care that it was this continent's night-cycle, and therefore hard to see anything at all.

He didn't care that there were indigenous predators watching him from a distance, or that the native humanoids had taken an interest in him as a source of entertainment.

He didn't care that the rain was slating down into his face, stinging his eyes, and filling his mouth every time he opened his inner lips to take a desperate breath. Nor did he care that the rain was turning the dangerously unused path into slippery mud. He had already slipped and fell into a ditch twice, covering himself and his clothes with mud.

He didn't care that he had ditched anything that wasn't attached to said clothes to gain a bit more speed, including his precious armour.

He didn't care that the mud was encrusting his shoes and legs.

He just wanted to stay ahead of the monster chasing him.

A year ago, he was enjoying the high life; his star was rising, his superiors, his family, and colleagues had all been singing his praise. Now, he was an exile, or would be, if he were ever to return home.

The monster chasing him was most definitely going to kill him for his crimes. It had been chasing him for two Terran weeks, constantly appearing where he would never expect it, barely one step behind him as he ran and flew through a dozen planets.

He could hear the snapping and cracking of branches, twigs, and dead undergrowth as he stumbled blindly along the path, brushing large green leaves out of his face every few seconds.

He could see a clearing ahead.

He would have to go around it to avoid being seen so clearly.

He hoped his pursuer was not as trained as he seemed to be.

His hope was a vain one.

Lightning snaked down from the black heavens, and struck a tall tree. Sparks flew off the tree as it was electrocuted and completely cooked from the inside out. Its great weight snapped with its sudden lack of inner support. The tree's corpse collapsed across his path. He cursed, and was about to clamber over when something hit his side. It felt like an entire starship had smacked him.

He was sent flying, and tumbled into the clearing he had been trying to avoid.

He could hear the near-silent footsteps of a trained hunter behind him as he scrambled across the clearing toward the other side where he might find some sort of safety.

There was a pause in the thunder, lightning, and rain.

In that terrible pause, there was a *pfft*, and suddenly white-hot pain flared in his leg. He fell, and slammed into the wet ground. A rib snapped as he hit the floor without protection, arms flailing hopelessly to protect himself from the floor.

A boot connected with his midsection.

"Why are you doing this?" he cried.

"Because of all that you've done," the hunter shouted over the returned crackling thunder and lightning.

The pursued craned his long neck round to see the hunter. The hunter was humanoid, wearing an armour-weave one-piece black body glove that showed off the thick muscles underneath; a thick leather equipment belt was at the centre of a web of dark straps, holsters, and pouches. A long, silenced bolt-action rifle was strapped to the hunter's back. What made the hunter even more sinister was the suit's hood. The eyepieces were rectangular and coloured a dim green that reflected the glare of the lightning; the hood was seamless, showing the outline of a human male's head.

There was a weapon in one of the human's hands, a blocky solid-round pistol with a silencer screwed onto the barrel. Like the rifle on the hunter's back, and the hunter's attire, the pistol was a matt-black —the kind assassins used. The silenced barrel was now pointing at the pursued's forehead.

"Who are you?" the pursued said through gritted teeth, trying to fight off the pain in his leg.

"You don't recognise me?"

"Of course not!"

The hunter lowered the pistol to point at his victim's legs, and squeezed the trigger twice. The pistol let out two more sharp *pfft* noises, and the pursued let out a strangled cry of pain. The human weapon was doing more damage to him than an energy weapon of similar size could ever do. The pain was overwhelming.

The barrel of the weapon was now pointing at the pursued's mid-section.

"Who are you?" he sobbed; the pain was so bad, he could no longer concentrate on keeping his emotions under control as he once could.

With the silenced barrel still pointing unwaveringly at the pursued's chest, the hunter's other hand reached up behind his head and began pulling at the hood. It slipped over his head, releasing the long, brown, unkempt hair that framed the strongly defined face underneath.

Second Yh'par'ban, once second-in-command to Lord Yh'reth'gar and a member of the bird-like Core species, screeched and clacked his beak in fear as he looked upon the face of Adam Caine.

* * *

Caine wasn't smiling, wasn't making any body or facial gesture that he was enjoying this situation.

"How did you survive? The last I saw of you, the air was escaping from Yh'reth'gar's escape craft, and you were heading for a very nasty death against an asteroid."

Yh'par'ban sighed, which sounded more like a gurgle in the rain that kept collecting in his open beak. He was dead; he knew that for a fact. He had tortured and beaten Caine, killing him and bringing him back to life; no matter how noble Caine was, there was no way he would let Yh'par'ban live a day longer. "I was able to get the other EVA suit from the closet you hid in. As for after that, I managed to find allies of my people to help me stay hidden."

"Why hide?"

Yh'par'ban was unsettled by Caine's serene calm; how long had the human envisaged this situation, planning out what he would do, how he would react? Was this situation going *exactly* how Caine wanted? What had Yh'par'ban released in Caine during those days of insane torture? Was this human even human anymore?

His claws started to shake with fear. Or was that the loss of blood kicking in?

"I hid because the Patriarch would kill me for not protecting his youngest son."

Yh'par'ban saw Caine shift slightly, and one of his eyebrows shot up, though there was still no other emotion on his pale face.

"The Patriarch?"

"Yh'reth'gar's father. I suspect even someone like you would think twice about attacking him. He is not someone you would want directing their attention on you, especially those he perceives to be weak."

"Do the Core know about Terrans?"

Yh'par'ban nodded. "At the moment though, the humans of this time are too strong militarily to be worth the effort of a full-scale invasion. With all the pirates and criminals picking away at your people's civilisation, however, it could only be a few years before the Patriarch deems your people week enough to be invaded and conquered." Yh'par'ban paused for dramatic effect, taking time to look into Caine's hard eyes. "And you are going to make sure your people are ready, aren't you? Your skills suggest you have the training to be a universal-class assassin. If I were to survive this, I would be checking the death notices every day." He sighed. "But I am not going to survive this. You could never allow it."

Now Caine finally smiled.

That smile was the most frightening thing Yh'par'ban had seen in his entire life.

It was also the last thing he ever saw.

One sharp *pfft* of the silenced weapon, and Yh'par'ban was dead, his brains blown out the back of his ridged head.

Adam felt no relief at having killed the being that had tortured him nearly a year ago. Ironically, thanks to Yh'par'ban's insidious ministrations, he would not have become the man he was today.

Adam felt sick, knowing he owed this creature a great deal.

Adam roared in frustrated anger, and emptied his silenced Walther P99's magazine into Yh'par'ban's lifeless body.

It was over.

He span, and stalked off into the jungle.

Ten:
What Happened Next

"To exorcise your demons is to rid yourself of all your fears and worries. I just wish my grandfather didn't take it so literally all the time. Though by what my mother told me, he had no choice in the matter..."
-Roath Caine.

January 4001ad.

MB7823.

It was a star system in the outer rim of the Milky Way galaxy, far from the eyes of the Terran Navy's patrols. A young system in universal terms, it had two even younger planets, one of which was a hot ball of dust, the other a jungle-covered nightmare with a burgeoning primitive race.

A crescent-shaped blue ship darted into the second planet's atmosphere, briefly lighting up with flames as its shields hit the ionosphere. It created a brief tail of fire like a shooting star as it plummeted to the ground.

It slowed and then hovered above the ground, before extending landing claws that sunk into the jungle floor. A sole figure stepped out of its hatch, covered in black skin-tight body armour, and armed to the teeth.

He climbed down to the ground, and then disappeared from sight.

* * *

It was on this backwater planet that Yh'par'ban met his demise.

The society that lived there was primitive, barely intelligent enough to create much more than rudimentary spears and fur wraps, much like Earth's ice age. Unlike that long-dead planet, though, this world was covered with jungle, and was frequently wracked with continent-stomping monsoons.

As he ran, he didn't care that he was surrounded by thick jungle foliage.

He didn't care that it was this continent's night-cycle, and therefore hard to see anything at all.

He didn't care that there were indigenous predators watching him from a distance, or that the native humanoids had taken an interest in him as a source of entertainment.

He didn't care that the rain was slating down into his face, stinging his eyes, and filling his mouth every time he opened his inner lips to take a desperate breath. Nor did he care that the rain was turning the dangerously unused path into slippery mud. He had already slipped and fell into a ditch twice, covering himself and his clothes with mud.

He didn't care that he had ditched anything that wasn't attached to his clothes to gain a bit more speed, including his precious armour.

He didn't care that the mud was encrusting his shoes and legs.

He just wanted to stay ahead of the monster chasing him.

A year ago, he was enjoying the high life; his star was rising, his superiors, his family, and colleagues had all been singing his praise. Now, he was an exile, or would be, if he were ever to return home.

The monster chasing him was most definitely going to kill him for his crimes. It had been chasing him for two Terran weeks, constantly appearing where he would never expect it, barely one step behind him as he ran and flew through a dozen planets.

He could hear the snapping and cracking of branches, twigs, and dead undergrowth as he stumbled blindly along the path, brushing large green leaves out of his face every few seconds.

He could see a clearing ahead.

He would have to go around it to avoid being seen so clearly.

He hoped his pursuer was not as trained as he seemed to be.

His hope was a vain one.

Lightning snaked down from the black heavens, and struck a tall tree. Sparks flew off the tree as it was electrocuted and completely cooked from the inside out. Its great weight snapped with its sudden lack of inner support. The tree's corpse collapsed across his path. He cursed, and was about to clamber over when something hit his side. It felt like an entire starship had smacked him.

He was sent flying, and tumbled into the clearing he had been trying to avoid.

He could hear the near-silent footsteps of a trained hunter behind him as he scrambled across the clearing toward the other side where he might find some sort of safety.

There was a pause in the thunder, lightning, and rain.

In that terrible pause, there was a *pfft*, and suddenly white-hot pain flared in his leg. He fell, and slammed into the wet ground. A rib snapped as he hit the floor without protection, arms flailing hopelessly to protect himself from the floor.

A boot connected with his midsection.

"Why are you doing this?" he cried.

"Because of all that you've done," the hunter shouted over the returned crackling thunder and lightning.

The pursued craned his long neck round to see the hunter. The hunter was humanoid, wearing an armour-weave one-piece black body glove that showed off the thick muscles underneath; a thick leather equipment belt was at the centre of a web of dark straps, holsters, and pouches. A long, silenced bolt-action rifle was strapped to the hunter's back. What made the hunter even more sinister was the suit's hood. The eyepieces were rectangular and coloured a dim green that reflected the glare of the lightning; the hood was seamless, showing the outline of a human male's head.

There was a weapon in one of the human's hands, a blocky solid-round pistol with a silencer screwed onto the barrel. Like the rifle on the hunter's back, and the hunter's attire, the pistol was a matt-black –the kind assassins used. The silenced barrel was now pointing at the pursued's forehead.

"Who are you?" the pursued said through gritted teeth, trying to fight off the pain in his leg.

"You don't recognise me?"

"Of course not!"

The hunter lowered the pistol to point at his victim's legs, and squeezed the trigger twice. The pistol let out two more sharp *pfft* noises, and the pursued let out a strangled cry of pain. The human weapon was doing more damage to him than an energy weapon of similar size could ever do. The pain was overwhelming.

The barrel of the weapon was now pointing at the pursued's mid-section.

"Who are you?" he sobbed; the pain was so bad, he could no longer concentrate on keeping his emotions under control as he once could.

With the silenced barrel still pointing unwaveringly at the pursued's chest, the hunter's other hand reached up behind his head and began pulling at the hood. It slipped over his head, releasing the long, brown, unkempt hair that framed the strongly defined face underneath.

Second Yh'par'ban, once second-in-command to Lord Yh'reth'gar and a member of the bird-like Core species, screeched and clacked his beak in fear as he looked upon the face of Adam Caine.

* * *

Caine wasn't smiling, wasn't making any body or facial gesture that he was enjoying this situation.

"How did you survive? The last I saw of you, the air was escaping from Yh'reth'gar's escape craft, and you were heading for a very nasty death against an asteroid."

Yh'par'ban sighed, which sounded more like a gurgle in the rain that kept collecting in his open beak. He was dead; he knew that for a fact. He had tortured and beaten Caine, killing him and bringing him back to life; no matter how noble Caine was, there was no way he would let Yh'par'ban live a day longer. "I was able to get the other EVA suit from the closet you hid in. As for after that, I managed to find allies of my people to help me stay hidden."

"Why hide?"

Yh'par'ban was unsettled by Caine's serene calm; how long had the human envisaged this situation, planning out what he would do, how he would react? Was this situation going *exactly* how Caine wanted? What had Yh'par'ban released in Caine during those days of insane torture? Was this human even human anymore?

His claws started to shake with fear. Or was that the loss of blood kicking in?

"I hid because the Patriarch would kill me for not protecting his youngest son."

320

Yh'par'ban saw Caine shift slightly, and one of his eyebrows shot up, though there was still no other emotion on his pale face.

"The Patriarch?"

"Yh'reth'gar's father. I suspect even someone like you would think twice about attacking him. He is not someone you would want directing their attention on you, especially those he perceives to be weak."

"Do the Core know about Terrans?"

Yh'par'ban nodded. "At the moment though, the humans of this time are too strong militarily to be worth the effort of a full-scale invasion. With all the pirates and criminals picking away at your people's civilisation, however, it could only be a few years before the Patriarch deems your people weak enough to be invaded and conquered." Yh'par'ban paused for dramatic effect, taking time to look into Caine's hard eyes. "And you are going to make sure your people are ready, aren't you? Your skills suggest you have the training to be a universal-class assassin. If I were to survive this, I would be checking the death notices every day." He sighed. "But I am not going to survive this. You could never allow it."

Now Caine finally smiled.

That smile was the most frightening thing Yh'par'ban had seen in his entire life.

It was also the last thing he ever saw.

One sharp *pfft* of the silenced weapon, and Yh'par'ban was dead, his brains blown out the back of his ridged head.

* * *

Adam felt no relief at having killed the being that had tortured him nearly a year ago. Ironically, thanks to Yh'par'ban's insidious ministrations, he would not have become the man he was today.

Adam felt sick, knowing he owed this creature a great deal.

Adam roared in frustrated anger, and emptied his silenced Walther P99's magazine into Yh'par'ban's lifeless body.

It was over.

He span, and stalked off into the jungle.

* * *

The rain slashed down at Adam like throwing knives.

The path was muddy, disintegrating as he marched through the jungle. The thunder and lightning had abated, moving off into the distance faster than he could believe. He chided himself for that kind of thinking –this was another planet, and thus its weather patterns could be nothing like those of Earth.

Correction, he mused, *there is no Earth, just an asteroid field where it used to be.*

The path wound away ahead of him, through the trees. The sun –or rather suns as the planet was part of a binary star system- was starting to rise, though he couldn't actually see them, the dark clouds above were starting to brighten ever-so-slightly as the morning came.

There was a howl that didn't belong to the wind; nor did it belong to the throat of an animal. It sounded like a man, or something close to it.

He knew that the planet was recovering from an ice age, much like Earth once had.

He stopped in his tracks.

I've got to stop comparing everything to Earth. Earth's gone, and the universe is a much different place than home. Nowhere was that more apparent than his current location: the strange, knobbly trees, the corpse of the bird-like Yh'par'ban he had left behind in the clearing two minutes ago, not to mention the alien tribesmen that were currently stalking him.

Even over the rain and the wind, he could hear the cracking twigs all around him as the not-so-careful tribesmen hunted him. He didn't consider them threats, though he reloaded his silenced P99 just in case he was wrong.

Guilt ran through him just then as the memory of what he had done only minutes ago burned in his mind. He remembered emptying the magazine of his pistol into the Core warrior's body, even after he knew the being had died. He remembered the rage he felt, and the emptiness it brought.

The realisation of his situation hit him like a hammer.

Yh'par'ban was dead, his last act of vengeance on those who had tortured him. Brag was gone, back to the Navy probably after Adam had dumped him out an airlock inside a space suit. Gold and Silver were gone, returned to a corporeal state after the destruction of their power source in the core of the Andromeda galaxy. Raymond and Hannah were living happily together on New Terra, with Sasha and Sapphire at school. The rest of the survivors were scattered throughout Terran territory. He and Eve were alone in the universe, and for the first time in a year, he had no real purpose, no goal in his life.

He was unsure what to do next.

A growl came from behind, breaking him from his thoughts, and he replaced his black hood, the green eyes glowing menacingly in the dark morning.

The world around him lit up via the hood's night-vision mode.

The tribesman, seven foot tall, with scales, vicious sharp teeth, and enough dodgy tattoos to cover half his body, was mid-swing when Adam spun round. It stopped right there, as if caught by some invisible force. Its face was slightly longer than a human's, with no nose and ears, except for dark slits. Its eyes were yellow, even with the green tint of the night-vision, and had thin black pupils that exuded cruelty. It wore leathery armour made of animal hide stitched together with what looked like cotton. The spiny protrusions on the crest of his head made it look a '50s movie monster.

The creature was alien, but even with the green-tinted world around him, he could see the shock and fright on the thing's face. His ghostly appearance was working in his favour.

Without a second thought, Adam shot the thing in its leg.

It howled in pain, and dropped to the muddy ground, clutching its scaly limb.

There was a responding howl from off in the distance, and Adam smiled. They were scared, though he knew that wouldn't last.

So much for not comparing, he mused, remembering a certain damned old fool saying something similar to a young blond-haired boy and two droids. *I wonder if I get my own Obi-Wan Kenobi, or if Silver was it, and gone the way of the Force the same as Alec Guinness.*

With the tribesman down, Adam turned and strode through the forest, the suit's enhanced systems picking up the sounds of the distant creatures baying for his blood.

He calmly walked down the path, taking in the spectacle of the rising dawn through the night-vision as he crested a ridge to look down on the clearing where he had left his ship. Rather than leave in the middle –the sensible thing a proper pilot would do would be to give the ship room to land- he had parked it under the trees at the edge of the large clearing, hidden in the shadows, where a young girl waited for him.

There was movement beside him. It was brief, but enough to notify Adam of the threat.

He fired the pistol at head height, and one of the alien tribesmen collapsed out of the bush, a large hole through its forehead. There was some more inhuman honking from behind the far bushes, and he could see silhouettes moving among the trees away from the muddy path.

They were still holding back, the dead creature just a scout to test him.

He quickened his pace, but didn't run. If they had any intelligence his running would alert them that he knew they were there.

He needed to get to the *Kara Marazov*, and fast.

They kept pace with him, and he could see their primitive attempts to threaten him, shouting and making noise at him.

He descended down the slope towards his shadowed ship.

A twig snapped quietly behind him, and he heard a wail of surprise as one of the tribesmen took a tumble in the mud and rain. He spun, and unscrewed the silencer, tucking it into the special pocket on his thigh next to the weapon's holster.

This should scare the shit out of them, without the thunder and lightning to cover the noise.

He squeezed the trigger and the weapon barked incredibly loudly, the flash and noise serving to light up the tribesmen sneaking up on him. The first tribesman went down, a gaping hole in its shoulder.

Two more shots, and two more tribesmen went down, howling in pain.

He didn't want to kill them, reasoning that they probably thought he was either a threat to their family grouping, or simply on whatever territory they had staked out in this region.

Another shot ricocheted off a piece of scaly armour, and sliced a vine in half that wrapped around the leg of another tribesman.

A knobbled spear made of wood with a crude stone blade whipped past Adam's ear, close enough almost to feel its wake against his hood. Its arrowhead buried in the ground, and was followed by several others, though none as accurate as the other had almost been. One buried itself in a tall tree trunk.

Adam turned to leave, but stopped when an ear-splitting groan roared across the jungle. Impossibly, it came from the tree. Even more impossibly, the tree began to move, at first shuddering and shaking, and then its branches began moving like arms. It looked like an enraged old oak tree with raggedy wrinkly bark and fraying strips around the upper branches.

How can a tree be alive?

The groaning continued, a thunderously deep affair that sounded the same as when a tree was felled in a forest.

Vines snaked out from the tree to wrap around the neck of an unlucky tribesman, and snapped its neck a little too easily for Caine's comfort. A branch swung down, and swept three tribesmen off their feet, before coming crashing down on two of them, killing them instantly.

The tribesmen, however, were not afraid. Well, as far as Caine could tell considering how alien they were compared to him. They were attacking and shouting –and probably swearing if Caine was any judge- the living tree, throwing their spears at it. The thing roared in pain when one spear stuck into something precious.

The tribesmen were ignoring Caine now, attacking the greater threat.

Caine moved to leave, only to have one of the branches swinging towards him. He dove for the jungle floor, ignoring the underbrush that scratched at him. He rolled under the branch, and came up on his feet in a second. He holstered the 9mm, and unslung the rifle on his back.

It wasn't an SA80 like he had used throughout the last year in this century, and in his previous career, but rather a metal-body Intervention sniper rifle. He was too close to use the sniper scope on top of the weapon, so he flicked it over to full auto, and slammed in a sickle magazine.

He brought the butt of the rifle up to his shoulder, and squeezed the trigger.

A hail of solid bullets peppered the tree.

It did nothing.

The staccato of bangs and the bright muzzle flares from the rifle frightened the tribesmen enough that it caused them to freeze in fear. Four more died when the tree roared and uprooted, its roots tangling around the tribesmen. It crushed them, eliciting bloodcurdling screams as their rib cages were flattened, and their organs turned to mush. The limp bodies were thrown away like rag dolls, crashing off into the darkness of the jungle.

Caine remembered the soft spot that had hurt the tree, and fired a burst of rounds into it.

The tree roared even louder, and reared up, finally ripping itself out of the ground. Soil was flung across the tribesmen, along with gibbering insects, and bundles of small plants and vines battered their armour.

The bullets and spears were hurting it, but they didn't seem to be doing overall damage. He needed something that would *destroy* the tree, not just hurt it. He had no incendiary devices, nor any grenades on him —he had only come out with the rifle and pistol.

He had to make a fire, and quickly.

Easier said than done, he thought, as a branch that was thicker than he was tall came flying towards him. He charged at it, hoping for a miracle, and jumped as high as he possibly could. The ground rushed past underneath him, and the branch filled his vision.

Then it sliced underneath him, the wake of its passing dragging him to the ground quicker than he was ready for. He crunched into a harsh grouping of alien brambles, though they were prevented from getting to his skin by the suit's thin armour. He rolled, and found himself entangled with nature's equivalent to barbwire.

Naturally, Caine's luck was not having a good day: the tree was now swinging *several* branches at him, probably now figuring that *Adam* was the greater threat.

"Bollocks," he muttered, trying to get his legs out from the tangle of brambles. He dropped the rifle, and pulled out a wicked matt-black combat knife that was very close to being big enough to be a machete.

With a few quick slashes, he was out of the brambles just in time to be lifted off his feet from another smaller branch. A rib gave way.

Always with the ribs, he growled inside his own head.

He hung on for dear life as the branch tried to shake him loose. He slammed the point of the knife into the bark, digging it in with all his strength. The knife held, and he managed to drag himself on top of the wooden limb, ignoring the pain shooting through his chest. Unfortunately, his situation didn't seem to have been improved. He clung to the branch, unable to do anything except keep his balance.

Then another branch crashed down on his back.

The armour held, preventing any more damage to his body. The branches twisted, and Adam suddenly lost his grip on his knife, and went flying towards the base of the tree's trunk. He landed on a soft patch of thick lichen, and rolled before the branches could swipe down on top of him.

The tribesmen were baying and growling at the tree. Whether it was for Adam's benefit, or they were goading the tree to attack them, he did not know; he knew it wasn't working because the damn thing skittered towards *him* on its largest roots. And then something grabbed his ankle.

He let out a quiet shriek as it dragged him across the ground towards the underside of the tree —the apparent source of the creature's roaring.

* * *

The tribesmen watched in horror as the interloper was dragged under the young Bilm Tree. Although there weren't many of the hunting party left, the interloper had saved their lives, and been afforded a healthy amount of fear and respect.

But now he was gone, taken by the Bilm to be fed upon.

The Bilm did not move.

It groaned and creaked as if suddenly ill. Then there was a hacking sound of metal on wood, and the Bilm groaned even more, its entire wooden form shuddering as if it was about to explode.

There was a high-pitched scream, and then the Bilm sagged, its top branches and limbs almost touching the floor.

More hacking noises came from the base of the trunk, and suddenly a blade appeared from inside a large wound in the wood. The hole became larger and larger as the blade kept hacking away at it until it was big enough for a person to pass through it.

The tribesmen gasped as Green-Eyes appeared from the hole, coughing and spluttering. The interloper removed the black face and green eyes, and revealed the alien underneath with his shaggy long brown hair, and steely gaze that held a thousand pains and nightmares. The blue blood of the Bilm was spattered over his black form, as if he had just wandered out of an animal slaughter.

"Cafreegar," one of the tribesmen said, invoking the name of their angel of death. The others all murmured in agreement, and dropped to their knees.

"Cafreegar?" Green-Eyes said with a confused tone.

"Cafreegar," the tribesmen repeated, this time pointing at Green-Eyes for emphasis.

Green-Eyes looked about to say something when his widened, and were looking over the shoulders of the tribe warriors.

There was a crash of several something's moving through the jungle, crushing the trees and foliage. There was a familiar roaring from several different directions, and the tribesmen turned to see a group of adult Bilm crashing through the jungle towards the corpse of their young. The biggest one, the mother, was ahead of the others, her bigger bulk and strength propelling her forward faster than the smaller males.

"Run!" Green-Eyes shouted, though none of the tribal warriors understood what he had said, they understood the intention behind it.

* * *

Caine watched the tribesmen bolt in the opposite direction the other tree creatures were coming from, shouting and yelping in fear. Without thinking about it, he tucked the hood into his belt, and bolted towards the *Kara Marazov*. When he didn't hear anything following him, he got suspicious and stopped. He turned and found the tree creatures just stood in a circle.

He swore he could hear one of them sniffing the remains of the first creature.

A chill ran though him when the biggest of the newcomers suddenly turned towards him.

"Oh, fuck me."

Although he couldn't see the hideous ringed mouth with its sharp teeth, he knew what it looked like, and could hear the hideous high-pitched roar come from the direction of the biggest of the creatures.

It charged towards him.

And he ran in the opposite direction.

It had taken a whole lot of effort to bring down what seemed now to basically be a child of the species. He had no intention of getting close to a whole group of adults with vengeance in their bark.

He opened a secret compartment on his belt as he ran through the foliage, eschewing the muddy path for a direct run at the *Kara*. From the compartment he slipped a small control device, a remote for the ship's systems. He clicked the power-up control, and then activated the homing beacon at the tip of the small triangle.

The big tree thing crashed through a thick tangle of vines that wrapped around the roots it was running on. It tripped over forwards, and tumbled down the slope leading to the *Kara*, just as the vertical crescent shaped ship's engines rumbled to activation, the ship's autopilot flicking power to the antigravs.

The tree creature somersaulted, and hit the ground with a mad bang that had more in common with the thunderstorm that was escaping onto the horizon in the distance. It rolled down the slope, and stopped in a heap.

A keening wail came from the top of the ridge, where four smaller creatures were waving their branches and other limbs in the air as if being blown upwards by a strong wind.

Not good.

The ground shook, and lights splayed across the area as the *Kara* hovered overhead. Its landing claws were still extended, and the ladder that ran up the port side of the lower main fin was open and ready to be used. The ship came lower and lower to the ground, pushing aside the jungle trees, and scaring the tree creatures on the ridge.

The bigger creature was regaining its footing alarmingly fast for something its size. It roared again, and rose up on its roots like a ballerina tip-toeing during a performance, except understandably more threatening. Caine figured it was probably trying to intimidate him somehow, though why it needed to given its size escaped him.

He hurdled a tree trunk and jumped with all his might, just as the tree creature dove after him, its incessant roaring almost drowned out the ship's engines overhead. Caine flailed and caught the bottom rung of the ladder, once again trying to ignore the sharp pain that spiked from his ribs.

Then the ship suddenly dipped toward the ground for a brief instant.

The ship registered its owner being aboard, and pushed the antigravs harder, bringing it back above the jungle canopy, where the not-yet-visible suns were highlighting the trees like light reflecting on top of a lapping ocean.

The rain was no longer pattering away on the giant leaves of the bigger trees, the clouds finally moving away with the rest of the storm.

Caine looked down to see what had made the ship dip, and stared with horror at the sight of the big tree creature clinging to the tip of the thick fin, roaring and bellowing at him.

Using its incredible strength, it used the roughness of its bark skin to act as traction on the smooth metal surface. It looped as many branches and roots as possible around the fin, then expanded several of the loops, placed them higher up, and pulled, before tightening them, and then opening the lower loops. It shimmied up the fin like this, inch-by-inch, until it was beside Adam, who was in the process of climbing up the ladder rungs.

Winds buffeted the ship, and threatened to pull Adam off the side of his vessel.

Somehow, he managed to hold on, wrapping his arms around the rungs themselves every time the wind hit him. The tree thing was unfazed, gripping tighter.

Adam tried to kick the branches away from the hull, but its grip was too strong.

He realised he had left his rifle on the jungle floor. He was only armed with the P99.

He unholstered it, and with one hand checked the magazine for rounds. It was half full, probably not enough, but there wasn't much choice without damaging or destroying the ship.

Gripping the ladder rung with his left hand, he leaned out, and aimed the pistol down.

He squeezed the trigger, and the pistol bucked, but the sound couldn't be heard over the wind and the noisy creature. The bullet tore a chunk out of the creature's side, but did nothing to dispel it.

He fired again and again, without any effect.

He was down to his last two rounds.

He aimed carefully, and took another shot just as the creature was shifting its weight to slide up the fin again. The shot severed one of the loops, and the thing slipped down again, howling with pain. The second shot severed another loop, and the creature suddenly fell backwards.

Unable to hold its weight with the lower loops, the creature fell through the jungle canopy with a defiant shout.

Caine breathed a sigh of relief, and holstered the pistol.

He clambered up the ladder, and in through the open hatch. He was breathing heavily, exhausted from the effort of the last few hours. His muscles ached, and his ribs hurt like a bastard.

He struggled to his feet after the airlock cycled shut, and stumbled through the claustrophobic corridor, up the ladder to the next cramped deck and to the cockpit. Set out in a square, the four high-backed seats were surrounded by interactive monitors and systems displays. The two front seats were closer together than the two behind, with the right one being the pilot's seat, a bank of flight controls in front, including an old-style flight stick and levers for the throttle and power.

In the co-pilot's chair there was a bundle of joy snoozing away blissfully unaware of the ship's movement. Her cute little green face was framed by vivid blue hair, and she was covered with the tartan blanket he had flopped carefully over her before they landed four hours ago.

He shook his head —little Eve could sleep through just about anything if she was tired enough. As quietly as he could, he sat down in the pilot's chair, and switched flight control over to manual, activating the sensors.

The sensors display monitor showed the jungle below. There were several humanoid life-signs running in the direction the tribesmen had disappeared, being chased now by larger readings that were almost indistinguishable from the rest of the jungle.

Damn, he thought, *once the creatures couldn't get to me, they went after the tribesmen.* Remembering the hideous mouth and the inside of the tree creature, he armed the ship's plasma cannons, and activated the auto-targeters. They immediately locked onto the tree creatures, as if sensing Adam's intention.

The deck hummed gently as power was fed into the energy weapons.

He goosed the antigravs, pushing the ship between the fleeing tribal warriors and the chasing tree creatures.

He flicked the weapons to active, and pulled on the cannon's trigger located on the flight control stick. Red pulses of plasma energy flew out of the crescent-shaped wings, and slammed into the jungle below.

Fires blossomed from the jungle canopy as the trees died.

* * *

The tribesmen stopped as the red fire fell from the sky. They couldn't see its source, but one suggested it was Cafreegar, saving their lives once again. They heard the hideous screams of the dying Bilm males, even as the female charged them, bellowing its kill-noise.

A flash of fire caught it in its midsection, and another burned its branches clean off. It shrieked in pain, before a wave of fire burned it from existence, vaporising its entire body. All that was left was a black pile of ash among the underbrush.

The tribesmen started dancing around each other, praising their angel of death.

* * *

Adam watched the fires die down, the sensors no longer detecting the signs of life from any tree creatures in a hundred-mile radius.

He slapped the main thruster control, and deactivated the antigravs, pushing the ship towards the horizon, the jungle flashing past underneath. He pulled back on the flight stick, the ship climbing towards the sky, away from the terrible jungle below, and the memories it held.

As soon as the ship left the atmosphere, the sensors went insane, blaring loudly, and flashing the screens red. There was something big in orbit, and it was locking weapons onto the *Kara*.

There was also a large group of smaller signatures swarming towards the ship.

Not to mention a communication coming in.

He ignored the comms, and focused on the ships.

The big one, he realised with no small amount of annoyance, was a Terran *Knight*-class battleship. However, unlike the black-hulled *HMS Fortitude* that he had encountered, this one had the standard Terran Navy deep blue hull. The ship's Friend-or-Foe beacon identified the ship as the *HMS Invincible*, a rather distressing name against Adam's chances of survival.

In all honesty, he wasn't worried about his safety, but Evelyn's. She was the world to him, and didn't want to lose her for any reason. She was just beginning to wake up, shifting under the blanket, her sparkling blue eyes looking out warily at her adopted father.

"Daddy?" she said groggily. "What's goin' on?"

"It's the Navy, Evie. They're in orbit."

The smaller signatures resolved into *Rhino*-class starfighters. There were thirty-six signatures, each being a starfighter, making up three squadrons. The odds were not good, no matter how well built the *Kara* was.

The Rhinos, weapons locks blaring for attention, were steadily surrounding the ship.

The communications panel lit up again.

He sighed, and answered the call.

However, the face that appeared on the comms screen was not one he had expected.

"Captain Mkdorn?"

"*Captain Caine,*" the familiar Navy officer replied. Janis Mkdorn was as serious as ever, with no hint of emotion on her stern face. She hadn't changed in the year since he had first met her. Her hair was tied back in a severe regulation bun still a pale brown like his own, and her stern gaze was filled with those piercing brown eyes. "*Power down your weapons, and prepare to be taken aboard the* Invincible. *You are under arrest.*"

"On what charge?" he snorted.

"*For the murder of Major Alyn Dunn, a Navy Intelligence operative, and the destruction of the Terran Navy warship,* HMS Fortitude."

"What's she talking about, daddy?" Eve whispered, but Adam shook his head. This was the part of his life that he didn't want his daughter to discover.

"There must be some mistake," he said to Mkdorn, feigning ignorance.

Mkdorn harrumphed, and shook her head.

"*Comply, Captain Caine, or we* will *take you in by force.*"

Adam sighed, and then nodded, deactivating the weapons system. Green energy filled the cockpit window as a tractor beam reached out and grabbed the *Kara*.

"Once your ship lands in our main hangar, disarm yourself, and come out of the ship." Mkdorn's gaze flickered to Eve. *"Both of you."*

"No," he growled. "She stays in the ship, where she'll be safe."

"Safe?" Mkdorn's face took on a quizzical look. *"From whom?"*

Adam replied, "From you and your people."

Mkdorn just shook her head. *"Comply, Captain,"* was all she said before she cut the transmission.

Adam leaned back in his chair, and gestured for Eve to come to him. She jumped up in his lap, and wrapped her arms around his neck.

"This isn't going to be fun, Eve. In fact, it could be very dangerous."

She looked into his eyes, in one of those weird moments where she seemed like a mature adult, and said, "I know you'll protect me, daddy. You always find a way." Adam was speechless, but the moment was gone, and she pressed her head into the crook of his neck and shoulder. He just stroked her soft blue hair, and watched helplessly as his ship was towed into the boxy battleship's main hangar.

* * *

Mkdorn arrived in the main hangar just as Caine's beautiful ship came into land on the glossy deck. A trio of landing claws extended from the lower fin of the blue crescent, and rested gently on the deck. A series of metal rungs flicked out of the hull to form a ladder from the port wing to the lower tip of the ship.

A small airlock slid open in the seamless hull, and Adam Caine stepped out, holding the hand of the little Mertik girl Mkdorn had seen in his cockpit.

Around her waited a full platoon of fifty troopers from the *Invincible's* company of the Fleet Protection Group unit, all dressed in their intimidating grey armour, plasma rifles held to their chests, their green fatigues a stark contrast in the gaps between armour plates.

The platoon's commander, Lieutenant Maydon, stood beside her, his grey helmet held under the crook of his arm, his rifle slung over one shoulder. He was holding a pair of force feedback cuffs, standard in the armed forces when transporting prisoners.

The cuffs had been Mkdorn's idea —she was aware of the kind of strength and speed Caine could call upon.

Caine descended the ladder, keeping a fatherly watchful eye on his daughter —she knew the time-displaced soldier had adopted the girl from the dispatches on the *Gold Royale* incident months ago.

When she had heard about it, she had immediately assumed he was unfit to be a father, but seeing the looks passed between him and his adopted daughter it seemed painfully obvious that Mkdorn had been wrong.

Mkdorn grimaced as she saw a blue liquid splashed over his form-fitting body suit; to Mkdorn it looked a hell of a lot like blood splatter, or arterial spray. Either way, it looked frightening on him, despite the tiny girl holding his hand as he slowly strolled toward Mkdorn. He didn't look happy, and the shaggy brown hair and angry face did nothing to help that image.

She nodded to Maydon, who stepped forward and snapped the feedback cuffs on his wrists. The bigger man did nothing to stop the officer from doing it, probably reasoning that any violence could accidentally get his daughter hurt.

She kept clear of him, however.

His eyes were simmering with rage, and he seemed to be shaking with anger.

The last time she had seen him this angry he had taken down an entire war fleet of massive warships, including an impossibly huge titan. She had no intention of even touching him.

"I am under orders, Caine," she said apologetically.

"I don't doubt it," he growled back. He glanced behind him, "Evie, hold on to the holster." She grabbed a handful of the black leather holster, and held on tight.

"I'm afraid the girl will have to be kept in separate accommodations, Captain Caine," Maydon stated.

Caine let out a low growl, and stepped nearer to Maydon, and said in a low voice. "You touch my daughter, and I *will* break all four of your limbs."

From where Mkdorn was standing, Maydon's face seemed to become paler than his pale grey carapace armour, though he quickly covered it up by sneering back at Caine, who was a head taller than him. The bigger man was not even slightly put off by Maydon's attempt; in fact he seemed to find it amusing. Then he sighed in defeat.

"Evie, stay with Captain Mkdorn." Eve was about to protest, when he said, "Now. This won't take long to resolve I'm sure."

Mkdorn hoped he was right.

* * *

Caine was taken to an interrogation room, the cuffs still on his wrists, and sat down in a solid metal chair. Unlike the interrogation rooms of his own century, which had bad lighting, uncomfortable seating, and a one-way window, this room seemed to be designed to be comfortable.

Says it all about the humans of this age, he thought, *they're all afraid of being uncomfortable. Everything's designed for comfort, no matter what the use of the room is intended to be.*

As such, the room didn't bother him, and in fact helped him calm down a little, but only a little. He was worried about what they were doing with Evelyn, and desperately wanted to break out and take her away from this warship.

But he couldn't now, not without getting her hurt, and not without having the Terran Navy on his back every step he took.

Or maybe it isn't the Navy; maybe it's someone associated with the Navy, he thought, remembering that the charges against him were those he had 'committed' against the devious and secret Kombat 3899 organisation. 3899 had been founded when Earth –or rather Terra- had been destroyed by an asteroid, reasoning that the Terrans should be the dominant species in the universe by any means necessary. It wasn't a view Adam shared, despite their trying to recruit him, kidnapping him, and eventually trying to kill him.

The door behind him swished open, and in stepped the two people he least wanted to be in the room with, though he knew had to be here.

"General Gardner, and Major Drummond," Caine growled.

The grizzled ancient head of Navy Intelligence didn't smile, but just stared at Caine. Caine remembered the old man from his sojourn on the *HMS Polly Jenkins*, and had been impressed at how old the man looked, and still seemed to be active.

Now, however, Gardner had lost a lot of weight, his hair was even thinner than Adam remembered and he seemed to be hunching. Adam also noted silently that the old man was limping slightly.

Command and the intelligence game takes its toll, he thought, repeating his Brigade Commander's fateful words after a joint service intelligence briefing. Nobody he knew emphasised this more than Gardner, who was leaning on the back of the chair on the other side of the white metal table in front of Adam. His uniform seemed to hang off his once barrel-chested form. He almost seemed ill, though Adam wasn't sure.

"*Captain* Caine," Gardner said with a deceptively strong voice, his voice as gravely as before. "First a Staff Sergeant, then a Commander, now a Captain. Life's been good to you, Caine."

Adam snorted. "Can't say the same about you."

Drummond slapped him round the face with the palm of her hand, though it didn't even sting him, and he barely moved his head. Drummond, however, frowned and shook her hand as the brief pain shot through it.

"What have you done with my daughter?" he demanded.

Drummond sneered, "She's safe."

Again, Adam snorted.

"There's no such thing as safe around members of 3899."

Drummond's eyebrows shot up her forehead, though Gardner seemed nonplussed by the statement. His eyes seemed cold beneath his pale wrinkly face, but there was something else: pride, or something like it.

"What, you think I didn't know you were their leader, Gardner?" Adam didn't actually know, but was simply guessing. Gardner, however, smiled and shook his head with amusement. If he had had a blank look on his face then Adam would have been wrong, but the old man was amused, and that wasn't a good sign.

Gardner nodded to Drummond almost imperceptibly, who then exited the room, leaving the two men alone.

"Is this the part where you get some big fucker to smack me around?"

Gardner shook his head again, though there was no amusement in his old face this time, only the cold hard stare. He finally sat down in the other seat, leaning on the table as if even sitting was hard to do.

"This is the part where we talk."

Adam leaned on the table as well, his hands kept rigidly in front of him by the force feedback cuffs, which were essentially two separate cuffs held together by jade-tinted lightning bolts that perpetually flashed in three uneven rows between the receptors. There was a slight tingling sensation constantly coming through his arms, though the energy made no sound.

"I have no intention of joining your organisation," growled Adam. "I thought I was pretty clear on that when I destroyed the *Fortitude*, and prevented your people from obtaining the power of Andromeda's core."

"Except now you have no choice but to accede to our demands," replied the other.

Adam looked at him incredulously.

"How are you going to arrest me without revealing the truth of what occurred? I mean, the *Fortitude* was supposedly destroyed several years ago, and your two girls, Dumb and Dumber, were reported killed six months before the Core captured me. For me to be arrested, and publicly charged you would have to reveal the cover-ups."

A sinister smile crept onto Gardener's lips, one that dripped with arrogance.

"We do not need to arrest you, Captain Caine, to get you to do what we want."

Adam instantly understood, and rage filled him, pushing his hands against the cuffs. The lightning intensified between the cuffs, and then pain began spread through his arms where the tingling had been jumping around, as if his veins were suddenly being electrocuted.

"Funny thing about these force feedback shackles," Gardner prattled on, "the technology was developed thanks to 3899. It's a funny story actually," he chuckled, and ignored Adam's glare. "Back when we first put the organisation together, our first field agent ran across a group of slavers hauling Rijiin slavers captured in the T'Kleth Halo. He discovered their use of the force feedback cuffs, and how they had developed them, and then stole them."

"Let me guess," interrupted Caine, "He left the slaves where they were, and then called in the Navy to destroy the entire operation."

Gardner's eyebrows twitched in annoyance.

"Indeed."

Adam leaned as far forward as he could on the table.

"You hurt even a hair on my daughter's head, and I will kill you, Gardner. And I won't stop at you either; I promise I'll bring down your crooked organisation, and expose you and your lies to the universe."

Gardner just sat there, scrunching his face as if mulling it over.

"You and I are very much alike," Gardner stated, despite Caine's apparent refusal. "Both of us were born on Terra itself; we've endured great hardships; and we both get the job done no matter what."

"The ends justify the means?" Caine retorted. "I've never believed that."

"But it does get things done, Caine."

"You obviously don't remember your history lessons as well as you think. Adolf Hitler, Benito Mussolini, Joseph Stalin, Osama Bin Laden all believed that the end justified the means. But all they really wanted was power, the end justifies the means speech was always just a cover for them to legitimise their horrific actions."

"Are you comparing *me* to your twentieth-century war criminals?" Gardner growled, straightening in his chair. "I am doing this for the good of the Terran Consortium."

Adam gave him a humourless smile.

"I'm pretty sure that's what *they* said as well."

This just seemed to get Gardner angry.

"Enough subtle remarks." He stood from his chair, the weakness overridden by supposedly righteous anger. "You are a Terran, and as such, you will comply with Terran military authority. You will do what we want, or I will indeed harm the little girl you refer to as your daughter. Naturally, I will not be the one to do the harming, but guaranteed it will happen if you do not help us."

"Fuck you."

Gardner chuckled when he saw Adam strain against the cuffs. The younger man's arms were shaking, and his face was reddening with sheer rage. Then Adam roared, and Gardner's eyes widened as Adam's hands spread further and further apart, the binding energy becoming more and more unstable.

Gardner backed away, almost tripping over his own chair.

The four-star General was shouting for Drummond to return, for anybody to return and restrain Caine. But Adam wasn't listening, his mind's eye seeing little Evie being hurt by these people.

He gave one last roar, his arms visibly shaking as the pain of the energy spread through him like a lightning rod in a storm. Suddenly the energy binding became unstable, and a bolt of jade lightning shot across the room, scorching the bulkhead next to Gardner's head.

Drummond, Maydon and two FPG troopers charged into the room at that moment, and stopped in their tracks when they saw Adam Caine stood in the middle of the room, his bindings gone, and his bodysuit smoking from the release of the energy.

Caine didn't give them a chance to attack.

He dove at Maydon, and body-slammed him against Drummond, who went flying backwards against the nearest bulkhead. The two troopers, armed with stun weapons, brought their guns up, and fired. The pulses from the exotic weapons struck Maydon and Drummond, knocking them unconscious. Caine rolled away, and came up between the troopers, and smashed the first across his exposed head, sending him to the deck.

Caine then spun, grabbed the other trooper's arms, and used the momentum of the previous actions to lever the unfortunate human on top of his compatriot.

All of this happened in four seconds, from start to finish, with Caine standing in the middle of the downed military personnel.

Caine dove for Gardner next, but the second trooper got his wits about him, and managed to catch him in the side with a shot from his stun gun. Caine stopped, and his legs started to wobble. But then he was going again, albeit slowly.

So the trooper kept shooting him, pumping shot after shot into Caine.

* * *

When he finally awoke, he was shackled with his arms out to either side; the shackles were attached firmly to the wall, the Navy personnel clearly taking no chances.

Adam was groggy, the effect of the stun blasts wearing off, and his vision was blurred, though it was quickly clearing up. He had a headache from all the energy that had passed through his body. He'd been electrocuted before, in Afghanistan, but this was something new —he could almost feel every single vein and artery in his body.

His feet had been shackled to the wall as well, and he was standing up, the majority of his weight hanging on his shackled arms, like a cruciform.

Somebody grabbed his chin, and pulled his head up.

He looked into the face of General Gardner once again.

"Welcome back to the land of the living, *Captain* Caine." He nodded to someone out of Adam's view, and Major Drummond walked in, followed by Captain Mkdorn holding Eve's hand.

"Daddy!" Eve cried when she saw the state he was in. She tried to run to him, but Mkdorn tightened her grip on Eve's hand, holding her back. Eve started crying, though she didn't make any noise.

Her little green face was wet with tears, and her bottom lip was trembling. She hugged Mkdorn's arm, who looked extremely uncomfortable with having to look after a young child. Or was it that she was uncomfortable with this situation? Adam didn't know, but hoped it was the latter.

The shackles were solidly locked to the wall, and he couldn't move.

His heart broke at seeing Eve so upset.

He turned his glare on Gardner, who wasn't intimidated.

"You *will* comply," said Gardner, a smug smile on his wrinkled face. When Caine didn't reply, he nodded again to Drummond, who unholstered the lethal plasma pistol on her hip, and then pressed the barrel against Eve's head.

Adam tried to break free, but he just didn't have any strength left to fight with. Mkdorn was protesting, demanding what was really going on, but Gardner just tuned her out, letting Drummond hold the pistol on her too.

Adam let out a long breath, and squeezed his eyes shut.

"Fine. What do you want from me?"

Gardner clapped his hands together, and finally had a genuine smile beaming away. He crossed the holding cell —presumably deeper within the Invincible than the interrogation room- and picked up a digipad waiting on the bed.

"This contains everything on the targets we want you to take out. They all belong to the same organisation, a group of warlords and lieutenants who used to work for a man named Garvion." Adam refused to show any surprise on his face –he still could not bring himself to tell Eve that the man he had killed in the mercenary enclave several months ago was in fact her biological father. He saw no point in it in all fairness.

"They call themselves the Emissaries of Power." Gardner called one of the ship's Navy security officers over to release the prisoner. When the officer did release the shackles, Adam fell weakly to the floor, his muscles still wobbly. The officer had to help him to his feet. "You have one week. The *Invincible* will leave you at the edge of Andromeda, and you can make your own way to them."

Adam made to go to Evelyn, but Drummond returned the barrel of the plasma pistol to Eve's temple. He scowled at the major, silently promising to kill her when he got the chance.

"You will see your daughter when you complete your task," Gardner explained.

"Daddy?" Eve half-whispered, the tears still streaming down her cheeks.

"It's gonna be okay, Evie. I promise."

Eve nodded, and seemed to fully believe, even if Adam was sure that Gardner and his people were going to double-cross him as soon as they got what they wanted. For now, he would have to play along until such a time he could extricate Eve from this situation.

"How long until we arrive?"

"Twenty minutes," answered Mkdorn. She was in full uniform now, with the peaked cap sat atop her head, and a plasma pistol on her hip. He wondered who that was for, and suspected that after having seen Gardner's disregard for life, she was worrying about being next. "I promise I'll look after your daughter, Adam. She can stay in my quarters." She glared at Gardner, making it obvious that if he contested *that* idea, she would give him hell. And as the *Invincible*'s commander, she could give him a *lot* of hell.

Drummond seemed about to protest, but Gardner nodded.

Mkdorn led Eve out of the holding cell, though not before Adam said goodbye from afar.

"I'll see you soon."

* * *

Thanagar II, Northern Hemisphere.

Eldron the Magnificent was out rowing, one of his few concessions to a normal life. His bodyguards were out on the shore, watching from afar, protesting his going out alone.

"Where's the fun in having your bodyguard with you on the boat when I'm trying to be alone," he had said with a big grin. It was a routine they had settled into every day. Every day they would argue about him going out onto the little wooden boat alone, and every day his bodyguard would relent under the pressure of his boss.

Today was no different, and Eldron, a junior lieutenant in the Emissaries of Power, could see the black speck of his stern Lakernl bodyguard. There were several other specks up in the sky, far in the distance, but he just waved them off as being birds.

He pulled on the wooden oars, an antique rescued from a Terran colony on Thanagar. The lake was still today, with no wind, a typical thing to happen around midday on that part of Thanagar.

In the distance, his mansion overlooked the lake, and he could see a couple of shuttles land, probably the prime minister of the local continent.

Something caught his attention out the corner of his eye: one of the specks got larger, and seemed to be cross-shaped, though it was still just a silhouette in the sky. Over on the shore, somebody was waving at the bodyguard, who then waved for Eldron to come back to the side of the lake.

Something was seriously wrong.

The speck was still getting larger, and getting larger faster. A hover car whizzed over the bodyguard, and raced over the lake towards Eldron.

Panic rose in him as he realised that the cross-shaped speck was not there for his amusement, and the hover car was coming to pick him up and take him to safety.

The cross became suddenly larger, and he could see it was a starship, coloured a brighter blue than the lake he was currently floating on. It wasn't a big starship, but he was in a wooden open top rowing boat, making him feel more vulnerable than ever before.

Orbs of coloured light appeared on the small wings, and he soiled himself as he realised it was weapons fire. Plasma pulses flashed down and took out the hover car in a blinding light of fire, and vaporised water.

Then the pulses hit Eldron and vaporised him and his entire boat.

The *Kara Marazov* rushed past the steaming spot in the lake that Eldron and his boat had occupied, the wake of the ship's passage left a brief gully in the water's surface, before climbing into the sky before anything could be scrambled to intercept it.

* * *

Thanagar II, *Southern* Hemisphere.

At the same time Eldron met his fate, his fellow warlord Uli the Foul was receiving his lunch and the midday post. His wife was outside in the garden, probably mating with the gardener again. He would have to sort that out after lunch.

But first, his lunch of a'Ratu bovine meat was placed on the big dinner table, still steaming. The greens were arranged in several fanned rows, with the meat in the centre.

His manservant, actually a female Kra Nal, placed a pile of hardcopy mail beside his plate. Before touching the food, he decided to get business out of the way. The first couple in the pile were letters from old acquaintances soon to be on Thanagar on business, all in his native language of Thanag.

The third was a chunky package, with no address, but with his name as the addressee.

His manservant frowned.

"[Somebody must have given it to the postal worker,]" she said in Uli's native Thanag, eyeing the package warily. She was about to take it off him, and dispose of it, when he decided to open it, thinking it must have come from his favourite mistress, an especially limber woman.

He ripped it open, and was greeted with a piece of paper with words written in Terran Standard that he couldn't read. He gave the Kra Nal the paper, whilst he picked up something that had fallen out of the envelope. His eyes widened as he realised what it was, even as his servant read out the card in Thanag.

"[It says, 'Fuck you Uli, love from a ghost'. What do you think that means, sir?]"

Uli just shook his head as the blinking red light at the centre of the explosive disk became just a regular red light, and the beeping stopped.

"[Oh, Gods.]"

Far above, as the *Kara* made orbit, the ship's sensors registered the explosion on the southern hemisphere that took out an entire mansion. Both Uli the Foul and Eldron the Magnificent were dead.

"Two down, seven to go," said Caine, piloting the ship, and activating the Faster-Than-Light engine.

* * *

Grt'Y.

The news of Uli and Eldron's deaths a day ago had brought out the mourners among the Emissaries, and two of them had gathered on Grt'Y, only a five-minute trip through the Linkways from Thanagar II. The planet was openly aligned with the Emissaries, and as such its government had put out a memorial procession through the largest main thoroughfare in the capital city.

At its head, leading the way to the memorial site was Ter-il-Fan-Dosh, the third-in-command of the Emissaries of Power. Beside his massive bulk walked Ghilop the Young, the youngest of lieutenants, armed to the teeth in case something happened, and constantly watching the buildings for signs of danger.

The youth of today, Fan-Dosh sighed inwardly, moments before a solid round blew out the back of his head, and sprayed the bodyguards behind him. Ghilop dove behind a gaggle of bodyguards.

It did him no good whatsoever, as an armour-piercing round punched through the guard, and struck Ghilop in the heart. Screams filled the city as everybody heard the loud gunshots echo through the buildings.

Nobody saw a figure dressed in a black bodysuit, with green eyes and a large rifle. Nobody saw him disappear, nor did they see the *Kara Marazov* racing into space, and away from the scene of the crime.

* * *

Honaka Prime.

Two days later, Hardmarch the Worried shivered in his hover limo. It wasn't cold, but he was scared witless. Four of the Emissaries' warlords were dead, and the news of it had hit him the hardest. He wasn't called the Worried for nothing.

The limo sedately skimmed through Honaka City, passing by at a nice relaxing pace.

Hona, the system's star, was shining high in the sky, without a cloud to stop its pleasing rays of light and warmth. The massive round buildings either side of the road reflected the sunlight beautifully. By all rights, it should have been an enjoyable day.

But he hadn't left his armoured limousine for thirty-six hours, hoping that whatever was going on would pass him by if he was protected enough. Two hover cars followed the limo, filled with armed guards, whilst outriders flew around on all sides on hover-bikes.

The limo came to a large traffic junction, and slowed at the hovering lights. The guards and bikes did the same, and stopped when the traffic stopped. Except the limo kept going, and then sped up and out into the stream of hover traffic coming in the opposite direction.

Hardmarch squealed in panic, and demanded to know what was going on.

The armoured partition between the driver's cockpit and the passenger compartment slid down, and the driver looked back at Hardmarch. He was human, not a Rijiin as was normal.

The human male grimaced.

"Sorry mate, but this is it for you." He turned away, then opened the driver-side door, and jumped out of the limo, landing on the roof of an airbus going in the opposite direction. Hardmarch dove for the cockpit, but was too late.

The limo slammed nose-first into a military transport that barely felt the impact.

Hardmarch was crushed inside without his guards ever having seen who did it.

* * *

Yargen V.

Grentlin the Tough jumped at every shadow, even though he was in his very own bedroom. The deaths of the others had made him that way, and now he was reduced to watching every single shadow, waiting for one to kill him.

He was the last of the lieutenants, and had been waiting for something to happen ever since the news of Eldron's death had come through. His guards were outside every entrance to his living quarters, even out on the balcony.

It was night outside on Yargen, and Grentlin had turned off his lights, so if something happened he wouldn't see it coming. There were rumours that the perpetrator was the ghost of one of the Emissaries' victims, earning the killer the nickname, The Ghost among the criminal world, in only a few days of operation.

There were two *pffts* of the wind, but he continued to watch the shadows, afraid of going to sleep.

Something metal and cylindrical was pressed against his temple.

He whimpered.

"Who's your boss?" a metallic voice asked. Grentlin could see a pair of green glowing eyes at the corner of his vision, but refused to turn around and look at it.

"I-I-I don't know. I've never actually met him." He whimpered again. "He calls himself 3899, and uses the Terran Navy communications network to keep contact."

"3-8-9-9?" the voice repeated. Then it started laughing, extremely hard.

"What's so funny about that?" wailed Grentlin, but the voice didn't answer until Grentlin suddenly found courage enough to call for the guards.

"They're all dead. And so are you."

There was another *pfft* of the wind, and Grentlin's brains suddenly decorated the right side of his bed.

"So the bastard lied to me," sighed Adam Caine.

* * *

Delta-Tango.

The system was a navigational nightmare, filled to the brim with asteroids, and larger and smaller chunks of rock spinning in random directions. Passages between the rocks were never the same from one moment to the next, and navigational repulsor craft were used to guide ships from the edge of the behemoth field to its centre, where a massive group of asteroids were interconnected with anchor lines, armoured passageways, thick bridges, and even zero-g airlocks.

Several asteroids had been cored out, and were converted into starfighter hangars, whilst some of the bigger rocks held warship hangars, workshops, and dry-docks. Small one-man worker craft darted between kilometres-long battleships, which dwarfed the smaller warships.

Off in the distance, at the very edge of the asteroid field, were great behemoth ships, the dreadnaughts and super-heavy carriers of the fleet, docked with a great network of station hubs and gangways.

High Admiral Jessica Scarlett, First Star Lady and commander of all Terran military forces, saw this view from her cavernous office, a sterile affair with rows upon rows of blue lights along two walls, each one denoting a treasured book or reading material belonging to her. She was a tall aged woman, far older than she looked, and dressed in her duty uniform, though it was open, revealing her white sweat-stained undershirt. She had once been beautiful, but a hundred years of service in the Terran Navy had dimmed that beauty a long time ago.

It had been a long day.

The self-proclaimed Emissaries of Power had been dismantled, its leadership destroyed, their hideouts and homes in the Andromeda galaxy exposed to the universe by a mysteriously silent and professional force.

The Terran Navy had gone into the Emissaries' home sector and cleaned up momentously. They had taken out their infrastructure, and made mass arrests. And yet, the intelligence behind the operation had been from some mystery source of General Gardner's.

Gardner himself entered the office, accompanied by the shaven-headed Major Drummond, who was as stiff as ever, though she was holding the hand of a six-year-old green-skinned Mertik girl, who seemed utterly afraid, with tears steaming own on her face. Her blue hair was unkempt, as if she had not washed for days.

The old man hobbled over to Scarlett's curving white desk, and leant against it. To Scarlett, he seemed to get older and older every time she saw the intelligence head.

"You made good time. Faster than would have been possible, even for the *Invincible*'s new engines."

"*Invincible* was already on its way here when the attacks on the Emissaries was underway."

"Convenient," she said, with an arched eyebrow, completely unconvinced by anything he had to say. "Who's the young girl? And why does she look so afraid of the two of you?"

"She's insurance."

"I'll say. The man coming after you is possibly more dangerous than anything this Navy has had to deal with in the last millennia." She strode over to her desk, and sat down in her over-stuffed chair. "That's why, when Captain Mkdorn called me, and informed me of the situation, I immediately invited that same man to this meeting." She nodded to something over Gardner's shoulder, and two green orbs appeared from the shadows.

Scarlett saw Gardner's hand shake before he grabbed it with the other to quell the nervous twitch.

Adam Caine, in his full black combat suit, a rifle with a bullpup design slung over one shoulder, and a silenced pistol in one hand, emerged from the shadows as silently as if he had not been there. Everybody, even Scarlett who knew he had been standing there, was taken off guard by just how menacing he seemed.

His daughter whimpered quietly, and hid behind Captain Mkdorn's leg, poking her head out to stare wide-eyed at her father.

Scarlett, herself a parent, saw Caine stop ever so briefly, and knew he was upset that he had frightened his little girl. She herself had had the same feelings when her children had first seen her dressing down several officers. But Caine was much quicker to recover than she had been, those glowering green eyes staring at Gardner, who would have taken a step back if the big sterile-white desk had not been there.

Drummond drew her sidearm, and pointed it at Caine's head. He did not look at her though. The eyes were staring straight at his cowering daughter.

"Close your eyes, Evie, and cover your ears. Keep doing it until I tell you to stop." Although the voice was modified to hide his identity, and sounded deep, and more mechanical, Eve still did as her father told, squeezing her eyes shut tight, and covering her ears with her little hands. Scarlett frowned, and saw Caine's gaze change to Drummond.

Scarlett saw a blur of motion, faster than she could track, and Drummond was down on the floor, a bleeding hole in the dead centre of her forehead, her face a rictus of surprise. Caine's pistol was there at shoulder height like it had been there the whole time, whilst the silencer smoked slightly.

A slight tremor ran through Scarlett as she realised that Caine was even faster than the stories she had heard, and hoped to the gods that he never turned his anger toward her.

Then horror filled her as the big man turned the silenced gun on Gardner.

"Caine, that's enough," Scarlett growled, hiding her fear. "You said you have the proof?"

Caine, without taking his eye and gun off Gardner, reached to something behind him, and produced a clean white Navy digipad. He gently tossed it onto the desk, and it slid to a halt in front of Scarlett.

She picked it up, and shook her head as she skimmed through its contents.

"This is a lot. Including how the General orchestrated the massacre of several high-profile criminals, as well as leading the organisation himself... Interesting."

"I figured it would take a lot to bring down Kombat 3899. Don't worry, I made copies in case they ever come after me again." He lowered the gun. *"Killing you would be putting you out of my misery, especially after your association with a man known as Gold."* Gardner was unable to keep the shock from his tired face, eliciting a dry chuckle from Caine. *"It was pretty obvious when both Gold's creatures and the* HMS Fortitude *turn up within minutes of each other to attack the* Gold Royale. *There was also the lack of surprise from your agents inside Andromeda's core, suggesting that at least some of them had been there before, or had been briefed on what they would experience there. Too many coincidences, don't you think, General?"*

"Quite," said Gardner.

Caine stepped right up to Gardner, inches from the older man's face.

"You will leave me and my daughter alone, or so help me I will come through on my promise to kill you." Then his head tilted towards Scarlett. *"And I won't stop with 3899. Any* Navy *interference will be treated just as harshly. Understand, Admiral?"* Scarlett almost laughed at the gall this man had at threatening the commander of the greatest military force in the existence of the Nineteen

Galaxies. But then she remembered just how much had been thrown at him, and how he had shrugged it off.

"Although I don't like being threatened, I'm not sure I have much choice." She sighed, and sagged, too tired to keep a stiff posture. "The Navy will not interfere in your affairs, as long as they are within the limits of the law."

Caine nodded an agreement.

"And if you or the Navy ever have need of me? Just call." He holstered the pistol, took the hood off, and tucked it into his belt, before picking Eve up into his strong arms. "You can open your eyes now, Evie," he whispered. He gave Scarlett a roguish smile before marching out of the office's main doors.

Scarlett watched after him, wishing she had been a century younger.

Then her own steely gaze turned to Gardner.

"So, Lenson, what do we do with *you*?"

Gardner gulped.

* * *

In the cockpit of the *Kara Marazov*, speeding out and above the asteroid belt that made up Navy Headquarters, and headed towards the star system's Linkway entrance.

"Where are we going now, daddy?"

Adam turned to his tiny daughter, and smiled, the worry of her seeing what he had done back in Scarlett's office gone. "I don't know. What do you want to do?"

She "umm"ed and "aah"ed for a few seconds.

"Let's go on an adventure," she said excitedly.

He chuckled, and pushed the *Kara* towards the blue tunnel swirling in space before them.

"Adventure here we come."

Eleven:
My Daddy (By Eve Caine)

I love my Daddy.

He is the greatest Daddy in the wholest widest world.

He saved me from the monsters.

He helps everybody.

We went to a planet with farms and farm people.

They needed Daddy's help to save them from the monsters.

There were loads of monsters.

They scareded the farm people, and hurt them.

Daddy said he'd help them, and he did.

He walked into the sand with his scary weapons, and his scary black uniform.

We could hear banging form the sand.

And then there was a loud bang and we heard a scream.

Daddy told me to stay with the farm people.

But I sneakeded out, and went in to the sand as well.

It was hot, and I needed a drink, but I kept going.

And going.

And going.

Until I found Daddy on his back in the sand.

His clothes were broken, and his weapons were broken.

And there was red stuff coming out of him.

He wasn't moving.

I was so scared, I ran to him, and hugged him, and shouted for him to be better.

There were monsters all round us.

None of them were moving neither, and they were leaking as well.

I screamed, and I screamed, and I cried for my Daddy to wake up.

But he didn't.

The farm people came. They said they heard me screaming.

I was still screaming when they took Daddy and me back to their home.

They said he was in a comb or something, but he would be awake soon.

I stayed next to him.

The farm people tried to pull me away, but I kept coming back.

I falled asleep at night, and when I woke up, Daddy's eyes were open.

I was so happy to see him, and he was laughing as well.

And the farm people were laughing and dancing in the street.

They kept saying the monsters were gone, and that everything was how it should be.

They said Daddy was a hero, and that he could have the house down the road.

Daddy told me it was our new home.

Ckeer Janoor... Ceer Madoor.

Can't say the name, but I was happy with wherever Daddy went.

Now I am at school, with lots of friends, and it's my birthday next month.

I love my Daddy so much I never want to leave him.

Love you Daddy.

Eve.
Xxx

Twelve:
Pretty Polly

"War has consumed our planet, but we have survived and thrived. We celebrate this day as the first of many in which we will explore the reaches of space, and strive to better ourselves as a race. This day marks the beginning of a new era for humanity. We should move forward, and, to quote Star Trek, explore those strange new worlds, seek out new life and alien civilisations, to go boldly where no human has gone before. Ladies, gentlemen, I give you the Icarus."

-Prime Minister's address to the world moments before the official re-launch of the *Icarus* (refit *Mayflower*).

2021ad.

One million tonnes of metal slipped through space at faster than light speeds, her cylindrical hull a stark white against the backdrop of the blackness of space. Consisting of two massive pods, connected by a thick ring of metal, it looked like a stunted version of a ballistic missile, with the nose chopped off, and a bridge/control centre jutting out on the upper side of the forward module. The rear module contained a massive bank of thrusters and sublight engines, as well as holding the ship's experimental FTL engine.

The underside of the ship was plastered in black re-entry tiles, with symbols and writing painted on the sides. Most of the paint had been nicked and scored, or even burnt off, but enough was there to be clearly identified.

In a square on the side of the slanted curving nose were four symbols, belonging to the navies and air forces of Great Britain and the United States of America, the builders and crew of the vessel.

Its commander, Rear Admiral Lonnie DaSilva, climbed the metal staircase to the anteroom that led to both the ship's bridge, and his personal office. Two Marines, one U.S., the other a British Royal, snapped to attention either side of the bridge doors. Although they wore different styles of black combat fatigues, the Marines both wore the ship's patch, with a unit patch belonging to just the ship's Marines stitched onto the sleeve below the first.

The two Marines were armed only with pistols, the American with a standard-issue SIG SAUER, the Brit with a Walther P99, which were holstered on their hips. DaSilva eyed those weapons, though made no comment of their presence outside his command centre.

He placed his palm on the blue biometric reader next to the doors. The computer recognised his DNA with a beep. The doors cracked open, and he stepped through. Originally, when he had taken command of the ship for its maiden voyage in its original configuration as Earth's first colony ship, *Mayflower*, the officers had had to wear dress uniform when on duty, but the aftermath of the Third World War had left ceremony a low priority, and now even the admiral wore combat fatigues.

Another fallout from the War had been the creation of a world government led primarily by the British, and thus DaSilva and his crew were no longer working for different allied governments, but one overall organisation: Earth.

As such, he was considered to be the premiere officer for space operations, and had been offered the position as chief of space operations. He had declined the offer, so as to stay in command of his ship.

Renamed *Icarus*, and refit, the colony ship was the first of a line of armed deep space explorer ships. *Icarus'* sister ships, the *Enterprise* and the *Iron Horse*, were in varying stages of development. The *Enterprise* was going through its final superstructure integrity tests at the International Space Station and Construction Yard, whilst the *Iron Horse* was conducting speed trials out from Proxima Centauri. Although all ships were under the authority of the new world government, many of the *Icarus* crew still wore the uniforms of their countries of birth.

Icarus had now been re-deployed by Parliament to explore the star systems surrounding Earth, whilst smaller, easily built craft explored Earth's sister planets. Currently, *Icarus* was heading towards a nebula newly discovered by Earth-bound telescopes.

DaSilva briefly stayed at the back of the bridge, watching as the graveyard shift bridge crew worked on the three-tier command centre, the massive wide viewports showing the stars streaking past at the speed of light behind them all.

Like so many ship commanders before him, DaSilva was a hard but fair man with a casual knack for command that bordered on brilliant, and a head of silvery hair cut short. His rank tapes were on the shoulders of his black Navy duty uniform, his peaked cap tucked under his arm, and a mug of coffee in his hand.

One of the junior officers finally noticed DaSilva watching them, and jumped out of his chair.

"Admiral on Deck!" she bellowed.

"Oh knock it off, Ensign," snapped DaSilva.

"A bit harsh wasn't it?" said a female voice behind him.

He turned, a smile on his aging lips, to see his unofficial executive officer standing in the doorway. She was, in fact, the inventor of the FTL engine currently pushing the ship at incredible speeds. It was DaSilva's idea to have her be the second-in-command, though the military hadn't officially endorsed it, keeping her as the ship's science officer.

"C'mon Polly, it's been seven years since we launched, and they still do it, no matter how much I tell them not to." He frowned. "Sometimes I wonder if they do it on purpose, or if someone put them up to it." His eyebrows shot up when Polly suddenly looked very guilty. "It was you, wasn't it?"

Polly suddenly found something better to do across the other side of the bridge, disappearing down onto the lowest of the three tiers, where the circular helm console was situated at the front of the bridge.

"I'll get you back, Jenkins," DaSilva called out.

Polly just shook her head having clearly heard him.

He stepped down to the second tier, and sat down in the central command chair, balancing the cap on the arm of the chair, and sipping his mug of coffee. The graveyard shift commander stepped up to the chair from his usual place at the communications consoles.

"Anything to report, Lieutenant Commander?"

"Nothing beyond the usual hand-over, sir. We are four hours from the nebula, and holding steady speed. No problems either."

"Good. Hopefully this should be an easy mission, not like that dragon thing we came across last month." He chuckled at the recollection of the crew's reaction to the massive creature that had attempted to mate with the *Icarus*. The doors at the rear of the bridge slid open to allow entrance to the day shift. "Graveyard shift is relieved."

"We stand relieved, sir," the shift commander stated. He snapped to attention, saluted, and then strode off the bridge. The day shift took over from the graveyard, and settled into their positions.

Polly was looking over the shoulder of the helmsman. Knowing her as DaSilva did, he knew she was checking on the FTL monitor.

It still amazed him that commanding a starship was becoming old hat. It wasn't long ago he was commanding the missile frigate *Reuben James*, sailing through joint operations with the Royal Navy, and space flight like this was purely science fiction.

"Admiral," the scanner operator called out, "I'm detecting a signal behind us."

DaSilva frowned.

"A signal?"

"Yes, sir. It's following us."

DaSilva jumped out of his chair. "Could it be a ship?" He felt himself getting excited. In the seven years he had been aboard the *Icarus/Mayflower*, they had yet to encounter any other space faring species, although there had been several planets with species that had not reached space yet.

"It's possible, sir, but we have no experience with other vessels other than our own so far. I have no way to tell if it is a ship, or simply an echo on our scanners." The officer looked over at the admiral. "It wouldn't be the first time, sir."

The scanner began beeping incessantly, then another, and then another, until the entire bridge was blaring for attention. Red lights flashed around the room, and the main lighting dimmed to tactical readiness.

"What the hell is going on?" demanded the admiral.

"Energy readings behind us are off the scale, Admiral," answered Polly, who had magically appeared beside the scanner displays, a bank of flat monitors around the console in question. "The readings themselves are like nothing I've ever seen before, and whatever they are they're getting stronger. I've pinpointed them to four-hundred kilometres off our stern."

"Them?" This worried DaSilva. "There's more than one?"

Polly nodded. "Yes, but I think they're simply two points within something bigger. Radar is showing a shadow of something. Looks like a vessel of some kind. Hang on whilst I get a picture." She tapped a few commands and one of the larger monitors on the bridge flicked on to show the stars streaking away from the aft of the ship. There was something following behind them, coming up closer.

It was a blood-red ramshackle affair, shaped vaguely like a bullet, although it was covered with ad-hoc spikes and fins, making it uneven, and asymmetrical. It was big as well, bigger than *Icarus*, and despite the unorthodox appearance, it looked more advanced.

Pulses of green light suddenly leapt from all over the red ship, and strobed at *Icarus*.

DaSilva was thrown forwards from his chair, crashing to the deck. He looked up to see the rest of the bridge crew sprawled on the floor as well. Smoke drifted from somewhere, and sparks sprayed from a nearby console. The red lights were no longer flashing, and the gravity plates seemed to be malfunctioning as he felt forty kilos lighter, and then forty heavier in the space of a few seconds. His stomach did flips at the abuse, and threatened to empty his lunch in front of the crew.

Metal screeched, and the ship shook again, this time it continued juddering underneath him, though thankfully the grav-plates were returning to normal.

"We've been hit!" somebody shouted unhelpfully.

"Thankyou for that," he returned, the sarcasm lost in the tumult of the ship's noises. "All stations make your damage reports."

Polly was first to make a report. "We've lost thrust, and the engines are non-responsive. We're drifting free. I don't know how, but we survived a pretty violent transition from light speed. I think the emergency dampeners we installed last month activated."

"Hull breaches in the engine module," another officer reported. "I can't reach the engine control room."

"Get someone to physically go down there to find out their status," ordered DaSilva, prompting one of the stand-by officers to bolt out of the bridge. "Any other bad news?"

"Reaction control thrusters are down as well," Polly added. "We are dead in the water."

* * *

November 4001ad.

The heavy smell of baking wafted through the building as the baker opened an oven, and scooped the food out and onto one of the treated wooden tables. The building was a primitive dome made of a local blast-dried mud-and-mortar mix, just like every other in the settlement. The domes were cream, and divided like any other house in the universe by equally cream walls that stretched to the ceiling.

This dome –the bakery- was larger than a normal residential dome, with a large area for the ovens and kiln, and a bulbous chimney to vent the steam and smoke. It stood on a small thoroughfare with several other large commercial domes that included a butcher, a vegetable store, and a blacksmith.

Although the settlement did indeed have advanced technology, it was used for things like food storage, transport and communications. They had chosen this life of primitive hands-on living.

A silhouette appeared in the main entrance to the bakery, and was chuckling.

"You really got it to cook?" the silhouette asked.

The baker, who wasn't really a baker, gave him a smile, and shrugged.

"Told you I could."

"You are a man of many talents, Adam Caine," nodded the silhouette. He stepped out of the light of the entrance, and into the softness of the bakery's overhead lights. The man was a green-skinned Mertik, the same race as Adam's adopted daughter, Evelyn . He was taller than Adam, though far thinner and less muscular, and was in fact the owner of the bakery, and had been a good friend to the small Caine family during their stay on Ckeer Najoor.

"Who'd have thought, eh?" Adam beamed, flashing his friend a roguish grin. "And you thought I was only good for killing monsters."

Relion shrugged helplessly.

"You blundered in and saved us from those things like some warrior of the old legends. What else was I supposed to think?" He wandered over to the table, and eyed the treacle tart Caine had made from local ingredients. "Smells delicious. *Looks* delicious too."

"It's a recipe I got off an old girlfriend when I was in the Marines."

Relion's face went blank, not understanding the term, though Adam did not explain, thinking it better to leave it a mystery. The baker didn't push the issue –they had been friends for two lunar cycles, and Relion had learned not to push Adam on his past, knowing his own past was not something to be proud of.

"Do you only do treacle tart?" asked Relion. "Or do you do other recipes as well?"

Caine gave him a sidelong glance and smile as he used a sharp implement to cut the tart into several slices. It was almost time for the end of the school day, the school being on the other side of the settlement, and the children would be coming home soon.

In the distance, a bell rung five times, announcing the end of school.

He smiled.

"I'm just not the baker type." He slid the slices onto a battered metal plate he had brought from his ship. The two friends blew out the flames of the ovens and kilns, the day's cooking over until the morning, and then locked the bakery up for the night, before wandering over towards the school.

The settlement would have been called a town in Adam's own century, with a central, much larger, dome acting as the town hall and general meeting place, and a stream running through it. There were two bridges crossing the water, and a ford at the edge of town. The settlement's commercial properties were all spiralled around the central dome, with the habitat domes scattered in large clumps around them. Off to the west, there was an ancient crater at the edge of the forest that bordered on the settlement, where the *Kara Marazov* had sat still for two months without flight.

Adam and Relion stepped across one of the bridges that lazily stretched across the rushing stream, their footsteps clunking on the timber structure. They strode through the adjoining residential area, and came upon the school, passing dozens of chatty children, excitedly telling their parents or guardians of their day at school.

There, at the low wooden gates, they found their own children waiting for them. Relion had three children, two boys and a girl, all of mixed heritage from himself and his Kra Nal wife. They were playing something that looked like hopscotch, giggling and laughing. Eve, her emerald skin vivid in the evening light, was dancing around the others excitedly, white ribbons wrapped round her head, waist, and wrists. Relion had mentioned it was a tradition for young Mertik girls or women to wear ribbons on the celebration of their birth date.

Adam remembered Relion's own daughter wearing ribbons when he and Eve had first arrived on Ckeer Najoor two months ago. Since coming to this farm planet, Eve had learned much of her Mertik traditions and culture, though Relion had admitted that he had not taught Eve or his own children about the darker parts. According to the baker, the planet Mertik was the centre of a large empire of criminals and warlords, and most of their race was raised in violence and crime.

Adam got the feeling that Relion had been talking from experience.

Eve noticed the two men watching them, and her eyes lit up. She bound over to Adam, and wrapped her arms around his right leg, and giggled even more. The tiny seven-year-old was full of endless joy, despite the hardships she had endured even before being rescued by Adam on Odyssey.

"How was school, Evie?"

"It was great, daddy." She paused for breath, and then spewed out everything in a super-fast collection of English –or Standard– words that Adam could barely keep up with. We learnt about plants and animals and then weplayed Tarik and I came second and then we had lunch and then we learnt abou this story and now we're out-here." Adam's jaw dropped at the sheer speed she had talked, and looked at Relion. The Mertik man just shrugged, and gave him a knowing smile.

Adam, the hand holding the tart behind his back to keep it out of Eve's view, put his right hand on her shoulder, and directed her back towards the way the two men had come. The group headed back, the two adults avoiding talking about birthdays so as not to tip Eve off.

They guided the kids to the central dome, the town oddly silent.

When they wandered into the central dome, and then into the main hall, they found dozens of people waiting there. They all shouted "Happy Birthday Eve!"

At first, Eve was taken aback, but then she started clapping excitedly, and began jumping up and down.

"Thankyou," she cried. The group, mostly the children from school who had slipped away before Eve and their parents, all gathered around, clamouring to tell her happy birthday in person. She grabbed Adam's trouser leg, a handful of it in fact. She wasn't scared, but seemed slightly wary of the others crowding in.

The parents of the children held them back, noting Eve's reaction.

Adam finally revealed the treacle tart behind his back, and Eve's eyes went wide, remembering that he had cooked it for her last birthday. He lowered the plate so that she could take a slice in her hands. She wolfed it down in seconds, and then burped, forgetting that there were dozens of people all around her.

"Pardon me," she said, before her father could make a comment.

The adults all chuckled, and the music started. The instruments were mostly homemade, and although the tinny sounds they made were odd, it was still a pleasing noise.

The party went on for a couple of hours, the children dancing with their parents, Relion seeing to the catering, whilst Adam watched from the sidelines, a big beaming smile on his lips. The smile lasted until somebody began calling out, "Captain Caine," a title that nobody had called him since the week he had arrived.

A young male Rijiin, barely out of his teens by human standards, came running up to Adam. He had come from a door at the back of the hall, which only led to the settlement's communications room.

"Captain Caine, there's a transmission being forwarded from your ship."

Adam sighed. For two months he had had no contact with the outside universe, content to stay on Ckeer Najoor with Eve. He had even considered making permanent resident. Now it seemed the outside universe wanted to contact *him*.

The wolf-like humanoid led Adam to the comms room, where the settlement's only *complete* concession to advanced technology lay: the holographic communicator, which was flashing a message in mid-air: HOLDING.

Adam nodded to the boy wolf, who then activated the channel, and left Adam in private. Unfortunately, the alien figure that appeared in the holographic projector's field was not all that surprising.

Adam sighed.

"What kind of trouble are you in now, M'Der?"

M'Der Tr'n, famous historian, and a member of the tall, skinny, pale-green-skinned Kra Nal race, suddenly had a guilty look on his naturally long, pointed face.

"*Since when do I need to be in trouble just to call an old friend?*" the hologram shrugged. Adam scowled, folded his arms across his muscled chest, and tapped his foot impatiently. *"Alright, alright,"* the alien conceded, putting his long thin hands up in surrender. *"So it's a lot. It's not my fault I keep getting into trouble; besides, that thing on Gorganath ten weeks ago was all down to that little bundle of fun you call a daughter."* He pointed a finger accusingly at Adam.

Adam nodded apologetically; the incident in question was the fourth time he had met the historian after their escape from the Saajil slaveship the first having been only a few days after the destruction of Andromeda's core. The Caines had met M'Der on the planet Gorganath, and Eve had accidentally destroyed a rare statue of one of their founders, enraging the locals enough that they came storming at the visitors with weapons, and chased them off the planet in a ridiculously long pursuit from their star system.

"Adventuring with you always has its downside, my friend," commented Adam. The Kra Nal was about to protest, but Adam interrupted him. "What's up this time?"

"Uh, I need your help," the other replied sheepishly. Adam rolled his eyes. *"It's a consulting job this time, and you'll be well paid. I promise this time —you will be paid; I know I promised to get you paid on Hoo, but you can't blame me for them not having enough money."*

"Nor any brains, since they'd been dead for fifty-thousand years." The big human frowned. "What kind of consulting could I possibly do in *this* century?"

"Actually, you would be consulting on technology from your century. A Tagarri mining fleet stumbled upon a large-scale stasis module in a large asteroid field in the outer rim of the Milky Way galaxy. Their initial scans revealed it to be of ancient Terran technology, relating to the era of mankind's first deep space exploration. They called the Terran Science Council, and me, and now I'm aboard one of two vessels the Council has sent to investigate."

"M'Der, I left in 2006, all that deep space exploration happened *after*."

The lanky historian shrugged.

"You are still the closest thing to an expert we have." M'Der waited for some kind of comment.

"I can't leave Eve on her own here, and I can't take her with me, because she's got school."

"Leave her with friends," the other shrugged.

Adam grumbled, "Send the coordinates to the *Kara*. I'll be on my way tomorrow morning once Eve is off to school."

M'Der nodded enthusiastically.

"See you soon."

His hologram jabbed the air with a finger, and was gone. Adam sighed, wondering how he was going to explain leaving Eve at home for the first time. He would have to leave her with Relion, hoping that the young girl would forgive him. After their many adventures (most with M'Der Tr'n dragging them into fantastic and dangerous places), it looked like this small town was going to be their home.

* * *

2020ad.

"Are the railguns operational?" asked DaSilva.

Somebody shouted in the affirmative from across the bridge, though he couldn't see whom it was through the growing smoke that was accumulating from a damaged power conduit. The bridge was tilted as once again the grav plates were malfunctioning, and were apparently being affected by a nearby gravity source.

Polly reasoned it was the nearby enemy ship's own gravity compensators and mass interfering with the *Icarus'* system.

"Lock onto their weapons system if you can," he ordered.

"Got it, sir."

"Fire when ready."

The deck vibrated, and DaSilva could hear the thudding of the rear railguns hammering at the big red ship. The technology, like everything else on the *Icarus*, was experimental: it was an electrical gun that accelerated a conductive projectile along a pair of metal rails that permit a large electric current to pass through the projectile; the current interacted with the strong magnetic fields generated by the rails and this accelerated the projectile toward its target at more than seven times the speed of sound.

They were accurate weapons, the best humanity had to offer.

DaSilva watched helplessly as the blurred projectiles stopped harmlessly before they hit the ship's hull. The other ship returned fire, the energy slamming against the *Icarus*.

The deck heaved, and DaSilva was once again thrown out of his chair. He smacked his head on the deck and passed out.

Fifteen decks down and far towards the rear of the ship, the officer the Admiral had sent down to investigate the engineering department came across a problem: the large doors that led into the engineering room were melted shut, and a readout from a nearby terminal declared the section uninhabitable.

He grabbed the radio from his belt, and clicked it on.

"Bridge, this is Johansson. There's no way into engineering." There was no reply. "Bridge?" All that came over the radio's small speaker was static, as if it were being jammed. "Can anyone hear me?" He was about to repeat this when something sharp stabbed through his back, and protruded out from his stomach. It was a serrated blade, covered in his blood.

The last Johansson heard was clacking and clicking beaks, and then his body went numb and everything went black.

A quartet of Marines —three U.S., one British- found Johansson's body sat upright against a bulkhead, blood pooling around him, his arms limp by his sides. There was something in one of his hands, and one of the Marines bent to pick it up. It was a small metal ball with lights flashing on it.

He frowned.

And then it started beeping.

The explosion blew out the melted doors to the engineering room, which, unfortunately, had been exposed to space by the last round of energy fire, suddenly exposed a large proportion of the ship to the vacuum of space. The explosion itself vaporised the Marines; the fire was then drawn out into the vacuum by the sudden rushing of oxygen towards the opening.

An engineer on Deck 7, heading to a burst power conduit with his toolkit, rounded a corner to find a group of aliens in front of him. At first, he mistook them for birds, but they stood like humans, with chunky red chitinous armour around their upper torsos and shoulders. Their rubbery skin was black as night, with a big black clicking beak and rather human inner lips, as well as varying sized crests on top of their heads. Their eyes were pure evil, a molten yellow and disturbingly thin, and they walked on clawed legs that were bent the wrong way, like a horse or chicken.

They carried wicked spiked rifles, whilst two of them wore black armour instead of blood red, with gold trimmings, and gold inscriptions. Instead of the spiked rifles, the two leaders, for what else could they be, carried long metal fighting staffs, tipped with small blades.

The engineer had only a few seconds to take this in when one of the red-armoured aliens raised its rifle, and shot him with a bright pulse of energy. It hit him in the chest, and vaporised a large chunk of flesh, bone, and internal organs. He was dead before he hit the deck.

Four sections over on the same deck, more aliens stalked through the corridors, killing indiscriminately as they went until they hit a large staircase leading to the next deck where a full squad of Royal Marines were waiting for them, rifles at the ready. Although communications were down, the Marines had heard the tumult, and even found an escapee of the massacre. They, a squad of US Marines, and a separate mixed squad of both nationalities, had stationed themselves around the area where the aliens were thought to be, lying in wait.

The aliens began climbing the steps to the next deck when the Royals popped out of cover at the top, and began blasting away with their SA80s down the stairwell. The black-armoured leader was torn to ribbons by the concentrated fire, as well as the two aliens either side of him.

Inhuman screeches reverberated up the stairs, though the Marines were not put off by it, still firing, and their weapons were incredibly loud in the confines of the corridors. A Marine took an energy pulse to the face, vaporising half his head. There was no blood, only smoke, and the retching stink of cooked flesh.

More pulses swept up the stairs, some stinging against the bulkheads, others slapping the rear wall behind the humans.

Another Marine was hit in the arm, almost burning it off completely at the elbow. He screamed and writhed around on the deck until another pulse shot out his throat, and silenced him forever.

Somehow, more aliens began to pour into the space at the bottom of the stairs; even as the Marines killed dozens of them, leaving a pile of corpses, more came to replace them. Another three Marines went down, one was spun around by a hit to the shoulder, which tumbled him down the steps, and onto the bayonet spike of one of the alien rifles. The other two were alive, but out of action.

"Pull back," the squad leader ordered. They fought a fighting retreat, dragging the wounded with them. The aliens rushed up the stairs, following the humans tentatively as they retreated back to the pre-arranged RV point at another staircase, only to find the corpses of the American squad. Aliens suddenly appeared from all directions, and cut the Royals down in seconds, even the wounded.

Polly, aware that DaSilva was still unconscious, began ordering the bridge crew to lock down the ship as best they could.

"Communications see if you can get a distress signal out."

"To who, Doctor?"

"To anyone that'll hear it," she scowled.

The officer nodded, and scrambled to carry out his orders.

Polly turned to the others. "Sensors, scan the ship, find out how many boarders we're dealing with, and keep an eye on that ship outside. Somebody use the CB radios to get in touch with as many Marines and other departments as you can." She remembered there were two Marines outside the doors. She jumped up to the rear doors, opened them to bring the guards in, and stopped in her tracks.

Fear and revulsion gripped her, and she froze to the spot.

The Marines were on the floor, smoking carbonised holes in their chests, with the bird-like aliens standing over them. The leader, clad in black armour that had the visible texture of crab shell, pointed at Polly with a bladed fighting staff, and gestured for her to step backwards.

Polly nodded; she was a scientist, not a soldier.

She put her hands in the air, and backed away from the doors. The red-armour aliens swept around their leader, rifles held parallel to the ground to point at the bridge crew. The bridge crew, all caught off-guard, just stood there dumbfounded.

The leader stayed close to Polly, apparently understanding that she had some kind of authority over the others.

It clicked and clacked its beak at her, gesturing with the staff, the point of which was disturbingly covered in human blood, which just made Polly tremble even more.

"What do you want from us?" she demanded, trying to still the tremors that threatened to encompass her body. The creature clicked and clacked again, forming unintelligible words with the pair of black lips inside its obsidian beak. It got angrier as Polly understood even less.

It jabbed the point of the staff into her stomach, bruising her but not drawing blood, despite her plain black fatigues being in between skin and blade. She still did not understand so it decided to raise the blade up, holding it up like he was about to throw a javelin.

His head disappeared in a spray of black blood.

Bullets put holes in the heads of four more before the bridge crew suddenly turned on the aliens, clubbing them with anything handy. The aliens screeched as the crew released all the frustration and fear of the last few minutes, and bludgeoned them to death before any of them could fire their rifles.

Polly turned slowly to her left, where the bullet that killed the alien leader had come from.

DaSilva was lying there on his side, blood dribbling from the cut on his forehead, sidearm in his hand, the barrel smoking, a grim smile on his lips.

"What did I miss?"

* * *

4001ad.

The *Kara Marazov* exited the Linkway, the brilliant blue of the subspace tunnel flitting away behind the vertical crescent ship. Light from the nearby star glinted off the ship's shimmering hull as it dove towards a large collection of starships that were hanging above a massive asteroid field, one not unlike that of Delta-Tango, Terran Navy Headquarters.

The Tagarri mining fleet was obvious to Adam, with the massive mining vessels at the centre. They looked like ramshackle coils, with four thick circles of metal connected by six giant prongs that made it look like a giant hand, with two diagonal engine banks at the rear. Of the ten mining behemoths that Adam could see, no two seemed to be exactly alike, presumably having had adhoc repairs and modifications. Banks of tractor beams pulled asteroids into the maws of the ships, and were broken up by lasers, electromagnetic devices drawing the precious minerals out of the rocks inside the rings of the ship.

The escort ships were built with a similar design, though they were far smaller, and had wing-like protrusions on either side of the ship, presumably to accommodate weaponry.

Bulbous, long ships that looked like fat metal fish trundled away from the sides of the miners, and docked with a similarly designed mass hauler that sat next to the Linkway entrance. Adam imagined that the bigger haulers would take the materials away once it was full to either sell on the local markets, or to whatever home base they had.

He skirted the *Kara* over the top of the asteroid field, and saw what he had come for: the two Terran-designed science vessels, hanging above a particularly shabby looking miner ship. Their hulls were coloured a deep navy blue, and were shaped like an ice-age stone blade, with long thin delta-wings that swept back from the point of the nose to the ring of powerful sublight engines at the stern.

There was a docking signal coming from the nearest of the two science vessels, identified by the ship's computer as the *HMS Hawking*. The other's ID was tagged as the *HMS Denning*, and both were designated as *Star Rider*-class.

The docking signal drew the *Kara* to the underside of the *Hawking*'s hull where there waited an airlock and docking clamps. A solid armoured docking tunnel extended from around the airlock, and Adam flipped the *Kara* onto its starboard half-crescent wing, activating the auto-docking system.

The tunnel latched onto the *Kara*'s portside airlock, and sealed the gap, pressurising it, and unlocking the airlocks on both ships. Adam, dressed in his comfortable combat fatigues, and with his treasured Walther P99 on his hip, locked the ship down, and wandered back to the airlock. Because the *Kara* was on her side relative to the other, a ladder was lowered into the tunnel, and Adam climbed up it and into the bigger vessel.

Stood with a smile on his long face, M'Der Tr'n was waiting for him patiently.

Either side of him stood two humans in light blue overalls, presumably members of the *Hawking*'s crew, since they had a black patch on their arms with the ship's name stitched into it in gold letters.

"Welcome aboard the *Hawking*, Adam," the Kra Nal historian beamed.

Adam, holding something behind his back, nodded his thanks, and then extended that same hand out in front of him. In it was a wedge-shaped object, wrapped in paper. M'Der's eyes lit up when he saw the wedge in Adam's hand.

"Is that what I think it is?" he gasped.

"We were at Evie's party when you called," Adam explained. "She wanted you to have a piece since you couldn't make it this year." In fact, M'Der had insisted during the previous birthday that Adam make *several* large treacle tarts, and had promptly eaten two of them. He had been sick the next day, but hadn't regretted it. "Sorry it's only a small piece this time."

M'Der shrugged.

"It's better than no treacle tart at all," he chuckled.

One of the *Hawking*'s crew cleared his throat impatiently, gaining the attention of the two friends. They gave each other a wry smile and a shrug and turned to the other two. M'Der made the introductions, gesturing to each as he went.

"Professor Pitr Mak, and Doctor-Captain Mykel Silk, this is Captain Adam Caine, owner of the private yacht *Kara Marazov*, and the consultant I brought in." The scientists nodded silently, but seemed to be deeply annoyed with the intrusion into their work.

"Doctor-Captain?" queried Adam.

Silk seemed to imperceptibly puff his chest up as if Adam had insulted the integrity of his title, no matter how innocently Caine had asked the question. M'Der, not wanting to see a conflict between the two after having seen Caine's skills before, stepped in.

"Doctor Silk was assigned by the Science Council as the *Hawking*'s commander, hence the title: Doctor-Captain. He is also the leader of this expedition." M'Der also mumbled something that only Adam could hear, "He's also my boss." One of Adam's eyebrows lifted far above the other, a smart-ass comment threatening to blurt out from his lips.

"We did not agree to your consulting on this project, Captain Caine," muttered Silk, who then shot a venomous glance M'Der's way. "But we were overridden by the Science Council, and a member of Navy Intelligence."

Silk didn't mention who the intelligence operative was, and didn't have to; Adam knew it could only be Raymond Sansky that had put in a good word for him.

"We better get down to business then, hadn't we?" commented Caine, a bit too chipper for the scientists, who glared at him, before leading the way into the ship proper. The ship itself was almost identical to the two Navy ships Adam had stayed on (the *Polly Jenkins* and the *Invincible*), with the clinically white walls, floors, and ceiling, and holographic images and panels hovering in shades of jade green before the walls.

They passed several crewmen dressed in the same blue uniforms, all of whom wore the same arrogant glare as the first two, sniffing as though Caine smelt bad, or was just an uncouth barbarian to them.

They entered a large round amphitheatre with a glowing table at its centre. Much of the lighting was dimmed, and a technician waited at the table's controls. Caine recognised it as a briefing room with a holo-projector –the *Polly Jenkins* had had something similar.

Silk nodded to the technician, who then tapped a few commands into the holographic control panel beside him. The large holo-projector flickered to life, and an image of a piece of technology appeared above the round table.

The lower half of it had black tiles instead of white hull, and Adam realised that the picture was in full colour, unlike his previous encounters with Terran holo-technology.

"I thought the Navy's holographic projectors were limited in what they could show?" pondered Adam.

It was Silk that answered, his voice filled with so much arrogance he was practically begging for a slap. "The Council's vessels are technologically superior to the Navy's. Even our *defences* are stronger than one of the Navy's new *Prophecy*-class cruisers."

"Arrogance is not a virtue," snorted M'Der, clearly continuing a previous argument.

"Whatever," snapped Adam. "What have you got?" He pointed to the hologram hovering over the table, which was striking a serious chord with him. Something from his past that he couldn't quite put his finger on.

Professor Mak nodded.

"As I'm sure you know, a Tagarri mining fleet discovered a piece of tech floating within the asteroid field we are currently above. The fleet's flagship is currently holding it with tractor beams." He briefly turned away from the hologram. "Unfortunately, the Foreman of the fleet has declared our operation frivolous and a waste of time, so he has given us another forty-eight hours before we have to take it ourselves."

"What is the tech?"

The image rotated, and Adam saw something in the white section of the technology. He asked them to zoom the image in. He gasped as he looked upon the Stars and Stripes, and the Union Jack.

And that was when it hit him.

"Jesus Christ, it's a part of the *Icarus*."

M'Der's jaw dropped as he remembered the name from his own research years before, though the scientists had blank looks on their highlighted faces. M'Der explained the conversion of the *Mayflower* to the *Icarus*, and the significance of the ship's place in human history.

"I'd have thought it would be taught to every school child," commented Adam.

The other two humans just shrugged nonchalantly.

Adam shook his head incredulously. "Anyway, what's a chunk of the *Icarus* doing here, and why has it only just turned up?" Despite the annoying scientists, Adam found himself getting excited about the prospect of what this could mean for Adam's own past: on Yh'reth'gar's flagship he had seen the wreckage of the *Icarus* itself, and even the fatigues he was wearing were from the ship. Not to mention he had taken a liking to the scientist responsible for its creation: Dr. Polly Jenkins. His heart began to quicken. Would he meet her again, after all this time?

"The sensor readings indicate cryogenics aboard," the technician reported, looking over the readings appearing below the image.

"Could be an emergency ejection module," Mak added, "with stasis pods to protect the crew. That would explain the cryogenics, and the fact that it is only part of the ship, rather than the whole thing." He looked at Adam accusingly. "*You* are the consultant, you could tell us."

Adam looked over at his friend.

"You didn't tell them?"

The historian snorted derisively, "They wouldn't listen to reason."

Adam sighed, and folded his arms across his muscled chest. "*Icarus*, or rather the *Mayflower*, was launched seven years after I disappeared in two-thousand-and-six AD. Stasis and faster-than-light technology was limited to fictional works and drawing boards, nothing more than pipe dreams. Rumour was, though, that they were testing some kind of new cryogenic system on healthy soldiers –but that was just before I left the military."

He ignored their incredulous looks, and stared at the hologram.

"If this is a stasis chamber, then its possible there were survivors, even after almost two thousand years."

M'Der nodded excitedly.

Adam smiled. "What are we waiting for then? Let's have a look inside."

An hour later, they were standing in the docking tube of the Tagarri flagship. The miners –humans evolved on a planet that wasn't Earth- steered clear of the visitors to their ship, except for a security contingent of four armed guards, and the Fleet Foreman himself. The Foreman was a bear of a man, his skin healthily pale from never having seen real sunlight, and dirtied by the primitive processes of the ship. His once-green overalls were just as dirty, though Adam could see no source of the dirt. The man's bushy greying beard stood out from his pale face, and gave him an air of command over the few others the group had seen.

Strangely enough, the Tagarri security contingent had not seen fit to take away Adam's sidearm, ignoring it completely. They, however, had small pistol sized lasers strapped to their wrists, making Adam wonder if they even knew he was actually carrying a weapon of any sort.

They were taken to an outer docking port, and stepped into the docking tube. The flexible tube folded out to the *Icarus'* emergency section. There was an airlock on the side of the section, just above the black re-entry tiles. The end of the tube latched onto it, and the doors cycled open.

The party stepped into the mouldy air, the mining barge's air scrubbers struggling to swap out the oxygen. Adam was stuck in the middle of the party as they entered the emergency module. There was a large round door that Adam recognised from his own experience on the *Mayflower* before its launch, and had a pretty standard wheel lock at its centre.

The others dawdled in front of the door, Mak fumbling with a hand-held sensor. The Tagarri were impatient to get back to their mining, glaring at their time-pieces, and giving each other bored looks, whilst M'Der was almost jumping on the spot with glee, excited at the prospect of getting to grips with real history.

Adam just rolled his eyes, and barged through the group, gripped the wheel, and twisted it.

The scientists shouted protests, but Adam ignored them, cranking the wheel counter-clockwise until the locking bars snapped out of their slides, and the door came loose. He pulled the door open, still ignoring the scientists' pleas to slow down, and check the area before proceeding.

He stalked into the corridor beyond, and his stomach suddenly felt like it was being torn apart. He stumbled forwards, and realised why: the emergency module had no active gravity, and he floated slowly forwards into the musty atmosphere. He was used to zero gravity, having experienced it a number of times since his arrival in the forty-first century. As he floated, he could see rows of frosted glass-fronted chambers. He pushed off a support girder and moved across the corridor to the nearest one, before wiping the frost and condensation off the glass.

He gasped as he looked upon the face of Polly Jenkins.

* * *

2020ad.

They made for the emergency module. The initial attacks had stopped, though the internal scanners indicated there were more on the ship, in the vicinity of the engineering section. DaSilva knew the ship was lost, and gathered what crew and Marines were left.

The Marines were ordered to make a vanguard and rearguard, the remaining senior soldier being a Colour Sergeant from the Royals called Graham.

Graham sent two Royals ahead to scout for obstacles. They left small clues behind as they went, usually in the form of a piece of debris pointing the direction they needed to go. The civilians, scientists mostly, were placed in the middle of the thirty-strong group. One of the Marines handed DaSilva an assault rifle from one of the weapon lockers on the bridge, making him an unofficial member of the unit. One or two of the Marines picked up the odd-looking rifles dropped by the aliens, uncomfortable with the decaying smell emanating from them.

Polly was at the centre of the group, trying to keep the hysterical civilians in line, whilst they moved quietly through the corridors.

There was a loud bang up ahead, and Graham and DaSilva ran forwards with the vanguard squad. The two scouts were crouched at a large intersection, with the dead body of one of the aliens between them, a bullet hole through its black forehead.

Graham, about the same age as the fifty-something admiral, knelt down beside the scouts, the closest of whom turned to him.

"This is the third one we've encountered, Colour," he reported, gesturing with his firing arm to the body. "They seem to be roaming the ship, almost as if they're lost, or they're looking for something."

DaSilva nodded. "Us, I expect."

"Or the ship's main computer database."

DaSilva paled at the prospect: the database had all their knowledge in it; ship schematics, the defences of the Proxima colony, and the location of Earth itself. If these aliens were an example of their entire race, then there was the distinct possibility that they could attack Earth.

The main computer needed to be wiped clean, to prevent the aliens from locating home, or gaining intelligence from the wreckage. When he looked over at the aging Colour Sergeant, he saw the same thoughts behind Graham's eyes.

"Keep them going to the emergency module, Colour," ordered DaSilva. Graham was about to protest, when the admiral cut him off. "I'm too damn old, Colour. You're a Marine and a commando, and more useful. Besides, the computer needs a flag officer's command codes to activate the wipe."

Graham deflated, seeing that DaSilva was going to be stubborn about it, and only being an NCO, he didn't have the authority to countermand him; at least that was what the flag officer hoped. He nodded, and then gestured to the two scouts to continue on. It wasn't far now. DaSilva stepped to one side to allow the passage of the rest. The military personnel saluted, the civilians nodded.

Polly didn't argue, she knew DaSilva well enough to know when his mind was set on something. She wrapped her arms around the admiral in a tight hug, before exchanging goodbyes. Despite it being a relatively simple task, there would be opposition to having the computer wiped, and would be near suicidal given the behaviour of the enemy so far.

DaSilva didn't look back, just pushed the rifle's stock into his shoulder and stepped into an adjoining corridor. He followed the corridor to where it ended at a staircase that lead down to Deck 8, near the main section of crew quarters. There were corpses littered about the place. DaSilva knew the names of every single one, having prided himself on learning the names of everybody under his command, just as he done on the *Reuben James*.

His mind wailed inwardly at the sight of so many of his people dead. There were no survivors; none were merely wounded. Some of the wounds inflicted on them looked as though they had been repeatedly slashed and hacked at like they were animals in an illegal slaughterhouse.

Nauseating guilt hit him like a wave at the realisation of losing so many of his crew.

No, dammit, he thought, *I won't give in now; not when the remainder of my crew still need me. I will not let* Icarus *become as tragic as its namesake.*

Something large broad sided him, tackling him to the deck. It was one of the aliens. The stench from it was like rotting meat, and it was wheezing heavily. The two rolled apart, and DaSilva saw it was one of the black-and-gold leaders. This one was wearing a long shimmering black cape that hung over one shoulder.

It was taller than the few that the admiral had seen, with old scars across the parts of its dark body he could see. Evil seemed to exude off of it like the cloak it wore, its eyes as molten as a lava flow. It had a wicked knife in its clawed hand, its blade slick with red human blood that still dripped onto the floor.

It charged at DaSilva.

He brought the rifle up, but it was too close to shoot. Instead, he used it as a stick, to smash against the thing's wrist. The knife didn't come loose from its talons, but it prevented the weapon from turning the old man into a shish kebab. Unfortunately, they were at the top of another staircase, and the two, overbalanced, tumbled down the metal stairs.

Bones cracked and fractured, bruises appeared, and blood leaked from cuts. They landed in a pile at the bottom, separate from each other.

DaSilva must have banged his head because his vision had blurred almost to the point where he couldn't tell what was floor, and what was the ceiling and walls. It was then that a big hand grabbed a handful of his fatigue jacket.

* * *

When the civilians and Marines entered the emergency stasis module, the scouts that had led them there approached Polly.

"Doctor Jenkins," the first said, making sure to keep his voice low so nobody could listen in. "We can't find Colour Graham."

"He never checked in with us when we came in here," said the second.

Polly groaned. She knew where the old Royal Marine had gone.

* * *

It wasn't the alien that picked him up from the floor –the black thing was gone, replaced by a very human figure. His vision clearing, DaSilva was shocked to find the big Colour Sergeant helping him to his feet.

Pain flared across most of his aging body, and he struggled to prevent it from overcoming him.

"Dammit, Graham, I ordered you to stay with the others."

The big Marine snorted.

"I'm as old as you, and I've been living on borrowed time ever since the Congo. Besides, did you really think you would actually be *able* to get down to the computer core by yourself?"

In retrospect, DaSilva knew he was right, though he was still angry.

He shook his head, let out a pained breath, and the two made their way to the core. They encountered nobody on their journey, though there were bodies of Marines, crewmen, civilians, and even a few aliens, all strewn against walls. Some were in seated positions; others were missing limbs, or were burned by laser fire.

Graham had to half-carry him, one hand holding his SA80 in a low firing position. DaSilva had one arm across Graham's shoulders. The two hobbled, Graham weighed down by the admiral despite his strength.

They came to the door of the computer core when they both heard the clicking of claws on the metal deck coming from several directions.

"Damn, they're coming for the core," muttered DaSilva.

They ducked through the door just as the armoured aliens appeared, weapons ready. DaSilva slapped the door control, and then shot out the control panel with his colt .45 to prevent anyone hacking the code.

They struggled to the centre of the room, where stood a tower of tera-byte drives, flanked by cooling towers that kept the core cool enough to work to its maximum performance. Graham took up a defensive position between DaSilva and the door, whilst the admiral leaned against the core, and opened the laptop-like internal interface that swung out from a black panel.

He quickly switched it on, and scanned through the main directives.

Something banged on the door, but it held.

The banging got harder and faster, and then stopped, causing DaSilva to pause in his long work.

"Crap, I'm not sure we're going to have enough time to complete this."

Graham nodded, grabbed something from his equipment vest, and stuck it to the door; it was a grenade, and the big man wired it to the door wheel as a booby trap. He stepped back, and kept his assault rifle trained on the same door, his gaze never straying.

A fizzing noise came from the door, and they both noticed the door was starting to turn a little red.

As DaSilva trolled through the directives, smoke began rising from the door in wafts, and then sparks started flicking from the red glowing blobs. The door was beginning to melt, the aliens using whatever laser weapons they were armed with to blast through the door. One of the heat spots touched the grenade off, cooking the explosives inside. The detonation took out the door, and four aliens on the other side.

Graham shielded his eyes from the flash of the blast, recovering quicker than even he thought possible. He squeezed the trigger, and let loose a pair of triple-shots that tore apart the chest armour of two aliens charging through the molten metal hole. Another shot took the head off another enemy.

The lights flashed quickly, like the strobing at the raves back home. Then DaSilva was beside Graham, his borrowed assault rifle thundering in the claustrophobic confines of the computer core room. The muzzle flash from both their weapons was so bright that neither soldier could see what they were shooting at; the chattering noise was so harsh that they couldn't hear the screams of the dying.

Something small and metal dropped between them, and rolled to a stop at their feet. It flashed red, the blinking counter light getting faster and faster.

The deck wobbled beneath them, and there was a great clanking of machinery. The two smiled to each other, knowing they had done their duty.

The grenade vaporised them and punched a massive hole into the centre of the ship, taking many of the aliens with them. Those that survived surveyed the wreckage left behind.

One of the royal guards watched the debris clatter around the wreckage.

"[This was wholly not worth the effort, and loss of life.]"

His companion, another black-armoured royal guard, nodded, his bird-like head bobbing as it did so. "[We cannot find the First. Do you think he is dead?]" When the first guard made no reply, he made his own assessment. "[We should retreat to the *Rage*, and inform the Patriarch his father is dead. He will not like it, but he is the heir to the throne. As royal guards, we must serve him as we would his father. I suspect he may want this primitive vessel for study; he does like his spoils of war.]"

The other guard nodded in assent.

They ordered the retreat back to their ship, leaving their dead behind.

* * *

The emergency module's thrusters pushed it away from the *Icarus* and the alien warship. The aliens didn't try to stop them, or were unaware of the presence of the escape attempt. Polly was at the controls in the central chamber of the stasis module. Most of the crew had been put into the stasis pods, with the Marines refusing to go in until the rest were secure.

She set a course towards Proxima Centauri. It would be a long, long trip to Proxima despite the fact that she would be in stasis the entire time.

She ordered the Marines to get into their pods, then did so herself.

As her eyes became heavy, and the sedatives kicked in, she was sure she saw dark figures moving around outside her stasis pod.

But I thought the Marines were already inside.

* * *

4001ad.

The Tagarri had agreed to take the frozen humans to the *Hawking*'s infirmary. Adam was about to accompany the unconscious Polly Jenkins when one of the Tagarri security guards came running up to him.

"Captain Caine," the young man said, slightly out of breath from the exercise. "There's something you should see in some of the pods we've just found." The younger man hurriedly gestured for him and M'Der to follow, who gave each other confused shrugs but followed nonetheless.

The young Tagarri guard led them to a small room of stasis pods that were slowly defrosting. Mak and Silk were there with a group of scientists from the *Hawking*, pouring over the readouts, and watching the bio-signs of the pods' occupiers.

"Okay, so what's all the fuss?" said Adam.

Silk nodded to the nearest pod, and Adam stepped up to it. He wiped the frost off the glass, and shock and rage filled him. He growled, and suddenly his Walther P99 was in his hand.

Before anybody could react, he squeezed the trigger twice. The two rounds crunched against the solid glass, impacting uselessly. Cracks spidered out from the impact points like a web, splitting the top layers of glass. Everybody flinched or jumped out of their skins, the scientists actually squealing.

"What the fernikking hell did you do that for?" shouted Silk. Adam was already attempting to open the pod by hand. When he couldn't, he turned to the Tagarri in the room.

"Open these pods, and kill the creatures inside. Don't let them wake up; not ever."

M'Der looked at his friend with shock.

Adam, his face a rictus of anger, turned to him.

"They're Core."

M'Der's face fell as he realised what Adam meant. The scientists, the shock wearing off, started shouting and swearing at Caine, calling him a barbarian oaf and other names that Adam didn't understand. He ignored them, though the Tagarri were moving to obey. They stopped in mid-stride when Silk shouted for them to stop.

"Explain this madness," he demanded.

Adam tried to contain the rage he felt at the sight of the being in the pod, and the idiotic scientist. But M'Der put a calming hand on his shoulder, and weariness set in.

"They call themselves the Core, probably because they believe themselves to be the core of the universe or something. Over a year ago I was captured –you don't need to know how- and they tortured my friends and I. They have no desire for anything other than to conquer every thing and everyone they possibly can. They scavenge and steal technology from other races, and they murder for fun."

Silk snorted.

"I think that is an exaggeration."

Adam glared at Silk, and started to move towards him, but M'Der put both hands on his shoulders to stop him. Adam turned back to his trusted friend, and the Kra Nal historian saw the sadness and grief that the Core creatures had invoked.

"Doctor Silk, I would suggest not questioning Captain Caine's veracity on this subject. I assure you, he is an expert." Silk sniffed the air as if he was royalty in the presence of a dirty peasant. M'Der put his hand on Adam's firing arm, having seen it raise slightly, and knowing full well that the human would indeed shoot the scientist. "I suggest you keep personal opinions to yourself. And Adam, do not do anything stupid, no matter how tempting it may be." This last comment he directed at both Silk and Mak with a sneer on his green lips.

"If you won't destroy them, then leave them in the pods, and study them that way," suggested Caine, worryingly gesturing with his pistol. Taking one last look at the Core soldier, Adam holstered his pistol, and stalked out of the room, accompanying the unconscious Polly Jenkins back to the *Hawking*'s infirmary.

After Adam had left the section, Mak let out a sigh of relief.

"What kind of madman have you brought onto this expedition, Tr'n?"

M'Der was still watching the door his friend had disappeared out through, and without turning round, he answered, "He's not mad, Professor; he's been through all kinds of hells that no human could possibly survive."

Mak frowned, "And yet he did."

"Adam's a survivor," M'Der smiled sadly. "He'll outlive us all."

And then he was gone from the room as well.

* * *

Polly woke to find somebody asleep with his or her head on her bed.

Wait, bed? I was in a stasis pod. Oh thank god —we've been rescued. It can't have been more than a few years since we went into cryo, so there shouldn't be any real difference.

The person resting against her bed, however, had disturbingly familiar long unkempt hair. He was wearing black combat fatigues, and despite being groggy, and her vision blurred, she could see a black Walther P99 holstered on his hip. His sleeves were rolled up in perfect military regulation size so as to cover his elbows, revealing muscled, if somewhat slightly scarred forearms.

She felt numb all over, although warmth was spreading across her body. The room she was in was a sterile white, and a single-bed medical room. But there were three-dimensional images and shapes hovering above her, and on the other side of the wall. Most of the text in them was gibberish, medical data that she had no experience with. There was a door leading to the head in one corner, with a larger door presumably leading to the rest of the medical ward.

She groaned involuntarily when she moved.

The sleeping man awoke, and turned his head towards her. The familiarity she felt turned to instant recognition, and she gasped.

"You?" she whispered, her voice hoarse from too long in the stasis pod. "How? Where? When?"

There was sadness in the man's eyes, and she could tell it was directed at her.

He sighed, and took her hand in his.

"My name is Adam Caine. You've been in stasis for... a while. You're on board the science vessel *HMS Hawking*, in its infirmary in fact. I... don't think you're ready to hear where and when you are."

She snorted, though what came out didn't sound like one. "I need to know."

He sighed heavily, and leaned back in the chair he was perched on, looking around at the room as if the walls would tell him the best way to let her down gently.

"According to the history files, you went missing in 2020ad. Well, you were discovered a couple of weeks ago, in the year 4001ad." He leaned forward again, taking her hand once more. "I'm sorry, but you've been in stasis for nearly two thousand years."

She couldn't form any words the shock was so intense.

Two thousand years? Why did nobody find us before? How could we have possibly survived for so long? These and dozens of other questions rattled through her skull as she tried desperately to process the information. Her breathing got faster and heavier, as she found it harder to draw a single breathe. She knew logically that she was having a panic attack.

The holographic images above her began flashing and beeping madly.

She lost consciousness within seconds...

...And woke up hours later, feeling much more relaxed. She suspected they had drugged her to keep her calm; she didn't mind the least bit. When she opened her eyes she found a very tall thin green-skinned man with a pointed head and chin, and an easy smile on his lips. She knew she should be scared, and panicking, but the drugs were keeping her calm, even inside her mind.

The tall green man spoke in English, nodding to her mysterious friend, Adam Caine. "He hasn't left your side for twenty hours now, not even to have something to eat or drink." When she looked over at Adam, she found that he was gently snoozing away.

"He's strong."

"He was trained to be."

"Trained?"

"He used to be in your Special Boat Service, and before that, he was a Royal Marine Commando. He's tougher than anything I have ever seen, and I'm a thousand years old, so I know what I'm talking about."

"SBS?" she whispered. "So he's from my time?"

The alien nodded.

"As I understand it, he disappeared from Earth fourteen years before the *Icarus* was attacked." Confusion and heartbreak set in, although she couldn't really feel it completely thanks to the calming drugs. "Staff Sergeant Adam Logan Caine; the classified files on him call him a war hero."

"You've known him awhile?"

The alien nodded again, a big smile splitting his face.

"I first met him on a slave ship where he rescued me. After that, we've been on a bunch of adventures, with his daughter in tow of course."

"Daughter?" she said. "I've missed a lot."

He sat down in the other chair on the opposite side of her bed from Adam. He went on to explain, in general terms, the history of what she had missed, at least as far as humanity went. He explained the discovery of the Linkways, contact with other species, the renaming of Earth to Terra, and the creation of the Terran Consortium and its Navy. He even told her about the Interior Wars, the Terran royalty and its government. And then he explained the few adventures he had had with Adam, enthusiastically talking about the big human's adopted daughter, and even the fact that the former soldier was the owner of a starship and a small residence on a planet called Ckeer Najoor. She took all this in, and realised that the drugs were wearing off.

The panic, however, did not return.

A grumbling noise came from the vicinity of Adam, who was waking up from his slumber. He was bleary-eyed from an hour of sleep, and gave her a smile.

"I'm sorry I upset you," he said.

She waved it off. "It's not your fault; I was a fool to think we could be rescued that far away from Earth or Proxima." She felt a sense of foreboding coming. "How many *did* you rescue from the emergency pods?"

It was M'Der who answered, "We found forty stasis pods; three were unoccupied. Of the others, we found twenty-three humans still alive, and two dead from electronic failure in their pods." M'Der threw a worried glance to his friend. "We found twelve aliens in total, though four of *them* are dead for sure. That reminds me, Doctor-Captain Silk is planning to leave within an hour, Adam. He agreed to let you stay onboard for now, and keep the *Kara* locked to the docking port." The seven-foot alien strode lithely towards the exit. "Don't forget to send a message to Ckeer Najoor, Adam. By the way, how did you convince Eve to stay in school when you were off gallivanting around the universe?"

Adam grinned, "I told her it was a job and nothing more. She seemed convinced."

M'Der snorted. "That girl's smarter than both of us. I'll try and convince the *Hawking*'s medical doctor to allow the other patients to see each other if they're up to it."

"As long as you don't tell him I need a haircut." He turned and winked at Polly, who had to stifle a chuckle at the camaraderie. "Everywhere we go he has to convince people I need a haircut."

M'Der was laughing out loud now, still in the doorway.

"I'll see you soon." He disappeared through the door, and then popped his head back in. "Oh, and Adam?"

"Yeah?"

"Get your damn hair cut."

Adam was about to make a witty retort when his friend vanished. He bit back a friendly curse that just made Polly burst out laughing. He threw her a mock glare, but it evaporated from his face as a beaming smile spread across it.

"Well. I better leave you to see to your colleagues, and send a message to my daughter." He planted a peck on her forehead, and smiled. "Welcome to the forty-first century."

* * *

Half an hour later, his message to Eve and Relion finished and sent through the ship's communications system, he found himself wandering onto the bridge of the *Hawking*. It was a sedate affair compared to the Navy equivalent, much smaller, but with more holographic displays and control panels lining the walls and making their own rows of consoles in the centre.

A single high-backed chair sat towards the rear of the bridge, Doctor-Captain Silk sat in it, staring out of the large wrap-around viewport ahead. The asteroids stretched out as far as the eye could see, and there was a holographic representation of the entire field hovering above the portside of the bridge, with indicators flashing identifications of minerals. There were a couple of dozen blips showing the ships of the Tagarri fleet and the *Hawking* and the *Denning*.

"Captain Caine," a voice said. It was Silk, finally noticing the big human standing on his bridge. Adam was worried that he was about to be thrown off the bridge for trespassing or some such. "What do you think of these new *Star Rider*-class ships?" It would have been an innocent question, if Silk did not look so bloody smug.

"Impressive," he nodded. "Aesthetically, it's definitely a lot more pleasing to the eye than the Navy's ships. The *Polly Jenkins* was nothing like this." He pointed to the holographic images hovering over the bridge crew.

"You served on the *Polly Jenkins*?" he questioned.

Adam didn't answer, cut off by a sudden alarm from one of the consoles nearby. He frowned, and looked over to the scientist manning the station. Silk was out of his chair immediately, and stepped up behind the dark-skinned man.

"Captain, I am receiving an emergency transmission from the Tagarri flagship."

Adam couldn't help but blurt out, "Emergency?" Silk sent him a filthy look that reminded Adam of his asshole of a father, though he didn't dwell on it for long. The communications technician pressed a few holographic controls, and an image of an audio wave that wobbled and spiked on the screen.

There was a great deal of static from the speakers, and there were words in Standard coming through. "Hawking... *attack*... Icarus." The voice, though distorted, sounded like the Tagarri Fleet's Foreman.

"Repeat that please, Foreman," said Silk nonchalantly, as if this were an every day occurrence.

The static cleared and the Foreman's voice was loud and clear.

"Hawking, *we are under attack by the creatures from the* Icarus *emergency section. Professor Mak opened their pods and they immediately killed him and his team, as well as the security team there. They've invaded our* Gorokk *barge, and have started killing my crew. We have sealed ourselves into the control centre. Please*, Hawking, *my security guards are not trained for this kind of violence. We need help*. Hawking *respond.*"

Adam saw that Silk had frozen, whether in fear for his own life or for other even less noble reasons, he couldn't tell. Either way, he was completely useless –he was a scientist after all, not a Navy man, or even a soldier. He shook his head, and leaned against a clear patch in the holographic controls.

"Foreman, this is Captain Caine. You have to hold on; I'm coming."

"*We'll be grateful for your help, Captain Caine.*"

"Help is coming." Adam turned to the communications tech. "Keep monitoring them, and calm them down if you can."

"Yes, sir," the tech answered automatically.

"Now see here," Silk started, shaking himself out of his frozen state. "You are a civilian consultant, and thusly have no authority on this vessel."

"You froze," was all Adam said in response, and then turned back to the tech. "You have a teleporter?" The tech nodded to a door off the bridge; Adam followed the gesture, and entered into a bay identical to the one on the *HMS Polly Jenkins*, with a large round disk at the centre of the room, and a holographic console to the side. A technician entered and stood by the console.

Adam jumped onto the disk, and unholstered his pistol, making sure it was fully loaded, and holding it out in front of him, in a combat ready position, pointing at the deck.

"Is the *Icarus* section still attached to the Tagarri flagship?" he asked. The technician nodded. "Teleport me into there if you can." Silk tried to protest, but his words were lost in the blinding white flash and ear-splitting noise of the teleporter. Seconds passed, and the familiar sight of one of the stasis pods replaced the *Hawking*.

It was open and empty, and there was no frost or condensation like before. There was, however, a weapons locker, with the weapons overlooked by the scientists, probably deeming them too primitive to pay attention to.

He smiled. There was some nice equipment, some of it slightly more advanced than those from his own decade. He grabbed a black equipment vest, and slipped it on, feeling how good it felt to be wearing a full combat uniform. He grabbed an assault rifle out of the locker. It was an HK-G36c, with a shortened barrel, a second vertical grip *under* that barrel, a light metal stock, and a small scope on the dorsal handle. It was matt black, and it had two-dozen clips beside it.

He slammed a magazine into the breach, pulled the action, thus loading the weapon, and flicked the safety off. He pushed the stock into his shoulder, and sprinted for the exit, his feet barely making a noise as his old –and new- training kicked in. There was no resistance when he entered the carbon-stained and dirty corridors of the Tagarri mining barge –the Foreman had called it a Gorokk.

There were Tagarri littered around the place, all with bullet holes peppering their bodies.

They took the Icarus *weapons*, he thought. *But, why? Why not use their own weapons?* He didn't have time to figure that out –they were Core, and they would die. He heard the clicking of talons on metal coming from around a cramped corner; the sound brought back bad memories he had not wanted to relive.

He pressed himself against the wall as hard as he could without making noise. The Core warrior –dressed in the black and gold armour of a royal guard– came around the corner, holding a P90 clumsily in its long clawed hands. It was looking at the bodies it passed; probably making sure they were dead.

Adam shred the thing's head with a burst from the assault rifle. The corpse dropped to its knees before collapsing, blood everywhere. Adam ignored the gore, and retrieved the P90; he flicked its safety on, and dropped it into a sack he had retrieved from the same locker as the HK –when this was over, he would have a decent armoury for the *Kara*.

* * *

On the bridge of the *Hawking*, Silk watched in awe as the 'consultant' moved through the Tagarri Gorokk. The first alien life-sign winked out in a few seconds. The open communications channel was also linked to other parts of the ship.

Just what kind of consultant is this man?

* * *

Adam silently moved through the ship, checking for survivors, and finding none.

He pushed the grief and guilt away, though he was disturbed to realise that the gore didn't bother him. To be fair, it hadn't for a long time, but he hadn't been exposed to this kind of violence since Odyssey Station.

He could hear the engines humming in the background, though there were no additional sounds to indicate the ship was doing anything but holding position in space. On the Navy's warships, their inertial dampeners kept the ship's engines from vibrating the deck too much. The Tagarri Gorokk, however, was far more primitive, and far more run down than the Navy ships, and thusly the deck vibrated quite badly, with a very un-rhythmic sound.

That was when the deck shook. It didn't feel like the previous humming and vibrating.

"*Captain Caine*," the communication technician's voice appeared over the Gorokk's internal speakers. "*The Gorokk is moving. I believe they are heading to the Linkway. And the sensors are detecting six of the aliens on the bridge.*"

"Trying to get back to their people," Adam nodded. He stopped. "Wait; you said six. I've only neutralised one so far. Where's the other one?"

"*Unknown, Captain.*"

Adam sighed, and continued his stealthy wandering, heading towards the control centre of the ship with directions from the communications tech. The tech informed him that the ship barge had a crew of forty engineers, sixty miners, twenty security personnel, and a seven-man command staff, including the ship's commander and the Fleet Foreman.

"How many Tagarri are detected?"

There was sadness in the tech's voice.

"The last one just disappeared, Captain."

Adam cursed loudly enough that he heard Silk gasp in the background of the *Hawking's* comms channel.

"Captain, they just disconnected the Icarus *stasis section."*

"Collect it if you can; use the *Denning* if need be." He ignored Silk protests, and simply added, "Get it done. We need that section's computer files with any data it has on the ship that attacked them." Silk protested that they already knew who had attacked them, but Adam was thinking that perhaps it could be an indicator of Core technological progress, though he didn't voice his opinion that the Core, as a race, were still out there somewhere.

"Captain, the command centre should be ahead of you."

"Acknowledged, *Hawking*. Go radio silent for now."

The channel clicked off, though he was sure that the Core had monitored the activation of the ship's internal comms. Indeed, the doors at the end of the corridor slid open, and two royal guard stepped out, human weapons at the ready. They saw Adam immediately, despite the fact that he dove behind a support girder.

They opened fire, spraying the girder with solid rounds that ricocheted in all directions, pinging off the walls dangerously. One nicked Adam's firing arm, taking a chunk out of his jacket and arm. He ignored the pain, and popped out of cover to fire on automatic.

The spray of fire obliterated the chest armour of the one on the left, knocking him backwards. The second royal guard took its hits in the stomach, and folded over, blood leaking onto the deck. It screeched, and then gurgled as it died. The second was groaning, its beak clacking, struggling to stay alive.

Adam got out of cover again, and then stepped over them. He pulled his sidearm out, and put a bullet in each of their heads to make sure they were dead. He wasn't about to take chances with the Core, especially the royal guards. He felt no guilt, no sadness, just satisfaction.

He crouched by the entrance to the two-tier command centre. There were no Core on the upper level, though that was purely because the cramped balcony seemed to have no computer consoles or interfaces. There were a few power conduits above it, but they seemed to be ignored by the intruders. The aliens themselves were stood at different consoles, presumably the ship's controls, and not paying attention to the noise that had occurred.

He watched through the small scope, and aimed the crosshairs over the Core at the helm controls. He was sure it was the helm, because the monitors showed the ship's motion and movement in space, along with a HUD that had other ships and objects in it. The creature bent over the console, then straightened, bringing its head back into the crosshairs. Adam switched to single-shot, and squeezed the trigger.

The shot blew out half the front of its head, splattering its brains across the helm.

The other creatures screeched, and turned to meet the new threat, but Adam was already charging across the balcony to the other side. The Core opened up with their captured weapons, and a firestorm of bullets followed him; the noise was deafening as dozens of rounds ricocheted off the balcony, creating a shower of sparks as it all pinged off the metal.

Adam dove forwards, and rolled to land behind a large wad of unused power conduits. More bullets panged off the conduits harmlessly until it went quiet –either the Core were reloading, or they were out of bullets.

He swung from cover, switching his assault rifle to full auto, and fired down into the command centre proper. Two of the Core were spun round, hit in the shoulders and chest, whilst a third collapsed to the deck, clutching the stub of its left leg that had been severed by a flurry of Adam's rounds.

The fourth was thrown backwards against the console it was manning, a look of utter shock on its hideous bird-like face, frozen in death. The fifth, caught completely off-guard by the sheer ferocity of Caine's attack, stood dumbfounded as the high-powered assault rifle took apart its chest.

Adam bound down the stairs, his magazine dry, and not enough time to switch it out for a new one, he jumped before he got to the bottom step, body-checking one of the wounded Core warrior into the wall, and smashed its head against the wall, leaving a slick trail of blood down the metal bulkhead.

The last one was still trying to slot the horizontal magazine into a captured P90, its long knobbly fingers having trouble getting to grips with the human weapon. This one had more gold gilding across its black armour, and a much more elaborate cloak than the usual royal guard. Either this was a leader among the guard, or it was what they guarded.

It dropped the gun, and slid a wicked knife from a scabbard on the back of its armour. Adam understood, and unslung the HK, setting it down gently on the deck. The thing also unholstered a stolen Colt .45, and placed it on the console next to it.

Adam slid a small combat knife out from his boot, and held it in combat position, with the sharp edge of the blade facing his opponent, and the point hanging below his clenched fist.

The two circled each other, snapping quick jabs and feints at the other. Each one was blocked precisely and expertly, the knives clashing for brief seconds before disengaging and circling again.

There was not much room for manoeuvring in the control centre, and Adam found himself bumping into the consoles.

He looked down at the last one, and saw the Colt .45 sat there. He sighed, shook his head, and picked the pistol up in his hand, to point it at the Core warrior. The thing looked shocked, and betrayed.

"Coward," it spat in severely stilted English.

Adam smiled mirthlessly.

"Idiot."

He shot the thing through the forehead, and then moved over to the two creatures still writhing around in their own blood, and finished them as well, still with no anger, no hate -just cold efficiency. He gathered all the captured weapons up, and placed them in the satchel, making sure to unload them, and switch the safeties on beforehand.

Which was when he remembered the helm console, and the images he had glimpsed briefly on the HUD. The Gorokk was heading straight towards the big Kkorrogg mass hauler near the Linkway. The Core had set it to go for the biggest target to maximise the destruction –if that thing exploded, the shockwave could potentially destroy half the mining fleet, along with the *Hawking* and *Denning*.

Adam ran to the controls, and tried to understand the Tagarri wording and symbols. He couldn't –languages were never his strong point: either in school, the Marines, or afterwards. The communications technician was no help either, so Adam started pressing random buttons and switches.

* * *

On the *Hawking*, Silk was still stood on the bridge, watching the comms tech, and the sensor displays. The flagship Gorokk with Caine aboard was heading directly for the Kkorrogg at the entrance to the Linkway.

The Gorokk didn't flinch from its path, even though Silk could hear Caine trying desperately to bring the ship under control, grunting as he struggled with the manual controls of the massive ship.

Most of the bridge crew were mesmerised by the scene outside the viewports as *Hawking* reversed. The thrusters suddenly flared on both ships, the two ships beginning their veering courses. But both were massive, too big and cumbersome for quick and tight manoeuvres.

Silk wanted not to watch, but some morbid curiosity within him made him watch.

The sensor technician counted off the distance between the two colliding ships.

"Two-thousand kilometres."

* * *

The crew of the mass hauler squealed and screamed in fear, cowering behind their consoles, despite it not making a difference whether they were there or anywhere else on the ship.

* * *

"One-thousand kilometres."

Silk closed his eyes.

* * *

"Five-hundred kilometres."

Adam roared as he poured all his strength into pulling the flight control bars backwards as far as possible. And then had an insane idea.

* * *

"One kilometre."

The sensor tech's voice wavered for a second.

"T-twenty metres."

* * *

In the control centre, Adam watched as the lights flickered badly, and his stomach lurched as the artificial gravity fields of the two vessels interfered with each other's, causing the gravity in the control centre to switch from full to zero-G to light and then heavy, pulling his body in different directions.

He kept his hand on the tractor control.

The counter read the metres, and hit zero.

The world shook, and Adam went flying backwards. The deck came up to meet him, and he bounced off the metal. For once, he didn't have any fractured bones, just a lot of bruising on his back.

There was an ear-splitting screech of metal on metal, whilst the deck rumbled and shook like it was in an earthquake. Sparks flew from conduits and the consoles, spraying Adam in tiny white-hot bits of molten metal. One bit his cheek, searing the flesh, but he didn't cry out in pain —compared to the bruises, it was nothing.

The consoles flickered as the data and power conduits were interrupted.

He struggled to his feet, fighting the shaking hull.

The monitors and displays showed that the Gorokk's dorsal sections were scraping against the top of the bulbous mass hauler. The tractor beam finally kicked in, and the Gorokk suddenly bounced up as the beam pushed against the larger hauler.

Sparks and fire flew from the underside of the clawed Gorokk, the thrusters shorted out, and the lights continued to flicker on and off, outside as well as inside. The Gorokk, its engines temporarily out of action, began to drift away from the bigger, sturdier ship, although thankfully it wasn't at a great speed.

The intercom was on the fritz as well, because the *Hawking*'s crew weren't responding whenever he called to them. He fished the handheld radio out of the pocket on his equipment vest, and flicked the channel indicator to the first.

"*Hawking*, this is Captain Caine. Acknowledge receipt of this transmission."

Static answered him, so he switched to another frequency, hoping the *Hawking*'s comms would pick it up.

"Hawking, this is Captain Caine. Come in, please."

Static again.

He went through another twelve frequencies before something other than static came out of the radio's small speaker. He could hear a voice in the background of the white noise, but couldn't make it out.

He flicked the switch to the next frequency, and the voice came through crystal clear. It was the comms technician on the *Hawking*'s bridge.

"*Captain Caine, can you hear me?*"

"I can," he said, relieved.

"*The Tagarri fleet is moving to intercept the remains of the mining barge you're on. Doctor-Captain Silk has ordered the* Denning *to teleport you off there in case there are any complications with the recovery.*"

"Why the *Denning*?"

"*They're closer, Captain.*"

"Understood," he sighed.

He felt a tingling sensation throughout his body, and white light filled his vision. The dying control centre was replaced by the sterile white room of a teleporter bay. This one, however, had a symbol belonging to the *HMS Denning*, and the crew seemed to be all smiles. They wore the same uniforms as the *Hawking*'s crew, but they seemed almost immediately to be more pleasant.

"Welcome aboard the *Denning*, Captain Caine," the ship's female captain beamed.

"Thanks for the rescue," said Adam. He stepped off the teleporter disk and almost fell over –his legs were a bit wobbly from the combination of the faulty grav plating, and the bruising on his back. The crew seemed a bit unsure of him at the sight of the big assault rifle in his hands, and the black combat gear he was wearing.

The young woman led him onto the bridge of her ship, which was identical in every way to the *Hawking*'s, except for the crew, who appeared to have a number of non-Terrans on board.

"Has the *Hawking* found the missing creature?"

She shook her head. Adam sighed, and then a thought struck him.

"Can you scan the interior of the *Hawking*?"

"Of course."

"Do it now, please."

* * *

Polly was with the other survivors. They were a sombre lot, lost in their own grief upon hearing that they were stuck here in the forty-first century. The remaining Marines were grouped in a corner of the sofa-filled lounge they had been given to meet each other, whilst the civilians were grouped together in another; the scientists were separate from each other and the others.

For Polly, the grief had subsided, and her mind was locked on the man she had obsessed over for a dozen or so years. She had tried to find him after his last brief appearance on the *Icarus*, but his description had only come up with a classified military file that even she had no access to; the alien historian had filled much of the blanks, including why he had kept appearing out of nowhere.

A clacking, and a quiet screech interrupted her train of thought; it came from behind her chair, and she froze, knowing exactly what it belonged to. She jumped out of her armchair just as the alien warrior opened fire on the Marines in the corner. It cut them down mercilessly, not sparing a single one with the captured P90 in its claws.

Screams filled the air, and panic ensued as everybody in the room scrambled to get out of the way of the advancing alien.

Naturally, that was when a bright white light filled the large lounge.

The light evaporated almost instantly, coalescing into a human figure at the centre of the room. The figure was dressed in black combat fatigues, an *Icarus* equipment vest, with a large satchel slung over one shoulder, and a big black assault rifle aimed at the alien.

The alien's magazine emptied, and found it had no more to continue. It pulled a knife from its scabbard, and advanced on Caine, evil menace in its molten eyes.

"Who are you?" demanded Caine, his aim unwavering. "What is your name and designation?"

The alien stopped in its tracks, taken off-guard by the big soldier.

"What does it matter to you?" it replied, its English better than the previous creature. "You are going to kill me with that weapon."

"I want to know why you attacked the *Icarus*."

"It was an inferior ship that needed to be conquered," it spat back. It stood to its full height, and swelled its chest with pride. "I am Kh'var'nash, leader of the royal guard to his majesty the First, Yh'reth'ten."

"Yh'reth'ten? That would mean he was the Lord's grandfather." Caine started laughing, to the point that he lowered the rifle. He was shaking uncontrollably, raucous laughter escaping from him, confusing both the alien, and those watching. "No wonder the Core hate humans; it was because *I* killed the Patriarch's father."

The alien's eyes widened with shock.

"The First is dead?"

Anger clouded its evil face, and it spat a feral snarl at Caine.

Its head evaporated under a barrage of bullets from the HK in Caine's hands. Polly had barely seen him move he was so quick to bring the weapon up. The thing's blood splattered over the pristine lounge in a circle around the corpse. Somebody vomited at the gory sight, losing his or her lunch quite spectacularly.

Polly just stared, slack-jawed at Caine's brutal action.

"That answered so many questions," nodded Caine, satisfied with the outcome. He turned to Polly at that moment, concern on his handsome face. "Are you okay, Polly?" And she finally saw the man she had seen on the ISS, and the *Mayflower* and *Icarus*, a man filled with pain but compassionate all the same.

Tears streamed down her face, and she broke down in his arms.

"You need to get away from all this violence, and mayhem," he whispered in her ear. She nodded silently, her head buried in his chest.

He wrapped his big arms around her, and held her tight.

"We'll go to a planet I know."

She looked sceptical.

"It's called Fayde; the cities are surrounded by miles and miles of grass plains and flat farmland. Last time I was there, it was great. Trust me, it's beautiful and very relaxing... Honest."

* * *

Although the Tagarri wanted to honour Adam for saving the two ships from destruction, he had fobbed them off on M'Der, who lapped up all the attention as he always did, smoothing over any problems anybody from the Tagarri and the Terran science ships had.

Polly had been given some sedatives by the *Hawking*'s medical doctor and been asleep for several days, giving Adam enough time to load her onto the *Kara*, and take her to the planet Fayde.

Groggily, she woke up, and found herself in a large double bed that was plumped to perfection. The hotel suite she was in was more like a five-star Hilton than what she had experienced in the past. Drapes hung around the bed like clouds, whilst plush furniture pieces littered the room.

There was a low, even pleasing, humming coming from somewhere in the suite. She slipped out of bed, and noticed that somebody had changed her clothes whilst she was asleep. She was wearing a pair of pretty standard polka dot pyjamas, and there was a change of clothes on a large wooden armchair up against the wall.

A cool breeze wafted through the suite –the doors to the balcony were open, the breeze gently waving the drapes and curtains back and forth. She changed into the overalls, and headed outside. She found Caine sat at a breakfast table, eating what looked to be marmalade on toast.

A steaming hot pot of coffee sat in the middle of the table, surrounded by a jug of milk, a small jar of sugar, and two pairs of mugs.

"Good morning," he smiled.

He was wearing loose-fitting primitive handmade clothes, presumably from his farm planet, and his hair was tied back. He looked nothing like the soldier she had seen on the futuristic *HMS Hawking*. He was relaxed, and laid back, and reading a holographic news report that hung over the edge of the table.

It was in English, and was a report on local politics, though she didn't understand what any of it referred to.

She looked to her right, and found the source of the low humming. It was Adam's ship, clamped to the side of the hotel, with a small gangway leading out to the ship's side hatch from the suite's balcony. It was a beautiful ship, just like M'Der had described. The reflection in the cockpit viewport, however, made her jaw drop almost off her face.

She turned slowly around, and gasped.

The city around her was massive, the spires of the geometrically placed buildings towering over everything below, each one different than the other whilst maintaining the same shades of greys and browns. There were no smaller buildings in between, just the sky-scraping towers that reached sharply into the blue sky, with giant walkways stretching the distance between them at regular intervals.

Roads snaked between the bases of the buildings, as big as the interstate highways back home in Iowa, though there weren't that many cars on them. That was mainly because all the traffic was in the air, flying in lines between the buildings, each one sat on a large polygonal disk, presumably an anti-grav device.

Above all this, starships of all shapes and sizes came and went from various points on the towers, thrusters and sublight engines flaring as they charged towards orbit, or slowed *from* orbit. None of them had the grace and beauty of Caine's ship, but it was absolutely amazing nonetheless.

"You made it all happen you know," said Adam, switching off the holo-projector in the table. "At least as far as the Terrans go." She looked at him questionably as he stood up and stepped up to the railing next to her. "You developed faster than light travel before the majority of the other races in the nineteen galaxies. Most still haven't because they depend on the Linkways." His eyes glazed over briefly as if remembering something from his own past. "Someone once told me that you were a... catalyst of sorts, both for humanity, and for other races they came into contact with."

She struggled to form an answer. "I... It's overwhelming."

He just smiled, a smile that reassured her no end, and sent strong warmth through her body and heart. She leaned her head on his shoulder, still watching the incredible spectacle of the city beyond.

"What happens after this?"

"After what?"

"After this little vacation."

"This is the forty-first century, Polly, anything is possible. Personally, I've got to pick up a heap of supplies from Fayde City on the next continent, and then head back to Ckeer Najoor. I expect M'Der will want to stay for a few nights there as well to make up for missing Evelyn's birthday. You could come with me if you want?"

She smiled, a beaming smile that spread across her beautiful face.

"That sounds nice."

Thirteen:
The Wrong War

"In the grim darkness of the far future, there is only war..."
-Warhammer 40,000 tagline.
"War is hell."
-*Full Metal Jacket.*

June 4003ad.

A few years ago, Rel Major was teeming with life. It was an ecumenopolis, a planet covered in cityscape from pole to pole, as well as being the capital of Craj Territory. But then the Core came, and the planet was levelled, and scavenged by Lord Yh'reth'gar's fleet. Not that anybody would have known who they were, or why they did it.

Ruins stretched as far as the eye could see, from one horizon to another, some still smoking even after six years.

This section of the planet-wide city was originally the home of the Craj government, but they had been the first to be hit by the Core's attacks, the skeletal wreckage of the government towering over the rest, throwing it all in shadow as Rel's yellow sun neared the horizon.

There were few survivors, and those that had survived, were hidden, afraid of another attack, never leaving the shadows of the sturdiest buildings, surrounding their fire-drums, and sleeping in their makeshift buildings. An attempt had been made by the Terran Navy to evacuate the planet, but raiders had intercepted them, and now the Navy rescue ship was in a pile of wreckage several miles from the Administration sector, at the end of the biggest boulevard on the planet, lying across a major junction.

At the opposite end of this road, with the Navy wreck barely visible in the distance, ran two figures, one chasing the other.

The first was a white-skinned fugitive Innnian, dressed in light grey armour that did nothing to help him get away from the human woman closing on him. He was huffing and puffing, sweat dripping down his porcelain features, staining the cloth under his armour.

His white face displayed the fright he felt.

He bound over a piece of rubble —a support girder of some sort. He looked behind him to find the human woman still chasing him. She was wearing a dark grey body-glove, small armour sections at vital points coloured an even darker blue.

She was carrying a stun rifle, the blue flashing orb a dead give-away in the centre of the short-barrelled weapon. She had both hands on the rifle, struggling to keep it steady so as to get a shot at the fugitive.

She jumped over the same girder, using her trigger arm to support her weight.

"Naroushka Dann!" she cried. "Stop where you are!" She swore when he didn't, in fact, stop in his tracks, just as he had ignored her shouts for the last hour from the moment he had started running. He fired back at her with his low-powered plasma pistol.

The pulse slapped against a column to his pursuer's left, dissipating ineffectually against the alien material.

The two fired at each other again, both missing just as badly as before.

Dann sprinted across a walkway bridge that spanned the distance between two buildings. The railings were degraded by weapons fire in a dozen places, big and small, but it seemed stable enough. He just did not want to look down at the ground far below. He wasn't afraid of much, but heights scared him. An odd choice then that he took the path up on the higher levels of the ruins.

He had hoped to lose his amateur pursuers.

They had followed him for three months now, desperate to get the two million credit bounty on his head, though he was worth less dead. He hadn't even committed a serious crime, just a high-profile robbery that went wrong, and a line of angry corporate bankers with a grudge.

Nobody had taken the commission except for a pair of amateurs.

He had heard rumours of a ghost that had taken out the entire leadership of the Emissaries of Power, and had decided that he wanted the amateurs after him rather than the alternative. The amateurs were good though, managing to track him somehow, using their odd ship to follow.

Where was it, though? And where was that tall, skinny Kra Nal that accompanied the human woman? He was usually not far away.

As he made it halfway across the bridge, a roaring filled his ears, and a shadow fell across him, and he knew without a shadow of a doubt that his previous questions had just been answered. Without stopping, he craned his thin neck to see the ship hovering beside the bridge, the blunt nose pointed toward him, thrusters pushing the ship sideways to match Naroushka's movement.

The ship was a private luxury yacht, though it looked more like a cargo shuttle, with three distinct sections side by side, the central hull flat and wide with the nose jutting out high, a wraparound cockpit viewport the only window into the thing. The massive bulbous engine nacelles were almost as big as the main hull, with big fan-like intakes, and a glowing blue exhaust strip on the sides that contrasted with the luxuriously cream hull.

The intakes were thumping away, spinning faster than Naroushka could keep track of, whilst the exhaust strips steamed away, the energy reacting harmlessly with the fumes from nearby broken power conduits. The air underneath the ship shimmered and blurred as the anti-gravs held it above the ground unwaveringly.

He charged across the rest of the bridge, and literally dove over the rubble obstructing the exit, rolling as he hit the pavement of the high-up walkways.

He recovered from the roll speedily, the human woman having some trouble with the rubble catching on her fancy body suit. He started laughing as he turned another ruined corner; he wasn't looking where he was going, until he rounded the metal. When he turned round, a big black elbow rushed into his face, and knocked him out cold.

* * *

Polly Jenkins saw Naroushka Dann go down, though she didn't see his attacker. He hit the walkway like a sack of spuds, eyes rolled up in his white head until only the pearl-whites showed. She pounded round the corner, rifle slack in her hands as her muscles began to give out from the running. She hated marathons. She took an intake of breath when she saw who was there.

* * *

M'Der slipped his ship around some more, pedalling the yaw to keep the ship's nose towards Dann and his new attacker. On the opulent bridge of his ship, M'Der Tr'n saw the attacker, and harrumphed when he saw the glowing green eyes.

"Dammit, I *knew* he was following us." He bashed the console with his fist in anger, and accidentally set off the music player, still set on Polly's human rock settings. The noise blasted his sensitive ears before he could swear and curse until he turned it off.

He sighed, and knew that the black-clad figure down on the walkway was going to have some words with him.

* * *

The black-clad, green-eyed figure was stood over Dann's unconscious form, one hand resting on the sidearm holstered on his hip, the other holding the strap of the big black assault rifle slung over his shoulder. The black form-fitting body glove had small armour plates in specific places, with micro-circuitry throughout to protect the wearer from EMP attacks, and to re-direct and absorb energy attacks.

Polly sighed.

"Adam; what are you doing here?"

"*Guess*," his mechanised voice grunted.

She planted her fists on her hips angrily. "You didn't think we could handle it by ourselves?"

"*Hmmm, let's see; you've been chasing a mere bank robber across two galaxies for three whole months, always one step behind. What do you think?*" He toed the body, looking down at the pathetic creature that had run his friends ragged. "*Besides, Evie demanded I watch out for you in particular.*"

"I don't need looking after," she said as defiantly as she could, though it just sounded petulant. "For god's sake, I'm older than you by a decade and a half –I should be looking after you."

Caine's mask twitched, and Polly knew for a fact that the big Englishman was smiling underneath that creepy hood. She found she couldn't look into the eyes of the hood without thinking about all her childhood nightmares, and the fairy tales of her youth where the big bad monster had eyes that glowed in the dark. She knew it was a personal choice for him, to scare his opponents, to put them off-balance in combat.

M'Der's ship, named *Red Stallion*, was still hovering nearby, its running lights flashing in the rising sunlight.

Caine pressed a small control on his wrist that she could barely make out. It glowed for an instant, and then continued to flash red. She heard a familiar hum somewhere nearby, but couldn't pinpoint it, nor could she place where she had heard it before.

"*You're friend's waiting for you,*" he said, throwing his free thumb over his shoulder to gesture at the *Red Stallion*. "*You should take him to collect the bounty before he tries to escape; unless you guys strung out the search for him because you like chasing him?*"

Polly growled at him.

"You are so infuriating, Adam; do you know that?"

"*So you keep telling me... regularly.*"

Hot air washed over her, followed by a shadow that encompassed both of them. The shadow moved past them, and she finally looked up to see the blue-hulled crescent of the *Kara Marazov*, thus identifying the familiar humming she had heard before. The control on Caine's wrist, she realised, was a recall device of some sort, for emergencies.

I never realised Englishmen were so prepared, she mused, but she didn't want him to know what she thought.

"So you came all this way just to elbow him in the face?" she called as he started to move towards his hovering ship. The *Kara* settled idly by the walkway, the hatch open above its port half-crescent wing. The ship's pale blue hull shimmered beautifully in the dawn's light, but she ignored it.

"*I just told you, I came to help you,*" he argued.

"I don't believe you."

"*Tough.*" He scrambled effortlessly over the railing, and onto the ship's wing without looking back. "*Besides, Raymond called, and asked me to investigate something in the Vaygar sector. Something about a missing Army transport.*"

"I still don't believe you."

He didn't hear her, or chose not to hear her.

He disappeared into the hatch, and the door closed behind him. She felt a pang of regret that she quickly pushed away, and returned to the unconscious criminal on the ground. She picked him up, and dragged him to the railing.

The *Kara*'s engines rumbled and it roared into the sky. Its wake bumped the *Red Stallion* a little, making Polly all the more infuriated with Adam's behaviour.

* * *

A week later, and Polly and M'Der had finally handed Naroushka Dann to the authorities on his homeworld. They were two million credits the richer, and neither had heard from Caine since he left them at Rel Major.

As the *Red Stallion* left orbit, M'Der called Polly to the ship's bridge.

"There's a transmission from the Navy Intelligence office on New Terra over the emergency channels."

She sat down in the co-pilot's chair, and activated the expensive holo-communicator on the main consoles in front of her. A small man appeared in three-dimensional form dressed in a Terran Navy Intelligence uniform, though not the standard peaked cap she had seen in the past. He was stood in a rather formal pose, almost uncomfortable even.

"*Dr. Jenkins; I'm Colonel Sansky, a friend of Adam Caine's, as you are. As you may know, I asked him to investigate the disappearance of an Army transport in the Vaygar sector. Unfortunately, I have now lost contact with Adam.*"

"Why can't you send a Navy ship to investigate?" she asked.

Sansky's hologram squirmed, distinctly uncomfortable.

"*The ship in question was declared lost sixteen years ago, and the Navy is refusing to send a ship to Vaygar because its deep in what used to be Okarnagan space. I asked Adam because I trusted him to get the job done, and he could defend himself against any Okarnagan warships, but now that he's missing as well...*"

"You have no-one else to send," she finished for him. She looked over to M'Der. "It's your ship: do you want to go looking for that big lug?"

M'Der, his thin, tall, bald head turned toward the hologram, said, "It'll be nice to be the ones rescuing *him* for a change."

"*Thankyou, both of you. I'll relay the co-ordinates to you now.*"

He signed off, and Polly felt a measure of smug superiority of being the one to rescue *Adam*, after his attitude the last time she saw him.

* * *

Filth fell from the sky.

Not all of it was dust or mud. Some of it was body parts and sprays of blood. An artillery shell had landed on one of the ammo supply trenches further down the line. Ammo hoppers were touched off, and a square kilometre of earth disappeared.

The company leader, a heavily muscled brute in a green uniform, shouted for the company to pick themselves up from the soggy bottom of the trench. He bellowed over the screeching shells, and the thunderclap of the resulting explosion. A mist of mud wafted across the trench, obscuring anything worth seeing besides the soldiers either side of them.

More artillery shells blasted down from the sky, detonating in the no man's land beyond the trench, the enemy range viewfinders unable to pierce the smog and dirt clouds that lingered over the quagmire.

The company commander's entire silky uniform was dark green with a black leather cross-brace over one shoulder and over his chest, and a silver-plated braid that was kept tight to the diagonal belt with tiny clips; the jacket had lines sewed into the front, with silver buttons lining the ends. He wore a faded maroon sash around his waist, with a curved infantry sword in its scabbard, hanging loosely from his uniform's belt.

In his hands he carried an advanced rifle, a keepsake of sorts from his previous life. His matted, mud- encrusted long hair was tied back at the back of his skull, out of his muddy face.

Two black-clad Elites, both armed with standard infantry rifles flanked him, and neither took their eyes off their charge. Nobody was under any illusion that he was a prisoner. They sneered at him even worse than they did the rank-and-file troopers –the commoners in other words.

Ears ringing, the soldiers in the trench realised that the bombardment had ceased. Everybody knew what that meant; nobody wanted it to happen.

"PREPARE TO REPEL!" the company commander bellowed.

Weapon safeties were switched off; magazines were ejected, checked, double-checked, and then slammed back into the breach. Somebody whimpered further down the line, whilst somebody else vomited up their daily rations. There were several curses, and whispered prayers along the line, none of which were rebuked.

Dark grey shapes moved through the fog.

"READY WEAPONS!"

Actions were pulled back and let go. Belt-feeds were pushed into the long-barrelled repeater guns, fed by a loader, and aimed by a gunner.

"AIM!"

Stocks were pushed into shoulders, scopes and sights ranged in. The dark shapes resolved into enemy soldiers.

The company commander, Adam Logan Caine, held his curved sword above his head, and then chopped it down forwards.

"FIRE!"

* * *

Vaygar sector was in the Spider Galaxy, far from Terran space, and extremely isolated from the civilised parts of the rest of Spider. The co-ordinates led to a star system at the distant edge of Vaygar sector, the Linkway disgorging the *Red Stallion* close to the elliptical orbit of the sixth planet.

Their target was the third planet, and already they could detect a vessel in orbit.

M'Der had been prattling on about some adventure he, Adam, and Evelyn had had on Gorrogath, or some such, one that had been particularly embarrassing for all concerned. Polly hadn't been listening to him until she realised belatedly that he was now silent as they approached the vessel.

Polly didn't recognise the ship itself, but the dark blue hull and the general design was a giveaway as to its Terran military origins.

"It's the *Gettysburg* alright," said M'Der, eyeing his instruments. "But there's no sign of power over there, or any sign of *life* for that matter. The transport's completely dead."

"Is there any sign of what happened to them?"

M'Der shook his head sadly, and they both continued to watch the big ship getting larger in the wraparound viewport. It hung ominously above the blue and brown orb of the third planet, no lights of any description, no engine emissions, nothing. The planet itself, keeping the transport in constant shadow, eclipsed the system's star, lending to the eerie atmosphere.

Polly frowned when she noticed the *Stallion*'s power consumption monitor.

"We're losing power at an incredible rate."

"What?" cried M'Der. "That's impossible; we refuelled at Ghil Station only two days ago —we should be good for another year. Something is drawing power off us." His eyes widened, jumping to the *Gettysburg* and back to his controls again. His fingers started to fly over the console, and the ship lurched. The *Gettysburg* seemed to dart to one side; and the *Stallion*'s engines ramped up to half sublight, the planet filling the viewport.

"What are you doing?" cried Polly.

He scowled.

"Something is drawing power from the ship's core; that's what happened to the *Gettysburg*, why there's no power there. And I think it's coming from the planet below; I'm landing the ship at what should be the source of the drain before we lose power and crash there. At least down there, we'll have air to breathe."

They passed the *Gettysburg*, and the forward shields began to light up as they hit the planet's atmosphere. The leisure yacht shook harder and harder, the inertial stabilisers struggling to keep up.

The friction against the shields became so great that flames licked across them until they obscured their view, forcing M'Der to fly via the instruments. Panic filled Polly as the flames continued for several very long seconds. The ship shuddered and vibrated some more, as if purposely scaring the living daylights out of her.

She considered shouting out, crying at the universe one last time before she died.

And then the vibrating stopped.

And the ship fell.

The power died whilst they were still kilometres from the surface, though they could both see through the clouds that a craggy dark mountain loomed up ahead of them. There was no sound at all from the ship around them, except for the hammering of the atmosphere against the hull, which whistled and roared despite the thickness of said hull.

The ship vibrated so hard that Polly was sure she could feel her brain rattling around in her skull. She found she couldn't concentrate on anything, not even the thoughts in her mind.

Something coughed either side of her, and then the lights flickered.

"The backup's kicking in," announced M'Der. He muttered under his breath, "Finally."

The deck hummed gently and then more forcefully as the ship's power was pushed around the conduits. The consoles flickered to life, and Polly caught a glimpse of M'Der pulling his long hand out of a small hatch beside him.

The engines coughed to life, but the massive, solid mountain continued to rush up to meet them.

Polly screamed.

* * *

The soldier next to Caine took a hit to the shoulder, almost obliterating the joint completely. He was thrown backwards into the back wall of the trench, screaming in pain. A man down the line literally lost his head from a solid round that splattered his brains all over his friends.

A primitive grenade, with a ticking timer, tumbled into the trench. One soldier picked it up, and was about to lob it back at the enemy when it detonated prematurely in his hand. It vaporised him, and the explosion tore out a section of the trench, flinging mud and body parts into the air.

One of the Elites was hit in the chest, and went down without a sound.

Caine, holding one of the native wood-stocked solid-round automatic weapons called auto-rifles, fired a burst out at the advancing enemy. Two figures dropped to the ground.

The enemy advance halted, too many of them killed or wounded by Caine's company.

A whistle came wafting down the line, and Adam knew what that meant: counter-push.

He jumped up onto the lip of the trench, followed by the remaining Elite. The rest of the company moaned, but followed suit anyway –insubordination was punishable by death in the Sovereignty's army.

The company, two hundred men, charged out into the no man's land between the lines. To each side of the company, the companies of other regiments charging as well, the combined roar of their war cries drowning out the *plunk-plunk* of distant mortars being fired. The mortars were dead on, falling among the other companies. The explosions threw soldiers into the air, along with tonnes of mud.

Screams of the dying echoed through the fog, but the battle-rage was upon them, and they continued on until they reached the enemy trench. The enemy were firing haphazardly over the lip of the defence works, most of the shots going wide except for a few strays.

The entrenched opposition were panicking as Caine's company let loose one final roar of defiance before jumping into the trench. Caine fired left and right with the auto-rifle until it clicked, the magazine empty. He didn't have time to change clips, so he dropped it, and started hacking and slashing with the sword.

Blood sprayed as he sliced the arm off a soldier, and splattered across his worn uniform. He looked for all the world like a warrior of old on some ancient battlefield. He was barely aware of what he did, moving faster than he thought possible, taking limbs off, and opening arteries. Some of his company looked at him with fright, seeing the blood and the sheer violence.

It was a while before Caine realised that the enemy were all dead, as well as dozens of his own men, some in the trench, some in the mud.

In the fog, Caine briefly glimpsed a familiar figure.

He whispered, "Polly?"

Then the artillery shells fell on them.

* * *

Polly opened her eyes.

She had passed out, though whether from the terror of hurtling towards a mountain, or from the gee-forces of the fall itself, with the ship's inertial dampers non-functional. Except, she had been dreaming, dreaming about a man with long hair in a nineteenth-century green military uniform.

Now, however, the ship was no longer moving, and the power had once again gone. Groggily, she looked over at M'Der, and found he was no longer in his seat. She remembered him saying something about his race –the Kra Nal- being more resistant to the effects of gee-forces, presumably because they had stronger heart muscles to keep the blood pumping effectively enough to counter the effects.

She called out weakly, her voice barely audible. "M'Der?"

"Here, Polly."

He was at the rear of the cockpit his head disappeared into an equipment hatch, fumbling around with something. He re-appeared holding two rugged rucksacks that looked very much like survival packs. Polly frowned, which made M'Der smile.

"Adam may be an overprotective ass, but he is definitely the universe's greatest survivor; so I took a page from his book, as you humans say. Now wherever I go, I go prepared. And since you came onboard, I've doubled up on everything, even survival packs." He threw the pack at her feet.

Confused, she said, "What are these for anyway?"

He pointed back out the forward viewports. When she looked out, she saw that the *Red Stallion* had landed on a small plateau on the side of the mountain they had been hurtling towards. Dark clouds hung about the top of the mountain like terrifying cliffs, throwing the ship into dark shadow despite the sun shining far in the distance.

391

John Charles Scott

But it wasn't the mountain or the weather that caught her attention.

Metres from the *Red Stallion*'s starboard nacelle sat a dozen identical vessels, with a mottled green and brown camouflage hull, the shape not all that different from the *Stallion*. They had four nacelles, two at the front, two at the back, that seemed to be designed to swivel to give maximum re-entry thrust.

Each one was dark, no power or running lights, just like the *Stallion*, and the *Gettysburg* in orbit, and probably the *Kara* too.

"Dropships," said the historian. "The Terran Army uses them to drop whole companies of infantry onto a planet's surface in a hurry. There's usually about fifteen or sixteen of them on a troopship like the *Gettysburg*." He scanned around the area. "Which there seems to be down here on this mountain."

Something moved outside.

It was eerily quiet up on there on the mountain, though she could hear the distinct thumping of distant thunder. Unusual, she thought, since thunder was a rolling noise rather than short sharp bursts.

Bizarre, she thought, though her attention was once again draw to what little she could see of the floor of the plateau. There was definitely something moving outside. More than one something, in fact.

"Let's go out and meet the neighbours," said M'Der. He had taken on a very Adam-like cheeriness about the strange situation they had found themselves. She struggled to get out of her chair, slipping the pack's straps over her shoulders. The two of them stepped out of the ship through the forward docking hatch that opened onto the rocky table.

The hatch clanked shut behind them.

The wind blasted them, and they struggled to keep their footing. There was no dust or leaves in the wind, the mountain having been scoured clean by the wind itself. The dropships were like silent statues, like the grave markers of some ancient war, the wind howling against their hulls.

Armoured figures appeared out of the gloom. Their armour and fatigues were identical to each other besides the wear and tear. Most of the plain green fatigues were faded almost to white, whilst the minimal white armour plating was dented and scorched in random places, and the metal was greying, the original sheen wearing off.

They were Terran Army soldiers, though they wore the Reconnaissance version of the Army's Mark 7 Personal Protection Armour. She had seen the like during her time chasing down Naroushka Dann.

What gnawed at her mind though was that not a single one she could see was young; all were leathery-faced veterans with snowy beards, and manes of silvery white hair. They were a bedraggled lot, unkempt and unclean. They looked as if they had been wearing their armour for months, even years; the *Gettysburg* had been missing for sixteen or so years, at least showing testament to the construction of their armour.

A heavyset soldier stepped forward, bigger than the others, and with a weary look to his aging face; she would have suggested that he had that look because of his time on this planet, but she had seen the same weariness in

Adam's face when the mention of war came into conversations back home on Ckeer Najoor.

Home, she realised, was indeed the small settlement on Ckeer Najoor. The people there had accepted her without question, simply because of her association to Adam and Evelyn. She felt a longing to be back there that she hadn't felt in a long time, since her childhood in Iowa.

The Army unit leader was holding his plasma carbine to his shoulder, the barrel pointed at the rocky ground. He seemed wary of the two new arrivals, as if expecting them to attack at any moment.

"I am Colonel MkFayden, commanding officer of the Terran 991st Reconnaissance Regiment. Just what the fernikking hell are you people doing on this planet?"

M'Der shrugged, "The same thing as you I suspect. Our ship lost power inexplicably; I'm guessing that's what happened to your dropships, and the *Gettysburg* in orbit."

"The *Gettysburg*'s still up there?" one of the other soldiers cried.

"She's dead in space; presumably the crew managed to get her on a stable orbit before they lost power." M'Der saw the hopeful looks on the faces of several soldiers around the colonel. "I'm afraid we detected no life-forms on board your transport before we too lost power."

"If they did not escape, how is it that you are here?" MkFayden looked at the historian questioningly.

Polly opened her mouth, closed it, and then opened it again like a fish. She wasn't sure whether she should tell them that nobody had really been looking for them before now, and that only one Navy Intelligence officer had heart enough to find out what had befallen the missing regiment.

"A civilian freighter picked up the *Gettysburg* and logged it with Navy Intelligence," M'Der lied. "They sent an outside contractor to search for you, but now he's gone missing, and so we're now looking for him and you lot." M'Der gave them a reassuring smile that did nothing to reassure them.

MkFayden frowned.

"This outside contractor. Is he a long-haired human, flying a blue crescent-shaped ship?"

M'Der and Polly traded suspicious glances.

"Yes," they chorused.

MkFayden nodded as if this answered an unspoken question, though he didn't elaborate nor make any other comment. He just span on the spot, and gestured for them to follow him. The other soldiers formed up in a loose square around the two newcomers, and they were led towards a set of giant bas-relief double doors set into the mountainside.

There was a smaller side door made of a pale blue metal with a dull glint in the grim weather. It opened, dim light shining out through the stone doorframe. The soldiers filed through the open doorway. Even with the light armour, they almost filled the door, stooping to get through.

But Polly wasn't looking at the soldiers; she was staring wide-eyed at the door.

She pointed to it, "Doesn't that look a lot like...?"

"Yeah," said M'Der, his voice barely a whisper.

They moved on, heading down badly lit corridors, light fixtures all connected with degrading sheathed wiring, and the corridors cut from the rock with precision instruments. They were a khaki colour, smoother than any metal surface, and had a dull sheen that reflected and gave the place a warm and welcoming feel.

MkFayden slowed his long pace so that M'Der and Polly caught up with him.

Although he was still wary, he seemed to realise that they weren't a threat, certainly not whilst surrounded by trained soldiers. His short carbine was now clipped to his belt, though he was resting his hands on the stock, keeping a steady stride down the tunnel.

"When we landed we found this facility almost immediately; it's been dug into the mountain, and extends throughout the entire rock. The locals call it Mount Duna: the thunder mountain. We've been here sixteen years, and we've mapped the entire place." They strode round a perfect ninety degree angle to find a much larger room, more like a lobby or foyer of some sort, with a far higher ceiling, and another large set of double doors.

Two of the Regiment stood guard either side of the doors.

They snapped to attention when MkFayden approached. The escort detail drifted away to the edges of the foyer, whilst the colonel led his two guests, as well as another officer with a major's rank pips on his chest plate, to the doors.

One of the guards waved his hand over the door control. The massive doors, the same light brown stone as the walls, rumbled open to reveal an even larger room. It was wreathed in shadows, at least until lights flickered on in the ceiling, illuminating what was inside.

From what Polly could see, there were two-dozen of them, all lined in rows of six, all facing the double doors. Somewhere above, there was a large door that led directly upwards. Polly gasped as the light fell on the objects proper. They were ships, crescent-shaped, with shimmering pale blue hulls, the same colour and texture as the small entrance door outside. They had horizontal wings equally crescent-shaped as the vertical fins.

"They're the same as the *Kara*," said Polly, her face a mixture of confusion and wonderment.

M'Der was shaking his head though.

"The wingspan is too long, and the whole ship is smaller than the *Kara*. If I had to guess, I'd say these were starfighters, whereas the *Kara* is more like a gunship of some kind." He turned to the colonel. "You said the ship you saw crashed."

MkFayden nodded.

"Where is he then?"

The Terran seemed apologetic; "His ship landed hard thirty-one kilometres from the base of the mountain. I sent an entire platoon out there to try and recover the pilot and the wreckage. When my men reached the wreckage, a unit from one of the local militaries was running away with him. I think they took some of his weapons as well."

"Locals?"

"This planet is divided into four large nations. Ever since we dropped onto this rock, we've been scouting the terrain around us. All four nations have been fighting over this mountain for centuries. They seem to be stuck in a war of attrition, like the wars of Old Earth. There are thousands of miles of trenchworks outside. At first, apparently they fought over the mountain; presumably they thought it was sacred. Now it seems, they've lost sight of that, and are simply fighting each other to be the greatest nation." He sighed. "I landed with four thousand men and officers, now I'm down to *two* thousand, and with no hope of ever getting out of this hole."

"Why do they think it's sacred?" asked M'Der who was still staring at the ships.

"What?"

The Kra Nal gestured to the surroundings, "Why do they think it's sacred? There must be something in this mountain that they originally wanted. All myths and legends have some basis in reality —it's only the passage of time, and the variety of people telling it that's changed it slowly over the years.

"Which means there may well be something in this mountain. Perhaps this is where the power drain is coming from. Have you found anything that could do it?"

MkFayden nodded, albeit somewhat reluctantly. He pointed to the ships, "We found these on our second day. There are twelve other hangars just like this throughout the mountain, all arranged in a distinct circular cone pattern, with tunnels directly to the outside world —launch tubes would be my guess."

"I'm guessing they all circle something important," suggested Polly.

MkFayden smiled, and led them back out of the hangar, and then headed down the opposite end of the foyer, with another set of doors. This one had scrawled writing above the doors, presumably indicating where it led.

MkFayden saw what they were looking at.

"Sixteen years and none of us have been able to decipher the writing. Then again, none of us are linguists; we're soldiers not archaeologists. It doesn't match anything in the database we brought with the command gear."

"Wait, you mean your equipment works?"

The big soldier nodded again.

"It's only the big power cores of ships and vehicles. And before you ask, our big communications devices are all powerless; all we have are our personal commlinks, which aren't much given their limited range. It's part of the reason why we've kept close to the mountain, as well as the food supplies abundant on this rock."

They passed through several hallways that seemed to lead to barrack rooms full of curious soldiers, all poking their heads through the open doorways. Polly saw that they were, to a man, old and grey like the ones that had escorted her and M'Der into the mountain.

MkFayden said nonchalantly, "Ignore them; the only time they get to see outsiders in this mountain are prisoners."

Polly's internal alarm went off at the bold mention of prisoners, reminded of the dark days of the United States' prisoner policies up until the Third World War when much of the country had been obliterated by massed missile strikes, including her beloved Iowa.

"Come on," said the big colonel. He led them down a long set of stone steps that wasn't lighted as well as what they had already seen, though there was a deepening eerie blue tint to the light the further down they went. Armed guards stood in rigid pairs either side of another large pair of doors.

The guards snapped to attention, though somewhat slowly due to their aging and abused bodies. One of them spun, and marched to a glowing panel to one side of the doors. He waved his gloved hand over the device. There was a rumbling grinding noise once again. The doors ground open, soft neon blue light spilled out from the widening crack, throwing the anteroom into stark relief, forcing shadows away from the guards, mixing with the anteroom's dim glare.

MkFayden nodded the two friends through.

M'Der was speechless.

Polly wasn't.

"Holy shit."

* * *

The whole world turned upside down. Men fell from the sky, parts missing. Screams would have filled the air if the shells were not still thundering down. Mud and shrapnel flew in all directions. More inaudible screams.

Adam had lost his weapons somewhere in the mud.

There was an arm next to Adam. Groggily, he realised it wasn't attached to anyone. He wanted to gag, but mud and dirt clogged up his nose and mouth. He couldn't hear anything –he was temporarily deaf from the pressure shock of the artillery strike. His head was spinning badly, and his stomach wanted to exit through his mouth. It had been a long time since he had experienced the numbing wrath of artillery.

Before this planet, it had been Kosovo, and still in the Marines –he had been trapped within a NATO airstrike, and forced to the ground, deafened by the intense pressure of the blasts. He had lost his equipment, nearly his life, only to wander through enemy territory, dazed and shell-shocked for three days. He was picked up purely by chance by a French commando unit on their own reconnaissance mission.

He had promised himself not to ever experience that again.

The ground stopped vibrating.

The artillery was done.

Which meant that their infantry would be on whatever was left of his company. A strong breeze began pushing the hovering bank of smoke west, away from the trenches.

Figures came out of that pall, charging with primitive rifles. They wore bright red, like the British during the Napoleonic Wars, with white cross-braces and black shakos. Like those that Adam now served, they were fur-faced, their hair trimmed neatly, and shaded multiple browns. He still couldn't hear them, but he could see the fear and anger in those furry looks. Fear for their lives, storming a possible enemy position, and anger at being forced to fight.

They reached the devastated trench, and jumped in.

Adam dove at the first, bringing him to the ground before he could get a shot off. The soldier squealed as Adam snapped his elbow into his throat. It closed his windpipe and he fell, writhing in the mud.

Caine rolled back to his feet, and spun, his kick sweeping the feet out from under the next soldier. A sharp kick to the man's neck snapped it, and Adam was moving on to the next target, weaponless, and deaf, ignoring the dead eyes of his previous victim.

He rolled again, snatching up the bayonet of the said victim. He held it point down like a combat knife, and deflected the blow of the next soldier's rifle barrel. There was a tiny spark where the metals scraped each other. Adam moved inside the rifle's barrel, and swiped the blade across his throat. Arterial spray splashed across Adam's arm, and he was onto the next one.

He kicked it in the face, crunching the nose cartilage up into its brain. The eyes rolled back, and he collapsed.

Green uniformed soldiers of Adam's company were suddenly among the reds, shooting at point blank with their Auto Rifles, and hacking with bayonets. Covered in filth, and just as shell-shocked as their captain, they still obliterated the enemy in minutes.

His hearing returned slowly, like emerging inch by inch from ocean water.

There was cheering somewhere, but his hearing hadn't fully returned yet, and so couldn't distinguish what was near and was far. The cheering matched his men punching their fists into the air, laughing and clapping hands on each other's shoulders and backs. Some of them were holding surviving enemy soldiers at gunpoint, grins on their faces.

They had taken the enemy trench.

Someone was tugging on his arm.

He turned.

His signals trooper, Sojun, was stood there trying to get his attention. He was wearing the chunky primitive radio set common to all signals troopers, the large microphone on the end of a thin metal boom so that it sat in front of his mouth. The boom was attached to a set of fluffy headphones, which in turn was plugged into the set on his back.

"Captain, the jamming from the mountain is interfering with the sets. I'm having trouble receiving a message from headquarters." He put his hand to one of the earpieces, listening to the incoming transmission. "I can't quite make out what they're saying, sir. Sounds like... *'Armour'*... *'Coming'*...and something about falling back."

Caine swore loudly and profusely.

"They're sending the armour up again."

He could already hear the rumbling of the tanks, the squeaking of their heavy metal tracks churning around the wheels, driving the armoured war machines forward. They came out of the smoke, great beasts of metal, turrets tracking round for targets. Large calibre cannons protruded from the box turrets, with pintle mount machine guns hanging from the hatches. Bed rolls and camouflage netting hung from the dull green armoured hides. They were similar to WW1 tanks, though Adam would never consider actually using the death traps himself.

They were as dangerous to its crew and the men fighting alongside them as to the enemy.

He could see at least a hundred of the damn things, trundling through the no man's land he and his men had fought through.

"Command is sending the armour in even though we haven't fully secured this trench." He turned to Sojun, "What's the count now?"

"Fifteen, sir."

"Fifteen times we've taken this trench, and the armour's pushed through behind us, only to be repelled by artillery. You'd think Command would learn from those mistakes. Not that those aristocratic prigs would know real military tactics if it came up and slapped them in the face." He shook his head, and took in a lungful of air. "FALL BACK! BACK TO OUR TRENCH!" He saw the dejected and betrayed looks on his men's faces. Sojun was crestfallen. Again.

He stayed behind long enough to make sure his surviving company left the trench, and retreated back to their own line. They slipped quietly between the roaring, growling tanks, barely aware of them as they leaped down into what was once their former positions.

The trench was barely that anymore, squashed by the ignorant tanks, and dug out by the artillery.

"Contact the engineer section; tell them they need to shore up our trench again."

Sojun nodded. He mumbled into his mic. There was a squawked reply that sounded like a curse, then silence. There was another series of muffled squawks, longer with peaked squeals. More curses. Sojun flinched badly.

"Sir, Command want you back at regimental headquarters immediately in full dress uniform. A staff tank is coming to pick you up." Caine nodded, looking down at his mud- and blood-caked uniform, and let out another choice swearword that made Sojun giggle, and several older soldiers nearby snort with laughter.

It had only been an hour since they first left the trench.

As the black-painted tank approached with a roar, he muttered to himself.

"Just another day in the trenches."

* * *

"What the fernikking hell is this thing?"

M'Der and Polly were staring up at the centre of the room. A massive pillar of blue fire writhed within a tall cylindrical forcefield that stretched from top to bottom of the cavernous room that itself was twenty storeys high at least. Invisible pipes of fizzing blue energy rolled into the sides of the monolithic column, feeding the fire.

And that was it.

The blue-lit walls were smooth, forming an equally monumental cylinder, broken only by one or two balconies. Only the balcony the two were stood on actually had a stone bridge that led to a ringed platform around the centre of the column. There were no consoles, no monitors, and no displays.

Nothing.

"We have found no way to determine what this thing is, beyond that it seems to be the power core to this place." MkFayden prattled on about the amount of power being fed through the place, though Polly tuned him out. This was her first scientific mystery since her arrival in the forty-first century.

She was going to solve this.

* * *

Sat on the high turret, ignoring the severe vibrations through the metal, Caine had perched himself on a thick roll of camo netting, grateful for the soft seating. The staff tank, painted black to distinguish from the regular machines; a rather ridiculous decision, but one well keeping within the Sovereignty's mindset.

The tank passed through bombed out farmsteads, and cratered fields of mud. That was all that was left of the Sovereignty's territory within forty miles of Mount Duna. Smoke rose from the horizon, probably another action further down the line.

Artillery duels thundered in the distance, out of view.

The tank passed a column of fresh-faced boys dressed in crisp starched uniforms, all carrying their polished new Auto Rifles, with every tenth man carrying a .30 calibre machinegun with long flash suppressors, newly stamped from the mass weapons manufactory at Bavna. The officer held a sword at parade rest on his shoulder, bellowing marching orders like they were going out of fashion, and wearing a stupid feathered bicorn hat.

Caine continued to watch the west, not wanting the discomfort of looking to his right where the surviving shadowing Elite sat, his head swathed in bandages. He had been hit squarely on the forehead by flying debris from the trench wall. Sojun, Caine's medic as well as comms specialist, had declared that the Elite had squealed like a little girl when he was being examined after the battle.

The Elite had said nothing except to mumble a demand to come along.

Two hours passed before the tank finally trundled into the regimental headquarters. It was actually a small town, built around an idyllic mansion at the centre. Vines crept up the bright brick walls to snake around the porthole windows, framed by steel guttering and topped by a tiled terracotta roof. Flags of different nations fluttered in the breeze on static white poles, casting long shadows over the even longer green lawn. It was all a lovely little slice of the high life.

There were a group of trussed-up ladies and gentlemen sipping tea and laughing at crap jokes, whilst others played bowls on the lawn. Opposite them, around the side of the building, Sovereignty Elites drilled with bayonets on their Auto Rifles. They were good in drill, but they weren't conditioned for battle like he had been. They were all family of nobility, joining simply to win prestige, unprepared for the horrors of frontline combat.

The staff tank drew the attention of everyone as it drove up the pristine gravel drive. It skidded to a perfect halt, the young driver eager to impress. A military aide waited stiff and impatient at the mansion's front door, flanked by a pair of Elites.

Caine jumped down from the tank's hull, his booted feet crunching in the gravel.

The aide looked him up and down with no small amount of disgust. Adam hadn't bothered changing his uniform, so all the blood, mud and sweat was stained on, at least until he could get it washed.

The aide, a balding tiny man in a gaudy white uniform, snorted derisively, spun and then led the way into the mansion.

Adam was taken to a fully stocked library where the regiment's colonel was conversing with the commanders of the other regiments operating in the sector. The library, and indeed the entire house, reminded him too much of his father's, a place he never wanted to visit by choice. He snapped to attention, and gave them his best salute. A salute that the Sovereignty military did not use.

The Colonel, a weedy bespectacled officer by the name of Kreejan, sneered at him. Caine had been forced into his regiment against the colonel's wishes. He nodded to the Elite by Caine's side, silently dismissing him.

He waited until the Elite had left before saying anything.

"You requested my presence, Colonel?"

"Yes, Captain."

If looks could kill, then the other colonels' contempt would have murdered the human ten times over. To his experienced eyes, however, they were all just as pathetic and weak-willed as the rest of the Sovereignty's officer class. They were too arrogant and pompous to realise that self-interest was counter to successfully winning a war. The local nations followed set rules of war. It was insane. Especially when those rules viewed common soldiers as nothing more than cannon fodder to be used for the glory of their officers.

He felt nauseous being in the presence of these butchers.

He had no choice, however.

He stood stock still at attention, staring straight ahead.

"I asked you here," the colonel began, "because our spotters saw something. A shape moving through the clouds towards Mount Duna." He was stood behind a heavy wooden desk gilded with gold filaments, and leaning on a writing pad. Maps were spread across it, of various areas in the region. Caine would have loved to get his hands on those. He himself only had a map of his immediate command, with no way to see beyond his own trench. It was a tactical nightmare as far as he was concerned.

"That's very nice for the spotters, sir, but what does it have to do with me?"

Anger rose in the faces of those around Adam, though his own colonel was definitely trying to rein himself in, aware of the orders from the supreme commander that this otherworlder was not to be killed.

The colonel forced his speech through his big, square white teeth.

"The supreme commander, in his infinite wisdom, has decided to pull you and your company from the front lines. You will be re-organised into a light company." Adam frowned; the supreme commander, an underwhelmingly uncharismatic midget, had forced Adam into his service because the human could not find the location of the *Kara* due to heavy concussion after the crash. The supreme commander had dangled the location as incentive for Adam to work for him as a line officer. Since then, he had been in the worst hell, fighting for his life, and fighting for the men under his command.

Now all that was pointless as they were probably going to be on guard duty, or some other crap job.

The colonel, unaware of what Caine was thinking, droned on. "You and your men will be given a mission of the utmost importance."

Here it comes, thought Adam, *guarding a pisspot*.

"Your mission will be to reconnoitre the mountain itself. The supreme commander believes that the mountain holds the key to victory, and you are the one unit chief that has proven his reconnoitring skills." He paused. "Well, Captain? What do you say?"

Caine was horrified to tell the truth: reconnoitring between the armour pushes and artillery duels in no-man's land was a suicide mission at best. Anybody sent behind enemy lines was never seen again.

"That's... marvellous, sir."

He felt sick.

The rest of the conversation was a blur to him, his thoughts returning to the mud and blood, and the evil smirk on the supreme commander's face. When he was dismissed, and handed the necessary papers to retrieve equipment, new uniforms, and the mission specs, he quickly walked out of the front door, and vomited in the flowerbed.

The staff tank had since disappeared, leaving him on foot, still dressed in his mud-encrusted uniform. Those still on the lawn looked at him with disgust. He ignored them, and left the mansion grounds with his head hung low.

The iron-wrought gates closed behind him.

He stood there for a moment, contemplating going back and killing them all, military or not. He'd be doing the lower class of their society a huge favour, and it would satisfy his own personal honour, to a point.

He was about to seriously consider it when a figure appeared ahead of him on the cobbled road. It was a woman, sitting cross-legged. It was Polly.

"Polly?"

She didn't hear him. She was staring intently ahead and above her, hands in her lap. He went to her, and reached down to place his hands on her shoulders. He gasped when his hands passed through her as if she wasn't there.

She wasn't there, of course.

It was a hologram.

But from where?

The hologram flickered and then disappeared.

Vainly, Adam reached forward again, as if to catch her and stop her from disappearing. In her place there was a brief flicker of something that looked a lot like a map. It was shown in the British OS style of maps, and seemed to be focused on a mountain, most likely *the* mountain.

Mount Duna.

A dot of light blinked in one specific location within the mountain.

He knew.

Polly.

Now he had a reason to go there.

* * *

Polly was sat cross-legged in front of the power core, watching the dancing random patterns in the energy before her. She was frustrated beyond words. M'Der had steered clear of her for fear of getting his head bitten off whenever he interrupted her train of thought.

She wasn't angry. Not really.

Frustration wasn't her best friend in the whole world.

In fact, the last few weeks had taught her that the natives, out there somewhere, had captured her best friend in the whole world. Adam. A man who had taken her into his home and welcomed her into his life without question, without reward. A man who had travelled through time and chosen to befriend *her*.

She rocked back and forwards, muttering to herself.

* * *

M'Der stood on an outcropping serving as a large balcony overlooking the southern face of the mountain. Beside him was Colonel MkFayden, both leaning on the rock outcropping that served as a railing.

MkFayden had been mildly amused to learn the identity of his new guests, though made no comment as to why he was amused. M'Der presumed it was because he wasn't actually too thrilled, or was not entirely aware of them.

"How have you survived here?" he asked, gently aware that he was being looked at by several of the soldiers as an intruder rather than a guest. Judging by their skittishness, he was sure it would not take much for things to change dramatically.

MkFayden snorted at the question.

"Believe it or not, we've survived mostly thanks to the political situation on this planet." The colonel shifted his plasma carbine so that he could rest against the rock without it getting in the way, taking on the air of a teacher. The attitude annoyed M'Der greatly, given his long age, and career as a historian –at least, before he had met Polly Jenkins.

"As I said before, the planet is divided between four nations," explained the colonel, and pointed in the four relative directions. "The Sovereignty, south of here. The Rina Kingdom to the west. Brana Kingdom to the northwest; and the Republic of Isa to the northeast. The Sovereignty is the biggest and strongest, though technologically more stunted than the rest; they were the nation to come up with their rules of war."

"Rules of war?" M'Der wondered how Adam had reacted to that knowledge after his experiences as a Special Forces soldier. "I've never heard of such a thing. I always thought the point of war was that the rules had already been broken."

The Terran nodded.

"So did I, but they've been at this for six centuries all told."

"Six centuries?" cried M'Der, his face aghast. "They've been fighting for six-hundred years, and it's still going?! How is that possible?"

MkFayden shrugged apologetically. "Every few years there's a small breakthrough in technology that pushes one of them ahead for a short while. At the moment, the Sovereignty is on top. They have a larger population to draw from, and more resources after they took some territory from the Republic."

"You said they were technologically stunted," M'Der pointed out.

The colonel gave him a knowing smile.

"Their current knowledge of military technology was stolen from a history text, which was in turn taken from an ancient Terran space probe that crashed here about a century ago. They have been bleeding it dry ever since then." He shook his head with a hint of a chuckle coming from his wrinkled lips. "Their military culture is a lesson in human history; their medical tech is limited to bandages and hacking limbs off. They have tanks, and semi-automatic solid-round personal weapons, as well as larger automatics. They use large artillery pieces that fire unstable munitions." He sighed. "Lately though, their tactics have begun to take on a more modern approach, at least in regards to small units. They still seem to use troops as cannon fodder."

He suddenly stood up, and handed M'Der a pair of digital binoculars.

He took them, and placed them against his eye sockets, training it to the spot where MkFayden was now pointing.

"One of my officers dated those trenches as being several thousand years old; since he served on a world like this, I'm going with his expertise." His face took on a thoughtful note, "This world seems to be engulfed in warfare, even before the intervention of outsiders. My thinking is that it will *always* be engulfed."

M'Der could only nod in agreement. He had been around for too long not to see the signs. He trained the binoculars on some old trenches, noting the rotten wooden support beams, and the ancient dried mud. The ground had started to sprout grass, untouched by the local war for a while. He could see torn rags of uniforms over corpses, and even one or two dirty white armour belonging to dead Terran soldiers.

More than ever, he wished he could see his friend. More than ever, he worried about him in that nightmare down there.

Adam would know what to do.

He'd know what to say. M'Der didn't, except to whisper something to himself.

"Be safe, Adam."

* * *

Polly muttered to herself.

"Be safe, Adam, please. Come home to me."

* * *

Come home to me.

His head whipped round at the whispered voice in his ear. There was nobody there, and no more noise. Just the wind, he reasoned.

Still disturbed by the hologram, Adam made his way to the armoury, holding the piece of paperwork with his own additions. He waved it in front of the clerk, using his imposing size to intimidate the anally retentive native. The shaking man disappeared, and then reappeared twenty minutes later and beckoned him round to the back of the warehouse-like structure.

There was a matt-black beetle-nosed troop truck idling around the back, with a line of orderlies packing the rear soft-top cargo section with his necessary supplies, including two crates of food, and a healthy stack of ammunition. When they were finished loading, one of the orderlies handed Adam the keys to the truck, and the return chits.

Caine screwed the paperwork up the moment he gunned the throaty engine. He shook his head at the fact that the truck was very much World War Two technology, and yet had its own local flavour, like the roof-shaped frame of the cargo section, and the thick-spoke wheels.

Dirty grey smoke poured from the exhaust that pointed up from the side of the nose, billowing into the sky. The engine roared, and Adam slammed his foot down on the accelerator. The truck lurched hurriedly forward, scattering the orderlies who had been stupid enough to stand in front.

The truck passed out of the armoury's grounds, and he turned onto the road, keeping his foot down as far as he could, just to be a nuisance to the neighbouring residences.

It was a two-hour drive back to his unit.

His mind wandered.

* * *

Consciousness returned to him, with the lingering feeling of unconscious movement still in his pained limbs. He snapped awake, and the fractured ribs in his chest throbbed with pain. He was lying in a hospital bed, in a ward that looked for all the world like the set of Blackadder Goes Forth. Except there were no other patients, empty beds stretching down each side of the ward.

A nurse, dressed in a blue-white dress and a piny, with a paper cap sat on the top of her furry head, approached his bedside, holding a tray.

"Good morning, sir," she said. Adam had never seen one of this species, though the furry faces seemed reminiscent of Ewoks; to be fair, he'd only seen a small portion of the nineteen galaxies. Everything about the place reminded him of the history texts he read as a child, textbooks on the First World War. There were even similarities to the medical displays in the Yeovilton Fleet Air Arm Museum.

Not a good sign.

The nurse seemed actually afraid of him, as if she had never seen a human before. Had he landed on a planet that hadn't reached space yet? What had Polly called it during one of their late-night discussions months ago? PLC. Pre-Lightspeed Civilisation..

"Where am I?" he groaned.

The nurse flinched, as if unused to the noise of his voice. Her hands, still carrying the tray of food, started shaking. She was truly scared of him, which unnerved Adam all the more.

The plate on the tray rattled gently.

He stretched out his arms, which were clothed in stripy pyjamas, and took the tray from her nervous furred hands. She flinched backwards when she released the tray, grateful for the sudden distance. He felt guilty when he saw tears forming in her big black eyes. She mumbled something incoherent, and then hurried out of the ward, leaving Adam alone to eat the delicious smelling breakfast.

By the time he finished, there were loud footsteps approaching. They stopped, and he looked up to find a large group of soldiers in bright red uniforms straight out of a Sharpe novel. They all carried feather-plumed bicorn hats under their armpits, with more gold braiding on their chests and shoulders than was necessary. One, a little runt compared to the rest, looked at him warily, a ridiculous amount of medals pinned to his chest. They all looked identical to the next, furry faces looking at him angrily.

The runt stepped forward.

"I am Marshal Sojun, supreme commander of the Sovereignty's military forces. You, otherworlder, will assist us." The commander's voice was a wheezing, weasley noise that sounded like it was being forced through a kazoo.

Adam looked at him incredulously, and then barked out harsh laughter. He never really considered that they seemed to speak the same language as he did, just taking it on faith as he did everything in this strange universe. However, the idea that they wanted his help for anything suddenly struck him as the funniest thing ever.

The runt got angry.

"Otherworlder; you were rescued from the strange blue contraption. As such, you owe us your life." An evil smile spread across his pug ugly features. "You will comply. And perhaps we will give you the coordinates of your contraption. Once you fight for us."

Adam frowned, and found himself bristling at being blackmailed.

"Fight?"

"We are at war with our neighbouring nations," Marshal Sojun said, taking on what he perceived as a commanding tone, but just sounded petulant. "The clothes and equipment you were found with were very much advanced military hardware. Thus, we came to the obvious conclusion that you are a soldier of some kind. Judging by your equipment, a very good one, yes?"

Adam didn't answer. He didn't need to. If helping them meant he got the Kara back, then he needed to do it as quickly as possible.

Knowing that they wouldn't understand the references, he said, "My name is Adam Caine, formerly of the Special Boat Service and the Royal Marine Commandos." He sighed. "I'll help you, as long as you promise to give me the coordinates when you believe I've finished my service to the Sovereignty."

Sojun smiled, and Adam knew beyond a shadow of a doubt from that smile that he would never see the Kara again. "You will be given a commission to Captain, and command of a frontline rifle company."

Adam frowned. Where did they get the human terminology?

Then Sojun slapped a large tome of a book on his bruised lap. Adam bit back a loud, insulting curse about the efficacy of his maternal parentage. It would do him no good when he was this vulnerable.

"What is this?" he asked instead, picking up the massive book in his hands. It was musty, and leather-bound, its pages yellowed with age, and the corners worn from much use.

"That, Captain Caine," smiled Sojun, "is the Rules of War."

Adam's jaw dropped in shock.

Who the hell puts rules on war?

* * *

Dressed in an immaculate green uniform, an infantry sword strapped to his belt, and handed a semi-automatic rifle the locals called an Auto Rifle, Adam was shipped to a desolately bare stretch of land riddled with trenches.

A war of attrition was what this was, nothing more.

Adam fought back the nausea that was caused by the sheer obvious waste of life: there were bodies strewn everywhere you looked, behind and in front of the trenches. Most were old, decayed, and sunken into the mud, but some still had flesh and uniforms on them. There were scatterings of destroyed tanks, and even one or two artillery emplacements that were catastrophically missing pieces.

A pair of black-clad Elite soldiers were tasked to his side at all times –Adam suspected they were there to keep him in line, and report his every move and word back to the supreme commander and the cronies that had appeared around Adam's bedside.

Adam and his keepers strolled into the underground command bunker that was to serve him. A young trooper awaited with one of the primitive local radio devices strapped to his back. He wore a similarly coloured dark green uniform as Adam, though with far less decoration, and a white stripe around one wrist. According to the Rules of War, the white band denoted a specialist trooper, either a heavy weapons trooper, or signals.

The trooper snapped to attention smartly, big black eyes wide at the sight of the otherworlder. It was the same reaction from everybody he met.

"Trooper Sojun, reporting for duty, Captain," the young Sovereignty soldier announced. Adam groaned inwardly. The supreme commander was sending his own son to spy on him?

"The Marshal's son." It wasn't a question, and the young Sojun wasn't surprised. "I'm Captain Caine, your new commanding officer until further notice. What happened to your previous CO?"

"He deserted, sir."

"Then he's a fuckin' idiot, and I understand why they sent me here."

One of the Elites growled at him, grip tightening on his Auto Rifle.

"That's not very diplomatic, Captain."

Adam smiled, remembering a quote from a Gaunt's Ghosts novel.

"Back home, the diplomatic corps wanted me to join them. I told them to piss off."

The Elites scowled, and stepped out of the bunker to stand either side of the curtained entrance. Adam watched them leave and turned back to see Sojun about to burst. He smiled as he realised the young soldier was trying to contain his laughter at the bad joke. When he couldn't take it anymore, he spluttered out a cough that spasmed into a full barking laugh.

Adam grinned.

Despite the nightmare of this world, he had made a friend.

* * *

A group of wounded drove the empty troop truck away from Caine's company, headed back to the headquarters settlement where the aid station waited for them. Caine's sixteen survivors were stood around in a circle, geared up in the fresh new uniforms, and new equipment.

Adam had ditched the sword in the command bunker in favour of a chunky eight-round revolver. He had requested Elite black uniforms for his unit, for stealth purposes, and because they were more like his well-worn fatigues recovered from Yh'reth'gar's flagship. The unit also had updated versions of the Rifles, and several other updated and modified pieces of equipment.

He looked round the circle at the others.

They had all been through hell together this last month. They had bonded, to each other, to their commanding officer. They had fought and won and lost, and trusted each and every member of the unit. As Adam did.

"I haven't told you yet why we're going out like this. We have orders to make a reconnaissance of Mount Duna during the next big armour push. Command wants us to see if we can find the prize that has eluded all four nations for the last six centuries." He strode into the centre, holding the gaze of each soldier in turn. "I won't lie to you; this will be incredibly dangerous. We have no idea what enemy forces will already be up there. Plus I have no doubt that Command will send others as well." He looked over Sojun's shoulder, and snorted. "Speaking of which."

Seven Elites approached, led by a tall brute with more muscle than Adam could possibly hope to achieve. The Auto Rifle in his hands looked more like a toy he was so big.

This is gonna be bad, thought Adam.

"I'm Elite-Captain Rojur," he growled, his voice a basso rumble. "Marshal Sojun tasked myself and my unit with assisting your reconnaissance mission."

"Are you trained in stealth tactics?" asked Adam. He gestured to his own unit. "I've been training my men in some of the basics of stealth warfare from my own planet. I won't have you giving our position away because of some stupid mistake one of your men makes."

"Deal with it," Rojur growled in his face. The two were face-to-face, though the top of Adam's head only came to Rojur's shoulders.

Adam grimaced, and gritted his teeth, ready to smack him on his arse when one of Rojur's subordinates shoved a piece of paper with Marshal Sojun's signature and identification wax stamp on it. It ordered him to accept the Elites into his unit and take them along on the mission, with Rojur on an equal footing as him.

Adam gripped his rifle tightly, and span on the spot, facing the mountain.

"Sergeant Sojun, with me. Lokul, take point; lead the way. Elite-Captain, spread your men as you see fit, just don't get in our fuckin' way." Lokul, the oldest of the survivors, jogged in the direction of the mountain, following his beloved commander's orders. Besides the newly promoted Sojun, he had shown the most promise in scouting, almost up to RM standards.

The mixed company fell into a loosely staggered line. Rojur trotted behind Caine, so as to keep an eye on the otherworlder. Silently he was impressed with the speed and limited noise made by the frontline troopers. And he was somewhat disturbed by Caine himself: he was making no noise, despite being bigger than his men —in fact, if Rojur didn't look right at Caine, he wasn't even entirely sure he was there.

This was going to be a hard mission.

* * *

Unpredictably, the trek through the no man's land between the trenches and the mountain had been eerily quiet. When they dropped into the trenches that only hours ago they had fought and died to take and hold, there was nothing, only the bodies of both sides, lying where they died, decaying fast.

Several of the riflemen muttered prayers to the dead, and were silently thankful they weren't among the rotting corpses.

The Elites looked at the corpses with disdain, as if they weren't worthy of anything other than their current situation. Rojur even spat on one of the riflemen's dead fellows, earning a glower from Caine, and whispered insults between the riflemen.

The mountain loomed up over them, like some giant about to squash them underfoot. Clouds drifted down from the valleys around the mountain, shrouding the team from view, and almost from each other.

In the distance, back towards the trenches, they could hear the rumble of a mass armour charge, and the muffled bangs of their turret weapons. Thunder rolled over the horizon, and the lights of the heavy artillery's muzzle flashes flashed hazily through the fog. Although the artillery was far in the distance, the tanks seemed to be closer.

Adam could hear the quieter cracks of infantry fire under all that.

The big push, so the Marshal had called it.

Adam shook his head, and that old familiar nausea returned at the thought of all those wasted lives. Sojun caught the look on his face.

Adam lowered his voice when his sergeant approached.

"Your father and his like have a lot to answer for, Sojun."

There was a sad smile on the younger man's face.

"Why do you think I enlisted, sir?"

* * *

It didn't take long for the wind to pick up the further they marched up the mountainside. It blasted across from the west, following the contours of the mountain to blast the recon team. Lokul found a cave that petered down into a tiny crevice at the back that was barely big enough to put a twig through, let alone the enemy. Night was descending rapidly there at the base of the mountain, forcing them to use the cover before it got too cold out in the biting wind.

The unit split into two, the Elites electing to camp at the cave entrance away from the frontline grunts. Lokul and Sojun sat with their captain around an oil lamp. The cold wasn't so bad at the back of the cave. The rest of the company were asleep, with two Elites standing watch.

"What's your homeworld like, Captain?" asked Sojun. He was staring at the lamp, thoughts straying away from the military life.

"Earth? It's not there anymore; destroyed by a mother of an asteroid years ago." He didn't bother to tell them about his time travelling, or the fact that

Earth, or Terra, had been gone now for over a century. "But when it was still there, it was beautiful. I miss it to a certain extent, though the world I live on now is just as beautiful. Plus my daughter is waiting for me there."

Sojun's long eyebrows lifted above his eyes, and he turned to Caine, surprise evident on his furry face.

Caine smiled.

"Yeah, I have a daughter. And a house to go back to if I ever get off *this* planet."

Lokul and Sojun seemed to look wistfully into the distance, as if remembering what it was like to have a home and a family. Lokul's wife and daughter had been killed during a particularly vicious artillery duel when stray shells had landed on local residences 'by accident'. And Sojun had voiced his own misgivings of his father in the privacy of the command bunker.

In fact, most of the survivors had endured suffering beyond the usual horrors of trench warfare. Two had lost their parents to those same trenches, three had lost brothers and cousins, and all had lost their hometowns miles away to the ravages of the war along different fronts.

A thought occurred to Adam –perhaps these soldiers would not necessarily want to continue working for the Sovereignty?

Sojun's radio suddenly squawked static. The signals trooper jumped at the sudden noise, but recovered quickly, scooping up the set and fiddling with the headpiece to lower the volume.

"Problem, Sojun?"

"Not sure, sir. I keep getting interference from a source nearby, but I can't pinpoint it exactly. It's definitely nearby."

"How bad is the interference?"

The young man shook his head. "It's just an annoyance."

"Maybe we can search for it on our way back."

He saw Rojur shift uncomfortably ever so slightly at the mention of the interference, as if he knew something Adam didn't. Something only Elites or Command would know. Something about Adam.

And suddenly he realised that the Elites weren't just out here to spy on Adam –they were here for the *Kara*. They couldn't advertise it over the radio because anybody could listen in and get to it first, so a team had to go out and make contact with whoever was guarding it.

"Get some sleep, both of you," ordered Caine, nodding to their fellow riflemen. They were all fast asleep, although Corporal Rogun was twitching soundlessly from a nightmare. Even when the two were asleep, Adam stayed awake, unable to sleep with the Elites so close, and so threatening.

The next day, they rose early, thankful that the wind had died down just before dawn. Dawn, in fact, tinted the mountainside red, sunshine spreading slowly across the rocks as the mixed unit trudged up the slope of the mountain, following Lokul's unerring lead.

More than ever, Adam wanted to get the hell off the planet. He could almost feel the hideous tension between the Elites and his men, and he noted the way those same Elites kept sending sweeping looks around them, as if looking for something.

The *Kara*.

They passed wordlessly through sentinels of dark rocks, climbed over mounds of shingle, all the while scanning the surroundings for any enemy or natural threats. At several points, Adam had seen flashes of white armour, but nothing else. He could feel eyes on him and his men.

Somebody was watching them.

* * *

Somebody was indeed watching them. An entire company of Terran soldiers, in point of fact. They watched from the shadows of crevices, from behind rock piles, even from the distance. Always watching.

They were under orders from Colonel MkFayden not to engage the intruders, despite the fact that there was indeed a Terran leading them, and they were all wearing the black of Sovereignty Elites, the secret police and all round nasty fernikkers reporting directly to the Supreme Commander.

Most were bone-weary, and every now and again they would knock a pebble loose that briefly caught the attention of the Terran.

Then one soldier tripped, and tumbled down an escarpment right into view of the natives. The locals were terrified by the appearance of yet another otherworlder, this one dressed in light battle armour.

Rojur, naturally, was the first to react, blasting the Terran with an experimental explosive round. The Terran's head detonated like an apple hitting concrete, splattering brain matter and blood across the rocks.

The Terran soldiers returned fire, only to realise that the Terran leading the enemy, and sixteen of his men had disappeared from sight. The aging company captain signalled for a platoon to move around and flank the black-clad opposition. There was a double click over the comms, and thirty men disappeared further round the mountainside.

Solid slugs panged off the rocks around the captain. They were bad shots, these Elites, and he could see them easily enough, trying to hide behind the rocks further down the mountain. Plasma flashed down at them from the soldiers' positions. The entire company fired at once.

Plasma disintegrated the rocks, melting them down to glass chunks.

The captain caught one of the Elites in the shoulder. The alien was thrown back by the energy round, the wound steaming instantly, cauterising it.

Three more went down, one missing a leg, the others with great big black carbon burns on their chests, a rictus of pain and surprise on their furry faces. He saw the biggest of them run away, in the same direction as his flanking platoon, whilst two Elites braved the fire to charge down the mountain, away from the Terrans and their frightening energy weapons.

The last one rolled out of cover, and blasted up the mountain.

One Terran jerked and fell back, his face a bloody mess. Another took a hit in his shoulder guard that spun him around, and exposed him to more fire that slammed him into the rock behind, a hole in his chest armour.

But, inevitably, the remaining Elite was hit with so much energy fire from the professional Terran soldiers around him that he was almost, but not quite, vaporised, leaving an ugly black burn on the ground.

"Medic!" he shouted, the man with the hole in his chest still sucking in air, the chest wound gurgling and spitting bloody air bubbles. The bullet had punctured his lungs. "Medic!" he shouted again.

The company medic scrambled over the rocks, medical pack dangling from one hand, his light recon armour festooned with pouches full of equipment. He crouched down next to the soldier.

"Hold him!" the corpsman ordered.

Captain Bayfield took the man's thrashing arms. He shouted for more help to keep him steady, swearing and cursing. Three of his command squad took a limb each, whilst others gathered around, watching nervously.

The dying soldier cried out in pain.

The medic tried to extract the bullet, but the thrashing just tore the wound further, adding more blood to get in his way. He swore, and tried to use a tiny suction pump to clear the obstructing blood. But it was no good. The blood was everywhere, staining the white armour and the green fatigues, turning them a dirty chocolate colour.

The soldier was crying now, not from the pain, but from the fact that he was dying. And he knew it.

"I don't wanna die, Captain," he whispered weakly. "Don't...wanna..." His head lolled to one side, and his chest gurgled once more before he stopped struggling. The three command squad soldiers looked ill. One turned around, and vomited.

Bayfield could hear a whistling now.

"What the fernikking hell is *that*?"

Then the mountain exploded.

* * *

"Found a door, Captain," Lokul shouted over the gunfire. Caine had drawn his riflemen as far from Rojur's men as he could, unwilling to shed Terran blood simply because they were wearing the same uniforms as those bastards.

Caine stumbled up to his point man. The door in question was big enough to let a man through, made of pitted pale stone, and had carbon scoring on it where somebody had tried to open it with explosives. They had failed miserably.

There was no handle to speak of, nor any other way of opening it.

Adam approached the door, and put his hand on it where the handle should have been on a normal door. There was a loud crack, the noise stone makes

412

when it moves after too much time sat still. Then the door slid open, disturbing a cloud of dust and cobwebs.

Then Adam heard the whistling.

Artillery fire.

"Everybody inside. Now!" he bellowed. Lokul led the charge inside. Adam saw the shells fall among the Terrans, watching as the inevitable body parts or worse were thrown into the air with the debris from the mountain.

It wasn't just one either. The air was filled with whistling shells and dirt, but Adam could see black shapes moving further down the slope. Elites. Battalions of them.

The Sovereignty were coming up the mountain in force.

Adam growled.

The Marshal had betrayed them. This was no recon –they had used Caine and his survivors to locate what they thought might be the mother lode of some mega weapon they could use against the other nations.

Adam swore. And then swore again.

A bigger shape was approaching through the fog kicked up by the artillery storm. The curtain of shells rolled further up the slope. He didn't have time to see who it was. He blasted it with a shot from his Auto Rifle, dropping it, and then dove through the door behind the last of his men. A shell hit the door just as Adam got clear.

The thunderclap shockwave knocked him against the wall, and then to the floor. Adam shook the concussion off, rolled onto his back, to find his men held at gunpoint, and a dozen plasma carbines pointed at his face.

"Thank Christ," he whispered, recalling Sansky's file on the 991st Recon Regiment. "Where's Colonel MkFayden? My name's Adam Caine, and I need to speak to him."

* * *

Bayfield was bleeding. He couldn't feel anything below the waist. He couldn't see much of anything either –dust had got into his eyes, and there was blood from a cut on his forehead leaking down his face.

When he tried to move, nothing happened. He looked down and found his legs were tattered ribbons of meat.

He started laughing.

For some reason, it was the funniest damned thing in the universe.

He was still laughing when a shell vaporised him and six of his men.

* * *

Rojur picked himself off the ground.

The bullet had hit him square in the chest just as he was off-balance. It had thunked into his ribcage with a pain he had not felt in a long time. Caine had disappeared into the mountain.

He had his orders.

He crawled up to what was left of the door, ignoring the battle behind him. The supreme commander had personally given him orders to infiltrate the mountain. He was not to be involved in the main battle, where two regiments of Elites would be assaulting the mountain's unseen guardians supported by an artillery battery, and two armour companies of main battle tanks.

Marshal Sojun had also given him orders to kill Caine, and detain his estranged enlisted son. The little puke had actually enlisted as a common trooper against his father's orders. He didn't deserve life, but orders were orders.

The door was gone, and the tunnel off to the right was collapsed for several metres. But the other direction was open.

He smiled.

Hard mission indeed.

* * *

Six companies of Elites were met with fierce resistance from two companies of the 991st. Solid rifles cracked, and plasma carbines fizzed back at them. It was a standoff for the most part. The Sovereignty tanks were stuck lower down, unable to get a decent grip on the steep slope. They just sat idle, banging tank shells up the slope that either fell short or too far.

The 991st were trained professionals, experienced by sixteen years of skirmishes on this nightmare world. The Elites were fanatics, loyal to their Sovereignty masters to the bitter end and numerically superior.

It was a slaughter.

It took the 991st three minutes to destroy the Elites.

Smoke drifted over the battlefield, leaving just the corpses. The shelling stopped, and the two company commanders sent scouts further down the slope. When they returned, they reported that the tanks had pulled back.

They called it in to the Colonel.

* * *

"You have one minute," MkFayden growled.

Caine was flanked by a dozen of the 991st, all armed with their standard plasma carbines.

"Are you a mercenary?" the older man demanded. "Or are you the one they came for?" Adam's eyebrows lifted up his forehead.

"They?" Adam's heart lifted. Had Raymond sent Polly and M'Der after him? If he had, he was thankful that they had ended up with the Terrans, and not stuck in his situation. He never wanted to see Polly involved in such violence. He was barely sure he wanted to ever be involved in *any* kind of violence, though he kept getting dragged into it over and over.

"Yes, your friends, the historian and the scientist. They are currently down in the power core, attempting to figure out a way to reverse it, or stop it completely. They are, however, a strange pair. She has not even left the core room except to go to the bathroom." He frowned. "No offence, Caine, but I will have to set a guard on you at all times. Your friends might trust you, but you are wearing the uniform of a local, and carrying their weapons."

"Understood, Colonel."

"Six Sovereignty Elite companies have been neutralised, but their armour has pulled back. I don't know what they are up to, but I do not have time to sit around and answer lots of your questions." MkFayden looked him up and down. "Your friends claim you are a soldier of some repute." He shook his head at the shaggy-looking officer in front of him, and then strode off down a corridor.

The guards gestured for him to move towards a blue-lit set of curving stairs.

Caine frowned; he could hear noises coming from the stairs.

The Terrans had disarmed him and his men, who were now being led behind him.

* * *

Polly heard footsteps behind her.

There was a groan behind her, and a thud like a sack of potatoes hitting the floor. She stood and spun to find her skinny alien friend on the deck, unconscious, and a huge walking mountain with a furry face. He was bigger than Adam, and far more muscled. His huge fists were balled up, and there was anger in those cold black eyes.

Despite being a local, he seemed to be unsurprised, or unimpressed by the raging blue column of energy that rose up impossibly high.

She was scared out of her wits.

She could see his intent to kill her, but she couldn't move.

He stalked over to her, heavy combat boots thumping on the stone bridge between the circular balcony and the staircase. He was a monster.

She couldn't move.

Adam had taught her basic self-defence, and taught her the confidence to use it. But she had never expected to be here, at the mercy of a psychopath. Chasing Naroushka Dann had simply been that: chasing.

Here she was cornered, without a weapon, and without any support.

Her hands started to shake.

He continued thumping towards her, slowly and surely, as if savouring the moment.

A black-gloved fist suddenly slammed into the side of the monster's head. It stumbled for a second, but recovered quickly, spinning around, with a massive fist swinging in a nasty backhand.

His fist sailed through the air, whooshing above a head full of shaggy brown hair.

Adam Caine stood there, in a fighting stance, and jabbed a punch into the monster's side. The thing grunted in pain, but made no other indication that it had affected him. It grabbed Adam by the collar, and threw him further down the balcony towards Polly. It drew a fat revolver from a holster on its torn uniform, and banged bullets back towards the entrance.

One hit the local soldiers coming behind Adam. The slug hit the soldier in the arm, the force of the large round knocking him backwards onto his ass with a cry. The soldiers around him ran to help him, giving him the medical attention he needed.

One dropped, a bleeding hole in his head.

The Terrans couldn't shoot back because the black-clad locals were in the way, forming a defensive cordon around their wounded.

The remaining six bullets missed everything, the pistol bucking badly with each shot.

And then Caine was on him again.

This time, he was faster than Polly had ever seen, twisting around the bigger man, and firing lightning quick punches and kicks into his opponent. The monster was big and strong, powerful enough to hurt. But Adam was faster.

He slammed an elbow into the thing's side, before spinning and ducking under a huge punch that should have taken his head off. He caught the arm, and twisted again, using the momentum to throw the brute over his shoulder.

It tumbled over, landing with a crunch.

But it just got back up again.

Adam leapt at it, but it caught him by the neck with one large hand, impossibly suspending Adam above the floor. It brought its other fist into his chest, letting go with the other. The human soldier flew through the air. He landed hard, and slumped down, unmoving.

The monster turned right round to look at Polly, hate in his eyes.

"Filthy human scum," it spat. It seemed that Polly was about to die simply because she was human.

The thing suddenly twitched, his arms splayed out, his face suddenly filled with shock and pain. He struggled to reach round to something in his back. He turned slowly round, still trying to remove the bayonet in his back.

Polly could see it now, jutting out of the walking avalanche's back, blood flowing freely, glistening in the weird light of the core.

Adam was standing there, triumphant, a feral smile on his face.

"Give Satan my regards," he sneered. He span and planted a hideously strong kick on the monster's chest. The thing went flying backwards into the air, and then tumbled down into the abyss below, screaming in frustrated rage.

Polly's fear evaporated into the form of hysterical tears, though even she couldn't tell if they were tears of fear, or tears of joy. She bound over to her greatest friend, and into his arms, and planted her lips on his impulsively.

They lingered in that soft and tender kiss for several minutes, neither sure if they should break apart for fear of it not being real.

When they did, she blushed, and became intensely embarrassed.

"Sorry, that was stupid of me. I shouldn't have done that." Before he could say anything in response though, M'Der groaned, waking from unconsciousness, and the kiss was almost forgotten.

Almost.

Adam was about to say something when MkFayden charged in, barely acknowledging the salutes of his men, and the two locals lying on the floor. He looked flustered, and agitated by something.

"Whatever you are going to do," he said, gesturing to the power core, "You had better do it fast. Those tanks were only regrouping. The Sovereignty commanders are sending every available unit up this mountain, and the other three nations have responded equally. There are thousands of tanks and infantry moving towards and up the mountain. After sixteen years on this rock, we are finally running out of time."

* * *

Marshal Sojun had ridden in a staff car to the frontline. The glossy black car had trundled along gently in the centre of a squadron of armoured vehicles painted in the same black. Ahead, over the driver's head, he could see the staging point where the armoured divisions waited to move.

The Sovereign had specified that the Sovereignty was to remain supreme above all others. That included those that supposedly dwelled in the mountain. The secrets of the mountain would then be the Sovereignty's for the taking.

Rules of war be damned, he thought as the staff car pulled up to the post's command tent. Elite guards stood at attention beside the massive canvas construction. The driver stepped out and opened the Marshal's door for him.

Sojun stepped out from the car, dressed in his full dress uniform. His bodyguards stepped out of the car behind him, holding their weapons as if they were in enemy territory –the best kind of ruthless bodyguard.

Elites and riflemen were running around among the tanks and troop trucks, dragging equipment and shouting orders.

He ignored the hustle and bustle of the staging point, and strode into the command tent where his command staff awaited.

* * *

MkFayden's regimental medic tended to Lokul, his arm wrapped in white bandages, whilst Adam, M'Der, Polly, and Sojun stood next to the power core, staring up at the thing thoughtfully, and silently. M'Der hadn't been silent when he saw Adam, whooping with joy, and picking him up in a crushing bear hug.

Polly filled them in on what she had found. Which was, in fact, nothing at all.

Adam shrugged, and stepped forward, trying to get a better look for something invisible –maybe a control panel hidden from view.

There was a flash of white light, and a booming voice sounded out around the core room. It was a mechanical voice, unemotional and slightly stilted by an unidentifiable accent. But the words it spewed were unmistakable.

"WELCOME ADAM CAINE."

* * *

Advance scout parties from all four nations appeared at different places on the mountainside. The Sovereignty recon elements were riflemen, marching in formation up the mountain as if they were on parade. Isa Republic troops didn't, at first, make it to the mountain, encountering the kilt-wearing Brana Kingdom scouts, slaughtered to a man. Rina troops, searching without any clue of where they were going, kept walking up the mountain without ever seeing anything but rock. They reached the summit some two days later, only to find nothing.

Clearly, Rina's forces were lacking in any tactical intelligence of any kind.

The 'barbarian' hordes of Brana, screaming their loyalties to their King, charged en masse into the bewildered Rina, hacking with swords and spears until the rivers of blood mixed with the rock and the grass and the mud, to literally pool into a field of blood.

Republic troops stormed the lower parts of the mountain in loose groups, or skirmish order as it was called in the Rules of War.

D Company of the 991st waited for them in the rocks, drawing the formations into gulleys and crevices where the Terrans firing from individual positions cut them down mercilessly. They were coordinated with personal comms, and the best damn regiment in the Terran Army.

There were thirty- thousand Isans coming up the mountain on the northeast side, followed by their own more advanced armour. They faced two hundred Terrans, who were armed with aging plasma carbines.

No matter how good the soldiers of D Company were the odds were distinctly against them.

Their captain, Godromer, ordered the signal to retreat.

After a half-hour of fighting at two kilometres above sea level, he had lost a hundred and twelve men, for a count of a thousand or so enemies. All told, they were good odds. But he called a tactical retreat all the same, backing up the mountain to the plateau where the dropships stood silently in the growing dusk. There the survivors waited with E Company.

Brigades of Sovereignty soldiers came up the south face, advancing like a tidal wave, blasting at anything that moved, even if it was just wind picking up loose dirt.

Two platoons from B Company hid themselves in caves in a small area, and waited until the enemy was all around them. They waited and waited, until their lieutenants shouted the order to engage. Ninety Terrans jumped out of the caves, and shot anything not wearing white armour and green fatigues. The platoons took down four hundred and fifty-three before they too were gunned down.

* * *

In response to the hit-and-run tactics, down on the muddy plains, the Sovereignty wheeled out their artillery batteries, and pounded the rock face ahead of the troops, paving the way, taking out any hidden forces that may or may not be there.

Unfortunately, F Company had taken on the same tactics as the two hiding platoons, and was obliterated by the falling shell curtain. None survived.

The remains of B Company —Bayfield's redeployed men- held all the remaining outer doors where they waited for those outside to re-enter the facility so that it could be locked down against the enemy.

G Company was the last into the mountain, fighting a battalion of Isans that had strayed too far from their own formations. The Isans were closing awfully fast as G Company had to keep running, turning and shooting, covering each other. In the background, the artillery continued to fire, despite the obvious distance. G Company lost men at an insane rate as they got nearer and nearer to B Company's positions.

Just as they thought they were about to be wiped out, B Company's heavy weapons —plasma cannons mounted on pintle tri-pods- opened up, spraying the battalion with enough energy to take down a destroyer. Pulses the size of a man's head vaporised anything they touched.

G Company —all four hundred and nine of them- filed in through the doors on the southeast side of the mountain. They stood inside the doors, and covered B Company as they packed up their heavies, and slipped through the entrances. The doors were slid shut, and clamped with whatever they could find.

The artillery shelling was nothing more than a distant muffled sound.

* * *

MkFayden re-appeared.

He was grim-faced, and there was blood splattered on his dented white armour, his carbine hanging from a clip on his belt. When Polly blanched at the blood, he explained that several of his men had been brought in wounded.

"We've locked the mountain down," he added. "But they are coming up in brigade strength, Caine. There are plenty of..." His voice trailed off when he saw the holographic control panel hovering in front of the younger Terran. The panel was not in Terran, however, but in some unrecognisable language.

It was not unrecognisable to Caine, however, who was tapping the panel with the speed of a man who knew what he was doing. The woman Polly looked just as confused as MkFayden, and the Kra Nal historian. The young local soldier seemed almost terrified by the hovering apparition of the control panel.

"How do you know what to do?" asked the Colonel.

Caine smiled.

"Despite the scary booming voice a few hours ago, this technology was built by the same people that built the *Kara*. Whoever the hell *they* were." He tapped some more controls, and the holographic screen changed shape, growing larger to show a cross-section of the mountain. "I learnt the rudimentary of the language back when I first started flying the *Kara*." Dozens of points were flashing along the slopes of the mountain.

"They're holo-cameras," he explained. "Presumably put there to give the facility a decent coverage of the area. It looks like the technology involved is similar to space telescopes. They have a coverage of about fifty miles." He turned to Sojun. "Where was that interference?" He had to wave his hand in front of the signals trooper's face to get his attention.

"S-Sorry, Captain." He reached for his radio, and realised that there'd be no signal inside the mountain. "We were walking north up the south face of the mountain, sir, when it hit; about two kiks south of the base, sir. I think the interference was a radio unit sending out white noise to block transmissions within a four kik radius."

"So they're protecting something."

"Your ship?"

Caine nodded.

"I presume that's where your men saw me. I definitely remember seeing them trying to hide in the distance." He shook his head, a chuckle in his throat. "White armour definitely does not make good camouflage." He studied the schematics again, and used one finger to double-tap on the depiction of the power core. The image zoomed in on the core itself, and a load of alien writing flickered around it, lines pointing to different parts.

Caine grunted, and tapped several places in a specific order that MkFayden did not understand.

Red suddenly began seeping into the blue power core above and underneath them, like blood spreading into water. In seconds, the core and its ancillary were glowing red, darker than blood. It looked evil and eerie to MkFayden, but he wasn't an expert on the subject.

"What just happened?" he queried.

"I've set it on reverse. Now it should be funnelling power into any power source not currently full. Five minutes, and your dropships will be fully ready to lift-off, if they haven't broken down with time. An hour, and the *Gettysburg* should be fully functional —again, as long as it hasn't broken down."

"What about all those starfighters in the mountain's hangars?"

Caine nodded again. "If I can get to my ship, I can slave their controls to the *Kara*'s, and run them like drones for a short while. But first, I've gotta get to my ship." He turned to MkFayden. "Start getting your people prepped for dust-off. And I mean everyone, including my men if they want to go."

M'Der injected himself into the conversation. "The *Red Stallion* has enough space to fit a platoon of your soldiers, Colonel. Since it hasn't been down long, it should be alright power-wise."

"I need a carbine," said Caine, "a pistol, and some power packs for both."

MkFayden gave him his own equipment.

"Good luck to you, Caine."

He nodded, and gave the others a stern look that quieted any protests from his friends and his men. He was going out alone. M'Der had seen his abilities first hand, and didn't argue. Polly felt heartache that he was going back out there after she'd only just got him back.

She and Adam held each other's gaze for a long time. He smiled sadly, and then bolted away, holstering the pistol and slipping the power packs into his empty pockets. Polly felt a tear dribble down her cheek.

For god's sake not again.

* * *

"My lord!" The signals officer cried out over the tumult of the command tent. Runners darted in and out of the tent, carrying messages from the front.

Marshal Sojun was stood at the map table, watching the updates translated into the tactical orderlies pushing the models representing different divisions. The battle was going well. News from the front was that the Isans had lost heavy casualties thanks to the mountain's guardians. Sovereignty battalions were also engaging both the Isans and the Brana, and making great headway.

This was the great battle that could decide the fate of all four nations —with the Sovereignty as supreme masters over all.

"My lord!" the officer called again. The young officer snapped to attention beside the Marshal. "My lord, the Elite unit you had guard the otherworlder's vehicle have reported that it has come to life."

Sojun's large eyebrows rose, shock in his black eyes. Then a smile spread across his furry features.

"Assemble a guard —I want to see for myself."

He waved off the protests from his command staff.

"NOW!" he bellowed. It was a surprisingly loud noise for someone so pathetic and small. But for Sojun it would be worth the trip. He wanted to see the thing for himself, especially if it was alive.

* * *

After the Terrans let him out a small doorway, and sealed it behind him, it took Adam an hour to work his way down the mountain as fast as he could, at least before he found himself confronted with some of the enemy who had enslaved him.

A squad of Sovereignty skirmishers appeared from out of the fog kicked up by their artillery. The same artillery had moved its curtain of fire to the east, where the Isans were engaged with Sovereignty troops.

Adam pulled the plasma carbine to his shoulder, and blasted the skirmishers. He dropped five of them with one precise shot each. The other five refused to engage, so Adam kept running, using the downward angle of the mountain to speed up his momentum, almost to the point that his legs couldn't keep up.

Somehow he managed to stay upright.

* * *

The corridors were packed with armed soldiers waiting to go out onto the plateau. Polly and M'Der were in the middle of them all, Adam's survivors electing to leave the planet, and travel on board the *Red Stallion*, freeing up any space on the dropships for the Terrans. They weren't armed, per MkFayden's orders in case any of them turned out to be spies.

They were grouped not far from the door since the *Stallion* was most likely to have started up first.

MkFayden had ordered M'Der to take his ship and get to the *Gettysburg*, and give him an assessment of the troopship. M'Der would take his job seriously.

The door was opened, and the soldiers poured out to find the plateau empty apart from the ships. It was strange, but nobody questioned it, pouring out towards the ships themselves. The ships' engines were whining as they powered up for the first time in sixteen years.

The *Red Stallion* was already ready, gently idling on the flat rock. M'Der led his motley crew to the converted cargo shuttle just as a horde of Sovereignty soldiers crested the edge of the plateau. They all stopped in their tracks when they laid their eyes on the ships, taken aback by the advanced technology.

The Terrans made no such mistake, blasting with everything they had. The pilots among the group jumped aboard the dropships, cycling them through the start-up sequences, and activating the small anti-personnel weapons on the sides of the ships' hulls.

The Sovereignty soldiers came up over the rise groups at a time, gunned down as they came up. But they kept coming. Dozens of Terrans dropped where they stood, hit by returning fire.

M'Der and co. ducked down behind the *Stallion*. Adam's survivors, with the old scout being led by the young signal trooper, followed, but they were frightened beyond belief. There was nothing that could fly on this planet, and this was a whole new experience for them. A terrifying one.

M'Der opened the forward door, the hull of his beloved ship highlighted by the plasma energy and muzzle flashes of the fire fight going on around them. He ushered them all inside, and even called for some of the wounded Terrans to join them quickly. Six of the armoured soldiers stumbled in through the hatch, which shut behind them. The locals tended to them, patching their wounds nervously.

M'Der and Polly finished the pre-flights, and received the go word from MkFayden. M'Der slammed the thrusters to full, and the ship leapt into the air on trails of white smoke and steam.

Thousands of local soldiers gasped in shock.

When the ship reached orbit, M'Der let out a long breath of relief.

The *Gettysburg* was waiting, its running lights on, and lights on in the windows and viewports. It was broadcasting landing procedures for the *Stallion*, and sending automatic transmissions to the dropships on the ground.

The main landing bay was open, and ready.

M'Der smiled.

It would be good to get back onto some kind of large starship.

* * *

Caine pounded down towards the coordinates given to him. He could see the upper fin of the *Kara*, and the cold blue glow of her upper and lower engine strips through the fog. Relief flooded through him like a tide. For the second time in the last month, he felt hope.

He stopped behind a large rock. He could see the patrols of ten Elites circling around the *Kara*, every now and again taking in glances of the otherworld ship.

They seemed to be random patrol patterns. Random at first, but he watched and saw that they were taking the same paths each time, making long looping circles around the ship.

He smiled.

This would be easy.

He crept closer, timing it so that the nearest Elite would be close to the rocks around the edge of their patrol. The Elite was almost passed the rock, when suddenly Caine leapt out of cover, snaked his arms around the Elite's neck, and dragged him silently behind the rock.

He slit his throat, and left the man to bleed, before doing exactly the same thing to the next three Elites that walked passed, piling the corpses out of view. The other seven's routes didn't take them near his rock, and there was no cover closer to the ship.

The Elites began to notice the missing men, and there were shouts from in the mist.

Adam shot the first with the carbine, hitting him in the face. It dropped, and Adam shot the second before the first hit the ground, taking it in the shoulder, and then blasting him in the chest to finish him off.

He sent three rapid-fire pulses that spun two more to the muddy ground. The last two dove behind the *Kara*'s lower fin, using the metal as cover, snapping shots around the edge of the fin that never came near to hitting Caine.

He just smiled.

"Computer," he called out. "Activate anti-personnel lasers, and neutralise two targets against lower fin."

There was a beeping acknowledgement, and a hatch opened on the underside of each small wing. A laser cannon dropped down from each hatch. Although the port weapon had no shot, the starboard weapon opened up, and sprayed rapid bolts of laser into the two hiding locals.

Adam stepped towards his ship.

The hatch above the port wing slid silently open.

There was a roaring engine sound, the noise of troop trucks and tanks approaching. Headlights bounced and bobbed in the fog. The Sovereignty had been alerted to the *Kara*'s activation. They were coming for the ship.

They were going to be very disappointed.

* * *

Marshal Sojun could barely keep the excitement in. There was a blue glow ahead, presumably the engines of the otherworlder's vessel. He fought to keep himself from giggling with anticipation.

His staff car and the armoured company around it approached the otherworld vehicle's position to find nothing but the dead bodies of its Elite guards on the ground.

Anger replaced the excitement, and Sojun stormed out of his car before the driver and bodyguards could even get out themselves. He raged, shaking a fist at the sky.

"DAMN YOU CAINE!" he bellowed.

He gasped when the blue glow got brighter overhead, and the blue-skinned vehicle descended vertically through the fog. It was more terrifying than the Marshal realised, its shimmering blue hull clouded by the grey fog.

Its engines roared as it descended, and tiny jets of mist or smoke the Marshal couldn't identify squirted out of dozens of tiny holes, keeping the ship in place. Searchlights glared from the wingtips, punching down over the tanks, which were in the process of elevating their heavy calibre turret weapons.

Two cannons poked out of the lower half of the wings, and four more out of the front of the wings, sat in pairs.

A squawk of static burst from unseen speakers.

"*Sojun; it ends for you and the forces under your command tonight.*" The Marshal recognised Caine's voice. "*I will stop you no matter how long it takes.*"

Sojun snorted despite himself. "As you humans say: You and whose army?"

"*This one.*"

* * *

There was a massive grinding noise from underneath the mountain. Colonel MkFayden was one of the last to board the dropships. The last count of his men after the massive firefight to hold the plateau was down to nine-hundred-and-forty-nine soldiers, with a third of that wounded.

The grinding noise was like nothing he had ever heard before. It rumbled beneath him, vibrating the ground under his feet. Stone scraped on rock. MkFayden turned to see one of the pair of massive hangar doors rolling open, dust billowing from the ancient entrance.

There was another noise that could be heard, over the roar of the last dropship's engines, over the opening doors, and over the thump of the distant artillery. It was a whining noise similar to starship thrusters.

And then mountain erupted, spilling twenty-four dozen of the blue starfighters into the sky, fully functional and flying at an inhuman speed. The noise was almost deafening as the cloud of ships formed up and rushed down the slope of the mountain, out of his view.

* * *

Sojun wailed as Caine's ship was joined by dozens of smaller versions of it that were pelting down the mountain towards his position.

His last thought before the *Kara Marazov* blasted him and his guard units into oblivion was the thought that his pathetic son would outlive him.

Damn you, Caine.

* * *

MkFayden watched as the alien starfighters obliterated everything on the mountain, showing no mercy to the butchers that had commanded and fought a six-hundred-year war, all at the beckon call of a dangerous soldier.

The colonel hung onto wall-mounted restraints in the dropship's cramped cockpit, watching the displays as the energy readings across the mountain almost overloaded the drop's limited sensors.

It was a massacre down there.

Not even the armour survived.

The mountain was pounded flat, devoid of anything that could be called life. The ships moved onto the plains, and the energy levels spiked horrendously high. Another massacre, this time taking out the remains of any artillery pieces or armouries.

By the time MkFayden's dropship landed in the main hangar, the *Kara Marazov* and its slaved starfighters were headed towards orbit at best possible speed. He jumped out of the craft, and ran to the magnetic containment field, along with anyone left in the hangar that hadn't been taken to the *Gettysburg's* main infirmary.

Below the cross-shaped starfighters, the mountain suddenly exploded and blossomed into a fiery mushroom cloud that slapped like open hand against the planet's ozone layer. The ozone layer spread the cloud and fire across the planet. In minutes, the planet was covered from pole-to-pole, extinguishing any hope of survival on that blasted planet.

Somebody cursed Caine for setting off something so huge.

"Not even Caine is that stupid," MkFayden corrected him. "It's probably some ancient booby trap in case the mountain suffered a major breach of some kind. Caine couldn't have known." Although he said it, he was still unsure about it. Though when he thought about it, he didn't actually feel any remorse for the planet below. It had taken a hellish sixteen years away from the lives of him and his regiment, and taken the lives of over three thousand of those men.

Screw them; they wanted war so badly they practically lived and breathed it. They just happened to cross a man who was an avatar *of war, someone they couldn't possibly hope to beat or control.*

The *Kara Marazov* slid slowly into the hangar through the magcon field, and settled onto a pair of small landing claws, sitting upright. A side hatch opened, and out stepped Caine, dressed in a fresh pair of real black combat fatigues, the sleeves of his jacket rolled up with military fashion. There was a patch on one sleeve from a starship called the *Icarus*, though MkFayden had never heard of a ship called that in recent history. Then again, he had been out of the loop for sixteen years, so it was possible there was one.

Caine clambered down the ladder rungs that suddenly protruded from the lower fin, and thumped to the ground, skipping the last two rungs. He barely seemed to acknowledge the fall.

He strode over to MkFayden, a grim look on his face.

Clearly, he had been deeply affected by the mountain's explosion. Destruction on such a scale was insane for any soldier, especially one who had fought to stay alive in the hellhole around the mountain.

"How many men did you get off the planet, Colonel?" asked Caine as he stepped up beside the older man.

"Just under a quarter of what I started off with sixteen years ago, and half of what I had before the big battle. A third of the survivors are wounded. Plus your friends are on board somewhere."

Caine nodded, staring at the spreading nuclear clouds.

"I think some of the secondary explosions from the battle pierced the energy core of the facility," said Caine, confirming MkFayden's suspicions. "I only wanted to destroy their main military line units to stop them warring long enough for someone to change things down there."

Caine leaned against the still-warm thruster of one of the powered down dropships.

"I've seen so much death and destruction, not just whilst on the planet below. I even saw the destruction of my homeworld. I wish I could stop it all; stop the wars, and the battles. But it always seems to turn to ashes." He sighed, and MkFayden saw in the man's eyes that he truly had seen horrors beyond war. "That's why I'm working on something. I'm putting together a way to combat a threat that I know is coming. It's just a matter of time."

"What kind of threat?"

MkFayden was curious now, though worried.

Caine continued to stare out the magcon field at the planet, "The threat is... an alien race known as the Core. There are several of us that believe a war with them is coming: a war to end all wars. My... special project will help to ensure that that war will be lessened, or at least reinforced." He suddenly turned to face the colonel, an earnest grimace in his eyes. "I need good, willing people to assist the project." He pulled a data chip from one of his chest pockets, and handed it to MkFayden. "On that are coordinates to a place I... acquired a few years ago. You and your troops are all welcome to go there."

MkFayden said he would think about it, though the offer was extremely tempting. He would have to check the validity of Caine's claims though. He contemplated seeing his family as well. But would they want to see him? Would they even recognise him after sixteen years? Or even care? His daughters would be in their thirties, and his wife would have moved on years ago.

"Just for identification purposes, the project is codenamed Lympstone," Caine added before disappearing again towards the *Red Stallion*, where his soldiers awaited. The *Red Stallion*'s crew also appeared, having returned from the ship's bridge. M'Der had had the unenviable task of using the *Gettysburg*'s teleporters to collect the corpses of the troop carrier's crew. He looked sickly pale and was a bit more hunched.

* * *

"So what now, Captain?" asked Lokul, still holding his bandaged arm. Lokul and the others didn't seem to have been affected too badly by the destruction of their world, having already decided to leave that hell behind.

"What do you want to do, Lokul? The Sovereignty is gone, so I'm not your CO anymore. I can take you to Ckeer Najoor, and find a place, or I can drop you off somewhere."

"I'm getting old, sir. As much as I enjoy scouting, I'd like to retire to a small farm of some sort." Several others, mostly the older veterans, asked to stay on Ckeer Najoor. The rest weren't sure what to do, or where to go, opting to go to Ckeer Najoor only temporarily. They all returned to the *Red Stallion*, with the exception of Sojun and Lokul, who asked to go with Adam on the *Kara*.

When everybody had retreated to the ships, Polly and Adam were alone next to the engine nacelle of the *Stallion*. Both shifted uncomfortably before either spoke.

"You were right to be overprotective before, Adam. Those fifteen months with you and Eve, I kept telling myself that I was going to get out and see the galaxy, that I could handle it like you do so well. But it was too overwhelming for me, and I guess I cracked in a weird sort of way, obsessed with catching Naroushka Dann."

Adam smiled.

"Believe it or not, my first few days in this century were spent in a cell. After that, I led a Navy attack on my former captors, and destroyed a titan and its accompanying fleet, all the while refusing to use contemporary technology and even clothes. If that isn't culture shock, I don't know what is."

He smiled again, a reassuring one that spread warmth through her.

"You know, that kiss was just a silly little thing," she blurted. "It was a release of all our worry and tension from the past few weeks; nothing more than that. Don't you agree? I mean, we are two completely different people: you're a black ops soldier and a war hero, not to mention a father; I'm older than you by a decade and a half, a propulsion science specialist without any modern knowledge. We are too different for anything to work."

He nodded, unwilling to show her anything of what he was really feeling.

She nodded as well, tears forming in her eyes, her bottom lip quivering, and then jumped into the *Stallion*.

Heartbroken, Adam loped to the *Kara*, and hopped up to the hatch, where Lokul and Sojun waited quietly, unwilling to enter further into the cramped ship without him.

"C'mon," he said quietly. "I'll take you to meet my daughter."

* * *

Ckeer Najoor.

Six days later.

Eve Caine stood at the edge of the field with Relion and his family. Uncle M'Der had sent word a while ago that her Daddy had gone missing. Another message had told her that he had suffered greatly in a harsh war like that of her dad's ancient homeworld.

Two ships descended from the bright blue sky, kicking up the dust of the small drygrass landing field. They settled down onto their landing claws, engines cycling down.

Black-clad soldiers with furry faces stepped out of both ships, followed by Auntie Polly, Uncle M'Der, and then Daddy from his own ship.

Eve, ten years old, shouted out "Daddy!" at the top of her lungs, and charged across the landing field to slam bodily into him, wrapping her arms around his waist.

"Hey, Evie. Did you miss me?" Polly's comments about them forgotten, Adam was all smiles, tickling his adopted daughter until she cried out with laughter. Adam saw Polly flinch at the sound, but decided not to react to it. He just kept tickling Eve.

"I missed you, Daddy," she said. He picked her completely off the ground in a big bear hug, her own arms around his neck.

"Missed you too," he whispered in her ear.

The two, followed by Sojun and Lokul, walked towards their home in the nearby settlement, along with Relion's family, and the soldiers of Adam's former rifle company.

The war temporarily forgotten, they were smiling and laughing, some looking forward to new lives, others looking forward to simply finally finding something approaching peace.

When Polly finally got to her small residential dome, she collapsed onto her bed, and cried herself to sleep.

* * *

Later that night, when everybody was asleep, Adam received a message via the *Kara*. Long ago, he had set up a hidden comms unit in his simple, uncluttered bedroom. The bedroom itself was unadorned except for a few badly painted drawings, each signed by Eve. They were arranged on one wall, lovingly placed opposite the large futon he had as a bed. There was a small wooden desk with several framed photographs of his family and friends on Ckeer Najoor.

He was sat on the edge of his bed, reading *Blood Pact* by Dan Abnett, when the digipad linked to the *Kara* was blinking rapidly, indicating an incoming transmission. The holographic projector activated at a tap of Adam's forefinger. A small figure appeared, hovering above the desk.

It was Colonel MkFayden, standing at parade rest.

"General Caine," he said.

"Colonel. I take it you've arrived at Lympstone."

"Yes, sir. The enclave was empty as you predicted in your mission notes, although its previous occupants left behind an old Navy frigate, plus two Rijiin equivalents. There's also enough spare parts to put together a squadron of interceptors until people can be trained on the use of the starfighters you recovered and sent our way."

"How are your men, Colonel?"

MkFayden's tiny image nodded. *"Most of them are enjoying living in a jungle after all that time inside a mountain. The wounded are recovering, though we had to leave the worst cases at Rokker Barracks. We have several recruits from Rokker though, and I have already made some discrete inquiries through Colonel Sansky as you advised."*

"Good, I assume Raymond was happy to see you?"

"Yes, sir."

"Any other business?"

"Yes, sir. We have finished repairing the damage you caused in the mess hall, and have recovered the remains you described outside one of the stepped temples." Holo-MkFayden grimaced. *"There wasn't much to bury, but there is a grave outside the enclave."*

"Thankyou, Colonel."

"Who was she, sir? The remains were identified as female, but not human."

"She was... an instructor of sorts. An enemy as it turned out." Adam shook the memory off. He had never wanted to check if his explosive device had done its job, not wanting to revisit the guilt of essentially murdering someone in cold blood. It had been necessary though. That's what he told himself anyway.

"This will be the last live transmission for a few months, sir, since the multitude of spatial anomalies and singularities in this area will soon prevent anything but compacted messages and data files from being transmitted out. I will send weekly updates, General. MkFayden out."

The hologram dissipated, leaving Adam with some hope for the future.

This was where it would all begin.

A new hope, he thought with a smile.

Fourteen:
The Last Nights of Fallus

"By Strength and Guile."
-Special Boat Service motto.

K-tor-ia watched his beloved world burn.

He stood on the balcony of the penthouse bedroom of his skyscraper mansion that overlooked the entire cityscape below. Once, it had been beautiful, but then a stranger had wandered into town, asking questions about Fallus Nine, and the operations K-tor-ia ran.

The first night, the stranger had only asked questions. The questions had been innocent enough at first, but had diverted into the kind that Police officers routinely asked in the course of an investigation. Nobody had moved against him in case it looked too suspicious –after all, Terran Navy Intelligence was keeping a close eye on K-tor-ia's operations, and it wouldn't do to kill a possible Intelligence slug on his first night on the planet.

The second night, several local thugs had gone missing, only to turn up in the morning with single bullet holes in their foreheads.

The third night, the stranger was spotted going into a weapons manufacturing plant owned by K-tor-ia. He sent his best men into the plant to smoke out the stranger. Four hours after his men entered, after screams and solid gunfire could be heard, the stranger walked out, and the plant exploded, taking six industrial blocks with it.

The fourth night, the riots started. Rumours spread of the stranger wearing a black armoured bodyglove, with green eyes. The rumours changed immediately though: the Ghost was here on Fallus Nine. The stranger and the Ghost were one and the same. The riots spread across the city like wildfire. At first, they were manageable, the corrupt authorities staying one step ahead of the civilians. But soon they degenerated into mindless mobs, and the first civilian deaths occurred.

The fifth night, the riots continued. The Ghost was not seen, but K-tor-ia's men began disappearing mysteriously, only to turn up dead, limbs broken with defensive wounds, and yet more solid bullets in their internal organs.

The sixth night, the riots turned worse. The rioters, with no real purpose behind them besides venting their anger and fear, began destroying buildings without pattern. The flames reached so high, that they could be seen from other nearby cities.

Tonight was the seventh night.

His men were gone, either dead, or too frightened of the Ghost to want to stay with K-tor-ia. Only his fearless personal bodyguards remained, armed to the teeth, and awaiting the inevitable moment when they would be called to do their duty to him.

K-tor-ia wept: one man had orchestrated this massacre like a professional, bringing his entire organisation to its knees. If it was the same man as he suspected, then this was not the first time he had done this either. He had had acquaintances in the Emissaries of Power when the so-called 'Ghost' had brought them down as well.

Suddenly there was a rumbling like an exploding volcano that vibrated the floor under his feet. And then the whole world tilted sideways, and K-tor-ia was flying through the air. Dust and debris coughed over him, and flames erupted nearby.

When he spluttered awake, his mouth was bone-dry from the dust, and blood was splattered over his face. He realised with horror that it was his own blood. Support beams were fallen from the ceiling, and his bodyguards were lying nearby; some of them were dead from the explosion and falling masonry, but at least one of them had a small round hole in their thick bony foreheads, blood leaking out.

He groaned.

Someone was standing over him.

His vision was blurred, but he could see a large figure with glowing green eyes.

The Ghost.

"Wh-who are you?"

The Ghost moved his arm, the blurred outline of a silenced pistol in one hand.

A mechanically enhanced voice boomed back at him.

"Name's Caine; Adam Caine."

Fifteen:
The First

Historian's Note: This story is set 6 months after the end of *The Wrong War*.

"Pirates are a scourge on our galaxy, always have been, always will be. I just wish they'd stick to pirating instead of conquering everything they see or hear. Bastards the lot of them. Somebody should shoot the lot of them... assuming we could find any of them."

-Anonymous Alliance senior officer.

January 4004ad.

A large refugee convoy, on its way to the Penpolllo Constellation in the Spider Galaxy from the ravages of the Dar-Greelar War in the M-561 Galaxy, was under attack.

They had been forced out of the Linkway by gravitic mines into one of the thousands of empty star systems in the Dark Galaxy. They had a large military escort in the form of the last remains of the Dar Remnant's armed forces: six battleships, nineteen cruisers, and a small number of boxy, misshapen frigates. Ramshackle cobbled-together starfighters flew sorties around the convoy, covering areas the bigger ships couldn't hope to cover.

The escort led the way into the star system, hoping to discover another Linkway entrance.

The convoy wasn't attacked until they were all fully into the system, a long line of starships of all sizes and shapes that were barely moving under their own power.

Then they came out of a nearby nebula, in great ships the colour of blood. Small Electronic Attack Gunships weaved in and out of the convoy, jamming transmissions, weapons locks, and even sensors. Three trios of blood-red frigates blasted down the length of the convoy, firing on the helpless civilian ships, too quick for the Dar military to counter attack fast enough.

Seven battleships, shaped like blocky metal sharks with fat backsides, moved out to engage the Dar force; all seven were ponderous beasts, though smaller than their Dar equivalents, and far more heavily armed.

Missiles and lasers streaked the space between the duelling battleships, the pirate vessels pounding the Dar mercilessly. Torpedoes flew lazily out, most missing, and some falling among the civilians.

The Dar command ship was crippled by a torpedo that punched through its weakened shields and slammed into its aft end, permanently wrecking its block of engines. The ship drifted lazily, her shredded back-end coming up and over. Out of the action, the ship bled escape pods like pollen in the wind. Each was blasted into oblivion as they left the tubes.

The convoy ships tried to run.

Something massive thundered out of the nebula.

And it was not alone.

Both dreadnaughts dwarfed the entrance to the Linkway, each taking up position at either end of the convoy, preventing escape to any direction, their weapons –turrets the size of frigates alone- tracking everything that moved. The rest of the pirates suddenly veered away from the convoy at maximum possible speed, leaving the Dar and their charges extremely exposed.

Blasts the size of small starships flooded down across the convoy, vaporising ships whole, or obliterating parts of them. Nothing survived. Nothing, that is, except for one.

On the bridge of the command dreadnaught, Rowlandos, Kra Nal emperor of pirates in all but name, stood with his arms folded across his skinny chest. Chrome-metal dreadlocks hung from his tall, pointed green head.

His number two, a human woman that called herself Hevskii, stepped up beside him.

"We have the package."

Rowlandos gave her a feral grin.

"Good."

* * *

A man and a woman sat on a farm.

The farm was dry and arid, its crops buried under the dirt, framed by strips of luscious green grass, impossibly standing against the glaring sun. The wind blew the pungent smell of fertiliser across the two from the bovine ranch over the ridge.

They were sat on a dry old log at the very edge of the farm.

They faced the white domes of the town in the near distance, the sun to their backs. They were both human, or looked it. She was petite and silver-haired, deep crow's feet spreading from the corners of wizened eyes. *He* was much taller, much broader, with knotted muscle, and shaggy brown hair. Faded scars marked his lightly tanned skin, but his face was used to much more cheer now than it used to be.

"Farming and family life seems to agree with you," she said with an ironic smile.

He nodded.

"The farm isn't actually mine; I just help out occasionally. As for family life, this planet is perfect –it's out of the way, the locals are warm and caring, and the future isn't quite as bleak here as it is out there." He pointed to the sky, indicating the heavens above.

She looked at him with ancient eyes.

"You're itching to get back out there," she smiled.

He shook his head. "I've been away from home enough times as it is; I don't want her to grow up without me."

"You can't survive this universe without those who love you, or those you love." He could see there was a sad smile on her face; something about that statement touched her in some way. He had a sneaking suspicion that her reason for visiting for the first time in years was to do with that statement.

He sighed, weary resignation.

"What's the mission?"

She looked sharply at him, realising that she had played her hand too much. The man knew her motives better than most.

"As you know, my people were once non-corporeal, shifting through time but unable to interact with what we saw. Time-watchers, if you like. And I told you that there are few of my race left alive." He nodded. "Well, there was a first; a progenitor. Much like your own people's Genesis legend, the First was supposed to be the mother of our race."

He frowned, knowing what was coming next.

"The First is real," he said with a smile, which prompted an excited smile from her as well. "I'm guessing you have evidence, or you wouldn't be here. And the fact that you're here means that this First is in trouble. You only ever come to me when there's serious trouble, or the world's about to end."

"True. And I'm sorry for having to involve you, but you are the best. You are The Ghost."

He chuckled. "The Ghost?"

She smiled.

"That's what they're calling you in the media. Nobody out there knows who you are so they started referring to you as the Ghost, and the name stuck. You really ought to keep up with the politics and news out there."

She paused before continuing. "Will you do this for my people? You'll be handsomely rewarded."

He blew out a big long sigh. "Sure; it's got pretty uncomfortable around here." When she frowned, he pointed to a group of figures in a nearby field, spreading sweet-smelling fertiliser by hand over the growing crops. At the centre, there was a couple fawning over each other, though the woman seemed to be doing it a bit stiffly, as if she were faking it. "They started dating about three months ago."

"Is that why there was such a large body count on Fallus Nine three months ago?"

The man didn't answer, and she wasn't really expecting one. "Where is this First then?"

"She was captured by a pirate group that call themselves the Idle Guns. They are the most feared pirates in the nineteen galaxies, well eighteen not including your friends the Core. A young Kra Nal that calls himself Rowlandos leads them. They have a massive fleet that operates throughout the so-called Dark Galaxy, and they're all just as vicious as he is." She handed him a digipad. "This contains everything I have on them."

"Evie doesn't like it when I go into these situations," he said. "She gets worried."

The immortal known as Silver smiled. "So tell her you've gone to help sick people."

He harrumphed. "Fine." He stood up from the log, brushing the wood detritus off his homemade clothes. He carried on walking, but stopped when she called out to him.

"How's Project Lympstone going?"

He looked angry that she knew, though somewhat unsurprised.

"You want in?"

She shook her head.

"It's fine," was all Adam Caine said before disappearing.

* * *

Two weeks later.

Harker Station hung in space like a cloud, sitting at a point where three Linkways spilled out into realspace —one of which was epically long and connected the Dark Galaxy with Andromeda. It was one of two large stations in the Dark Galaxy, the other being Fort Sentinel that enforced the Terran Navy's quarantine zone around the Y-40 galaxy.

Harker Station was shaped like a knife, with the long blade pointed down, and the thin handle-like command tower pointing up. Ships were docked with the command tower, whilst others floated in holding patterns around it. Some came and went, disappearing into the galactic Linkway to head to Fort Softfire in Andromeda, whilst flights of four starfighters each disappeared into the Dark Galaxy, flying recon missions into the Idle Guns' territory.

Commander Ment Grokail stood in the circular operations centre of the station. He was stood around the central holographic status display table, watching a three-dimensional representation of the idiocy outside.

A civilian heavy freighter had bumbled out of one of the Linkways, on fire, and calling for help. It was refusing to stay at the outer edge of Harker Station's weapons range. Grokail had ordered it to remain out there in case it was another trick by the Guns. It wouldn't be the first time.

The freighter was bleeding coolant and atmosphere, and its entire cargo hold was exposed to the vacuum of space. The holographic representation showed the *HMS Guardsman* —a frigate- manoeuvring into position beside the freighter, attempting to control its erratic flight with tractor beams. The tractor beams were too strong, however, and the freighter began to break apart under the stress.

The *Guardsman*'s crew de-activated the beams, and teleported the limited freight crew over in one sweep, moments before the larger ship tore itself apart, spilling debris into the ether. There was no explosion —the core had lost complete power beforehand, and thus had nothing to react to in the ship's violent death.

The *Guardsman* veered off, avoiding the debris.

Grokail was a whip thin human losing his hair, and about as physically intimidating as a cheese sandwich. He had served in the Navy for forty years, commanding space stations. He ordered the destruction of the ship's wreckage before it began interfering with the station's operations, or even caused accidents.

The *Guardsman* moved to a safe distance, before opening fire on the wreck, vaporising the hull plating and bulkheads. The flammable coolant was lit off as well, briefly creating a long trail of flames that were put out almost instantaneously by the vacuum around it.

For all intents and purposes, the freighter no longer existed in any form.

The *Guardsman* turned slowly back to its original position before the freighter appeared, a shuttle launching from its tiny shuttlebay.

* * *

Five minutes later, and Grokail was stood on a balcony overlooking the station's main fighter bay. The blocky shuttle landed on the glossy black deck with a loud *thunk*. The hydraulics of the landing claws hissed, and the craft settled, surrounded by Rhino starfighters, and a squad of Fleet Protection Group soldiers armed with a combination of plasma and stun rifles.

On board the shuttle, four figures dressed in ragged clothes were seated in the passenger compartment: two men, two women, but only one was nonhuman. The pilot sat comfortably in a big soft flight chair in the cockpit. The four were alone in the back, the *Guardsman*'s commander unwilling to send any of his Army complement with them.

Rowlandos, Hevskii, Toddorov, and Heidi Gabs were all pirates, the cream of the so-called Idle Guns. Row, as referred to by his fellow Gunners, had to keep adjusting his metallic dreadlocks, so they wouldn't catch on the illegal command implants in the back of his head. Hevskii had a bored expression on her long face, arms folded across her chest. Heidi was glaring at Toddorov, her long black hair tied in braids emphasising her sculpted features. Todd, a tall, gangly idiot with a big nose, was making clucking and mooing noises to calm his nerves. Row and Hev were ignoring Toddorov, but Heidi was getting angrier and angrier.

"I really hope that Styre's information is good on this one, Row," Hev whispered, so the pilot couldn't overhear the conversation. "We are seriously in the klop here. If we're recognised by anyone other than your contact we'll be shot on sight, and we don't have any experience in fighting ground combat. We're stuck here without our ships."

"I know," he replied, in as reassuring a voice as he was physically possible. "Besides, Styre is confident that this shipment is there. You saw the data at his briefing, you know this could mean billions of credits for the Guns."

"True," she allowed. "But trusting a Navy senior officer to just hand it over and let us out stroll out the front door is an insanely bad risk. I said that before, but you didn't listen. Doesn't mean I won't back you up."

They sat there, the shuttle's engines humming as the anti-gravs kicked in, and the shuttle glided into the bay.

Heidi hadn't really wanted to be part of this mission. But Row had demanded she come. In fact, Heidi had been turned on by Row's forcefulness, even going so far to suggest they go to her expansive quarters in the Guns' main base. Row had gone pale at the suggestion, and made some excuse about needing to water his plant.

Toddorov was still mooing, and with every passing second, the rage on Heidi's face got worse and worse. Why did Row have to bring the idiot? He was a good pilot, one of the best even, but he was just so gods-damned annoying.

Cluck.

He did it again.

Cluck.

And again.

Cluck.

He did it again and again until she could take no more.

As the shuttle settled onto the deck, and the door folded open, she roared and lunged at him, grabbing the nearest loose object to hand.

* * *

The shuttle's doors folded open, and the pilot disembarked, along with two of the raggedy refugees. The other two were not coming out, so two FPG troopers went in, and found a severe-looking human woman trying to insert a digitalised flight manual into the rectum of a bruised man.

They had to be kept apart, and then dragged out of the shuttle. The troopers struggled to wrestle the woman.

"Knock it off!" the one with metal dreadlocks shouted.

The two 'combatants' stopped still, and relaxed, though the woman still had the look of insane rage on her. Despite the shredded, patched, and pungent refugee clothes she wore, she clearly looked capable of harming or killing her fellow 'refugee'.

* * *

Grokail, still stood on the balcony, shivered.

He recognised the four pirates all too well, though he didn't let on to anyone else as to who they were. He knew why they were here though. He wasn't *that* stupid that he didn't know what they were doing.

He called the FPG squad leader to bring the 'refugees' up to him immediately. By the time they all arrived —and the troopers left them alone- Grokail was a gibbering mess. He knew damn well what these people were capable of.

"What in all the gods' names are you doing here, Rowlandos?" he hissed. "You know there are standing orders to kill most of your group on sight." He noticed the sidelong glance Rowlandos and his number two shared, though made no comment on it. "I know you're here for the drug shipment we confiscated last week."

"It belonged to a competitor," Row shrugged. "It would generate a lot of capital for us."

"You have a debt to pay to the Guns," Heidi growled from behind him. Hevskii sent her an evil glare to shut her up. Grokail nodded, knowing full well that they would try to take the confiscated shipment without his help anyway. He gestured behind him, and led the way.

Row nodded imperceptibly to Heidi, who then broke off from the group and disappeared down a different corridor to the rest.

"I'm afraid that our cargo bay is full; we're re-supplying Fort Sentinel in a few days, so we've had to store the items we confiscate in several of the holding cells unfortunately. Which means we'll have to pass some of the criminals we have locked up. Perhaps you'll see somebody you used to work with."

There was a sudden ear-splitting squeal of noise that pierced their internal comms speakers connected to their skull implants. Row and Hevskii immediately glared at Todd, who was waving his hand over his right ear, evidently trying to get a signal. It took him a few seconds to realise what had happened, and why they were staring at him, when Row slapped across the back of the head.

They shook their hands angrily, and then moved on, leaving Toddorov to trail behind them out of arm's reach from the others.

They passed through the security checkpoints, the three pirates nervous as they approached each checkpoint in turn, eyeing the armoured FPG troopers. Each time though, the troopers barely registered their presence, their featureless helmets staring straight ahead, plasma rifles held diagonally against their armoured chests.

When they entered the cells, a half-squad of troopers bolted passed ahead of them, armour chinking, weapons held at the ready. They could hear their helmets' comms clicking acknowledgements to some unheard question. There was shouting ahead, and then a loud wet squelch, and a trooper suddenly came flying backwards out of one of the cells. He slammed against the wall with a loud crack. It was a solid hit, but the trooper was still moving, although blood was indeed dribbling onto his chest armour.

There was a feral growl from the cell itself.

"That looks like it could be fun," said Todd, a little too cheerily. Hevskii batted him over the back of the head with one hand. "Dammit, that hurt."

"Good," she said, a humourless smile on her lips.

"Let's have a look shall we?"

All of them, Grokail included, looked at Rowlandos with something less than enthusiasm. He just grinned in return.

* * *

Heidi passed the large ready room, avoiding contact with the Starfighter Command officers, and their Navy counterparts, waiting for the call to action. Nobody seemed to pay much attention to her despite her raggedy look. She made her way to one of the station's main ship bays.

The bay itself wasn't that large, with a squadron of Rhinos hanging amongst launch racks that themselves hung from the shadow-encrusted ceiling, deck crew swarming over the fighters. There was also a Navy gunship with part of its superstructure exposed to the air, the holes scorched black by weapons fire. She recognised the ship having survived a skirmish with the Guns.

Work drones buzzed overhead, and her attention was drawn to a starship locked into an impound cradle.

It was an alien starship, the same size as the Navy gunship, although it had a sleeker profile, and its hull was coloured a mottled green camouflage colour, as if it was used for ground combat. The hull plating was corroded in places, caused by a spatial ion storm, adding to the camouflage colours. Its vicious, angular profile was reminiscent of canine predators of old. It seemed almost menacing. It was disturbing. She loved it already, a wicked grin spreading across her face.

Looking around, she made sure nobody was watching, and moved across the gantries that filled the space between all the ships.

Stencilled on the side of the ship was the name *RMS Before Dishonour*, though it was worn in parts. She had no idea what RMS could stand for, nor did she really care. Despite the ship's apparent condition –looks could be deceiving as she well knew from Row- it would make a nice addition to the Idle Guns' fleet.

* * *

The occupant of the cell was a monster.

He was a human male. He was as tall as Rowlandos but with rippling muscles, shaggy brown hair, and dozens of scars that stood out rather starkly against his slightly tanned skin. Apart from the scars, his skin was slightly ruddy, from labouring under a hot sun. But he had the look of a soldier, a damn good soldier judging by the multitude of scars on his naked torso. There were livid purple bruises on his chest and arm where the troopers had hit him to subdue him.

His thick arms were held together at the wrists by neural force feedback restraints that had little black electrodes attached to his forearms. For now, the feedback cuffs were holding him at bay, using his own strength against him to send energy feedback through the small electrodes on his arms to his nervous system. Every now and again, the tiny electrodes flashed a brilliant blue as he struggled against the cuffs.

Toddorov was making stupid animal noises to keep his nervousness at bay.

But worst of all, was the look of shocked recognition on Hevskii's face upon seeing the scarred human. It was usually a cold day in hell when something actually surprised or shocked her.

"You know this monster?" asked Grokail, having also seen her look.

She nodded, but stayed silent.

"The Ghost," said the Navy officer. "We're holding him for the deaths of half a dozen of the Emissaries of Power. Not to mention he's wanted by Navy Intelligence for the deaths of two of their officers, and the destruction of a Navy battleship."

Toddorov stopped his nervous gibbering, and his jaw almost fell off his face in horror.

"Th-the Ghost?"

He started making noises again, this time louder, mooing and baaing as if that would truly help. This actually seemed to annoy the prisoner, making Rowlandos wonder just how effective the neuro cuffs would be against this monster in full rage.

"Why is he wearing those?" he asked, pointing to the restraints as the remaining guards eased back out of the cell, and activated the forcefield, leaving him behind the glowing field of energy.

"We originally put him in standard non-lethal restraints, but he managed to break them and knocked out fourteen of my crew before we had to stun him. Even then it took eight shots to bring him down. In all my years I've never known anybody as psychotic as him."

"Is he truly psychotic, Grokail, or is it that you're just afraid of him?" Rowlandos queried. He saw out of the corner of his eye a tiny smile tug at the Ghost's lips, but it was gone in an instant.

Grokail didn't answer, so Rowlandos stepped toward the forcefield. Despite the presence of the energy field, neuro cuffs, and heavily armed and armoured guards, Hevskii put a hand on his arm to try and keep him away, but it was no good.

"*Are* you psychotic?" the pirate leader asked.

The big soldier looked him up and down with a hunter's eye, gauging his movements to see any telltale signs of what he could be. Rowlandos and his Guns had a reputation for viciousness and ruthless, but this man made them look pathetic, seeming like a predator more than anything.

"Who wants to know?" he demanded.

"My name is unimportant, I merely wish to know *what* you are. For curiosity's sake," he added as an afterthought.

"Well then, for curiosity's sake," the man snorted. "Have you ever heard of the Special Boat Service?" Row shook his head, which prompted a chuckle from the big man. "Look it up when you get a chance. Then come back and ask me who or what I am."

Row smiled.

"Show us to the shipment, Grokail. I want to be out of here as soon as possible."

* * *

Heidi had managed to get past *Before Dishonour*'s antiquated, but incredibly sophisticated, locking mechanism controlling the nearest airlock to her position. The doors clanked open, revealing a darkly lit corridor beyond.

She stepped through, and suddenly she became aware of someone or something to her left. It stepped out of the shadows as if it had been there the whole time, glowing blue. It was a hologram, holding a holographic gun, with sanded down features, and no eyes. Despite its holographic nature, she was sure the weapon could hurt her.

It racked the action on the weapon, and then tapped a comms device on his wrist.

"*Intruder alert,*" it said, before reaching towards her.

For the first time in decades, Heidi Gabs screamed.

* * *

The shipment was exactly as Styre had predicted. There were big bricks of the Slash drug sat in a nice pile in the cell packaged in some kind of cling-wrap. It was all stacked in a very tall looking pile.

"Balls," Row muttered under his breath. "We can't carry all that in one go."

"You and your people are going to have to be quick," warned Grokail. "I can keep your visit a secret only for so long before questions start being asked. There's going to be enough questions about the destruction of that freighter, which, by the way, was officially attributed to the Idle Guns."

"So we need to get this to a ship in a hurry," the pirate leader nodded thoughtfully. And then a grin spread slowly across his lips. "We'd need some help, wouldn't we then? And there just happens to be a muscled soldier in the cell back there."

"No," said Hevskii, a little too forcefully.

Row frowned.

"Why the hell not? We could use him, now and in the future. He could be very useful if he's as dangerous as you believe."

"He's the wrong kind of dangerous," she replied. "At least not the kind of dangerous we need. The Ghost takes out people like the Idle Guns. Don't you remember the Emissaries of Power? And what happened to them? Look at your friend Hardmarch –The Ghost drove his limo into the front of an armoured truck just to kill him. He's insane."

"As opposed to a bunch of pirates that control a galaxy with zero habitable planets?"

Hev shrugged and let out an exasperated sigh.

Row was still nodding thoughtfully when an alarm blared for attention. It was coming from down the corridor, from another cell, and he was willing to bet the alarm had been raised in regards to the so-called Ghost. Grokail bolted down the corridor, leaving the three in lock-up.

Row turned to Toddorov.

"Use your subspace communications implants to contact Suggy and Styre; we're going to need as many of them at the rendezvous as possible. When we get there."

Toddorov nodded, and squeezed his eyes shut. The link connecting the three's short-range comms implants suddenly squealed with static.

Row slapped him round the back of the head.

"Oops, sorry boss got the wrong implant there." He raised one arm up slowly, and the static changed pitch as Toddorov tried to reach the right subspace channel. He kept his elbow high, and placed his wrist on top of his head, his hand acting as a fin, pointing it this way and that.

"Pratt." Row shook his head whilst Hevskii rolled her eyes.

He continued that way for a few seconds, the static whining and squeaking as his hand moved around like a demented jester in a royal court pretending to be a shark. Then the static ceased, and Toddorov finally sent the message.

He put his hand down, and Row slapped him round the back of the head once more.

"What was that for?" Toddorov whined.

"For being such a gods-damned idiot; you can stay here with the shipment, whilst we go and see to our new ghostly friend."

Toddorov harrumphed, rubbing his head, and grumbling to himself.

* * *

One of the troopers was unconscious already; his head was slumped against his chest, his person in the same place as the last trooper only minutes ago. The Ghost was still in his cuffs, and Grokail was standing there, holding a fallen plasma rifle, his hands shaking too much to be able to fire accurately.

This was the scene when Row and Hevskii returned to the cell.

There was a tray of uneaten food splattered on the floor of the cell, presumably the reason why the forcefield was turned off. Grokail hadn't shot the assassin yet, but the way his trigger finger was shaking, it was only a matter of time.

"We'll take him off your hands," suggested Row.

Grokail shot him a worried look, torn between keeping him away from the likes of the Idle Guns, and letting him off the station so he wouldn't keep beating the *shicta* out of his troopers every five minutes. The man was a prisoner for a damned good reason, after all.

"Fine, you can have him, but leave the cuffs on until you're off the station."

The Ghost never gave Grokail the satisfaction.

It started off as a low hum, the electrodes on the big human's arm flashing brighter than ever. Then there was a low growl from the assassin himself, starting off like a distant rumble, and then getting louder and louder until it became the sound of an avalanche. The veins on his bulging arms were standing out, and the arms themselves were shaking. His face was a rictus of pain and rage, using the energy from the cuffs to fuel that rage.

With a roar, and a screech of metal, the cuffs smashed to pieces, and the assassin was finally free. A piece of the cuffs flew across the room like a missile, and lodged itself in the last guard's shoulder splattering the wall with his blood. The man glared knives straight at Grokail.

He stalked toward the station commander, his footsteps impossibly making no sound at all as he moved, a product of black ops training, or worse.

Hevskii stepped in his way.

"Warrant Officer!!" she shouted.

He stopped, and stared down at Hevskii, his face looking as though he had just been slapped hard across the cheeks.

"Calm down, Warrant Officer," said Hev, placing a comforting hand on his massive biceps. He took a deep breath in, blew it out, and Row saw utter calm sweep across his features.

He turned to Row. "You need an extra pair of hands?"

"Row you can't!" complained Toddorov. "He's just a bloodthirsty beast."

Rowlandos grinned wickedly just as two large hands whipped round Toddorov's neck.

* * *

Row wasn't smiling anymore.

This Warrant Officer had moved so fast, Row had barely seen him move. One minute he was just standing there, the next he was letting Toddorov's unconscious body drop to the deck. Grokail acted foolishly, pointing the rifle directly at the Ghost's temple so that it was pressing against the skin.

An arm flashed upward, catching the barrel of the rifle. The Ghost ripped it out of Grokail's hands, breaking a couple of the smaller man's fingers in the process.

"Just get your damned shipment, and get out of here," the Navy officer whimpered. "We're even, Rowlandos. The next time we meet you will be treated as the criminal you are. And if I ever see that monster again, I'll-"

"Run like a little girl," growled the topless human. "Right now."

The Navy officer began to back away slowly, before bolting out of view.

"My ship's impounded down in one of the hangars."

"What ship?"

"The *RMS Before Dishonour*."

* * *

Heidi wasn't killed, thankfully, but instead taken to the ship's command centre. According to the holographic soldier that had surprised her, she was being led to the ship's temporary commander, probably another featureless hologram.

She was pushed rather forcefully onto the bridge to find that it was manned completely by more holograms. There was even one sat ramrod-straight in the central command chair, staring straight ahead.

"Welcome aboard the *RMS Before Dishonour*," the one in the command chair said without a hint of emotion. Its head didn't turn. "The General will be with you shortly." She flinched as it raised a glowing arm to point at a screen to her right, hanging from the low ceiling of the bridge. On it were four life forms. There were several concentrations of a substance she knew to be the Slash stash, bobbing along among the life forms.

It was Rowlandos, Hevskii, and presumably Toddorov, though she didn't understand why there was a fourth life form. She shrugged, hoping it was actually Rowlandos or Hevskii, and just a sensor echo. They were being chased, the bio-signatures reading like Army FPG troopers, and there were pulses of energy whipping between the two groups.

"Hurry up, Row," she muttered to herself.

* * *

Plasma energy flickered up and down the corridor.

Bolts of energy slammed against the walls as the three ran with the loot. The Ghost was using Grokail's rifle to shoot back, though not to actually kill, simply to keep the troopers ducking. They ran out onto a large gantry that overlooked the hangar.

He pointed to an unfamiliar mottled green warship locked into a bright red impound cradle further along the hangar.

"You fly in that thing?" Row asked. "You're braver than I thought."

The Ghost just glared at him, still lugging Toddorov's unconscious body over one shoulder, the rifle in the opposite hand. He had a large quantity of the drugs in a satchel strapped over the same shoulder as the rifle. For some reason, the troopers were now holding back, out of sight, as if waiting for reinforcements.

He led the way across the gantries, until they came to the *Before Dishonour*. One of the airlocks was open, and the emergency lighting was on inside. He barrelled through without even stopping, charging through the ship until he reached the bridge, whereupon he found a female human, and TX-2, the ship's command hologram program.

Row and Hevskii gasped when they saw the holograms crewing the bridge. Heidi stepped beside them, belatedly seeing Todd's body.

Not again, she thought, staring at the cold, lifeless eyes.

"How is this possible?" gawped Row. "Command holograms were outlawed decades ago."

"The *Before Dishonour* is a very old prototype that was built a number of years ago to see if holograms could be used to man a ship in emergencies. The project was finished, but unfortunately proved too expensive to run, so they locked it all up in a hangar, and I stole it." The Ghost turned to the crew. "Departure stations. Get us out of this impound cradle, even if you have to blow it up, then plot a course to the nearest Idle Guns starship on long-range sensors, best possible speed."

The holograms all nodded, bobbing their heads as they set to work.

TX-2 stepped down from the command chair, leaving its commander to retake his seat. The oversized chair actually seemed to fit him comfortably. Row and the others dragged the drugs and Toddorov over to one side of the curving triangular bridge.

"Engines are at optimum efficiency, sir," the hologram stood at the engineering console reported.

"Good. Helm, get us the hell out of here."

"Acknowledged," the glowing pilot nodded.

The ship shook as it tried to free itself from the surrounding metal cage.

"Use the port and starboard laser cannons to cut us out."

It took only a few minutes for the weapons to cut the *Before Dishonour* free, and return to their standby position. The impound cradle shattered, falling apart, the cut ends glowing orange where the lasers had sliced them up.

"Battle stations," ordered the ship's captain. "Raise shields, and power up *all* weapons."

The gunship reversed out of the wrecked cage on just its manoeuvring thrusters, before turning slowly and carefully to face the hangar exit. The ship's sublight engines roared to life, vaporising the gantries and cage behind it, before rocketing the ship through the hangar, and out into space.

Navy ships, including the *Guardsman* and its three brethren frigates, *Kennedy*, *Woodhouse*, and *Thunderheart* thundered towards the escaping vessel.

"FTL drive activating," the helmsman announced. Through the forward windows, everything suddenly rushed past them as the ship leapt to faster-than-light speeds, and away from the pursuing ships. It was only a matter of seconds before they also jumped to faster than lightspeed, and would be right behind the *Before Dishonour*, guns blazing.

Seconds passed before the ship dropped from lightspeed.

Almost instantly, the ship shook from impacts.

"Railguns, General," TX-2 reported from behind the weapons controller. The rank produced a confused frown from Hevskii, who mouthed the word *General*. "From a *Groll*-class starship -the *Barren Prince*, mercenary ship out of the Spider Galaxy. The *Guardsman* has dropped out of FTL speed ahead of us, as well as the *Kennedy* and *Woodhouse*."

"Load missiles into the launchers, and lock onto the *Guardsman*'s weapons systems only. We don't have time to try and destroy her. Helm, take us directly at the *Barren Prince*, full sublight speed, and be ready on the emergency thrusters." The helmsman nodded, and carried out its orders, turning the ship to point at the *Barren Prince*.

Row's jaw dropped.

"You can't seriously believe you can take on even a small Navy fleet, *and* a *Groll*? Especially not in this tiny gunship." The Ghost glared at him, making Row realise he had overstepped his bounds as a passenger on somebody else's vessel. He stepped back, remembering Hardmarch, and the Emissaries of Power. Heidi was having none of it, though.

"Even if we survive, they'll just hunt us down whenever we come back into their patrol space."

"Then don't come back," the ship commander growled, shutting her up.

The *Barren Prince* opened fire with all its railguns then, throwing man-sized projectiles at the *Before Dishonour* at close to the speed of light. But *Before Dishonour* was moving straight toward the alien battleship, its profile much smaller now, and moving at greater speed every second, the railgun rounds either missing entirely, or simply ricocheting off the shields at too shallow an angle to do any harm.

"*Guardsman* is firing," TX-2 announced. The ship rocked again, this time sending the three Idle Guns to the harsh metal deck. Only Row bothered to get up, the others knowing full well they would back down there soon enough. He managed to keep his feet, however, watching as the *Barren Prince* got larger and larger in the forward windows.

It wasn't moving, probably believing that if the *Before Dishonour* rammed it, it wouldn't do much in the way of damage, especially if it had its shields fully up.

"Can you see the Navy ships?" Heidi whispered to Hevskii.

"I'm not made of eyes, you know," Hev replied, raising her voice just a little too loudly, earning an irritated look from the Ghost.

The *Before Dishonour* was now so close to the *Barren Prince* that it was possible to see the individual windows and viewports along its hull, and even make out the firing railguns, which had picked up their rate of fire in response to the gunship's ramming action.

* * *

In the *Barren Prince*'s control room, the captain wailed in terror as he suddenly realised what the smaller ship was trying to do. To save his ship, he gave them what they wanted, and began manoeuvring procedures, slowly rolling and yawing two point three million tonnes of starship out of the way of the charging gunship.

* * *

"Emergency thrusters, full ahead, and ninety degree roll to starboard, NOW!"

The helmsman acknowledged the order, and rolled the ship to the right, bringing the *Before Dishonour*'s keel parallel to the *Barren Prince*'s left flank, skimming above the bigger hull like a dive bomber pulling out of a bombing run.

A high-yield missile from the *Woodhouse*, losing its speed from the sheer distance, skipped off the rear edge of the *Before Dishonour*'s shields and slammed into the *Groll*'s midsection. It detonated on the hull, crumpling its shields, and sending feedback energy through the emitters.

Explosions rippled along the *Barren Prince*'s starboard side, vaporising hull plating, crewmen, and weapons alike. The secondary explosions triggered off in one of the railgun magazines erupted, and blew a massive chunk out of the side of the ship, severing power conduits and energy matrices.

The battleship's engines died, and the wreckage began to list lazily to one side. By some stroke of luck it's listing brought it between the gunship and the pursuing Navy, protecting them for the precious few seconds needed to jump through the Linkway.

* * *

The commander of the *Guardsman* slammed his fist into the railing surrounding his command pulpit, shouting with rage at being so close. The *Before Dishonour*'s commander had executed an insane manoeuvre, one that he could never have predicted, and one that never should have worked.

He continued to mutter to himself long after the enemy gunship had disappeared into the Linkway, and into Idle Guns territory.

"Damn them."

* * *

As the *Before Dishonour* exited the Linkway in a system of Rowlandos' choosing, Row asked their saviour to set course for coordinates he provided, where the Idle Guns had a station inside a massive unstable nebula. Suddenly the sensors blared for attention, and four blood-red battleships appeared out of the nebula that encompassed the entire star system directly on top of the *Before Dishonour*.

Hevskii was disturbed by the brief look of horror on the Ghost's face at the sight of the red warships. She had never found them to be particularly scary, although she had been the one flying them. The red was Rowlandos' idea, to 'honour' the Guns' benefactors. The ships themselves had been a bulk buy from a factory in the Spider Galaxy's western quadrant, as well as a large contingent of smaller ships and parts. The rest, including the dreadnaughts, had been built right here in this system, in the cobbled-together shipyards.

Rowlandos only smiled at the appearance of the four ships, his eyes closed as he was now in contact with someone via his implants. When he opened them again, the Ghost was looking at him with a questioning look.

"That's our escort," he said, using his chin to point at the huge warships.

"Styre came through once again," Heidi said with some surprise.

Hevskii pointed to the other three ships.

"And Chainsaw, Tech, and Suggy as well."

The two women watched as Row stepped up to the command chair.

"Welcome to the Idle Guns, Warrant Officer."

The big human gave him a stern look. "Ghost is fine."

Row nodded, and held out his hand. The bigger man took it without a smile.

* * *

The *Before Dishonour* was escorted into the blue and red swirling nebula, travelling slowly as it passed through the mass of energy clouds. The big battleships travelled in a square formation around the gunship, trailing at a distance.

They flew round a swirling pillar of concentrated energy too dangerous to pass through. An indistinct rectangular shape appeared ahead, just a dark shadow amongst the colours. It became larger and larger as the ships drew near. Other starships flitted around them, some unmanned work drones, most warships.

A Tagarri mining ship suddenly burst from the clouds, moving into the clearing with its long prongs poking out first, followed by its circular hulls. Two small Tagarri escort ships flew beside it, running interference for the command ship as it left the Idle Guns' home base.

The big shape resolved into a massive construction yard, dwarfing the habitats, weapons factory facilities, repair yards, and labs that hung either side of it. It wasn't the facilities that was the most worrying, however, was what was *inside* the main construction yard.

Although it wasn't finished, and its bow and stern jutted out each end of the rectangular structure, its size was unmistakable: a titan.

The Ghost swore.

Row smiled.

"Our pride and joy, and the first of a fleet that can match anything the Terran Navy can throw at us."

"You're planning on going up against them," said the Ghost. "It's been my experience that they have the firepower to take down titans if they really need to."

"The only reason they haven't is because they don't know we have one," the pirate leader replied. "And it's not just for the Terrans. With a titan, we can expand our territory indefinitely, and assist our benefactors more readily"

"Benefactors?"

Row didn't reply to that, instead giving the holographic crew instructions for docking with the habitat station. The gunship slowed, spun, and slipped into a set of docking clamps, latching onto an extending airlock tunnel.

They exited the ship, still carrying Toddorov, and were met by a team of security guards at the other side. They were all dressed in civilian clothes, carrying a more primitive version of the Navy's plasma rifles, with less armour plating, and more glowing pipes.

The Ghost, now dressed in plain black military combat fatigues that had a starship unit patch on one shoulder that had ICARUS sewn into the primitive picture, suddenly found half-a-dozen rifle barrels in his face.

"What is the meaning of this?" he demanded.

"A test if you will."

Unfortunately, the Ghost understood what was expected of him. One of the guards lowered his weapon to apprehend him. It was a serious mistake, and the guard realised it too when the Ghost grabbed the rifle, ripped it from his hands, and slammed it into the next guard's face. The guard went down, and the Ghost kicked the next in the stomach, and then spun and kicked the first in the face.

He was a flurry of kicks, blocks and punches that brought the guards down so fast Row barely had time to blink more than once before it was over. He was astounded by the sheer speed and ferocity it frightened him, thoughts of Hevskii's warning of how dangerous he was flashing through his mind.

He gathered himself, and started clapping.

This Ghost would make a nice addition to the Guns.

* * *

It was another week before the Ghost was let out of his assigned quarters in the habitat station. The *Before Dishonour* was powered down completely, though he had retrieved some of his equipment and clothes.

Adam Caine stared at himself in the mirror, wondering just what the hell he had been thinking coming on this mission.

Because Silver asked, he thought. He had left the *Kara* on Ckeer Najoor, and received the *Before Dishonour* from Silver, a gift to Project Lympstone -so she had told him. Evelyn had understood why he had had to go on this mission, and had even been happy for him. He was helping a friend, after all.

His kit lay on the plump comfortable bed in his small quarters, spread out uniformly. It was a habit he had gotten into from day one of basic training, all through commando training, and his career. He hadn't left the habit behind, still doing it even at home on Ckeer Najoor.

His SA80 was out on the small metal desk, the small scope detached. Several sickle magazines lay in perfect order beside it, with a holster containing his favoured Walther P99, the silencer tucked into a loop on the side of the holster.

The door to his temporary quarters opened, and in stepped Hevskii and Rowlandos. Although he hadn't intended for them to see the kit and weapons, he didn't much care. If they found him out, most of these people were only trained for space combat, piloting starships. Except for a few security guards, they weren't a match for him.

Rowlandos just looked at the kit curiously, his hands clasped at the small of his back trying to look imperious, as if his unofficial title of emperor had gone straight to his head. Hevskii, on the other hand, was furious.

"HOW THE HELL DID YOU GET THOSE PAST THE WEAPONS SCANNERS?! TELL US NOW, OR WE'LL HAVE YOU THROWN OUT OF AN AIRLOCK!" Her delicate porcelain face was flushed red with rage, filled with promises of pain and retribution.

Adam just smiled. "That's the problem with modern technology; the weapons scanners are only designed to scan for modern energy weapons, and blades. Solid-round weapons don't show up on those contraptions."

"And why did you not inform us of the weapons?"

Adam snorted derisively, shaking his head in incredulous amusement.

"Come on," said Row, waving a beckoning arm. "It's time you saw our operation in... well, operation." He nodded to the rifle on the desk. "You won't need that, but you're welcome to bring the pistol." In a flash, Adam had the holster strapped to his hip, loosening the clasp so it was easy to remove in a hurry. Row noted this with a certain amount of wariness.

After a week cooped up in the quarters, Adam was grateful for the escape. Row led the way out of the room, Adam between him and Hevskii. Two security guards flanked them, staring straight ahead with the rifles lowered.

The group moved down several corridors, and took several cramped but open elevators that flashed past ramshackle levels and half-built hangars. The station was in disrepair; Adam figured that the Guns' money was going towards their frighteningly red ships rather than towards the upkeep of the station.

A long glass tunnel led them onto the massive construction yard, where the command centre sat over the partially built titan, the massive windows overlooking the midsection and bow of the monstrous vessel.

"We shouldn't bring him into the command centre, Row," Hev whispered to her leader. "We still don't know his intentions, or why he was so willing to come along with us. He could be a Navy plant for all we know."

"He could be," Row whispered back. "Then again, he could be a genuine friend to us."

Hev glowered at him from a distance, wandering off to stand in front of a large holographic status display that showed the nebula around them. Row led Caine to the windows, ignoring the angry looks from the command centre's crew.

"You said before you intend to expand," said Caine.

Row nodded, glad to be talking to an outsider about his plans.

"A war is coming, one of epic proportions in which our benefactors will have to take territory from the Navy. As such, we, and others like us, will have to pave the way for them. In fact you're just in time to meet them." He pointed to a shape far out beyond the stations and starships. The shape resolved into a starship, one Adam had seen before.

It was red, much like the Guns' ships, but instead of the pirates' modular regular-shaped ships, this one was cobbled together out of spikes and blades.

Adam felt a tremor in his hand, and had to tuck his hands in his pockets to avoid them being seen. It wasn't fear he felt, but sheer anger, rage beyond comprehension.

Out there, coming towards the pirates, was their benefactor.

It was a Core cruiser.

* * *

Caine was shooed away to a control room overlooking one of the larger hangars. Hevskii was there, along with Heidi Gabs, both angry at having to baby-sit the newcomer. He ignored them, watching the red spiked shuttle slide into the hangar.

It settled, and a figure stepped out of a side-door.

Caine's fists bunched in his pockets, and he tried desperately to use his shaggy hair to hide the anger showing on his face. The figure was one of the bird-like Core, dressed in black armour and gold lining, with a long flowing black cape.

It's either a royal guard, or a member of the royal family, he thought. *So much for the Navy believing there was no more Core to threaten them. If Rowlandos and Yh'par'ban are right, then the Core are gearing up for a big war. Just like I suspected.*

He could hear the two pirate women whispering to each other, though still loud enough that he could hear what they were saying. It sounded like they were referring to what he had come here for, in spite of the Core's presence, and the implications of Rowlandos helping them.

"The prisoner is giving us trouble again." This from Heidi.

"So deal with her," came Hevskii's reply. "Just don't kill her; Row wants to negotiate for her ransom personally. If he finds out she's been damaged in any way he may put his new friendly assassin to good use."

"If he's so scary, why don't we put the assassin in the same room as the little scab, and scare her into cooperating?" Heidi's suggestion, originally scoffed at by the other, quickly became a good idea.

So they took him down to the cells.

When they got there, there was a cell with a little girl, around Eve's age of ten and a half, with golden blonde braids in her long hair, and a cute little chequered dress that made her look like Dorothy from *Wizard of Oz*. She was slightly dirty, though there was a washbasin and a toilet in the corner.

Heidi banged on the paint-chipped bars, getting the girl's attention.

Adam was disturbed by the wisdom in the young girl's eyes, and the fact that she was a *human* girl, something he wasn't expecting this far from Terran space. She was small, with blonde pigtails and red ribbons in her hair. She wore a red dress, though most of her appearance had dirt, or worse, smudged all over her.

Although she was tiny, especially compared to Adam, she was smiling knowingly, as if she were in control of the situation, not her captors. She sat cross-legged on the floor, her fingers interlaced in front of her.

She watched Adam from behind the bars.

"You are the Ghost," the girl said. "Why do you not wear your green beret?"

Adam was taken aback by the question. How could she possibly know? But he didn't show it; there was no emotion on his face, though he leaned against the bars. "I haven't worn commando green in years."

451

"True," the girl smiled. It was truly unsettling, and Adam felt the desperate urge to run out of the cells screaming. He could feel the air turning cold, and his breath was starting to show. The hairs on the back of his neck stood up on end, usually an effect of static electricity nearby.

"What are you?" he demanded with a frown. "You're one of the Star Mystics, aren't you?" She smiled, something that turned his face pale. "I met one of your kind on Fallus Nine, just before... just before a lot of people died."

"Yes, this is true." She leaned forward. "Fallus Nine *was* something of a mess, wasn't it?" She jumped to her feet rather gracefully, and put her hands on the bars, brushing his fingertips as though flirting with him. It made him nauseous, jerking back from the touch.

"I thought the Star Mystics limited themselves to one star system in the M-561 Galaxy?"

There was sadness in those young eyes of hers, and she slumped.

"We did. But the Dar-Greelar War consumed our home, and we were forced to leave with the refugee fleets. I am... I am the last survivor of the fleet attacked by these pirates." Tears rolled down her face, and yet the rest of her face was blank, no emotion showing through at all. The salt-water ran down her cheeks in streams. "I have seen into your mind, green beret. I know what makes you tick."

Heidi cackled with laughter.

"If you think this man is going to help you in some way, then you are no Star Mystic I have ever heard of before." She jerked a thumb at Adam. "He kills anybody who he thinks is against him." Adam frowned at the comment, wondering where the hell Gabs had got her corrupted information. Wherever it had been from, he wasn't going to openly dispute her claim. Perhaps it would just add to his supposed reputation within the Idle Guns.

If they didn't know his true personality, then it was a good bet that they had no idea why he was amongst them. Which was a blessing. Then he noticed the girl looking at him with a curious look on her face. He could see a shape glowing under her skin. It was an elongated four-pointed star, and it seemed as though a piece of glowing metal had been inserted under her forehead.

She was reading her mind, reading his intentions.

He tried to shut her out, using what little Diamond had taught him about psychic warfare, which wasn't a whole lot apart from concentrating your mind down to one single innocent thought. His combat suit's hood had psychic shielding embedded into its electronics, preventing mental intrusions. But that suit was hidden inside his shielded bag, waiting for the time when he would have to fight the Guns.

He shook the thoughts off, focussing on something she already knew: green berets.

She smiled again, and again Adam felt nauseous. More so, because he knew she could see what he was thinking. Unfortunately, the combination of the young girl and the green berets had him thinking about Evie back home.

"Evie?" she whispered.

Reflexively, he knifed a hand through the bars, and slapped her round the face. The impact was forceful enough to throw her to the floor, rubbing her cheek as though it had only been a slight tap.

He heard her voice in his head.

I have seen your spirit, Adam Logan Caine, and I need your help. I believe that you have been sent to retrieve me from these pirates, but I sense you have other plans involving their benefactors.

He growled unintelligibly at her, and then marched out of the cells, Heidi hot on his heels, who was quite pleased at his reaction, as if just confirming his fraudulent reputation. When she was satisfied that the Ghost had done what they had 'asked' of him, she allowed herself to respect him. Fear and hate were the most powerful tools in the pirating business.

"Nicely done indeed," she commented.

"Piss off," he said in reply.

She let out a bark of laughter.

* * *

Rowlandos and his benefactor's representative secluded themselves into an empty pilot's briefing room. The bird-like creature, dressed in black armour, and cradling its long flowing black cape in one claw like he was an emperor, glared at him with beady yellow eyes. He always glared at anything that wasn't his own race.

Row clapped his hands together dramatically.

"So, what can I do for you and your masters?"

"*Your* masters," it reminded him, its voice filled with the clicks and clacks of its black beak, and a long talon pointed at the Kra Nal. "You serve us in all ways. That was your agreement to us."

Row sighed. "And what can the Idle Guns do for you, Commander?"

"We have a task for you and your ships." It slapped a digital data disk onto the table, which skidded perfectly into place in front of Row. He picked it up, and clicked it into the reader. The holographic projector sputtered to life, and then died. Row kicked the table, and the projector flared back to existence, spurting an image out to hang above the table.

It was a large Alliance starship, a dreadnaught in fact. According to the intelligence file it would be travelling through the Dark Galaxy on a shakedown cruise after its recent completion from the Alliance's primary shipyards at Fullina.

"We want it destroyed. It is the first of a new series of Alliance vessels that could be a threat to us in the future. Perhaps you could make use of your new asset." This brought Row up sharp.

"How could you possibly know about that? I've had him held in quarters for the last week until today."

"We have our sources," was all the creature would say on the subject.

Row's eyes narrowed in his long head, but knew better than to pursue it. If he did, the response would either be extreme violence, or complete silence, neither of which were appealing to him.

"I'll see he gets some action," he nodded.

"Indeed," the Core Commander said nonchalantly. "My ship and I will accompany you on this mission."

"Afraid we can't get the job done?" sneered the pirate.

"Afraid you'll capture the ship for yourself."

"It could be useful," replied Row, returning his attention to the hologram, a knowing smile on his thin green lips. He was looking at the holographic ship like a starving man finding a feast, even licking his lips at one point. Ideas were tumbling through his head.

"And your new titan won't be?" The question broke his reverie.

"The titan is barely usable at the moment. A fully functional dreadnaught could be of value –for us, and for you. At least for now."

The creature relented, making Row wonder if that had been the Core's plan all along. Although many of the main troops and commanders were not known for being especially bright, their combat tactics and overall scheming seemed nigh-on impossible to predict or counter. The Patriarch, it seemed, really was a genius.

"Keep the dreadnaught then. Assuming you can keep it intact enough to use it again. As I said, my ship will accompany your fleet during the mission. We will not be part of your command structure during combat; however, we *will* be joining in if we feel the need to."

"Of course..." he started, watching as the alien commander stalked out of the briefing room. "...Master."

* * *

Another week later, a black-clad figure stalked the corridors of the Alliance dreadnaught *Unrelenting Spirit*.

Armed with a humming plasma carbine, the woman behind him walked as quietly through the corridor as she could, nervously eyeing her surroundings. She was frightened beyond belief, cursing herself for opening her big mouth, and landing her in this situation.

She cursed again when she realised she'd lost sight of her mission partner. Again.

She had to keep her eyes looking directly at him otherwise he would disappear. This last time she had blinked, and he had been gone. That had been five minutes ago, and still no sign.

"Where the hell are you?" she hissed.

She felt something metal and cylindrical press against her neck. She froze, and cold sweat dripped down her back. Her hand shook rattling the carbine she was holding. An electronically enhanced voice growled from behind her.

"If I was an Alliance trooper, you'd be dead, or worse."

She turned.

Green eyes glowed brightly in the dark passageway, reflecting dimly off the curved architecture. She hadn't heard a single noise to indicate that he was there. Even when he moved into her sight, she still heard nothing.

"Fernikking hell, you scared the living daylights out of me."

"*Good.*"

She wasn't certain, but she was sure that there was a hint of smile underneath that near-featureless black hood. The suit had been a surprise, hidden among the belongings taken from his ship. Row hadn't chastised him –it was the suit that had become part of the Ghost's story. But Hevskii had kicked up a storm, shouting and swearing to the heavens and anybody who would listen.

Nobody understood her viciousness towards the Ghost, nor why she had called him Warrant Officer upon their first meeting. His military rank? Whatever he was called, he was certainly proving his worth aboard the *Unrelenting Spirit*, and adding to the legend of the Ghost.

"*Now stay close,*" he ordered. "*I didn't want you on here, but Rowlandos ordered you to spy on me, so stay fucking close, or so help me god, I'm going to kill you before the Alliance can find you. Understood?*" He was leaning close to her now, the glow of the eyepieces filling most of her vision.

She nodded wordlessly.

He span, and strode off, Heidi trying her best to keep as quiet as possible, and keep her wits about her. Once again, however, each of his strides made no sound whatsoever, and she had a hard time picking out his silhouette in the shadows of the unused corridor.

Silently, she cursed herself again for volunteering for the mission.

Ahead, the Ghost had discovered an exposed power conduit next to a working computer control terminal.

* * *

On the bridge of the dreadnaught stood Far Commander Pio, watching the ship's progress on all the monitors arrayed around him and the bridge crew. Alliance Military Command had tasked him with the shakedown cruise of this magnificent ship, though he had hoped to command it permanently.

Despite a large crew complement aboard the *Unrelenting Spirit*, it was still a skeleton crew compared to what the ship should be running with. There were simply not enough trained officers and enlisted to fly it fully, at least not yet.

The ship itself was performing well.

They were currently flying through the Linkway, on their way to test their new sensor arrays in the Dark Galaxy, a place filled with spatial anomalies in horrendous amounts –definitely somewhere to test the worthiness of the great ship's scanning abilities. Not only that, but it would be a test of its defences this close to the infamous Idle Guns' territory.

After a brief stopover at the Terran Navy's Fort Softfire, and the arrival of a Terran observation and advisory team, the *Unrelenting Spirit* had dove into the Dark Galaxy at full speed.

The Terran team had set up shop on the ship's bridge, with their leader, a Brigadier General Sansky, always hovering near to Pio, as if the Far Commander needed a Terran chaperone.

They're always interfering in Alliance business, he thought. Although General Sansky wore the uniform of the Terran Army's Tactical Support Corps, Pio knew the man worked for Navy Intelligence. The Alliance's own intelligence network was no slouch, and Sansky was well known to them as recently promoted to the post of Senior Deputy Director of Navy Intelligence.

"Commander," one of the bridge crew shouted. "Internal sensors have just gone offline."

"Again?" exclaimed Pio. He was exasperated with the system's failures, made worse by the fact that the crew had still not found the cause for it. Sansky twitched uncomfortably, as if he knew what the cause for it was.

"Sorry, sir."

Pio let out the seething anger through his clenched teeth, folding his long upper tentacles across his rounded chest.

Then the lights died.

"What the frikta was that?" he shouted.

Sansky still did not seem surprised at the turn of events, though Pio saw a little fear in the Terran's eyes.

"Sublight engines are shifting out of phase, Far Commander," the engineering officer shouted. The deck shook, and there was a loud banging sound from further back in the gigantic ship. Alarms blared, and the Linkway outside was shaking —or rather, the ship was shaking violently enough that it looked like it was.

Pio's three stomachs quailed at the abuse.

"Get us out of the Linkway, now! Before we get stuck in here!" he bellowed.

The engines whined as the helmsman fought against the ship's shaking to drag it into the nearest Linkway exit. The lights flickered on and off, and the consoles died. But the ship's momentum carried it slowly out of the Linkway, moving away from the slight gravity pull of the subspace network.

The massive dreadnaught listed and drifted in space.

"Report!" he demanded. Beside him, the Terran general was clinging onto the nearest railing. The gravity net was malfunctioning, and there was no noise from the engines anymore. The ship was dying.

"*I assure you, the malfunctions are only temporary, Far Commander,*" an electronically altered voice said from behind Pio. Something metal pressed against his back for a brief second. He spun to find two humans standing there. One was holding a common plasma carbine, the other covered head-to-toe in a full black bodyglove.

Pio had heard the stories.

"The Ghost."

"*Indeed.*" He was holding an odd-looking weapon –a solid-round pistol with a silencer attached to the barrel. An odd sight in this day and age to be sure. "*I am afraid I will have to relieve you of your ship, Far Commander.*"

The figure seemed to suddenly notice the Terran General.

"*Raymond? What the fuck are you doing here?*"

"I could ask the same thing, Adam."

"Adam?" murmured the human woman behind the Ghost.

Pio started chuckling. "Despite the stories over the last few years, I seriously doubt that even you could capture the entire crew of the *Unrelenting Spirit*, even a skeleton crew."

"*I don't have to.*" He pointed over Pio's shoulder, out of the enormous forward viewports. "*I suggest you surrender to the Idle Guns, immediately, Far Commander. Although I have no wish to kill unnecessarily, the Guns have no such restraint.*"

Outside the ship, two dreadnaughts lumbered into view, along with a host of battleships, cruisers, and a cloud of starfighters. Hanging back away from the pirate fleet was a lone red cruiser, covered in spikes. Sansky was staring at it with mortal dread.

"Is that-?"

"*Yes, it is,*" replied the Ghost. "*It's a long story.*" He turned back to Pio. "*Surrender.*"

Pio looked around at his distraught crew, and the look of resignation on the faces of the Terran Tactical Support officers. He nodded sadly.

"*You and all your crew evacuate the ship in the escape pods. You'll be left alone if you head straight for Harker Station. You have my guarantee. Just ask Sansky here.*"

Sansky just nodded, still staring wide-eyed at the spiked cruiser.

The crew filed out, Pio and Sansky last. The Ghost nodded to Sansky once, and the bridge was empty. Heidi moved to the communications console, and signalled the Guns' fleet.

* * *

Rowlandos boarded the *Unrelenting Spirit* aboard one of the many generic shuttles from his command dreadnaught. He strode onto the bridge surrounded by security guards, metal dreadlocks jingling, hands clasped behind his back, maintaining his favoured emperor pose. He towered above the others, though he was skinny as hell.

Heidi and the Ghost were waiting for him, stood at the centre of the bridge, the consoles flickering to life as the Ghost's temporary commands revived the ship. The sensors showed the escape pods heading back into the Linkway, and the Guns' ships leaving them alone. Row had been against that part of the plan, but the Ghost had convinced him that the escapees would take back the story of how the Idle Guns captured a full dreadnaught without ever firing a shot.

"This is truly remarkable," smiled Row. "Well done everyone."

* * *

Idle Guns' home base.

Two days later.

"Did you really beat him?" one of the exotic dancers purred, stroking Todd's neck and cheek. They barely wore anything, save for string bikinis. Toddorov had taken a shine to them instantly, and they to his large wallet. He had regaled them with a wonderful tale of how he had beaten down the one-man army known as the Ghost in hand-to-hand combat the day before.

The girls had oohed and aahed along with every detail of every punch and kick.

"I really did beat him," he beamed. The girls stroked him even more. He shut his eyes as they walked, thinking how much like heaven this was, especially given they were headed for his quarters in the habitat stations.

The two girls stopped, and wrapped both arms around him.

"Tell us again how you defeated the mighty Ghost?"

He could see they were simple, but obliged, slipping from their perfect embrace so he could use his whole body to tell the story once again. He was jumping about, swishing an imaginary sword, and throwing targetless punches, when he got to the best bit.

"I had him on the ground, and he said, 'please don't hurt me, Toddorov, I promise I'll never be mean to you again.' And I was like-" he looked up as he realised they weren't paying attention, their eyes wide as they stared at something over Todd's shoulder. Horror shuddered through him. "He's behind me isn't he?"

They nodded.

He turned.

CRACK!

* * *

The two new ship captains of the pirate organisation Gattus and Gurbelldunf stepped into the mess hall in the Idle Guns' nebula-bound station. Something smelled extremely good, but neither knew what it was.

Two of the senior members were sat at one of the many tables, throwing nervous glances at each other. Manko and Chainsaw made to leave when Styre appeared from the kitchen brandishing a tray with plates. He laid the plates of food out in front of them, whilst Gattus and Gurbelldunf stood far enough away that Styre didn't notice them.

"Sit," Styre Blixtsnabb growled. Manko and Chainsaw sighed, and sat back down, grimacing at the thing steaming merrily away on their plates.

"What the hell is it?"

Manko poked it with his fork, wondering if it was about to jump off the plate and eat *him*, whilst Chainsaw looked ill. Gurbelldunf barfed up his lunch.

Styre replied happily.

"It's cripes on toast. Naturally."

* * *

The door opened, there was a crack of knuckles on somebody's face, and Rowlandos came flying backwards out into the corridor, a green and brown blur. The floor was, unfortunately, rather solid, as was the wall he hit after bouncing off the deck, not as Row had intended.

Heidi now stood in the open doorway, arms folded across her chest, rapidly tapping her foot. She did not look happy.

"What, no kiss?"

She followed the punch up with a rather hefty kick to his midsection, knocking the wind out of his lungs.

"That's good," he wheezed, "I don't need my stomach anyway."

Heidi harrumphed, span, and stepped back into her quarters.

"Not even a goodbye?" he groaned, cradling his stomach.

He was suddenly aware of a pair of booted feet barely a metre from his head. When he looked up, he grinned. Wearing his trademark brown leather bomber jacket, he looked like he had just been thrown out of a bar during a brawl.

Hevskii shook her head.

"Noobtard. When are you gonna learn to stop flirting with that woman?" She held out a hand, and pulled him to his shaky feet.

"Can't help myself," he chuckled, belatedly realising how painful it was to laugh. The two strode down the corridor, side-by-side. "We're only a few minutes from the arrival of this week's drug shipment. Any news on it?"

Hevskii shook her head.

"Not yet." Row could see something was bothering her, though didn't question her until they reached the main hangar. Repairs were taking place overhead in the docking cradles –the results of the latest skirmish with Alliance vessels trying to reclaim the *Unrelenting Spirit*.

"I don't like it, Row," Hevskii admitted as they stared up at the ships above them. "Your new ghostly friend has been keeping secrets from us this whole time. I mean he won't even let us go onto his ship besides that one time when he rescued us. Now all he does is talk to that freak-job in the cells, and study history files."

"What about it? You asked him to get her to co-operate, and she is for the most part. What exactly were you expecting?"

"I think he's a spy sent by the Terran Navy. We don't know anything about him besides the stories we keep hearing from around the known galaxies. All of those stories are about him taking out warlords and criminals. Criminals like us. He has to be working for the Navy."

"We're not in their territory," Row shrugged, watching as a Guns cruiser was released from the repair cradles, and guided back into the main hangar.

"Besides, if the Navy had an operation going against us, our contacts would know."

"But one of these days when they're pissed off enough, they'll come looking for us. We've caused too much trouble in this galaxy for us to go unnoticed for long. Idle is too big to ignore, especially since we took the *Unrelenting Spirit*." Row shrugged again, earning himself a slap round the back of the head from his number two.

The lighting dipped, and the emergency alarms blared loudly for attention. The station had just gone to full combat alert. Row grabbed a technician who was charging past to get to his battle stations.

"What's going on?"

The technician was frightened, and not of the pirate.

"A Terran Navy gunship squadron just appeared outside the station, my lord, and our scout ships near Harker Station picked up a massive Terran fleet coming through the Linkway. They're being led by the *HMS Alexandria*."

The technician bolted, away from Row, and out of view.

"*Alexandria*?" worried Hevskii. "That's Vandergrift's flagship." Her eyes narrowed, looking at Rowlandos. "What were you saying about the Ghost *not* being a spy?"

Row turned to Hevskii.

"Find the Ghost, and deal with him if you can. Take whatever security guards you need. And kill that Star Mystic while you're at it. As you say, she's proven too much of a liability. I'm going to get every ship I can up in the air in case these Terrans really are after us."

As Hevskii turned away, he added, "Oh, and destroy his ship whilst your at it. No sense giving him an escape route." Hevskii nodded; she was satisfied at last that she was proven right about her grumblings.

Row was already headed towards the outer docking facilities, where his dreadnaught awaited.

* * *

The senior officers' mess hall was filled with shouts as the ship captains jumped up from their seats, and charged to the exit, leaving poor Styre standing there in his apron, holding a plate of food.

"What's wrong with cripes on toast?"

He harrumphed.

"There's just no pleasing some people."

* * *

Row arrived on the bridge of his dreadnaught to find alarms blaring, emergency lights flashing, and crew running about. His ship's XO was bellowing orders so he could be heard over the tumult.

"Lets get these ships going, XO," ordered Row.

The Rijiin warrior nodded, and flashed a feral toothy grin, revealing the sharp wolf-like fangs underneath his lips.

Holograms descended around Row, showing the rest of the fleet mobilising in record time, the other dreadnaught lumbering out from between the collection of stations and construction yards. Battleships prowled out into space, whilst the smaller ships clouded around them all like locusts.

"Status on the scout ships near Harker?"

* * *

The piratical scout ships were in pieces, brushed aside by the giant form of the *HMS Alexandria* –a *Crusade*-class dreadnaught in the service of the Terran Navy, and flagship of the Seventh Fleet's Taskforce 7-Gamma. The entirety of 7-Gamma swarmed around it: 3 battleships, 15 cruisers of varying classes, 5 frigates, 23 destroyers, and four dozen starfighter squadrons. Five battleships and three cruisers from the Fifth Fleet, as well as a dozen Alliance battleships now under the command of Far Commander Pio joined these ships, accompanied by those vessels seconded to Harker Station.

Ment Grokail, his command staff, and most of his senior crew were arrested for their collaboration with the Idle Guns pirates. They were remanded into custody aboard the *Alexandria*, and kept under guard.

The wave of ships swept through into the next Linkway tunnel, pouring through like a cloud of steam drawn into the crack in a window.

7-Gamma blasted pirate ships to pieces as they moved through the Dark Galaxy, pummelling automated defences spread throughout the Idle Guns' territory. Several lone ships were dealt with, having been preying on passing freighters.

The massive fleet swept the tiny lifeless galaxy clear of major pirate infestations, all within one day of the *Unrelenting Spirit* being captured. They were earlier than the Idle Guns realised, Navy Intelligence having falsified records and communications out from Harker and the surrounding area so that they were unsuspecting of what was really going on.

And what was really going on was that the combined Navy and Alliance fleet waited in the Linkway to flood into realspace at the word of Sansky's undercover asset.

* * *

That undercover asset, namely Adam Caine, arrived in the cells fully armed, and carrying the satchel and limited equipment he had brought from the *Before Dishonour*. He shot the guards on duty, the big black assault rifle in his hands thundering away. The muzzle flashed blindingly, and two more guards went down.

Adam, dressed in the bodyglove once more, kicked in the door to the young Star Mystic's cell.

"C'mon, I really was sent to get you out of this place."

461

"My people sent you?" she asked.

"A woman I know as Silver sent me to retrieve you. Do you know her?"

The girl shook her head, something he hadn't been expecting. He was still wondering why she didn't know Silver when Hevskii appeared with a bundle of fresh guards. Adam brought the HK-g36c up to his shoulder, and squeezed the trigger on full-auto.

The guards went down in a hail of bullets before anyone had a chance to react. Hevskii just stood there, wide-eyed with shock at the sheer brutality of the noise, and the accuracy of the shots.

"We need a hostage to get out of here safely. Which I intend for the both of us to do."

"You will not use me as a hostage, Adam Caine."

The big man frowned. "How do you know me?"

"Don't you know? I'm the reason you came here. I am the one your friend Silver refers to as the First."

"Huh?"

* * *

On board the *Before Dishonour*, a timer counted down. The holographic crew were nowhere to be seen, nor was any console activated, apart from one in the small engineering room, at the base of the glowing core.

The timer was counting down from one hour, though it was almost finished by the time Hevskii appeared in the jail cells, reaching ten seconds as she revealed herself to Adam.

The activated console was wired into the core, with explosive devices attached around the entire room. This was why there was only a holographic crew, not because it was cheaper to run.

Silver had gifted six identical gunships to Adam's Project Lympstone, with the most rundown one being assigned immediately to the Idle Guns mission.

The timer hit zero, and the core overloaded.

The energy touched off the explosive devices, and the entire ship suddenly detonated in an instant. The explosion took the main hangar bay with it, vaporising ships, docking cradles, hull plating, and even technicians unlucky enough to have been working on those same ships.

The blast tore out a massive section of the station itself, making it look like a half-eaten egg. Bridges between it and the other stations were snapped by the sudden movement, and starships already outside the hangar but not far enough away were shredded by massive chunks of debris. Others further out were only peppered, although it interfered with some of the older shield and sensor systems.

Fuel lines and energy conduits were severed between critical systems.

All because of one small gunship.

* * *

Rowlandos saw the devastation and knew that Hevskii had been right all along. He slammed his fist into the nearest console, and then the nearest crewman, who stumbled over the railings of the command balcony, and tumbled down to his death below. Rowlandos glared at anybody who dared complain about the mistreatment, shutting them up instantly.

But he couldn't worry about the remains of his station.

He knew the Terrans were out there somewhere.

* * *

Adam stared at Hevskii, dumbfounded as the deck shifted beneath them.

"You're *the First*?" he exclaimed, his voice altered once again. *"How? I thought the Star Mystic was the First."*

Hevskii shook her head.

"No, we picked her up only a few weeks ago from a refugee convoy. Rowlandos was going to ransom her back to her people for a substantial amount." She paused, thinking seriously about how to phrase her next words. "About four and a half years ago, I was in the midst of time-watching the fall of the last Mertik Emperor when I was dragged back to the present, and became corporeal with no means of returning to my immortality. I had hoped that my people might find me and rescue me, but there was no such luck."

"Why have you been such a bitch towards me then?" queried Adam.

"Because I recently discovered that *you* were involved in the destruction of the Andromeda power core. And given your reputation for the death and destruction that follows you around, it was an intuitive leap to assume that you were directly responsible."

Adam's cheeks blushed, though thankfully his face was covered by the black combat hood, thus covering his embarrassment. This woman was clearly who she said she was: who else would know that kind of information?

"My bad. I shot down a Terran Black Ops battleship, and detonated its power core that collapsed your people's time-watching abilities. I'm sorry that it happened, but there was no alternative. That power was about to fall into the hands of some very nasty people —I wasn't about to let that happen."

Hevskii, though not entirely satisfied with the answer, let it go for now.

The deck shook violently then.

"Secondary explosions," said Adam.

"From what?" asked the young Star Mystic that was now stood somewhat close to him.

"The Before Dishonour *was named for an old saying. 'Death before dishonour.'"*

Hevskii nodded in understanding at the implication.

"We have to get off of this station."

"Do you have any fighter-bombers with changeable ID broadcast codes?"

"Of course," replied the pirate-cum-immortal. "There are several in the starfighter hangar on the construction yards."

"*Show us.*"

He slipped a comms device from a pouch on his belt, opened a specific channel, and then transmitted a single codeword.

"*Hammer.*"

A reply squawked through the minute speaker.

"*Anvil.*"

Adam smiled.

"We need to hurry."

"Why?" the two females asked simultaneously.

"*Because in about three minutes, the Terran Navy is sending its best anti-pirate taskforce into this star system. And then all hell will break loose. That's why we need the changeable broadcast codes. Otherwise we'll be seen by the Navy as just another pirate vessel.*"

"Great," muttered Hevskii as she led the way out of the body-stricken cells.

* * *

Rowlandos was about to demand a status report from the stations, when the Linkway suddenly spat out a starship, then another, and then another, and kept spitting until the silhouette of a Navy dreadnaught pushed its way out of the nebulous clouds that surrounded the base.

So this was the *Alexandria*.

He was shocked to see so many ships.

Three *Knight*-class battleships charged forward, spearheading the formation of twelve of the Alliance's shiny, pristinely curved battleships. Behind them came the *Alexandria*, surrounded by cruisers, frigates, destroyers, and starfighter squadrons.

Farlander and *Washburn* split left all of a sudden, whilst *Underwood* split right, each taking a wing of the Alliance formation. A pair of torpedoes suddenly streaked from every single battleship.

Thirty torpedoes –designed for high damage, and to combat bigger starships– suddenly streaked in at the Idle Guns battleships. The fat torpedoes detonated among the red ships, ripping them apart like they weren't there. Only one of the ten battleships survived, and it was bleeding coolant, debris, and hull plating.

The smaller ships were in chaos, trying to avoid the wrecks, and at the same time, attempting to avoid the now incoming fire.

The Terran and Alliance battleships moved out and away, splitting off from the ships behind to come above and below the rest of the fleet. The cruisers *Flatland*, *Shaper*, and *Protocol 42* led seven destroyers –*Requiem*, *Restoration*, *Brightstar*, *Storm in Heaven*, *High Charity*, *Thunder*, and *Dreamer*- straight towards the unfinished titan and its undersized construction yard.

Rowlandos watched in horror as the fast ships darted through the chaos of his own group. He bellowed for someone to shoot the smaller ships down, but the dreadnaught's starship-sized weapons batteries were too slow and ponderous, and the smaller ships slipped through.

Explosions rippled around the Terran spearhead as they fired upon anything that moved around them. These ship were accompanied by a wing of Rhino fighters that flew in flights of four, manoeuvring around each ship, and taking out enemy starfighters.

Dreamer was clipped by an errant energy blast from the command dreadnaught, its armoured prow gone in a flash of light. It tumbled end-over-end until it slammed lengthways into the construction yard around the titan, gouging out a long canyon across the top of the structure.

Row was horrified to see flames pouring across the construction yard.

Dreamer's friends came within range of the titan, the destroyers pulling ahead to keep out of the cruisers' weapons range. A firestorm erupted along the top of the moon-sized starship and its cage, but the damage was purely cosmetic, the smaller ships' weapons not strong enough to take out a titan by themselves. But they obliterated the construction yard, breaking it apart so that the rig floated away from the ship.

The horror continued as the other Idle Guns dreadnaught sped ahead of Row's command ship, firing on the *Alexandria*. That ship, however, had a lesser range than the command ship, and so did no damage to even the Navy vessel's shields.

Alexandria, pride of the anti-pirate/smuggler community, had no such restrictions. A hail of ship-sized energy rounds flew across space, and encompassed the other vessel. Her shields were brought down far too quickly for Row's liking. Then the battleships joined in with their torpedoes, sending wave after wave of lethal projectiles into the dreadnaught's hull. One battleship –the *Underwood*- was hit by the dreadnaught's return fire. The energy stripped its shields and vaporised its outer hull, before touching off its munitions, and detonating the entire thing within a second of being hit.

The Guns' dreadnaught disappeared in a wave of energy and missiles as the *Alexandria* and the Alliance ships pounded it into oblivion. The big ship didn't explode at first, instead breaking in two. Then the massive unstable engines imploded, tearing a brief rift in the space/time continuum. It sucked two of the unfortunate Terran cruisers in with it, including the *Guardsman*, previously seconded to Harker. What was left just span and bled metal, still heading in the direction the engines had been taking it.

He shouted to the communications officer.

"Tell the *Unrelenting Spirit* to get its backside into this fight immediately!"

The officer frowned for a few seconds as it listened to the reply from the other end.

"They say they can't, my lord!"

"What?!"

"The engines just shut down by themselves."

Rowlandos smashed his hand against his XO's face, sending the Rijiin warrior sprawling across the deck.

"GHOST!" he shouted to the air.

* * *

"You did what?" Hevskii looked at him incredulously.

Adam could feel the vibrations from the battle outside resounding through what was left of the station around them. They had had to double back at one point because the hangar explosions had cut off one of the corridors with debris.

They were moving through the officers' mess hall when a human in an apron popped up with a primitive plasma pistol in his hand.

Adam blasted him with the assault rifle, throwing the man back into the wall. The corpse slipped to the floor, his blood streaking down the wall with him.

"Poor Styre," said Hevskii, with a twinge of regret in her voice. They moved on through another door that led around the obstruction.

"*I said I re-wired the* Unrelenting Spirit*'s control systems to power down the engines whenever the ship's weapons were brought online during combat. Far Commander Pio gave me the specs before this mission started.*"

Hevskii was laughing her ass off at thought. "You really are full of surprises, Caine."

"*Got a sense of humour too, if you can believe it,*" he muttered, though it sounded strange with the altered voice. "*Not that most people would notice it.*"

"I'm guessing you're referring to someone in particular?"

He nodded, "*She's dating someone though, for the last three months.*"

"Next you're going to tell me you have children," Hevskii chortled.

Caine stopped in his tracks.

"*A daughter.*" He pointed to the young Star Mystic. "*About the same age as you actually. Well, Mertik women hit puberty a lot younger than most humanoid races, apparently. You should see the tantrums she has.*" He shuddered, and then moved on, ignoring the shocked looks on the faces of his two new companions.

Two ship captains –the two new ones- appeared around a corner ahead. They seemed lost, and now were frightened at the green-eyed killer coming towards them with a big assault rifle. They balked, and sprinted in the opposite direction. Caine let them go, wanting to get off the increasingly unstable station.

* * *

Rowlandos' bridge was falling apart. A girder had fallen from the ceiling and turned two of his crew into red paste. Sparks were flying from consoles, and his holographic tactical overview had malfunctioned completely.

The status reports from the rest of the ship were much the same.

Alexandria had turned its guns on the command ship whilst the smaller ships took care of everything else. So far, the Terrans had left the titan alone, believing it to be no threat at all, at least not next to the fighting ships.

The command ship's engines were dead, several large power conduits having been severed in the initial bombardment. The two ships had passed each other, exchanging punishing broadsides. Then the *Alexandria* had re-tasked its guns and pounded the pirate vessel's engines.

Weapons were down, and life support was on emergency supply.

There was a fire down on the lower command deck, blocking the entrance to one of the escape pod sections.

"Abandon ship," he ordered. "All hands, abandon ship."

The ship rocked again as the *Alexandria* came around for another round.

He needed to get to the titan, and power up its defences. Even if it couldn't move, he could at least push the Terrans and Alliance ships away to give his benefactors time to bring their own fleet in.

The sensors had last recorded the Core cruiser moving towards the Linkway at full sublight speed, away from the engagement. He hoped they were calling for reinforcements. The alternative was unthinkable.

The cruiser *City of Avarice* was hit amidships, and listed the wrong way, into the side of the pirate command ship, tearing a massive chunk out of the dying dreadnaught.

Row ran to the nearest escape pod hatch, and dove in. He slammed the hatch closed behind him, ignoring the fists banging on the outside to let some of the crew in. He ejected the pod from the ship, and the tiny craft fired out into space.

He got a good look at the battle around him.

It shouldn't have been such a slaughter, but one man had put a crux in his plan, and ruined everything for him. He flipped the controls over to manual, and directed the craft towards the titan.

* * *

Alexandria thundered over the debris of the pirate command ship, sweeping in a wide semi-circle around to the titan. The construction yard was still tumbling away from its former charge. Occasionally parts of it would hit the other station constructs, tearing hull plating off into space, and dragging unsuspecting crewmen out.

The Alliance battleships were mopping up the pirates after the one-sided battle, scouring the wreckage, either for survivors to arrest, or ships to disable. The *Farlander* and *Washburn* moved ahead, blasting any wrecks to pieces too big for the ships' shields to deflect.

Rowlandos' pod slipped into the titan's command deck hangar, settling on the glossy black deck. He was met by the titan's construction foreman, who had thankfully been onboard the great vessel overseeing the construction of the ship's command systems.

"How far along are we?"

"She'll fight, sir, but we still can't move. The engineers haven't fixed the structural integrity problem, so even if the engines were working we'd tear ourselves apart just trying to move a few metres."

Rowlandos nodded, and then shot the foreman through the head.

"You're behind schedule," he commented, stepping over the corpse. The deputy foreman was horrified by the casual brutality. But the pirate 'emperor' had a look of insanity on his long face. The deputy foreman snapped to attention, trying not to look at the ruin that had once been his boss's head.

"Get my ship moving," growled the pirate. "I don't care what it takes." As he walked by the deputy foreman, he suddenly pressed his face into the smaller man's. "If you do not I *will* kill you and a dozen of your closest relatives. Understood?"

The engineer nodded enthusiastically, and turned to start bellowing orders to the engineering crews nearby.

That's better, thought Rowlandos.

* * *

Hevskii led them into a large hangar bay that was mostly empty.

A pair of small fighter-bombers sat there, deck crew pouring over them.

"There aren't enough pilots to fly all of our starfighters and bombers," Hevskii explained. "Either of these two are big enough for the three of us."

"The nearest."

Caine charged across the hangar, ignoring the shocked expressions on the deck crews. At first they didn't do or say anything, but then they recognised that he was carrying a large weapon, and thus was a threat.

They charged at him with anything handy.

Hevskii saw it coming a mile away.

Caine squeezed the assault rifle's trigger, knocking three of the crew back with one long blast. Blood splattered across the deck, and the rifle roared. Two more went down, and another and another until there were no more standing.

Hevskii and the Star Mystic were frozen with fear at the sheer ferocity of the attack, and the brutal noise of the weapon in Caine's hands.

"*Come on,*" he said without turning, no hint of emotion in his altered voice. When they didn't follow, he did turn, about to ask what was wrong, when one of the horrendously injured deck crew reared up behind him.

Caine grunted as something was stabbed into his back just above his hip. He made no other sound as he span, wrenching the makeshift weapon out of the wielder's hands. He slammed the butt of his rifle into the alien's long nose. The cartilage of the nose was pushed violently up into the thing's brain cavity. Its eyes rolled up into its sockets, and it collapsed to the floor.

So did Caine, his legs wobbling.

The two women rushed to his aid, taking an arm each. Hevskii scooped up his assault rifle, and wrapped the sling around her shoulder. She took one of his arms over her shoulder, and the three stumbled to the closest fighter-bomber.

It was twelve metres long, with two fat reverse delta wings, a blunt nose, and a rectangular cockpit canopy; a modified civilian version of the Terran Navy Rhino.

Hevskii, still holding Caine up with all his equipment, directed the young girl on how to open the cockpit canopy, and commence a quick-start of the engines. When the girl couldn't do it, despite her mind-reading talent, She leaned Caine against the dark metal fuselage, and jumped up to the cockpit.

She heard a grunting sound from below, and turned to see Caine gripping the sharpened implement in his back. With a roar of pain, and a squelching noise, he ripped it out of his back. It fell from his hands, and he once again collapsed to the floor. Hevskii jumped down, and ripped his combat hood off.

His face was pale, the white skin showing the red marks of old scars criss-crossing his neck and one cheek. He was sweating profusely, and even shaking a little.

"Give me something for the pain," he groaned. "I'm a better flier than you." She was about to protest. "I've you see you fly small ships in the simulator, Hevskii, or First, or whatever you're called." His voice was weak. "Now," he hissed.

She wanted to say something else, but it wouldn't form into actual words.

She rummaged through the cockpit's med kit, and pulled out a small re-usable injection tool, shaped distressingly like a gun. She pushed a tiny capsule into the base of the pistol grip, and then jabbed the needlepoint into his neck. There was a hiss, and the liquid chemical was injected into his blood. She pulled the tool away, and the needle was automatically ejected, along with the empty chemical capsule.

He gasped, and he stopped shaking. He blinked away whatever pain was left, and jumped to his feet. He stripped off the bodyglove down to the waist, and stripped the blood-soaked shirt off. Hevskii's eyes widened at the amount of older scars across his body.

She pulled bandages from the med kit, and tightly wrapped them around his midsection. The bandages made him a bit stiff, but it was enough to keep him going for now.

The station rocked again.

"We need to get out of here," he said.

He re-dressed his bodyglove, and pulled the hood back on, so he was once again the Ghost, frightening and strong. The rest of his equipment, including the rifle, he slung into a small cargo compartment underneath the cockpit, and locked it down.

He struggled to get into the cockpit, the bandages constricting his movements, but settled into the forward pilot's chair. Hevskii sat in the second seat behind him, with the young Star Mystic on her lap.

At the flick of a switch, the canopy lowered down, and locked into place.

Adam looked around him, noticing that the controls were a simplified form of twentieth century controls, with a flight stick between his knees, a throttle stick by his left hand, and easy-to-read readouts.

He flipped the antigravs on, and the craft hovered several metres off the deck. The landing claws retracted, and he slapped the throttle stick forward.

The fighter-bomber roared out of the hangar into space.

* * *

HMS Alexandria.

Raymond Sansky stood beside Commodore Garrison in the command pulpit. 7-Gamma's commander, Vice-Admiral Vandergrift, had elected not to join the taskforce, having had some trouble with Fleet Admiral Shischko for leading ships in the field, rather than commanding them from Fort Softfire as taskforce commanders were supposed to do. So Garrison had been ordered to command *Alexandria*, and had invited Sansky to the bridge.

"Commodore," an officer cried out. "There's a pirate fighter-bomber on an intercept course with us."

"What is its weapons status?" demanded Garrison.

The officer shook his head, "Their weapons are powered down."

"Could be a trick," pondered the Commodore. "A last ditch effort by Rowlandos to gain some kind of revenge: load up a fighter-bomber full with high-explosives, and detonate the whole thing inside our starfighter hangar, setting off enough secondary explosions to severely damage *Alexandria*."

Sansky was shaking his head now.

"What about the ID broadcast code?" he asked.

The officer in question looked somewhat confused.

"General, the ID code is not the same as any known pirate or Navy ship."

"Identity?"

"The code identifies it as the *Millennium Falcon*."

Sansky barked out a laugh, earning a bemused look from Garrison.

"You're undercover asset?" said Garrison. Sansky nodded, still chuckling.

Then the world suddenly tipped to one side.

* * *

"They're transmitting landing coordinates," reported Hevskii. She was acting as Caine's co-pilot despite having a ten-year-old girl on her lap, fingers flying over the controls around her. Caine was concentrating on weaving the heavy fighter through the debris leading to the massive *Alexandria*.

"Got it," he grunted as he banked to port and slipped around the wing of a pirate battleship. He was sweating again from the effort, struggling with the flight stick, swearing in various languages he had learned on missions every now and then as a piece of debris came close to scraping the fuselage.

The coordinates popped up on the holographic HUD that danced around on the cockpit canopy's front transparent pane.

"What the f-" Hevskii tried to say something else when the cockpit was suddenly filled with a blinding white light. "Holy mother of the gods." The three were temporarily blinded by the light, blinking profusely as they tried to return their vision. The young girl was crying at the abuse, a stark reminder that no matter what her abilities, she was still a little girl the same age as his daughter.

She clung onto Hevskii tight, tears streaming down her cheeks.

Adam's vision returned, though there were retinal afterimages at the edges.

He swore when he saw what had caused the light.

The *Alexandria* was rolling to port, flames pouring out of its side. Another beam of white light scoured down the dreadnaught's keel as it tried to manoeuvre. Her shields were nowhere to be seen, and the beam weapon gouged out a long scar. The massive ship's lights flickered briefly.

He followed the direction of the beam, to its source: the titan.

* * *

Rowlandos was cackling with insane laughter as his titan began the process of tearing the *Alexandria* apart with its massive beam weapons. The engineers had done a grand job in getting the ship going in under an hour, although the engines were still giving them problems.

Rowlandos wasn't going to punish the engineers, threatening them was just a way of motivating them, though the foreman's death was his frustration at the loss of his fleet. But with the titan, he could start afresh, begin a new empire.

"Sir," the former deputy foreman called out. "The beam weapons are overheating."

Rowlandos growled. His threat to kill the engineers might actually have to come true.

Suddenly a torrent of sparks flew from every console, conduit and display on the bridge. Everything went dark.

"The weapons overheated," a helpful voice said in the darkness.

Row sighed.

* * *

Sansky was clinging onto the railings of the command pulpit for dear life. *Alexandria* was still trying to manoeuvre out of the titan's weapons range when the call came for all safe.

"All safe?" he cried.

"Their weapons have overloaded their power systems, sir," an officer shouted as a way of explanation. "They're dead in the water."

"Good," said Garrison. "Destroy it before they can repair it."

The weapons controls were once again alive with activity as the *Alexandria*'s heavy plasma batteries launched a wave of energy at the floundering titan. Explosions rippled along the moon-sized hull, and flames the size of cities spilled into space. Hull plating was vaporised, and electrical discharges played along the debris. The titan was ripped apart at the seams, broken into pieces that fell away from each other slowly.

"Life signs?" asked Garrison.

The sensor operator replied in the negative.

Sansky frowned, "What about the... heh, the *Millennium Falcon*?"

"It just landed, General," replied the starfighter control officer, looking over his large control board. "The co-pilot requested immediate emergency medical assistance for the pilot." When the controller looked up Sansky was gone.

* * *

The cockpit canopy opened, and the three clambered to their feet. Adam put one foot on the edge of the cockpit fuselage, and tumbled to the hangar deck, landing awkwardly on one side. There was a loud crack as his arm snapped, but there was no cry of pain.

The medics appeared with a hover-gurney, rushing to Caine's side.

"He's unconscious!" one of them called out.

There was blood everywhere.

"Somebody stop that fernikking bleed!"

"The extra blood's waiting for us in the Medical Ward!"

Hevskii and the young Star Mystic watched on in barely concealed horror and pain as their saviour was treated by the medics. They poked and prodded his unconscious form, using a cellular regenerator to partially close the wound.

Sansky barrelled into the hangar, demanding to know how he was, though the medics just shouted for him to back off and let them do their work. They took Caine and the gurney to the medical ward, his three friends following silently behind.

They were not allowed to see the surgery. The operation, such as it was, took five hours –a long time indeed for modern medical techniques and technology.

The doctor, tired and weary from the long surgery, strode out of the central medical chamber where the surgery had taken place. There was red blood on his medical scrubs, and he was scrubbing some of it from his arms. There was a resigned look on his face. Clearly he was unused to injuries of this type on the large dreadnaught.

"What's the prognosis, doctor?" demanded Sansky. He too was tired, his face drawn, and his uniform pulled open. His peaked officer's cap was flicking around nervously on the tips of his fingers.

"Well," the doctor began. He looked over to the Star Mystic, wondering if the young girl would steal his thunder and announce the result of the surgery. She was silent, still holding onto Hevskii's arm like it was her saviour. "The surgery was a success," he said with a tired smile. "We got to your friend just in time. We've repaired the wound, stopped the bleeding, and set his arm."

"What's the bad news then?" queried Hevskii.

"Nothing serious," he assured them. "But he'll have to rest up for the next couple of months to give his wounds the chance to fully heal. Plus the pain drugs he took before had damaged some of the muscles in his torso. He will fully mend, but it will take time. Does he have anyone to look after him?"

Hevskii and her young charge smiled knowingly.

"We know someone who'll look after him."

* * *

Adam woke up in muted pain. It stretched across his midsection when he tried to sit up from a lying position. Impossibly, he was in his own bed, in his own bedroom, in his house on Ckeer Najoor. The last he remembered was falling unconscious in the *Alexandria*'s starfighter hangar.

Someone was asleep on the side of his bed.

"Polly?" he said weakly.

She awoke, bleary-eyed, her long raven-black hair a mess.

"Hey you," she smiled.

"How did I get here?"

"General Sansky brought you here on board the *HMS Hyperion* –a frigate I believe. He said your friends the First and the Star Mystic have been taken back safely to their own peoples, if that means anything to you."

He nodded, and regretted the action immediately, his head pounding.

"And what are you doing here?" he asked.

"What do you mean?"

"We, uh, we haven't exactly been on friendly terms on recently," he pointed out. "I didn't figure you for the Florence Nightingale type."

She smiled again, which made his heart flutter. She was beautiful, no matter how bad her hair was, and no matter how bad the pain was. Or was that the pain talking?

"Does it matter? The *Hyperion*'s doctor told me to look after you, and your little daughter practically demanded it of me." She chuckled. "She certainly has grown in the last six months. Like her father, she's become somewhat stubborn."

As if she were listening to the conversation, Evelyn suddenly bound into the room. She had indeed grown up, and out, her figure starting to curve a bit more now that puberty had set in. She was giggling like she was six again, though, and jumped onto the bed to hug her father.

He groaned as she squeezed the more painful parts of him.

"Oops, sorry, Daddy," she chuckled, letting go.

"You've gotten stronger, Evie," he grumbled.

"Nah, you're just getting older, Daddy," she said innocently.

His jaw dropped, and he complained, "You see the abuse I get from my own daughter?"

Polly burst out laughing, "What do you expect from a Caine?"

"These next two months are going to be hell aren't they," he said as the realisation hit him. They both nodded in response.

Polly put a reassuring hand on his shoulder. "Face it, Adam; it's about time we got to look after *you* for a while."

Sixteen:
New Frontiers

Historian's Note: This story is set 18 months after *The First*.

"I never saw a wreck and never have been wrecked nor was I ever in any predicament that threatened to end in disaster of any sort."
-Attributed to Edward John Smith, Captain of the *RMS Titanic.*

Present day.
(July 4005ad)
"What a load of crap."
Adam Caine looked at Polly like she was mad.
"What's a load of crap?"
Polly gestured to the pompous windbag up on the podium. He was a near-human native of Zoltra IV, more overweight than any normal human (or Terran) could physically be, his pinstripe pink suit barely able to contain the sheer mass. Adam had called him Mr. Creosote when he first saw him, though Polly didn't understand the reference. The fat executive was droning on about the great ship behind him.

"All this pomp and etiquette," she said. "When the *Mayflower* was launched, there were a couple of generals and the President, and that was it."

"These guys own a multi trillion-credit company, Polly," Adam explained. "They're allowed to do whatever the hell they want to at the official launching of their own ship. It's all about marketing, same as it ever is with these guys." He was still staring at the city-sized vessel with something akin to dread. In fact, he'd been doing it ever since he had laid eyes on it.

The ship was made up of two giant blue clamshells, the upper shell thicker and longer than the lower hull, both connected by a sandwiched oval that looked like the negative of an Oreo. This was the successor of the *Gold Royale*, a ship that had been home to him and his young daughter for many months before its destruction at the hands of the *HMS Fortitude*.

Cold shivers sparked down his spine.

He hadn't wanted to be here, but Polly had been invited after her identity as being the founder of human lightspeed technology had been discovered a month before. She had been invited to bring one other with her, and she had chosen Adam because of his familiarity with the new ship and the company that owned her. She had claimed that the trip to another galaxy on the *Kara Marazov* would do him some good after two months cooped up on Ckeer Najoor.

His wounds from the massive battle in the Dark Galaxy were healed, though occasionally Polly noticed him having difficulty moving, as his muscles were still occasionally quite stiff.

Polly harrumphed, realising that he was right.

"At least it's got a solid name," she commented innocently.

He looked at her incredulously.

"You didn't study history much before you came to this century, did you?"

She shook her head emphatically. "I always used to nod off to sleep in history class, and after I left school I never bothered to concentrate on the past, rather on the future. My head was always filled with things about engines and-"

"Boys?" Adam finished for her with a wry smile. She slapped him gently on the arm, earning a gentle chuckle from him.

"So what's so important about the name? *Titanic* sounds like a rather good self-explanatory name."

He sent her a withering stare.

"It's the *Titanic*." Her face was completely blank. He kept his voice low so as not to panic anyone nearby. "*Titanic* was a famous cruise liner belonging to a private company called White Star. It was the most expensive, most impressive, most luxurious ship of its time, even reputed to be unsinkable. But in 1912 it struck an iceberg, and sunk into the ice-cold Atlantic, taking almost two thousand people with it."

"Why was it famous?"

"*Infamous* is more the word. White Star lauded the ship as the greatest ever built, and the media kicked up a shitstorm afterwards for the sheer stupidity of the design, and the upper-class mentality that killed so many commoners. My great-great-grandfather and his second wife were aboard when it went down."

Polly blanched at the thought, but tried to turn her concentration back to the speaker on the podium.

The *Titanic* itself was behind the obese speaker, obscuring the view of the gas giant below. The ship was tethered to an orbital docking facility that hung far above the swirling menagerie of the rocky, uninhabited planet designated M-29013AX1 by the Terran Science Council. It had been kept top secret by the company, at least until the *Titanic* was launched and made public.

The speaker wound down his long-winded speech.

"Once again, the company and crew of the *Titanic* thanks you for attending the launch of the ship, and welcomes you all to a free tour of the vessel." He made an elaborate bow, or one he thought was elaborate as his overflowing stomach got in his way.

The large group of visitors -dignitaries from several worlds the ship would visit, celebrities, military officers, business rivals, and even several survivors of the *Gold Royale*- were herded towards the large docking tunnel that led to the ship itself.

When the group was led through into the giant entrance lobby, he was disturbed to find it almost identical to the *Royale*, even down to the golden gilding of the grand staircase. The carpet was a soft peach affair, and there were dozens of exotic plants scattered around the entire lobby.

The rest of the ship wasn't much better, adorned with all sorts of eyesores and unnecessary luxuries. Adam briefly wondered if he had been on the farms of Ckeer Najoor too long, living in the simplistic lifestyle that he had enjoyed for several years now. Not that he was complaining; it was an ideal place to live.

The tour split into four groups, with different kinds of visitors in each group. Adam and Polly were part of the group that were led to the lower section, and the bridge. There the crew were busying around, preparing the ship for launch, with its alien captain stood at the command pulpit, overseeing everything from his position on the central command deck.

He turned to greet the visitors with a smile on its four mouths, showing the big square white herbivore teeth between huge lips. Polly seemed taken aback by the species, but Adam was intensely curious.

The captain, an officer's peaked cap perched on its domed head, and wearing a similarly designed uniform as Brag Franks once had, extended a luminous green tentacle to the nearest of his new visitors.

"Welcome aboard the *Titanic*," he said. The visitor didn't respond immediately, but a look of strong determination passed over the woman's face. Adam knew the look –she was about to get violent. She pulled her free hand out of a bag, and produced a small device.

"NOBODY MOVE!" she screamed. Everyone on the bridge froze. "I'VE PLACED HIGH-YIELD EXPLOSIVES ALL ACROSS THIS SHIP! IF I DON'T GET JUSTICE FOR MY HUSBANDS, I WILL DESTROY THIS SHIP AND EVERYONE ABOARD!" She held the little device –which had a big red button on it- above her head so that it could be clearly seen. Then she pulled out a rather large disruptor pistol and started waving it around. There were screams and cries of fear, and everybody immediately dove for the floor.

Everybody except Adam.

"Adam, get down," hissed Polly, who was lying face down on the cold hard deck.

"Get down," the woman with the detonator growled. Adam could she was desperate –he'd dealt with people like her in Bosnia.

"What do you want justice for?" he asked in a soft voice so as not to aggravate her. "Why do you want justice for your husbands?"

"What does it matter to *you*?" she cried. Then she did a double take. "You!" She pointed the gun at him several times. "You and your friends dragged me off the *Gold Royale*, but didn't save my three husbands. Why didn't you get them as well?"

"We had minutes, maybe even seconds to get off the ship with as many people as possible," Adam replied, his voice calm and collected. He had long since gotten over the guilt of not rescuing as many people from the dying *Gold Royale* a long time ago, and was not about to let this woman bring that back. "There was no time to hang around and search for survivors; those creatures were everywhere, and the ship was falling apart around us. I am truly sorry, but there was nothing more I could have done."

"You lie!"

The gun in her hand was starting to shake as she got more and more angry, and yet Adam, despite his dishevelled, rough appearance, was getting calmer and calmer. Nervous perspiration beaded on her pale forehead, and her eyes were bloodshot. She was close to completely snapping. She was staring intently into his eyes, never noticing that he was inching closer to her.

The gun finally pressed against his chest, and she suddenly realised just how close he had got. It wasn't a good sign –it meant that her sense of reality was warped, and that whatever grief she was feeling had fully taken over.

"Stay back," she warned, her eyes staring at the shaking barrel. "I want the company to reveal the real truth about how the *Gold Royale* was destroyed. Not the garbage they released to the media."

"You know they can't," he said. "The Navy classified it all Top Secret. You signed a confidentiality clause with the company *and* Navy Intelligence, same as me." He started to raise his hand towards the gun, speaking in an even softer voice. It calmed her down, and the shaking hand stopped vibrating. His hand closed on the gun. "You don't need to do it this way. Justice will be served; I promise you."

In truth he didn't care; this woman had been prepared to kill innocents, including someone that meant too much for him to lose. He was only trying to calm her down so that she might not go through with it, and reveal her backup.

Two shifty humans stood up, anger on their faces. They were dressed in identical black clothes, looking more like comical bank robbers than intimidating thugs. They threaded their way through the prone visitors and crew.

They were inexperienced, Adam could tell by the way they walked, and only paid attention to her rather than him. Not only that, but they had come within Adam's reach. He tugged on the energy pistol, and it came free from the woman's hand. He span and slammed the pistol butt into the first thug's face, before twisting the man's swinging punch, and wrenching his shoulder out of its socket in one swift move.

He brought the butt of the pistol down onto the back of the thug's neck, knocking him unconscious. Adam pushed the blacked out man into his compatriot, the other man dodging quickly out of the way of the dead weight... straight into Adam's large fist.

His nose crunched under the impact, and he staggered back. The thug recovered quickly, taking a long right hook at what he thought was Adam's head, but was instead just air. Adam had ducked under the punch. He then raised his forearms up in a Kaysi move, using one hand to grip the thug's punching wrist, and the other to ram an elbow into his carotid artery, briefly pinching the nerve, and rendering him unconscious as well.

The woman suddenly seemed intensely grateful that she hadn't opted for the violent way, and dropped the detonator. Adam watched it tumble from her hand with wide eyes. It span continuously, end over end, until it hit the deck right on the detonate button. There was a beep as the button depressed.

Roars of explosions reverberated through the hull.

The entire ship lurched badly, sending Adam and the woman to the deck.

The entire world vibrated.

Screams rent the air.

Sparks flowed from everywhere around them. Bulkheads buckled, girders and metal beams fell from the ceiling. Holographic displays flickered, and consoles exploded from the intense feedback.

* * *

The crew of the orbital facility watched in horror as the *Titanic* spewed plasma and flames into space, as it started drifting away from the facility. The station commander shouted down the comm for all ships to begin immediate rescue operations. The ship was caught in the grim planet's gravitic pull.

The rescue ships were too late.

* * *

The alien captain of the *Titanic* was gibbering in utter fear, hugging its knees to its rubbery chest, all four mouths sobbing. He had been fine until someone had announced that all escape craft had been destroyed, and all shuttles had been sucked out of the shuttlebay when it depressurised extremely violently.

"Great," Adam muttered. The bridge was a mess —beams and girders had crushed or sliced apart most of the bridge crew, along with several a-list celebrities. Adam and Polly had been lucky to get survive without a scratch, although the woman terrorist hadn't been.

Adam stepped over the red wet stain that had been the woman with the detonator, and charged down the battered steps to the lower command deck. The massive bubble forward viewport was untouched by the damage.

Thank god for small favours, he thought. Polly and several others were right behind him as he bound up to the large helm pulpit. The helmswoman was dead, her arm crushed by a collapsed bulkhead, and her most of her face burnt beyond recognition by a flamed out secondary console. He threw the bulkhead off her, and dragged her body out of the pulpit, placing it on the deck as respectfully as possible.

"Polly, get one of the remaining crew over here," he said, jumping into the high-backed chair in the helm pit. He surveyed the controls, and thanked every god under and above the sun that they were generic controls. Polly appeared with a senior steward who had apparently been serving the bridge crew with refreshments, most of which had splashed on his pristine white uniform.

"You, what's your name?"

"Uh, Karrrigann, sir," the old human replied.

"Karrrigann, get on that console." Adam pointed to the shield monitoring station. "Tell me what kind of shielding we have, and give me a damage report."

The steward was a little confused that a civilian was ordering him around, but Adam gave him a withering stare that brooked no doubts. He nodded and jumped back down to the appropriate station.

"Shields are gone, sir, and the navigational deflector is fluctuating badly. Hull plating is compromised, and we've got hull breaches on twenty decks. Sublight engines are down as well."

Adam swore rather colourfully.

He activated the manoeuvring thrusters, checking the thruster status display. "Crap, the thrusters aren't strong enough to fight against the planet's gravity." The control sticks started to wobble badly as the ship began to scrape against the upper atmosphere. He turned to Karrrigann, "Open communications on all available channels." The deck shook again, this time more violent. "Keep telling the orbital facility our status."

He turned to Polly. "Find some way to strap in or secure yourself, Polly."

"Can you really fly this thing?"

He shook his head. "This ship isn't flying, it's falling. I can control it at least a little." When Polly moved to the second chair in the pulpit behind him, he tapped the intercom. "All hands, this is Captain Caine. Stay away from all main power conduits and anything liable to explode. The pressure and heat from entering the atmosphere will badly damage the ship, so stay as close to the centre of the ship as you can."

Here we go, thought Polly.

* * *

Flashback 1

Calhoun County, Iowa.

1994ad.

"Here we go, Polly."

Her mother held her as she climbed up onto the wooden fence. The fenced pen contained forty head of cattle, the pride of Polly's dad's ranch. Dust kicked up by the cows' hooves filled her nostrils, and threatened to blind her if she wasn't careful.

Daddy was on the other side of the pen, a red handkerchief around his mouth and nose, and black sunglasses protecting his eyes. To Polly's young eyes, he looked like he was about to rob the railroad express that passed through the nearby town every day.

Daddy was checking the cattle for any injuries before the buyers turned up.

She waved at him, and he waved back enthusiastically.

"Love you, Daddy!" she shouted over the mooing and stamping.

"Love you too, sweetheart!" he shouted back.

He was still waving when the fence suddenly collapsed, and her daddy disappeared between the cows. She screamed and screamed, and her mother had to pull her off the fence before she could jump in to save him.

Tears streamed down her face, the dust drying them in seconds.

She slipped out of her mother's grip, and charged round the outside of the pen to the gap that had appeared in the fence. The cows, seeing the broken fence, all stampeded out, smashing the fence to pieces, and running into their dry field. Her brother dragged her away from them until they were gone whereupon she darted into the pen.

On the dusty floor, bloody and battered, lay her father.

She shook him, and screamed for him to wake up, not entirely understanding the concept of death.

"Daddy, wake up! Wake up!"

She barely felt her mother grab her once again.

"Come away from him, Polly!" she shouted, tears streaming down her own cheeks. "Polly, please! Polly!"

* * *

Present day.

"Polly!"

She snapped out of her disturbed reverie at the sound of Adam's voice.

"Polly, are you with me?"

She gave him a forced smile. "Always." But he smiled as well, filling her with unexpected warmth.

"I need you to keep an eye on the sensors, if you can," he said, pointing to a particular part of the console to her right. "Tell me what kind of planet we're about to hit."

She scanned the sensor readouts, though her familiarity was nowhere near as accomplished as Adam's always seemed to be. It scared her sometimes at just how much he knew about this century, even if he had been here longer than her. She knew it had something to do with his specialised training both during his time with the SBS and his time on a mystery planet he had nicknamed Lympstone.

"If I'm reading this right, the atmosphere's mostly made up of methane and nitrogen."

"Great," he muttered again. "So we could end up igniting the entire planet's atmosphere when we make re-entry. And here I was not wanting to destroy a planet this week."

"Maybe next week," Polly said flippantly. Her voice sounded strained, obviously somewhat scared by the prospect of crashing into the surface of a planet. He desperately wanted to turn round and hold her until everything was all right. But everything wasn't all right, and they had to land the ship as safely as possible to get out alive.

"Set the inertial dampeners to full," he called to Karrrigann. "Pump as much power as you can into them and the structural integrity field."

"I'll try, sir, but there isn't much left." He too was strapped into his console's chair, bouncing up and down as the ship shook, holding on for dear life. He looked pale, at least to Adam's eyes, though there were a few debris-strewn metres between them.

He's a steward for god's sake, Adam, he thought, chastising himself, *you're the only one with military training and crisis management experience. You can't expect everyone to behave the same as you.*

"Just do what you can, Karrrigann," he said as reassuringly as possible. The steward seemed to be reassured for a short time, but Adam knew it wouldn't last. "Nine seconds to atmosphere proper," he announced over the intercom. The ship started to rattle badly as it neared.

Adam suddenly had an insane idea.

He flicked a few controls.

"What are you doing, Adam?" asked Polly, even as the ship began a slow roll. "If we don't get a decent re-entry vector, we'll burn up before we hit the ground."

"We need as much metal between us and the atmosphere, so I'm rolling us to have the stronger upper hull take the brunt of the damage."

"We're not going to make it," she complained.

Adam was about to say something, the horizon still diagonal in the massive forward windows, when he was suddenly slammed forwards painfully into his restraints. The alien leather straps strained under his muscled bulk, and cut into his chest. Metal screeched, and there was a roaring sound as the planet's atmosphere rushed past the hull.

Alarms shrilled and red warning lights flashed on every working console.

The ship was going in.

* * *

Still watching helplessly, the orbital facility crew saw the *Titanic* plummet. Shockingly, it suddenly started rolling onto its back, though nobody seemed to know why it was doing that. The commander of the station, stood rigidly in the operations centre, watching the holographic footage on the main holo-table.

The ship hit the atmosphere badly, still in the midst of its roll. It jerked as it slammed nose first into the upper atmospheric layer. Parts of it, including what looked to be the sublight engine nacelles, were torn off, leaving a trail of fire and debris behind the ship.

"Life signs?" he asked.

The sensor officer tapped controls on his console, frowned, and then re-checked his readouts. The frown continued as he triple-checked his readings.

"Sir, I can't get a reading from anything down there. The ship's impact with the thermosphere somehow ionised the planet. It's temporary. But for now, I can't even determine that the ship is even there."

The commander growled in frustration.

* * *

481

Gas jetted out of a fractured conduit, and a fountain of sparks sprayed over Karrrigann. He yelped, covering his face with his arms as the little specks of heat burned his skin, and singed his uniform.

Consoles exploded along the back of the command deck, killing several of the surviving visitors. Polly didn't want to look at what was left.

"Hull breaches on all decks of the upper hull!" she shouted over the roar of the noise. "Conduits to the upper hull are losing containment. If they're not stabilised, they'll blow out, and we could lose a third of the ship."

"We don't have time," Adam shouted back.

He pushed the ship further into the atmosphere. Red blips began appearing around the graphic representation of the ship. They were major damage sections. The deck buckled badly around the humans, breaking in places like a Californian earthquake. More gas poured from broken tubes.

A fire broke out briefly in the lowest deck of the bridge, encompassing a pair of crewmen attempting repairs.

Without shields, the ship's outer hull was stripped free, despite its strength.

"We're descending through the mesosphere," Adam called out. His teeth were rattling, and he felt like he was being slowly shaken to death. More red blips appeared on his main display, this time indicating several thruster modules.

Damn, that's going to be a problem.

He siphoned power from the damaged ones to the remaining modules. It wasn't a great compromise, but enough to make some kind of difference. The ship was picking up speed as it went further into the gravity well.

Fire filled the viewports, forcing Adam to rely on the instruments alone.

Polly was screaming.

"Passing into the stratosphere," shouted Adam, fingers flying over the helm. The fire abated almost instantly from the viewports, though they were blackened by smoke from the fires.

He wished he couldn't see.

There was a mountain range ahead, looming through the clouds, upside down as Adam saw it. Several peaks spiked out higher than the rest. Adam swore as he realised the ship was headed through the range instead of above it. He activated the thrusters, ponderously rolling the ship one hundred and eighty degrees to the right way up.

His eyes widened as he projected the course the ship was taking.

He removed his restraints, and jumped out of the chair, perilously ignoring the shaking of the ship around him. He slapped the restraints on Polly's chair as well.

"EVERYONE OFF THE BRIDGE RIGHT NOW!" he bellowed. Behind him, the mountains got larger, and one in particular became ever so clearer through the windows. Karrrigann and the other survivors saw what he was looking at, and bolted to the nearest doors, leaving Adam to struggle with Polly's restraints. In the end, he simply found a jagged piece of debris, and sawed through the restraints.

She was confused, even as the proximity alarms shouted for attention.

He grabbed her, pulled her out of the chair, and picked her up in his big arms. She clung onto him with all her strength, and finally got a good look at the mountain tip speeding directly towards the bridge.

Adam charged at the closest door, diving through at the last second, and slapping the door controls. But he continued to run, Polly in his arms, pounding down the deck, a screaming noise chasing them. She couldn't tell if it was her screaming, or the metal behind them.

And then the world went black.

* * *

Flashback 2

Calhoun County, Iowa.
2000ad.

A young girl of fourteen sat on one of the picnic tables strewn around the courtyard, her head buried in a book on theoretical mechanics –a somewhat complicated reading for someone so young. She was engrossed, despite having already read it several times before. So engrossed was she, in fact, that she didn't notice the boy hovering nearby, fiddling with the hem of his crimson school football jacket.

"Uh, hi," the boy said nervously.

The girl yelped loudly, dropping the book.

She turned to see who had made her jump out of her skin, and butterflies suddenly filled her stomach. She found she couldn't say much of anything, her mouth refusing to work. Her cheeks flushed red, and her started to shake. She slipped it into her pocket, embarrassed beyond reason.

"I, uh, I was wondering," the boy stammered. "That is, I was wondering if anybody had asked you to the dance on Friday."

"N-no," she replied, stammering just as much, "nobody's asked me yet."

The boy seemed to be relieved, the colour returning to normal in his face.

"Well then, would you go with me? I mean, you don't have to, but I'd really like you to. And I really like you."

"I'd love to go with you, Gary."

"Wicked," said young Gary, a big smile on his handsome face. He leaned down and impulsively kissed her on the lips. The kiss lingered for a long time, longer than she thought possible.

My first real kiss, she thought, heat flashing through her. He stroked her cheek with one hand, and then their lips parted. Both were grinning like idiots, cheeks crimson. Everybody around them was staring at them, some disgusted that two geeks were kissing in public, some laughing joyfully, others simply agape at the public display of affection.

"Are you doing anything for the rest of lunch?"

She shook her head.

Nervously, he sat down next to her on the bench, and wrapped an arm around her shoulders.

"So," he said with a smile, "what are you reading?"

* * *

Flashback 3

Angel Islington.

2005ad.

Polly and Gary, newlyweds, walked hand-in-hand into the VUE cinema lobby. They were here to see the new Batman movie whilst they were on their honeymoon —Gary had been raving about it since seeing the trailers. The holiday had been spectacular so far, a whirlwind of museums, sightseeing, and long fantastic nights in bed. Today, they had decided to have a lazy day: shopping, and then the cinema.

In a month's time, they were both off to college, but in different states. So they had got married, they were both eighteen after all, and taken a month-long honeymoon/holiday in England.

They bought their tickets, and walked into the long wide thoroughfare that led to each cinema screen. Gary kissed her on the cheek, and disappeared into the men's toilets, still juggling the large coke in one hand. She chuckled.

She jumped when someone tapped her on the shoulder.

When she turned, she was surprised to find a large man standing there, holding her phone. In the excitement of explaining their marriage to the ticket vendor, she must have dropped it. He was wearing a blue polo shirt with the VUE company logo on the left breast, and a nametag under the badge.

A D A M were the letters printed on the tag, though the polo shirt seemed too small for him, stretched over large muscles, scars evident on his exposed forearms. His sandy-brown hair was just starting to grow out from an obvious military cut, and he seemed ill at ease in his freshly pressed new uniform, still fidgeting occasionally.

"You dropped this, ma'am," he said sheepishly, holding her phone out. He said it in a very military way as well, as if addressing a female superior officer, just as her daddy had when she was little.

"Uh, thankyou, mister...?"

"Warrant Off-" he caught himself; she presumed he was about to give her his rank. Instead, he pointed to the nametag. "My name's Adam, ma'am."

"Adam. Thankyou again for returning my phone. I'd lose my head if it weren't attached to my body." She dropped the phone into one of her shopping bags and smiled. He returned the gesture, and strode away without another word.

She was shaking her head when Gary re-appeared.

"What's wrong, babe?"

"Dunno," she frowned. "Something off about that man." She shook the thought off, and slipped her arm under Gary's, fiddling with a lock of her short jet-black hair.

"Hey, what were you saying this morning about this new project of yours?"

"The FTL drive?"

He nodded.

"Well," she said, leaning towards him conspiratorially, "It starts off with the ILY matrix."

He frowned. "ILY?"

She grinned, and kissed him on the cheek.

"I Love You."

* * *

Present day.

A banging sound woke Polly up from her unconscious trip down memory lane. Why had she been dreaming about that cinema? She hadn't thought about Gary for a long time, but it wasn't her ex-husband that stuck in her mind. It had been the usher that returned her phone.

"My god," she coughed, her voice hoarse from the screaming. "We knew each other."

Adam, startled by the sudden noise, span sharply, having been tapping on a piece of bulkhead. They were in a dark corridor, the lights barely illuminating them. It was claustrophobic, to say the least; one end of the corridor was sealed off by a wall of twisted and burnt metal, whilst the other had a door that would barely budge. She had woken up on her side, Adam having put her in that position.

"You're awake," he said. Worry was etched into his face. "God, I was worried you weren't going to wake up."

A frown scrunched her forehead.

"How long have I been out?"

"About an hour." He crouched down next to her, and checked her over. "You should be alright: only a couple of bruises and scratches from flying debris. Though you may want to change your underwear at the earliest opportunity."

Panicking, she looked down, but felt nothing, nor saw anything. When she looked up, Adam had a teasing smirk on his lips.

"Made you look."

She knew it was his daft attempt at cheering her up, and she even felt a smile try to tug at the corners of her mouth, but she shook it off. It was wholly inappropriate given the circumstances.

"That's not funny," she growled.

He looked like he had been slapped hard in the face, and recoiled from her, standing up. He offered her a hand to pull her to her feet, but she batted it away, and struggled to stand. She coughed again, this time slightly longer.

"I'm sorry, I was just trying to-"

"I know what you were trying to do," she interrupted, "but it's not appropriate for this situation." She scowled at him, though how she thought that would intimidate someone like him was beyond her. She brushed his hands away when she stumbled slightly; her legs were still weak from whatever had happened to them –she was still drawing a blank as to what exactly had happened after they escaped the bridge into the corridor.

She looked around, realising that this was a very different corridor.

He saw what she was looking at.

"We're about a hundred metres aft of the bridge."

"What the hell happened?"

Adam was looking around, avoiding eye contact with her all of a sudden.

"The lower hull hit a spire of that mountain range. The impact smashed the forward sections in, though if it hadn't been for the tough hull, we would never have made it alive. And then, of course, we crashed, though I don't know what condition the rest of the ship is in. Can't imagine there's much left after the hits we took." There were scratches and bruises all over his arms where his cotton-equivalent shirt had been torn, and was that blood on the right side of his back?

"Thanks for cheering me up," she sneered. There was cold sweat running down her back, and she tried to avoid the dark look that clouded his face. It wasn't a look she wanted to see.

"I'll try to curb my enthusiasm from now on," he growled. He was still ignoring the wound on his back, the one that he had spent two months lying in bed trying to heal. He kept scanning the corridor with his eyes, all the while noticing Polly's own eyes trying not to imagine the walls closing in on her.

"We need to get to a console," he added, all business again. "Find a way out of this ship, and off this rock. The internal sensors are at the heart of the ship so they won't necessarily be harmed."

"How do you know all this?" she cried.

He shrugged. "I just do."

"That doesn't scare you?"

He gave her an amused grunt. "In this universe I've seen and experienced far worse, and I'll take any knowledge or luck I can get." There was a humourless smile on his lips, accentuated by his shaggy hair tied back. "Guess it's the enlisted man in me, but I never turn down a spot of good luck."

He pointed to the dim lights on the ceiling and floor that gave the corridor an even eerier feel. "Emergency lighting is on, so there must be some kind of emergency systems going." He started feeling around the door that lay between them and the rest of the ship. The door's emergency power supply was gone, crushed by an errant piece of debris.

He managed to dig his fingers into the small line between the two doors, and pulled on each door. They shifted a little, but nothing more happened. Sparks flew from the door's hydraulics, and the doors slammed shut, Adam barely getting his fingers out in time. It snapped shut with a bang.

"Shit," he swore. He backed up a pace or two, and then slammed the sole of his foot into the door, as if kicking it would open it up by magic.

The doors slid open with a strained hiss.

Polly was agape.

Adam just grunted, "See what I mean?"

The corridor beyond wasn't much better than the previous one, buckled and distorted. The lights were as dim as before, although this one was far longer, and littered with several dead bodies.

Two wore the uniforms of the ship's crew, whilst the third and fourth were civilians, their faces a rictus of surprise and sudden pain. Polly didn't look, just stared straight ahead at Adam's back as they picked their way through. Each had a large bloody hole through their chest, and a long piece of metal was embedded in the doorframe, blood all over it where it had passed through all four in quick succession.

They made it to the other end of the corridor that turned left onto a t-junction, following it right until they came across a fizzing and static-filled console screen. It had been knocked out of its mounting, hanging from its own wiring.

He grabbed it, and gave a sigh of relief.

"Passenger computer interface is the same as the *Gold Royale*. Good it means I can..." he didn't finish the sentence, so intent was he on cracking through the ship's computer. He kept making stupid little noises as he worked his way through the system. "Ah ha!" he cried, making Polly jump out of her skin. "Sorry," he added, without entirely meaning it.

"This ship," he reported, "is fucked."

She gave him her best withering stare.

"The engine room's completely gone, most of its lying about five miles behind the ship. Engines are gone completely, no thrusters, nothing. Which means we have to find a way off this ship as well as the planet." He looked around the corridor, ascertaining where they were by checking a map on the small screen in his hands.

"We're not far from the crew's secondary shuttlebay." He dropped the screen, letting it hang there again, and strode in the direction they had originally been moving.

Polly struggled to keep up, her legs far shorter than his, and less muscled.

"What about life-signs?" she asked.

"Some," the reply came. "Intermittent at best, although there was a large concentration of bio-readings down in the main lobby. I think they're visitors trying to get out."

"But this planet has a methane-rich atmosphere. The minute they open the outer doors they'll die, and any spark could burn out the inside of this ship."

"Yeah, but there's nothing we can do about that. I'm not going to feel guilty about this ship going down, or anyone else who dies on it. Got enough of that crap to last a lifetime already."

After five minutes of seeming random wondering, they came to a pair of thick generic doors, marked with alien lettering that Polly didn't understand at all, but which Adam did. He forced the doors open through sheer strength of willpower and muscle.

"Fuck me," he growled when the doors opened.

There wasn't much left of the secondary shuttlebay. It was burned and charred almost beyond recognition. There was a pile of shuttles and pieces of shuttles in one corner, where the force of the ship stopping had thrown them forwards.

Flames were roiling from a ruptured fuel line, spreading across the shuttlebay like waves in a falling tide. There was nothing left that even resembled a useful vehicle.

She was in total agreement with Adam.

"Fuck me."

* * *

Flashback 4

2012ad.

Houston, Texas.

The stars shined with not a cloud in the sky. The sun had fallen behind the horizon six hours ago, and now Dr. Polly Jenkins was stood staring up at the monolithic structure that towered above her into the night sky. Floodlights were beamed onto the sides of the vehicle inside the structure's gangways and permanent scaffolding.

The vehicle itself was lit up like the statues in Houston's city centre, its ghost-white hull lined with black heat shielding. Its long delta-wing shape was dwarfed by the terracotta-tinted main fuel tank, which itself was saddled by two thin grey rockets.

Freedom was written in big black letters above a standard depiction of the Stars and Stripes. *Freedom*'s cargo hold was closed now, but it had been open the day before to receive the experimental Faster Than Light Drive, that Polly herself had designed. This would be the first official test of the device outside of her lab at the Kennedy Space Center. The whole world was watching this test.

The space shuttle *Constellation* would be taking her and a team up to the ISS in two days time to monitor the trial from orbit, with the *Freedom* following twelve hours later.

Constellation was currently parked in the distance, on its launch pad, its nose pointed to the sky. *Freedom*, however, was still moving, the skyscraper-sized tracked carrier slowly making its way to the second launch pad.

She was stood beside it, just staring up at the *Freedom*.

"Penny for your thoughts?"

She smiled as the tall naval officer stepped up beside her.

"The same as always Admiral," she smiled.

Lonnie DaSilva, the main proponent for getting her FTL Drive into action, had recently been promoted to Rear Admiral and immediately been pushing NASA to accept any and all technology from outside their own sphere of influence. Polly Jenkins' FTL Drive had been that technology. Six months of official testing in laboratories, and he had practically demanded that a live test be made in space with one of the new generation of shuttles.

"You're worried about the tests?"

"I'm not a military or NASA scientist. Even if these trials go right, I won't be involved in the process afterwards."

"If these trials go right, kid, there'll be a fleet of starships with our names on them within a couple of months." She smiled at his calling her 'kid', something he had not yet got out of the habit despite her insistence on being called anything but 'kid'. "I guarantee it. Besides, if they try to leave you out, they'll have to go through me first."

They both chuckled.

Comfortable silence permeated between them, watching the *Freedom* being moved until DaSilva spoke up.

"How's your husband taking all this anyway?" he asked.

She couldn't but snort, "Gary isn't taking it very well. What with my late nights, and then my twenty-four hour sterile period before takeoff, he's getting frustrated. I can't say I blame him; I miss him, but this work is so important to this country, to this planet."

"You wish he understood."

She nodded, plunging her hands into the pockets of her blue overalls.

"I wish he was more like your wife."

"I'm a twenty-nine-year Navy veteran, she hasn't had much choice," he joked, and then turned to her, putting his long arm around her shoulders, drawing her into a fatherly hug. "All we can do, my friend, is hope for the best. Life will find a way of sorting things out; you'll see."

* * *

Present day.

"So what do we do now?" cried Polly, staring accusingly at Adam. He was sat up against the wall opposite the shuttlebay entrance, staring into the fires of the dead auxiliary craft.

He blew out a frustrated breath.

"I have no idea. The shuttles were pretty much Plans A, B, and C."

"Well that's just fucking brilliant, isn't it?" she shouted, her voice gaining pitch with every other word. Adam could tell she was venting some fear, presumably claustrophobia, given the confines of this hellhole. "We're stuck on this fucking planet, in this fucking ship, and you, the master covert ops soldier, have no clue as to how we get out of here?!" She stopped pacing, and shouted straight at him, her finger waggling like some parent punishing a child. "Why the fuck not?!"

Adam was somewhat taken aback, not just that she was laying all this on his door, but that she was swearing at all. Foul words never left her tiny mouth, at least not in Adam's presence. It was a shock to hear her swear so vehemently, and so angrily.

"I just don't, alright?" he replied. He rested his head back on the wall, still staring at the burning shuttlebay.

She harrumphed, and plonked herself down next to him.

"Why do you never talk about your past, Adam?"

He frowned at the change of subject though went along with it.

"I do so talk about it."

"No, you don't; only what you've experienced here in this century."

He sighed, knowing that she wouldn't let up. "Before I was kidnapped from our century, my life was pretty shit. My father was a billionaire who believed I should have followed in his footsteps, become one of the aristocracy, and lived the life of a poncy lord, looking down my nose at everyone. My oldest sisters were pretty much of the same mind." Adam smiled, remembering something. "I am technically the seventeenth earl of Cambridge. My father was in such a fit of rage when I told him I was enlisting in the Royal Marines as a common grunt."

"What about your mother?"

"The same as any mother when their only son joins the armed forces: worried beyond belief, and proud as hell. She tried to get my father to pull strings and get me a plum assignment after I was tortured in Afghanistan."

She frowned. "Why didn't you?"

"There's no such thing as a plum assignment in the Royal Marines."

She chuckled, "That's what Colour Sergeant Graham always used to tell me."

Adam's head suddenly snapped round to look at her. "You knew Graham? He was a *Colour* Sergeant?" There was a smile on his lips. "Kept telling him to take a promotion."

"So he could become a Warrant Officer like you?"

He shook his head a bit too enthusiastically.

"The Warrant Officer rank was only honorary. I was a Staff Sergeant; the honorary rank was for when I ever needed to commandeer troops or equipment without being an officer."

It was her turn to frown.

"Why not just become an officer?"

Adam snorted with laughter at the thought.

"Because that's what my father wanted; he wanted me to become a proper officer, serving in some office somewhere going to posh dances and balls, not dirtying myself with violence and actually defending the country." He shook his head. "I wanted to *earn* my career, not buy it. My father could never see the point of me working for money when he already had millions."

"So why have you never talked about this before?"

He gave her a sad knowing look as she sat down beside him.

"Because that's not my life anymore. My life is here, in this century, on Ckeer Najoor, with Eve... and with you."

She looked at him sharply, and he was smiling nervously.

"I...I'm not very good at this sort of thing," he stammered, a bizarre reminder of her first few moments with her ex, Gary, a nasty comparison by any standard. "I love you."

She'd been expecting it, but still felt some shock.

She didn't say anything more, instead leaping onto his lap and pressing her lips to his hungrily. He relented, wrapping his arms around her torso, and pulling her closer, returning the kiss just as passionately. They remained lip-locked for several minutes before coming up for air.

"It's about time," she said, a tear glistening in her eye. "I've been waiting for you to do that for months and months."

He was speechless, staring contentedly into her beautiful eyes. He snapped out of it, confusion on his unshaven face. "What do you mean?"

"Adam, I have loved you for so long. I'm so sorry for treating you the way I have; I was scared that you wouldn't reciprocate." And then the tears flooded out. "I was so scared you wouldn't love me." He wrapped her in his arms, and held her tightly. "I didn't want to get hurt again." She sobbed for a few long moments, nestling her head in the curve of his neck.

When she looked up, he was smiling.

"I think it's fair to say that I've been in love with you since I first met you on the ISS." He stroked her porcelain cheek until her tears dried up, and she was calm. He whispered in her ear, "I love you, Polly, and I'll never leave you. Never."

* * *

Flashback 5

2012ad.

Houston, Texas.

Having deposited her kit bag in the kitchen, she looked around for a sign that Gary was here. The lights were on, and she could smell recent cooking. Traffic had been light through Houston's city centre, and she had made good time from the mission debrief at Cape Canaveral.

The entire journey had been filled with excitement for the brilliant outcome of the FTL tests conducted on *Freedom* and the ISS. *Constellation* had brought her and her science team down to Kennedy two weeks ago, after *three* weeks in space.

But the excitement and exhilaration of the tests was mixed with the bizarre sighting of the man on the ISS. His face was familiar, but his sudden appearance, and his even stranger bright light-filled exit, had her curiosity stretched to the limit. All she had dug up on him –using his likeness- was a newspaper article on the missing son of some obscure British aristocrat. The name had meant nothing to her, but the face was still familiar, and even her insanely high military clearance was not enough to dig up information on him.

Her arms were still sore where the medical staff had run tests on her to determine if she was hallucinating. Since the rest of the ISS crew and science team had seen the man as well, the tests had taken the majority of two weeks.

Now she just wanted to fall asleep in her bed next to Gary.

If he was here.

The dishes had been left dirty on the table, and there were two plates, both with food eaten and discarded remains. Two long candles were still smoking in the centre of the table, the lights in the dining room dimmed to a soft level. Had he put together a dinner for her, but gotten impatient and ate without her? No, there were two sets of used cutlery and crockery. She felt nauseous when she saw smudged pink lipstick on the rim of one of the glasses.

I'm gonna be sick, she thought, *and then I'm going to kill him.*

She made it to the sink before her stomach tightened suddenly, and she vomited up a day's worth of digested food. She held her head over the sink for several long minutes in which she dry-retched three times before reaching for a glass of water, and swishing the vomit taste out of her mouth.

Unsteadily, she left the glass next to the sink, and stumbled to the stairs. The soft-carpeted staircase was littered with items of clothing hastily thrown there in the throws of passion.

She avoided the clothes like they were the plague, stepping over them. She could hear giggling, and the odd bump or two. She stopped midway up the stairs, the nausea returning. She fought it off, and continued to the landing, passing the photos of her with her father.

She gently pushed open the bedroom door, and whimpered.

Gary was there on the bed, with his secretary, Belinda, in mid-coitus.

"Oh my god," she whispered, covering her mouth with one hand.

Gary suddenly whipped round, guilt and surprise on his face. The young girl underneath him squealed with delight, unaware that his wife was stood there. When she did, she squealed again, this time shocked to find her there.

"Mrs. Jenkins, I am so sorry," she cried, pulling the bed sheets over her naked body. "I-" The young girl looked from her lover to the scorned slightly older woman, neither of which was paying attention to her. She ran from the room, and barged past Polly, who was too tired to stop her.

"Polly," he started to say.

But she screamed at him, "DON'T EVEN TRY TO TELL ME HOW SORRY YOU ARE! DON'T EVEN TRY TO CONVINCE ME IT WS AN ACCIDENT, OR THAT IT WASN'T YOUR FAULT!" She yanked the wedding ring off her finger, and threw it at him, her voice hoarse. "GET OUT! JUST GET OUT! I NEVER WANT TO SEE YOU AGAIN!"

He bolted out of the door, a stricken look on his face.

She collapsed in sobs and tears.

* * *

Present day.

"To hell with this."

Adam pulled Polly off his lap, and put her down on the floor. She had a stunned look on her face as if she had been slapped in the face. He jumped to his feet in one incredibly swift move, and then pulled Polly to her feet effortlessly.

"What do you mean, 'to hell with this'?" she said, a little testy. He leaned over and kissed her on the cheek.

"I mean, I am *not* going to sit here and wait to die. There *has* to be another way off this ship; especially not after what just happened between us. We are *both* getting out of this place, if I have to get out and push this damn ship into orbit."

The anger gone, she gave him a wry smile.

"I'd rather you didn't go out into that atmosphere," she said, a hungry smile on her lips and in her eyes, grabbing a handful of the front of his shirt. "I want you in one piece."

"Yes, ma'am," he smiled in return.

He slipped his hand in hers, and they walked down the corridor, she following his lead. She pointed to the small control panel that was strapped to his wrist like a watch.

"Can't you activate the remote for the *Kara*?" she asked. The *Kara Marazov* was currently docked at the orbital facility along with all the other VIP ships. Although he knew it wouldn't work, he tapped the recall control anyway.

"We're too far out of range," he said, shaking his head. He let out a groan, "Why didn't I think of that before?" He slapped his forehead with the palm of his hand several times, chastising himself for not thinking of it before.

"What? What didn't you think of before?"

He was looking around for something.

"I think I can patch the recall device into the ship's comm system, the only problem is I don't have the technical expertise." He was looking at her expectantly.

She shrugged.

"I can give it a go, but I don't have as much experience as you do with alien technology. So far, I've only helped repair the machines back home on Ckeer Najoor, and they were mechanical backhoes and pumps, not advanced computer systems."

"Then we'll both give it a go," he said. "We have to try." Taking her hand, he led her down yet another corridor, away from the shuttlebay, but away in a new direction. "We need to find some kind of hardwire access to the ship's comms system. There should be an engineering station up here somewhere. I hope."

"How can you be so confident?" she asked.

He smiled, "I'm a master covert ops soldier, remember?"

As they strode down the corridors, her little legs strained to keep up with Adam's loping steps. Her muscles began to ache from the effort, unused to it after two months of sitting by Adam's bedside.

They passed through a twisted and buckled corridor that had been blackened by a ruptured power conduit. Adam swore when he saw what he was looking for: a sparking computer terminal, the screen of which flickered constantly, and only showed an emergency message in bold red characters. It wasn't what they were hoping for.

Of course, neither was the rumbling noise coming from behind them.

"What the hell was that?" she whispered, as if the noise might hear her.

"Sounds like an energy overload somewhere behind us," replied Adam, who was staring in the direction of the rumble. He leaned around the corner to look down the previous passageway and suddenly leaned back to look at Polly, eyes wide with shock.

"Run," he said.

Heat blasted across them as the air in the corridor was suddenly heated up. Adam grabbed her, and rather than letting her run, he scooped her up in his powerful arms, and slung her over his shoulder. She screamed for him to put her down, but he just ran, pounding down the deck. She stopped complaining when a wave of flame suddenly engulfed the console they had previously been using.

It roared and screamed like an animal as it curled towards them, her jiggling up and down on his shoulder. It sped closer and closer, the flames barrelling towards them in their mad dash for survival.

The flames got so close that she could feel the wash singe her newly grown-out raven-coloured hair.

He shouted through the roaring of the flames, though she could only make out, "Hold on tight." She could almost hear her nervous heart beating over the sounds of the rolling fire, although it was beating so hard in her chest that it felt as though it was going to explode.

Then they were suddenly flying through the air, passing through a doorway that closed behind them with a grunt of effort from a pair of throats that were nonhuman. A spurt of flame jetted several inches from between the two doors before disappearing as the two armoured doors shut the flames out just barely in the nick of time.

Adam and Polly were on the floor, his big arm still wrapped protectively around her midsection, and they looked up to find two of the uniformed crew standing over them.

"Thanks," coughed Adam, reluctantly relinquishing his grip on Polly. She felt her heart flutter at his almost unnoticed gesture.

"You must be Captain Caine," one of the alien crewmen grunted. He was a walrus-like native of Fayde, blubbery cheeks and whiskers all, although much trimmer than Adam had described them as a race. The other was a feline that naturally walked on all fours as opposed to the humanoid Caitians in the Yarr Halo, although it seemed as though the alien feline could choose to walk on two legs as well.

The Fayde crewmen held out a flipper-hand and levered Adam to his feet, who automatically dragged Polly to hers.

"What's the situation?" he asked of the crewmen.

"We've found several civilians, Captain," the feline answered, gesturing with a dirty-blonde paw away from the steaming door behind them. "So far, we haven't found any more of the crew, though what's left of the computer claims there are more roaming the rest of the habitable sections of the ship. But the readings flickered too badly to get an accurate head count."

"I'm not sure we can trust the computer entirely," suggested Polly, her heart rate slowly returning to normal, though she was aware that her face was still white as a sheet at the near miss. She felt Adam's hand slip into hers, reassuring her even more when his thumb started idly stroking the back of her hand.

"I need to get to the ship's communications arrays," Adam said with some authority. "If I can tap the recall device in this," he explained, holding up his wrist and the strap on it, "to the *Titanic*'s comms arrays, then I can call my own ship down and get us all out of here." Now that they were walking, he turned to the feline, "How many of you are there?"

"Forty-three," it purred in response.

There was a somewhat shocked look on Adam's face.

"Why? Is that a problem?"

"Hopefully not," he said. Polly could see in his eyes that he was already working out how he was going to fit forty-five people into his tiny little ship. When he escaped from the *Gold Royale*, he'd apparently only had about twenty survivors to contend with. Polly had quite obviously seen the inside of the *Kara Marazov*, and was sure there wasn't enough space for that many people. However, like Adam, she didn't voice that fear.

"What was that explosion?" she asked instead.

The feline, an engineer by the tiny red trim of his uniform's collar, replied, bobbing along casually on all fours. "One of the passengers tried to activate the ship's main power after she was advised that it could have catastrophic feedback potential. We were about to head to the bridge as part of the tour when the ship crashed; the visitor in question was stupid enough to claim that she was an engineer and decided to try and repair the engines." The feline jerked its head backwards towards the door slowly getting smaller behind them. "You saw the results."

There was a commotion ahead, and Polly was the only one aware of how Adam's stride lengthened to put himself slightly ahead of her, his arm moving ever so slightly in front of her. She frowned but once again it showed her just how much he obviously cared about her.

The commotion was a bodyguard of some sort restraining one of the other civilians, with a sharply dressed female alien, a scolding righteous look on her face, such as it was trisected by two bright blue cranial ridges that ran above and below each of her diamond eyes. When she saw Adam and the others walk in on the situation, she glared with contempt at the shaggy-looking human.

"Who in all the nineteen galaxies are *you*?" she sneered.

Adam gave her a false grin. "Santa Claus; why is that man being restrained?" He pointed to the man in question.

"He attempted to assault my mistress," the bodyguard said with a rather monotone mechanical voice that sounded all too much like the combat stealth suit Adam used to wear.

Adam folded his arms across his chest, his eyes narrowing, looking straight at the bodyguard. Then his eyes widened and shifted to the bodyguard's 'mistress'. "I thought androids had been made illegal by the interstellar courts decades ago," he said authoritatively. "The pathways of their artificial brains were incapable of comprehending emotions so they went mad and started killing people."

"How the hell do you know that?" Polly whispered to him, leaning closer to him at the same time.

He whispered back, keeping his voice low enough so that only Polly could hear him. "Remember when you first woke up on Fayde? I was reading some news articles on the subject when you came out onto the balcony."

She shrugged, not entirely remembering what he had been reading that first time she had seen Fayde, overwhelmed as she had been by the sheer magnitude of the buildings around and above her.

"Let him go," Adam growled to the cold-faced android. It turned its emotionless face to its mistress for confirmation, who was still glaring at Adam.

"No," she said, stepping in front of Adam. "I want this man arrested and punished," she said accusingly to the two crewmen either side of Adam and Polly. They just shrugged nonchalantly, mumbling something about being only engineers.

"Tough," said Adam, deciding the matter for her. He stepped towards the android, and placed a large hand on its well-tailored sleeve. It let go of the relieved civilian, and then instantly clamped onto Adam's hand. Using its enhanced strength, it threw Adam over its shoulder to smash into the corridor wall. He grunted, and then rolled out of the way of the android's foot that smashed down where his head had been a split-second before.

But the android was quicker than he could imagine, striking out with its other foot almost immediately without over-balancing itself. Its foot caught him in his midsection, and flipped him over onto his back, a sharp pain emitting from his ribs.

"Why always the ribs?" he muttered under his breath. He scissored his legs, and caught the android's ankle between his and twisted his whole body so that the momentum put even the enhanced android a fraction out of balance. To Adam's obvious horror, the android barely wobbled. He kicked out just as the android stepped forward, clipping the android's knee.

Amazingly, the knee gave way, and Adam was up on his feet, ignoring the pain that sparked through his side. He stamped down on the knee again, before the android could react with its faster reflexives. The knee, an apparent weak spot, folded under his foot, though the metal of its endo-skeleton sent jolts of pain up his leg.

The android tried to regain its balance by shifting its weight to the other foot, but Adam was on it, pushing all his weight and strength against the other. The two collapsed onto the floor.

There was a combat knife in Adam's hand, the empty scabbard tucked under the straps of his Ckeer Najoor-borne leather boots. Polly hadn't even seen him move his arm, much less produce a serrated-edged blade. He plunged the knife into the android's armpit, eliciting a squeal of revulsion from its mistress, and indeed several others.

The android jerked and convulsed, and then went completely rigid.

Adam breathed a sigh of relief, and stood up, groaning when the pain jabbed through him quickly. Polly helped him to stand to his feet.

He was muttering to himself.

"Damn it; I've been idle in bed for too damn long. I got beat by a damn robot."

"He's an android, Adam; I'm amazed *any* human could beat him." She smiled at him, briefly suppressing any negative comment he had on his lips. "Just goes to show, that even when you're injured you can take out a mechanically enhanced android bodyguard."

Adam chuckled despite the seriousness of the situation.

He gave the rest of the civilians a glance before settling his gaze on the android's mistress. "Any questions?"

Wisely, the woman shook her head.

Naturally, somebody felt the urge to scream.

When Adam turned towards them, the person in question was an abnormal white colour, shock and fear on their face, though Adam had a tough time telling if the alien was male or female. The person in question was staring at a bright blue blood stain on the carpet floor, a bloodstain that had drag marks leading away from it. Right into a darkened corridor with no lighting.

Adam harrumphed.

"'Cos crashing the ship would just be too easy by itself," he grumbled. "Now we've gotta deal with some ravenous, murderous beastie-thing. Where've I heard that one before?" He turned to Polly, and kissed her gently on the cheek. He sighed, "I'll be back in a minute." He handed his wrist-mounted device to her. "Get this to the communications array if you can; I'll meet you there." He leaned down again, his mouth up against her ear. "I love you." Then he was gone. She noticed that the knife previously stuck in the android's armpit was gone as well.

"Be careful, Adam."

* * *

Flashback 6

2013ad.

Proxima Centauri.

The first thing they noticed was the red sky. Proxima's star was a red dwarf; as such it tinted the landscape in all directions with a crimson that was easy on the eyes. It was almost identical to the scrub and bush fields near around Calhoun County. Some wag had already erected a makeshift flag showing the Stars and Stripes and the Union Jack in the same image. She turned slowly on the spot, taking in the tall weeping willow-like trees, the long grass in the far fields, even the small winding river that would be the basis of the new colony's water supply.

Behind a small smattering of trees stood the bulbous form of the *Mayflower.* The stark white hull reflected the red sky brilliantly at midday. The colonists and the ship's crew were disassembling the massive central module of the ship; the metal plating, computers, and wiring of the module had been designed to be reconfigured to make habitable buildings to live and work in. It was all designed for exactly that.

"Taking a break?" a familiar voice chuckled.

Lonnie DaSilva was not a big man per se, but at that instant, he partially blocked out the sun, reaching down to her seated position with a flask of water, purified from the nearby river. There was a big grin on his face, his own skin slightly pasty from the day's efforts.

"You too, huh?" she smiled back. He parked his behind on the rock beside her, and took a swig from his own flask, smacking his lips as he swallowed the refreshing liquid.

"Is it going well?" he asked, gesturing to the skeletal superstructure. She knew that he knew how it was going, but it was just his way of starting the conversation, attempting to steer it towards what she knew he wanted to discuss.

"Out with it, Lonnie," she smiled.

He chuckled again, shaking his head.

"Polly; a week ago we landed Earth's first faster-than-light purpose-built starship to create Earth's first off world colony. Four weeks before that, we witnessed the reappearance of a man who literally disappeared into thin air from the bridge of that same ship. I know you've been trawling through the computers searching for information on the man, even *after* we left Earth orbit."

"I-" she tried to say something, but found she couldn't deny what he was telling her. "You're right." She snorted. "I've been having dreams about him." She saw DaSilva's thick eyebrows rise up his face, almost to his greying hairline. "Not those kinds of dreams. Just dreams about all sorts; for some reason, most of them were in London, but I don't know why, I haven't been to London since my honeymoon." Both became very silent when she mentioned the honeymoon. DaSilva had been there to pick up the pieces of what was left of Polly's personal life, and had seen how she had discarded that life, and thrown herself into the construction and launch of the *Mayflower*. That period had tested their friendship to the limit.

"You know when we put the command and engine sections together we're going to have to give the ship a new name. The colonists have already claimed *Mayflower* for several other things, and if this new version of the ship is going to be mainly for defence and exploration, we need something a bit more..."

"Manly?" she interjected.

He barked out a brief laugh, earning some confused looks from a group of colonists who were huffing and puffing with the exertion of carrying a pile of small metal plating between them.

"What about *Icarus*?" he suggested.

"The man who flew too close the sun? Isn't that a bit of a bad idea?" DaSilva shrugged.

She just sighed, knowing full well that his mind was already made up about the subject. "*Icarus* it is then."

He took another swig of water, before standing up again.

"C'mon, Polly; we better get back to work before the colonists start complaining again." He leant an arm across her shoulders as she stood as well, and the two strolled towards away.

* * *

Present day.

"So who iz zat demon anyvay?" one of the VIPs asked, English —or rather Standard- clearly not being their first language. "My pardon. My Terran iz not, uh, very good. I meant soldier, not ze demon."

"He's..." she fought for the right words as they filed through winding corridors. "He's my partner." It was a somewhat odd way to put it, but to her it sounded right.

The feline engineer led the way for the group, padding along on the carpeted floor. Polly wasn't far behind, trying to avoid any actual contact with the VIPs. The one actually attempting to talk to her, complete with a comically long moustache, was half-decent, with a bit more knowledge and common sense than the others —though not much more.

"I think he's a beast," the android's mistress sniffed. "People like him should be exterminated, and prevented from breeding."

"Adam Caine is the greatest hero this universe has ever seen, or will ever see." She stopped, turned, and jabbed a finger into the woman's collarbone. "If you even knew the things he had done, you would be worshipping the ground he walked on."

"Like you, you mean?" she sneered.

Polly let out a growl, and stormed off, keeping pace with the feline engineer.

"Why did he go off on his own?" purred the engineer.

She smiled at him, though inside she was still somewhat disturbed by the fact that he looked like an over-grown ginger tabby cat. Ignoring the innate reaction to pet him, she replied, "Because he works best alone. That's how he operated in the SBS."

"SBS? That sounds like a Terran military abbreviation."

"Special Boat Service. They were the best and most secret my world had to offer, if memory serves."

"My people are mostly engineers and artisans," he said softly, "If one behaved such as your partner, they were cast out of our society, never to be seen again. Violence of any kind is abhorred. I-" he paused, having some difficulty with even the thought. "I am sorry; it is hard to see for someone raised as I was."

"Adam's been around that kind of violence since he was sixteen years old. He's good at what he does, even if what he does isn't very nice."

"I recognised the name when he was speaking over the intercom. It is a name spoken with reverence on many worlds that I have visited since leaving my own."

"Just don't tell him that, or it'll go to his head," she chuckled. The engineer purred loudly, a very pleasing sound to her ears; she hoped it was his people's version of laughter. Either way, it was preferable to the prigs behind them, who had started arguing among themselves about why they should be following Caine and the ship's crew. She tuned them out, and judging by the twitching of the engineer's larger tall ears, he was too.

"Your partner seems confident that this plan will work," said the engineer's colleague. "How does he know so much about everything?"

Polly sighed. "I wish I knew, but I'm not even sure *he* knows where the knowledge comes from."

"That sounds somewhat disturbing," the feline commented.

"Adam would say it was luck."

They came to a large room that had once been some kind of mess hall for the crew. Tables, chairs, crockery, and cutlery were piled up against one wall where the ship had stopped suddenly, and everything not bolted down was thrown forwards. Unfortunately, the only other exit was buried under all the dining detritus at the other end of the hall.

"Is there another way through?" asked Polly.

"The kitchen has a staff and supply access around the back," the feline's companion answered. They all looked to the left at the main double-door entrance to the kitchen. Flames licked out from between the doors, and there were scorched corpses among the debris of the hall.

"That's a no-go, then," snorted Polly. "I suppose we'd better get that debris cleared pronto then." She and the engineers moved towards the tables and chairs, pulling them away from the doors. The VIPs stood far away from the action, sniffing the air and folding their arms in defiance. Polly growled at them to help out, but they refused, earning a few muttered swearwords from her.

They were huffing and puffing by the time they got the entrance cleared. The feline turned to her. "How do you think Captain Caine is doing?"

"I wish I knew."

* * *

Adam was once again in the thick of it, striding silently down a corridor he thought the creature had disappeared down. There were small blood droplets along the carpeted floor; he was following the trail through several sections that hadn't been entirely finished. They looked like crew quarters judging by some of the furniture.

Knife in hand, he crept around, waiting for some sign of the creature, until he came across another trail that crossed over the first.

No, not another trail, he realised, but the same trail simply crossing over itself.

Clever girl, he thought, just before the slobbering thing came bounding out of the shadows, claws unsheathed.

The remains of the VIP it had killed were still lodged in its rows of fangs. He rolled under the creature's charge, its claws scraping his arm as it passed over him. He slashed at its belly with the combat knife. Steaming hot blood sprayed over his arm, sending a dull ache through him.

He grunted, the blood burning his skin like a bad case of sunburn.

The creature smashed into the opposite wall, whilst Adam leapt to his feet. The creature was large, bigger than the Odyssey monsters, with a sand-coloured armoured hide, no neck to speak of, and no nostrils. Its six eyes glared evilly out from beneath armoured eyelids. It picked itself off the floor with six muscular legs each ending in a trio of obsidian-streaked claws bigger than each of Adam's hands.

It reeked of fresh meat and sulphur.

It was a native of this world, armoured against the harsh atmosphere outside the ship.

Armoured, so it seemed, everywhere but the thing's underside, the least inaccessible part of the animal. And it was an animal —there was no sentient intelligence behind its darkened eyes.

The creature snarled, and tensed, its muscles shivering as it leaned back. With a roar, it launched itself across the corridor, fangs and claws outstretched. Adam dropped suddenly, ducking under the leap.

With a squeal, the thing smashed headfirst into the metal bulkhead. There was a squelch and a hideous cracking noise, and the creature slumped to the floor. Adam toed the thing's side with his boot, but it didn't move. It was dead, for sure. Its head was at too steep an angle for anything less, armoured or not.

"Stupid sum'bitch; knocked itself cold." He shook his head, and chuckled, wiping the blood off the knife on the carpet.

He sighed, wondering why that had been too easy a hunt.

When he turned away he heard a quiet growl.

The growl got louder, and there was something scratching behind him. He was sure it was further down the corridor than the fresh corpse.

"There's more than one?" he whispered. He glanced behind him, and what he saw filled the corridor, even shrouded in the shadows. Fear and adrenaline pumped through his system, and fuelled his arms and legs as he bolted.

The larger animal howled as it realised its prey was getting away.

* * *

Polly heard the howl, and it chilled her to the bone. She saw the scared looks on the faces around her, even the ones she wasn't entirely sure she knew how to read, given their alien nature.

"We need to hurry," she suggested, picked up her own pace. Having heard the monstrous howl echoing through the ship, nobody argued. Although she didn't say it, she hoped desperately Adam was okay.

* * *

"Shitshitshitshitshitshit," Adam was cursing as his arms and legs pumped as hard as he possibly could. He could hear the things behind him, their collective foul breath making him cough uncontrollably.

They probably breathe methane, he surmised.

"Shit, why didn't I think of that before?"

With every last bit of will he had left, he tried to outpace the creatures, an idea forming in his head.

* * *

Flashback 7

2015ad.

Calhoun County, Iowa.

She had dreamed of what it might be like to come to this place, but she had avoided the actual coming here for the three months since the hostilities had ceased. She had hoped to see something... anything.

But there was nothing around except for a field of glass. According to the readings the *Icarus* had taken from orbit –right after the mysterious stranger had appeared and then subsequently disappeared- half of Iowa had been levelled by a nuclear device, fusing the elements in the ground into one gigantic sheet of black glass.

Although the glass had absorbed much of the radiation, she still had to wear a radiation counter on her belt to be safe.

She didn't care that China had wanted the plans for the *Mayflower* and the *Icarus*; she didn't care about any of the politics that had combined to bring about the Third World War. She dropped to her knees, and sobbed, rivers of water flowing from between her fingers as she covered her face from her companion.

She felt DaSilva put a comforting hand on her shoulder.

When the wracks of sobs stopped, she tried desperately to search around her for any sign that this had once been her childhood home. But all she saw was the featureless obsidian mass.

"I'm so sorry, Polly," he whispered.

"I brought this on us," she croaked. "If I had never designed that engine, none of this would have happened. All these millions of people would never have died because China and its allies wanted a piece of my invention for themselves."

He crouched down beside her.

"This is *not* your fault," he said sternly. "This is the fault of greedy and paranoid politicians. You can't blame yourself for their reactions to the technology. It's not like China wasn't involved in the *Mayflower* project anyway: we have several Chinese scientists living on Proxima Centauri." He sighed heavily. "Look, King Charles has requested our presence at Buckingham Palace. He and the Prime Minister seem to think that we could help establishing a new world government."

She looked at the radiation counter on her belt.

"I wanna stay here for a bit longer. We've got time."

"Sure, Polly."

They looked out at the glass fields together.

"Hey, you know the Navy is already putting together the space frame of the next *Icarus*-class starship. They're calling it the *Enterprise* of all things."

* * *

Present day.

By the time the bedraggled group reached the access corridor leading to the communications array, many of the passengers had regained some of their composure —no creature had attacked them, and they had all started to believe that it had just been in their imaginations that anything had made that bloodcurdling noise.

They were bickering when the feline engineer called for a stop whilst he and Polly sorted the comms array out.

They waved them away like they were servants to them.

Polly breathed a sigh of relief when the two entered the access corridor; glad to be away from them all at last.

That, however, was the least of their problems, as they discovered upon stopping outside the door. It was warped, probably by super-heated gases, and fused shut.

"How the hell are we going to get through *that*?" she blurted.

The engineers grunted, admitting they were stumped, until one of them spotted an emergency engineering kit lying just under a torn piece of bulkhead. The engineers muttered to themselves, attempting to turn a part of the welding tool in the kit into a cutter. Sparks leaped from the tool and the feline yelped, jumping away from the thing like it was about to kill him. A patch of his fur was singed clean off, on his paw, leaving a bald spot behind.

He hissed and spat at it as if it were a predator, hurling a stream of hissed curses at the tool itself.

"Will you cut that out?" the other engineer whispered, so as not to alarm the VIPs, though his tone was harsher than he had obviously intended, because embarrassment passed across his face.

"Sorry," the other purred.

They set to work on the door, holding their forearms across their eyes as much as they could to prevent the actinic flash from ruining their eyesight. Polly had to cover her own eyes, though she wasn't fast enough to prevent a big green retinal afterimage from jumping up in her vision.

The feline cursed again.

"This is going to take a while," he shouted over the fizzing and sparking.

* * *

Adam vaulted a railing and dropped two levels into the auxiliary engineering control pit, not realising just how high he had been. The lighting had failed down there, and the emergency lighting was intermittent at best.

A sharp pain jolted up his legs as he hit the ground later than he thought.

"Crap." He rolled; he hoped that the fall hadn't done anything more than jarred the bone. Then he heard the thing he'd hoped he'd lost. The big creature's head appeared above him where he had leaped the railing, sniffing the air, and casting its head from side-to-side. It let out a howl, and was answered by a dozen more.

"Crap."

Apparently one of them heard him because there was a growl from nearby, and one of the creatures' heads suddenly popped around from the corner of a console to his left. Six eyes blinked at him, and drooling dirty fangs glinted in the half-light.

"Crap."

It dove at him, faster than he thought possible. There was nowhere for him to actually go except forward, so he leaped at it, knife drawn back to deliver a killing stroke. The methane creature had barely started to bring its claws up when it and Adam slammed into each other, tumbling to the grilled metal floor in a bundle of muscled arms and armoured legs.

Claws sliced at Adam's arms, drawing thin amounts of blood. Adam returned in kind by stabbing the knife into its suddenly exposed abdomen, and slicing open its belly. Gore-wrapped entrails spilled out, and it screamed, the shrill noise piercing his ears.

Adam lashed out with his foot automatically at the sound of a scraped footfall behind him. His boot connected with the forehead of the creature sneaking up behind him. There was a crunch, and a rush of breath being let go. The creature slumped to the ground, motionless.

More howls erupted from the remaining animals.

Three more of the smaller ones jumped down into the pit, ready for attack. One roared and charged, bounding along the floor effortlessly on its strong limbs. Adam used all his strength to heave the corpse he had tousled closely with on top of him. The charging creature bundled into its dead compatriot.

Adam sliced its throat open.

The rancid hot blood spilled over his leg, heating it up a great deal. It wasn't burning, but it probably wouldn't take long to do so.

The other two creatures, seeing the carnage wrought by Adam, backed away into the shadows, hissing at him like cats. His judgement of why they did it was re-evaluated when the biggest one pulled its vast weight over the railings, blotting out any of the emergency lighting, and leaving Adam in pitch-black.

"Crap."

It dropped towards him.

* * *

The doors squealed as they parted, the engineers letting out very human whoops of joy. They piled into the control room, along with the uninvited VIPs, who were more intent on saving their own necks from the unknown creature than caring about etiquette in the face of fear.

More than one of them gave a moan of despair at the state of the control room. Half the place had been scorched black by a flash fire. Part of the control consoles had been permanently damaged, sparking occasionally when power tried to pass through its conduits.

The engineers went to work on the console, whilst the VIPs cowered by the large window that was wrapped around the central communications array jutting out of the room and outside the ship. The view outside was spectacular, the ship apparently having stopped its crash-landing close to the edge of a high cliff, overlooking a massive dry valley of dust and methane-plants. It was reminiscent of a family trip to Death Valley, or the rocky desert outside Area 51 in Nevada.

It was not an inviting comparison to say the least. Oddly enough, the thought of being exposed to that harsh an atmosphere actually chilled her.

There was another bone-chilling howl that reverberated through the ship around them. Someone in the crowd whimpered; someone else sobbed openly. The two engineers exchanged worried glances –the sound had been closer.

"Hurry," she hissed to them.

"What the *sten* is that thing?" one of the VIPs whined.

Polly shook her head.

"It's only a guess, but I'd say it was a native of this planet. Anything weaker wouldn't be able to survive for more than a few seconds outside in that environment." She was still staring out onto that horrible landscape, ignoring the looks of contempt and fear on the faces around her. There were shapes moving around out there, far in the distance. They were closing, drawn by the downed starship; she could see dust rising far on the horizon.

That's not good, she surmised.

* * *

"Whoof!"

Adam smashed against the wall of the control pit, the console screens giving way under the impact. The wind rushed out of his lungs, leaving him struggling for breath. The biggest creature had backhanded him after landing in the spot he had just vacated. It snarled and came at him immediately, smashing a tower of monitors out of the way in its rush to get at him.

The five remaining smaller beasts had stayed away, though whether that was through fear of him, fear of the dominant beast, or simply staying back to watch the show, he didn't know. He didn't really want to find out.

He scrambled up onto the next level of the control pit, and rolled hard, narrowly avoiding the claw that attempted to skewer him like a shish kebab. It roared in frustration at not getting him, and tried again with the same claw and its partner, sparks tinkling off the metal. The methane-beast kept roaring, pulling its bulk further upright until it was on its back legs.

Adam grinned, seeing an opportunity to get away from the creatures.

Unfortunately, it meant getting closer first.

Worry raced through his mind as he briefly thought about not seeing Polly again, or indeed Eve, if this didn't work. Then again, his overall plan would likely backfire... literally. But Polly and Eve were forever on his mind, his new life as a family man, as something that a certain young Royal Marine would never have dreamed of. Staring into the jaws of the beast in front of him was a massive reminder of just how much his life had changed.

The beast raised its clawed limbs back to strike.

Adam leapt to his feet, and charged straight at the creature. He jumped and dove over the railing at it feet first. Normally, the size of the creature would be too intimidating, too huge to contemplate doing what he wanted to do. He planted two feet squarely on its chest. For a minute split-second, it seemed like nothing happened and he would just flop to the ground.

But the creature toppled backwards, limbs cartwheeling, and its eyes wide open in surprise. It gave a squeal of shock, and fell back into the control pit, Adam riding its chest like a surfboard until it rebounded off the central console. He used the momentum of the fall to carry him over the other side of the control pit. He flew over the railing and crashed into the opposite wall, once again winding himself.

He groaned before picking himself up, amazed that he had managed to hold onto the knife through all that.

Chest heaving from the effort, he ran from the control room, barring the door from the other side as he exited. Almost immediately, he heard and felt banging on the other side, trying to follow him.

Next stop, life support control.

* * *

"Got it!" the feline shouted excitedly.

The power conduits finally pulsed with power, lights flashed rhythmically as the ship's remaining emergency power was pumped into the comms array. An erratic beeping and whistling issued from the undamaged control console.

She handed him the wrist device, and he used an interface to connect the two. One of the central comms pylons lit up, and pulses of white light began strobing along its length. The console's monitors began showing a series of waves passing away from the wreckage of the Titanic. The waves flew into the atmosphere on the display, pulsing up towards space.

The engineers held their breath as the representation of the comms waves flickered, died, pulsed again, and then died again. They both let out a growl of frustration. Another whimper came from the VIPs.

"We're stuck here," someone groaned. It only took a second for Polly to realise that it had been her that had said it.

* * *

Life Support Control was not too far from the auxiliary engineering control.

The doors, like so much of the ship, were deformed, though thankfully were not as bad as some. With a little applied pressure, Adam wrenched the doors apart. The room was barely lit, though it hadn't been scorched or destroyed like much of the ship around him.

The consoles were marked for each of their purposes. He found the one he was looking for, and flicked it on, hoping that it was hooked up to some kind of emergency power source; the screen spasmed to life with a sputter of static, giving him a comprehensive list of the life support systems. He selected 'environmental composition', and pulled up the environmental manufacturing options.

He brought up a list of elements, and selected the one he needed. He then activated the distribution console, and selected the area around the auxiliary engineering control room, highlighting whatever wasn't flashing red with damage.

The word PUMP appeared on the screen in big crimson letters.

He tapped the screen, and heard a hissing sound. He couldn't smell anything, but then methane had no smell, so the creatures wouldn't necessarily be aware of it.

He snatched up a portable palm interface, and bolted from the room, aware that he'd been still for too long. There was some scratching behind him as he left; the creatures were on the move again —straight towards him.

Crap.

The big one was in the lead again, although its back armour was cracked where it had fallen on the central consoles in the control pit. He pocketed the palm device, and picked up a fallen pole that was burned and deformed, but was a perfect javelin.

He backed down the corridor, hoping they wouldn't attack before he was ready.

They didn't seem to be in a hurry to kill him, which made Adam nervous. What were they waiting for? Were they afraid of him? Or were they simply checking him out, looking for a weak spot?

There was a clicking behind him, echoing from a cross junction not far ahead. Adam knew that sound. It was bone claws clicking against metal floors.
Crap.

Five more of the damn things appeared from the side corridor, whilst another two stalked towards him from the opposite direction. Although they had slightly different colouring to their armour, they were identically built, with the same beetle armour, multiple eyes, and slavering jaws.
Double crap.

Every single one of them drew back on their haunches, preparing to strike.
Triple crap.

Adam ran, pumping his limbs as hard as he could, the pole still in one hand. The ambushers pounced, all at the same time. Adam dropped to the floor, skidding under them as all seven smacked into each other at the same time. They all fell into a mess of flailing limbs and growls of frustration.

Adam jumped to his feet, and hurled the pole just like a javelin, diving through the nearest doorway. It sailed past the concussed pile, and missed the largest creature by a hair's breadth.

It flew on, until it panged off the metal wall.

All it took was one spark.

The methane Adam had pumped into the immediate area ignited. Red-hot flames washed down the corridor, cooking the animals alive as the flames rolled through the corridor, scorching everything they touched, roaring like a lion. The wave flashed over the creatures, incinerating every single one of them like an overgrown oven.

Adam huddled in a corner, staying as far from the flames as possible, but the walls and floor were heating insanely quickly. But he couldn't move yet: the spot he was hiding in was the only part that *wasn't* on fire. He couldn't move without getting cooked.

The flames licked closer, the heat so intense he could barely breath. The fire was using up all the remaining oxygen in the area, and was starting to heat the air itself.

He shouted Polly's name as loud as he could, and felt the fire wash over him.

* * *

Polly span at the sound of something in the distance.

There had been a low rumbling noise, followed by the lights flickering for a second. She could feel vibrations pass through the deck beneath her feet. But there was something in the noise, something whispering her name...

She shook the thought off, putting it down to the stress of her situation.

There was a pained howl that followed when the vibrations and distant rumbling finished. It was replied to by dozens of muffled, barely audible cries. Something bad had happened, and that something filled Polly with hope: Adam was still out there, fighting.

They all sat there in panicked silence for long minutes, the engineers still fumbling over the comms array, trying unsuccessfully to boost the signal of the wrist device. But there was too much damage, and the tension in the room was getting worse as they all began to imagine what might happen to them.

After an hour, one of them couldn't take it anymore.

"Oh my gods," said one of the VIPs. "We need to get out of here." He was becoming consumed with panic at the realisation that perhaps they were not going to survive. "Gods, we have to get out of here." He bolted for the door, barging past the others, and back into the corridor. The others shouted for him to come back before he was killed by whatever made the noise.

The moment he was beyond the door, and out of sight, there was a snarl, and he screamed. A loud wet squelch accompanied the scream, and blood splattered over those standing nearest to the door. His head bounced back into the room.

The entire room suddenly filled with terrified screams as one of the creatures filled the doorway.

Then there was a thumping noise, and the creature suddenly turned its head to one side. Something man-sized smashed into it, knocking it away from the door.

There was another wet squelch, and an even wetter gurgle followed by more silence.

The group, Polly included, watched the door with morbid curiosity, wondering what had knocked over the creature. Their answers, and in Polly's case prayers, were answered. A man walked into the doorway, covered in steaming hot blood, his clothes burned black and his skin reddened by what looked to be sunburn. His long shaggy hair was singed, making it uneven and ragged.

There was still a knife in his hand, dripping with the slightly acidic blood of the creature.

"Adam," she cried. The knife slipped from between his fingers and clattered on the floor. He wrapped his big arms around her, and squeezed her tight to him. Tears started to form, though they were tears of joy at seeing him again. "Please don't leave me like that again," she whispered.

"Never," he said.

He looked up and saw the dust trails that were no longer on the horizon. Each had a small black dot at the base of the trail, each one another of those creatures. He pulled out the portable interface, and patched into what was left of the sensors.

He smiled.

Something was coming down through the atmosphere, something moving at too controlled a rate to indicate another falling starship, or even a piece of debris. It was a ship. Help was coming.

The sensors detected several more creatures inside the ship, and hundreds more only minutes away outside on the planet surface.

He hugged Polly tighter, even as another of the methane-beasts rounded the doorway, a snarl on its lips, and darkness in its eyes. He was exhausted, too tired and burned to fight another of the things. He used his arm to block Polly's sight.

"Don't look."

The creature pounced just as a bright white light filled the room.

* * *

The pain never came, death never struck, and Adam, Polly and the other survivors suddenly found themselves surrounded by Terran Navy medical personnel. They were in the hold of a large cargo shuttle, sat on the teleporter pad.

The medics rushed to Adam, who seemed to be the most injured, bandaging what they could until they reached the larger starship in orbit. The shuttle didn't take long to reach its mothership, all the VIPs thankfully silent, aware of how close they had come to death.

The ship could be seen out of the cockpit's wraparound window.

It was one of the majestic new *Diligent*-class battleships, bigger than the *Knight*-class, with more curves to its blue hull. Because of the way the star system's sun flashed its light all over the beautiful ship, Adam couldn't make out the name of the ship painted on its side.

But when the shuttle slid into the main hangar bay of the ship, he started to laugh spectacularly loudly at something Polly couldn't quite see that was situated on the bulkhead high above them; something he had a better view of. She could see the corner of a coloured unit patch through the small viewport, presumably belonging to the ship they had been rescued by.

Polly finally saw what Adam saw as they were escorted out of the shuttle and onto the hangar deck, and began chuckling as well. A confused Navy captain –a female Rathgar- stepped forward with a smile on her mottled face.

"Captain Caine, Doctor Jenkins. I'm Captain Flakenrix. Welcome aboard the *Enterprise*."

* * *

Adam immediately requested that they be let back to the *Kara* to return home. Neither wanted to hang around long, despite the warmth of Captain Flakenrix's hospitality. They wanted to get as far from the planet as was humanly possible. Adam's light burns had been healed in record time by the medics on the shuttle, though they didn't bother to give him a new set of clothes.

They said goodbye to the two *Titanic* engineers, and Captain Flakenrix, before boarding the *Kara*, and setting a course for home. When the ship plunged into the Linkway, Polly reached over and activated the *Kara*'s autopilot. Adam looked at her like she was mad, but she grabbed his shirt, and pulled him into the small bunkroom, a hungry look on her face.

When she woke up in the morning, she felt wholly satisfied, and very much in love. But the attention of her love was no longer in the bed with her, though it was still warm to the touch where he had been lying.

"Adam?" she queried.

He appeared in the doorway of the bunkroom, something in his hand. At first she mistook it for another knife, but there were two looped handles at one end. He handed her the pair of scissors.

"What're *they* for?" she said.

He squirmed, embarrassed all of a sudden, but managed a smile.

"I think it's about time I had a haircut."

Seventeen:
Evie's First Adventure

Historian's note: **The main body of this story is set two years after** New **Frontiers.**

"Sod off!"
-Breneth Caine, when asked about her mother, Evelyn.

January 4004ad.

Rowlandos had his face pressed against the glass of the escape pod, the vision of his dying titan twirling as the pod span. The manoeuvring thrusters were faulty, and the limited computer had trouble keeping the pod in a stable flight pattern. The stars twisted and bucked, making even his alien stomach lurch.

Nausea swept over him.

The Navy ships surrounded his survivors, latching onto the spiked red warships like Fesai Limpet Tigers. *They're taking prisoners. Great.* Even now, he could see the Terran starfighters running patrol patterns around the bigger ships, protecting the boarding tunnels and troop shuttles from any fortuitous pirate.

His breath steamed the glass, obscuring the action.

There was a flash as a red frigate was torn apart by the energy weapons of three Navy gunships, whilst a motley assortment of red-splotched fighter craft were corralled towards a hangar bay, bleeding flames.

The escape pod dipped into the nebula clouds, away from the action and the prying eyes of the Navy. He sat back onto the grav-couch, and fumbled around for something to eat. He was hungry, and thirsty. Losing a titan could do that to you.

But he would do things differently next time.

There was a rack of bottles under the padded couch. He pulled one out, and was delighted to find that it was a bottle of red Argus wine; incredibly strong stuff, and incredibly sweet. He uncorked it, and took a swig.

"Ah," he said with gusto, "the good stuff."

* * *

Two weeks later, salvagers in the Betrella Star Cluster rescued the escape pod; when the door was opened, Rowlandos fell out, drunk as a skunk, and collapsed in a heap.

"Wasssssssuuuuuuuup?" he slurred with a stupefied grin.

* * *

"A Comprehensive history of the Nineteen Galaxies, Volume 8: The Core War."
-Written and compiled by M'Der Tr'n.

Strangis Forgan Kror.
Situated in the Triangulum Galaxy, it was an oddity to say the least. The planet itself was barely a thousand kilometres across its largest equatorial diameter, but its atmosphere was vast, currently measuring at over twenty thousand kilometres across at time of writing. There was no evidence to suggest that this phenomenon was artificial (like Potri Regular), nor was there anything that indicated how it could possibly occur naturally. Officially, the planet was classified as a gas giant, though the planetary body was habitable to a certain extent.
The atmosphere was filled with cottonbud clouds in the upper half, and evil, dark storm clouds in the lower. Magnificent floating cities drifted lazily through the clouds, usually in groups of up to a dozen, though even this could change depending on the elements and planetary politics.
Each city, governed by individual councils and an overall police force, flew on hundreds of ancient anti-gravs, the technology of which was beyond the understanding of its current occupants. Interstellar vessels came and went like any other planet. Unfortunately, the introduction of outsiders a hundred years before also brought the dirtier element of a previously peaceful society.
Hover-bike gangs moved in to the larger cities, claiming the streets as their own. Although they seemed to have no agenda besides chaos, they were a blight on the planet. Coincidentally, around the same time, agents of the Mertik Vianok (secret police) appeared to start operating on the planet.
Although officially, and historically, the Core War began with the tragic events on New Terra and at Fort Zeus, many closest to the situation believe that it was on Strangis Forgan Kror that the War truly began. The events on the bizarre planet were the precursor that started the ball rolling, as humans say.
My friend —my greatest and most trusted friend- Adam, has always believed that the conflict would always happen, no matter what events came before.
Perhaps he was right, perhaps not.

* * *

Now.
January 4007ad.
"Yeeehaaa!" she squealed, the sheer delight evident on her face. She goosed the hover-bike's throttle, and clung to the handlebars as tight as she could, relishing the intense adrenaline rush as the bike dipped under a long walkway. She ignored the shocked looks on the faces of the pedestrian crossing the bridge. She ignored the howling of the wind rushing past her ears.

Forgan City, the largest of Strangis Forgan Kror's floating cities, was the busiest, though that wasn't saying much. There were maybe two-dozen spacefaring vessels in the air, with only twice that number of anti-grav vehicles visible. She ignored all of them, occasionally skirting some of the bigger ones emblazoned with their company logos. There were sirens barely audible over the roaring wind and the whine of the bike's engine beneath her.

Her passenger clung desperately to her, his arms tight around her midsection.

"Slow down; you're going to get us killed!" he shouted over the tumult around them. His voice was drowned out by a sudden rush of wind from the wake of a starship lifting off from a nearby platform. His protests continued as she weaved around a limousine.

He looked behind them, and saw to his horror that they had by no means lost their pursuers. What was worse was that it was no longer just the hover-bike gang chasing them. Far behind the gangers, gliding lazily above the air traffic, a pale blue starship hung like a star, its main hull a vertical crescent. Fear coursed through him like a flashing jolt of electricity.

"Your father's behind us!" he shouted. This time she did falter, the hover-bike dipping again briefly before she regained control and whipped it round a traffic control tower. Both of them could see the controllers shaking their fists angrily at them. She also snuck a glance behind and above, and cursed. This was going to be bad.

"We'll be fine," she lied.

There was a loud fizz followed by a bang and a hover-car suddenly dropped from the sky, smoke pouring from its engine housing: the gangers had opened fire with their personal firearms. They loosed off energy rounds left, right, and centre, shooting at random; that or they were lousy shots.

The energy came faster and thicker now as more and more bikers joined the fray. All were howling, waving their firearms above their heads, racing each other to get to the prize. Most of them were tattooed, with enough piercings to be able to open their own jewellery stores. Each of their bikes were customised, unique and considered untouchable by anyone but the owners.

Until now.

Upon arriving on the planet, Evelyn had grabbed Thrigor by the hand and the two had slipped away from their school group to kiss in an alley. It had been exciting for both of the thirteen-year-olds, full of rushing hormones. Then she decided to defy her rather intimidating father by snatching a hover-bike belonging to the local gang, and jumping on. Thrigor, seeing the very angry faces of the gangers, jumped on too, and they had sped off.

Now they were being chased, and Eve seemed to be pushing the bike down towards the deck. The buildings rushed past them at breakneck speed. Walkways came perilously close to turning them into bloodstains as the bike got faster and faster.

"What are you doing, Evie?" Thrigor asked, trying not to scream his head off with sheer terror as Evelyn pushed the bike further and further into a dive. The engine squealed loudly, and it vibrated badly. The vibrating became a juddering, and the bike started to pull to the right.

More energy rounds flashed down at them; one hit the bike's engine exhaust, and blew off an exhaust pipe. The pipe spun away, and bounced off a communications stack, replaced on the bike by a trail of grey smoke that plumed up at the chasing gangers. They coughed and spluttered as the smoke billowed over them.

Another energy round flew past Thrigor's head so close he could feel the heat singe his long bright yellow mane of hair, and even hear the sizzle of the energy round as it passed his blue head.

Evelyn suddenly levelled the bike, and the handlebars were shaking badly. She was fighting with the handles, struggling to keep it from just spasming and crashing into the nearest large object.

"We're going down, Three!" she shouted, using the nickname she had given him when they were ten.

"We're what?!"

"We're going down!"

"Fabulous," he muttered under his breath.

There was a bar up ahead with neon lights marking the doors, windows, and the huge bold sign over the window. More bikers were parked outside the bar, their bizarre range of vehicles clamped to the metal walkways outside. The parked bikes rushed beneath them, the steering vanes caught on one, and then the two were suddenly flying forwards through the air.

Right before they smashed through the window, they both took a leaf out of her father's book, and said in unison, "Crap!"

* * *

When Evelyn Cassandra Caine woke up, her head was pounding, her ears were ringing, and her nostrils were assaulted by the foul smell of the bar. She was lying on a long wooden table, Thrigor's hand wrapped round hers. They were on their backs, looking at the high ceiling adorned with biking memorabilia.

Thrigor turned to Eve, who was trying to catch her breath, making her bosom rise up and down. Similar to his own race, Eve's race –particularly the women– matured at a far earlier age, usually around the ten-year-old mark. As such, Eve's frame had filled out a bit, although being still only thirteen it hadn't been much. Both of their hormones had been racing since the day they had met.

Eve caught him looking at her chest, and blushed with both anger and excitement. She glared at him, though still held onto his hard blue hand.

There was shouting and swearing all around them, and a fight had broke out somewhere in the back. They had apparently only been unconscious for a few seconds, because the bikers that had been chasing them had only just finished parking their vehicles.

There was a man at the table they had landed on, a Kra Nal male, with long metal dreadlocks that had seen better days. The man himself had swirling fresh tattoos on his arms and what she could see of his chest.

He was skinnier than Uncle M'Der, and far drunker. In fact, he was so drunk that his slurring speech was incomprehensible, and he smelled of stale sweat and too many hours sat in the same spot with the same type of drink. The smell of alcohol on his breath was beyond foul.

"Wha' 'id ya do t'me beer?" he managed. He was looking down at a smashed beer mug, the handle still in his long-fingered hand. His purple beer was splashed all over him and the table, and there was a forlorn look on his long face.

Someone grabbed her hand, and pulled the two teenagers off the table. It was an older Mertik woman, her blue hair whitening at the temples slightly. She had a hard worn face, like that of her father's, having seen too much violence, although there was a bitter darkness behind it from too many years without warmth or love.

She smiled, but there was no warmth in it or her eyes.

She seemed completely oblivious to the bar riot gaining momentum around her, as if it didn't faze her in the slightest.

"You must be Evelyn," she said, her voice a flat monotone.

"How do you know my name?" Eve asked suspiciously.

"I know a lot of things," came the reply. "I know that you are the adopted daughter of Adam Caine, and I also know that your biological father was a mercenary commander called Garvion."

The name meant nothing to Eve, but she was sure daddy would know. He knew everything, much to the chagrin of Polly, the closest thing she had to a mother, and the love of daddy's life. She wondered when they were going to get married. After two years together now, it would be about time.

"I'm sorry," replied Eve finally. "I have no idea who or what you're talking about."

The woman gave her a sad smile, and slapped a 'friendly' hand on her shoulder, before disappearing from view.

"Who was that?" asked Thrigor.

Eve just shrugged.

"Dunno; I think she knows my dad though."

"Wha' 'id ya do t'me beer?" the drunk Kra Nal repeated. He actually seemed to raise his head, his bloodshot eyes seemingly alert for an instant. His eyes looked over at something outside. They turned, and there was a large rush of wind that invaded the bar, followed by an ear-piercing whine.

Eve's face dropped as the *Kara Marazov* descended down into view, its anti-gravs crushing dozens of the parked bikes. It swivelled vertically to face the bar, and Eve could see into the cockpit. Daddy was there, anger evident on his face even from that distance, with Polly trying to calm him down.

The drunk saw the ship, and his eyes widened.

"You!" he slurred. Fear twisted his features, and he suddenly bolted upright. He pointed to the two kids, and then to the *Kara*. "Is he chasing you?"

516

They both nodded.

"Come with me if you want to live," he said, and he started walking quickly towards the door. His course zigzagged around the riot, narrowly avoiding flying glasses and unconscious bodies. He kept bumping into tables, and belching loudly. The two teenagers followed at a distance, squeezing each other's hand to make sure the other was still there.

The gangers that had been chasing them before appeared behind them, rage on their faces, and an assortment of weapons in their shaking fists.

The three barged out onto a service walkway around the back of the bar. The walkway was empty and drenched in the shadows of the buildings that reached up into the sky either side, obscuring it except for a sliver of blue far above them. The tall metal buildings were monolithic from their viewpoint, inducing mild vertigo in the two children; neither was used to buildings higher than two stories, and the huge height of these was overwhelming to say the least.

They were led to a grilled staircase that wound up the side of the left building, passing several other similar walkways at regular intervals, their shoes clanging on the metal as they did so.

Clangs further down the stairs told Eve that the gangers were still in hot pursuit, still shouting angrily now that she had destroyed one of their bikes, and that the Kara had destroyed even more.

Her muscles were aching from the effort of pounding up so many stairs, and the crash before. In fact, her legs and arms felt like they had been badly bruised from smashing through the forcefield that passed for a window in the bar below.

"Where are we going?" demanded Thrigor, wheezing loudly. Despite working on his parent's small farm, he was unused to this kind of exertion.

"I have a ship," the drunk shouted back, although to the teenagers it sounded more like, "have a dip," though barely. He too was wheezing, though more from the drink than because he was physically unfit, his long legs loping four steps at a time.

"A ship?" wailed Thrigor. "How's that gonna help?"

The drunk just threw a *tsk-tsk* noise back at him.

More energy rounds panged off the railings, melting the metal around them. Thrigor yelped loudly as one passed in front of his face to splash harmlessly against the wall to his left. Another skimmed the back of his leg; it burned a hole in his trouser leg, and scorched the back of his actual leg. Pain leapt through him, and he stumbled to the floor of one of the landings between cases.

He shouted for them to keep going, but Eve stayed, holding out her hand.

"My dad says you should never leave behind anyone, let alone someone you care about."

Thrigor smiled weakly.

"You care about me?"

She shrugged. "Maybe."

Before he could say anything more, more energy rounds flashed up around them.

"This isn't the place for this," she said, sounding more like an adult than he realised she had the potential for. He could only agree as the gangers got closer and closer. And the presence of the Kara was forever at the corners of their vision, as if waiting to see what might happen.

Thrigor was extremely aware of Adam Caine's reputation, not only as a soldier, but also as a fiercely protective father, and it made him pause for thought whenever he was around Eve. Which, between school and an after-school job on the fields, was almost all the time these days.

"Come on, come on!" the drunk shouted without stopping.

The two teenagers tried their best to follow, but his long stride pushed him far ahead, leaving them behind. The gangers, however, were closing faster and faster, and getting angrier and angrier. Some of them were banging knives and metallic clubs on the railings, vibrating the entire structure.

They ran and ran and ran, trying to ignore their burning muscles.

Both of them stumbled, and a ganger appeared behind them, brandishing a wicked looking energy pistol, with a short knife attached to a bayonet lug under the barrel. He advanced slowly up the stairs, growling like an animal.

Eve stopped, turned, and slipped past a stunned Thrigor.

Eve tried to remember the lessons daddy had taught her about self-defence, which essentially boiled down to avoiding violence of any kind at her age. Although, when she pushed him, he had relented and begun to teach her, Polly, and several neighbours basic martial arts.

But he had also taught her over the years that improvisation was better than skill, and luck could save you more than anything else in a fight.

So she grabbed the railings, and swung her legs forward, planting them on his chest. Despite her smaller stature, she had momentum and speed on her side. He went flying backwards and smacked his head on the corner railing. He slumped to the floor, blood trickling from the back of his head.

Fear and guilt ran through her as she realised what she had done, or what she had possibly done. Daddy made it look like it was an easy thing to do, but it wasn't. She didn't know if he was dead, but she still felt horrible, her guts twisting in a huge knot. She felt nauseous, in fact.

She was barely aware of anything, just the enormous amount of blood.

She could feel someone pulling on the sleeve of her jacket, but she ignored them, staring at that blood. Someone called her name, but she ignored that as well. She just couldn't take her eyes off that blood pool.

She felt Thrigor's arms wrap around her.

Her legs moved automatically when he started pulling her up the stairs.

She didn't fight it.

In fact, before she knew it, they were on a large platform on the corner of the building, looking up at a rust bucket of a starship. It was a ramshackle affair, with corroded wing tips, a half missing upright stabiliser fin, and barely twenty metres long from nose to tail. There was wiring hanging down from the engines at the rear, and the cockpit bubble was visibly cracked in several places.

"Look at this piece of junk," Thrigor exclaimed.

"She's a good ship," protested the drunk, before a piece of hull plating comically fell off the rear end. "No matter what condition she may be in."

"That's reassuring," Thrigor muttered.

"Just get on," the drunk growled, before jumping up the boarding ramp at the rear of the vehicle. Thrigor was left to manhandle Eve, who was still staring off into space. He had seen that look before on some of the shell-shocked military veterans that had made Ckeer Najoor their home.

The ship's engines were already powering up by the time the boarding ramp sealed shut. They coughed and spluttered, and Thrigor felt the ship lurch as it lifted off the platform in stops and starts. At one point the whine of the anti-gravs cut out, and the ship skidded along the platform. And then it dropped off the edge, falling down, no anti-gravs, no engines.

There was drunken cursing from the cockpit, and the sound of metal clanging on metal —apparently their new friend was trying to beat the consoles into submission with some kind of heavy tool. Thrigor helped Eve to the cockpit door to find the drunk wrestling with the controls, and attempting to smack the throttle lever forward with a large metal wrench.

The ground was rushing up to meet them.

"Uh, that ground is getting pretty close," commented Thrigor, pointing beyond the nose of the ship.

"I know that," shouted the pilot. He banged the console, the lights of the controls came on, and the ship started to slow down. One of the console monitors showed the distance indicator counting down, the numbers slowing along with the closing ground.

The anti-gravs finally fully kicked in, and the ship stopped in mid-air.

"Three?" a soft voice asked. Thrigor turned to find Evie starting to come out of her stupor. "What's going on? Where are we?"

"We're on a starship," he answered. "I think those gangers are still behind us; I hope they don't have any ships of their own, or we're totally screwed."

"Well then, we're totally screwed," the pilot shouted, trying to orient the ship so that it was parallel with the platform they had just left. The power level indicators were incredibly low, and warning signs flashed brightly on all consoles, lights and sirens competing with each other for attention.

He flipped a few switches, and the engines began humming loudly as power was shunted to them. The ship jumped forward, and the engines began growling loudly, and continued to rise in volume. The noise rose to a deafening level, before the ship finally picked up some real speed, roaring down the main avenue. Air traffic swerved to avoid it as the ship sped on.

Another warning siren and light brought their attention to the consoles, and something slammed into the rear end. More warnings and sirens, and a growling noise came from the engines that sounded none too healthy.

The sensors showed dozens of contacts behind them, more joining them every second. There was an unfamiliar sensor contact behind all of those, maintaining distance. Even without the sensor information, Thrigor and Eve knew it was the *Kara*. They weren't worried about that for now; the gangers appeared to have a collection of starfighters, light freighters, and aerofighters.

They all followed in a chaotic formation, vying and racing to get first shot at the running ship. The one functioning rear mini-camera showed them even bashing each other to get in front, and the north south pointed star behind them, the picture barely showing its shape from a distance.

The city authorities were attempting to contact the pilot and his new crew, but the drunk just ignored it to the point of turning off the external comms. The ship blasted out into the open-air, passing beyond the city's circular rim. Ahead of them was the nearest city, a massive chunky white disc with a forest of tall buildings sat in the centre. Further beyond that were another two floating cities, peeking out from behind the white clouds. And the sensors showed a dozen more at varying distances from Forgan City.

The gangers were right behind them as the drunk pulled the ship into a steep climb, pushing the ship towards the blue sky.

From a distance it looked like a trail of insects flying to a new source of food.

In the rust bucket ship, Eve and Thrigor could only watch as the drunk Kra Nal pushed the shaking vessel further and further towards space. Thrigor popped his head up into the bubble of the cockpit to look back at the rear of the ship.

"We're on fire!" he complained.

"I know," said the drunk.

"But we're on fire!"

"Thanks for the information, but I'm a little busy trying to keep this thing in the air." He was frantically trying to monitor each and every damage warning in the ship, whilst also trying to avoid the laser fire from their pursuers. The starfighters among the chasing group were already locking their heavy weapons, their strike wings separating for combat mode, and missile ports sliding open.

The small freighters were holding back, the sensors indicating multiple missile locks.

The aerofighters among the group, however, were struggling to maintain pursuit, the small jet-propelled craft designed only for combat in the air around the cities. Some of them dropped, their pilots blacking out and losing control.

A trail of smoke plumed out behind the rust bucket, and even a few pieces of hull plating flew off.

"This is really not good," Thrigor shouted. The ship was roaring inside and out, struggling to get out of the planet's atmosphere. "Aren't we going a bit too far just to escape some angry bikers?"

The drunk shook his head emphatically.

"These people don't give up. Ever."

The shaking became violent enough that anything loose was thrown to the deck, and wiring came loose in the main hold. Sparks splashed down over the floor like a waterfall. Thrigor and Eve were thrown to the deck; they didn't bother getting back up.

The ship was suddenly hit, lurching as if it had been kicked up the backside. Eve and Thrigor, on the floor of the main hold, were suddenly thrown forwards into the bulkhead. Smoke started pouring into the hold from a leaking conduit. Although they managed to get it shut down manually, the two were still coughing and spluttering.

"Hold onto something," the pilot said, "the transition to space is going to be rough on the artificial gravity."

He wasn't kidding.

As the ship passed from the atmosphere, the ship's artificial gravity suddenly decided to malfunction, and the two teenagers were suddenly floating weightlessly for a few seconds. When the gravity came back, they dropped comically and painfully back down.

"Forty seconds to Linkway entrance."

The two returned to the cockpit, though Thrigor had to crouch in the small hatchway to the side of the rear seat whilst Eve took that rear co-pilot's chair.

Eve, however, was slightly enjoying finally being able to be at the controls of a spacefaring ship. Daddy kept telling her that she wasn't old enough to handle the Kara, even with him in the second seat. Black space was all around them now, with no orbital facilities, and only one or two large starships were present in orbit, though the one she could see seemed to be a Tagarri Gorokk mining ship.

The Linkway was ahead, pulsing brightly in the darkness of space.

"Twenty seconds," the pilot called.

The chasing ships were right behind them, starfighters either side of the rust bucket, and the light freighters trundled along after them. Several of the fighters ran out of fuel, and drifted, no lights, their pilots banging on the cockpit bubbles to warn their compatriots. One of the freighters was too slow to move out of the way of them, and subsequently smashed into a fighter; both vanished in a bright fireball.

"Ten seconds."

The Linkway filled the forward view from the cockpit.

An Alliance warship suddenly thundered out of the cloudy blue entrance, its curved white hull reflecting the light of the Linkway and the system's sun.

The wake of the visiting warship bounced the smaller ships around like fowl on a river. The rust bucket rolled and bucked but never bounced off course; the ganger starfighters were not so lucky, tumbling back out into space, struggling to control their flight.

The drunk flew his ship past the Alliance warship, and then down one of the five Linkways that branched off from Strangis Forgan Kror's Linkway entrance/ exit, although it was random at best with the failing computer.

Although the light freighters were keeping up, they weren't within firing range, and couldn't maintain a faster speed. For now, they were safe.

* * *

As if on cue, the drunken pilot had fallen asleep the moment they were safe, snoring loudly in the forward chair. The ship, apparently named Jewel of Perdition, was on autopilot, though the computer refused to tell Eve what the destination was.

Thrigor stood up, and reached an arm around her shoulders, gazing up at the Linkway passing by the *Jewel*. There was no other traffic in this Linkway tunnel besides what was following the Jewel at a distance.

"You okay, Evelyn?"

She glared at him. Evelyn was the name on her adoption papers, something to make the bureaucrats happy; even daddy didn't call her that, but Thrigor did, and was the only person in the known universe to call her by her official name. She didn't berate him for it though. She liked it. She liked him.

"I... I never killed a man before."

"It wasn't like you were trying to kill him, or even trying to hurt him. Besides, he would have killed both of us if you hadn't; and he may not even be dead. You don't know."

She smiled, and nestled her head on his chest.

"My dad always says that killing is the last resort, although he never says that violence is never an option."

"Your dad used to be a professional soldier; it's what he's best at." It wasn't an insult, and Eve knew it for what it was: a statement of fact; one she was proud of.

They stayed in those positions for a short silent while, comfortable but very tired.

"How come your father hasn't done anything yet? I was expecting him to swoop in and rescue us from this nightmare."

She shrugged.

"Maybe he expects us to do this by ourselves," she replied nonchalantly. "I guess I wouldn't be the daughter of Adam Caine if I couldn't handle a bunch of gangers."

"Maybe not," he said, leaning down next to her face to kiss her passionately on the lips. "But I'd still love you either way."

* * *

The drunk was temporarily coming out of his stupor at just the wrong time.

He heard the name 'Adam Caine' and rage and despair filled him.

His daughter, his mind wailed. *How was that possible? The coincidence is insane; oh god, that's him in the blue ship behind us. What do I do? What do I do?* The thoughts filled his head, even as he fell asleep again.

* * *

Eve hadn't even realised she'd fallen asleep, but she found herself jerking awake at the sound of an alarm. The blue of the Linkway had gone, replaced by the black of space, and the twin spheres of a binary star system.

The sensors were going haywire, trying to keep track of dozens of contact. The monitor was filled with hundreds of dots of varying sizes, with garbled information flickering next to the symbol.

Pulses suddenly flashed past the cockpit bubble, and missiles streaked in straight lines, exhaust trails left behind.

"Oh my gods," Eve whispered, "we've wandered into a battle. In fact, not just any battle." She pointed to one side of the battle, where blue-hulled ships were in formation. "Those are Terran warships."

"And those are the Idle Guns," the pilot said, a tinge of sadness in his voice as he pointed to the large fleet of red starships. He let out a torrent of curses and swearing directed at someone called Toddorov. He also had some choice words to say about Eve's dad.

Eve and Thrigor's eyes widened, and shock filled them.

"You know Adam Caine?" she asked.

The pilot, no longer drunk, smiled, laughter lines crinkling the edges of his bloodshot eyes. "I know him as The Ghost. He destroyed my fleet, my station, my entire pirate operation."

"I knew I'd seen those dreadlocks before!" Thrigor suddenly shouted excitedly. "You're Rowlandos, pirate emperor." Something flashed brightly to their left, a pirate frigate exploding. Behind them, the ganger light freighters suddenly became the target of a horrendous amount of firepower from two of the Navy cruisers. The freighters were torn apart by the sheer force. And through the debris field came the *Kara Marazov*, engines blazing.

"I was," he growled. "Until I met your father."

"Yeah," she sighed, seeing the Kara hanging back, "he does that."

Rowlandos suddenly flipped the Jewel over onto its top, before pulling it into a climb that took it towards the outer edge of the nightmare that was descending on this star system. He was having trouble keeping the evasive manoeuvres fast enough and unpredictable enough to keep the ship out of harm's way. Energy rounds from massive battleships fizzled past the Jewel, heating the hull enough to make its passengers sweat.

When they finally made it out of the hot zone, there was a message from the Terran command ship demanding they identify themselves, and a demand of surrender.

"I think you should surrender to the Navy," said Eve.

"I'm with her," Thrigor added.

Rowlandos snorted, but said nothing more.

There was a transmission coming through from the pirate fleet. Rowlandos piped it up on the comms screen, the blank monitor replaced by a face he wasn't expecting.

"Todd? Who the hell put you in charge?"

"I did," the former idiot replied defensively. *"When you and Hevskii disappeared, we all thought you were dead; Heidi didn't want leadership, and nobody else was senior enough. So I was elected to lead."*

"What happened, they all misplace their brains just before electing you?"

Anger passed over the new pirate leader's face, contorting his goofy features, the red skin an odd contrast to his scruffy blonde hair. The screen was briefly distorted by static, and the image of Toddorov wobbled as if his ship had been hit badly. Sparks flew down in rivers behind him.

"Very funny," he growled. *"Surrender now, or we will open fire on your wreck of a ship; that, or the alien ship behind you might do it for us. Then again, the Navy are now aware of who you are."*

"What?"

Shock filled all three of the *Jewel*'s motley crew.

Missile lock warnings blared for attention, and laser batteries began thumping pulses towards the *Jewel*. They all missed, but two came close enough to fry the ship's electronics enough that barely anything would work except for life support and limited comms. The ship began drifting, listing so that the intense space battle came into full view ahead of them.

The Terrans had started powering forward from their static position. There were seven battleships of different classes in their fleet, accompanied by six cruisers, and thirty-two frigates, destroyers, and gunships. All of these surrounded the *HMS Valkyrie*, the Navy's highly publicised new starfighter carrier. It was twice as big as the standard *Knight*-class, with enough hangar space to carry fourteen squadrons of starfighters.

The swarm of Rhino fighters sped into combat with their pirate counterparts, dancing, juking, and jinking. The pirates were flying an ugly assortment of patched-together craft that looked as badly built as the *Jewel*. They were torn apart in minutes.

The Terran warships thundered towards the pirates, who had –predictably- started to turn tail.

"Toddorov never was very bright... or strong," commented Rowlandos.

Neither of the teenagers said anything; they just watched the god-like battle.

The Terrans were slaughtering the pirates once again. Despite not being part of the fleet, Rowlandos felt guilt and anguish at seeing the Idle Guns being trounced by the Navy once again. He was powerless to do anything about it.

The battleships obliterated a dozen red cruisers before pounding on their enemy equivalents. It took no more than two minutes for the Idle Guns' fleeing battleships to break apart under the massive firepower. Only one remained, the one with more communications masts than the others: the command ship.

The *Valkyrie* hung back, its starfighters ganging up on the other remaining smaller capital ships, using their sheer number to overwhelm the targets. Explosions rippled everywhere, filling the space with fire and debris.

It was over far too quickly for Rowlandos' liking.

The Terrans had captured the enemy command ship.

"So what now?" asked Eve. "Are you going to kill us?"

Judging by the look on the former pirate emperor's face, he was thinking about it.

Unfortunately, his decision was made for him.

A blue fin poked up above the lower rim of the cockpit bubble, and then continued to elongate, and widen, reaching upward like the pinnacle of a church steeple. Then the chevron-shaped cockpit rose up, and behind the transparent window sat the human who had ruined Rowlandos' life; his hair was much shorter and neater, and he had a neatly trimmed thick beard, but it was definitely *him*. There was another human beside him, a woman who looked both worried and angry —assuming that was possible for a human.

A voice came through the cockpit comm speakers.

A hauntingly familiar voice.

"Jewel of Perdition, *this is the* Kara Marazov. *Prepare to be boarded.*"

"Or what," said Rowlandos, "You'll destroy us?"

Rowlandos saw shock pass over Caine's face, but it was gone like the good soldier that he was. Then the anger was there; Rowlandos was fully aware of the speed and strength Caine was physically capable of —he had no trouble believing his ship was no less dangerous.

He sighed, and stumbled out of his seat, pushing past Thrigor to get to the small emergency hatch in the ceiling of the small hold. There was a clanking noise as the two ships connected, and a hiss as the seal was established. A whirring sound let him know that the ships were fully connected.

The hatches opened, and a big fist suddenly came flying out of the hatch. It connected with Rowlandos' face, and he fell to the deck, his nose broken, and blood dribbling from the nostrils.

"Ouch," the Kra Nal muttered.

Adam Caine dropped noiselessly into the hold. Unlike the last time he had seen Caine, Rowlandos noticed he was slightly leaner, and wearing primitive homemade clothing. There was an air of menace about him that made Rowlandos quake inwardly. But Caine just growled at him, and moved past him.

"Daddy!"

The big human wrapped his arms around the green-skinned teenager in a big bear hug, lifting her off her feet; she was laughing joyfully. When he put her down, his attention suddenly turned to the young boy, and the menace returned.

"You." He started towards the boy, who was very much afraid. The boy backed away until he bumped against the bulkhead. But before Caine could move, his daughter grabbed his arm.

"Daddy, it was my idea to run off." Despite the softness of her demeanour and voice, he seemed unconvinced. "I've never been off on my own before; I know I'm only thirteen daddy, but I just wanted to have a little fun."

Rowlandos snorted. "So you stole a ganger's bike on Strangis Forgan Kror?" He shut up in a heartbeat when Caine glared at him.

"I'm sorry, daddy," she said, putting herself between her rather dangerous father, and her teenage boyfriend. Clearly she knew he would never hurt her, and used it to her advantage. "I promise I won't do it again."

He blew out a long breath, a grumble forming in his throat.

"Alright."

He gestured to the hatch, and the two teenagers slunk quietly up the ladder, and through the open portal to the other ship. As soon as they disappeared, Row found himself slammed helplessly against the bulkhead, his feet dangling off the floor, and Adam's forearm pressed hard against his throat so he could barely breathe.

Row gurgled, trying to form words.

Caine pushed his face close to Row's, a snarl on his lips.

"If I ever see you again, for any reason, you will die horribly. Do you understand?"

Row gurgled but didn't nod. Caine yanked on one of the metal dreadlocks. Row gurgled again, much louder this time, and with far more pain involved than he thought possible.

"Do. You. Understand?"

Rowlandos nodded, and in seconds he was gasping for air and lying on the floor. Caine was gone, and the hatch was shut. There was a humming, and a whine as the other ship rocketed off.

"Damn you, Caine," cursed Row hoarsely.

* * *

"Who is Garvion, daddy?"

They had returned to Strangis to rendezvous with the rest of the school trip they had detoured from. Polly was still in the ship, whilst Thrigor was having a dressing down from one of the teachers.

The wind had picked up as father and daughter stood side-by-side underneath the wing of the *Kara*, looking out at the city around them. She had told him about the ganger on the stairs, and how she had frozen up with guilt and fear. Adam hadn't said anything, but he looked sad, as if disappointed with himself for not protecting her from that experience.

"He was your biological father," he replied sadly.

She nodded. "He was the mercenary you killed when you were training with Diamond." He looked shocked that she remembered the man. "It wasn't exactly a pleasant experience, daddy," she said, slipping her arm under his, "and the nasty ones are always the ones you remember most."

Adam was about to say something, apologise for not telling her before, or something that could have made things better, but she was way ahead of him.

"It's okay daddy, I know why you did it. And I know why you kept it all from me. Daddy, I understand, and there's nothing to forgive."

He smiled down at her, "When did you grow up so fast?"

"When I got a boyfriend."

Polly approached, a grin on her face, fingering something on her ring finger. She held her hand out to show Eve, and the young girl gasped. And then she started to giggle. She ran into Polly's arms, and hugged her tight.

"Daddy proposed?" she asked excitedly. "How? When?"

Polly told her. "Well he proposed just before you disappeared." She pointed a mischievously accusing finger at her, a sly smile on her lips. "He was very un-Adam-like in fact, nervous and stammering. He was even sweating." She cuddled up to Adam. "It was all very romantic."

"So does that mean you're my mum?" asked Eve. Polly thought she was taking the piss, but the straight and completely innocent look on the girl's emerald face dissuaded her of that notion.

"If you want me to be," answered Polly.

Eve giggled, and threw herself literally into her parents' arms.

"Thankyou."

Eighteen:
The Bodyguard

Historian's Note: The events in this story take place eleven months after *Evie's First Adventure*.

"My father? He's the greatest being in the universe... he just didn't know it back then. Never did, in actual fact, not even now during these tumultuous times when nothing is as it seems, and the idea of nations is meaningless."
-Prince Lucien.

December 4007ad.

M'Der Tr'n was complaining.

"When I said we should have a different kind of bachelor party, playing golf was not what I had in mind." He was standing there, his naturally gangly long body clothed in the ridiculous outfit of long socks with the trousers tucked into them, a chequered tank top, and a flat cap. "Raymond's party was a blast."

Raymond Sansky halted his swing mid-strike, sending the little white ball skittering across the grass erratically, stopping barely metres away. He frowned and grumbled.

"You started a fight with a hover-bike gang," he cried, turning to his Kra Nal friend. "Then when the fighting got tough, you left Adam and I to fend for ourselves whilst you flirted with one of the local women."

M'Der grunted.

"She stiffed me as well."

The other three men looked at him with shocked expressions.

"Stiffed me on the money," he growled. He stepped up to the centre of the marked area, and pushed his spiked tee into the soft ground. The sun was high in the sky, illuminating the luscious green course beautifully. Far overhead, silent starships raced across the sky, dark specks against the natural blue, far above the peppered fluffy white clouds. It was almost just like Earth, except for the massive grey moon on the horizon, and the nine others visible around it in the daytime.

He placed the ball on the tee, setting his feet in the right position, and then swinging the club. It connected with a loud thwack, and the ball flew into the air, arcing down the fairway. Someone harrumphed at the perfect shot, and M'Der chuckled to himself.

"Anyway," he continued, stepping out of the way of Relion's tee-off. "As best man, it should've been my choice where we go."

"You agreed with my decision," complained Adam Caine. "You were excited when I mentioned I wanted to come to this sports planet."

The Kra Nal historian sighed, slipping his chrome golf club into the shoulder bag provided by the course's Central Management Centre. "When you suggested we come to this beautiful place, I assumed we'd be going to see the hover-bike races, or the fights in Grey Sector's arenas, possibly even this atoll-to-atoll endurance boat race I heard about in the hotel lobby."

He suddenly noticed something being passed between the others.

"What's this?" he complained.

Raymond, embarrassed, cleared his throat, and hid the credit note behind his back. Relion fidgeted under the tall Kra Nal's penetrating gaze. It was Adam that answered him, twiddling the golf club around in his hands.

"We, uh, we bet each other how long it would be before you started complaining about the sports activities."

"Adam and I lost," Relion harrumphed. The Mertik baker shook his head in defeat. "Sorry."

M'Der's eyes narrowed. "Sorry you made the bet, or sorry you lost?"

Relion just shrugged, eliciting a snort from the others around him.

"I bet the women are having more fun than we are," M'Der sniffed. "Polly always had a better imagination than you, Adam. At least you got your damn hair cut." There was a loud swipe, and Relion made a half-decent shot that whistled down the fairway towards the green. The white ball plonked softly into the darker grass. Raymond let out a curse, and started muttering to himself.

"Stop muttering, *General*," Adam grinned. He turned to M'Der, "At least I've got hair to cut." Raymond kept muttering. Adam chuckled, turning to the others, "I think it might be a good idea to try a different sport after this hole." Enthusiasm overtook him all of a sudden. "How about cricket?"

The others all groaned.

The wind kicked up, and one of the ships that were passing far overhead came closer and closer at breakneck speed. It was a Terran Navy shuttle, one of the heavily armoured models used to carry dignitaries. It was the standard navy blue hull, although it had ostentatious gold lettering and bordering.

Adam cursed.

"It's from the *St. George*."

Raymond and M'Der swore, throwing down their golf clubs.

The grass shifted wildly as the shuttle slowed, spun, hovered, and then dropped onto the fairway, the wake abating. The rear hatch swung open, and a large group of Terran soldiers filed out in two lines. They wore black armour and black fatigues, each carrying a matt-black plasma carbine. A Navy officer strode out between the two lines of Hunters, hands clasped at the small of his back like some imperious ruler. The snot-nosed young officer wore the *St. George*'s unit patch on his sleeve, with too much gold braiding and lanyards for someone so young.

"What's the *St. George*?" asked Relion.

Adam's face had fallen, answering in a growl. "The *HMS St. George* is the home of the Terran royal family; it's a floating palace, although officially it's classified as a titan. As far as I know, it's the biggest ship ever built by the Terran Navy. Has a whole battlegroup of Navy ships protecting it."

"Your monarch isn't much more than a visible figurehead, is she?" Relion asked Raymond, who just chuckled, and nodded. "So who's St. George?"

Now Adam smiled broadly.

"St. George was the patron saint of England, my home country." M'Der snorted when he saw the distant look on Adam's face, and the smile still twitching at his lips. The historian knew he was thinking of the life he had been forced to leave behind, or at least the parts of it he hadn't been running from.

The Hunters surrounded the quartet of friends in perfect parade formation, and snapped to attention, their boots muffled by the grass of the golf course. The runt in uniform stood in front of Adam, oblivious that a flag officer stood nearby.

"Captain Caine, your presence is requested in the throne room of the *HMS St. George*. You have a personal invitation from Her Majesty Queen Leya herself. She's waiting for you, Captain."

"I'm not at her beckon call," replied Adam.

"All Terrans serve the monarchy," the junior officer sniffed. He carried himself as if he had a silver spoon stuck up his arse, and yet his eyes seemed nervous, like he was making sure he knew where the Hunters were to bail him out of trouble.

Raymond cleared his throat, and stepped up beside Adam, glaring down at the short officer.

"Adam Caine and his family are citizens of the planet Ckeer Najoor; that planet –and the one we are currently stood upon- are far outside Terran territory, and outside the Terran Navy's jurisdiction, or any of its allies."

"I have my orders," the runt said stubbornly. "Who, sir, are you to question them?"

Raymond got up in his face. "I am Major General Sansky, Executive Deputy Director of Navy Intelligence." The uniformed runt quaked as he realised just how screwed he would be. "You will take us to the Queen, and on the way explain why the Terran Navy is breaking the rules of foreign planets!" Raymond's voice had slowly risen in volume, his anger evident. Something Adam could never get his head around when dealing with Raymond: after all the things he had seen and experienced as a former field agent, Raymond Sansky was still as naïve as he had been nearly eight years ago.

"Y-y-yes, sir!" the Lieutenant stammered. He fidgeted on the spot, the prior arrogance gone, replaced by outright worry. He was sweating profusely, the stains showing through quickly under his armpits, the perspiration glistening his brow. He hesitated, and then spun on the spot, stumbling as the grass slowed the spin. His cheeks reddened as he marched away towards the shuttle.

Raymond followed, and the three others rushed to catch up. Adam leaned in as they walked. "What the hell are you doing Raymond?" he whispered.

"Keeping them off balance, Adam. Just stick with me." There was a hurt look on the bigger man's bearded face, as if it was his job to do the leading and the talking after so long being in charge one way or another. "They came down wanting to bully us into doing what they want; now we're the ones doing the bullying, and it'll keep them guessing."

* * *

The *HMS St. George* was huge, reminding Adam of a photo negative of Yh'reth'gar's titanic flagship. Like any other military Terran vessel, it was a dark blue colour, though there were patterns on the hull chased with gold armour plating that shone under the star of the planet's system. Its shape was reminiscent of the ships that escorted it, though it lacked the doorstop-shaped armoured prow, instead a long neck extending from the upper bow of the ship like the head of a swan. Giant engines protruded from the aft, only the two biggest actually symmetrical and of the same size. It was a truly magnificent sight.

The military shuttle was escorted into the hangar by a flight of four red-hulled Rhinos, who flew in a perfect diamond formation all the way down to the hangar deck. The landing clamps clanked out, and the shuttle settled onto the shiny black deck with a loud hiss of hydraulics. The Hunters filed out in pairs, silent as the grave, followed by the runt in uniform.

The four friends warily exited the shuttle.

Raymond didn't seem surprised by the cavernous expanse of the hangar bay around them, though Relion looked at it like it was the most amazing thing ever.

The red starfighters lifted off again, and powered out into space.

* * *

They were brought in front of the Queen herself, whose throne room was devoid of anyone but several officers and her bodyguards, all of whom stood either side of the golden throne itself. The bodyguards glowered at the newcomers as if they were a new threat to protect the Queen from.

The Queen was clothed in a long dress that seemed to be made from the hide of some large lizard that glistened and changed colours with the bright lights around her. Her gold crown was identical to that of Adam's own time, inlaid with sparkling rubies and glittering emeralds.

The formal announcer was about to call out the names of the four newcomers when Raymond and Adam both glared at him, shutting him up.

"Staff Sergeant Caine," the Queen called. There was a sad smile on her ebony lips, and something slightly more sinister in her twinkling eyes. The bodyguards inched closer to their Queen as the four friends were pointed to a spot in front of the throne. The big bodyguards were far taller than any human. Their muscles bulged under carapace armour that only added to their size.

M'Der saw what Adam was staring at, and whispered to him.

"The Terran King or Queen is always protected by a group of abhumans who have lived on a high-gravity deathworld called Ar's Paradise. Lifeguards, if you can believe it, who are raised on a planet where nature is more dangerous than most in this universe. They're dedicated to protecting the monarchy like no other."

"Thanks for the reassurance," muttered Adam.

They stopped as one under the sneering scrutiny of six officers wearing Admiral stripes of varying grades, along with a dozen civilians who were probably part of the royal family. Adam recognised one of the admirals as being the Rijiin female that commanded the *St. George.*

Raymond stepped forward, and bowed to the Queen; the nearest of the Lifeguards twitched perceptibly, wary of the man, though the Queen just gave him an amused look. She had aged a little since the last time Adam had seen her: she was no longer the confused and overwhelmed teenager, and very much the strong young woman.

"And you are?" she asked. Her legs were crossed, and she held herself up straight, her hands folded in her lap.

"Major General Sansky, your majesty. Executive Deputy Director of Navy Intelligence, ma'am."

"Adam's greatest ally," commented the Queen. "I didn't invite you, or the other two. Just Caine." She beckoned Adam forward with one dark ringed finger. The leader of the Lifeguards twisted his head round to look at the Queen, his features indistinguishable underneath his black helmet. The Queen nodded, and the guard relaxed slightly.

"What do you want, Leya?" demanded Caine. Every visible face dropped at his brashness, shocked at his attitude towards a monarch.

"Such boldness."

Caine was angry. "You are not *my* Queen, nor am I a citizen of the Terran Consortium, or a foreign dignitary, so I don't have to show any kind of respect, especially after the last time we met. Now you basically kidnap the four of us off a planet not aligned with you or Terra. Respect is the last thing on my mind." Despite the featureless helmets, Adam was certain the Lifeguards were tensing, waiting for the order to strike him down in a second.

"I need your help," the Queen said, though her demeanour didn't change at all.

"The last time you said those words, I was nearly killed by a Tyrannosaurus Rex that I'd already killed, nearly torn apart by a reality altering weapon, and... YOU FUCKING USED ME!"

The Lifeguards snapped forward, stalking towards Caine, flexing their large fists.

Raymond saw the menace in Adam's eyes, and knew what was coming: Caine was about to enjoy this, despite the size of his opponents. The former Marine was suddenly a flurry of arms and legs, twisting, as the first Lifeguard swung low at him. The large fist swished past Adam's midsection, and his own fist crashed down onto the soft space between armour plates at the neck.

The Lifeguard grunted and slumped to the floor. The next guard kicked out, trying to sweep Adam's legs out from underneath him. Adam leaped above the kick, and came down on the guard's knee, where the armour plating separated at the knee. The guard made no sound, but hit the floor and didn't get back up; the remaining three guards backed off, disturbed that they had badly underestimated Caine.

The Queen waved them away, a knowing smile on her lips.

It was a test.

Damn her.

"As I said," she smiled again, "I need your help."

"Tough shit," he growled. He turned to leave.

"If you don't," she called out as strode away. "You'll regret it."

Adam stopped in his tracks, and gave a dry chuckle, shaking his head.

"You can't be serious."

"I'm the Queen of Terra; I'm always serious. And as for why you'll regret it: the *HMS Raj Kochhar* is currently in orbit of Ckeer Najoor with orders to destroy your home settlement if you do not comply with my request."

"Are you fucking kidding me?!" Raymond saw the dark rage cloud Adam's face, and wondered just how safe the Queen was. He put a hand on Adam's shoulder to curb whatever violence was building up within his friend. Adam didn't resist it, his jaw working to release some kind of words, but nothing more came out.

To Raymond, the gathered Navy and Army officers looked decidedly guilty, and somewhat uncomfortable. It was a sign for Raymond that the Queen was acting without approval from her military advisors, though none of them were brave enough to speak out directly.

Wetness glistened in Adam's eyes, his rage palpable.

The last time he had seen this rage was in the untamed barbarian he had seen eight years ago, raging against the creatures that had tried to lock him up. Then, the Core creatures had unleashed Adam's nightmarish rage within. Now, he was tempered, wiser, older, and far more aware of what he was capable of. Raymond, after discovering Adam's survival onboard the *Gold Royale*, had researched Adam's past, and was horrified to discover just what kind of military operations the man had conducted. It just made him that much more frightening.

Like now.

"You're going to protect me," the Queen smiled coldly.

It said a lot to Raymond that Adam was restrained by only a light hand on his shoulder: Adam trusted him a great deal, even in the throes of his rage. Although his voice was shaking, Adam spoke in a whispered voice.

"Raymond, get M'Der and Relion back to Ckeer Najoor on the *Red Stallion*. Tell Polly and the others about this, and then start making calls to anyone you can think of to find out what the hell is going on."

Raymond sighed.

"Okay, Adam. I hope you know what you're doing."

Adam just nodded.

* * *

Ckeer Najoor.

A week later.

The *HMS Raj Kochhar* slid out from behind Ckeer Najoor's second moon. Its wedged blue hull powered forward, the light from the system's star glinting off its shape. Engines flared brightly, and gun turrets swivelled. A squadron of Stickleback bombers disgorged from its hangar bay, and took up formation around the sleeker *Woomera*-class cruiser.

The ship's commander, a young captain distantly related to the royal family, was stood on the bridge of his brand new ship. The order had been passed down directly from the *St. George*'s commander. He had had to re-read the written orders several times before it sunk in, and even then he had felt sick to his stomach.

But orders were orders.

His crew said nothing, but he saw the looks on their faces.

"Targets plotted and locked, Captain," one officer called.

"Thankyou, tactical. Helm, put us in geo-synchronous orbit with the target settlement." He ignored the condemning looks on the helmswoman's face, but was glad the crew were continuing with their duties; he was not so sure he would be as quiet if he were in their positions.

He sat down in his high-backed command chair, reviewing the holographic displays that hovered in a semi-circle around him.

His XO was standing by the side of the chair.

Neither of them spoke.

There was no need.

* * *

"The boys are late," Hannah Spears-Sansky said. She, Polly, Eve, and Relion's wife Felp were in Polly and Adam's domicile, cleaning up the mess from last night's party. Most of the visitors had gone home the previous night, leaving the four alone.

The town was quiet; it was the local equivalent of a Sabbath day, the settlement recovering from several other celebrations the night before.

"Worried?" smiled Polly.

"About two of the most dangerous men in the universe?" Hannah returned the smile. "Always, though I wouldn't be so worried if that historian friend of yours and Adam's hadn't gone with them."

"M'Der? He's harmless." She caught herself. "Sometimes."

"They'll be fine, Mummy," Eve said from the other side of the room. Hannah saw the almost hidden smile on Polly's lips.

"What were you talking about last night?" said Felp, tucking a long strand of bright red hair behind her ear as she picked up some paper streamers. "Your husband was giving Adam something special for the wedding."

Hannah grinned. "You'll love it, Polly. It's a..." A loud roar interrupted her as something passed over the town. The four women rushed outside to see the

Red Stallion thunder overhead, and land in the small field set aside originally just for the *Kara*. Except that the *Kara* itself was nowhere to be seen.

Dread filled Polly.

Without thinking, she held Eve's hand, and the two ran to the *Stallion*'s landing spot as it kicked up a cloud of dust. The blunt-nosed former cargo shuttle touched down on the compacted baked dirt, the engines whining as the ship powered down. The ship's starboard personnel hatch slid open with a pneumatic hiss.

M'Der, Raymond and Relion stepped out.

But no Adam.

* * *

HMS St. George.

The Lifeguard roared as his left hook swung over Adam's descending head. Caine rolled, and snapped a hard kick to the unarmoured guard's ankle. It snapped painfully. The guard roared, falling flat on his face. Adam pounced back to his feet in a ready stance but his opponent was down, clutching his leg.

The other Lifeguards had barely seen Caine move –just a flash of motion.

The commander of the Queen's bodyguards had demanded that Caine be tested for a week so that the guards could get the measure of his skills. Unfortunately, Caine had put fifteen of them in the *St. George*'s infirmary, all with varying injuries, and all with a greater, healthier respect for the newcomer.

Commander of the Guard Rorg approached Caine as he took a swig of water, and towelled off the sweat that had perspirated during the three sparring matches so far that day. He winced from a bruise on his leg, inflicted by the second opponent. Rorg was especially large compared to the rest of the guards, though his large features were softened by age, his long straightened hair greying.

"You are... different to the other Terrans," the huge man said, his voice a perpetual low rumble. It was a reminder that neither man was truly considered to be Terran -certainly not by birth. "The way you fight is beyond any military training I have ever seen. The speed you move with is faster than I thought humans were physically capable of."

Adam looked embarrassed.

"I've had some extra training, *after* my military service."

Adam didn't elaborate that the training had consisted of weeks of alien martial arts, insane endurance training, being thrown down the side of an active volcano, and running through miles and miles of hostile jungle hunting bizarre predators. Nor did he elaborate that he had killed the woman who had trained him, or at least that was the hope; he had never bothered checking, nor did he want to.

It wasn't something he had dwelled on for a long time, and wasn't about to start now.

A civilian dressed in a long-tailed tuxedo entered the training room, turning his nose up at the sweating injured soldiers all around him. His big bushy white mustachio wiggled imperiously.

He addressed Rorg, though in a manner that clearly aggravated the huge Ar's Paradise native. "Commander, the Queen wishes to know if Staff Sergeant Caine can perform his duties as her personal bodyguard to your satisfaction."

Rorg grumbled, throwing as much disdain for the servant into his answer. "Tell... *Her Majesty...* that the Staff Sergeant will do a better job than twenty of my Lifeguards." Despite his 'imprisoned' status, he felt pride at the huge warrior's respect and admiration. He did, however, notice the sarcastic stressor when Rorg said *Her Majesty*.

Something worth looking into, he thought.

The manservant bowed slightly, as if trying to give the abhuman Lifeguard commander as little respect as possible within the confining protocols of his own lowly profession. He then left the soldiers to themselves, scurrying out in a hurry.

Adam was shaking his head. The aristocratic behaviour of many of those he had encountered on the *St. George* was a sad reminder of his own upbringing in Cambridge, under the baleful eye of his father.

"You do not approve?" queried Rorg. The other Lifeguards looked over, interested to hear Caine's opinion on the matter.

"I just thought that after two-thousand years of so-called democracy and liberality, humans would be beyond petty things like caste. It's one of the reasons I enlisted as a regular Commando, instead of as an officer." The huge abhuman's thin eyebrows lifted for a very brief second at the word commando.

"All societies have castes," replied Rorg, folding his massive arms in front of his solid chest. "Even my own; it is the way of nature –for the rich, greedy, and selfish overprivileged to seek command over others, whilst the poor, selfless, and enslaved are forced to serve them."

"Then why do you and your people serve the Queen? Ar's Paradise isn't within Terran territory, and there is, as I understand it, a big difference in culture between your people and the Terrans."

Rorg bowed his head in shame. Adam noticed the others doing the exact same thing. "We owe a great debt to the Terran monarchy for saving our world from a natural disaster. We had nothing of value to give in return so our leaders promised to send our best hunters and warriors to protect the King or Queen until he or she deems the debt paid."

Adam snorted. "And you can't get out of the deal?"

Rorg shook his shaven head. "The Queen told me herself that if we didn't comply she would personally undo what her predecessors did to save my people, thus turning my planet back to the dangerous place it was before."

"So you're as much a prisoner as I am."

Rorg didn't say anything; he didn't have to, the answer was clear –Leya was bullying useful people into helping her, even going so far as to threaten to kill their loved ones, and everything they hold dear.

The other Lifeguards were exchanging knowing looks, though Adam had no idea what they were thinking.

"The Queen is hosting a formal ball in the main ballrooms in six hours," Rorg commented. "Are you sure you wouldn't like to use some of the armour the armoury provided?" He pointed to a pile of shiny black armour off at the edge of the room.

Adam smiled.

"Thankyou for the offer, but I'm quite happy wearing the fatigues I retrieved from my ship. Same goes for the Heckler Koch and the Walther." Adam gestured to the neatly folded black military fatigues on a bench, a matt-black assault rifle and 9mm pistol laid next to them with extra magazines, and a long combat knife in its scabbard. "Besides, I won't be wearing just the fatigues." He didn't elaborate on that either, deciding to keep it a secret to himself and nobody else.

"As you wish Staff Sergeant."

Caine smiled. "Adam."

"Ragar," the other replied.

The two shook hands.

* * *

Couples danced in concentric circles, twirling and giggling as they mixed, span and chatted through slow, multiple-partner routines, all in concert with each other, rehearsed over days of practice. They played through the dance by a nine-piece orchestral group, who utilised bizarre alien instruments as well as the human traditionals.

Groups of dignitaries from dozens of non-aligned and allied worlds were gathered together, talking over drinks and canapés, sharing jokes and witty anecdotes. Fine tuxedoes were on display along with layer-cake dresses designed by the most expensive dressmakers of the nineteen galaxies. Some wore the military uniforms of their represented worlds, whilst others wore the black and gold of the Terran Navy.

Rorg's Lifeguards stood at the very outside of the gathering against the walls, keeping an eye on the proceedings in general when the Queen was announced as she entered the cavernous ballroom, flanked by Rorg and Caine.

The announcer cleared his throat, and spoke into a small mic on his little dais.

"Her Majesty, Queen Leya the First."

The guests clapped politely, and bowed to her as protocol demanded. However, all of them eyed Caine disdainfully, seeing the combat uniform as inappropriate for such an event. He rested his hands on the butt of the HK that was slung from one shoulder, draping down in front of him where he could easily get at it in a hurry.

Underneath the loose-fitting black fatigues he had added the stealth suit underneath for a bit of extra insurance in case he actually had to defend the

Queen; then again, the blasted woman would never have brought him here if she didn't think someone was going to make a move.

The guests continued to bow as the Queen and her new bodyguard passed them. The band had stopped playing as well; their instruments limp in their hands.

Above it all, Adam was amazed to see rings of floating chandeliers lighting the entire room, the light catching the dozens of regal paintings of Leya's greatest ancestors, even Elizabeth II and her world-shaping son, Charles III.

The Queen nodded to each dignitary in turn, ignoring the glower from Caine as she stopped to talk to the Damoc Empire's ambassador to Terra, exchanging false pleasantries.

A trio of Terran civilians wearing gold sashes and royal brooches, however, distracted Adam. They were sneering to each other, looking over at him with the same disdainful looks as all the aristocrats seemed to give him. They muttered something that they thought Adam couldn't hear about his dubious parentage... something about apes in a zoo.

Caine speared them with a frightening glare, and the three scurried off to find more alcohol. He felt no satisfaction at the sight, knowing that either they'd be back to make some hastily thought-up retort, or someone else would.

It was going to be a long night...

* * *

An hour of mindless talking and dancing went by before anybody broached the subject of why Caine was wearing primitive clothes, and carrying primitive weapons; and why he was protecting the Queen of all people.

The owner of the question was a red-cheeked young Naval officer with the royal broach on a red sash, presumably indicating that he was a lower member of the royal family.

I'll bet he got his commission because of it, Adam thought, unable to help being cynical. *Although judging by the rank stripes on the sleeves of his dress uniform, he commands a starship; probably one of the ones escorting the* St. George.

The pudgy, balding officer was clearly inebriated, slurring his words, cheeks red, and having trouble standing up straight.

The Queen had seated herself in the throne at one end of the ballroom, raised up slightly on a stepped metal platform. Nobody had approached her as she sat up there, overlooking the whole proceedings. She was smiling and waving, mostly at the band, though even that was false to Adam's experienced eyes.

Adam hadn't even noticed the drunken idiot approach; he'd been intent on the rest of the crowd for those who weren't drunk, and very much alert.

"So what's a scruffy ruffian like you protecting Her Majesty, my favourite cousin?"

"You should ask her," he growled.

"I'm asking *you*," the officer said, stabbing a wobbly finger at Adam's solar plexus. "What makes you so special, *Sergeant*?" Adam ignored him; or at least, he tried to: the officer wouldn't let up. "Hey, I'm talking to you." The idiot was getting angry now, pissed off that a lowly commoner was snubbing him.

He pushed Adam gently. Out the corner of his eye, Caine saw Rorg take a step toward the officer, though whether it was to assist Adam, or prevent him from doing something violent. Caine continued to glare at him, but the man was in too much of a drunken stupor to realise just how much on the edge of a precipice he was.

So the drunk pushed him again, this time much harder. Adam didn't budge, never losing balance, and continued to glare at his 'attacker'.

He said through gritted teeth, "Please refrain from whatever you have planned."

"Or what?" the other slurred.

"Or I'll hurt you."

The drunk laughed stupidly loudly, attracting the attention of the many guests within view. They all looked interested in the proceedings like hyenas circling a campfire, waiting for a moment of weakness to strike.

The Queen's cousin, however, just pushed Adam again.

Controlling his anger, Adam slowly turned to the Queen, who seemed to be mightily amused by it. She nodded, and Adam saw a twinkle of mischief in her eyes.

Damn her, she's enjoying this.

The drunk, seeing that Adam was turned away from him, and having seen the Queen's nod of approval for his own actions, threw a hard punch directly at Caine's head.

Adam didn't even turn his head, his eyes meeting the Queen's.

He caught the punching fist in the palm of his hand with the hard slap of skin on skin.

Shocked beyond belief, the officer tried to throw a punch with the other hand, forgetting that his glass of wine was still there in his fist. But the punch never got past his own head.

Adam suddenly span to face him, and kicked him high in the chest, sending him flying backwards onto his arse. A shocked gurgle escaped from his lips and the wine glass emptied its purple-tinted contents onto his dress uniform.

"You low-born bastard," the drunken officer snarled, his similarly sashed and sloshed friends picking him off the floor. "I challenge you to a duel." He was pointing viciously at Adam, his finger curling where the bigger man's hand had briefly crushed his fist.

Unfortunately, his finger was the first to go.

Caine darted forward so quickly only Rorg seemed to see him move, grabbed the accusing finger, snapped it with a quick twist of his wrist, and then slammed his other forearm into the man's face. Blood spurted from his opponent's nose, and bruises immediately welted up around his eyes. Without letting go of the broken finger, he then delivered a solid punch to the man's throat, letting him fall to the ground gagging and spitting blood.

Adam returned to his position in front of the throne, glaring at the Queen.

There was a gasp of shock from several light-hearted guests, and Adam suddenly span, snapping the Walther out of its holster too fast for the human eye to see.

The shot was louder than anyone expected, catching all by surprise.

The bullet blew out the Queen's cousin's brains, splattering grey matter and chunks of bone over a female dignitary wearing a white meringue dress. The Queen's cousin collapsed to the floor, the tiny one-shot plasma pistol that had been aimed at Adam's head falling from his lifeless hands.

The Walther's barrel still smoking, Adam bellowed to the crowd.

"PARTY'S OVER! GO BACK TO YOUR QUARTERS! THERE'S NOTHING TO SEE HERE!" The crowd made to move, but then stopped, and Adam felt something cold and metallic press against his back.

He twisted slowly to find Rorg standing there.

"I'm sorry Adam, but there's *everything* to see here."

* * *

A figure stood in Polly's doorway casting their shadow across the living room of the domed home she shared with Adam and Polly.

Her heart skipped a beat.

"Adam-?" the sentence died in her throat when she realised it wasn't him.

The person was, however, dressed in the local variant of sandstorm gear, including a hemmed design that looked like a circled squiggly line to anyone that didn't live on Ckeer Najoor; the design indicated that he was a resident of the Loor Province, site of the informal capital city. The gear was only used when crossing the Jilo Plains, a huge stretch of medium desert between Loor Province and Polly's home settlement, Rino.

He was a messenger, bringing messages, parcels, and other such items from Loor City's spaceport.

"Dr. Jenkins?" He stepped into the living room, and pulled several envelopes and a pair of brown-wrapped packages from the pack on his back. "Sorry to disturb you; your daily mail." He placed them on the kitchen table, and pulled out the electronic device he used to keep track of packages. She placed her thumbprint on the device, and he disappeared, leaving her alone.

Hannah had taken Eve, Sasha and Sapphire for a walk with some of the neighbours, and M'Der and Raymond were almost permanently stationed in the *Red Stallion*, trying to find answers via the comms systems.

So Polly was alone.

She sunk to the floor, and sobbed until her tear ducts were red, raw and dry.

"Please come back to me, Adam."

* * *

"Why are you doing this, Ragar?"

Adam didn't turn around until the big Lifeguard released the pressure of the barrel from Adam's back. He turned slowly, so as not to alarm the bigger man, and was alarmed himself when he saw the strange weapon that was pointed at him. Rorg's big meaty hands made it look like a tiny twig, but it was still easily identifiable.

He took an involuntary step back.

It was the same damn weapon a fanatic had attempted to use on the *Gold Royale* to assassinate the Queen. Unfortunately, the weapon had backfired and killed its wielder, and attracted the attention of a mischievous reality-altering alien, almost costing Adam his life at the hands of a dinosaur he had previously killed.

He did not want to be near the damn thing if it decided to backfire again. Nor, in fact, did he want it fired *at* him on purpose. He had too much to lose now.

"Why are you doing this, Ragar?" he repeated.

"It's like you said, Adam," the huge man replied finally. "Ar's Paradise should be free of Terran influence, now and forever, not enslaved to the will of the Terran monarchy." Adam was about to plead for his new friend to stop now while he could. But Rorg seemed as if he was reading his mind. "I cannot stop this, Adam; I will not. There is no other way except this."

"There's always another way," pleaded Adam. "Petition the Terran Parliament for official membership like the Rijiins or the Rathgar, or request aid from the Alliance. Make your people an interstellar race by themselves. Anything but putting a gun to the Queen's head, or worse."

"No, my people will only be free through grand, dramatic actions; it's the only way anyone will take us seriously."

"If you go through with this, *nobody* will take you seriously. Dammit man, this is all they need to go storming onto Ar's Paradise and forcibly enslave all of your people under the pretences of putting them under arrest."

But Rorg was set on his path, and Adam could see the stubborn righteousness in the other's dark eyes.

Adam just nodded and sighed.

"Then I'm sorry."

Rorg's face was awash with shock as Adam was suddenly gripping his wrist, barely a blur of motion. He gripped the weapon arm with vice-like strength, and then twisted, at the same time squeezing with his fingers and palm. The movement accomplished what he had intended: the wrist snapped with a painful crunch, and Rorg dropped the bizarre weapon, letting it fall to the floor.

Adam's world suddenly turned upside down, and filled with stars as something large hit him in the side of the head. He found himself on the floor, trying to blink away a possible concussion. One of the black-clad Lifeguards was standing over him, his fist balled tightly.

"Stay down," it grumbled.

"No chance," Adam returned.

With both feet, he kicked at one of the knees nearest. It collapsed with a sickening crunch, and the Lifeguard fell to the floor, grunting from the pain. The Lifeguard's buddy stamped down towards Adam's chest incredibly quickly, putting as much of his weight into it as possible.

The large size-16 foot crashed down on the floor.

Adam rolled, and flicked out a blurry foot that connected with another knee. This time the owner dodged the majority of the hit, though Adam's combat boot still clipped his foot, off-putting his balance. This was followed by a kick to the chest that sent the Lifeguard flying backwards into another guard, the two tumbling to the floor.

Adam was up on his feet in an instant, a flurried blur of precisely aimed blocks, kicks, and punches that downed all but Rorg and another Lifeguard.

Rorg was still open-mouthed with utter shock, whilst the remaining guard charged at Adam, not heeding Rorg's warnings.

Adam slipped the HK from where it had rested at the small of his back, and slammed the butt into his head, flooring him along with the others.

The civilians were all still in the room, backing away in screaming fear to the sides of the room since the Lifeguards had sealed the doors shut for the time being. Most cowered behind upturned tables or their equally terrified spouses and bodyguards. Those military officers still in control of their bodily functions had gathered around the Queen's throne in an attempt to protect her.

Unfortunately, without any weapons of any kind —having been left in their quarters for an official diplomatic function- they were of no use to the Queen except as living shields.

The Lifeguards began picking themselves up, rubbing their heads as if to get rid of the grogginess. They looked up to find Adam with the butt of his assault rifle against his shoulder. They tensed themselves, preparing to charge him all at once.

"Don't," he warned them. "You will die."

"For freedom," one of them snarled.

They charged.

Nobody, not Rorg, the Lifeguards, the guests, or even the Queen herself, were prepared for the sheer thundering noise the assault rifle roared out. But Adam was oblivious as he slaughtered the Lifeguards, solid rounds bursting through their meagre body armour. Each guard was killed with an incredibly precise burst of three bullets each, all within split seconds of each other.

The ear-splitting rattling didn't stop until the Lifeguards were back down on the floor. This time they didn't get back up, and Adam felt a great sorrow well up in him. These people had been fighting for something good, and he had had to kill them because the Queen was holding the lives of his own family above his head.

He tried to fight off the overwhelming urge to turn the assault rifle on the Queen, spinning round, and aiming straight at her head. There was a collective gasp as the entire room held their breath, morbid curiosities making them watch even though they knew it could only end badly.

Adam's jaw worked under his beard, and the thought of killing her became very tempting. But Polly and Eve's faces came unbidden to his mind, a huge reminder of why he was here, why he simply didn't pull the trigger and end the Queen's miserable life once and for all.

He lowered the rifle, and let it hang once again in front of him.

His hands were shaking uncontrollably with rage.

When he looked up he found that she was smiling at him.

Bitch.

* * *

Rorg was taken to the *St. George*'s infirmary under heavy guard and heavily sedated by the doctors; some of the Army guards dealt the prisoner several kicks and punches meant to 'subdue' him.

The Queen decided to visit him whilst he was restrained, and was accompanied by the Rijiin admiral that commanded her flagship. The Admiral brought along a contingent of handpicked soldiers from the *St. George*'s gold-plated Army regiment. They were ordered to wait outside the infirmary.

Rorg was in and out of consciousness, the sedation only enough to knock out a standard human rather than a giant like Rorg.

"A...Adam," said Rorg, his voice weak.

"Ragar," Adam nodded emotionlessly. Despite the previous betrayal, he hated seeing the noble warrior being clamped to the bed like that, unable to move. The big warrior refused to look the Queen in the eyes, even though she was glaring knives at him.

The admiral's gaze was impenetrable, though she seemed to be reserving judgement, making Adam wonder what kind of deal existed between the Rijek and the Terran Parliament.

"Why did you do it, Ragar?" the Queen sneered. Adam could barely believe what he was hearing: she was genuinely angry that the people her ancestors had essentially enslaved wanted their freedom. She seemed to be taking it as a personal betrayal that her Lifeguard Commander had led the 'rebellion'.

"Ar's... Paradise... should be... a free world," he struggled to say. "Terran oppression has been... left unchecked... for far too long. Terra has lost... its way from the old times."

"Terran oppression?" the Queen said incredulously.

"The old times?" said Adam.

Rorg nodded weakly.

"The old times when humanity sought... sought to better itself. I...I read the stories from centuries ago, when... where humanity explored the universe, seeking out new life and... new... civilisations. They went where nobody had gone before them, always exploring." He paused as he tried to fight off the sedation again, his eyelids falling closed as if they were the heaviest objects in the world. He never saw Adam's strangled reaction to his exact wording. "Terrans have... lost their way."

"True," Adam admitted. "Modern Terrans believe in their own superiority, because their technology surpasses any other race, and always will."

There was a small smile on Rorg's lips before he finally fell asleep; the IV drip in his arm finally knocked him out.

The Queen sighed, shaking her head.

She turned and strode away, head held high.

Adam let out a growl as she disappeared with the golden guards.

The admiral stayed, looking at the large Lifeguard Commander with affection and pain. Adam frowned.

"How long have you been married?"

Shock showed on her wolf-like features. Her swept-back ears flattened briefly before she rallied herself.

"How did you know?"

Adam smiled.

"I've seen the way you look at each other, and the fact that Ragar mentioned his *ar'il'arlo* when we were training. If memory serves, that's a Rijiin phrase; means soul mate, I think." She gave him a slight wolfish grin. "Which can also mean wife or life-partner on one of the more obscure mountain-continents on Ry." She looked at him with what he hoped was respect: Rijiin facial expressions weren't entirely familiar to him.

"You are full of surprises, Caine," she said.

He accepted the compliment with a nod, but wasn't sure what to say.

"I need to see that weapon Ragar had," he stated instead.

She nodded reluctantly; she was still the *St. George*'s commander, and thus loyal to the crown, but she clearly saw something trustworthy in Caine. She beckoned him to follow her, keeping her eyes and ears out for anyone who might see them, or where they were going.

"The weapon and all the Lifeguards' artefacts were taken to the morgue lock-up." She kept her voice as a whisper as several crewmen passed by, each one snapping to attention and throwing a hasty salute. The admiral gave them formal nods, barely sparing any of them a second glance.

"Why does this floating palace have a morgue?" Adam wondered.

The Rijiin shrugged, a very human gesture.

"The designers of this ship deemed it necessary; looks like they were right." She pointed to one side as they entered the cold sterile morgue. The bodies of the Lifeguards he had slaughtered were being pushed via rolling chrome drawers into individual storage lockers by a pair of medical technicians. The doors were then shut tight, and a forcefield flashed into life across the whole wall of lockers.

The techs noticed the two standing near the doorway, and asked if they needed any help.

"We'd like to see the weapon the prisoner was carrying. It should be in the morgue lock-up." The techs nodded immediately, and one of them moved away to retrieve the item. He returned with it in a small metal box, and set it down on one of the cold metal autopsy tables for them to see.

The admiral pressed her thumb against the lock reader. The lock clicked, and the lid slid open with a hydraulic hiss. The cylindrical weapon was held tight by a clamp in the centre of the box. The clamp released the weapon, letting it sit loose.

Adam picked it up, and held it in front of him so that both of them could see it.

"I've never seen a device like this," she admitted.

"It's Muntarian technology."

"I've never heard of the Muntarians."

He gave her a sad smile. "You wouldn't; their civilisation was destroyed ten years ago by the Core not long after Rel Major fell. What little was left of their technology was scavenged by the Core; they used reality-inversion energy to power their weapons and ships. According to survivors I spoke to, it only took one hit from a lucky shot to destabilise one of their starships; the ship's drive inverted the space around it, and took half their home system with it. And then there's the chain reaction with other nearby devices."

She was looking at him with shock again.

As an explanation he said, "Then-Major Raymond Sansky was stuck undercover with the Core when they attacked Muntaria. He saw the whole thing." Trusting that he was telling the truth, she seemed to be looking at the weapon in Adam's hands with a newfound fear.

"I'll have some forensics experts brought over from the *HMS Lancer*, and then get them to find a way to safely dispose of that thing." She was pointing at the thing when a female voice growled menacingly from behind them.

"That would be a very bad idea, Admiral."

* * *

Adam was somewhat shocked to see that the two medical technicians were shimmering, as if a curtain was being flapped in front of them, their visage blurred and indistinct except for the pale colours of the generic uniforms.

A crisp emerald colour began suffusing itself into the blurred image.

When the effect dissipated only a second after beginning, Adam was shocked to discover a Mertik woman standing in front of him, replacing the medical technician completely. Adam didn't voice his concern that it was the same holo-technology as Raymond Sansky had once used –the visual effect was the same as Raymond had described some time ago.

But the woman shocked him more.

Her features were familiar to the point of recognisable; and yet, he had never met the woman.

"Who the fernikking hell are you?" demanded the Rijiin. A feral snarl escaped from her throat, and her lips pulled back to reveal her mouthful of carnivore fangs.

"Who I am is not important; who I work for is."

"Mertik secret service," Adam guessed. Though he didn't know the exact name of the planet Mertik's spy agency (it was a generic term after all), Relion had furnished him with a few stories of his own time spent running from them.

"And you are the invincible Adam Caine," the woman said, a sadistic smile on her pale green lips. Although she had an incredible facial structure, her face was worn from age, and the stress of her job had lightened her blue hair considerably.

"Invincible?" he snorted.

"Yes, it seems every time you are thrown into a fatal situation, you come through it alive, or close to it. We've been watching you and your family: the *Gold Royale*, Andromeda's core, the Emissaries of Power, Ckeer Najoor, even that massacre on Fallus Nine."

At the mention of Fallus Nine, Adam lost all curiosity, seething with anger. That had indeed been a debacle, but he tried to avoid thinking about the sheer amount of death he had instigated on that damned planet. He didn't need some spy reminding him of it.

The rage, however, subsided when his brain finally made the connection he had been looking for. But it was impossible; there was simply no way the universe was that small.

"You see it don't you, Caine?" she smiled. "The similarities in our facial structure are unmistakable, aren't they? Especially now she's growing up, her features are more prominent."

The Admiral leaned in closer to Adam.

"What's she talking about, Caine?"

Adam sighed.

"This is my adopted daughter's biological mother." He looked to the aging Mertik woman, who nodded for confirmation. "What the fuck are you doing here?"

"What, no questions of disbelief? No demands to know how I know? I should not be surprised I suppose; I'm sure *Evelyn* has told you about our brief encounter on Strangis Forgan Kror."

"Yes, but she never knew who you were."

It was then that Adam remembered the other spy, who had circled around to stand behind and to the left of the Mertik woman. The other was also a Mertik, although he was bald, the shaven blue stubble indicating it was by choice. He was harsh looking, stern sneering features with dark dead eyes: a sociopath –he was the real danger.

The Mertik woman's eyes flickered to her left for a second, using her peripheral vision to check her partner was there.

Adam kicked her in the chest blindingly fast.

The air exited her lungs with a loud *whoomph*. She went flying backwards into the forcefield protecting the cold storage lockers. The field flared brightly for a second as she made contact and bounced to the floor.

The sociopath reacted quickly, firing the plasma pistol in his hand as he dove behind a metal girder. The shot went wide, ricocheting ineffectually off the autopsy table. Adam immediately brought his assault rifle up, blasting at the spy in return.

One round clipped the sociopath's leg, blowing out a chunk of bloody meat.

The spy squealed in pain, clutching his leg, and dropping the weapon.

The woman, however, was picking herself off the floor, looking at Adam's rifle with fear. Adam approached her, barrel pointed down at her.

"Who the hell are you working for?" he demanded.

She started laughing, with a knowing glean to her eyes.

"Maybe you should ask the Queen's beloved uncle."

She slapped a small control on the sleeve of her jacket, and she was snatched away by the embrace of a bright red teleport beam.

"DAMMIT!" Adam shouted; he stamped his foot down ineffectually in the spot she had disappeared from, his boot hitting the metal deck of the morgue. He needed to know what she knew. But she was gone.

Now the sociopath was laughing, his voice tinged with pain and wet gurgles.

He was holding something in one hand.

A detonator.

Adam grabbed the admiral, and slung her over his strong shoulder despite her indignant screams of protest. He charged at the open exit, hearing the sociopath still gurgling with insane laughter. He was partially through the door when the explosives went off.

The noise was overpowering, cancelling out everything else with a deafening roar. The shockwave smashed into them, throwing them headlong into a bulkhead ahead of the flames. Adam managed to twist his body so that he would shield the admiral from the bulkhead, crunching against the metal wall.

He grunted, and let go of the admiral.

Her fur was singed in places, but she was alive and breathing.

* * *

Queen Leya, however, was raging.

Golden-plated guards had escorted Adam and the admiral to the Queen's personal chambers. She was sat behind a behemoth of a wooden desk, the high-backed chair towering above her head; her beautiful ebony face was contorted with yet more rage. When the two new allies appeared her anger was directed towards them.

"You blew up the morgue!" she bellowed. "It contained all the evidence we needed to understand what is happening here."

Adam didn't reply at first, just glaring at the Queen's uncle who stood by her side —he was pretty sure it was the same uncle she had been afraid of when she made her desperate visit to the *Gold Royale*.

"We did not cause the explosion, Your Majesty," the Admiral said with conviction. "Two Mertik agents were responsible; one teleported away before the other set off the explosives. Mr. Caine," she continued, avoiding using his rank he so clearly refused to use himself, "saved my life."

"Mertik agents?" the uncle snorted. "Preposterous."

"Funny you should say that," said Adam. "One of them told us that we should ask Your Majesty's dear old fucking uncle about their involvement." The uncle in question tried to splutter a protest, but Adam cut him off with an evil glare. "My guess is you're still in bed with whatever's left of 3899, who in turn decided to ally with the Mertik's spy agency. They used Rorg and his Lifeguards to instigate their rebellion, and then used the Mertiks to clean up the mess as best they could."

The uncle's mouth opened and closed several times like a fish as he tried to deny Adam's educated guess. Adam, however, had hoped that he was wrong; that Kombat 3899 had indeed been disassembled seven years ago. But the Uncle's face said it all.

"Uncle?" the Queen asked, her anger now directed at him.

He opened his mouth again, but nothing came out.

"Lock him up in the ship's brig," ordered the Admiral, looking at the gold-plated soldiers around them. They nodded, and circled around the royal in question, snapping force feedback cuffs on his wrists, and led him away. The Admiral went with them, and what officers had been in the room left Adam alone with the Queen.

"It's time you were straight with me," he growled.

The rage lifted off her like a veil, and she broke down crying.

Adam didn't budge an inch, although a small part of him felt pity towards her. He couldn't tell if it was another of her tricks to get something out of him that she wanted. How could he trust her after all this time, after all she had done?

A small voice in his head shouted at him to show compassion to another human being, but the soldier still in him railed against it.

For god's sake, Caine, he thought, *she's just a girl. Help her; go to her.*

"You were right," she sobbed. Her shoulders shook uncontrollably, and she tried to speak through the sobs. "I am so sorry, Adam, I should never have involved you in this."

Adam stepped around the side of the desk, unslinging his rifle, and laying it down gently on the wooden surface. He kneeled next to her gold-chased chair, taking her hand in his. Her eyes were red raw now, and her cheeks wet from the tears.

"Give up your throne," he said. "Take yourself away from this life. Or better yet, demolish the monarchy and you'll never have this problem."

"It's not as simple as that."

"It never is," he retorted.

"I... I have a son."

"Oh."

"Oh?"

"Surely that's a greater incentive to get out."

She sighed. "Like I said; it is not as simple as that."

"It's always a simple choice when it comes to our children: protect them at all costs. Right now, your best chance is to get away from all this. Besides, it's not like the monarchy *rules* the Terran Consortium; you've got Parliament for that."

"But it still means something," she whispered.

"After today I wouldn't be so sure. All those foreign dignitaries saw the Terran Queen attacked by her own Lifeguards, and defended by a human with no allegiance to Terra. They aren't going to think highly of the Terran monarchy from now on. Whoever sponsored Rorg's rebellion got what they wanted: the monarchy on the rocks."

The flat monitor screen on her desk flickered to life, and the face of a uniformed officer appeared.

"Your Majesty; a pair of officers from the *HMS Broken Bow* are requesting an audience with you. They claim that they have come in response to the attack on your person."

Leya frowned, and the officer shrugged.

"*Their* words, Majesty."

She sighed, and nodded.

"Show them in." Adam stood up, and snatched up his rifle, bringing it up in a ready stance in front of him, barrel down. "Are you sure that's necessary?" she asked.

"As well as being named for a town in Oklahoma, the *Broken Bow* is currently seconded to Navy Intelligence." He didn't add that he had received a communiqué from Raymond warning him that a certain former general of their acquaintance was aboard the *Broken Bow* and headed to rendezvous with the *St. George*. At the time of the transmission, he had thought nothing of it, but after the attack it seemed to make sense, as well as the Intelligence officer's current assignment aboard that ship.

As expected, the two officers strode purposefully through the door.

One was a Navy captain, bedecked in the black dress uniform of his calling, with medals pinned to his chest, and enough gold braiding to strangle a man. He carried his peaked officer's cap under his arm, his stride stiff as a board.

His companion wore a different uniform to the last time Adam had seen him.

Dressed in a black duty uniform, his arm showed the unit patch of the 21st 'Hunters' Regiment; *Colonel* Lenson Gardner looked far more intimidating than he had once been, though his face was still gaunt and unhealthy, his wispy white hair almost completely gone. But the steely determination was still in his grey eyes just as it had always been.

Caine's hands tightened on the assault rifle.

Gardner didn't recognise him at first; after all, Adam had always appeared to be a shaggy primitive before; now he had short hair, a beard, and looked older and wiser than he previously had done.

"Caine," he growled, when he finally recognised the Queen's new bodyguard.

"*Colonel*," Adam smiled without humour.

"Majesty, what is that man doing here?" demanded Gardner. He said it with such little respect that Adam had no doubt as to who had supported her in the past, and as to what their relationship still was. Anger seethed within him at the thought of Gardner escaping the justice he so richly deserved; he was continuing on the mission he had been chastised for: leading the ultra-secret Terran-supremacist Kombat 3899.

"He is here at *my* request," she sneered back.

Gardner clearly wanted to say something more, but he kept looking at Adam as if the younger man was preventing him from saying more.

The two officers shared a knowing glance, as if something unspoken were passing between them. They both nodded, and Gardner tapped a comm-bead sat in his ear canal. Adam frowned at the movement –who was he contacting? And why? Surely the *Broken Bow* was too far away to establish infantry-range communications devices?

The *Broken Bow*'s captain pulled something out from under his peaked cap tucked under his arm. A device of some sort.

"Sorry, Majesty," the captain said.

Alarmed, Adam brought his assault rifle up to his shoulder, and his finger tightened on the trigger, demanding he put the small device down. In the split-second before Adam could pull the trigger, the captain depressed the blue glowing button on the round device.

There was a piercing squeal that vibrated in Adam's ears, and only then did he notice that both of the two officers were wearing some kind of earpieces –selective noise cancelling technology most likely.

Adam found he could barely move, and felt something heavy pressing on his mind, as if the noise was driving him into unconsciousness. Which of course it was. His finger twitched, and the rifle barked.

Adam was unconscious within seconds, unaware of what damage his rifle had done before his eyes closed. His last vision was of the Queen slumping in her chair, blood dribbling from her ears.

* * *

"Thrice-damned bastard," spat Captain Lockwall, *Broken Bow*'s commander.

The burst of solid rounds had hit him in the shoulder, blowing out the joint, and splattering blood across the wall behind him. Gardner just stared at the ruin of Lockwall's shoulder; he was pale with shock at the violence and noise Caine's weapon had just shown it capable of. Even unconscious, Caine was capable of anything.

He snapped himself out the stupor, and tapped the comm-bead in his ear.

"Gardner to A Company; the Queen and bodyguard are incapacitated, commence Operation Regicide."

"*Acknowledged, Colonel,*" came the crisp reply. "*Operation underway; all units are go.*"

"Get a medic up to the Queen's personal office; Captain Lockwall's been severely injured, and we have two high risk prisoners up here."

"*Medics and an escort are on the way, sir.*" The line clicked closed, leaving Gardner to attempt to stem the bleeding from Lockwall's injuries. Caine and the Queen were unconscious, and currently no threat, the sonic disabler having done its job admirably. The device used high-pitched sound to interact with the target's nervous system, and knock them out.

"A good start."

* * *

Adam awoke hours later, his head pounding like he had had a bad night of drinking with plenty of illegal spirits. He moaned; even the slightest movement gave him pain. He struggled to get his limbs to move; his arms and legs ached as if they had been numbed, and then allowed to re-circulate the blood through them.

His strength returned in waves, getting stronger over the minutes.

He blinked his eyes quickly, pushing away his blurred surroundings to once again see the Queen's office around him. Leya was on the floor next to where he was lying. She was moaning, still unconscious, whispering her son's name in some incomprehensible bad dream. She wouldn't be much use for a while.

There were two pairs of black-clad Hunters stood at the ornate double doors, plasma rifles at the ready. For some reason neither Adam nor Leya had been tied or restrained in any way, presumably their captors believing they wouldn't need to if they were unconscious.

This was confirmed when the Hunters began looking at each other, and shifting uneasily, their faces unreadable behind their black helmets.

One of them stepped forward, and seeing an opportunity, Adam pretended to still be groggy, muttering and cursing like a drunkard. The Hunter, clearly a new recruit, stepped closer, checking to see if the prisoner was all right –a rookie mistake.

Suddenly, Adam grabbed the end of the plasma rifle's barrel and pulled hard, flipping the heavy trooper over him but maintaining a hard grip on the rifle. The trooper went flying over Leya, crashing into the desk with a startled shout.

Adam was instantly up on his feet, ignoring the lingering pain of the sonic weapon, rifle in hands. He spun the rifle around, the Hunters unsure what to do.

Adam shot them.

The rifle was powerful, slightly more so than the standard Army weapon. It produced a pulsed ring of swirling purple energy that slammed into the target, producing a loud zap with each shot. The pulse smashed the black armour to pieces, leaving a smoking ruin and carbon-scored body underneath.

The Hunters were dead two seconds after Adam attacked the first.

It was only then that Adam realised that there was a siren going off in the distance, muffled by the doors and walls of the private office. He opened the doors to find the standard lighting replaced by red flashing warning lights.

"Uh-oh, that's not good."

He went back to Leya, and shook her awake.

She screamed in pain as the same sensations that had hurt his tough body racked her own. Tears ran down her cheeks anew, and she curled up in a foetal position. But they didn't have time. Red lights like that probably meant some kind of catastrophic meltdown of the reactors, or the ship was under major attack —which was improbable given that the ship had headed back into Terran territory when it had left the sports planet behind. The only thing big enough to attack it was another titan or a super-heavy carrier, which were few and far between.

What did Gardner and the *Broken Bow*'s involvement mean?

Could this whole event be the start of another of the infamous Interior Wars that had plagued Terrans up to a thousand years ago? He hoped not —with the Core now a major threat, an Interior War now would leave the galaxies open for the Core to just take.

But 3899 were after the Queen herself.

Would they really go so far as to destroy the *St. George* to take her out?

Adam didn't know.

He was, however, pleased to see that the Hunters guarding them had held onto his weapons and ammunition. Energy weapons could be dampened in modern warships; 21st century solid-round weapons couldn't. He ditched the plasma rifle, and snatched up his equipment.

He slammed in a fresh magazine since the previous one had only one round in it left over from the brief fight in the morgue, and the burst that had clearly hit something when he fell unconscious: the blood was still splattered across the wall. Racking the slide, he realised that the helmets of the Hunters were squawking with static.

Somebody was trying to get in contact with them.

Two Hunters came charging through the doors, probably posted down the corridor.

The rifle roared, and tore their armour apart.

Before they could hit the ground, he grabbed Leya and bolted through the open doors. Her protests of still being in pain fell on deaf ears, the two stumbling through the red corridors. He had no real clue as to where he was going until they almost slammed into Admiral Vo'par, Adam's new Rijiin ally.

"What the fuck is going on, admiral?"

She shook her head. There was blood caked around her ears.

"I take it you were hit with the same sonic device," stated Adam.

She nodded.

"Gardner," they both said simultaneously.

"Is Her Majesty all right?" asked the admiral. Leya was dazed and confused, unable to focus entirely, occasionally whimpering from the pain she was still experiencing.

"She will be eventually," he sighed. "So what *is* going on?"

"Platoons of Hunters began teleporting onto the ship from the *HMS Broken Bow*. They slaughtered the Queen's household guards, the royal family, and whatever foreign dignitaries were around. I don't think they've found Prince Lucian yet, so thank the gods for small mercies I suppose." She looked around, searching for any targets or attackers. "I haven't found access to a terminal yet, but I think the reactors have been set to overload. It'll destroy the entire ship, and probably take out the Linkway around us."

"We're still in the Linkway?"

She nodded.

"Great; and I suppose the escort fleet is nowhere to be seen."

She nodded again.

"Crap." He didn't like what he was about to suggest because it would mean that once again he would put his life in mortal danger for somebody else's cause. But thousands could be in danger —the titan was too big to use some of the smaller, older Linkway tunnels, so had to use the main ways, and if its reactor overloaded it could invert and tear a massive hole in the space-time continuum and disrupt the major spacelanes. "We need to stop the overload."

She nodded yet again.

"If for nothing else," he said, "the destruction of this ship would erase any physical evidence of what went on here. How do I stop it?"

"We need to get down to the engineering section," Vo'par replied.

"There's no we," he stated. "*I'm* going down; you're taking the Queen to my ship, the *Kara Marazov*, wherever it's been impounded by your crew. If I can't stop the overload you get the Queen, Prince Lucian, *and* your husband off on the *Kara*, and head to Fort Zeus; you'll be safe there. Also, you need to contact the *HMS Raj Kochhar* and tell them to leave Ckeer Najoor orbit immediately."

She nodded.

"I need a map of some kind."

She handed a standard digipad previously tucked into her belt. "One of the Hunters was carrying this; it should help with getting around on this ship."

"Thankyou."

He didn't say goodbye, just ran in the direction the pad told him was the quickest way to the engineering decks. The route took him through multitudes of corridors, and down several of the more public elevators criss-crossing the behemoth vessel. He even had to listen to the dull tones of the elevators' orchestral music as they took him from one deck to another.

It took him fifteen minutes to reach any kind of sign telling him he was on an engineering deck, and another two minutes to find a way onto the main engineering deck. There was an intense rumbling vibrating through the deck underneath his feet, becoming stronger the closer he got to what he hoped was the reactor.

He had encountered no Hunters thus far, though there were a few of the crew with plasma burns and carbon scoring marring their corpses. None of them were alive, killed by pinpoint accurate kill-shots as only special ops soldiers like the Hunters could manage.

He was careful to stay silent, avoiding dislodging any of the corpses.

As much as I would love to see the Terran Navy fighting against itself, he cursed inwardly, *another Interior War, or civil war, or whatever they call it, would inevitably drag me back in, not to mention putting Ckeer Najoor squarely in the crossfire.*

The engineering deck, when Adam finally reached it, was massive, reminding him all too much of Yh'reth'gar's hellish version on his flagship. This one, however, was sterile; gangways and walkways made of transparent material with strong metal railings that reflected the glare of the alarm lights.

The main reactor sat at the centre of a massive square cavern, a giant glowing tower of energy contained by a network of forcefields and a lattice of armoured buttresses. The reactor's glowing energy was growing brighter, almost cancelling out the red light of the warnings.

The heat was just as intense as the light, although Adam was sure it wasn't real heat, but radiation.

Which wasn't good.

A pulse of energy almost took his head off when he stumbled on the corpse of a senior officer. He had looked down, and the pulse whipped through the space his head had occupied previously. He dove behind a big console, the plasma pulses fizzing against the other side of the console.

The holographic displays flickered as the power was temporarily interrupted.

By his reckoning, there was a dozen-man squad situated on different levels. They'd been waiting for him. But with the radiation rising, they couldn't possibly have been here the whole time. Unless their armour protected them, or someone was keeping a teleporter locked onto them.

Neither option was particularly helpful for Adam.

Although if they continued shooting at the console, as they seemed intent on doing, they would eventually melt right through it.

He slowly, and very carefully, poked the barrel around the end of the console, sighting on the flashes from the barrels of the firing plasma rifles. He shifted the aim a bit higher and to the right and squeezed the trigger. There was a sharp explosion as the single bullet pierced the power pack of the plasma rifle and detonated the energy within. There was a bloodcurdling shriek cut off by a loud gurgle.

He ducked behind cover before anyone could get a bead on him.

Several of the muzzle flashes were coming from one particular direction: a large balcony overlooking the entire cavernous deck, surrounding a glass-walled office, presumably belonging to the ship's chief engineer.

There were four distinct muzzle flashes on the balcony.

He set the assault rifle to auto-fire, making sure he knew where each one was. Gripping the rifle tightly, he spun and stood at the same time, maintaining the spin, and squeezed the trigger. The long burst roared bullets across the span of the engineering deck, taking out all but one of the four Hunters.

A ricochet that pinged off the railing in front of him, and took off his left ear underneath his suddenly smashed helmet hit the survivor. He went down screaming, ignoring the bodies of his buddies, and clutching the raw bloody stump that had been his ear.

Adam was down behind cover before any of them could get a fix on him again. Plasma pulses burst against the other side of the console, this time fewer in number.

He could hear muffled shouts of alarm around him; the Hunters had clearly underestimated their prey.

Unfortunately, Adam had done vice versa.

Whilst he had been concentrating on the squad on the balconies, another squad had hidden themselves and then followed him as stealthily as they could, waiting to pounce on him.

The big boot of the squad sergeant caught Adam in his ribs, though for once they didn't give way under the impact. A rifle butt caught Adam square around the back of the head.

He blacked out.

* * *

When he came to, his head pounding from once again being knocked out.

I'm not cut out for this shit anymore, he thought, *I'm getting old.*

Yet again, he wasn't restrained.

This time there were voices around him, and he couldn't feel the reassuring weight of his rifle in his hands, though his hands refused to work properly –they must have hit him hard on the back of the neck for his arms to be numb. They hadn't taken his Walther though.

He groaned.

The voices became louder as his hearing returned fully.

"Ah, Caine, you're awake."

"Where am I?"

"We haven't moved you, Caine." The voice was familiar. Gardner. "And we won't move you; you're going to see first hand what will happen here." Gardner swept an arm out, gesturing to the glowing power core. "We are going to leave you right here," he smiled. "You'll be praised as a hero for trying to stop the reactor from going critical but ultimately failing."

Adam snorted.

"What would you know about heroism?"

His head was clear now; he wanted Gardner to keep talking so Adam could prepare himself for the close-combat firefight that was about to ensue. Several of the Hunters had removed their helmets as the radiation from the power core was interfering with their helmets' sensors and visor-displays.

Good, he thought, *they're vulnerable.*

"When people understand that what 3899 did here today was for the good of all Terrans, they will label us heroes, Caine. *Heroes.*"

"There's nothing heroic about starting another civil war, Gardner." Adam was slowly, inch-by-inch, moving his hand to his unclasped holster. "You'd kill millions of your own people just to gain some more power for yourself and your friends."

Anger clouded Gardner's aging face.

"I am doing this for the good of mankind."

"You said that before. And that's still what Adolf Hitler said just before he invaded Poland. As did Josef Stalin, Saddam Hussein, even Lex Luthor."

Gardner frowned. "Who are they?"

"You really need to read a history book; or a bloody comic."

Gardner was still frowning, crouched next to Adam. He wasn't in a position to see Adam's hand moving slowly over the holster, unclasping the flap, and loosening the pistol inside.

"The point is they all used fear, violence, and intimidation to gain more power," continued Adam. "They were never interested in doing what was right for their citizens or for the rest of humanity, but they told everyone around them that that was why they were doing the horrible things they were doing."

Gardner snorted with no small amount of contempt.

"And you think I'm doing this for *personal* gain?"

"Maybe not you. But I'm willing to bet that the people that replaced you as Alpha-1 isn't military, and is using 3899 for their own personal gains. Look around you: I know you've never had many scruples, but *murdering the crew of this ship,* hundreds of royal family and foreign dignitaries? I can't believe even *you* would be a party to that."

The old man actually hesitated for a few uncertain seconds, clearly thinking about what Adam had said. But it wasn't long before the steely determination returned in his wizened face.

"No. I am doing this for the good of Terra. End of discussion." He stood up, and finally noticed what Adam's hand was doing. Adam was squeezing the trigger before it even left the holster. The matt-black boxy pistol barked and flashed, the barrel barely out of the holster when the round left the chamber.

The bullet blew out a chunk of Gardner's leg.

He shrieked as loudly as Lockwall had, the leg armour holed completely through. He collapsed towards the deck, his arms flailing for something to hold onto. He accidentally caught the arm of the Hunter next to him, and gracelessly tumbled to the floor.

Adam shot the squad sergeant through the eye, and blew the brains of two other Hunters in quick succession within two seconds. The Hunters were stupefied for a second.

Adam kicked out the legs of the nearest standing Hunter, who toppled with a muffled curse. Adam shot him through the soft armpit flex-armour. He screamed, and Adam shot the next one, and the next one, and the next one, until the squad of Hunters were just corpses. Gardner was bleeding, clutching his leg.

Adam, wary of the other Hunters that were probably nearby, finally stood up, and stamped on Gardner's leg where the bullet had wounded him. Gardner roared with pain. His face had gone paler than ever, either from the shock or the blood loss. Or both.

"Tell me how to shut off the reactor overload." He pointed the gun at the bridge of Gardner's nose, pressing the barrel into the skin, and against the bone underneath. The old man gritted his teeth. "Tell me how to shut the reactor off, Gardner," he repeated angrily.

"Frag you, Caine."

Adam kicked the wound again.

Sweat poured from Gardner's wrinkled old face, but he refused to give in. Adam sighed, and grabbed Gardner by his collar. He dragged the wounded man across the engineering deck, scraping him across the grated metal floor, earning a few unintelligible curses.

He dumped him against the main railing surrounding the power core, and then held him upright, facing the pulsing core.

"Tell me, or I'll throw you head first into the weakest part of the core." They could feel the heat from the core —the overload's radiation leaking in part because some of the containment forcefields had been taken offline. "TELL ME!" Adam didn't really care if the ship blew, as long as he and the Queen weren't on it when it did; after all, someone might carry through her threat to annihilate his hometown of Rino if she died along with her flagship. "TELL ME!" he bellowed again, pressing the Walther into the back of Gardner's neck.

The old man was struggling for breath, and looking at the core with no small amount of fear.

"NOW!"

Gardner mumbled something Adam didn't quite catch.

"What was that?"

"I will do it myself; just please let go."

Adam relented, and the old man collapsed back onto the deck, wheezing loudly.

"You are psychotic, Caine," said Gardner.

"No; I'm just trying to protect the lives of my family and friends." He still held the pistol on the other, whilst Gardner struggled to hurry to his feet. The old intelligence officer stumbled across to one of the main control consoles. He began frantically stabbing at the controls, the humming and beeping of the console audible over the throbbing vibrations of the power core.

Gardner's eyes went wide for a second; fear setting in, as he was sure nothing was happening to the forcefield containment system.

This is not how I wanted it to end, thought Adam, glaring at Gardner for dragging him into this once again. *I love you, Polly.*

There was a high-pitched squeal, and a flash of light that filled Adam's vision for two-hundredths of a second.

The forcefields were up –but would they hold?

Adam looked at Gardner; the old man nodded as the heat began to lessen almost immediately. Blue sparkles flashed in a set cylindrical pattern around the core, marking the barrier between Adam and eventual doom.

He took his eye off the colonel for a second to glance at the contained core.

There was a fizz of energy, and Adam suddenly smelt something burning. He looked down at his chest to find his fatigues were badly burned. He slipped them off in a hurry, revealing the black advanced combat suit underneath. The suit steamed, but was untouched, the energy having been dissipated by the suit's electronics.

Adam looked back at Gardner to see the officer pointing a plasma pistol at him. There was a dumbfounded look on his face, staring at the pistol, and then staring back in horror at Adam.

Adam shot him through the shoulder of the arm holding the gun. The pistol fell to the floor, followed by Gardner. By the time Caine got to him, he was already unconscious. He turned to the console Gardner had used, and activated the engineering deck's comms.

"Caine to *Kara Marazov.*"

There was a brief pause as the computer connected.

"*Vo'par here, Caine,*" came the answer. "*Your ship gave me a little trouble when I entered it, but I am still alive so that is probably a good thing by all accounts. I have the Queen and my husband, but we have not yet left the hangar. The sensors detected the core containment fields restored to normal. I assume that the overload has been prevented.*"

Adam nodded, more to himself than anything. "Yes; I have Colonel Gardner here unconscious. He'll need a medic, though the Hunters in the engineering deck won't."

"*Oh? You managed to subdue them?*"

"No. I killed them."

There was silence for a few seconds.

"*What about the rest of the Hunters? It would take the entire regiment to slaughter all those crewmen and civilians.*"

"That would depend on where the *Broken Bow* is. Is she anywhere nearby?"

"*Affirmative, but she's moving away at full speed.*"

"Escaping. Ah, let them escape. They failed. That's enough for me."

"*As you wish.*"

He tapped a few more commands into the console. "I've just sent out a distress signal. Hopefully your escort fleet will pick it up and come get us. I'll be up in a second to help you take the others to the Infirmary after I've dumped Gardner there as well."

"*Acknowledged.*"

Adam signed off, and turned to the man that caused him so much pain and grief.

"Come on you old bastard, let's get you to the Infirmary so you can go to prison."

* * *

It took seventy-two hours for the escort fleet to return, in which time Adam and Vo'par managed to stabilise Gardner, and treat his wounds as best they could. Rorg refused to talk to either of them, just lying in bed, staring up at the ceiling. The Queen, once recovered from her physical ordeal, had taken Prince Lucian and retreated back to her chambers, also refusing to speak to the two.

Vo'par kept apologising profusely for not being able to get in contact with the *Raj Kochhar*, to call off any attack.

Adam spent much of the three days trawling through the computer, using Vo'par's access codes to read some of the more classified and secret files available. He had found something interesting in the communications server —something that left him seething with anger.

On the bright side, he managed to get a message to Ckeer Najoor, if only a brief one to keep it scrambled and undetectable.

Shuttles and other small ships docked with the outer hatches, whilst heavier craft slid into the hangars, and disgorged engineering and Army teams that spread through the ship immediately. The medical teams were teleported in and arrived in the Infirmary within seconds, finding Caine sat beside the bed of Commander Rorg, reading a book downloaded from the computer.

The chief medical officer of the *HMS Orion's Sword* was shocked —he had seen the corpses littering the ship. Adam didn't care.

"Will Gardner live, doctor?"

The doctor, having completed the surgery not long after arriving, nodded.

"Good," said Adam. "Then he can stand trial for what he's done here."

"He is the one who did all that outside?" the doctor stammered, clearly unable to believe it.

"He wasn't alone," said Adam, throwing a sidelong glance at the holographic computer terminal he had been using before. He moved over to the computer console. "Computer, locate Admiral Vo'par, current commander of this vessel."

The floating holographic screen flickered and gave him a location of her whereabouts: on the bridge. He reached over, and opened a communications channel to Vo'par directly.

"Caine to Vo'par."

"*Vo'par here; go ahead.*"

"Admiral, now that the relief is here, I think it's about time we got some real answers."

"Agreed, but how?"

"Meet me outside the Queen's chambers ASAP."

"Understood."

* * *

Vo'par was already waiting when Adam strode round the corner. She was taken aback by his appearance –his fatigues gone, he had opted to wear the entire combat suit, even the green-eyed hood and black gloves. She had brought one of the escort ship commanders, Captain Brokker of the battleship *Orion's Sword*, a tall, broad man who had apparently served with Vo'par for several decades.

The doors were locked.

"Why do you think the answers will be here, Caine?"

"You'll see," he said, and forced the door open.

The Queen was sat behind her desk, giggling with her eight-year old son, Lucian. The boy was tall for his age, though still just a child, with toffee-coloured skin, and shaggy dark hair.

When she looked up to see the door forced open, she recoiled.

She called her child minder in, who ushered Lucian into the next room, and sat back in her big chair, eyeing the three that had entered: Vo'par was a mess, her fur ruffled and matted, her uniform dirty and bloody, with Brokker in fresh duty overalls, his officer's peaked cap sat tightly on his head, the peak almost covering his eyes.

"Adam," said Leya. "What is the meaning of all this?"

Adam sighed, and approached the desk. He placed his hands on the desk, letting his recovered assault rifle bang against the wood.

"We are here for answers, Leya. Actually," he corrected, "I'm pretty sure I already have the majority of the answers, I just need the others to hear it from you."

"Answers to what?"

"To this whole catastrophe; to some questions that have been bugging me for the last eight years... Alpha-1."

Her eyes widened for a brief second. It was very brief, but Adam saw it.

"It never occurred to me that it would be you who took Gardner's place. Then again, who would suspect the Queen herself?" He threw her a humourless smile. "This was the plan all along wasn't it? The Hunters come smashing through here, slaughtering everyone they could find. But they spared you."

"Don't forget, they spared you and the admiral as well."

"True, but I was with *you*; they couldn't very well kill me and not kill you without it looking suspicious. Admiral Vo'par was spared because she was a trusted ally –although you didn't expect her to be against you; nor did you count on Rorg being her husband." He paused, not for effect, but because he was trying to gather his thoughts, making sure he got it right.

"This operation was a chance for you to clean house, so to speak; you knew about your uncle's deal with 3899, so you made your own, and managed to get yourself in as their leader. You wanted the Hunters to eliminate all your enemies in one fell stroke –then you'd only have to contend with the military and Parliament."

"If that's the case, Captain Caine, why bring *you* into it?" It was Brokker that spoke, looking intently, but not accusingly, at Adam.

"An insurance policy in case Gardner or someone else in 3899 decided to take her out as well. She blackmailed me into protecting her so that I would do my very best to keep her alive." He leaned further forward on his hands, glaring at the Queen, who tried her best to look impassive. "So, now that your big plan has been exposed, and you're up the kybosh, what's next?"

Leya tried to glare at him.

He didn't even find it a little disconcerting.

And she knew it: he'd faced down far worse beings.

"You're only one man, Adam," she sneered. "What can you possibly do?"

Adam was somewhat taken aback –he had originally believed that despite her actions she was still the naïve young girl he had met eight years before, desperate for the approval of others. She had become a manipulative, double-crossing bitch, grabbing power where she could.

"Ckeer Najoor's administrators are currently in talks with the Alliance to become a protectorate. As I understand it, it should be finalised within a week. Attacking the planet would draw you into a conflict with the Alliance, something the Terran Parliament doesn't ever want."

Leya deflated in her chair, but her eyes still glared at him.

"What do you want, Adam?" she sighed.

He stood up straight.

"For me: Ckeer Najoor is to be left alone by you and your government, as am I and my family."

"Family?" she asked.

"I was supposed to be married this week." The answer brought a shocked look to her face and Admiral Vo'par's. "Your idiot officer dragged me away from my bachelor party when you arrived at the sports planet."

"Who?"

His eyes narrowed. "It'll be a cold day in hell before I tell you anything about her."

Leya nodded, suitably chastised.

"Also," he continued. "Commander Rorg and his people are to be released from their debt, and be accepted as an ally of Terra if that's what they desire. Otherwise, they are to be left alone to live as they want. And... Kombat 3899 is to be disbanded forever." She nodded in agreement, and he turned to Vo'par. "Admiral?"

The tall Rijiin stepped up beside him.

"I too wish 3899 disbanded. But I would also like this ship to be handed over to the Terran Navy to serve as a frontline capital ship. Since the royal family is effectively only two people, there is no longer a need for this ship to be the family's home." Leya's face darkened, but she said nothing. "Also, Captain Brokker is to be made its commander if he so chooses, and the promotion to Commodore that goes with it. I am resigning my commission, and going to Ar's Paradise with my husband. Oh, and we'll be taking the remains of the Lifeguards with us."

"Anything. Else?" said the Queen through gritted teeth.

"Yeah; I'm leaving."

The three turned to leave, the two officers already out of the door when the Queen called him back, her voice pleading with him, like she had pleaded with him on the *Gold Royale*.

"Adam, could I have a word in private, please?"

He sighed, and turned around.

"There's something you should know about Lucien."

"He's my son," Adam realised.

She nodded, the shock evident on her face.

"How long have you known?"

"Since I saw him a few moments ago. The resemblance was uncanny. I'm assuming that you always intended to tell me..." he left that hanging in the air for her to finish or answer.

"I... I didn't know how to tell you."

He snorted involuntarily. "For almost eight years?" She looked down into her lap, the guilt on her face obvious. And yet, he felt nothing: no guilt, no sadness, nothing in relation to the boy. "Don't expect me to come rushing to your side just because you've suddenly decided to tell me we have a son together."

Even from across the room, Adam could see tears welling up in her eyes. He remembered that she had once wanted him to be her Prince Consort –was it more than royal obligation? He found he didn't care about that either. All he wanted was to return home to Polly and Eve, to get married, and be a father and a husband.

"I'm sorry," he added. "Goodbye, Leya."

* * *

Leya watched Adam leave the ship through as many cameras as she could find that were still active and accessible. His face was never seen from the cameras, as if he knew she was watching him. He still clung to the assault rifle like a professional soldier, barrel down, the stock tucked into his shoulder.

The tears streamed down her ebony cheeks; marring what little make-up she had re-applied after the attack.

She loved him –despite not having spent much time with him, she had been in love with him from the moment she had met him on the *Gold Royale*, his actions then and now only making her feelings for him stronger. Her shoulders shook as she sobbed. Her own actions were absolutely unforgivable; she had organised the murder of thousands of crew, relatives, and even foreign dignitaries. She was no better than those that had hounded her and Adam for so many years.

The doors to her right opened, and Lucian came running in.

His face fell when he saw her crying.

"Mummy, what is wrong?" he cried. She swivelled her chair to face him and he jumped into her arms, resting his head on her shoulder.

"Nothing is wrong, Lucian; I am just tired is all."

He seemed to accept this as all children accepted what they were told by their parents at that age.

"Who was that man before, mummy? The big one with the big gun?"

"He..." she faltered. "He is a hero."

"A hero?"

She nodded.

"The greatest our people have ever known."

* * *

The *Kara Marazov* left the ship at great speed, not stopping for the Navy escort's temporary patrols of the star system the *St. George* had ended up in. Adam sent a brief message to the *Red Stallion* on Ckeer Najoor and another to an undetectable destination before it slipped into the Linkway tunnels and disappeared from the Navy's sensors.

* * *

Ar's Paradise.

One week later.

Reti'l Vo'par, formerly an admiral in the Terran Navy, stepped off the shuttle with her wounded husband. Thousands of his people –now calling themselves Paradisians in the wake of their freedom from Terra- were gathered to greet him around the starport, waving and cheering so loudly that the tumult was almost deafening.

Rorg was a hero to his people.

Reti'l could see the first of the Terran shuttles and starships rising into the sky, emptying the nearby Terran Army base of its soldiers and personnel.

The high-grav world was free to do what it pleased, as the married couple was.

Rorg held his fist up high above him, and the crowd roared.

A human in a military uniform neither recognised stepped out of the crowd to greet them. He was old, with a thick grey moustache, and a green beret on his greying shaved head.

He had a big smile on his face, though.

When the noise of the crowd had died down a little, he spoke.

"Admiral Vo'par, Commander Rorg. I'm Brigadier MkFayden."

He stuck his hand out; there was a digipad in it.

"Major-General Caine sends his compliments."

* * *

Ckeer Najoor.

Adam brought the *Kara* past the retreating *HMS Raj Kochhar*, ignoring the messages being sent to him from the cruiser. The small alien vessel plunged toward the planet below, its shields lighting up as it hit the atmosphere, leaving a flaming comet trail behind it. To anyone watching it looked like a meteorite passing harmlessly through the upper atmosphere.

He swung the *Kara* low over the forest that bordered one side of Rino, skimming bare feet above the treetops. The *Stallion* came into view, parked in the middle of the area designated by the town as the landing bay, a large depression in the ground; a crater from an invasion of bizarre large animals some years ago.

The *Kara* hovered briefly before touching down between the *Stallion* and the forest. He powered down the engines, but didn't immediately get up; instead, he just sat there and looked over the town laid out several hundred metres away, seeing the white domes of varying sizes. He could see the school in the distance, over the small river that passed through Rino; to his right he could see the smoke coming from Relion's bakery, and the heat rising from its roof. The residential domes surrounding it were alive with colours, the continent experiencing the beginning of its hot summer. Flowers were sprouting from dozens of window boxes, and grass sprang in the middle of town, where the children played under the shadow of the domed town hall.

Most of all though, he could see his own residential dome; Polly had her tools and gear stashed in the corner of the fenced off back garden they had grown together.

He was home at last.

He exited the ship, and climbed down.

He was still wearing the combat suit, though he had left his weapons in the *Kara*, where they belonged.

He took in a deep breath of the fresh air, and smiled.

God, it's good to be home again.

They were all waiting for him: Polly holding Eve's hand, Hannah and Raymond waiting with a parcel, M'Der entertaining their two daughters, and Relion's children as well. Some of the townsfolk were out as well, waving at Adam, grins on everyone's faces.

Eve dragged Polly out from the welcoming committee and ran into Adam's opening arms. The trio hugged each other tight, unable to say anything.

"Welcome home, my love," Polly finally whispered in his ear. There were tears of joy in her eyes, although her eyes were already reddened from previous bouts of crying. Raymond had said as much in his reply to Adam's last message.

"I missed you both," he said. He held them tight. They were all smiles, grinning like idiots. "I'm so sorry I messed up our wedding plans, Pol."

"It's okay, Adam; it was hardly your fault. On the subject of the Queen, is everything...?"

He smiled.

"Yeah. Everything's great; the Queen is on her own; 3899 are gone –at least for now; Gardner is in prison; and the *St. George* is now officially a frontline capital ship for the Terran Navy. I believe as well, that the Alliance has formalised the agreement between them and Ckeer Najoor's Administrators. So... all in all, pretty good."

He let go of them except to hold their hands.

Raymond and the others approached tentatively. Once upon a time there had been something between Adam and Hannah, but for him that had been a lifetime ago. He had been a different person back then, and there were no romantic feelings between them.

Sasha and Sapphire ran to stand beside Eve, whispering excitedly about things Adam couldn't hear. He let go of Eve's hand to shake Raymond's.

"I want you to know Adam, that because of the Queen's actions I have requested a transfer to the Navy proper. Scarlett has already told me the position is mine: Vice Admiral in charge of Naval Operations in the New Terra Sector. I can affect real changes, and still be close to Hannah and the girls." Adam noticed that the girls in question were grinning at the thought: clearly, they had formed an indelible bond with Raymond as his stepdaughters.

"Congratulations, Vice Admiral Sansky," Adam said with genuine pride.

M'Der came rushing over, having just been approached by a minister from another town.

"Adam; it's all set."

Adam's grin was huge, and he looked down at Polly, who was confused as hell.

"Wanna get married?" he said.

Her brow furrowed.

"When?"

That grin again. He looked from Polly to the newly arrived minister.

"Right now."

* * *

Raymond and Hannah's wedding present to Adam had to be opened a little early, though he used it immediately. It was a uniform: a Royal Marines Commandos uniform to be exact, with the rank chevrons of a Staff Sergeant, and all the medals and campaign markers that Adam had once worn. Raymond had dug it up from some bankrupt museum on the edge of Andromeda, and had the uniform restored fully for this day.

"How do I look?" asked Adam. Relion had brought out one of his wife's mirrors for him, and he found that the olive greens fit him better now than they once had done a long time ago.

"You look like a hero," smiled Relion.   Raymond and M'Der nodded approvingly.

Outside it was one of the most beautiful days possible in Rino: the sun was blazing down with enough of a breeze and enough fluffy white clouds to make it an amazing day. White-winged gulls warbled as they hovered in the breeze. The ocean, two miles downstream from Rino, lapped peacefully at the sandy shore.

A musician played quietly on a shryl —not that different from bagpipes— whilst the guests stood in rows with the alien minister stood at the head of the aisle in between the groups.

The *Stallion* and the *Kara* were being used as changing rooms for the couple-to-be, each one with their nose pointed toward the proceedings.

Adam, M'Der, Relion, and Raymond stepped out of the *Kara*, and strode over to stand in a row in front of the minister. Hannah and Relion's wife stepped down from the *Stallion*'s entry ramp, followed by Polly.

Polly was petite and astonishing, with her straight medium black hair tied back in a ponytail. She wore a bright white suit with laced sandals to walk in the sand. She carried a bouquet of flowers picked from the town's gardens with a huge smile on her face.

It was the perfect day.

Polly stepped up beside Adam, slipping her hand into his.

She whispered to him, "I love you."

"I love you too."

The wedding began in earnest. The minister cleared all three of his throats.

"Dearly beloved, we are gathered here today..."

Nineteen:
Wildcard

Historian's Note: This story takes place eighteen months after *The Bodyguard*.

"We can't stop here! This is bat country!"
–Raoul Duke
"Cheese it!"
–Bender Bending Rodriguez

June 4009ad.

The smell of heated metal hung in the air, mingled with the odours of sparking arc-welders and repair tools. Sparks flowed down from above like a waterfall, dissipating when they hit the floor. Shouted complaints of protest rose up from around the underground hangar, along with a flurry of colourful curses and oaths.

The darkness hung over the hangar like a huge cloud, the massive doors keeping the light outside away from sensitive circuitry.

A whole plethora of starship designs were on display in the hangar: three hundred all told; a number that included one hundred and fifty professional racers, forty-two mega-corporation-sponsored craft, two dozen private racers, as well as representatives from several military navies, including the Terran Navy, Alliance Fleet, and even a representative vessel from the Tagarri mining fleets.

The *Kara Marazov* sat to one side of the hangar, underneath a large, open gallery for onlookers and well-wishers. None of the deck crew touched her, steering clear of the alien craft as if it had the plague, or was haunted. Word had got out that the ship was there, and the rumours began of how the ship was connected to the faceless Ghost character. The other pilots looked at the ship with suspicion, also giving it a wide berth.

Adam Caine wasn't happy either.

"You know, when I said let's go away for the summer, I didn't mean enter the universe's biggest and most popular interstellar starship race of all time."

"That's what you said yesterday," his wife Polly pointed out.

"And the day before that as well," added his daughter Evelyn –as she liked to be called now she was older.

He stuck his tongue out at both of them, before returning his attention to the rest of the hangar. Several onlookers gave them odd looks, as if the three were mad. Then again, they were sat in deckchairs, watching the rest of the ships being prepared with a somewhat cheery mood compared to the sombre and serious faces around them.

Everyone was taking it seriously... except the Caine family.

* * *

Commentary Transcript

Draf Rogtar: Welcome, ladies, gentlemen, and multi-gender species, to this solar year's Grand Interstellar Race. Tomorrow marks the one-hundredth anniversary of the race's first start; as such, we have several special guests this year to mark the special event. On my right, I have with me my usual co-pilot on the Terran racing circuits, Arlen Gran.

Arlen Gran: G'morning, Draf.

Draf: As I was saying, we have some quite amazing guests today: four-time Interstellar Champion T'i'l'ik of Grathe; former Terran circuit champion Mack Tanner, and Lieutenant Commander Maryna Del Vio, chief engineer of the *HMS Enterprise*.

T'i'l'ik: (*translated from his native language*) [Thankyou for this opportunity, Draf, Arlen]

Tanner: Good morning, guys.

Del Vio: Morning gentlemen.

Draf: As the preparations continue for tomorrow, we will have a look around the main underground hangar, have a talk with some of the pilots and crews, and go over some of the statistics of previous years, as well as the records of some of tomorrow's racers and ships.

Arlen: Let's begin with the pilots shall we?
(*They all nod eagerly.*)
Up first, we have last year's champion, Guilio.

Draf: That's right Arlen. Last year, Guilio took his ship, the Ark 1-XV, on a massive victory, four hours ahead of second place. Can he repeat his amazing success with his Ark 2-XV? We'll find out soon enough. This year, we have rumours of a brand-new type of engine being used by Guilio and several others of the professional racers. Commander, any thoughts on this?

Del Vio: I've been reviewing the specs handed in by all the racers, and the engine Guilio has installed along with fourteen others, looks like it could be quite the trick. Its design is compact enough to be fitted into a small ship, but still powerful enough to give it more speed than larger engines.

Draf: So this year could be a close call?

<u>Del Vio:</u> Indeed
(They all nod again)

<u>Draf:</u> So, with fourteen pilots ahead of the curve, what about the rest of the professional pilots, anyone?

<u>T'i'l'ik:</u> [Well, Draf, we have all twenty-two teams from the Grobo Eternity race, as well as forty racers from the New Tarla Touring Championship, and the hundred racers of the Red Star Endurance Test that finished for this year last solar month.]

<u>Tanner:</u> And that's not including the amateur racers.

<u>Arlen:</u> Aye, this year we have a record number of racers from the amateur circuits, as well as a record number of privately owned ships that have not entered before.

<u>Draf:</u> As well as representatives from the biggest of the nineteen galaxies' mega-corporations.

<u>Del Vio:</u> Not only that, but I can see small ships from seventeen different militaries.

<u>Draf:</u> This year is certainly going to be one of the more interesting ones I've commentated on. So... favourites anyone?

<u>T'i'l'ik:</u> [Well, I hate to be predictable and boring, but I would have to go with Guilio. He has the right ship, and the experience of previous years to use it on this course.]

<u>Del Vio:</u> Indeed. Though what interests me is a small privately owned yacht designated as the *Kara Marazov*, under the ownership of the Caine family. The ship is a design I have never seen before, of a species' technology I do not recognise. But it looks like a powerful vessel. I believe that this could be the wild card of the race.

<u>T'i'l'ik:</u> [Wild card?]

<u>Tanner:</u> An old Earth gambling term, where a card could be unknown, and is thus unable to predict –hence, wild card. I have to disagree with you though, Lieutenant Commander; this year Plior Corporation, owners of the ill-fated *Gold Royale* and *Titanic* liners, have shelled out a large sum on their new starship, the *Plior Runner*, with an ex-racer at its helm.

<u>Arlen:</u> The Terran Navy's team has a good chance this year, with their new and improved Stickleback bomber having its weapons replaced with extra manoeuvring thrusters and extra sub-light engines.

<u>Tanner:</u> I have spoken to the pilot of the *Plior Runner*, and he says that he *really* wants to win.
They are silent for one minute before anyone speaks.

<u>Draf:</u> (*coughs*) Uh, thanks, Mack. That was very... insightful. Let's go live over to Rada in the hangars...

* * *

25 hours later.

Adam watched the camera-drones float by overhead, red lights winking as they captured everything on film, or digital files, whatever visual recording technology they were using. He heard some of the commentaries being played live on the audio devices of some of the deck crews, and once heard his name being squawked from the small speakers, though paid it no heed.

They were now only an hour away from when the hangar would open, and the ships would lift into the sky of the sports planet. The family was back in the ship, though only Adam was in the cockpit, running final flight checks whilst the two girls were still asleep. The race started early in the local morning; Adam had already been awake for two hours.

"Good morning sleepy head," he smiled without turning round.

Polly was stood behind him, stretching, rubbing the sleep out of her eyes. As was her wont when they were on the ship, she was wearing long cotton two-piece pyjamas that buttoned up at the front.

"How do you always know it's me?" she smiled back.

"I could hear you yawning from in here," he chuckled. He spun the seat around to face her, and snaked his arms around her waist, bringing her chest in line with his face. He looked up at her, adoration clear as the day.

"You were up early," she said, looking over the controls. "Finishing the flight checks?"

He nodded. "I was awake early and didn't want to wake you."

She smiled sleepily, and kissed his forehead.

"I love you, Mr. Caine."

"I love *you*, Mrs. Caine." She kissed the tip of his nose, and slipped out of his strong embrace, sitting herself down in the co-pilot's chair, and watching the frenzied activity of the hangar around them. The ships were powered up, ready and raring to go, and the deck crews were making the final external inspections.

"So how many ships have you scanned since you woke up?" she smiled.

He tapped a command into his console, and a hologram flickered into life above the co-pilot's console. The display flickered through several long lists of the ships around them, their classifications, size, mass, engine type, and so on, listing immaculate details of each and every ship.

"This ship never ceases to amaze me," she said appreciatively.

"Aye, she's a beaut alright."

"Have you ever thought about checking just where it's from? Or what species built it?"

He nodded. "Yeah, but it came to a dead-end."

"A dead-end?"

He chuckled, "The race that built this ship and the starfighters in that mountain hangar we found was killed off hundreds of millennia ago; the records call them The Builders, though that's it. No real name, no description of what they were, nothing; very bizarre." He shrugged. "Another mystery of the universe to be solved for another time."

She smiled, and crooked her head on her shoulder, looking over at him.

He saw her staring at him, and felt a flutter in his stomach. He was still as much in love with her as he had ever been. And she was still as beautiful as the day he had first met her –that he could remember; she still claimed they had first met briefly in a London cinema- on the International Space Station.

"If anyone could solve the mysteries of the universe, it'd be you," she chuckled, bringing her knees up to her chest.

"Not on purpose," he replied.

"Have you reviewed the official course yet? The one that was issued by the organisers?" she asked idly, still sleepily looking at him. He gave her a smile that said it all: he didn't think much of their chances. She knew him too well. "That good, huh?"

"The official stuff is pretty vague: riddles about the dangers we're supposed to face, with a map that looks like it was made by Yellowbeard the Pirate." She frowned at the film reference. "Never mind." He checked the chronometer in the centre of the command console. "Which reminds me; I'm meeting an old friend, in a couple of minutes, who claims to have more detailed scans and plans of the race's route."

He slipped out of the chair, and planted a kiss on her forehead.

"I'll be back in a few minutes."

He was wearing a pilot's flight suit that Polly had picked out from one of the surplus uniform stores on the sports planet's surface. All three of them had one: sandy coloured overalls with multitudes of zipped pockets, and a colourful unit patch hand-made by Relion's wife with a stylised version of the *Kara*, and the name wrapped around the outside of the circular badge.

Despite the internal warmth of the flight suit, he still had to grab a furred bomber jacket from the tiny bedroom he shared with Polly. He quickly made his way through the small airlock, down the ladder rungs that extended from the side of the lower fin, and away from the ship to the outer edge of the massive ledge.

As he had anticipated, it was cold in the hangar: the place was too vast to heat artificially. The doors were open this morning, for the ships to launch, and take their designated places at the starting line in orbit.

Indirect sunlight shone down from the mouth of the doors above, highlighting the curves and edges of the ships beneath. As he watched, the Terran Navy Stickleback bomber rose into the air, using its antigravs to lift its fat self out of the hangar and into the sky above. Two more ships followed it, flying in its wake, both gaudily coloured like overly bright bees.

The Stickleback bomber roared into open air, and disappeared from view.

Down below, Adam saw a rickety old ship that looked like it could fall apart at any moment being worked on by its crew. They were cursing and swearing oaths of violence at each other, and at the ship, demanding it to work.

Even above the tumult, Adam heard the soft footfalls of someone trying to sneak up on him. He smiled.

"You're late."

The woman behind him let out a snort of annoyance.

"I'm nearly a hundred thousand years old, and I still can't sneak up on you. Why is that?" Adam turned to see Hevskii approaching with a digipad in her hand, and a crooked smile on her lips. She hadn't aged a day since the last time he had seen her; then again, she probably hadn't aged for thousands of years.

Her hair was shorter now, and she had lost weight –the product of assisting her people build a new home for them. She too was wearing flight overalls, although he noted that hers had Idle Guns patches stitched to the arms and shoulders.

"Missing the old days?" he said, pointing to the patches.

She shrugged. "It was all I had."

"What are you flying, anyway?"

She pointed down into the morass of ships, to a small vessel that had eight, curved blade wings pointed forward like a striking octopus. Like the *Kara*, its hull shimmered seamlessly between two shades of the same colour; in this case, green.

"Scary looking thing."

"We based much of the design on the *Kara*," she replied. She held out the digipad, and he took it gratefully.

"Do I dare ask how you got those scans?"

"Despite the organisers of this race wanting nobody to be able to take home the exact details of this race's locations, there is always someone who will take clandestine scans or hidden holo-cameras on their ships. Besides, I flew a few years ago as a representative of the Guns, back when criminal organisations were allowed to compete."

He rifled through the scans, noting some odd terrain features.

"They like to keep it interesting," shrugged Hevskii.

He turned back to look at her ship, and noticed that it was somewhat too small to survive a long journey from her people's new homeworld. He pointed that fact out.

"Your friend Silver is currently commanding a starship in orbit: it's parked with rest of the larger starships. Similar design as my racer, but a hell of a lot bigger and more heavily armed." At Adam's frown, she gave him an ironic frown. "A lot of pirates out there."

He started to walk away, when he turned back.

"What did you call the ship?"

Her smile turned even bigger. "Since names are important when it comes to vessels, we decided to give it the strongest and most invincible name ever known to the universe." That smile again. "The *Adam Caine*."

Adam was slack-jawed, staring off into space with shock. It was two full minutes before he realised Hevskii had already left his side to return to her ship. When he did come out of his stupor, he noticed that there were dozens of people watching him.

He cleared his throat, and muttered something about watching the ships taking off, despite nothing launching at that precise moment in time.

* * *

When Adam clambered back into the *Kara*, he was slightly bewildered by Hevskii's admission. Was that how people saw him? Invincible? Naming a ship after him seemed odd at best.

He shook the thought off when he saw Polly getting dressed in the bedroom, her flight overalls only on up to the waist, the sleeves tied around her waist. She was wearing a sleeveless dark tee shirt that left nothing to the imagination.

"Did you get it?" she asked when she noticed him standing in the doorway.

"Yep." He held up the digipad, though he was still staring.

"Stop staring," she said, though she blushed. She moved toward him, and wrapped her arms around his waist, placing her chin on his chest to look up at him.

"I can't help it."

They heard a snort behind them. "Please; get a room."

Evelyn strolled out of her even tinier bunkroom, yawning and stretching. She was dressed in the flight overalls, leaving it baggy, as was her wont. Despite having grown into a beautiful, attractive young woman, she was still shy about her appearance. It was something her boyfriend, Thrigor, had been very pleased about; he had a hard enough time worrying about what Adam thought of him without having to deal with the attention of other young men.

Adam had warmed to the boy almost instantly; he just enjoyed winding him up.

"Good morning, Evie," he smiled. She glared knives at him.

"Evelyn, Dad, remember? I'm not a baby anymore." She punched him lightly on his arm to let him know she was just playing. He nodded sadly, and then suddenly picked her up in a big bear hug, making sure she didn't hit her head on the low ceiling. She squealed, giggling as he tickled her relentlessly.

"No, no, Daddy, please don't," she cried through the tears of laughter. He put her down, letting her wipe away the tears.

"Breakfast?" He produced a bag of pastries he had picked up from a mobile vendor pushing a cart on his way back from his brief meeting with Hevskii. "We can eat on the way up."

They all sat down in their seats in the cockpit. Adam handed the bag to Polly so she could dish out the soft pastries whilst he took the controls. He called to the hangar control, and requested permission to undock, and head for the start line in orbit. Permission was given, and the docking clamps holding the ship down were released with a clunk.

The ship's anti-gravs automatically kicked in, and the *Kara* hovered above the deck. Adam goosed the manoeuvring thrusters, and the ship coasted forward slowly, limited by the hangar's rules. He pushed the ship up higher, keeping the *Kara* vertical so as not to feel the temptation to put it into full sublight burn.

The ship's warning alarms went mad as dozens of ships locked their sensors onto the *Kara*, trying to see what the ship was about. They would have no luck whatsoever: the *Kara*'s strange hull prevented those kinds of scans.

The ship passed through the giant open doors and out of the hangar.

Several others rose with them, engines flaring.

Adam set the autopilot to the coordinates race control gave him, and the ship drifted gently up into the sky, giving Adam time to take one of the proffered sweet pastries, and slowly eat it, enjoying the view.

"Isn't this where you came for your 'bachelor's party'?" asked Polly between mouthfuls.

He nodded with a wry smile.

"Yeah; we'll have to come here on a proper holiday one day." He glanced behind him, "Maybe we can bring Thrigor as well." Evelyn's face lit up with a big smile. He finished off the pastry just as the *Kara* broke into space. There before them, the starting line was stretched out through space, a long double line of flashing marker buoys.

All around, *outside* the buoys, were hundreds of big starships, thousands of people watching the event from the motherships of the racers, or simply there to watch. Adam spotted the big Terran Navy battleship somewhere along the middle of the right side of the start line. The sensors identified it as the *HMS Enterprise*, pride of the Navy, and captained by the Navy's first Rathgar CO, Flakenrix, an old friend of Adam and Polly's.

The *Kara*'s autopilot brought them to a position far towards the back, somewhere between the professionals and amateurs. Hevskii's ship appeared beside them.

All the ships were organised into rows, with the *Kara* sharing a row with five others.

A line of other ships was floating up from orbit, taking their places in the starting line, falling into place. According to the live feed from the control ship, there was only one more ship to achieve orbit, and take its place.

Sure enough, the rust bucket Adam had seen earlier trundled up from the lush blue-green planet below. It stalled, drifted, and then regained speed, diagonally inserting itself into the starting line facing the wrong direction.

A tug from the control ship turned the ship so it was facing in the right direction, for all the good it would do them if the ship's engines died again. As it was, Adam could see the glow of its sublights flickering.

"They look like they won't survive ten minutes with those engines," Polly commented. Since before their wedding, she had managed to catch up with contemporary engine technology, to the point where she was even fixing local hovercraft and vehicles back home in Rino. Their back garden was filled with junk she used to fix things.

"I wouldn't put it past them to survive. Sometimes the unlikely can happen."

She smiled over at him, "We're living examples of that."

Evelyn just rolled her eyes behind them.

* * *

Draf: Well, ladies and gentlemen, here we are, we have seven minutes before the start of this race, and the excitement is becoming intense. All of us here are on the edge of our seats, waiting for the command to go. As always, our commentary box is situated on the race control ship.

Arlen: That's right, Draf. Right now, we've got an amazing view from in front of the starting line, looking back down the race grid, and the ships all gathered above the sports planet Arkat.

T'i'l'ik: [It is truly inspiring.]

(Commentary drivels on with the participants repeating their previous statements as to their favourites for winning. At twenty seconds to go, Draf Rogtar brings the commentary back on track)

Draf: There's the twenty-second countdown, people! *(He bangs the table excitedly with his fist)*. Ten seconds. Nine. Eight. Seven. Six. Five. Four. Three. Two. One. And we are go-go-go for the one hundredth Grand Interstellar Race!

Arlen: Guilio is out in front already, speeding away towards the first obstacle: the Firehead Nebula, where FTL drives are inoperable due to EM interference, and prevents navigational sensors from getting more than trace signals and fixes. It is a test of navigational skills, and situational awareness.

Tanner: It certainly is.

<u>Draf:</u> *(Looks at Tanner despairingly)* That's some kind of insight you got there, Mack. As you can see, ladies and gentlemen, the race is in full swing. Guilio leads the start, with Firok second, Arlkep in third, the *Plior Runner* in fourth, and Feorn, the Prince of Zorb in fifth place, making up the podium places for this first leg.

* * *

Adam threw the ship into a decent speed when the lights on the marker buoys turned to green from red. The ships around the *Kara* all shot forward together, albeit not as quickly as Adam's ship.

The huge tumult of ships plunged between yet more green-lit buoy markers. The sensors registered the Firehead Nebula before they could see it, a static mass millions of kilometres ahead of them. Polly was manning the sensors, Adam the controls, and Eve was just sitting back and watching the spectacle of her parents fly.

Adam goosed the throttle, and rolled the ship onto its side, before skimming over the back of the Terran Navy's struggling Stickleback bomber.

"That nebula is huge, Adam," said Polly as he righted the ship, and darted between two others. She was right; it was three light-years across, and the sensor information coming off it was far worse than Hevskii's scans were indicating. Then again, the *Kara*'s technology was more advanced than most vessels. "That thing's filled with pockets of flammable and unstable gases."

"Great," muttered Adam. "Can you detect any passage through?"

She nodded. "Yes, but once we pass into the nebula itself, the sensors are going to be limited to short-range only."

Like a great fog bank, the nebula loomed ahead of them, stretching around so far they couldn't see the end properly. It was, like its name suggested, fiery, swirling patterns of reds and oranges mixing in with each other like a giant fire. The nebula didn't even stay in one shape, its edges always roiling and writhing, as if trying to get loose of the main clouds.

A blue-and-red chequered ship with engines on the end of its long wings roared past, briefly rocking the *Kara*. It blasted past four more ships before disappearing into the clouds of the nebula.

There were squawks over the open comms channels as pilots unfamiliar with the course panicked at not being able to see four feet in front of their faces. Warning alarms blared briefly, and the sensors showed some bizarre readings within the cloud, something that Hevskii's previous scans hadn't detected.

Polly looked worried, and confused at the same time.

The readings were erratic, and popping up all over the massive cloud

The *Kara* was still two minutes from the cloud perimeter.

Hevskii's ship was still outside the perimeter as well, though closer than the *Kara*. He tapped the comms controls.

"This is the *Kara Marazov* calling Hevskii. Do you copy?"

"*I read you, Caine,*" came the voice. It was filled with static interference from the cloud's bizarre properties. "*I'm about to pass into the nebula. After that, communications will be impossible.*"

"Understood. We're detecting some unusual readings coming from the nebula; the *Kara*'s sensors can't identify them, and they're everywhere." He transmitted the details to her, and heard an audible gasp down the line.

"What? What is it?"

Her reply was garbled at best.

"*Those...* <kzzz>*... old times...* <kzzz>*... star dragons. Stay...* <kzzz> *anomalies...* <kzzz>*... good luck.*" Then the line went dead, and Hevskii's ship disappeared sooner than they had thought into the nebula. Adam found himself unable to say anything helpful, just looking at his wife and daughter, as if to say, *what the hell have you got me into?*

"Star dragons and anomalies?" he said, an incredulous tone to his voice.

"Sorry, daddy," Eve cringed.

He rolled his eyes, and throttled down so as not to rush headlong into danger, making sure Polly had her eyes on the sensors. Following the marker buoys, they plunged into the cloudy nebula.

* * *

It was just like being stuck inside a fogbank. Nothing was discernable, and phantom shadows kept morphing into nothing, whilst the blurred outlines of other ships hurtled past, either off course, or recklessly taking the path at speed. Adam felt intensely claustrophobic, despite the bright colours of the nebula. Lightning flashed in the distance, although it was too distant to actually tell if it was indeed lightning or a random flash of light. The nature of the cloud was such that it felt like the whole world was closing in on him.

He shook the panic off, trying not to remember the small box he had been forced into for days on end in the furnace-heat of Afghanistan.

The marker buoys were spread out, out of visual range of each other, and only detectable from certain vantage points around the previous buoys. It was a bizarre way to run a race, but then the nebula was dangerous to those who didn't keep to the path, making it ideal for an endurance race.

Polly had detected the first one as they passed through the outer layer.

The ship shook again when something impossibly huge rushed past, its outline long and curved... like a crocodile. Or worse. But it was gone in an instant, leaving Adam to wonder just what the organisers of this race were holding back.

Polly swore all of a sudden.

"What?"

"The markers are gone." There was panic on her beautiful face as her fingers raced over the alien controls. "The next set of marker buoys has disappeared. Whatever that thing was that passed us took them out."

"Probably ate them," mumbled Eve from behind them. Adam turned to rebuke her, but saw she was more terrified than her mother was, trembling in her seat as if suffering from hypothermia.

"We can turn back, if you want, Evie," he said softly.

She seriously thought about it before shaking her head. "No. We've only just started, and I want to finish this race. Don't you, daddy? Mummy?" Adam and Polly nodded, the former picking up the stylised digipad given to him.

"What are you looking for?" asked his wife.

"You said there were lots of unstable pockets of flammable gases and the like. Could you plot a course around them that isn't part of the course? Away from the markers, and the other racers so that we don't attract the attention of whatever the hell that was." He started flicking controls on his right. The lights dimmed and several of the controls and readouts in the rear of the cockpit cabin all died out. The humming underneath them, coming through the deck, softened down.

The ship was in stealth mode.

Polly frantically connected the ship's computer with the information on the digipad, bringing the reams of data up on one monitor, the *Kara*'s sensor data on another. The console beeped, and she pointed to a raggedy line that stretched out before the ship's icon.

"There," she said. "There's some kind of natural eddy through the nebula. It's empty of any volatile materials, and I'm not reading any interference from it."

"No interference?" he said, incredulous. "That can't be good."

He slammed the ship forward all of a sudden, pushing them all into the backs of their chairs. The clouds flitted past randomly until the ship broke through into the calm eddy. They could see the sides of it rise up like a fiery canyon.

The interference disappeared as Polly had said it would, though it baffled all three of them as to how it could be that way when the interference affected systems at a significant distance *outside* the nebula. So why wasn't it affecting the ship inside the calm spot? Adam had a funny feeling they were going to find out after too long.

"Adam, this eddy is getting longer, running parallel with several others popping up."

Hevskii's garbled warning came back to him at that moment; now he knew what had created the eddies.

He wanted this section of the race to be over quickly.

"How long to the other side of the nebula?" he asked.

Polly checked the sensors. "Six hours."

Adam swore.

* * *

Draf: Wow! Did you see that explosion? That was impressive.

Arlen: Yes, that was pretty amazing Draf. It looks like two of the amateurs crashed into each other moments before entering the Firehead Nebula, igniting some of the gases, and engulfing twelve others. Rescue ships are being despatched as we speak.

(A technician walks into the commentary bay, and hands Draf a digipad.)

Draf: This just in: we have received confirmed reports that contact has been lost with dozens of the marker buoys inside the Firehead Nebula. There has been no reason given for this, except that they are already attempting to warn the racers of the danger. Unfortunately, most if not all of them have already passed into the interference of the Nebula, with the first ones emerging within the next two hours.

Del Vio: I have also had a report, Draf, from the *HMS Enterprise* that they have been asked to assist in any rescue operations safe enough to operate in or around the nebula.

Arlen: Indeed, commander, this is certainly hotting up to be the most exciting race ever. Wouldn't you agree, Mack?

Tanner: Sure.

Draf: *(incomprehensible muttering)* Yes, well... thanks for yet another detailed insight, Mack.

Tanner: You're welcome.

Draf: *(sighs)* Let's go over to Klawdier who is live onboard the main pit stop vessel, in the process of interviewing the deck crews of the different professional teams. Klawdier?

* * *

They were taking it in turns to pilot the ship for a couple of hours each, to the end of the eddy, despite it growing in length towards the other side of the nebula. It was Eve's turn at that point; Dad was in his bunk catching some shut-eye, and Mum was fiddling with the upper sublight engine after noticing a slight imbalance with one of the power conduits.

So Eve was alone, finally getting to fly her father's ship after so many years not being allowed to.

There was still no sign of any other ship, or the marker buoys laid out for the race.

Eve wasn't worried: her parents were confident about the calm eddies being their way out of the nebula and onto the rest of the course. What she was worried about was the impossibly huge thing that had destroyed the buoys in the first place, and had passed the *Kara* at faster speeds than the ship was capable of.

Hevskii's warning had mentioned star dragons.

Her father had told her of the dragons of ancient Earth, breathing fire, and eating multitudes of people. They were the size of houses on Earth; it seemed in space the dragons were bigger than the biggest battleships.

That was when she saw two orbs ahead, baleful and glowing.

She froze, letting the ship continue on in a straight line. Fear gripped her like she had never known before; it was a primal fear, like the fear brought on by childhood fears. She couldn't move, couldn't speak, tears gathering in the corners of her eyes.

The orbs —or rather the giant eyes- didn't move, but they blinked, and she nearly voided her bowels at the thought of the size of the creature that owned a pair of eyes that big. She tried to call out for help, even as the ship got closer to the distant creature, but her voice caught in her throat, only giving out a tiny squeak.

"D-dad-daddy..." she whimpered. She cleared her throat, never taking her eyes off the creature's emerging outline. "DADDY!" she screamed.

Adam was in the cockpit in a second, and she heard a gasp from him.

He grabbed Evelyn out of the pilot's chair, and placed her gently in the chair behind. He grabbed a blanket and wrapped it round her. She was trembling, and her green skin had paled considerably, cold sweat permeating her forehead. Her eyes were blank, staring straight ahead.

"Evie? Evie!" He tried to shake her out of it. His voice was soft and reassuring, snapping her out of her stupor. She was crying, reminding him, and herself, that she was still only a sixteen-year-old girl, no matter how much her Mertik biology matured her physically.

He let her go so he could take the controls, throttling the engines up farther. Polly rushed into the cockpit, and went straight to Eve, wrapping her arms around her adopted daughter's shoulders, whispering to her gently.

Evie watched as her father ran the ship straight at the creature's outline.

It came out of the surrounding nebula, a dragon of the old days, with a long snout and even longer mouth filled with giant razor-sharp teeth. Nostrils the size of the *Kara* flared at the end of its snout, with its deep-set eyes glaring behind far behind them above its mouth. The giant head connected to a long straight neck that blended in with the rest of its body, four muscular, powerful limbs swept back against its flanks, with a tail that stretched to a point, longer than the entire body before it. A line of small fins ran down the length of its spine, whilst its entire body was covered head to tail in shimmering multi-coloured scales.

He realised he had seen one before —an infant, judging by the size of this one- on Ckeer Najoor, when he and Eve had first arrived on the planet, and he had been asked to save the planet from a multicultural horde of bizarre monsters rampaging across the landscape. He hadn't realised the thing was a star dragon though.

Shaking off the memory, he pushed the ship at the thing's grinning mouth, before running it along the spine when it snapped its jaws at him, the finned spine flashing past the cockpit. The tail waggled about as the dragon began turning round.

The wake of the movement battered the *Kara* around, bumping it out of the way of the tail attempting to swat at the small ship.

"Hold on," he said. "I don't know if this is going to work or not."

"If what is going to work?" cried Polly.

He punched up some numbers on a monitor that didn't make a lot of sense to Polly or Eve, but had Adam working furiously to compensate for the cloud's interference. The sensors screamed for attention as the star dragon gained ground by sheer dint of its size and power.

Its jaws open wide, it closed to the point where the *Kara* was just inside its mouth, struggling to get free.

Its jaws clamped shut with an ear-splitting crunch.

* * *

Adam was aware of the headache before he was aware of anything else. He was coming out of unconsciousness, sprawled across the control console, waking up with the mother of headaches.

He groaned, and was aware of Polly on the floor beside him.

His headache forgotten, he picked her up, and sat her down in the co-pilot's seat. Eve was clinging to her own chair, still trembling. Sparks flew from the consoles, and the monitors were dark, along with the lights.

He could feel the ship drifting, and the stars were moving slowly past the cockpit until the Firehead Nebula was visible in the far distance. He could see dark shapes moving out of the nebula, away from the course, and towards an unknown destination.

"I can't believe that FTL hop worked from *inside* the nebula."

"Me neither," he admitted, his voice a pained groan. He didn't notice the shocked expression on Polly's face at his admission. He shrugged nonchalantly. "It was an FTL hop or get eaten by a giant space lizard."

"Well, we've had no official condemnation from the race organisers, so I can only assume that what we just did wasn't against the rules."

He snorted.

"That's something I guess." Eve was still trembling uncontrollably behind him. "Pol, can you get us back on the course? And then onto the next obstacle?"

She nodded, and told him to take Evie back to her own bunk. He left her to it, lifting her up gently in his powerful arms, and carrying her into her tiny bunkroom. He laid her down on the thin bed, and pulled the covers over her. She was still awake.

"Daddy," she whispered. "Can you tell me about your home?"

He frowned. And odd question to be sure.

"I don't need to; you live there as well, remember?" He placed the back of his hand on her forehead, checking to see if she had a fever. She didn't. She was in shock, at least temporarily. He knew it wouldn't be permanent, although she'd have nightmares for weeks.

"No, daddy," she smiled weakly. "I mean your home. England."

"Oh," he said in understanding. The main lights flickered back on, and the engines began to hum again. Adam felt the tiny movement as the inertial dampeners compensated for the sudden movement of the ship.

"Well," he began; "England, or at least the part I was born in –Cambridge- was a beautiful place…" he carried on telling her everything he could remember about England, Earth, his crappy apartment in London, and even some of the brighter spots of his time as a Royal Marine. When he finished, he realised she had fallen asleep.

He kissed her on the forehead, and pulled her duvet up to her chin, leaving her to snore gently.

He returned to the cockpit, and slumped into the co-pilot's seat, glancing over the sensors as Polly flew the ship towards the line of marker buoys now visible outside the nebula, leading away towards the Linkway entrance in the system.

Over the previous days before the race's start, ships belonging to the race organisers had seeded the course with millions of the marker buoys to light the way.

"So what position are we in?" asked Polly, looking intently ahead at their destination. There were no ships in view, nor any on the sensors. Adam checked the live status feed from the race control ship. He started laughing.

"We're first."

* * *

Draf: And look at that!

Arlen: Wow! This is a first ladies and gentlemen; one of the racers –the *Kara Marazov* piloted by the Caine family- has just used an FTL hop to jump out of the Firehead Nebula. Nobody has ever managed this, despite it not being against the regulations of the race.

Draf: Commander, there's no need to look smug.

Del Vio: Sorry, Draf.

Arlen: Well, it's a bizarre event to top off a bizarre section of the course this year. With reports coming in from the race control ship of massive life-readings and possible explosions from within the nebula, it is indeed the most exciting race yet.

T'i'l'ik: [Well, as we can see Arlen, with the *Kara Marazov* in first position and already close to entering the Linkway, and the other racers yet to appear from the nebula, this could well be the year of the wildcard.]

Draf: As always, we will be here to bring you, the viewers, live commentary on this the exciting one hundredth Grand Interstellar Race. And now, here's a word from our sponsors.

* * *

They had a full twelve hours before they were due to exit the Linkway, following the marker buoys through the tunnels. The next obstacle was another navigational nightmare: an asteroid field of immense proportions, and the home of some nasty spatial anomalies that played havoc with the sanity of pilots who dared to go in there.

But that was hours away yet, and the ship on automatic whilst Polly and Adam got some sleep and some alone time.

That is, until the warning alarms blared throughout the ship. Adam was up in an instant, slipping on a baggy shirt and trousers and running out the bunkroom door before Polly was even out of bed.

The proximity alarm was going nuts, declaring that the ship was about to be hit by something massive. Not just one something either, there were dozens of them, of varying sizes as well.

"That's *so* not good," he muttered.

The first one blasted past the *Kara*, and snapped at the small ship with its monstrously huge jaws.

"More of these things?" he cried.

Polly was muttering about being woken early, her voice croaky, as she stumbled into the cockpit. She looked up, and froze.

"Oh no, not again."

"Yep," he replied, distracted by trying to fly the ship so none of the star dragons would smash into them, or try to eat them again. "There isn't another Linkway exit until the course leaves it. Which means, I'm going to have to slow down, and let them pass." As he said that, another slid past silently. It was the one that had tried to eat the *Kara* earlier. It was bigger than the rest, as if it were the leader, or the alpha-male.

The mass of star dragons, no longer interested in the *Kara*, wasn't just a random mass. Adam could see some of the smaller ones flying circles around each other as if they were playing hide and seek, or some child's game. The bigger ones –the ones with tentacled antennae trailing from their skulls- moved to protect the pups: the mothers of the family.

"It's a herd," he smiled. "A herd of dragons." He shook his head in amazement, chuckling to himself, despite Polly's continued worried look.

The proximity alarm blared again as the small pups flew towards the *Kara*. They spun and twisted around the tiny ship, as if showing off to Adam and Polly.

They never hit the ship, though there were a few close calls when their tails flicked past the upper and lower fins and washed their wake over the ship, bouncing it around.

"I wonder why they aren't trying to eat us like they did before?" he said, almost to himself. He looked at Polly, who was still yawning and rubbing the sleep from her eyes, and the answer struck him like lightning. "Because they were waking up," he said out loud. "They woke up grouchy, and lashed out at what they perceived as their wakers. But why did they wake?"

"Does it matter?" asked Polly.

He shook his head. "No, I guess not; I was just curious."

Polly had a knowing smile on her luscious lips. "Trying to solve the mysteries of the universe?"

"Not just yet. Let's finish the race first."

Stuck in the middle of the herd, the ship swept noiselessly through space, surrounded by the giants of deep space.

When Polly finally relaxed, she said, "I wonder how the others are doing?"

* * *

Flight Lieutenant Ludder was kicking the engine block of his Stickleback bomber. Through sheer luck he had stumbled into an eddy of calm space within the Firehead Nebula after abruptly losing contact with the marker buoys. Unfortunately, something huge then swiped his ship off course. Systems failures in the thrusters prevented him from manoeuvring the craft properly.

So the ship just drifted until it dropped out of the relative bottom of the nebula.

When it emerged, he sent out a distress signal, and then slipped to the rear of the compartment, crossing where the bombs would have usually been racked up. Which was when he started kicking the engine.

The computer warned him not to try to fix the engines in that manner, and repeated the warning until he started ignoring it. Then the warning changed.

"Warning: proximity alert. Incoming starship."

He swore and jumped back into the cockpit, strapping himself into the grav-couch, and grabbing the flight stick. He looked up, beyond the cockpit bubble canopy, and sighed heavily.

"Perfect."

The bomber was thrown into shadow as the *Enterprise* rumbled above him.

"I will never live this down."

* * *

Feorn, Prince of Zorb, was steadily going mad.

His speedy private yacht had been disabled when a careening fellow racer had stumbled out of the foggy nebula, and struck the yacht's port circular wing, tearing it off, and taking half the ship's engines with it. They were stuck inside the nebula, and had witnessed the exodus of the massive creatures.

Unfortunately, his sanity was barely attainable at the best of times.

He was ranting and raving at the universe for preventing him from becoming the winner of the race. When his veteran pilot tried to talk some sense into him, Feorn shot him through the head.

Then he turned the weapon on his chief steward, who lurched at him to take the energy weapon off him. The chief steward fell back, his chest a charred mess.

"Damn your eyes, all of you!" Feorn raged. "I want to win this race! How can I do that if you are all working against me?" He shot the co-pilot and another steward before sitting back in his gold-plated command chair, huffing a sigh of frustration. "Got to do everything myself."

One of his harem wondered in just then, and screamed in fear and revulsion.

Feorn shot her as she tried to make a run for it.

He made sure everybody was dead: nobody could witness him losing this race. He then pulled the pilot and co-pilot out of their chairs, and sat down in the main control seat. He hadn't flown since he was a child, but how could difficult could it be?

He was still sat there two hours later, having found no way to control the ship that he could discern, when a piece of debris from the ship's own wing slammed into the unshielded bridge, and killed him.

* * *

The *Plior Runner* made it out of the cloudy nebula without incident, the pilot noting the wreckage of other ships as he passed, including some of his competitors.

He smiled at the thought of being closer to winning the race than ever before. The Corporation would be immeasurably pleased.

* * *

Guilio, Firok, and Arlkep were jockeying for position around each other, overtaking one, then another, before being overtaken by the one behind the first. They went on like this throughout the race, most notably inside the Firehead Nebula, where the clouds made it almost impossible to see who they were overtaking, or who had just overtaken them.

When all three exited the nebula, a pointed eight-winged craft blasted past them at a terrifying sublight speed, eliciting useless shouts and swearing from the professional pilots.

* * *

Hevskii grinned as she entered the Linkway, and tried to put a call through to the *Kara Marazov*. But there was no answer.

What could they be doing, she wondered?

* * *

"I think it's stuck," announced Polly.

Adam had stopped as soon as they saw it: one of the dragon pups, having been playing with one of the race's marker buoys like a cat playing with a piece of string, had got its front paw jammed in the inner workings of the buoy. The other pups were keeping their distance from the trapped pup and the buoy, suspicious of a trap.

The adults of the group looked on with interest, their own paws too big to pull the pup free, or break the buoy apart without hurting the youngling.

"I'm going to go out there and help it," announced Adam.

"Are you insane?" cried Polly.

"It's stuck, Polly. The others can't help it, but I can. I can break the buoy apart with a laser cutter from your repair kit without hurting it." He was already out of his chair, his mind made up. But Polly was having none of it. She got out of her own chair, and stepped between him and the cockpit door.

"You can't go out there in one of those flimsy EVA suits."

"Why not?"

She looked at him incredulously. "It's. Deep. Space. One tiny scratch and you'll lose your atmosphere; with those creatures floating around out there they could eat you, and you won't have the *Kara* around you to protect you. And let's not forget, that this Linkway is being used for a high-speed interstellar endurance race. There could be other starships coming through at any moment, and they may not be as friendly as the dragons."

He smiled, slipped his hands either side of her head, and kissed her passionately. She melted in his arms, angry yet wholly unwilling to let go.

"That's not fair," she said when they finally came up for air.

"I'll be fine," he said.

* * *

Floating out in space, in a flimsy sealed EVA suit, Adam was muttering to himself. From the cockpit of the *Kara*, it didn't look so huge out here. But now that he was out there, in a spacesuit, surrounded by creatures that ranged up to the size of carriers and battleships. Then the swirling Linkway over that, and he was thoroughly intimidated, and suddenly understood the concept of vertigo.

He swallowed what fear he could, and pushed off from the *Kara*'s hull, diving across the space until he bumped into the cylindrical marker buoy. The dragon pup had caught its paw in a manoeuvring vane, and couldn't get free.

Adam was distinctly aware of the eyes watching him as he pulled out the laser cutter from the belt of the EV suit.

He found it odd that none of them had made a move to stop him. Surely they would be jittery about having an unknown being near their child? And why did he have the overwhelming urge to help the stricken pup? He could almost hear it mewling pathetically.

Wait, he thought, *I* can *hear it making a noise.* He looked up at the cute little wingless dragon, and saw that its jaws weren't moving. *Idiot, sound doesn't exist in the vacuum of space, even in the Linkways.*

He grunted as the realisation occurred to him.

Polly's voice filtered through his helmet's comms unit.

"What's wrong?"

"I think they're telepathic," he answered. He looked back at the mothers of the herd, who were hovering nervously; exactly like human mothers having to stand back and watch firemen pull their children out of a well or some such. "Which would explain why I had the overwhelming urge to rescue this pup."

"You think they implanted the need into your head?" she asked worriedly.

"Probably didn't do it on purpose; at least I hope not."

He activated the laser cutter, and began the slow process of carving the offending pieces of metal away from the pup's paw. All the while, he tried to think calm, soothing thoughts, hoping that the pup would pick up on it. It seemed to work for a while.

But then the entire herd became agitated; the psychic vibrations were audible even to Adam's blunt mind. They all turned to face the direction they and the *Kara* had come from. One of the other racers was coming.

More than just one.

Adam could see several distant dots along the Linkway. So could the dragons; they took up a defensive formation around the pups and the *Kara*. The dots were getting larger, getting closer. Adam blinked, and Hevskii's bladed octopus ship slammed between the dragons, roaring past before the creatures had time to react, disappearing the other side of the herd without stopping.

Unfortunately, the three behind her were not so fast, or nimble.

* * *

Firok and Guilio were trying desperately to catch up with Arlkep, who had pulled ahead of them moments ago. They were trying everything to close the gap. Firok even resorted to firing a grappler at Arlkep.

The grappler's claws dug deep into the opponent's hull.

Sparks flew from the grappler arm, and the lights dimmed on both ships as the strain drained their energies. Then Guilio panicked at the massive sensor readings congregating farther down the Linkway. He twitched the controls only slightly, and his extra sensitive, ultra-manoeuvrable ship twitched with it, suddenly rolling towards Firok.

The two ships connected only briefly, but it was enough to send both careening off in separate directions. The grappler chain snapped, and parts of it flew into the engine intakes of Firok's racer. Arlkep's ship, suddenly released from its tug-of-war with Firok, jumped forward, and straight into the armoured flank of one of the dragon males.

The ship was smashed to pieces, explosions igniting the ship's atmosphere as it bled out into space. The dragon didn't even notice it, like a flea crashing into the leg of a human.

Firok's ships went into an uncontrollable spin that created so much gravity force inside the cockpit that Firok himself blacked out. The dragons moved to avoid the ship, trying to get their younglings away, which were intensely curious, as all children are.

The ship carried on like that for days.

By the time anyone found him –two days later- Firok was dead: the force of the spins had pooled blood in the wrong part of his brain, preventing it from reaching his vital processes, and even his vital organs.

Guilio's ship, however, was under partial control.

He managed to twist his damaged ship so that it missed the claw of an attacking dragon by inches, only to have the back claws shear off one whole long thin wing, taking the starboard sublight engine with it.

The ship twisted again, this time impossibly fast.

It tumbled towards the trapped dragon pup.

* * *

"Damn it," Adam cursed.

The wrecked racing vessel was tumbling straight towards him and the pup, spewing debris and flames. The pilot had punched out, leaving the ship on a deadly course.

He didn't know why, but he instinctively reached around the pup, and pulled himself on top of it, so that he was between the ship and its head. He squeezed his eyes shut against the inevitable pain.

Something roared, and there was a hard vibration through his helmet.

The ship never hit.

He turned slowly to see the racer in the death-grip of one of the male dragons, clamped between its jaws.

"Gordon Bennett," he said, breathing a huge sigh of relief. He patted the pup on the crown of its large head, and then slowly dragged himself back to cutting the offending piece of metal off its paw.

"Adam, are you alright?"

Polly's voice was filled with genuine concern, and he looked around to see the *Kara* hovering nearby, Polly in the cockpit trying to get a better view of him. He waved with a smile, hoping she could see he was fine.

He chuckled.

"I'm fine, Pol."

He returned to his work, and had the pup free in only a few minutes. When it was freed, it nuzzled him, sending a psychic cooing to him that was pleasant, reminding him of the tribbles of *Star Trek* from when he was a child.

He stroked the top of its head, and he could feel more intense psychic emotions feeding through into his mind from the dragons surrounding him.

The pup put on a burst of speed, and returned to its mother, leaving Adam afloat in space.

"Come on home, Adam. Maybe we can catch Hevskii up."

He held onto the marker buoy as the dragon herd began 'swimming' off in their original direction, leaving Adam with a sense of psychic euphoria, their wake bobbing everything around, even in the vacuum void of space. He felt intensely serene as he just floated there, watching the herd disappear down the Linkway.

He sighed, and then pushed off from the buoy, grabbing the *Kara*'s port wing, and pulling himself into the airlock. The outer door shut, and the inner door opened, allowing him to remove his helmet with a hiss of equalising pressure.

Eve was waking up by then, and fully clothed this time. They entered the cockpit and found dozens of ships blasting past them.

"Shall we?" Adam smiled, taking his place in the pilot's chair.

He slammed the ship forward at an impressive rate of knots, catching up easily to the big group of racers ahead of them.

"This should be fun," he said, as he dove the *Kara* into the pack.

* * *

Arlen: Are you seeing this, people?

Draf: We certainly are, Arlen. For those of you just joining us, the camera drone following the *Kara Marazov*, the ship previously in first place, picked up a mass of creatures identified as the legendary lost star dragons flying through the Linkway between obstacles one and two. The *Kara Marazov* was then seen stopping, and its pilot, Adam Caine, leaving the ship in an EV suit to assist an injured star dragon.

Arlen: And in the process, losing their first place position.

Draf: Yes indeed. Whilst this was going on, nearby Arlkep, Firok, and last year's winner, Guilio were all involved in a fatal crash that destroyed or permanently crippled all three ships. It seems that only one of the pilots survived, although we have to confirm which one.

T'i'l'ik: [This Adam Caine must be truly mad to give up his easy first place position simply to help an animal in distress. Either that, or truly heroic.]

Del Vio: Judging by the news articles being generated on the man, I would be willing to bet on the latter.

* * *

"You're going to get us all killed," said Polly. She was gripping the armrests with white knuckles, and talking through gritted teeth. Eve was similarly distressed. Adam couldn't blame them: after all, he was throwing the *Kara* around the asteroids as if he had not a care in the world.

"You're the one who suggested we catch up with Hevskii," he complained. Polly couldn't answer for a second as Adam rolled the ship, and dove across the path of two asteroids on a collision course. The asteroids came uncomfortably close to squashing the family of three.

"Yes, but not get us killed in the process."

The asteroids whipped by, and Adam was rolling the ship in another direction to dance across the surface of a monumentally huge asteroid, avoiding the upright rock formations, and passing over gaping craters the size of battleships.

"We won't get killed," he snorted.

As he said that, the asteroid dropped all of a sudden, replaced by a small field of micrometeorites that were being pulled inexorably towards the gravitic anomaly that had sprung up to ensnare the big asteroid.

That was the real obstacle; not the massive collection of asteroids themselves, but the unstable and unpredictable gravitic anomalies created by the mixture of unknown metals contained within the rocks. Gravity masses ranged from the strength of suns to that of 0.1 Terra normal –barely any gravity at all. Unfortunately, the gravity fields projected by the asteroids regularly connected, and could randomly do a number of things. It was said that if enough of the asteroids came together, they could rip a hole through time and space.

Adam pumped as much power as he could into the shields, and pushed through the swarm of micrometeorites.

The shields lit up like an umbrella bombarded by rain, each hit a splash of small blue ripples. It wouldn't hurt the shields, but cumulatively, they could eventually overwhelm them.

The marker buoys had been seeded in a wide circle from one Linkway entrance back to a second leading to the next objective. But travelling in a flat circle was impossible in the asteroids, especially ones that could suddenly change course at a moment's notice.

He kept the course straight, pushing towards the upper slice of the asteroid's elliptical plane, a path that currently had no big rocks on it, though that would change dramatically in a heartbeat. He held the speed high, aware of how reckless that was. But he didn't want to be slowing down, and giving the gravitic anomalies a chance to form and affect the *Kara*.

The rain of rock continued for several long seconds, until finally they escaped into the large space between two huge rocks.

The ship suddenly lurched forward, the sensors registering a hit from behind.

One of the asteroids had suddenly changed course to ram the *Kara Marazov*, pushing it forward faster than its previous speed. Another big rock loomed up ahead of them, this time spinning like a super-fast planet. The spinning planet's gravity mass strengthened, the sensors registering massive amounts of movement from the asteroids around it.

The sensors began registering masses of gravitic anomalies in all directions.

"Oh, crap," Polly muttered, keeping her voice low so as not to alarm Eve, who was struggling keeping her panic down at normal levels. Polly pointed to the asteroids ahead, as lines of them were dragged by the biggest asteroid towards a bizarre orbit.

The *Kara* was still being pushed along by one of the asteroids. Adam didn't want to activate the FTL inside the field, as there was no guarantee they wouldn't smash to pieces against one of the rocks during the run-up to lightspeed.

The ship rumbled and vibrated madly, the family's teeth chattering at the abuse.

In response, Adam slammed the throttle to full, pushing them back into their seats, and eliciting a yelp of surprise from Polly. He skimmed the top of the huge gravity-defying asteroid ahead, using the gravity mass as a slingshot.

The ship's speed indicator rocketed sky-high, as the combination of the ship's engines and the gravity mass before them pulled them forward faster and faster. Warning alarms blared for attention as the ship went faster than it was technically designed for. Creaks and groans came from around the ship. Adam was pushing the ship harder than he ever had before, even when they had escaped from the destruction of the Andromeda galactic core.

"Adam!" Polly shouted over the increasing noise. He wasn't paying attention, focused on the task at hand.

Suddenly the big planet-like asteroid shot past underneath, the vibrations and creaks and groans stopped, and the ship was blasting up above the elliptical plane of the field itself. They looked over the never-ending field to see several metallic shapes moving through the asteroids: the other racers.

Several fireballs erupted among the asteroids as some of the racers made a wrong turn, or were caught in a sudden gravitic anomaly and sent them off course to smash into something.

Polly was scouring the sensor read-outs.

"I've found the marked course." She sent the coordinates to Adam's monitors who dove the ship back down, and levelled out just above the asteroid field, as if hovering above an ocean of rock. He followed the course laid out by the marker buoys, and put the course into the ship's computer, and flicked it over to autopilot.

He sunk back into his seat, and breathed a sigh of relief.

"Eve, where did you put that digipad with all the race's rules?"

"It's here, Daddy," she said, holding out the digipad in question from where she had it stashed in a small locker at the back of the cockpit. "Why do you want it?"

"'Cos I've got a bad feeling we're breaking the rules by being up here."

As it turned out, they were breaking the rules, and received a transmission from the race organisers that they would be penalised if they didn't return to the course laid out by the marker buoys.

When the transmission disappeared, Eve stuck her tongue out at the blank screen and blew a raspberry.

Adam sighed, and plunged the ship back into the asteroid field, this time, pumping power to all shields so that it was even all around. He hoped it would protect them.

* * *

Arlen: Wow, that is different. The *Kara Marazov* briefly elected to break out of the asteroid field and be given a penalty in added time on their total, instead of staying in the danger zone.

Draf: You've got to admit though Arlen, that if the pilot had stayed in that part of the asteroid field, the ship would have been pulverised, or worse.

Arlen: One of the many downsides to this race: there are plenty of lethal dangers to contend with.

Draf: Which to many is the whole point of this race. Okay, ladies and gentlemen, we are down to two hundred racers out of the three hundred plus that we started with. Some have survived; some are, unfortunately, no longer with us. But that is the excitement and risk of the race. Your thoughts on the rest of the race, fellow commentators?

Del Vio: I still believe that Caine and the *Kara Marazov* could feasibly win, despite the handicap of a time penalty. That ship is of a design unknown to any species, and could possibly still have a trick or two yet to use.

T'i'l'ik: [I have to disagree. This pilot calling herself Hevskii is familiar to me.]

Draf: She was a former pirate for the Idle Guns in the Dark Galaxy, according to her file. She was given clemency for turning stateside against the Guns' operations.

T'i'l'ik: [Incredible. A pirate. Then I believe *she* will win this race.]

Draf: Interesting hypothesis; Mack, your thoughts?

Tanner: Well, someone's going to win there's no doubt of that.

(Complete silence for one minute)

<u>Draf:</u> Uh, I don't think that was quite what we were looking for, Mack. *(Tanner nods).* Moving swiftly on, let's go down to Arke Ramion, who is currently visiting the *HMS Enterprise* whilst it is assisting with the rescue efforts. Over to you Arke...

* * *

The *Kara* bounced again as the last asteroid came a little too close for comfort, ricocheting off the ship's shields as they made the run to the Linkway entrance and off to the next obstacle. According to the data file of the course, the next obstacle was, in fact, a trinary star cluster —yet another navigational nightmare to overcome.

The marker buoys stretched out ahead of them, and into the Linkway.

"Well, Captain Caine," Polly smiled. "Take us in."

"Yes, ma'am," he replied with an equally big smile. Eve, back to her old self now that they were out of the insanity of the asteroid field, just rolled her eyes. Her parents could be so embarrassing, making her wonder constantly if other teenagers were similarly embarrassed by their own.

"How long to the next obstacle?" she asked instead.

"About two hours; it's several systems over from the asteroids."

"Are trinary star systems common?" she said. Her curiosity wasn't entirely uninterested, as she had to write an essay on binary stars when she returned home to Ckeer Najoor. Sometimes it paid to have a renowned scientist for a mother.

"Not in this region of space, and especially not given the varying ages of the stars involved." She was looking at the details given by the race organisers, frowning at some of the inconsistencies compared to Hevskii's subtle scans.

"What do you mean?"

Polly smiled, grateful for the rare moment to be able to use her knowledge from her time on the exploration vessel *Icarus*. "The stars in a star system are usually the first thing to be created, and then the gravity mass of the star or stars pulls the materials in to make the planets. It's the same no matter how many stars are in the system. The only difference is that sometimes the elements in one star make its gravity mass heavier, and therefore begins drawing more elements away from its siblings, changing the size and composition of both."

"Surely that's what happened here?" asked Eve, who was also reviewing the almost incomprehensible official documents of the racecourse. "Each star drawing from another, leaving one smaller than the others?"

Polly shook her head.

"According to Hevskii's scans —which are really detailed by the way- these stars are of different compositions, and different *types* of stars."

"So that couldn't happen in nature?" asked Adam, who had switched the ship over to autopilot, and was now leaning back in his chair, looking over at his beloved wife and daughter.

She shook her head emphatically.

He sighed loudly. "Great, something else that'll probably blow up in our faces."

She grinned, "Mysteries of the universe remember?"

Again, he sighed, a little too melodramatically for the two women to take him seriously.

"I suppose we better get something to eat then."

* * *

Hevskii was struggling with a trio of oddball racers, one professional, the others owned privately by individuals. All three were a match for Hevskii's ship, in terms of speed, and they were each equally as armoured and shielded, so brute force wasn't an option either.

The others were still trying the brute force option though, occasionally rolling into the shields of their opposition, the shields sparking and overloading until they dropped in a hail of sparks and shakes.

Her ship was only like the *Kara Marazov* on the outside, the cramped cockpit reminiscent of a starfighter cockpit, with a long bubble canopy overhead, and controls all around with easy access at a moment's notice. She wore a starfighter helmet, which held her comms, and a holographic HUD projected onto the canopy.

The four ships, including Hevskii, followed the marker buoys out of the Linkway and into a pilot's nightmare. She had piloted this obstacle before –more than once- but somehow the readings she was getting were different this time. The three huge stars loomed around the Linkway entrance like giants waiting for prey to make a run out of a cave opening. Each was a different colour, denoting three completely different types of star: a red giant, a blue dwarf, and a main-type yellow star. It was a bizarre combination to Hevskii's hundred thousand plus years of galactic experience.

She was just wondering what it was that she couldn't quite put her finger on when one of the private yachts suddenly opened fire with illegal hidden weapons on one of the others. The shields of the victim were still recharging from another ship-to-ship contact; the lasers of his attacker punished the ship's aft engine block, annihilating vital components, including the coolant tanks and the antimatter regulators.

The victim ship tumbled forward, carried forward by its own previous momentum. It kept tumbling, but no pilot bailed out, and Hevskii could detect no life signs. She slowed, wary of being near the ship if it blew.

Which it did.

Except the trouble didn't stop there.

The ship, flooded with antimatter from a leak in its engine housing, tumbled into the middle of the three suns, and suddenly imploded, the antimatter engine ripping a devastating hole in the space-time continuum. Normally, the hole would disappear within seconds, but with the gravity mass of three stars in incredibly close proximity, it stayed open.

It also got larger.

"Oh, no," she whispered, remembering the last time something like this had happened.

The destruction of the ship and its antimatter engine inverting was about to unleash the most terrifying force in the universe: a quantum singularity –what the humans called a 'Black Hole'.

She reached for the comms activation panel.

* * *

Draf: Gods preserve us. I have never witnessed this happening in this race, or any other, but it seems as though one of the leading ships of the competition was fired upon, and destroyed. Its engine inverted reality around it, and has created the beginnings of a black hole in the centre of the trinary stars.

Arlen: Look, there are survivors.

(Gasps of shock all round the commentating room.)

Draf: The camera drones are detecting an emergency transmission from the ship flown by former pirate Hevskii. They cannot detect where the transmission is directed, or who received it.

Del Vio: The *Enterprise* is already en route to rescue the survivors.

T'i'l'ik: [I think someone else is going to get there before the *Enterprise*.] *(Points at screens)*

Draf: Ah. So once again, the *Kara Marazov* is going to attempt a rescue.

Arlen: Let's hope so, Draf.

* * *

The *Kara* slipped from the Linkway, and almost immediately, the ship began bouncing around. Adam had answered Hevskii's distress signal, and pushed the ship once again to its limits.

The black hole had widened considerably since Hevskii's transmission, the accretion disk already big enough to swallow a full battleship.

"How can it have grown?" he asked.

"The combination of the three stars' gravity masses must be acting as a catalyst, feeding it so that is grows in size, and draws in more and more." She looked down at her readings. "I've found the other ships," she said. "At the moment, Hevskii is furthest from the centre, whilst two others are being pulled in. Neither of them can last as long as Hevskii at the moment, or us for that matter."

Like a gaping maw, the black hole seemed to roar as it drew light and energy from the three stars around it, creating a swirl of the three primary colours. Adam realised that he was the only one who had heard the roar, making him wonder if he was just imagining it.

He pushed the ship closer to the growing accretion disk, wary of the horrendous amounts of energy being thrown around. What looked to be lightning was erupting from the accretion disk, and hitting the massive red giant that dwarfed everything –literally everything.

But it was shrinking fast, along with the other two, the blue dwarf already starting to darken as its materials were consumed piecemeal.

The whole vista would have been beautiful if it wasn't so utterly deadly.

He pumped more power into the shields, hoping it would be enough against the super-strikes of lightning. The ship rattled and vibrated even more as it closed with Hevskii's ship. Eve whimpered at the sight of the black hole tearing the stars apart, and Adam was reminded briefly of how they met above another such singularity in Odyssey Station. He wondered if that was the connection she was making, or simply terrified of what might happen to the *Kara*.

"Hevskii, are you all right?" he asked over the comms.

"*For now, Caine, but my engines are starting to struggle. They're not as advanced as yours.*"

"The *Enterprise* is on the way for rescue operations. We detected their signals about thirty minutes behind us."

"*Thirty minutes?*" Hevskii's disembodied voice cried. "*Those others won't survive that long.*"

"I know." He clicked off the comms, and pushed the *Kara* into the small accretion disk. "Sorry, you two, but I'm not going to stand by and watch those other two racers be pulled into that damned thing."

Polly seemed to be okay with it; she would have said something if not. But Eve was once again in shock, her green skin paling. Adam swore, and told Polly to take her back to her bunk again, and calm her down if possible. Eve resisted at first, but then relented when Adam turned in his chair, and put his hand on her arm.

"It's going to be okay, princess," he said softly.

She nodded, and the two women disappeared, leaving Adam to fly the ship single-handedly, the way he liked it.

He pushed the throttle further, closing the distance with the asymmetrical curved ship closer to the singularity. Its running lights were gone, the glow of its three engine strips fading as it began to run out of energy.

The accretion disk passed underneath, the hole of the singularity in the centre of Adam's viewport along with his first rescuee.

This is such a bad idea, he told himself.

A piece of hull plating from the second, less endangered, racer slammed into the Kara's rear shields, pushing it perilously close to the ship Adam was about to rescue.

"Polly?" he called.

She came rushing in.

"I need you to handle the tractor beam whilst I manoeuvre us next to these guys, please." She sat down in the co-pilot's chair, and brought up the tractor beam controls, activating the ship's small tractor. Adam hailed the ship in trouble.

"This is the *Kara Marazov*, do you copy?"

"We... <fzzzt>...you Kara... <fzzzt> ...trouble... <fzzzt> communications and propulsion."

"Punch out," Adam said, "We'll tractor you to us."

"Can... <fzzzt>... tractor the ship?"

"Negative; there's too much pull from the singularity. You're going to have to abandon ship. I'm sorry."

There was a long pause, although Adam could hear a long sigh through the comms speakers.

"Acknowledged."

The engines were struggling to keep the *Kara* in one place, the gravitic pull of the black hole getting stronger by the second as it expanded beneath the ships. A random lightning strike passed perilously close to the two ships, bouncing them around, and briefly shutting the electronics down.

The ship powered back up almost instantly, but the ships had already drifted an incredible distance, sinking towards the event horizon. The lightning-energy strikes were more frequent closer in, although thankfully none of them hit.

The cockpit canopy of the other ship shot off the hull of the ship, and the pilot was sent rocketing out into space. The tractor beam shot out, but was intercepted by a piece of debris from the second ship further away, dragging the chunk of hull towards the *Kara* in a hurry. Polly managed to disengage the tractor beam, and let the chunk of hull fly away on the gravitic currents. But the pilot was being pulled away as well, flapping his arms, and kicking his legs, as if that would help him, fully aware that his ejection seat's emergency rocket was faltering.

It stopped altogether, and flew past the body of his ship, which was still stuck on autopilot.

Just as the pilot seemed about to be pulled forever into the black hole, Polly snagged him with the tractor beam, and pulled him in to the small airlock on the port side of the ship. She held him there, giving Adam time to suit up in his EV suit, and pull the pilot in by hand.

The coughing and spluttering pilot was dragged into the cockpit. Adam placed him in one of the two rear chairs in the cockpit, and wrapped a blanket round him: the pilot had clearly spent all his money on his ship instead of his EV suit, and was suffering a small amount of vacuum exposure. He was a Kraj, one of the last of his species from Rel Major. His normally grey skin was almost white with shock, although it was starting to return to its normal colour.

"Thankyou, Captain," the pilot groaned.

Adam nodded at the acknowledgement, and returned to his seat.

He was just in time to see a wing from the other stranded ship slam into the Kraj's ship, shearing through the cockpit where the pilot had sat, and gouging a canyon along the spine of the ship.

The ship broke apart, and was instantly sucked into the vortex below.

Adam turned the *Kara* to face the other racer, and pushed the throttle, now suddenly fighting completely against the gravitic current. The ship, a pointed rocket of a thing, was struggling just as much as the first. It was missing its left delta wing, and was spinning, its right engine still keeping it 'afloat'... just barely.

It was starting to lose the struggle when Adam brought the *Kara* alongside. Polly latched the tractor beam onto the ship's main body. The thing started to disintegrate instantly, torn apart by the tractor beam's strong energy field. The pilot punched out, and Polly disengaged the tractor, instead focusing it on the pilot.

The figure of the pilot was waving its arms and legs frantically.

Adam couldn't see any air tanks or survival gear attached to him: another racer who wasn't prepared for the worst.

The figure stopped jerking all of a sudden, and a liquid flowed from his chest.

Adam slammed his fist into the console, making Polly and the Kraj pilot jump.

"Drag him anyway, Polly. At least we'll be able to give the body to his family or friends. He deserves that much at least."

Polly pulled the impaled pilot into the airlock with the tractor. Adam reset the autopilot, and leapt from his seat, followed swiftly by the Kraj. Adam looked at him curiously, but the pilot just shrugged.

They managed to drag the dead body of the impaled pilot through into the ship. He was indeed dead, blood frozen around the wound in his chest. His peach skin pale and his eyes open in shock, his mouth was stuck in a rictus of pain and surprise. Adam closed the pilot's eyes and mouth, and laid him to rest under a blanket next to the airlock door.

When they returned to the cockpit, Polly was worriedly attempting to fly the ship, and not having much luck.

"The singularity's still getting stronger," she cried.

The ship was whining and groaning, the engines having a hard time keeping it in place. He jumped into the pilot's seat, and switched off the autopilot. The engines whined as he pushed the ship to full throttle, and bounced towards Hevskii's ship.

"Are you sure about this, Adam?"

"She's one of the oldest living beings in the known universe, and Silver would never forgive me." Hevskii's ship was struggling now, and it was starting to slip backwards, the engines blazing.

The comms channels were alive with all sorts as other ships began piling out of the Linkway, and flying around the singularity, avoiding the gravity wells of the dying stars, and ignoring the rescue operation taking place. Polly attempted to contact them to help out, but none of them were interested in risking their lives, and passed by. The Kraj pilot had a few choice curses to send at them.

Eve turned up then, sleepy again, and rested from her shock. She didn't say anything about the Kraj or the licking edge of the accretion disk still visible through the triangular cockpit window. She sat down in the spare fourth seat, and watched as the eight-pointed ship was latch onto with the *Kara*'s tractor beam.

But there was a problem.

Hevskii's voice came through the comms channel loud and clear:

"Caine, my ship is falling apart, and my ejection system is fried. I can't even manually open the cockpit canopy."

Adam swore.

"Then I'm going to have to come out there, and cut you free."

"What? Are you insane? You'll be killed."

"I've been out there once already, I can handle it." Polly, however, wasn't entirely convinced –she knew her husband well enough to know even he wasn't entirely sure, but also that he wouldn't let a friend die if he could do something about it.

He raced back to the airlock, still wearing the EV suit, and stepped in. Before he could close the helmet, or the door, Polly appeared and planted a long passionate kiss on his lips before handing him the laser cutter he had used earlier to free the dragon pup.

"Please come back safe," she whispered.

He smiled, that Han Solo smile he had when he was up to mischief. "Don't I always?"

The airlock cycled closed, and the outside door opened. Adam tied a long, strong cord to his suit, and the other end to a bracket in the airlock itself. Making sure it was tied well enough, he pounced out of the ship, and towards Hevskii's vessel. The small thrusters on his suit propelled him forward at an exponential rate until he grabbed the nearest of the eight pointed wings, ducked under and latched onto the cockpit canopy.

Hevskii was sat inside, having donned an emergency EV suit, waiting impatiently for him to do something.

He dragged out the laser cutter, aware of the tidal forces battering the ship and himself on their way to the centre of the black hole. The laser cutter made mincemeat of the canopy's metal edges, but still it took a long time.

The canopy came away as soon as he finished cutting, smashing into one of the upper wings, and tearing off large piece of the hull in the process. Hevskii unhooked herself from her ejection seat, and floated up to meet him. Which was when the tractor beam cut out. Adam knew it was the engines diverting power to stay 'afloat', the ship's computer making the sacrifice to keep the ship whole and intact.

He grabbed Hevskii just as her own ship's engines gave out, and the ship suddenly flew out from beneath their feet, whisked away by the intense gravity field, and tumbled into the singularity gracelessly.

The gravity field pulled them around the *Kara* until they were behind the ship. And Adam found it too hard to pull them along the cord. Although it was tested for several people to hold onto at any given time, he didn't have the strength to pull the pair of them up the cord to the *Kara*, and fight against the gravity of the black hole beneath and behind them.

He activated the suit's comms.

"Polly, take the ship away from the gravity field: we can't pull ourselves to the ship because the gravity is too strong." Even to him, his voice seemed strained. He was holding onto Hevskii with all his not-inconsiderable strength, but she was starting to slip. So he tied part of the cord to her suit.

"Okay, hold on tight now."

The cord tugged them away as the *Kara*'s sublights blazed furiously.

Adam had always suspected that the universe had a sick sense of humour, and of course, a morbidly comic sense of timing. One of the other racers coming out of the Linkway slashed past the two suited friends, and its wake somehow –only the gods knew how- ripped Adam off the cord.

Hevskii whipped her arm out, but was too late as he flashed past behind her.

Adam could hear Polly's screams over the comms.

"I love you," he whispered, before he was out of the suit's pickup range.

His suit got torn from yet more debris, taking his air supply with it.

As the carbon dioxide build-up knocked him out, he swore he saw something huge move past him. But then the blackness overtook him, and he was out.

* * *

<u>Draf:</u> Oh dear gods.

<u>T'i'l'ik:</u> [That just is not fair.]

<u>Del Vio:</u> Figures it would take a black hole to kill a man like Adam Caine.

<u>Tanner:</u> Wow. That's one hell of a way to go out.

<u>Arlen:</u> I hope the *Enterprise* gets there soon.

<u>Del Vio:</u> They will.

* * *

Polly was still screaming when the *HMS Enterprise* ploughed from the Linkway. The Kraj pilot –calling himself Kraka- had wrestled her away from the controls when she started pushing the ship back towards the black hole. Eve was comforting her mother, whilst the newly retrieved Hevskii joined Kraka in piloting the ship.

When they landed in *Enterprise*'s starfighter hangar, Captain Flakenrix was waiting for them, her face grim. Polly wasn't really aware of anything going on around her. A Navy medic appeared, and looked her over, but announced that she was only in shock, and would be fine soon enough.

Polly's screams were down to whimpers as if she had been badly hurt.

Eve was in shock as well, but she realised that it had taken a black hole –the universe's most destructive power- to defeat him. As it should have been. The two survivors of the Caine family consoled each other, not speaking to any of the Navy crew or even the two pilots that had temporarily taken control of the *Kara*.

Hevskii, however, refused to believe that even a black hole could kill Caine. She sent a brief message to her mothership, requesting aid in searching for its namesake, though she knew it wouldn't arrive for hours.

Both Hevskii and Kraka declared that they would use the *Kara Marazov* to search for Adam. Flakenrix offered them the services of the *Enterprise*, for all the good it would do them.

Everybody was shocked when Flakenrix announced that the man in question was no longer to be found on the *Enterprise*'s sensors, although there was a trace of bizarre energy leading away from the black hole and toward the second Linkway entrance.

Hevskii frowned.

* * *

Wake up, Adam.

He woke up in a panic. The blue swirls of the Linkway passing him by was all he could see at first, and for some reason his helmet was off. The voice he had heard had been familiar, but his mind was too filled with the grogginess of recovering from oxygen depravation to remember where it was from.

He sprang to his feet, and wobbled a bit. He accidentally took a deep breath... and realised that there was air around. His already groggy mind refused to believe that there could be air there. He was standing on some leathery hull, not recognising the long, giant bony spine leading away along a tail.

A man-sized figure stood near him.

His eyes refocused on the man, and his confusion became more intense.

"Graham?"

Colour Sergeant Graham was wearing the forest camouflage and a green beret of his calling, his hands clasped at the small of his back, and a big grin on his bearded face. There was something wrong with his eyes though, completely blank and devoid of emotion.

"You're not Graham."

Of course not, a voice said in his head, a voice that sounded just like Graham's. The faux-Graham's lips moved in sync with the voice in Adam's head, but there was no actual sound.

"If I had to guess," he said, looking around at his surroundings properly for the first time, "I'd say you were a psychic manifestation of the star dragon I'm standing on: presumably the herd-father. I heard part of your call before in the Nebula."

You are more perceptive than you give yourself credit, Adam.

"Deduction more than perception," he replied. "Though I'm still curious as to how I'm breathing when we're in space, even the Linkway. Obviously, you and your kind have a way of doing it, but humans need oxygen to survive no matter where they are. Simple biology."

We...'dragons', as you call us, do not need oxygen as you do. We do, however, perspire something similar to oxygen.

"So I'm breathing in dragon sweat? Gross."

It's keeping you alive, said faux-Graham. He stepped closer, though he cast no shadow from the light around them, whilst Adam had dozens of shadows flickering into existence at random points around him.

"True; do you mind if I ask why you rescued me? Going so close to the event horizon of a black hole couldn't be too good for your health."

We dragons are tougher than you know.

"I don't doubt it."

Graham started slowly pacing around Adam, who found he could not move his legs —he didn't know if it was from his previous unconsciousness, or the dragon's psychic interference, neither of which were appealing.

You are the chosen one, Adam Caine: the Strand, messiah, saviour, whichever one you like, you are destined to do great things in this universe.

"Great, another whack job. I'm not any kind of chosen one; I just want to grow old with my family. All this talk of destiny is a load of crap —we all choose our own destiny, and there is no other force behind it. We make our own way: human, dragon, Rijiin, Kra Nal, even Core."

There is a great darkness coming, Adam.

"I know. That's what Project Lympstone was created for."

I am not referring to your resurrection scheme. Soon, a great darkness will descend on you, but one that will have great repercussions for the universe, your friends, and your family; but most especially for you. Adam, there are choices and decisions ahead that could affect the destinies of trillions upon trillions of this universe's inhabitants.

"So what am I supposed to do?"

Although the faux-Graham showed no emotion, he sighed, and Adam felt a deep rumble from the leathery skin under his feet.

You have suffered greatly over the years, Adam, and despite your family life, and the passing of several cycles without violence, there is still a great reservoir of anger and rage within you, an unprecedented one for a physical being so young.

"Young?"

Faux-Graham smiled, though still there was no emotion in his eyes.

Yes, I recognise that among the younger races your physical being can be aged by harsh experiences. It is the way of things I am afraid. Graham stepped towards him, and took Adam by the shoulders; though the hands were noncorporeal, Adam felt a shiver run down his spine. *Adam you will be faced with a choice soon; if you choose to go down the darker path, you will be forever damned. We dragons have seen it. Your friend Silver calls you the Strand; we refer to you as the Centre, because every decision you make affects the universe as if you were its centre, moving in the direction you go.*

"So what you're saying," Adam replied sarcastically, "Is that if I have a piece of toast on the wrong day, it could be the end of the universe as we know it?" He felt a thundering rumble pass beneath him, and remembered just how vulnerable he was standing on the back of a behemoth dragon herd-father. It probably wasn't the best idea he had ever had in annoying one of the largest creatures he had ever heard of.

I know that you will not at this moment take this warning seriously, Adam, faux-Graham started again, *but you must remember it in the months to come.*

Adam nodded, though Graham was right: he didn't take the vague warning seriously. How could he with so little details about when or where, or how?

The dragon suddenly erupted from the Linkway and into the vacuum of space, and Adam found himself catching his breath as they arrived in a spectacularly beautiful star system. A ringed gas giant sat not far from the Linkway, surrounded by at least a dozen large moons, all framed by a dwarfing, swirling nebula that resembled angel's wings. This was all thrown into stark relief by the bright blue star at the centre of the system some way off.

And of course, there were marker buoys leading from another Linkway entrance to above the gas giant's rings.

Big ships lined the last section of the buoys, all pointed inward. A massive space station hung above them, lights by the millions, and covered by hundreds of communications masts and arrays.

"It's the finish line," said Adam. "How did you-?" He looked at faux-Graham questioningly, but there was an approximation of a smile on the psychic manifestation's lips. "I didn't think beings such as yourself were interested in the minutiae of humanoids, and other lower beings." It was Adam's turn to smile.

It's important to you.

Adam shrugged. "Polly and Evie wanted to compete in this race; they sort of conned me into it."

You have gained more than a few admirers during the course of this... competition. That includes myself and the rest of my species when they hear of your bravery and selflessness.

"Where's the-?"

Just as he said it, the *Enterprise* burst from the Linkway behind the dragon and almost collided with the great beast. The warship ploughed past the dragon, giving it a wide berth until they stopped.

They have detected your presence on my back, Adam. You should prepare to return to them. Faux-Graham pointed toward the *Enterprise*, and several seconds later, a small blue dot detached from the bigger vessel.

Graham began disappearing.

"Wait; I need to know. Why did you pick Sergeant Graham to interact with me?"

'Graham' smiled again.

Because he was the closest thing you have ever had to a loving, caring father. Family is important to my people, as it is to you personally. The manifestation snapped to attention, and saluted perfectly. *Goodbye Adam Logan Caine; I hope it will be my pleasure to see you again someday.*

The faux-Graham finally disappeared, leaving Adam alone on the back of the dragon.

"Me too," he said, before donning the suit's helmet –which had been sat idly by where he had lain before.

The *Kara Marazov* came into view, speedily making its way towards him. When it finally reached him, he was indeed ready to return to his family, somewhat shaken by the experience.

He didn't even realise that there was no gravity on the dragon's back until he jumped towards the *Kara*. Someone was waiting in the airlock for him, their arm extending to grab him. He bounded off the back of the dragon and onto the wing of the ship.

He took the hand of the person waiting for him, and they pulled him in. As soon as the door was shut, the helmets came off, and Polly wrapped her lips around his. Her eyes were red-rimmed from crying, but relief was slapped all over her face.

When they finally released each other from their lip-locked embrace she slapped him hard. The noise sounded louder in the tight confines of the small airlock, and stung just as much.

"That's for leaving me like that." Then she hugged him tight. "Why have you always got to be the brave one? Why is it always you that risks his neck to save others from disaster?"

"I'm sorry, Pol. It's just the way I am."

She sighed melodramatically, and started playing with his beard, stroking the hair like it was a pet.

"Just one of the many reasons why I love you," she smiled finally. The inner door opened, and three people waited on the other side, expectant looks on their faces. Eve leaped into her father's arms; her own eyes were rimmed with a dark green where she had been crying as well.

"Shall we win this race then?" he smiled.

Everyone collapsed against the walls in relieved laughter.

* * *

<u>Draf:</u> I do not believe this! The *Kara Marazov* has rejoined the race having been rescued by the *HMS Enterprise*. According to the race rules, this is permitted.

<u>Arlen:</u> Even if they don't finish first, this has been the most fantastic story in this race.

<u>Del Vio:</u> The race hasn't finished yet gentlemen.

<u>T'i'l'ik:</u> [Yes, this race has been the most exciting I have ever seen. Although much of the course has been destroyed, and I suspect the owners will have some answering to do to the Terran Navy, I hope next year will be just as exciting.]

<u>Arlen:</u> Let's hope so, T'i'l'ik.

<u>Draf:</u> Well, let's watch the last leg as the *Plior Runner* leads the pack towards the finish line, with the *Kara Marazov* closing.

* * *

The *Kara* passed three more ships in the desperate dash for the finish. They disappeared behind them as Adam pushed the ship harder and faster. Weaving through the throng of other ships making similar dashes.

The *Plior Runner* was up ahead, the only thing between them and first place.

There were dozens of larger starships lining the last stretch, facing inward toward the course. The *Enterprise* hung far above the marker buoys, whilst the dragon herd-father had again disappeared.

Adam tried pumping as much power into the engines as possible, but he could only get as far as coming within spitting distance of the *Plior Runner* when the pilot of the leading ship slammed on their afterburner and jumped forward a fair distance.

Polly and Eve were urging Adam to go faster, but the *Kara*'s engines were too badly damaged from fighting the gravity of the black hole.

"Dammit, he's going to win," Adam cursed, just as the *Plior Runner* crossed the holographic barrier that marked the finish line. The hologram dissipated, and vacuum-rated fireworks exploded all around, filling the area with a rainbow of colours.

The *Kara* passed through a cloud of sparkling blue lights before speeding through the finish line as well. Everybody in the cockpit cabin let out a wronged sigh of defeat, sitting back in his or her chairs in shocked disbelief.

"That's just not fair," exclaimed Eve. "That just is not fair."

"No it's not," replied Adam in a soft voice. "At least the race is over." He turned to the others. "If I go near another event like this, somebody shoot me please." Hevskii and the Kraj pilot both chuckled. Polly just looked at him sidelong, as if to say, *you told me so.*

But Eve wasn't very happy.

She was grumbling about the unfairness of it all, despite Adam's reassurances that second place in the greatest and most dangerous of all races in the known universe was no bad thing. Neither was surviving the horrors of what had happened during the race.

They were directed to dock with a large platform sat on one side of the space station. The *Plior Runner* was already docking up, thousands moving to greet the pilot inside the huge spherical forcefield. The pilot was hoisted above the crowd, passed along to the stage, his face split with a huge grin, waving his arms in the air.

Adam noted the collection of suit-wearing prigs on the stage, some of which were the same men who owned the *Plior Runner's* company. He wondered just how fixed the race was: the owners of the racer making sure he won by using their inside knowledge and connections.

He shook his head almost imperceptibly at the thought of such corruption even here at a supposedly clean race.

He docked the *Kara*, and the temporary five-member crew were escorted around the cheering and jeering crowd by several race marshals. None of the crowd paid a blind bit of notice to Adam and his motley crew, too intent on watching the race winner being dragged to the stage.

One of the race officials dressed in suits raised his arms, and a deafening squeal pierced the air –speaker feedback being too close to a mic pick-up. The crowd went deathly silent, and a marshal brought a tall pole with a pick-up sat on its peak. Speakers hovered in large towers above the crowd. The suit's voice was carried over the entire bubble.

"Ladies and gentlemen; welcome to our closing ceremony. Unfortunately, this will also be the *last* closing ceremony." There was a wave of grumbling and shouts of disbelief from the crowd. "After the disastrous events of this year's race, it is only right that this be the last." More grumbling.

The suit sighed, and looked at the human pilot of the *Plior Runner.*

"As such, we have a last minute change to the rules." There was a big white grin on his purple face. "As you all know, the *Plior Runner* crossed the finish line before everybody else, thus earning first place." Roaring cheers went up, and the pilot of the ship in question waved enthusiastically to the crowd.

"But," the suit continued, "as part of our new rules, we as the management and official of this race have decided to award deduction of time to one of the other racers. As such, this time puts them in first place, *ahead* of the *Plior Runner.*" He turned to his left, just as the crew of the *Kara* arrived on the stage, followed by several other racers still in their flight gear. "Captain Caine, step forward."

Adam had a stunned look on his face.

Two other men in suits stepped towards him, carrying a large silver gilded cup between them.

The first suit picked the mic pick-up off the stand, letting it tumbled to the ground.

"Adam Caine, for the most incredible –and somewhat insane- acts of bravery we have ever seen in our lifetimes, we award *you*, your crew, and your ship the winning trophy. Congratulations, Captain."

Adam was still shocked, but took the cup in one big hand, looking at his reflection in the polished sides. Eve held the other handle, looking at it with awe and excitement. She looked up at her father with a big grin on her green face. The roar of approval was immense, almost deafening. Flags flapped in people's hands, scarves and pieces of clothing were thrown into the air in celebration, and cries of whoops of joy resounded inside the forcefield bubble.

Then the first suit put the mic pick-up in front of Adam and asked him what he thought of the honour.

In true Adam Caine style, he said, "Nice."

* * *

Draf: Wow, I did not see that coming, Arlen.

Arlen: Me neither, Draf, but he is totally deserving of the trophy.

T'i'l'ik: [I too believe that this is indeed appropriate. The human Caine has shown bravery above and beyond any call of duty, and has shown a sportsmanship like few others before him. He is a credit to his species.]

Tanner: Excellent.

Draf: (*Open-mouthed expression for a second*) Well, we're stood here on the stage, attempting to get closer for an interview with one of the main protagonists in this bizarre tale. It seems, though, we will not be able to get much closer. Perhaps Commander Del Vio could help us? Wait, where is she?

Arlen: She was here a second ago. Look, there's Captain Flakenrix from the *Enterprise*.

Draf: Captain! Captain Flakenrix, may we have a word about the race?

Flakenrix: Of course, mister Rogtar, I am a big fan.

Draf: Thankyou, madam Captain. First, though, do you know where commander Del Vio is? She disappeared a few minutes ago, and we haven't seen her since.

Flakenrix: I am sorry, but is that some kind of joke?

Arlen: I don't follow.

Flakenrix: Lieutenant Commander Maryna Del Vio was killed two years ago in a shuttle accident.

Draf: Then who in the nineteen galaxies have we been talking to for the last three days?

* * *

The psychic manifestation that looked like Maryna Del Vio smiled. The manifestation hung above the crowd, shrouded from view but still watching nonetheless. It wasn't much effort anymore to pose as the human Del Vio, though truthfully the herd-father was beginning to enjoy using psychic manifestations to walk among the lower beings.

His interactions with Adam Caine were intriguing.

Just being around the chosen one was exhilarating.

Despite his ancient old age, the herd-father felt young beside the Earthman. The chosen one would have to bear some more observation. A smile spread across Del Vio's features before the manifestation dissipated completely.

* * *

It took a week of interviews and congratulations before the Caine family were finally allowed to leave the space station.

They said goodbye to Hevskii and the Kraj pilot, and left the station aboard the *Kara*, managing to avoid the attentions of the *Enterprise* and Silver's big starship, the *Adam Caine*. Adam himself wanted to avoid talking about his experiences with the star dragons, and especially the herd-father. He didn't know why, he just did.

"So," he said when they were finally into the Linkway, "where to now? We've still got another week before we need to start heading back home."

"You want to go somewhere after all that back there?" Polly exclaimed.

He nodded. "Nothing extreme."

Polly's eyes narrowed. "You already have somewhere in mind, don't you?"

He threw her a big grin. "M'Der recommended a paradise planet in the inner Andromeda systems. Beaches far as the eye can see, blue skies with the most amazing sunsets, and palm tree villas to beat any posh mansion."

"Sounds good; what's the catch?"

"Catch?"

Polly gave him a withering stare.

"M'Der recommended it," she said. "That probably means that it's a jungle deathworld with native tribes out to kill any interlopers that turn up."

Adam tried to say something, but found he couldn't.

Eve appeared between them.

"So what are we waiting for?"

Twenty:
All Fall Down Part One: The Burning House

Historian's Note: This story is set one year after Wildcard.

"In all trust there is the possibility of betrayal."
—Anon.
"Only the dead have seen the end of war."
—Plato
"Some mother fuckers are always tryin' to ice-skate uphill."
—Blade

I have faced gods and monsters.
I have walked across galaxies, and stridden through suns and stars.
I have seen the end of worlds and civilisations.
I have witnessed pain and suffering on an unimaginable scale.
I have brought death and destruction to my enemies.
I have lived a thousand lives.
I have faced terror and fear.
I am your sword.
I am your shield.
My name is Adam Caine.
And this is the end of my world.
-Introduction paragraph to *The Book of Caine*, a part-fiction novel by Roath Caine.

June 4010ad.
Darkness spread across Fullina like wildfire in slow motion, pressing like a wave across the planet, pushing over the continents, blanketing them just as much as the already dark oceans and the terminator line.

Fullina was a hive of activity like any other planet serving as the capital of a great star empire. The Alliance of Independent Worlds —or just Alliance- held sway over hundreds upon hundreds of worlds and growing larger every year. Its government was based on Fullina, and during this long night, the governmental buildings were alive with the sounds of treaties being made.

One treaty in particular would have been cause for concern.

"Thankyou, Premier," the green-skinned politician smiled. The two men shook hands, and the deal was officially done.

"I am pleased to bring Mertik into the Alliance, Representative. It will be my honour to see members of your people in the halls of the Alliance government."

* * *

Ckeer Najoor.

The captain of the heavy freighter *Regal Sandwalker* was yawning. Despite his love for the quiet planet below, the run to Ckeer Najoor was always a dull affair, monotonous and slow.

He was sat in his ultra-comfortable command chair on the ship's circular bridge, watching out of the forward windows, his feet up on the railing around the chair. He sipped at a hot caffeine liquid supplement from a beige mug, letting the vapour fill his nostrils; it was gods-awful stuff, but it sure as hell kept him and his crew going on the long shifts.

His bridge crew were setting about the process of final landing procedures to the small spaceport outside Loor City on the surface. The big ship was currently oriented parallel with the planet's surface, preparing for atmospheric entry. There were three ships on their way out of the atmosphere, with another ahead of the *Regal Sandwalker* awaiting permission to land via the tight flight path.

"There's that damn interference again," the sensor operator announced. He was jabbing the ancient console with several fingers from all four hands, hoping that the captain would actually fork out for a new console, or a new ship.

"Probably interference from whatever they're doing around the system's sun," the captain said idly, scratching his rotund belly. "Whatever the hell that is," he muttered.

"Wait, I'm picking something up."

"Probably just a sensor echo of that ship down at the star's orbit again."

"No, there're several large masses moving towards us and the planet."

The captain frowned, heaving himself to an upright position in his armchair, and activating the chair's holographic displays. The floating readouts flickered badly, before resolving into a dozen metallic objects that revealed no identification whatsoever.

"Energy readings are spiking off the chart!" the sensors man suddenly shouted. "They're firing at us!"

The *Regal Sandwalker* took a direct hit to its midsection, energy fire from the largest of the warships breaking it in two. The two halves fell out of the sky, parts of which burned up in the atmosphere. The crew were alive long enough to send out a distress signal.

The *Regal*'s captain had just enough time to feel the pain of the burning spilt liquid on his face before his bridge was obliterated in an instant.

However, other ships were destroyed, or shot bad enough that they simply tumbled into the planet's atmosphere, too heavy to fight the gravity below. The attackers showed no mercy, destroying the one or two satellites in orbit, along with several private yachts.

Debris rained down on Ckeer Najoor's settlements.

* * *

The Caine family, however, were temporarily unaware of the sudden attack.

They were driving in a rented hover speeder, the wind rushing through their hair, the sun beating down from behind fluffy white clouds far up in the sky. They were returning from a long weekend in the planetary capital, Loor City, a holiday before Evelyn went to college in the big city.

They were all smiles as the open-top hover car skimmed along the Jilo Plains. In the distance to their left were the Black Mountains, ominous on the horizon despite the bright sunlight. To their right, a haze of green-blue where the ocean wasn't too far away: Adam wasn't going to risk skimming along the old mail trail through the middle of the Plains where the heat reflected off the sand could kill a man not protected.

So he drove the speeder through the outer Plains, close to the ocean.

It was only another ninety miles to Rino, their home, short change for a speeder.

They were all looking forward to returning home, during the town's informal version of a 'Sabbath' day, when everybody would be out in the gardens relaxing, and generally having fun.

Thrigor, the young blue-skinned boy that Evelyn had essentially kidnapped to be her boyfriend several years ago, was fast asleep in one of the two backseats, whilst Evie was idly stroking his long bright yellow hair.

"Can we have some music on please, Dad?" shouted Eve over the rushing air.

"What like that noise you tried to push on us last week?" he said back. He shook his head. "No way; I like metal but that was just gibberish with a vague tune injected into it." He looked in the rear-view mirror to see her sticking her tongue out at him.

"Thrigor likes it," she complained.

"Only because you told him to," said Polly, her mother. She received a stuck-out tongue as well, though Evelyn had a big grin on her face so Polly stuck her own tongue out.

Evelyn had grown taller than Polly in the last few years, though Polly was never especially tall anyway, less so next to her husband. Even sat down, he seemed to tower over all of them. Once possessing long scraggily hair, Adam was now older, wiser, with shortened brown hair, and a neatly trimmed beard that he liked to think made him look like a young Obi-Wan Kenobi; Polly disagreed, and teased him for it mercilessly.

"Are we there yet, Obi-Wan?"

Adam's eyes narrowed when he looked over at her, keeping his hands on the steering wheel.

"Soon," he grumbled.

Polly chuckled. Adam couldn't help but still be completely and totally in love with her, and was still very much attracted to her. She had changed her hairstyle in recent months, having had strips of it bleached, but she was still the petite beauty he first met on the ISS. She had an athletic frame, thin sculpted face and soulful eyes that Adam could melt in every time he looked into them.

She placed her hand on his as he pushed the throttle lever forward a little.

He smiled, and drove the craft between a pair of sand dunes.

* * *

In orbit, the sinister warships moved into geosynchronous orbit above the major settlements, including Loor City. Massive pulses of energy slammed down through the atmosphere and obliterated city blocks in seconds, turning the metal into molten lava.

Hover cars were vaporised on the streets and paths, short-range aircraft were smashed to pieces in the air, or knocked out of the air completely.

The River Loor boiled, cooking the sailing vessels and their owners still on the water at that time of day. Onlookers were burned to death by the superheated steam, whilst those aircraft lucky enough to avoid the actual plasma bursts, suddenly found themselves contending with the extreme temperatures of the steam. Some pilots were boiled alive, whilst others managed to escape unharmed only to slam into the sides of ruined buildings hidden in the cloying fog.

This scene was repeated on a lesser scale across the planet, whole communities wiped out in an instant. The fires of the attacks spread through the dry fields, catching alight whatever the flames touched.

Soon enough, the planet burned.

When the big ships' weapons batteries stopped firing the planet's surface was almost completely obscured by smoke plumes. By chance, or fate, only the Jilo Plains was kept clear, the bizarre wind patterns preventing any smoke from drifting aimlessly across the sand dunes.

Military-grade dropships descended into the atmosphere, through the smoke, carrying a large contingent of soldiers. Each one landed at a large settlement disgorged its cargo, which then slaughtered every living being on their personal scanners before re-embarking on the ships and heading for another village or town.

Two dropships, both midnight black flecked with blood-like spatters of red across their hulls, landed at the small village of Rino...

* * *

Adam could see the horizon change colour almost instantly. It went from a hazy blue to a menacing grey colour, although it was still a way off. The temperature rose several degrees, forcing him to expend more of the hover car's power through the air conditioners.

He didn't say anything at first, not wanting to alarm the others.

He pushed the throttle lever forward a bit more, skimming round a particularly large sand dune on their left. There were flashes of energy in the far distance; at first he thought it was lightning created by the extreme heat and pressure of the desert, but it was too uniform and constant.

Weapons fire, he realised. *Except no hand weapon could be so noticeable from such a distance.* Although he didn't think it was possible, he came to only one conclusion: orbital bombardment. *But how*, he thought? *The traders that come here are all reliable; none of them would give up Ckeer Najoor's protected secret surely. Besides, it's a protectorate of the Alliance.*

He was sure he wouldn't like the answer; not that it mattered when the defenceless world was under attack from orbit. Where the hell was the Alliance in all this? They were supposed to be protecting this planet.

The first sign that Adam and his family were truly in trouble was a loud whistling sound, followed by a roaring sound as something large passed close by overhead, the wind battering off odd-shaped surfaces.

Eve screamed as a giant fireball slammed into the ground ahead of them. Mini fireballs dropped on the hover car, pinging off the chassis, and spraying flames outward. Polly was quiet, but there was panic on her face as larger chunks of flaming debris hit the sand all around them.

It rained fire, and Adam did his very best to avoid it. He swerved the hover car around a pillar of fire and smoke as wide as the car was long. The engines whined louder, straining to turn properly at such a fast pace.

"Adam slow down, we're going to crash," Polly warned.

He swerved again, this time careening the floating vehicle around a large chunk of hull plating with the name *Regal Sandwalker* stencilled on it. Adam felt a moment of lament: the *Regal Sandwalker* had belonged to Garth Marelighter, a direct descendant of his youngest sister.

The rain of fire was getting heavier and thicker as more ship parts fell to the ground, flattening dunes, and making craters.

Adam darted behind one of the larger dunes in the area for cover, only to have a huge piece of debris bounce off the sandy slope and crash into the side of the hover car. It turned the vehicle over, and then over again.

Adam was the only one to be thrown out of the hover car, landing in the soft sand with little pain. The car was upside down, though it would be a simple task to right it again. Adam crawled to the vehicle, glad that the rain of fire was now petering off. Another fireball ricocheted off the top of the massive sand dune, and slammed into the ground beside the car.

The shockwave tipped the vehicle back over, and smashed down on top of Adam's crawling form.

* * *

Once the rain of fire was no longer detected, one of the dropships parked in Rino dusted off, and roared through the smoke-filled sky until it hovered over the battered hover car. The side doors slid open, and figures dressed in thick combat armour and dark visored helmets roped out and down to the ground.

They spread out in tight formation, running low with their slim, forked energy rifles pointed at the ground.

Their leader checked the vitals of all four of the car's occupants.

"The two males are dead," he announced through his comms unit to the waiting dropship. "The females are both alive and well."

He nodded, listening to instructions from some unseen source.

He nodded again and motioned to his unit, who pulled the two women from the battered hover car and roughly threw them onto the dropship before jumping onto the craft themselves. The VTOL engines roared back to life, and the ship kicked off into the sky, leaving the sand scorched and clouds of dust puffing up in its wake.

* * *

Polly had heard the unit commander, and her world had come crashing down. Her bottom lip trembled, and tears streamed down her soft cheeks. Eve was holding on to her, but her eyes were vacant. She knew Adam and Thrigor were dead: Thrigor's neck was broken, his head twisted too far round for him to be alive.

There was vomit down Eve's top from when she had seen Thrigor lying there in the wreckage, and she reeked of bile, stomach acid, and their previous lunch. Eve had been talking about moving in with Thrigor, getting their own place once they had finished college in the city.

Now Three, as they all called him, was dead, that happy future gone in an instant.

But worse, Adam was gone. Polly could see his upper body sticking out from underneath, lifeless.

She couldn't believe he was gone.

He couldn't be gone: he was Adam Caine; he had survived everything the universe had thrown at him and then some —including a black hole and a war of attrition on a primitive planet. How could he have been killed by a simple car crash? Why would the universe be so cruel?

The soldiers holding her prisoner stared at her and her adopted daughter, but were silent, occasionally glancing at each other. None of them were agitated, or at least didn't show it so far as Polly could see.

The soldiers themselves were wearing dark desert fatigues under darker flak jackets, with webbing and the usual combat accoutrements, including a wicked-looking combat knife strapped to their hips. They had no unit patches, but their darkened helmets had jagged red designs along the sides, each one different for every ten soldiers. They seemed human enough, though none of their skin was showing to confirm it.

She would normally have cared for the details: who they were, why they were there, or what they wanted.

She didn't care.

Adam, the love of her life, was dead.

* * *

Adam Caine orbited Ckeer Najoor's sun.

Or rather, the starship *Adam Caine* orbited it.

It was sleek and powerful, with a long hull, large curved engines, and a pointed vertical wedge-shaped prow that made it look like it could plough through the oceans of a planet. Its beautifully handmade hull was coloured a faint metallic orange; though the colours were obscured by the bright star it was orbiting.

The light from the star shone off its starboard side, small solar flares occasionally licking against the powerful shields, flaring them for brief seconds.

The ship was approaching a dark metal structure hanging above the star's corona. The structure's dark brooding asymmetrical shape was being battered by larger solar flares, attracted by the strange metals.

The *Adam Caine* glided smoothly towards it, its wings in glide mode for the time being. Sensor towers protruded from just behind the prow, scanning on every available frequency and setting.

"Beautiful isn't it?"

M'Der Tr'n looked at Silver as if she was completely mad, although that had been the same opinion he had formed of her when they had first met before this little expedition.

"Quite," he said, arching a hairless eyebrow, unconvinced. "Not sure why though." Silver had constantly either ignored or been oblivious to his sarcastic comments for the nine days he had been aboard the *Adam Caine*. In fact, the entire crew were like it, Silver being the only one that had so far showed any kind of sense of humour. He was seriously looking forward to some downtime in Rino with the Caine family.

The ship, laughable as the name was considering the namesake, had rendezvoused with his *Red Stallion* in orbit of Silver's new homeworld, and immediately jumped into the Linkway headed for Ckeer Najoor.

A rogue trader vessel had detected an unknown structure after they had suffered a brief navigational malfunction that brought them into the star's outer orbit. They had contacted Loor City, who passed the information on to the Terran Science Council, who in turn passed it on to M'Der and Silver's people separately.

Silver had brought her people's flagship to investigate the apparently familiar writings.

M'Der, over a thousand years old, felt positively young standing beside Silver and the others of her ship. He couldn't explain why, but he just saw them as ancient beings whose souls seemed close to dying, strung out, yet their physical bodies refused to give up.

They were stood in the observation dome, watching as the floating building was drawn closer and closer by the ship's tractor beams, being pulled out of the dangerous lower orbits.

The building was ominous, frighteningly so.

M'Der hadn't entirely been convinced this was such a good idea, but Adam had told him to play nice with Silver's people.

"Best you get to your ship, historian," said Silver, in a tone that brooked no argument. "Our science team will be aboard shortly."

M'Der nodded.

He left the bridge of the ship, grateful for the brief respite. It had been three days since he had even bothered to try and make casual small talk with passers-by in the corridors of the ship, though he passed several of the human-looking immortals. Most of them were permanently sombre, as if their recent transformation from non-corporeal to corporeal had doomed them to a hellish existence. They all walked around in a myriad of clothes, products of observing different cultures over centuries, all with a dark foreboding on their pale faces.

It was a stark contrast to his bright and cheerful homeworld.

But the *Red Stallion* was his home away from home, filled with all the luxuries common to his home planet.

The tall, lanky Kra Nal strode lengthily into the *Adam Caine*'s sparse, softly lit hangar bay. There was a group of multi-coloured, pale, sour-faced trouts that were milling around underneath the *Red Stallion*. The former cargo shuttle overshadowed them as the entry ramp folded open.

"*Welcome, sir,*" the ship's computer announced when it detected his presence nearby. It's A.I. was exceptionally automatic, and tailored for the ship's recent luxurious refurbishment. It was a female voice, mechanically altered from the voice of M'Der's eldest estranged daughter.

"Good morning, computer." He stepped up the entry ramp into the inviting small foyer that led to the bedrooms, engine room, dining room, kitchenette, and the state-of-the-art cockpit. He heard footsteps on the metal ramp behind him as he stepped through to the cockpit. He sat down in the armchair-like command chair, and activated the command station.

One of the science team appeared behind him.

"Everybody is on board," he said in a monotone voice.

"Thankyou... Platinum, is it?"

The man nodded glumly, but then disappeared from sight, leaving M'Der somewhat perplexed by the whole experience.

"The hell kind of name is Platinum anyway?" he muttered, wishing desperately he was on Ckeer Najoor's surface, with Adam, Polly, and Eve, enjoying the sunshine, and the brilliant company they always offered, as well as the celebrations that seemed to happen for one reason or another every local weekend.

He remotely closed the entry ramp, before powering up the incredibly powerful engines. He smiled as the deep vibrations hummed through the *Stallion*. He cut in the anti-gravs, and hovered the ship above the deck, waiting for the hangar doors to open above.

The doors cycled open like a corkscrew, the forcefield flashing into existence.

He goosed the engines, and the ship roared out of the hangar, through the forcefield, and out into the bright orange-tinted space. He twisted the ship around to face the dark structure, running it above the hull of the massive ship and past its armoured prow.

The dark structure was even more ominous up close, its lines and right angles orange that brought the eye line away from the shadowy recesses. It reminded M'Der of so many childhood fairy tales where the brave hero warily approached the dark castle.

The place was indeed a dark castle.

The ship's sensors were showing readouts with numbers and elements scrolling so fast down the screen that he couldn't keep up. There were still no life-signs, and no signs of power, but the thing was made from several unknown alloys of hundreds of different combinations of other materials each.

He scanned the structure for somewhere to land or to latch on to, and found an opening that looked like an empty cargo bay, though he couldn't be sure. It was asymmetrical like the rest of the station, with nooks and crannies that were all cube-shaped but at varying sizes. There was a subtle wrongness to the whole place, as if it had been designed to be off-putting, and distracting.

There was no forcefield in the bay, so he called down to the team to make sure they were wearing EV suits for the time being.

He set the *Stallion* down on the floor of the bay; he was sure he had heard a crunching noise when the landing struts settled, though it was probably the creepy place playing tricks on his imagination.

"We're down," he called through the intercom.

They acknowledged in return, and he felt the entry ramp thump down onto whatever floor was beneath the ship. He flicked on the visual sensors on the outside of the ship, and watched as the team spread out from the *Stallion*'s ramp. They were cautious, stepping carefully, and sweeping their portable scanners around like torches.

The ship's spotlights lit the cavernous cargo bay, throwing a multitude of shadows in all directions from the bizarre collection of shapes and sizes.

"*It smells of charcoal in here,*" one of the science team announced over the intercom.

"*And abandoned memories,*" said another.

M'Der rolled his eyes at the description; they had a flair for the melodramatic when they wanted to be, a trait that annoyed him greatly.

The sensors bleated at him, drawing his attention to something.

There was a weak sensor ghost shifting position on the opposite side of the structure to the *Adam Caine*, closing with the station and the *Stallion* inside. It read like a starship, but the echo was too faint to get a clear scan on.

He activated the ship's external communications, and attempted to contact the *Adam Caine* since they had a much more powerful set of sensors. But there was nothing on the channels, just static. The noise from the speakers was a hideously obvious indicator: someone was jamming the *Adam Caine*'s communications.

He tapped the intercom connecting the suits to the ship. "Science team; get back on board right now. The *Adam Caine* is being jammed by something approaching this station." He ignored their protests that they had only just started. "Just do it, or I'm leaving without you."

They protested more, but it wasn't as heartfelt as before, and their footsteps were already ringing on the ramp. When the consoles read that the ramp was closed, M'Der bumped the throttle, and pushed the ship out of the cargo bay, leaving the mystery behind.

Platinum entered the cockpit at that moment, without his helmet.

"What is going on, historian?"

"I think there's a warship sneaking up on the *Adam Caine*; but with their communications jammed, and the star playing merry hell with sensors, they may not know they're about to be attacked." The cargo bay shrunk away from the chunky ship. "If I'm wrong, we can quite easily land again and carry on where you left off."

Platinum –M'Der still couldn't take the name seriously- nodded in agreement, stripped his suit off, and slipped into the co-pilot's chair, activating the dormant console. Whatever gripe he had with the so-called immortals, they certainly knew how to get on with the job.

"I am detecting an engine signature," declared Platinum. Some of the science team, stripped of their EV suits, filtered into the cockpit, sitting down in the six auxiliary seats. "I do not recognise it though."

It came into full view as M'Der swung the *Stallion* out and around a prominent large section of the structure.

He still didn't recognise the ship, but he got an almost point-blank view of it as it roared past the station, almost slamming into the *Stallion*. Its hull was black as the starfield behind it, covered in seemingly random stripes of red. Nearly a kilometre long, it was squat and butch, with two forward fat arms, and a chunky back end. It bristled with gun batteries and missile ports; a warship.

It coasted past the *Stallion* without a single weapons lock or sensor scan.

The large converted cargo shuttle was no threat to the big warship, and thus worth their attention. That, or they had something far worse than destruction in mind.

He spun the ship around, and raced after the bigger vessel.

The *Adam Caine* was definitely the target.

* * *

Get up, a voice said in his head.

He recognised it, but it was too far away.

His entire world was pain and suffering. He couldn't move and pain speared through him at the slightest twitch. He couldn't see anything, although there was a distant pinprick of light that moved whenever his eyes twitched, so it wasn't that he was blind, just without any light.

Sounds were muffled, as if his ears were covered by something.

His throat was hoarse, not from screaming or talking, but from not being used. Why would his throat not be used? And why was he in such incredible pain? He had experienced it before: massive crushing pain in his chest where his heart had stopped for too long to be healthy. His muscles were burning, though some of them had no feeling at all. One of his legs was completely pinned, and numb, despite the feeling returning to the rest of his body.

Afghanistan had been the last time he had felt like this.

Not even his tortures ten years ago compared to this.

He felt like death warmed up, literally.

He groaned, and tried to move. More pain. He tried to move only one arm. More pain. He tried to the other. Even more pain. He moved his head to one side, and saw a series of flashing lights in the dark. They winked and twinkled at him like stars in the night sky, though these ones were blue.

He smiled, and found sand had clogged his nose and mouth -making him cough and splutter badly enough to turn his throat raw. He was wheezing from the effort.

He stretched his arm as hard and as painfully as he could, and flicked the flashing lights with a shaking finger.

Nothing happened.

He swore.

Loudly.

He flicked another light.

There was a whine of building energy, and suddenly the crushing weight lifted. There was a loud humming noise above him, and blinding light slashed in at him, despite the large shadow now over him. The sunlight reflected in off the sand, spearing his eyes as bad as the grains of sand.

The pain in his chest was beginning to lift, and there was a huge ache throbbing in the leg he couldn't previously feel, the blood finally flowing through the abused limb. He could taste the metallic tang of blood in his mouth, and despite the heat of the sun beating down on him, he could feel something warm and wet on the damaged leg.

When he looked down to assess the damage, he stared into the lifeless eyes of a blue-skinned young boy. Nausea overwhelmed him for a brief second, but he fought it down for later.

The boy was dead —his head was bent at too much of an angle to survive- and grieving would only make things worse. He himself needed to survive. He forced his muscles to work, and dragged himself out from under the floating vehicle. He blacked out twice from the pain, but still hauled himself out from the shadow into the burning sun.

He leant on the vehicle, and got unsteadily to his feet. His left leg was almost useless, a large gash horizontally where the battered hover-car had been leant. The muscles were almost cut through completely, and he could tell the bone underneath was bruised.

It would take a long time to heal from these injuries.

But he was no longer concentrating on his own injuries.

Adam looked out at the landscape around him and saw hell had come to Ckeer Najoor. Fires burned wherever he looked, some close by from starship hull fragments that had fallen through the atmosphere, the rest from fires on the horizon, and one in particular that burned from the direction of Rino settlement.

It reminded him too much of the pictures from the Gulf War of the Iraqi Army setting fire to the Kuwaiti oil fields.

He looked around.

Where were Eve and Polly?

If Thrigor was dead, where were his wife and daughter?

Logic asserted itself: the family hover-car was once an offworld unmarked police vehicle he had bought with a dozen others for the residents of Rino. All police vehicles, no matter how small, carried some kind of visual and audio recorders in their control consoles.

He limped round the vehicle, and accessed the craft's recorder.

What he saw chilled him to the bone.

The figures that corralled Eve and Polly moved like professionals –not special ops, but definitely tightly disciplined and well trained. The unit commander said something into his comms device that the audio recorder didn't pick up.

Wherever they went, they didn't go into orbit –the recorder showed the orbital dropship skimming off across the desert towards Rino.

They were taking his family to his home, but again why?

If they were doing that, it meant it was personal. But who? He didn't recognise the soldiers, their uniforms, or the markings on their factory-standard drop ship. He would need the *Kara*, and his weapons caches that he had hidden outside his hometown.

He opened the first aid kit in the beat-up hover-car, and slapped a pain-repellent patch on his leg. Next came the dermal regenerator, a fat tube that spread a wave of blue light across his wounds to knit the arteries, muscles and skin back together. It was monstrously painful, though he gritted his teeth and pushed through it. He blacked out again.

When he came to, the regenerator was still in his hand, but the bleeding had stopped, and the wound was closed. He didn't even remember finishing the job.

He flicked the ignition switch, and found to his surprise that it started, the engine humming to life, albeit not quite as harmoniously as it once was. Luckily, the crater the *Kara* was hidden in wasn't far from his location.

He stowed Thrigor's body, laying him neatly and respectfully across the backseat, jumped back into the driver's seat, and slammed the throttle full forward. The hover-car lurched, and jumped to full speed, squashing him into his seat.

He ran the car above the desert sand, skimming between the dunes at a pace that would have had Polly crying with terror.

He came at the forest bordering Rino from the west, taking him away from the town, and closer to the thicker parts of the woods. He didn't want the car picked up close to town, and give away that he had survived, if this could be called survival.

The thick woods grew ahead of him, appearing from the sand as if the trees had sprung up there and then. The massive jula trees, taller than Canadian Redwoods and chunkier than English Oak, were wrapped in vines and shadowed the underbrush around them. Grass and ferns stretched out past the trees, clashing in bizarre patterns with the desert sand.

He parked the car in the shadow of a particularly gnarled jula tree, hiding it beneath a giant dead root. He pulled Thrigor's body out of the back, and laid him to rest in a soft patch of dead leaves, shifting him into a stereotypical funeral pose.

"I'm sorry," he said, then left the body and the car where they lay.

* * *

Wake up, a voice said.

Evelyn struggled to open her bright blue eyes, though she could feel her adopted mother stroking her long blue hair. Polly was whispering in her ear, attempting to quietly wake her up without alarming her.

The acrid stench of burning meats, heated stone, and charcoal assaulted her nostrils, whilst her ears were subjected to almost nothing: there was barely any sound, except the click-click of personal comm units on silent mode. She could also hear boots scraping on the dusty ground, and muffled objections to something she couldn't make out. But it was so quiet: there were no sounds of wildlife, no air traffic, nor even the howl of the wind.

It was eerie.

And it was about to get eerier.

When her eyes finally fluttered open, she looked up from her position resting on her mother's lap, and looked into the eyes of herself. Or rather, what she could possibly look like at the age of fifty-plus years old.

"You," she growled.

"I am glad you remember me, daughter."

Anger clouded Eve's beautiful face.

"I am not your daughter." Polly and Eve both struggled to their feet, though Polly's eyes were still somewhat vacant. Eve looked around at the soldiers surrounding them: most were looking outward, protecting the inside of the circle, whilst four were ready with their weapons, their helmets looking directly at the two Caine women, wary of any move they made, or might make.

"I gave birth to you," the elder Mertik said angrily. The intervening years since their first encounter on Strangis Forgan Kror had not been kind to her. Her green face had lost any semblance of brightness, now just a dull shade of olive. Wrinkles creased around her eyes and mouth, and her eyes had taken on a dull tiredness. Her hand occasionally shook uncontrollably, a sign of some lifelong habit.

"That's all you did. You and Garvion abandoned me when I was young. Adam Caine rescued me, and gave me a home and a family. I don't care that he is not biologically my father, nor even the same race as me; it doesn't matter. He is my father, and this is my mother." Eve gestured to Polly, who hung limply on her arm.

There was a dark look in those dull eyes.

"Blood is blood. You will obey to your people's demands."

Eve looked at her incredulously.

"My people abandoned me just as much as you did; nobody bothered to claim responsibility for a Mertik orphan. None of my own people wanted to take care of me, or offer me a place to call home." Eve rested Polly back on the floor, and then got up in the older woman's face.

"You abandoned me, why? Because you were afraid of Garvion? Or was it that you just couldn't handle the responsibility of raising the love-child of a known criminal mercenary?"

The elder woman took a step back at Eve's fury, briefly showing regret and remorse in her haunted, tired eyes. But the four inward-looking mercs took steps forward, their energy rifles coming up a bit further in front of them, preparing to fire.

The elder Mertik waved them down, and the hardness returned to her face.

"I don't have to explain my actions, then or now, Ayanka."

Eve didn't need the woman to explain that that was her name from before Odyssey Station: she just didn't care what the woman called her. She was Evelyn Cassandra Caine, now and forever, daughter of Adam and Polly Caine.

"You wiped out *thousands* upon *thousands* of innocent people across this planet, murdered anybody you come across, and you *won't* explain your purpose here? This planet is protected under the Alliance's Protectorate Treaty."

The older woman smiled, that same humourless smile that sociopaths gave people when they want to be left alone, the smile that chilled you to the bone. It meant something awful, it meant the end of her world.

"As of a week ago, the planet Mertik is now officially a member of the Alliance of Independent Worlds. As such, the Mertik secret service is being integrated into Alliance Intelligence. Thusly, we have been given access to this planet and some very interesting technology." She produced a pair of odd-looking devices. Both were matt grey, and curved like the rim of a hat, with blue circuitry inlaid into the outside of the curve. The circuitry flashed every now and then, as if on standby.

The woman nodded to the four inward facing mercenaries.

They stepped forward quickly.

One grabbed the insensate Polly, whilst the other three made to grab Eve.

The young girl slapped a high kick into the throat of one of them, sending him reeling back, clutching his damaged larynx. The sounds coming out of his throat were hideous pig-like snorts. She didn't want to think about what was underneath those helmets.

The other two were too quick for her however, and had both their free hands wrapped around her arms in an instant, clamping so tightly she couldn't move at all.

She was breathing hard from the ineffective effort of her resistance. The old woman approached her cautiously, holding one of the devices in each of her hands. She clipped one to the back of her head, and the circuits glowed an eerie red colour. She winced as wires fed from the device and pierced the skin under her hair. Eve was sure she knew where the second headpiece was going.

"What demands did your people have?"

The elder Mertik smiled again, that same humourless one. She started marching towards Eve, an intense look in her eyes.

"We are not here for you or this wretch you call a mother; though that is a personal bonus for me."

Eve's eyes widened as the older woman slapped the second headpiece around the back of her head. Pain viced through her skin and then her brain, lancing through her like molten lava.

Her last thought before she blacked out again escaped her lips.

"Daddy?"

* * *

Adam found the first weapons cache an hour after leaving behind the hover-car and Thrigor's body.

It was essentially a pit dug out of the ground, covered over with a tarpaulin and piles of branches, leaves and other natural detritus. It was blended with the rest of the forest around it, almost invisible, but Adam knew where it was.

He pulled back the tarpaulin, revealing the weapons and ammunition underneath.

When they had married, and he had given up the violent aspects of his life, Polly had demanded he either destroy the weapons or hide them where only he could find them. So he had chosen the latter, splitting them between four sites around the forest.

This one had the assault weapons: HK assault rifles and P90s he had liberated years ago from the wreckage of the *Icarus* escape module. There was also enough ammunition to take on an army. But he would need some other pieces to be able to fight these people, whoever they were.

The next cache was two miles distant through rough terrain. He'd left the P90s in the pit, and kept one of the HK, as well as fifteen clips, and a spare change of camouflage fatigues he had kept hidden there. He'd fashioned himself a makeshift ghillie suit, and pasted mud on his face to hide his skin next to the brown of his beard and hair.

The next cache had explosives in it, all packed in damp-proof secure containers. He scooped some of them into a satchel, camouflaged it to blend in with the rest of his appearance, and melted into the forest once again.

He was methodical, silently picking his way through the underbrush of the forest floor, snapping no twigs, barely moving dead leaves, and staying in the deep shadows.

The third cache, closest to Rino, held the last few things he was after.

He pulled back the tarpaulin.

He gave a grim smile.

The high-powered sniper rifle and life form scanner disappeared under his ghillie suit as well.

For the first time in a long time, he was on the hunt.

* * *

"It's firing!" announced Platinum in a monotone voice.

"I can see that," replied M'Der.

The enemy ship was still powering towards the *Adam Caine*. The smaller warship's engines were flaring, and its gun batteries all swivelled towards the bigger ship. M'Der tried to catch with it, but it was too powerful, and had too much of a head start.

Then it opened fire on the *Adam Caine*.

Fat pulses of bright energy lanced from the batteries, and pounded the shielded ancient vessel. The energy splashed against the horrendously powerful shields. It raked the *Adam Caine* from bow to stern before the other could even flinch.

The bigger ship began to turn and bring its own batteries to bear.

Beams spiked from its weapons, lashing out at the smaller ship, but they weren't effective, designed to take on big ships and not smaller ones the beams ricocheted off the fast-moving vessel.

The dark warship was behind the *Caine* now, pounding its rear shields mercilessly.

M'Der brought the *Stallion* around the combat zone, not wanting to get between the two warring starships, both capable of blowing the former cargo shuttle to pieces without breaking a sweat.

He kept trying to contact the *Caine*, but the enemy ship was still jamming them.

Then the warship finally noticed the *Stallion*.

A pulse of energy flashed past the cockpit windows. The energy passed by so close to the shuttle that it fried the ship's electrics. The cockpit was pitch black except for the light pouring in from the nearby sun, and the immense amounts of weapons fire.

The battle lasted for a few minutes more, until both of the big ships were drifting without power. There were occasional flashes as internal explosions wracked through their innards.

The back-up power suddenly kicked in, leaving M'Der wondering just why it had taken so long to come on.

The consoles came on, but the lights were only up to a dim level, keeping them in semi-darkness.

"Life-signs on the *Caine*?" he called.

Platinum and the others were instantly working the controls, furiously tapping the consoles. He himself was running diagnostics on the ship's engines, making sure everything was working, as it should be. There were some glitches in the RCS modules around the ship, but the main sublights were still working at reasonable efficiency.

Debris filled the space between the ships. The chunks of hull plating were slowly moving towards the star below, finally being pulled by the gravity well into the super-heated embrace of the sun's corona. The smaller ship, now just a hunk of metal, was being pulled as well, its small size easily affected by the well.

Random bursts of thruster fire spurted from along the hulls of both ships, the surviving crews trying to save their precious hides from falling into the flames.

M'Der pushed the engines a little to test them, and found that he had moderate power considering how badly scorched the ship had been. Visual sensors were gone, along with most of the ship's more sensitive scanning equipment. Some of the communications equipment had experienced malfunctions, although some of the most basic systems were still functioning off of the backups.

He guided the *Stallion* around the pieces of debris being taken down, grateful for Adam's flying lessons when a large chunk of metal came almost too close to the hull. M'Der had twisted the ship painfully fast around it, and boosted the throttle to come speeding out from behind it, essentially slingshotting around the detritus.

The *Caine* was starting to slip away as well by the time the *Stallion* was close enough to it to see the damage done in detail, and see the individual windows and viewports along the ship's hull. The ship's engines weren't glowing as brightly as before, and only on one side of the great vessel. Great big black scars ran along the ship's flank, exposing the ship's innards to space. The ship's internal lights were flickering, and the external running lights were completely dark.

Whatever power the *Caine* had, it clearly wasn't enough to sustain any kind of operation. In oceanic terms, the *Caine* was sinking.

"Life-signs?" he repeated, a bit more forcefully.

Platinum frowned.

"It is a jumble in there; I am picking up confusing readings. Some of them are my own people, but there are life-signs I do not recognise, nor does your ship's computer." He continued frowning, his dull eyes glued to the monitor.

"But there are survivors?" suggested M'Der.

Platinum nodded, and the others agreed.

"Good; we need to get in there and rescue them."

The immortals all looked forlorn, and very much did not want to go on board the *Caine*. Their race really was not mentally or physically used to any form of violence, and it was starting to show on the now-worried faces of the immortal science team. Apparently, in that regard M'Der was actually more experienced.

Not that he considered it a good thing.

"Find me somewhere safe to land or dock," he snapped.

They nodded, and began conferring with each other, pointing to different points on a computer-generated image of the *Caine* on one of the monitors. Platinum plotted the final idea into the computer, and sent it to the navigation computer, letting M'Der fly the ship towards an airlock on the port side of the command section.

He slid the *Stallion* beside the airlock, and let the autopilot finish the docking manoeuvres. There was a loud clunk as the ship connected with the airlock, followed by an equally loud hiss of air. The air seal read pressurised and the airlock began cycling open.

M'Der moved to the foyer, and turned to his left, picking up a readymade 'adventure' pack, as he liked to call them, filled with a personal scanner, luxurious MRE bars, torches, a pair of compact energy pistols, as well as an assortment of gadgets for opening doors, climbing elevator shafts; you name it he had a gadget for it.

He waited for the airlock to open.

Platinum shouted something that sounded like, "Wait, there's something on the other side," but M'Der wasn't listening.

He strode forward on his naturally gangly, long legs, and manually opened his side of the airlock open. He had it halfway when the door suddenly smacked violently into his face and threw him onto his back.

A grouchy, gravely voice barked in an incomprehensible battle-language.

M'Der thought he recognised the language, or at least the sounds being made.

The first mercenary through wore dark desert fatigues with red scribbles on it, its blank glossy helmet obscuring any facial features. The second, however, had had his ripped off, leaving a mangled ruin around his thickly muscled neck.

The face, or at least the species, of the warrior was unmistakable.

M'Der couldn't believe his eyes.

Despite the cut above his eye bleeding profusely, he refused to believe that this was anything but his own fevered imagination.

A dozen more of the mercenaries barged through the half-opened airlock, weapons at the ready, and began growling and barking orders at the immortals in the cockpit.

The one without a helmet, a terrible sight indeed, stepped to M'Der's side, and crouched down next to the Kra Nal historian. In the ship's dim light he looked all the more terrifying to behold.

With bright red skin, leering ugly triangular face, and two small horns sprouting from his forehead, the soldier was no mere mercenary.

M'Der breathed the name quietly, as if it would make it not true.

"Okarnagans."

* * *

The corpse dropped silently to the ground, its throat blown out by a long-range sniper round. Its counterpart turned to see what all the fuss was, and had his head blown off with an equally accurate shot for his trouble. His corpse joined his friend's in a pile at the edge of the dusty crater.

Adam prowled forward out of the forest, sniper rifle in hand.

He lay down in a prone position at the lip of the crater, and slipped the barrel of the rifle over the edge, sighting through the high-powered scope.

At the base of the sloping crater sat the *Kara Marazov* in all its glory. It was powered down for the moment, and had been for several days since he and his family had been on holiday in Loor City.

He had a set of basic controls strapped around his wrist to control the ship remotely if he ever needed to in an emergency. He touched the power control first. Below, the ship came to life. The soldiers, spooked all of a sudden, jumped around, their energy rifles flicking left and right, searching for a target, or some sign of the ship's owner.

Adam sighted on the calmest of the soldiers, who was a lot less jerky and presumably more experienced. He firmly squeezed the trigger. The rifle bucked, but there was barely any sound, the silencer and flash suppressor doing their job.

The squad leader's head disappeared in a spurt of blood, brain matter and bits of helmet. His squad began blasting the slopes of the crater, firing at a presumed invisible foe. Whoever was in charge of this operation had decided that their most inexperienced unit was put in charge of defending a powered down starship.

This would be their first blooding.

And Adam made sure it was one they wouldn't survive.

He pulled the action back, ejecting the spent shell casing, and slammed it forwards again, the gun's mechanism slotting a fresh round into the chamber.

Another squeeze of the trigger, and one of the rookies flew backwards, a hole in the chest plate of his armour.

Rack, push, squeeze, buck, and the next one was dead as well, his throat gone.

Another shot, another dead.

He carried this on until they were all lying dead in the dust.

He stood up and strolled down the bank of the crater until he was stood beside the lower fin of the *Kara*'s smooth crescent-shaped hull. The ship hummed loudly, beckoning him in. But he wouldn't be flying her just yet.

He needed the ship's sensors.

He climbed up the ladder rungs that extended out of the lower fin, and slipped through the now-open small airlock. The ship woke up fully around him, the lights flickering on, and the cockpit coming to life.

He sat down in the pilot's chair, and activated the sensors.

The monitor in front of him showed him a wire layout of the town of Rino, just beyond the field north of the crater. There were hundreds of life-signs, as well as two large vessels tentatively identified as military-grade dropships.

There was almost a perfect circle of unfamiliar life-signs surrounding several others. Among them were two Mertik females, and a human female. Polly and Eve; but who was the second Mertik?

Adam found he knew the answer without much thought.

He had met her in the morgue of the *HMS St. George*.

Evie's biological mother, an operative of her people's intelligence service.

There were a couple of the unfamiliar life-signs surrounding Eve, so close they had to be holding her.

What worried him most was that there were no other life-signs from the rest of the town. There were extreme heat blooms from burning buildings, and the small hydropower tower at the river was leaking water into the outer edges of the town. Every single building was a ruin, blasted apart by either random or targeted firing from orbit, even his own home.

There was nothing left to call home, except the ship he was sat in.

He brought out a digipad and used it to link with the *Kara*'s sensors so that he could use them remotely.

He tucked it into his webbing, and looked around at the ship.

"I have a job for you my old friend."

* * *

Eve was still standing when her vision returned.

Not by choice mind. She was still being held upright by the mercenaries either side of her. The device was putting immense pressure on her brain, and she kept seeing flashes of other places, events she had never been involved in.

Her 'mother' smiled.

"Those are my memories you're seeing, Ayanka."

"My. Name. Is. Evelyn." She struggled desperately to say it, but it came nonetheless.

The older woman frowned.

"Hmm, you're stronger than I realised. Caine taught you well."

"He taught. Me. The value. Of. Strength and love.... Bitch."

The other made a *tut-tut-tut* noise.

"Such language is unbecoming of a Mertik woman."

"But mass. Murder. Is?"

That humourless smile again. "That was necessary," she said, but her face suggested anything but. "The ends always justify the means."

"And what end. Do you have. In mind. For my father?"

Anger passed over her face, and Eve began to feel it through the device, suggesting to her that the device had some kind of psychic link or network between the two. If she could just use against her 'mother' she could free herself. After that though, what then?

She focused her own rage and hate in her mind, and attempted to visualise sending a bolt of lightning at the other woman.

She cried out when the device suddenly sent an electric shock through her head.

The shocked cry seemed to wake Polly up though, and one of the surrounding mercenaries had to hold her, as she started moving towards Eve. Her mum whimpered as the mercenary held her wrists a bit too hard. Something crunched under the strong grip.

Eve was about to shout for her to be let go when the device shocked her again.

"Don't question me again, Ayanka. You won't like the consequences."

Her 'mother' went for the pistol on her hip, but was stopped when the helmets of the soldiers around her squawked with interference from their comm sets.

The unit commander approached her.

"Ma'am," he began, his harsh voice muffled by the helmet, "we've lost contact with our recruits unit."

The woman frowned. "The unit guarding Caine's ship?"

He nodded, the helmet bobbing.

As if to punctuate the point, there was a whine of powered up engines in the distance. Then the whine grew into a roar, and the *Kara Marazov* came powering out of the smoke, and roared above their heads. Small arms fire chased ineffectually across the sky, and it disappeared into the smoke once again like a wraith.

Eve used the confusion to grab the plasma pistol on the belt of the mercenary holding her. His grip had relaxed on her arm, and she pulled the trigger whilst it was still in the holster. The plasma pulse flashed into his leg, and he collapsed screaming onto the floor. She held onto the pistol as he fell, and shot the other in the chest multiple times. She shot two more mercenaries and then pointed the barrel at her 'mother'.

But the operative just smiled, this time with an evil humour.

"You really think you can shoot me?"

Eve nodded, and squeezed the trigger.

* * *

M'Der was dragged into the cockpit and the immortals were herded into the bedrooms.

He still could not get over it.

The Okarnagans' clan-fleets had been supposedly extinct since their harsh war with the Terran Navy, where they had been supposedly wiped out, and their homeworld of Okar destroyed by orbital bombardment. It was a sore point in Terran history, one of those events that the Navy would never be proud of.

Except, that it turned out they had survived somehow.

M'Der suspected they had had outside help; given the reports of the sheer amount of attacking Navy ships there was no way they could have survived without help from some technologically superior race.

"How did your people survive?" he blurted, ever the historian.

The Okarnagan just leered at him with big yellow eyes.

"Keep your mouth shut," it spat in accented Standard. He –and M'Der was pretty confident it was a he from the shorter horns- tapped the mic strapped to his throat; he growled and spittled something in his own language. The airlock filled with another round of stinking Okarnagans, who herded a dozen or so of the *Adam Caine*'s surviving crew, including Silver, the ship's commander, who had been bound and gagged, presumably because she had resisted against their capturing her.

It was yet another example of the flesh-and-blood Adam Caine's strength and influence among those around him.

The Okarnagans pushed Silver into the cockpit with M'Der, and the rest were goaded into the remaining bedrooms.

The helmetless Okarnagan pointed to M'Der.

"Fly this *ragta*."

"Ragta?"

M'Der received a hard punch to his ribs that broke under the harsh impact. He tasted blood in his mouth, and found he had bit his tongue. Green blood dribbled out from between his lips, spilling onto his long chin.

"You mean the ship?"

He received another punch to the ribs, and was sure another bone had broken.

"I'll take that as a yes then. But why should I?"

The helmetless Okarnagan pulled out an old energy pistol from the webbing on his uniform, and nodded to the nearest soldier. Platinum was dragged through into the cockpit, though he wasn't showing much in the way of emotion.

The Okarnagan leader put the stunted muzzle of the energy pistol against Platinum's temple, and blew out the immortal's brains, leaving the mindless corpse to fall sideways to the deck.

"Fly this *ragta*, or I will carry on until there is nobody left but us and you."

M'Der saw Silver nodding almost imperceptibly to him.

"Fine. Can I at least get some kind of bandages?"

The helmetless one just sneered at him, and pointed to the controls.

M'Der sat down in the command chair, and disengaged the airlock, breaking free from the *Adam Caine*, and pushed the ship out of the debris field. The *Caine* began falling faster into the sun, but the *Stallion* was already moving away at top speed.

"What destination?"

"Ckeer Najoor," the Okarnagan replied.

* * *

The Alliance cruiser *Far Light*'s lights darkened as it was hit by another barrage of energy. The ship hung in space, unmoving, as the Terran Navy warship *Wolf Brother* thundered past. Starfighters flashed around them, exchanging fire at tremendous rates. Other, bigger starships, fought desperately further afield. This was the first time the two sides had fought each other in decades, and it was going in the Terrans' favour.

"Vice-Admiral?"

The voice was getting on his nerves.

"Vice-Admiral Sansky?"

Raymond sighed, and turned from the holographic tactical display on the *Wolf Brother*'s bridge. He looked at the young grating Ensign with his best withering stare. The young woman seemed to visibly shrink in front of him.

"Yes, Ensign?"

"Sir, I was monitoring the communications channels, and found something odd."

"Odd, Ensign? This is a Navy starship not a civilian ship; be more specific."

"I... Yes, sir." She held out a digipad for him to take. "We received an automatic distress signal on an old civilian channel. It came from a hauler called the *Regal Sandwalker*, citing the old Merchant Navy code for being under attack. I think..." her voice trailed off as she saw the shocked look on the admiral's face.

"The *Regal Sandwalker*?" he asked. "What planet and star system?"

"There's nothing in our records, sir."

A dark look passed across Sansky's face. He spun to face Captain Crown, the *Wolf Brother*'s commander.

"Send to all ships, cancel the exercise."

Crown frowned, but carried out the orders.

"Ensign, you just became my favourite person; see if you can get a comms line through to Far Commander Laro." The Ensign nodded, and several tense minutes later, the Alliance senior ship commander's face appeared in holographic form in place of the tactical readouts.

"*Why have you broken off the exercise, Vice-Admiral?*" the hologram questioned. The war exercise had been dreamed up by the senior fleet admirals of both the Terran Navy and the Alliance Fleet to better military relations between the two powers. Sansky had been vocally dead-set against it, and had been given command of the Terran side as a result.

"We've received a distress signal from a nearby star system, Far Commander."

The alien's face took on a grave tone, and his voice heavy with sadness.

"*We know, admiral,*" the alien replied. "*We are under orders to ignore it.*"

"Orders?" Sansky asked, incredulous to what he was hearing. "What kind of orders prevent you from answering somebody's distress call?"

The alien seemed to shrug, despite only being a head. "*Our secret service gave us explicit instructions.*"

Sansky sighed, knowing all about the intelligence business.

"Fine; would you object to us answering the signal?"

The holographic head shook.

"Be my guest, admiral."

Sansky nodded, and disconnected the feed.

"Communications; tell all ships to form up on the *Wolf Brother*. Captain Crown, set a course for the coordinates of the distress signal. It's not in our charts, but there is a planet there. Spin up the FTL if you please."

* * *

Eve's finger didn't finish squeezing the trigger.

It held steady, almost at the point of firing, but nothing happened. She tried to move her fingers, even her arm, but nothing happened. She couldn't move anything, in fact, not her arms, legs, head, nothing.

She whimpered as she realised what the device was doing, and who was doing it.

"It's a mind control device," her 'mother' told her, an evil smile on her lips, "but not just controlling the mind. It taps into the cerebral cortex, and accesses the central nervous system, allowing the controller to move the other person's body as if it were their own."

The mercenaries aimed every weapon they had at Eve's head, whilst one of them flopped Polly onto the dusty ground.

"Mummy? Are you okay?"

Polly nodded, coughing up a mouthful of dust.

"I'll live."

The older Mertik woman cackled with delight. "Not for much longer."

There was an explosion nearby, followed seconds later by another. Two fireballs erupted in the distance, visible even through the dust clouds, and fogbank of black smoke.

The commander of the unit surrounding Eve shouted into his helmet comms, demanding to know what was going on. No reply came, and the commander became more and more frustrated. He then started shouting to someone in orbit, and demanded they tell him what was going on.

Eve didn't hear the reply, but the commander began shouting and swearing, waggling an accusing finger at the Mertik woman.

"It's not my fault your dropships were destroyed," the elder woman said back to him. "Perhaps you should have put better security on them."

The commander replied in heavily accented Standard.

"Damn you, woman. This whole operation has been a massive waste of resources."

"You are being handsomely rewarded, commander. You cannot back out now."

"The chieftain shall hear of this!" The commander strode away, still shouting into his helmet comms, demanding updates from orbit.

The mercenaries all twitched, exchanging uneasy glances.

But the Mertik woman just continued to smile.

Eve felt a sensation of heat pass through her, and her arm was suddenly moving, the gun still in her hand, her trigger finger slackened. She was horrified to find that the gun was now pointing at Polly's chest. Polly had a look of shock on her face, though she occasionally sent pleading looks to her captor.

But the spy was enjoying the situation a little too much.

Polly and Eve had both seen that kind of psychotic glee in the looks of those attempting to kill them, or worse. It was a darkness neither one had wanted to see again, especially given their own experiences with Adam.

"N-n-no, please don't do this," Eve stammered. Her hand was shaking from the effort of resisting, and there was a blinding headache piercing her brain under the skull as if she had been stabbed.

* * *

The *Red Stallion* entered orbit at around the same time that this was happening. M'Der was terrified by the sight of so many sinister warships orbiting his friends' planet; the sensors told him that all of them were throwing weapons locks at the *Stallion*, and the communications console was alive with dozens of transmissions demanding to know who they were, and what they thought they were doing.

The helmetless Okarnagan barked into his own comms device, and allayed the demanding transmissions, although the weapons locks continued unabated, as if they were testing M'Der's resolve, or that of the Okarnagans aboard.

"Take us towards the flagship," the Okarnagan spat, pointing towards the largest of the warships. "And prepare this ship for landing in their main hangar."

M'Der could only nod as the leader threateningly fingered the energy weapon in his meaty clawed hand, continuing to let him know who was in charge.

Of course, that sneering smug look only lasted a few more seconds.

M'Der had always assumed that the universe itself had a particularly nasty sense of humour when it wanted to. Usually, it came against M'Der and his friends. Today was not one of those days.

"There's a major spatial anomaly," Silver announced as she glanced at the sensor readouts. Her eyes widened as she realised what it was. "Ships coming out of FTL speeds."

The HMS *Wolf Brother* was the first to arrive, followed almost immediately by thirty-three other Terran Navy vessels, including, M'Der noted with some hope, four of the *Knight*-class battleships.

The *Wolf Brother*, one of the new *Valkyrie*-class starfighter carriers, opened its hangars and unleashed fifteen squadrons of Rhino starfighters whilst its forward batteries battered the nearest Okarnagan warship. The ship's shields collapsed, and then the ship itself broke in half as the Rhino squadrons fired a multitude of missiles that raked it from bow to stern.

The other black-and-red starships spun on their upright axis, swinging round, and unleashing their own torrent of firepower that splashed harmfully against a dozen of the Terrans. The *Knight*-class battleships –*King's Herald, Wisconsin, Super-Six-Four,* and *Protocol 19*- thundered away from the formation of the other ships, straight towards the big enemy flagship.

M'Der watched as the Terrans engaged the Okarnagans wholesale.

Except, that the Terrans weren't aware of who they were facing. As he thought this, one of the Okarnagan warships rammed the *Super-Six-Four*'s tail end. Both ships were locked in a tight spin, still exchanging pummelling salvos. They clipped two Terran *Hightower*-class cruisers, both of which went tumbling away, trailing fire and debris. Despite their decent training, the Okarnagans were still as rabidly fanatical as they had been centuries before: even if they lost, they would take the Terrans down with them.

The Okarnagans aboard the *Stallion* were all standing stock-still, staring with awe at the violent and bright spectacle outside the small ship. M'Der had immediately refused to land on the flagship whilst it was engaged with the Terrans, and pulled the *Stallion* back out of the warzone.

He subtly opened the communications whilst his captors were distracted.

Unfortunately, they weren't distracted enough.

One of them noticed M'Der and dove for him, clamping its hands around M'Der's spindly wrists. But M'Der had already activated the comms.

"*Red Stallion* to Terran units," he shouted. "Be aware that you are facing Okarnagan forces!" He was struck across the back of the head, and he started feeling woozy.

After what seemed like a lifetime, he heard shouting and swearing from behind him, and several flashes of energy impacts. When he finally turned round, he realised that the Okarnagan holding him had stopped and been knocked unconscious, or dead –he couldn't tell which. As had several others.

He turned to find a half-squad of Terran Army Fleet Protection Troopers standing behind his chair, having apparently teleported in and incapacitated the kidnapping aliens.

"Good to see you fellows," he grinned, before sinking to the floor.

* * *

Sansky had heard the desperate call from M'Der Tr'n's ship, and had immediately ordered a boarding party to assist the historian with whatever trouble he was having.

The Okarnagans? Hadn't High Admiral Geletti's forces wiped them all out a over thousand years ago, along with their homeworld? Despite M'Der Tr'n's many vices, though, he was one of Raymond's most trusted allies, and wasn't prone to tall tales in serious situations.

"Pour it on," he ordered. "Everything we have. Destroy those ships."

Crown nodded, and started shouting orders over the thumping vibrations of the *Wolf Brother*'s weapons.

"The Okarnagans," he muttered to himself. "Why are they here?" He span. "Communications. Put me through to the *Red Stallion*." Outside, the cruiser *War Anthem* was disabled by a lucky shot to its engines. Its lights darkened even as the starship was hit from three different directions, and darkened forever. Sansky felt every death, and regretted this action, despite what it could mean in the long run.

The Okarnagans were indeed as fanatical as he remembered from the history lessons during his time at the Academy. They were throwing themselves at the Terrans with such ferocity; the Terrans were hard-pressed to keep them back, and keep them at distance, where their superior firepower would be more effective.

"Communications established, admiral."

"Thankyou." He turned to the holographic console beside him, to find the old, wizened features of the woman he knew as Silver.

"*Vice-Admiral Sansky; it is good to see you.*"

"Silver. What the hell are you doing on the *Stallion*?" He shook his head. "Never mind."

"*The Kra Nal historian was assisting us with our efforts to search a ruined space station down by Ckeer Najoor's star. Unfortunately, the Okarnagans attacked us, and my ship was destroyed. Many of my crew did not survive, and those that did were brought aboard the* Red Stallion."

"I am sorry to hear about the *Adam Caine*. It was a good ship."

The image nodded, though Sansky saw no emotion in her stony face. He could never understand Adam's fascination with Silver and her race of immortals: despite their human appearance, they were anything but, and it disturbed Raymond greatly.

"*Thankyou, admiral. You should know though, that they only came after us because we were a heavily armed starship —a threat to them. Their apparent goal is to capture a specific person.*"

Sansky's eyes widened. He didn't need to be told who they were after.

"Adam. Why do they want Adam?"

"*Why does anyone want Adam? More than likely they require his services.*"

"They razed the entire planet, simply to hire him for a job? I doubt it."

"Well, they seem to be purely mercenaries, so maybe there's someone else who wants him."

Sansky wasn't sure either way; in any case he didn't care.

"Starfighter control. Send two squadrons down to the surface, and do fly-bys of a town called Rino. Tell them to be on the lookout for the private vessel *Kara Marazov* as well; specs are in the computer."

"Sir, the *Protocol 19* is breaking up."

"Damn."

On his tactical displays, he saw the indicator for the battleship wink out of existence, taking two of the enemy with it. There were four of the Okarnagan warships left, the others obliterated. One of them was attempting to make a break for it, but the Terrans were finally in a position to beat the Okarnagans back, and started pounding the escaping ship mercilessly.

"I want prisoners," Sansky announced. "This Okarnagan resurgence will need an explanation."

There were several nods, one of which was the commander of the *Wolf Brother*'s Fleet Protection Group unit.

Two more of the sinister warships blinked out of existence, leaving the flagship by itself, still holding its own against a pair of cruisers, and half a dozen small destroyers. The flagship moved closer to the *Wolf Brother*, obviously identifying the biggest ship as the Terran flagship. They were moving a bit too fast for Sansky's liking.

"Captain," he warned.

"I see it, sir." Sansky hid a smile at Crown's irritation; Sansky knew Crown could do his job better than most, but he was still the admiral.

The *Wolf Brother*'s entire collection of weapons arrays suddenly opened up on the Okarnagan flagship's bow, whilst the speeding warship returned fire. The blows were immense, flashing across the distance faster than anything possible, shields flaring randomly. Crown muttered something about not wanting to play chicken with poultry masters, and ordered the *Wolf Brother* to a different course to prevent collision.

The enemy flagship pounded the carrier's port shields horrendously, except that her port and starboard shields were the strongest to protect the starfighter hangars from damage. *Wolf Brother* took the punishment easily, and returned the favour with its own weapons, as well as giving the rest of the fleet the opportunity to pound on the enemy ship as well.

The shields crumpled first, before the energy weapons began pulverising hull plating and inner bulkheads, turning it all into molten slag. Fires raged from exposed corridors and air vents, whilst more and more was peeled away from the ship's superstructure until it began listing to one side. Its engines sputtered and died, then cracked and fell apart.

The ship was still going on momentum alone, essentially a moving debris field, its remaining weapons running off emergency reserves in a last ditch attempt at vengeance. But it was all for naught as it slammed five minutes later into Ckeer Najoor's closest moon.

Sansky gave a sigh of relief.

"All ships, stand down from battle stations, begin search and rescue operations."

* * *

M'Der sighed a relief when he awoke on board the *Wolf Brother*, surrounded by Terrans instead of vicious Okarnagans. Silver had explained the ship was part of Raymond Sansky's fleet. The memory of who the Okarnagans were after spurred him out of the medical bed.

"I need to see Vice-Admiral Sansky right now!"

* * *

Adam gently lowered the body of another sentry to the floor.

Its throat was plastered with blood where he had blown out its larynx from nearby with his silenced pistol. He had taken down seven others like it, and removed the helmets of all seven. They were all of the same species, though he had no idea who they were; they looked exactly like the old cartoons of Beelzebub.

Whatever species they were, the seven sentries were dead.

As would the rest be in a matter of minutes.

He clambered up onto the domed house that had once belonged to Rino's local cloth merchant. He was dead now, his burning carcass visible through the hole in the roof. His house was the only one that still had a generous amount of structure left. The rest of the town was skeletal remains, in more ways than one.

He didn't want to think about the death and destruction around him, the friends he had lost in one fell swoop of energy blasts. It was a nightmarish scene, and a nightmarish thought.

But his family were still out there, still alive.

The *Kara*'s sensors had indicated that they were still alive, still breathing.

Speaking of which, he thought.

The *Kara* rushed past overhead, and commenced a pre-programmed attack run on the positions around his family. Energy blasts tore into the dirt, sending more clouds of dust into the air. The mercenaries dove to the floor as the *Kara* passed close enough to almost hit them with its lower fin.

He slipped into a prone position, and pulled the sniper rifle round. He brought the butt to his shoulder, nestling it tightly. He slowed his breathing, and looked through the high-powered scope.

He frowned, seeing Eve standing with a gun pointed at Polly, and her biological mother stood nearby, growling and staring evilly at the two. Mercenaries were scattered around, although one or two were injured and still on the floor.

What the hell?

At least he had his confirmation as to who had hired the mercenaries: Eve's biological mother, an agent of the Mertik secret service. He sighted in on the woman, and noticed the light flashing off something metallic on the back of both Eve's head, and that of the elder Mertik woman. A psychic device maybe?

He wouldn't put it past the woman.

He centred the scope back on Eve to see what she was doing. Her hand was shaking, and her emerald face was darkening with the effort of some immense physical strain. He could see the finger tightening.

With no small amount of horror, he realised what was happening.

Please don't do it Evie, he thought. He willed her not to, but her hand shaking more and more violently. She was losing the fight against the psychic device. And he was too far away to help her.

Please don't do it, he willed, sighting in on her hand even as he thought it.

Tears were streaming down her cheeks, even as she pulled the trigger.

Adam's finger automatically tightened on his own trigger, tears streaming down his own cheeks.

* * *

Eve's hand was shaking badly as she fought the mind control. Her finger still tightened on the energy pistol's trigger, but she refused to pull it, despite the woman claiming to be her biological mother shouting for her to do it, and do it now.

Her finger pulled the trigger just as a whipping whistling sound filled the air.

The pistol in her hand discharged and her hand suddenly exploded with immense pain. Half her hand was gone, a bloody mess. The pain was so bad she could feel herself beginning to pass out; there was dark green blood everywhere and she was screaming involuntarily.

But then she saw her mummy, lying on the floor, a large plasma burn on her chest. Eve whimpered and collapsed next to Polly, unaware of the cries of pain from her biological mother, who had also collapsed to the dusty floor clutching her hand.

"Mummy," she cried, the tears streaming down her cheeks creating clotted wet patches in the dust underneath her. "I'm so sorry mummy, I'm so sorry." Eve lay next to Polly, who used a weak hand to wipe away her daughter's tears. She was whispering to Eve, telling her everything was going to be okay, that it wasn't her fault.

There was a sudden bloodcurdling scream as one of the mercenaries was pulled backwards into a thick bloom of black smoke, followed by a hideously loud snap of bone. This was succeeded by a flash of metal that lodged itself in the neck of another mercenary, who dropped like a sack of potatoes, blood leaking down his dark uniform.

The next two mercenaries lost their heads –literally- when armour-piercing solid rounds blew their brains out the backs of their helmets. Then a sniper rifle came flying out of the smoke to strike another of the soldiers and sent him flying backwards into a wall that knocked him out.

Both fear and hope filled Evelyn as her beloved father emerged from the smoke, a silenced pistol in his deadly hands, and his favoured old assault rifle slung over one shoulder. He was dressed in combat fatigues, and wore a camouflage ghillie suit that obscured his facial features, and his outline, making him look almost like a running bush.

But there was fury in his eyes.

It was a fury she had seen before when she was very young.

He unslung the rifle and it barked. Two more mercenaries were torn apart, splashing the ground with their blood. The last two were dead before the first two had even hit the ground, one of them losing a limb to the sheer amount of bullets fired at them.

The unit commander was the only one left alive.

He jumped at Adam.

It was his last mistake.

Adam simply lashed out with one long roundhouse kick that snapped the mercenary commander's head around too far to be considered healthy. The body dropped to the dirt lifelessly, and Adam surveyed the wreckage of his assault.

All that was left was the elder Mertik woman.

She was on the floor, holding her own hand. It was proof that the metal devices were indeed psychic, transferring Eve's pain of losing her hand to the other device psychically. He tried desperately not to think about what he had done to stop his daughter.

He slung the rifle, and pulled out the pistol, unscrewing the silencer and replacing it in its pocket on his webbing. He strode over to the woman, and placed the barrel of the gun against her temple.

"WHY ARE YOU HERE?"

She muttered something in response.

"WHY?"

"We were under orders."

"FROM WHO?!"

She murmured something else. He heard what she said, and refused to believe it. It couldn't be. How could it be possible for *them* to be involved in this? They were so far away, so far removed from him and his life now that he had almost forgotten they existed.

"You're lying," he said.

He shot her through the head, and left her corpse where it was.

He was horrified to find that Eve had stopped moving. Her eyes were closed, and her head was resting on Polly's belly, which was when he saw the plasma burn on his wife's chest.

"Nonononononono," he cried, running to her. Eve still had a pulse, but she wouldn't wake up. To his horror, he remembered that she had been carrying the other psychic device when he had killed the Mertik spy. "Nonononononono," he repeated, holding his daughter to him. "What have I done?"

"What you always do, Adam," Polly whispered through struggling breaths. "You made a difference my love; my Obi-Wan Kenobi." She stroked his beard with a shaky hand as he lifted her into a sitting position, her head against his chest. He didn't entirely hear her, his thoughts drifting around the idea that he had essentially destroyed his own family in a matter of seconds.

Familiar shapes rushed overhead in formation, big green birds that swooped around in circles and kilometres-wide holding patterns: *Rhino*-class starfighters, mingled with a pair of *Stickleback* bombers.

The Terran Navy was here.

But he didn't care, his family was dying; his daughter was unconscious, possibly in a coma, and his wife was dying from a plasma hit.

Polly was barely holding on. Tears were forming in her eyes, and blood was dribbling from the corners of her mouth. Every now and again, she coughed, and more blood escaped.

Her gingerly kissed her on the forehead.

"Please," she whispered, "sing me that favourite song of yours." Her voice was hoarse with pain and damage, and her eyes were closed. There was barely any strength left in her fragile hands as he encompassed them with his own much bigger hands. He lowered his voice, and held his mouth next to her ear.

"Here's forty shillings on the drum for those who'll volunteer to come
To 'list and fight the foe to-day –Over the hills and far away.

O'er the hills and o'er the main. Through Flanders,
Portugal and Spain
King George commands and we obey –Over the hills and far away.

When duty calls me I must go to stand and face another foe
But part of me will always stray –Over the hills and far away.

O'er the hills and o'er the main. Through Flanders,
Portugal and Spain
King George commands and we obey –Over the hills and far away."

When he finished, his voice was barely audible, and her hands had no strength in them. His hands shaking badly, he reached to her neck, and felt for a pulse. He whimpered. There was none, not even a faint one.

Tears streamed down his cheeks again, and his whole world was obliterated.

"Please," he begged. "Please don't leave me."

* * *

The battered *Red Stallion* dropped through Ckeer Najoor's atmosphere incredibly quickly, faster than its escort of Rhino fighters could keep up with. It streaked through the sky like a comet, ignoring the re-entry protocols. It emerged from the normal cloud layer, its nose and forward parts of the engine nacelles blackened.

M'Der was at the helm, with Silver in the co-pilot's chair, and Sansky holding on for dear life in one of the auxiliary chairs in the cockpit. Wearing his duty uniform, his peaked officer's cap had fallen off during the bumpy ride down, and hadn't bothered to retrieve it. He had insisted on riding down on the *Stallion*, with a squadron to escort them.

The Okarnagans onboard had been taken into custody immediately, and Silver's people currently inhabited the *Wolf Brother*'s large medical bay, being cared for by the starfighter carrier's medical staff.

Only the *Wolf Brother* seemed to have come through the engagement intact, the other twenty-nine surviving vessels having suffered some form of battle damage. Sansky knew he would have a lot to explain to Fleet Admiral Bartleby, his commanding officer. Then again, the Alliance had a lot to answer for as well.

Sansky could now see the devastation wrought across Ckeer Najoor's surface. What he had taken to be cloud cover across much of the continental landmasses was in fact smoke from the ruins of the settlements. He remembered the descriptions of hell from history lessons as a child, and found that it wasn't all that much different from the planet's current description.

My friend is down there, he thought, *down there in that hell*.

There was a platoon of FPG troopers ready to disembark from the rear of the ship at a moment's notice.

The sensors started blaring a warning as something came out of the smoke and took up an escort position beside the *Red Stallion* above and behind it. M'Der was surprised to find that it was the *Kara*, its computer on autopilot. There were no life-signs onboard, though there were on the planet surface, located in the street outside the Caine residence.

One of the life signs —an older female- suddenly winked out, and the second female's life sign was bizarrely weak, like it was in a coma or some similar condition.

M'Der increased speed, and the *Kara* easily kept pace.

He landed the ship down the street from the life signs, and jumped out of his chair, barging past the platoon of soldiers, and bounding down the ramp to the dusty, smoky outside. Sansky wasn't far behind him, with the soldiers trying to keep pace with their admiral, slowed down by the bulk of their armour and weapons.

They almost ran straight into the back of the admiral when he stopped dead.

M'Der and Sansky were stood, transfixed at the scene before them. Tears were flowing from M'Der's tear ducts, streaming down his long cheeks. His bottom lip was trembling, and he was frozen to the spot.

Sansky wasn't much better. He pulled his retrieved hat off, and it slipped from his fingers.

There was horror on their faces.

"Oh my gods, no," M'Der murmured.

In front of them, Adam was cradling the body of his wife, his daughter not far away, most of one of her hands missing. There were bodies everywhere, and Adam was dressed for serious guerrilla combat, his expertly used weapons lying on the floor by his knees.

M'Der and Sansky slowly walked towards the grim visage.

"Adam?" the historian said softly. The former soldier was holding on to Polly like she was asleep, rocking back and forth on his knees, whispering in her ear, his eyes vacant. He sidestepped around Adam and Polly, and checked on Eve. She was breathing shallow breaths, and her pulse was good, but her eyes wouldn't open, and she wasn't responding to any outside stimuli, at least for the moment. Her skin was pale from blood loss, and M'Der felt nauseous at the sight of her destroyed hand. He called over the FPG unit's medic, who immediately called for an emergency teleport to the *Wolf Brother*.

Eve disappeared in a blinding flash of light.

M'Der gingerly approached his friend, and placed a long-fingered hand on one shoulder. Adam flinched, and his whispering stopped.

"They're gone, M'Der. They're both gone," said the human.

"Eve's still alive, Adam," the other replied softly. "They've just teleported her up to one of the Terran ships in orbit where she'll received medical care."

"They can't help her," whispered Adam. "I killed the spy, but she was wearing a psychic device linked to one on Eve's head. I think I killed Eve's brain."

It sounded like some insane fictional story if it had been from someone other than Adam. He wasn't prone to exaggeration or wild flights of fantasy, but even so, M'Der had a hard time believing it.

Of course, when he saw the body of the spy in question he realised there was something metal around the back of her head, with dormant inlaid circuitry across it. Not so difficult to believe.

He didn't want to think about what had happened to Polly, and the rest of the town.

"Adam; why did they did they want you?"

Adam shook his head, and mumbled something. M'Der didn't hear what he said over the noise of the passing starfighters overhead, even after he repeated it, and the broken human didn't seem to be about to repeat himself again.

"Adam, where are the rest of the people? What happened to the rest of Rino?"

"Dead," the other replied. "Murdered."

M'Der didn't know what to say; the normal commiserations and platitudes seemed empty and hollow given that it was his friend lying dead in Adam's arms, and the corpses of people he had known (and loved) for close to a decade. Rather than open his big mouth, he stepped away and returned to Sansky's side, who was keeping a respectful distance, and conversing with Captain Crown in orbit.

The FPG soldiers were giving Adam a wide berth, though none could explain why.

Sansky angrily closed the communications channel, his face almost steaming with hot anger.

"What is it?" M'Der queried.

Sansky's jaw worked silently, trying not to swear and curse loudly or disrespectfully in front of his men, and in front of the devastation of his friend's home and family.

"The planet Mertik was recently accepted into the Alliance as an emergency member, apparently not long after certain officials of their government were murdered some weeks ago: officials who were stubbornly against Mertik joining the Alliance."

M'Der frowned. "You think joining the Alliance was just a ploy to get in under the Protected Planets Treaty? Join the Alliance, and they could move freely within their territory? Seems a bit much for this one operation they were barely a part of."

"Who knows? Maybe they're in league with a renewed 3899?" Sansky said light-heartedly. His face fell however, when he realised that someone was listening in on their conversation: Adam. "Gods no."

M'Der turned to see what he was looking at, and saw Adam looking back at them.

"He heard us."

There was a fury in his eyes that only M'Der had seen once before: on the Saajil slave ship, ten years ago.

Adam gently lowered his wife's body to the floor, and then bolted towards his house, weapons jangling from his ghillie suit. There was a loud whining sound as the *Kara* –temporarily parked next to the *Stallion*- began powering up, and was already humming as its engines pushed it forward. Adam scrambled up the side of his house, and leapt off the roof just as the *Kara* thundered past, landing perfectly on the port wing.

The beautifully dangerous ship then roared into the sky, Adam entering through the small airlock above the wing.

The ship disappeared into the haze of smoke, leaving M'Der and Sansky stunned and in shock.

M'Der felt sick for what he too had done.

"Gods, I hope he doesn't find the Wrath Stone in there."

Sansky looked at him with horror on his face.

"The what? Are you insane?"

M'Der shook his head, "No, but Adam is right now."

TO BE CONCLUDED....

Twenty-One:
All Fall Down Part Two: The Wrath Stone

Historian's note: The main part of this story is set two weeks after *The Burning House.*

"While there's life, there's hope." —Cicero
"I am ready to meet my Maker.
Whether my Maker is prepared for the great ordeal of meeting me is another matter."
-Winston Churchill's epitaph
"Our destiny is frequently met in the very paths we take to avoid it." —Jean de La Fontaine
"Carry on my wayward son, there'll be peace when you are done." -Kansas
"Never surrender." —words to live by.

January 4000ad.
Ten years ago.
M'Der Tr'n, Famous Historian, had been quite comfortable in his little cell by himself. Every now and then, the Saajil would come into his cell and kick him a couple of times, insulting his mother and the memory of his homeworld. He'd had worse in his thousand years of life, adventuring around the nineteen known galaxies, or at least the eighteen that weren't forbidden to traffic.

His last meal was sat in a battered ceramic bowl, barely touched.

They had been feeding him some protein slop that barely had any taste, and looked like it had been eaten already. But it was palatable, and in all fairness he didn't mind it. The cell was pretty disgusting, with only a bucket for a toilet, and nowhere to sleep besides the floor.

For the moment, he was more interested in the commotion outside.

The door was suddenly flung open, and a dozen of the armoured midgets threw a large Terran into the cell with him.

The Terran wasn't moving, and made no noise as the Saajil slavers disappeared. He was wearing basic black fatigues, the kind military forces wore during night ops, and he had long unkempt brown hair.

Who was this man?

His question was answered, in more ways than one.

Caine, as the man had called himself, had then supposedly killed the little runt commanding the slave ship, and disappeared out of the door. There was a clamour and shouts of pain and alarm. There was a flash of red light, and a roar of anger from a human throat.

M'Der's eyes widened, and he jumped to his feet, bounding out of the cell, to find the corridor empty except for a grouping of dead bodies. There was barely any blood, necks snapped the wrong way or simply too far round to be healthy.

There was something held in the hands of one of the corpses.

M'Der's eyes went so wide he was afraid they would fall out of his sockets.

"The Wrath Stone," he said, his voice an awed whisper. It was dormant, and still beautiful; it was why he had been on Proxima, looking for a way to get the Stone back to Gorrh where it belonged. Then the Saajil had captured him, and taken the damned Stone away from him.

This Caine had clearly touched it, releasing the Stone's power into him. There were screams from down the corridor; he grabbed the inert red Stone, and sprinted out of the cells area. There was blood splashed everywhere on the walls, Saajil torn apart like dolls, limbs strewn about like clothes in his old apartment.

M'Der was terrified beyond reason, and yet something compelled him to follow the trail of blood and destruction. He felt nauseous at the sight of the rent bodies and the gore; it had been centuries since he had seen that kind of violence.

He picked up one of the helmets from the bodies, and dropped the darkened red gem inside. It was about the size of his head, although it was preternaturally dark as if no light could pass through it or reflect off it.

He needed Caine to return the Wrath power to the stone.

But first they would have to get out of this ship. The Terran, or whatever he referred to himself as, didn't seem to be heading in any particular direction, just aimlessly slaughtering every living Saajil in sight.

That was what the power of the Wrath was: ancient rage-enhanced strength and willpower, directed by an age-old intelligence that twisted the host's subconscious thoughts and whims. This Caine's subconscious was clearly filled with thoughts of rage and battle.

Clutching the Stone, he precariously stepped around the bodies, noticing that the Saajil corridor signage indicated that Caine was headed for the ship's command centre. He doubted Caine knew where the command centre was on a Saajil slaver ship; another indication of the ancient intelligence set loose from the Stone.

He hoped that he could return the Wrath back to its prison.

When he found the command centre, it was filled with bodies, as with the rest of the ship, and the stink of torn bodies and gore filled his sensitive nostrils making him gag involuntarily.

Caine was nowhere to be seen, though there was a sliding door opening and shutting jerkily against a corpse missing its head, the body preventing the door from closing. Beyond the door more bodies were evident leading away to another part of the ship.

He had a rudimentary knowledge of the Saajil written language, and their temperament in regards to layouts and such. He looked over the command centre and found the navigational console, hoping to make sense of where the ship was.

It wasn't easy; the Saajil didn't maintain a particularly coherent filing system, nor did they seem to believe in any kind of security coding algorithms. It was almost too easy to get into their computer, and discover the ship's whereabouts in the universe at large.

He brought up a star chart, and plotted the course of the ship, from the orbit of Proxima Centauri, where he had been snatched looking for the Saajil and the Stone. The course took a circuitous route around the Terran core systems from Proxima, certainly explaining M'Der's lengthy stay. But the ship had made a stop to Holy Terra itself, or at least the ruins of its sister planet, Mars.

The ship had then begun a slow, cloaked and hidden, route towards the Sol system's Linkway entrance. The ship had dropped into emergency autopilot mode since Caine's internal attack, and the computer had put the ship into orbit of Titan, one of Jupiter's moons. Somewhere down there, he thought, is a nice little mining colony.

The ship was now idling.

He tried contacting the colony below, but nobody answered; or at least nobody could hear the ship's transmissions.

There was huge Terran Navy activity down by the rocks that had once been Old Earth, including one of their biggest ships, the *HMS Cerberus*. Salvage vessels were present, and starfighter squadrons were conducting regular patrol sorties. He wondered what they were up to, and found he didn't care at that particular moment.

He'd had enough trouble with the Terrans to last a lifetime.

He set the ship's course for the nearest planet where he had an apartment: Fayde.

The ship hummed beneath him, and came to life. As a result, the navigation console lit up with reams and reams of navigational data, indicating the ship's movement towards the Linkway. The lights were dim, indicating the cloaking device was still active, and had been since picking up Caine from near Earth.

There was a pause in the background noise, as if all the instruments around him had stopped at the same exact instant. It was almost like the beeps and whistles had become one and the same.

M'Der turned round, and saw to his dismay the brutalised form of the Saajil ship's commander, missing an arm, and with blood oozing from his mouth, eyes, and ears. He was hobbling, and his breathing was ragged.

"You. Get away from that console." He held a vicious looking sidearm in his remaining hand; the hand itself was shaking badly, his short stature unable to cope with the immense amount of pain. M'Der did as he was told.

"What is that thing?" he said, pointing to the Stone in the hook of M'Der's arm.

"It's called the Wrath Stone, one of the prison stones, holding the essence of one of the worst criminals in ancient times."

The Saajil was about to say something else, when he started gasping for air. A big Terran-pink hand was wrapped around the midget's throat, squeezing tightly. Suddenly the Saajil's head snapped round too far. The corpse slumped to the floor, its life extinguished, leaving M'Der alone with the possessed Caine.

"The Historian," it said in a freakily modified version of Caine's normal voice. It chilled the Kra Nal to his very core, a racial memory from the dawn of his people's sentient existence. "I half suspected one of your people would be here, responsible for this. Who would have thought that it would only be a half-famous historian?"

"I'm not afraid of you, demon," M'Der shouted.

The Caine-Wrath thing laughed a booming laugh that was punctuated by background screams, as if the laugh briefly showed a glimpse of the hell that awaited him.

"No, that is probably true, Kra Nal. But you are afraid of the human inhabiting this body, yes?"

That's an understatement, thought M'Der. Caine was a human black ops soldier, possibly from another time if he was any judge, and therefore intensely dangerous, even before his gory transformation into a violent killer.

"So what?" he said defiantly.

That laugh again.

"You, and all your people, will die by my hand."

With that, the Caine-Wrath roared, and leaped into the air, arms extended like those of a striking lion, or wildcat. M'Der held the Stone up in front of him, and the two tumbled to the floor in a pile of twisted limbs.

Caine was unconscious when M'Der came round. The Wrath Stone was still in the helmet where he had left it, but now it was glowing again, the criminal's essence once again restored after Caine had touched the Stone mid-leap, therefore downloading the consciousness back into its receptacle.

M'Der's head was pounding from the hit, and found that he was once again falling into unconsciousness. When he awoke once again, the command centre was bathed in the writhing blue light of the Linkway outside.

He pulled himself to his feet, ignoring the unconscious form of Caine beside him. He left the Stone where it was, unwilling to touch it or even look at it. The swirling blue-white Linkway dissipated around the ship, and the slaver vessel emerged into realspace. He had been out of it for several days judging by the fact that they were now approaching the planet Fayde.

He stole himself into one of the escape pods, which was extremely technologically limited, and punched the eject button, forcing the tiny two-man craft out into space before Fayde's Police ships could find him and confiscate the Stone before he could hide it.

As the planet grew in the forward viewport, with Fayde City's star-scraping spaceport closing awfully fast, he began to mentally plan what he would do. His people would need to be contacted, and the Stone returned to its tomb on Gorrh.

Caine would need to be watched closely.

Very closely.

* * *

Now.

June 4010ad.

They came with the rising of the sun, erupting from the clouds like a swarm of locusts. Red-and-black darts flashed from the sky spitting death down on the capital city, missiles streaking through the air on thin grey trails of smoke.

Screams rent the air, mixing with the hideous whine of diving bombers. Balls of fiery explosions filled the streets, and tracer fire stitched across the sky as the anti-air defences woke up. This lasted for only a few minutes until beams of energy lanced down from orbit and with pinpoint accuracy blasted the AA towers to pieces.

The air was chock full of strafing fighters and speeding munitions. The clouds lit up from above as a monumental battle took place in space –a very one-sided one as the wreckages of several planetary defence force vessels slammed bodily into the countryside around the city from orbit.

When the return fire ceased, the fighters moved into a holding pattern above the smoking, skeletal city.

Massive dropships landed in formation along the main thoroughfare, their noses pointed inward; troops marched in perfect rows onto the road, and snapped to attention. The noise from the thousands of feet slamming on the floor was a deafening as an artillery barrage.

Forty thousand throats bellowed at once.

"ALL HAIL THE CHIEFTAIN!"

The final dropship landed at the head of the parade. An armoured figure draped in black flowing stepped down the ramp, a six-foot broadsword in one hand, and a stylised helmet in the other. A cadre of individually black-and-red bodyguards who marched in time with him flanked him either side.

A hobbling servant brought a microphone stand out to him, and was kicked for his troubles. The Chieftain smiled, revealing triangular chrome-metal teeth.

"Soldiers of Okar!" he bellowed. When he spoke, his amplified voice rang out across the city. "We have conquered this planet in the name of our forefathers!" The crowd roared with approval. "This place is ours and we will continue to take more for as long as we draw breath!" More roars. "Tomorrow, we shall once again declare war on Terra's children!"

The response shattered every window in the city.

* * *

Now.

I love you, Adam.

Polly looked at him with a universe of beauty and love behind her eyes.

I love you too, he replied.

* * *

The rage roared and bellowed.

It smashed its non-existent fists against the side of its cage, its face reddened beyond comprehension. It charged at the walls of its prison, slamming itself again and again into the invisible cage. It screamed the names of its hated enemies, and spat curses and oaths at everyone and everything in existence.

The rage cried and wept at being kept locked up.

It roared again before slumping to the floor of the cage.

* * *

Sweating, Adam Caine awoke with a cry.

His bed was empty, the duvet crumpled against the far bulkhead. *The bed was soaked with cold sweat, and the holographic pictures were shaking as if in an earthquake —which was impossible on board the Kara Marazov.*

His hair and beard were matted to his face, and the bed sheets were stuck to his back.

He slipped out of bed, and pulled on a fresh pair of underwear, followed by a nondescript set of grey overalls. Leaving the mess in the small bunkroom, he stepped into the four-seat cockpit. The communications console was alight, dozens of messages waiting for him to view them.

Most of them were from M'Der or Raymond.

They were scared.

They were all scared.

Scared of what would happen if the rage of Adam Caine was unleashed upon the universe. He was going to show them all what it meant for him to be unleashed, for rage to devastate the nineteen galaxies.

He would show them.

What was that light coming from Eve's room?

Guilt and grief swept over him at the thought of what he himself had done to Evie. The entire scene kept playing over and over in his brain: the shot that took Eve's hand away too late to save his beloved wife from being shot.

Tears streamed down his cheeks for about the hundredth time in the two weeks since he had raced from Ckeer Najoor in a blind rage. That rage had subsided somewhat since then, having no target to rail against.

The red light shimmered from beneath Eve's old bed.

He could hear an evil cackling from the recesses of his mind, a vague suggestion of some long-past misdeed of his.

He bent down and pulled out a glass box.

There was a red orb inside, pulsating with light that hurt his eyes. The evil cackling grew louder as he opened the box. He reached into the hardened transparent container, and touched the perfect sphere.

Pain flashed up his fingers, and he suddenly felt the most intense rage he had ever known fill his every being.

A voice in his head spoke to him. A familiar voice.

Hello Adam. It's been too long since we last saw each other.

* * *

The young woman, for she had no other way to identify herself, was trapped in the medical ward. The medical technicians –mostly human mixed with one or two non-humans- refused to tell her anything about who she was or why she was in there, beyond the fact that she had been seriously hurt, and lost her right hand.

The doctors were even less circumspect, though they seemed to hide it better.

She didn't know her own name, nor even what species she belonged to: the medical technicians and nurses claimed she was a member of the Mertik race, though that was all they supposedly knew.

She had been refused access to the computer –the ship's computer, she corrected herself, she was on board some kind of starship. All of the medical staff had a military unit patch with H.M.S. Wolf Brother emblazoned on them, though she had no idea what it meant, nor what the HMS stood for.

All she knew was that she was a teenager, and that she had green skin, and long bright blue hair.

She kept having phantom pains in her nonexistent hand.

It hadn't been replaced with a biomechanical version yet, and she still couldn't look at the stump, despite not knowing what happened.

Whenever she went to sleep, she dreamed of a bearded human man with a vaguely familiar face. But she didn't know who he was, or what he was to her.

She slumped in defeat on her bed, consigned to not knowing anything beyond the four walls of the medical bay.

The doctor, a tall human woman with amazing facial bone structure, and blonde hair tied into a severe bun, approached her bed, holding a large diagnostic digipad.

"How are we this morning, young lady?" she asked, though there was no humour in her voice, or her face. She'd been stretched to the breaking point by an influx of battle casualties to the ship, though nobody would tell the young woman what had happened. Most of those casualties had gone back to their duties, patched up and healed, except for some of the worst cases.

"Still a blank," the young woman replied with a shrug.

The doctor nodded sympathetically, and placed the digipad in the pocket of her long white medical coat.

"I am afraid that you are being released from my care. You and four of my critical patients are being transferred to the HMS Musgrove for transport to a medical facility on Caldona III near the Alliance border, and your homeworld."

"Musgrove? Caldona III?"

"The Musgrove is a dedicated naval medical ship currently assigned to this particular taskforce. I am not sure of the particulars of Caldona III itself, only that the Navy base there has a specialised facility dedicated to your predicament."

The young woman nodded silently.

Predicament, she thought, bemused by the term, what a hilarious word to use, as if this is somehow something trivial. I just wish I knew who I was, or where I came. Who are my parents? Are they around somewhere nearby? Or are these Navy people as much in the dark as me?

She hoped Caldona III would yield some answers.

* * *

"What is the Wrath Stone?"

M'Der frowned at his friend, who sat on the right side of his big metal desk in his office. The Wolf Brother's engines pulsated quietly underneath them, the holographic projections of the ship's tactical displays turning the normally pristine-white an emerald green.

"You know the legend, don't you?" the Kra Nal scoffed.

"Something about the worst kind of evil trapped in a small orb."

The historian nodded. "The Wrath Stone and the other six Stones are the original evils, the embodiment of the Terran and Rijiin seven sins. They were super-criminals bent on death, destruction, and corruption on an intergalactic scale, all immortal and all as powerful as Adam. It took three millennia to track them all down, and destroy their physical bodies, entrapping their essences in the orbs my people call the Havakai –the Sin Stones."

"Why is this all important?"

M'Der sighed heavily.

"Twelve years ago, somebody stumbled onto the Havakai in their tomb on Gorrh, the tomb world. They stole the one, the leader of the seven, and took it away to several different places over as many months. I and several others were asked to locate and retrieve it." He sat back in his chair, fiddling with the zipper of his borrowed Navy overalls, acutely aware of the two Army guards posted outside Vice-Admiral Sansky's office.

"I discovered the Wrath Stone on Proxima, and was about to return it, when I was captured by the Saajil. I was placed in a cell with one Adam Caine." He saw Sansky perk up at the mention of their greatest ally and friend. "Adam somehow released the essence trapped in the Stone, and was briefly possessed by the criminal Hadjkai."

Raymond Sansky nodded, "So that's how he killed the crew of that Saajil ship, and why he had no memory of it: it wasn't him." He leaned forward, resting his elbows on his big desk. "It still doesn't explain why you decided to hide the Stone onboard the Kara Marazov. Or why you didn't just take it back to Gorrh."

M'Der, agitated by the question, slipped from the chair, and stood by the large floor-to-ceiling viewport that looked down the length of the Wolf Brother's main hull.

"I don't know. Gorrh became hostile territory after that Jalic Incursion fiasco. Eve's room on the Kara seemed the last place anyone would ever check."

In the reflection of the large viewport, M'Der saw Sansky's face cloud with anger.

"So what you're saying is that if Adam is once again possessed by this Hadjkai, the embodiment of Wrath itself, in the state he is currently in, he could destroy this entire universe."

Sadness and guilt swept through the tall, lanky alien.

He nodded.

"I'm afraid so."

Sansky growled, and slammed a closed fist down on the top of his desk.

"We need to know where he's going, M'Der," he said, the accusation in his voice evident. "Although after he heard our conversation about Kombat 3899 being a possible suspect, I can guess where he'll go first."

* * *

The rage smashed and smashed against its cage once again, renewing its need to escape. It could feel the anger, and the hate boiling up; it could feel the warmth of the Wrath building up outside, seeping into its invisible cage.

It roared and bellowed with laughter as it realised just how close it was to escaping once again.

A voice spoke to it.

Hello my friend, you are released from your prison as I was.

* * *

Grunhardt Prison was no joke.

It stood at the centre of a massive mountain range on a barren planet at the edge of Terran space. It was a forebodingly dark and grim place at the best of times, and downright inhospitable at the worst. It was home to the very worst of humanity's law-breakers: mass murderers, sexual offenders, and traitors to the Terran government.

It was built like a castle, and fortified like the strongest of Terra's military installations despite its remote location.

Lenson Gardner, formerly CO of the defunct "Hunters" Regiment, and former Head of Navy Intelligence, heard and felt the rumbling first before the other prisoners of his maximum-security prison wing. The ancient forcefield projectors rattled in their brackets, the energy fields fizzing and crackling under the pressure. The lights shut off, with only the blue forcefields illuminating the cells.

Gardner backed away from the edges of the cell.

The ceiling of the corridor outside the cells collapsed almost noiselessly, the thick, armoured metal melting and falling to the floor like molten lava. It crackled and hissed like a bag of snakes, already cooling in the cold air of the cellblock.

He knew what this meant: he'd heard about the attack on Ckeer Najoor through his limited amount of remaining contacts within the Navy. The attack had set off political outrage against the Alliance, even so far as being publicly condemned for their inaction by High Admiral Scarlett herself. But Gardner didn't care for the politics of the situation anymore; he was far more interested in the news of the casualties.

Adam Caine –a constant thorn in his side for close to a decade- had lost his entire family: his wife dead, his daughter comatose and not expected to come out of it at last report. Caine himself was now missing, presumed to be out for revenge.

He wasn't disappointed in his assumption.

A burst of engine coolant super cooled the molten metal, and a dark figure dropped down noiselessly to the floor.

Gardner was horrified by the visage of Caine's black stealth suit, the glowing green eyes of the headpiece lending an even greater eeriness to his appearance. The old, world-weary former intelligence officer backed away from the forcefield. His bones ached and his muscles refused to move very fast.

"Caine."

"Gardner." His mechanically enhanced voice was frighteningly deep, and Lenson swore he could hear screams in the background, but he just assumed that it was coming from somewhere else in the prison. "I have come for you. It is time you and I had a reckoning."

Gardner found he couldn't back up any further, standing against the metal wall as he was.

"Wh-what do you want?"

Caine stepped up to the forcefield, and held his right hand out palm forward. There was a surge of electrical discharge from his hand that leapt out and struck the field of energy. For a moment nothing happened.

Then the powerful forcefield flickered, and died altogether, leaving the cell in darkness except for Caine's glowing green eyes.

"I want you to assist me in my vengeance."

Gardner couldn't help but laugh.

"You want me to assist you? After all that's happened between us? Ha-ha-ha-ha! That's a good one!"

Caine grabbed him by the throat, and hoisted him off his feet. Gardner swore silently; Caine was really going to kill him this time: he had no friends or family to hold him back now, nobody to appeal to his conscience. Gardner had never felt so vulnerable before, his feet dangling in mid-air.

He had never felt so old, so helpless as he was in one of Caine's hands.

He tried to speak, but his throat was still constricted. He couldn't breathe and his vision was starting to go red around the edges.

"What do you want from me, Caine?" he finally managed.

That frightening chuckle again, surrounded by dying screams.

"I am not Caine, Lenson Gardner." Caine –or whoever- ripped his headpiece off with his free hand. His bearded face was now marred by a black flame tattoo that reached up from under his collar and spread to a point across the bridge of his nose. But his eyes, they were truly terrifying to behold: they were a deep dark red, the colour of blood; but it wasn't one shade of red. Several different shades of red mixed and swirled around his eyeballs like a Linkway tunnel. It wasn't natural, and the swirls kept making the vague shapes of skulls and blades. "You may call me Mr. Wrath," he chuckled. "Or better yet, you may use my real name. I am Ruga'forn Belag Hadjkai, once of the Kra Nal, and formerly interred in the Wrath Stone on the planet Gorrh."

He put Gardner back down on his feet, and let go, leaving the aged man to rub his bruised neck.

"Gorrh? The tomb world?" the old man scoffed. His brief humour dissipated in a heartbeat at Hadjkai's evil glare. "It is a forbidden world for a damned good reason; nobody goes there except to bury the dead."

"Exactly."

Gardner nodded in understanding, though he hoped he didn't find out how this was going to be accomplished.

"Come, Gardner. We will use Caine's ship to begin my plan."

Gardner's eyebrow shot up.

"I assume you have a plan." His already aged voice croaked from his abuse. Some of his old confidence returned though. "I'd hate to go into this without a plan."

An angry humour passed over Hadjkai's red eyes. It didn't reassure Gardner at all.

"I have been planning this for centuries. Do you not think that that is enough time to plan revenge so sweet you can almost taste the sugar in their blood? After all, there are more than tombs on Gorrh."

Gardner frowned at the idea.

Caine –Hadjkai- stalked back out of the cell, and climbed back onto the roof of the prison, reluctantly assisting Gardner to do the same. The Kara Marazov was waiting patiently, her lower fin hovering inches above the solid metal of the roof. Gardner felt a slight apprehension at the thought of going near the dangerous starship after all his dealings with Caine.

Hadjkai had no such qualms, jumping up the ladder rungs like they were barely there. He disappeared into the airlock above the port wing, leaving Gardner to climb up.

Halfway up, he looked around, and found that the prison was in ruins. The guard towers had been slagged worse than his cellblock roof, and alarms were ringing across the entire compound. In the dark distance, he could see a suggestion of the mountains ringing the prison, forming yet another barrier for prisoners to get past in any bid to escape.

Only a single spotlight was on, pointed at the Kara Marazov's upper fin, lighting the shimmering blue hull against the night sky.

None of the prison's defences or offensive technology activated as he entered the famed little ship, making him all the more worried about being onboard the Kara. Nobody seemed inclined to try and escape either –Gardner suspected that was down to the appearance of the Kara, and the legend that went with its owner.

He arrived in the alienised cockpit to find Hadjkai already in the pilot's chair, using Caine's knowledge to fly the ship.

"Sit down," the possessed man ordered.

Gardner did as he was told.

"So what's first?"

Hadjkai grunted. "First we need to pick up some things from my shopping list."

* * *

"Where the fuck am I?"

Adam stood on an ash waste, the sky dark and filled with forked lightning, and the ground soft with the burned ashes of the dead. The horizon was too far in the distance, and there were no landmarks of any kind in visual range. The last thing he remembered was touching that red orb.

"*This is what it feels like to be me,*" a voice said.

"Who are you?"

"*You released me,*" it said. A figure appeared before him. It was himself, except that the copy of him was tattooed with black flames, and his eyes were a disturbing red colour.

"Who are you?" Adam demanded. He charged forward, and wrapped his arms around the other, only to find the other wasn't there anymore. He was behind the big human, his arms folded across his chest, and a highly amused look on his face.

"I am you," it answered.

"Bollocks."

"*Okay, so I'm just using this appearance; although I am currently inhabiting your body right now. This is your subconscious.*" He gestured around him to the ash waste they were stood on. "*You are currently stuck here with no way out anymore.*"

"Fuck you I'm stuck here."

Adam dove at the copy of himself.

The evil copy disappeared into thin air, a deep frightening chuckle remaining in the air for a few seconds afterward.

* * *

The *HMS Wolf Brother* slid into orbit of the Kra Nal homeworld not long after, the ship passing through its defence net with permission and an escort of two of the Kra Nal's starships. The ships were spindly things, almost flower-like with great spinning power cores at their centre and petal-shaped wings and hulls surrounding them.

The *Wolf Brother* was ordered to remain in orbit, weapons offline and starfighters remaining in their hangars.

Only one ship was allowed to go anywhere near the surface, and it belonged to one of the Kra Nal: M'Der.

He and Sansky, as well as a bodyguard of two Fleet Protection Group troopers, were sat in the cockpit once again, on their way to meet with the head of the Kra Nal Justice Ministry.

"How long since you've been home," asked Sansky? The ship passed into the cloud layer above the capital, the city still unseen below them.

"Forty-three years."

Sansky stared at him with disbelief; he was barely much older than forty-five himself, and found he already missed his home on New Terra after only a month in space. Then again, M'Der was over a thousand years old, and didn't necessarily measure time the same way as he did.

M'Der, however, had a knowing look in his eyes that spoke volumes: as much as he loved his homeworld, he really did not want to come back here.

The clouds parted before them, and one of the troopers gasped. The capital looked like a collection of giant flowers, metal and gleaming even in the cloud-shrouded light, petals fanned out in seemingly random shapes. It seemed as though there were no buildings, yet the sky was filled with small aircraft, coming and going from all over the city. As they approached closer, the humans realised that each 'flower' was itself the size of a city, the tip of the highest petal invisible among the cloud layer. The *Red Stallion* was directed to land on the roof of the Justice Ministry's headquarters.

The Ministry was located within one of the larger horizontal 'flowers', the largest of the petals covered with two-tone Justice vehicles, their flower-like hulls much more hardier than the delicate vessels that had escorted the *Wolf Brother* into orbit.

The *Stallion* landed with a thump, the hydraulics of the landing claws hissing painfully as the ship touched down too fast to compensate fully. A gaggle of overly tall Kra Nal waited at the edge of the marked landing area. Two of them wore long sleeveless robes that billowed in the breeze, their four companions dressed in carapace armour, stun pistols on their hips, and tall helmets on their stretched heads.

The four visitors descended the entry ramp unarmed, as instructed. The FPG troopers had complained on more than one occasion about that fact, though Sansky had shouted them down.

One of the hardy Justice Ministry aircars launched into the sky, sirens screaming, lights flashing. The four approached the Kra Nal welcoming committee.

"Welcome to the planet Kra, Vice-Admiral Sansky," the tallest of the welcomers smiled. "It is not so often that a Terran Navy flag officer of such high esteem visits our wonderful planet."

"Given the circumstances, can you blame me?" asked Sansky in as polite a tone as he could.

"No. I suppose not. I am Minister F'Ler Ka'n, head of the Justice Ministry." Sansky saw a knowing glance pass ever so briefly between M'Der and F'Ler, almost as if they shared some great embarrassment —and it had come at the mention of F'Ler being the head of the Ministry. Had M'Der been involved with the Ministry? F'Ler gestured to his colleague. "This is Deputy Minister R'Gar Lr'n, he heads up the Special Operations Division, among which are the units dedicated to protecting and guarding the Sin Stones."

"Then you are aware of what has transpired on the Alliance-protected planet Ckeer Najoor?" asked Sansky. They stood facing each other, two small lines of professionals like an old game of rugby.

F'Ler nodded. "Yes; your Admiral Scarlett has asked me and several others to join her on Fullina to meet with the Alliance's Premier." He directed his gaze back to M'Der. "We are also aware of M'Der Tr'n's failure in regards to keeping the Wrath Stone safe and secure."

M'Der hung his head low in shame and guilt, though nobody bothered to explain anything to Sansky. "Are you aware of the person that Wrath has taken over?" said the admiral.

Ka'n waved it off. "This... Adam Caine is a mere human like you? I would be more worried if the creature had taken over a Kra Nal."

Now it was Sansky and M'Der's turn to exchange knowing looks.

"Adam," Sansky explained, "Is officially considered to be a super-soldier in the eyes of the Terran military. He is dangerous at the best of times, and frightening at the worst. He's a time-traveller from the dawn of my civilisation's reach into space."

"Our friend Adam is the Strand, according to the *B'morans*."

Sansky frowned, though once again nobody explained anything to him, they simply stared at the two friends with shocked looks on their long pale green faces.

"The chosen one?"

M'Der nodded.

"But..." F'Ler seemed completely taken aback, his previous aloofness gone. "You shall have all the assistance you require, Vice-Admiral. Any request you need from us, please do not hesitate to ask Deputy Minister Lr'n."

He nodded to the visitors, and then hurried towards a waiting shuttle, leaving them to watch him go.

A bit more enthusiastic than his previously mute behaviour, Lr'n clapped his hands together with a smile on his lips. "So, where do you want to start?"

"An official briefing on the Stones would be a good place to start. Then we can discuss tactics and strategies on how to properly handle this situation with all the facts."

Lr'n nodded.

The four visitors were taken off of the monumentally huge landing platform, and taken through more normal surroundings of dull military-esque corridors, with zero decorations, and plenty of coded signs indicating the location of specific parts of the Justice Ministry's headquarters.

Like the flower-shaped city from above, the signs and the surrounding structure's architecture looked almost too delicate to be anything other than decoration. But there was an obvious strength lying beneath everything, just like the fragile-looking Kra Nal that inhabited the planet.

They were brought past dozens of uniformed Kra Nal, all tall, all spindly, and all uninterested in the newcomers. They were escorted to a sterile-white semi-circular amphitheatre, semi-circular rows of stepped seats surrounding a small circular stage, and a waist-high holo-projector.

Lr'n stepped onto the stage, and fiddled with the controls.

The lights dimmed, and the holo-projector sputtered to life. Like Terran holography, it was somewhat limited in its capacity, only capable of one colour: standard emerald green. Images of alien lettering flashed to life around the four visitors.

The two FPG troopers —not usually a part of high-level briefings- were slightly unnerved by the whole experience, remaining almost invisible.

Lr'n began his practiced briefing, clasping his hands in front of him like a teacher.

"Around a hundred thousand years ago, our race was young and naïve when we began our own industrial revolution, our technology advancing too quickly for our society to handle."

Hand-drawn sketches and paintings appeared among the myriad of holograms, showing Kra Nal in primitive clothing about to commit unspeakable acts, as well as crude drawings of riots and shouting and screaming Kra Nal. Sansky was feeling his impatience rising, though he knew better than to interrupt.

"Chaos was abundant across our planet, with no real leadership, except for seven brothers who used the riots and unrest to further their own criminal enterprises. The eldest and most dangerous of these was called Hadjkai. Each of the brothers used a different series of methods to rule their subjects, corresponding to one each of what you humans refer to as the Seven Deadly Sins."

A grainy old photograph appeared holographically, with seven similar looking Kra Nal all huddled together, all smiles like it was a family picnic, though Sansky could see a dead coldness to their eyes, despite it only being a static picture.

He remembered the last time he had seen those kinds of eyes: kneeling before Lord Yh'reth'gar beside his new friend Adam, awaiting death at the hands of his Second, Yh'par'ban. It was not something he wanted to repeat.

"These so-called super-criminals were at the head of our technological advances; many, though, were unsavoury and violent in nature. Among these advances was the creation of devices that could transfer the consciousness of a person from one body to another, ripping apart the original mind, and inserting the invader's own." Lr'n sighed, and deflated slightly. "Despite our extremely long lives, the brothers were intent on living forever."

Sansky couldn't help himself.

"These devices helped them put themselves into newer bodies to keep them going for another thousand or so years," he said, nodding in understanding.

"Precisely, vice-admiral." He swept a long arm across a series of moving holograms, video files from the dawn of their electronic age. "At first these devices were huge and bulky, taking up an entire space equivalent to a modest residential hab. It took two centuries before the devices became portable-"

"When they became the size of stones," the human interrupted. Lr'n glared knives at him, but it was a half-hearted effort at best.

"Yes, indeed," he replied distractedly. He pointed to a hologram that separated from the rest and hovered above the projector: one of the Stones. This one was of a different shape, slightly more ovoid than M'Der had initially described the Wrath Stone.

"After a reign of almost forty thousand years, the Kra Nal people rose up against the immortal brothers, and trapped their consciousnesses in seven devices they dubbed the Sin Stones. They then placed each one in individual compartments in a small area on the surface of the ancient tombworld Gorrh." Holograms of uniformed Kra Nal and holographic blueprints of the Ministry's various types of craft appeared in random sequence around Lr'n and the projector. "The Justice Ministry was created as the planet's police force, with the Special Operations Division tasked with any military matters, and the protection and imprisonment of the seven Stones."

A junior officer entered the room at that point, hurriedly stepping up to the small stage, and handing Lr'n a flimsy hardcopy message. But his long face only frowned with confusion at the information contained on it. He stepped down after the junior left, and handed Sansky the hardcopy.

"The *Kara Marazov* has been sighted," said Lr'n.

Sansky nodded, though he was just as baffled.

"On Korana Minor, where several tonnes of medical equipment and medical supplies were stolen in one robbery."

M'Der frowned. "Medical equipment."

"A bio-resequencer; a gene-splicer; six infant incubation chambers; six adult incubations chambers; a portable quantum scanner; three tonnes of bio-meme polymer. There are some other things here that I have no idea what they do."

He handed the page to M'Der.

"Uh-oh," the historian said. "I know what Hadjkai is doing."

Sansky and Lr'n looked at him inquisitively.

"He's trying to clone Adam."

* * *

Adam ran and ran across the barren ash desert.

There was nothing to see, except ash being kicked up by his heavy footfalls. He was angry, terrified, claustrophobic, and agoraphobic all in one big hit. He was panic-filled, running tirelessly towards the red sky and the black horizon that never got closer.

Then a figure appeared, quickly getting larger and larger as he ran toward it. It was female, and somewhat petite, but it resolved more and more into a disturbingly familiar outline until the red sky glinted off each agonising detail.

"Polly."

Adam stopped, still ten metres from her, unable to believe what he was seeing. She was perfectly intact: there was no plasma wound on her chest, no blood and soot plastered across her face, nor any smudged tears running down her perfect cheeks. She was wearing the uniform of the Icarus, the emergency craft of which he had rescued her from almost nine years ago.

She was smiling.

"Hello Adam," she said, her Midwest American accent as vivid as ever.

"You can't be real. This is just my subconscious, or some screwed-up version of it anyway." She kept smiling, and stepped slowly closer. Adam felt his heart race a mile a minute, but the memory of what had happened to her still lingered in the forefront of his mind, or rather the parts of his mind he wasn't already in.

"I am as real as this place," she said calmly. Even in here, she was still his voice of reason, still his conscience and calming influence, and his one true love. "Right now, I am the part of you that represents your soul. You need to get out of here, and stop that creature from going through with whatever it is he's doing. You need to reclaim your body."

"How can I possibly do that when I'm stuck in here?" he complained. He fought down the overwhelming urge to run into her arms, and kiss her soft lips. He remained stock still on the spot he had stopped on. She came so close he could smell her strong perfume, the one she liked to wear when they went out for a romantic evening. But he still stopped himself from touching her.

"Anything is possible, especially for you." Again, that big warm smile. "You're Adam Caine."

Then she disappeared into thin air, leaving her perfume behind.

"No," he whispered. A growl emerged from his perceived throat, getting louder and louder as he strode forward with heavy steps. Rage filled his every being, and the growl turned into a roar.

He charged forward, bellowing like a lion, until he ran into an invisible barrier. He bashed his fists against it, all the while still roaring and raging. He found it started to become malleable, and charged at it.

At first, it only caved a few centimetres, but then he felt a surge of rage and hate, and he pushed and pushed, roaring his hate at the world, the barrier becoming as soft as linen in front of his anger.

It ripped, and suddenly white light blasted the red sky and ash waste away.

Adam finally smiled, though it was anything but humoured.

* * *

Gardner was terrified.

He was crouched as best as his 140-plus old body would allow, hiding behind a clutch of bushes that ran round one whole side of the compound below. There were patchy-uniformed mercenaries slowly patrolling the compound, occasionally stopping to light a tobacco-filled tol-stick, and take long drags from it. They weren't especially heavily armed, but they didn't look soft either.

The compound itself was sunk into a large pit, a perfectly circular hole the only indication that anything was down there. Although he couldn't yet see into the hole, he knew there was a habitat the size of a small mansion down there, with escape tunnels, a shuttle hangar, and even a collection of alien-designed pools. High walls surrounded the equally circular garden, topped with security lights and scanners.

He knew all this because the compound had been a safehouse for Kombat 3899 some years ago, but was now in the hands of a private enterprise, after Caine's spectacular takedown of 3899 two years ago. The compound, however, was still the same as it had been before, with the same security, and the same paths of patrol.

Gripped tightly in his hands was an old custom plasma rifle, modified with a large scope, and a chunky flash suppressor wrapped around the long silencer. It felt good to be handling a weapon again: before joining Navy Intelligence, he had been an Army sniper, one of the best.

But that was a hundred or so years ago.

Now he was old and decrepit, and terrified out of his mind.

There was an alarmed shout from somewhere he couldn't see. It was time. He pulled the scope to his eye, and swept the rifle around. The nearest guard whipped his head around at the noise, his back finally to Gardner.

Despite his trembling hands, Gardner kept the powered plasma rifle steady, the crosshairs in the scope centred on the back of the guard's head. He squeezed the trigger almost effortlessly, and the guard's head disappeared in a cloud of red vapour. The lifeless body dropped to the ground.

He was already searching for another target.

Another guard, another shot, another dead body.

Two more were sat in a crow's nest on top of the armoured wall, tol-sticks falling from their shocked unmoving mouths. Their weapons were coming up as Gardner shot them both through the chest —they were too far away for him to get an accurate headshot.

There was an explosion that overloaded the scope's night vision and infrared, the fire blossoming from the underground mansion.

Seconds later, Hadjkai-Caine came running across the grass, dragging a bespectacled human male, who himself was carrying a suitcase, his legs almost unable to keep up with the bigger, faster human.

Hadjkai-Caine filled his recovered scope for a brief second, and Gardner felt his finger begin to tighten on the trigger. But Caine sped out of view, and then bounded over the bushes, straight past Gardner, without so much as a sideways glance.

The *Kara Marazov* came hurtling out of the sky, and landed inside the walled complex, kicking up leaves and dust into the air.

"*Get in, Doctor,*" Hadjkai growled at the simpering human. The scientist —whom Gardner recognised from his time with 3899 as a Dr. Paverson- seemed to have already wet himself, judging by the patch covering the groin of his trousers. He clambered up the ladder rungs, and into the ship. Hadjkai turned on Gardner, putting his tattooed face close to his. The older man almost voided his bowels and bladder then and there.

"*I know you were going to shoot me just then, Lenson Gardner. I won't forget it.*"

"What makes you say that I had any intention of doing such a thing?" Gardner asked. He fingered the trigger of the rifle in his hand, ready for action, despite the terror he felt at being so close to someone so universally dangerous, who was so ready to kill him.

Hadjkai seemed about to laugh when his eyes flicked to one side. Gardner frowned, his curiosity getting the better of him, and turned round to see what the creature was looking at. But there was nothing there but bushes and spotlights.

"Something wrong?"

Hadjkai looked at him sharply.

"*Nothing is wrong.*"

He jumped up the ladder, several rungs at a time, leaving Gardner flabbergasted.

* * *

He had seen a figure, a shadow, just in front of the bushes surrounding the underground mansion complex. He had heard a voice. He had *his* voice. He refused to believe that anyone could have escaped from the mind-prison he had devised.

You better start believing fuck-face, an invisible voice said as Hadjkai entered the *Kara Marazov*.

You will never have this body back, Caine. I am stronger than you.

And yet I escaped.

Yes, but not for long. Your kind is obsolete in this universe. You have no place here. You should have stayed in the twenty-first century.

There was a dry chuckle from the wall beside him.

If you have access to my memories, you know that is not a reality. You are in my body. I am taking it back. You cannot stop me. And once you are gone, I will destroy your brothers. Another chuckle. *The memory thing works both ways. Your kind is also obsolete; you fuckers should have died out millennia before I was even born.*

A vision of a bearded Caine appeared before him and then flickered away again. There was a lingering smile before he disappeared.

It is my destiny to rule this universe.

There was a weary sigh.

And it's mine to stop people like you. I know that now.

* * *

Caldona III.
HMS Musgrove.

The young woman watched the blocky hospital ship disappear from view above the terminator line, obscured by the sudden rising of the sun over the curved edge of the planet. She watched the planet through the viewports, and decided it was beautiful: the huge green expanses surrounded by equally large lush bright blue oceans.

It was definitely a place she could call home.

"Two minutes to landing at Caldona Base, ma'am," the Terran pilot called from the forward section.

"Thankyou," she replied politely. She didn't know why she needed to be polite, only that it seemed the right thing to do. She looked around at the empty seats, wondering why she was the only one onboard besides the pilot.

The shuttle descended through the atmosphere effortlessly.

When they reached the main base, there was a large shuttle on the huge landing field bearing the markings of the so-called Alliance of Independent Worlds –she had read that her people had recently become a member of the Alliance. The symbols on the sides of the shuttle marked it as belonging to something called the Naval Criminal Investigative Service.

Whatever that was.

Her curiosity was mostly focused on regaining her identity, and on discovering whom the man in her dreams was. He was human, tall, incredibly strong, but not of this universe. She didn't know how she knew that, just that it seemed right. When she saw his face, he felt a deeply intense bond, yet couldn't describe what kind of bond, or why it was important.

The shuttle touched down with a clanking and hissing of its landing claws. The de-pressurisation system hissed, and the shuttle's side-door slid open, a ramp extending to the hardtop. She grabbed her bag –still full of clothing and a memory-heavy digipad from the Wolf Brother and Musgrove's quartermasters–and descended the ramp.

A young medical student named Lukas, a handsome young man similar to her own age, greeted her with a warm smile.

"Welcome to Caldona Base," he said.

"Thankyou," she replied as cheerily as she could.

"I'll show you to your quarters that you've been assigned for the duration of your stay here." He gestured to the edge of the landing pad, past the Alliance shuttle to where a large set of doors awaited them. The shuttle seemed ominously quiet, though she figured its owners were somewhere else.

Lukas began a lecture on the various medical facilities in the base, pointing at different Terran-designed buildings in the distance. It was all extremely interesting and he presented it in a very entertaining way, but the young woman was paying more attention to the Alliance shuttle.

There was something ominous about it all.

The *Musgrove* shuttle suddenly launched into the air with a roar of thrusters, leaving the two alone on the pad with the remaining shuttle. She heard loud footsteps from behind her.

She turned and looked into the eyes of a frightening being.

He was bird-like, with black rubbery skin, a large beak that could snap bones, a ridge over its head, and evil yellow eyes sunk back into its head. She recognised it, a distant and blurred memory of pain done to someone else, but could not remember where or who. She didn't need the memory to know that this creature was pure evil, and something to be very afraid of.

He was pointing a plasma pistol at her.

It talked with a set of black inner lips, its beak clacking as it talked.

"You're coming with me."

* * *

Fullina.

"Members of your intelligence service attacked one of your own protected planets! A planet, I might add, that was put under your protection to protect it from elements of our own damned intelligence service!" High Admiral Scarlett's face was crimson with righteous anger, her rage palpable from a distance.

Premier Du'Gon'ik'La'Lon'ik'Far —Du'Gon for short— shrunk back into his chair. Several of his bodyguards fidgeted warily, eager to put the alien in her place, but aware of how politically and militarily powerful she was, as evidenced by the four hulking armoured Terran Army bodyguards watching over her.

Minister F'Ler was by her side, though his own anger paled in comparison to her, even as he towered over her.

"The operation was illegitimate," Du'Gon whimpered. His cabinet was arrayed around the arguing group, though none seemed interested in what the Terran had to say. "This government had no knowledge of the operation, nor of the involvement of the Okarnagan mercenaries."

Scarlett stopped her rant, glanced at F'Ler and frowned.

"We never mentioned the Okarnagans, Premier."

Horror spread across the fat little alien's face, and he shrunk even more into the large high-backed seat. His cabinet had expressions of outrage and disbelief slapped all over their faces, all of them staring at their elected leader.

"You must have," the Premier stammered. His bodyguards stepped forward to flank their master, though made no move to arm their weapons.

"I am in agreement with the High Admiral, Premier," declared F'Ler. "We never made any mention of the involvement of the Okarnagans. In fact, we were not sure you would believe us since the Okarnagans have long since been missing from our regions of space."

"Who paid you, Premier?" Scarlett demanded. "I noticed that the planet Mertik was accepted into the Alliance in record time. Clearly somebody wanted to... 'Grease the wheels' as they used to say. Who was it, Premier?"

The Premier was silent.

"Are you aware of the planet that was attacked?"

The Premier shook his head.

"Ckeer Najoor." She produced a small holo-projector that immediately lit up, and showed a holographic representation of Ckeer Najoor. "A small peaceful planet with thousands of small farmsteads and only one small city. According to the Terran fleet that responded to the distress signal, an agent of the Mertik intelligence agency led the Okarnagans, using their new association with the Alliance of Independent Worlds as a cover. The reports stated they were after one man: Adam Logan Caine, a time-traveller from Terra's twenty-first century. We do not, however, know why they were after him." She paused to take a deep breath. "He survived, and slaughtered his attackers, with the loss of his wife, daughter, and the planet he called home."

"C-Caine?" the Premier stammered. He was sweating profusely, which for an alien from a lava-covered world was extremely difficult. "You mean The Ghost? The super soldier?"

Scarlett nodded.

The Premier looked at the ground thoughtfully, weighing his options.

"It was the Mertiks. They paid me, and then they paid the Acceptance Committee to accept them into the Alliance. But I had them spied on anyway. The Okarnagans were only pawns, someone to blame the attack on. I do not know what they were called, but the pictures I was sent before my last spy died was of black bird-like beings in red chitinous armour."

There was a confused frown on F'Ler's long green face, and most of everybody else's.

But there was horror on Scarlett's face. Her voice sounded scared.

"The Mertiks and the Okarnagans are working for... The Core?"

* * *

Sansky looked at the hologram like he was about to have a heart attack. More than likely, he was about to suffer from one.

"How can this be, ma'am?" he said, though his voice sounded almost like someone else's given his shock. The figure before him was stood holding a digipad, almost at full scale above the holo-projector in the briefing theatre that had been turned into Sansky's temporary command centre for the taskforce.

"The Premier's description could be no other," Scarlett replied.

"What I meant, Admiral, was how could the Core be controlling the Okarnagans and the Mertik? They couldn't have slipped a fleet past Fort Sentinel at the exit from the Y-40 galaxy, could they?"

"Since the destruction of the Core fleet above the ruins of Terra, Fort Sentinel has been upgraded with the latest in our scanning technology. But then if Caine is right, the Core had some... supernatural help in getting past Sentinel ten years ago, then perhaps they did this time as well."

Raymond sighed, crossing his arms thoughtfully.

"From my own experiences, I wouldn't put it past them."

"My worry is what is their endgame? What do they hope to achieve by capturing Caine? And what comes after that?"

He shook his head.

"According to Adam, Lord Yh'reth'gar was the youngest of seven royal sons. I suppose it's possible that whoever in the Core is behind this might be after revenge. Although it seems a bit like overkill for one man, despite Adam's strength."

"*We received a report from i'lim Minor, an independent ally of ours in Andromeda. Their last report was cut off mid-sentence, but they described ships that were very similar in size, shape, and colour to the Okarnagans that attacked Ckeer Najoor. It looks like they are on the move once again.*"

"What do you need me to do?"

Scarlett's hologram sighed, and put the digipad out of view of the camera.

"*Keep on with this Caine-Hadjkai problem, Raymond. I'm depending on you to handle this. I'll be commanding a mission to confront the Okarnagans directly in Andromeda aboard the Atlantis.*"

"Good luck, ma'am."

Scarlett nodded.

"*To us both, Raymond.*"

M'Der looked at Sansky. "So what now?"

"We need to get to Gorrh before Hadjkai does."

M'Der's eyes narrowed, "Why didn't I think of that?"

Sansky just rolled his eyes.

* * *

I'lim Minor.

The Chieftain surveyed the devastated landscape below as the dropships began to lift off from the surface. He was stood with his face into the wind on a high escarpment that overlooked what was left of the capital city.

He smiled, showing his metal teeth.

One of his lieutenants snapped to attention beside him, managing to deftly avoid the billowing cape.

"Chieftain! There's a message from the forward scouts."

"Let's have it then, warrior."

"They claim that our Far Rider Fleet has either been slaughtered or captured by the Terrans. They do, however, claim that the *Pa'kai* used the Mertiks to control the Far Riders into capturing a Terran."

"Just one?"

The warrior nodded, but didn't quake in the presence of his Chieftain's anger.

"According to the scouts, this Terran is a *super*soldier —even the Terran Navy is afraid of him. They claim that the Far Riders destroyed his world."

"Then they have doomed us." The Chieftain balled his fist and punched it into the palm of his other hand. "The Terrans will surely strike sooner whilst we are still not strong enough to conquer them. Where is this supersoldier now?"

"The scouts believe he is headed for the ancient tombworld of Gorrh, although they do not know why."

The Chieftain nodded.

"Then that will be our next destination."

* * *

The *Kara Marazov* blasted through Gorrh's atmosphere, followed by a control-slaved freighter devoid of life. There was no pursuit: Hadjkai had destroyed the Kra Nal Justice Ministry vessels hiding behind Gorrh's dead moon. They were just pieces of metal flotsam, no threat to him, or to his work.

The freighter was a rental, though he had no intention of returning it, and had decided to slave the controls to that of the Kara's so as not to have to use a crew that could betray him.

The doctor was imprisoned in the secondary bunkroom, the one that seemed to be made up to be a young girl's room. Caine's memories indicated that the room belonged to a teenage daughter —or had until recently. The memories were fading fast, Caine's unbreakable personality having broken free from its subconscious prison.

Even now, he was still seeing hallucinations or manifestations of Caine around him, alternating between glaring at him and sending sadistic smiles his way.

He was jittery, aware that any minute Caine's image could appear and severely distract him from his task. The problem was there wasn't much he could do about it: Hadjkai's control over Caine's body was slipping every moment.

The *Kara Marazov* and its charge flew effortlessly through Gorrh's atmosphere, the larger ship trailing long condensation trails as it followed. They passed over thousands of giant tombs, many topped with skyscraping statues of long-dead conquerors and dictators.

The ships lowered below the lip of a long valley that finished in a spectacular dead-end of rows upon rows of stepped tomb entrances.

The freighter, under Hadjkai's control, spun slowly, and touched down with its manoeuvring thrusters roaring to keep it from just falling out of the sky. Landing claws extended, and the ship crunched heavily to a stop on top of a collection of tombstones on the valley floor. Hydraulics hissed, and gaseous coolant poured from the engines, an old leak in an old ship.

The *Kara* touched down with effortless grace, its curved claws making almost no noise as it landed on an artificial platform of stone.

Hadjkai shepherded his two 'guests' out of the ship, and onto the platform below.

"*You two; use the freighter's cargo lifters to carry the equipment into that tomb.*" He pointed to the largest entrance that opened onto the platform.

"And if we don't?" asked Paverson.

Hadjkai grinned evilly. "Guess."

The human scientist blanched, and scurried away, leaving Gardner to watch the psychotic murderer stride towards the tomb in question.

Dammit, there's got to be a way to beat him.

Gardner sighed, and hurried after Paverson.

* * *

Hadjkai, ignoring the visage of Caine walking imperiously beside him, strode into the darkness of the tomb, following the central passage, holding something in one hand. It was too dark to safely traverse the tunnels without assistance.

He reached to his left, and felt for a metal device he knew from his escape. He flicked something, and the tunnel filled with bright white light. The myriad funeral etchings lining the carved stone tunnel reflected and shaded it eerily, though the lights and shadows didn't affect Caine's image.

He strode on until he came to a large artificial cavern. The walls were covered with runes and warnings of dire threats.

There stood seven plinths in the centre of the room, all set in a circle. Each one had a perfect sphere cradled in flower-like tendrils holding them securely. Each was a different vibrant colour, but one was missing: Hadjkai's.

He pulled the dull red sphere out, making sure he only touched the metal cradle currently holding the sphere, so that he wouldn't touch it and transfer his consciousness back to his former prison. He put the sphere and its cradle onto the claws of the plinth, and stepped back.

"*Soon my brothers, we will all be free once again. I promise you.*"

One of the cargo lifters rolled into the cavernous room, and deposited the incubators in one corner. Gardner was at the controls of the remote machine, watching as the tracked vehicle retracted its loading crane, and turned round to leave the room once more.

Gardner gave him a quick glance over one shoulder then followed the cargo lifter out.

Paverson entered, bringing another lifter in with him.

Using the crane, he placed a pallet of the materials he needed to create what Hadjkai had in mind. He moved to the sides of each incubator, and began plugging them into the cargo lifter's over-sized power core. Each hummed to life, the internal lights and computer displays flickering to life.

A few minutes later, Gardner arrived with the rest of the equipment on the backs of two more cargo lifters. The crane worked quickly to deposit the equipment and supplies, and Gardner powered them down in another corner.

Paverson was quick to connect everything up to a central set of large computer console screens. Holograms leapt to life around Paverson, and he began manipulating the three-dimensional representations of DNA strands and other biometric data.

"This should take a day to physically create the foetuses, and begin the growth process. It should be another twelve hours after the process has started and you'll get your first fully grown clone." He wasn't even looking away from his work. He was completely engrossed in his work –it was a trait that had made him a top choice for Kombat 3899.

"*Excellent doctor,*" smiled Hadjkai. He continued staring at the empty red sphere, though every now and then there were still flicks of his head as if he were seeing something at the corners of his vision.

Gardner wondered what it could be, then silently remarked on how ironic it was that his career had taken a few changes since meeting Caine: first as the head of Navy Intelligence and Kombat 3899, then as a super-max prisoner in Grunhardt, now as a lowly cargo lifter operator.

Life had a sense of humour, and Gardner had yet to see the punch line.

"Soon my brothers. Soon." Hadjkai was clearly muttering to himself.

Gardner found himself, for the first time in his very long life, betting on a hope.

Come on Caine, come back and do what you do best.

* * *

Caldona III.

The creature continued waving the energy pistol, pointing to the Alliance shuttle.

"Why are you doing this?" the young woman asked.

"Because the Patriarch demands your father's head."

"My father?" she wailed. "I don't even know who I am, let alone who my family might be! Who is the Patriarch? And why does he want my father dead?"

The creature backhanded her across the face with one large hand that sent her sprawling. She let out a yelp as the hit split the inside of her mouth. She was on all fours, spitting blood when the creature spoke again.

"The Patriarch is the master of all masters. He is our god and emperor, and he will rule this universe in this life, and the next."

The barrel of the energy pistol was against her head.

"Get up filth," the bird-like creature growled. "Get. In. The. Shuttle. I will not tell you again."

The young woman picked herself up with Lukas' help, and they struggled towards the shuttle. Lukas seemed seriously alarmed that the shuttle belonged to the Alliance, though he didn't voice his concern. He suddenly tripped over a crack in the landing pad, and accidentally dragged the girl down with him.

As she hit the ground, her foot lashed out at the alien's ankle.

The creature went down as well, and the girl jumped on him, wrapping her hands around its wrists. It swore and cursed in its harsh, clicking language, and snapped its beak at her face.

Its taloned finger twitched accidentally during the struggle, and the pistol flashed close to her face. Pain erupted through her head, and she reeled backward, clutching at her eyes as if they were on fire. They felt like they were, but she could still see.

Images flashed through her head: the man that had haunted her dreams in various familiar settings, with love in his eyes, and strength in his heart.

Memories began flooding into her brain as she remembered more and more of her forgotten past.

She began hyperventilating, panicking as the memories weren't all good: living in fear for weeks on Odyssey Station, the destruction of the *Gold Royale*, the collapsing of Andromeda's galactic core. But the worst one appeared last: a gun in her hand pointed at a woman she identified as her adopted mother, the gun going off just before a rifle round turned her hand into a bloody mess. Tears streamed down her cheeks as she remembered everything.

"I remember," Evelyn Cassandra Caine whispered.

"Then you will be prepared," the alien clicked. The energy pistol was in its hand, and once again pointed at Eve's head. "My master, the Patriarch, will make a great prize of you. And he will have his revenge on Adam Caine for the death of his youngest son."

There was a loud twang of metal hitting something biological and less sturdy. The alien's head snapped forward, and it pitched forward onto the landing pad face-first.

Eve looked up at Lukas, with a grateful smile on her face.

Lukas dropped the digipad he had used as a makeshift weapon, and helped Eve to her feet.

"I-I have never done that before. Violence is unheard of on Caldona Base."

"You get used to it," she snorted.

"So who are you then? The Base's commander has no clue either. His superiors kept it classified."

"My name is Eve Caine. Or at least it was."

"Was?" he looked at her questioningly.

She looked at the base, and yet seemed to be looking far away into the distance. She gave a long sigh. "I killed my Mum. I can't go back to that life; I don't want to, as much as I love my Dad. He'd never forgive me. To be honest, I'm not sure I can forgive myself."

She looked at the Alliance shuttle.

"Maybe this is an opportunity to start afresh, as you humans say."

"You're only sixteen."

She shrugged, "I had a good teacher."

"Then I'm coming with you."

She smiled. "Sorry, just me."

She retrieved the energy pistol from the unconscious warrior and then vaporised the body. She ignored the shocked look on Lukas' face, and then limped towards the Alliance shuttlecraft. She stroked the letters NCIS and decided it was a good place to start.

* * *

Kra Nal homeworld.

Raymond Sansky strode through the halls of the Justice Ministry in full duty uniform, with M'Der in tow. The two bodyguards had been sent back to the

Wolf Brother after the arrival of the rest of Sansky's taskforce direct from Ckeer Najoor.

"Where are we going?" asked the historian, though Sansky had his doubts on just what his friend had been before either had met Adam Caine.

"To the *Wolf Brother*, and then Gorrh. Captain Crown is anxious to get under way."

"The Okarnagans?"

"Their fleet is still at I'lim Minor; the *Atlantis* battlegroup is moving towards them, though there is no guarantee that they will be there in time to catch them."

"Why is the *Wolf Brother*'s group being sent to Gorrh, and not to assist in the fight against the Okarnagans? I would have thought the Terran Navy would be eager to get to grips with them."

"Yes, but both myself and Scarlett agree that what's happening on Gorrh is just as important. You know how powerful and influential Adam is. Something needs to be done. If your people had their way, they'd cover the whole thing up from the rest of the universe."

They both strode through to the gigantic landing platform above the Ministry's headquarters.

A shuttlecraft awaited them, its pilot already finishing his prep.

The shuttle took them up to the massive starfighter carrier, *Wolf Brother*, still accompanied by two of the Kra Nal's Justice cruisers, and now joined by the surviving starships of Sansky's original taskforce.

The *Super-Six-Four* remained in orbit at one of the Kra Nal's repair stations, whilst *King's Herald* and *Wisconsin* flew above and below the carrier. The rest of the force consisted of four cruisers, nine gunships, a modified pair of destroyers, and a multitude of starfighters still in their hangars.

The Terran ships disappeared into the Linkway, followed quickly by the Kra Nal cruisers.

Raymond hoped it would be enough.

* * *

HMS Atlantis.
Orbit of I'lim Minor.

The massive *Crusade*-class Dreadnaught dwarfed everything around it, but all that was left were the accompanying Terran fleet: two starfighter carriers, twenty battleships, forty cruisers, and eighty destroyers, frigates and gunships.

Atlantis' bridge was quiet, High Admiral Scarlett, her aide Lieutenant Commander Gorsson, and *Atlantis*' commander Commodore Ty all stood round a holographic representation of the planet below.

"There's nothing left, my Lady," announced Ty. "The planet's been scoured; bombarded from space. If I had to guess, I would say they used mass drivers to throw asteroids from orbit: anything not destroyed by the impacts would die from the nuclear winter."

The petite First Star Lady folded her arms across her chest.

"Are there any survivors?"

Ty shook her head. "None, ma'am."

She sighed. "Is there any sign of where the Okarnagans went?"

"No, ma'am," replied the taller woman. "And none of the prisoners Vice-Admiral Sansky captured would know either, since they weren't a part of this destruction."

"Contact any nearby bases, see if they have any weird ship movements near their sectors."

Gorsson hurried off to the communications controller on the other side of the massive five-storey bridge. For an hour, he was chattering enthusiastically, until he returned to the senior officers with a digipad in one hand.

"My Lady, none of the local bases have detected anything. However, the *HMS Klaus Reigart* sent out a distress signal ten minutes ago; before the signal was cut off, the ship's XO described the ships as black with red detailing. They were in the Linkway, and the attackers were heading in the direction of Sector 478 in the Small Magellanic Cloud."

"The direction of Gorrh," noted Ty, pinching the bridge of her nose.

"Precisely, ma'am."

Scarlett turned to Ty. "Prep the fleet, set course for Gorrh. Maybe we can head them off."

Ty nodded and moved away to her crew.

"Do you think they're headed for Gorrh, ma'am?"

Scarlett shrugged. "If they're working for the Core, then there's a distinct possibility."

Beneath their feet, the massive Dreadnaught came to life; the distant rumble of the engines could be briefly heard over the hustle and bustle of the ship's bridge. Scarlett watched with pride as the crew of her flagship went about their daily duties.

Soon, she knew, they would be tested.

Gorsson approached again, a confused frown on his face.

"My Lady, we just received a report from the commander of Caldona Base."

"Oh?"

"Apparently they were due to receive a patient from the *HMS Musgrove* and the *Wolf Brother*. The base commander confirms that the shuttle from the *Musgrove* landed, and delivered the patient. Unfortunately, the patient never made it off the landing pad. An unknown alien attempted to kidnap her."

"Her?"

"The record lists her as 'unknown Mertik female.' The base commander was under Sansky's orders to keep her identity a secret. He adds that there was an Alliance NCIS long-range shuttle on their landing pad for several hours before the patient went missing along with the shuttle."

"More mysteries," she harrumphed.

* * *

Gorrh.

A day later.

Adam woke with a hangover. His head hammered at itself with a ten-tonne weight, whilst his entire body felt like it was being burned along his veins and arteries. He cried out, and writhed around, only to find his wrists and ankles clamped to a table.

Dammit, not again.

He was thankful, however, that his body was once again his own.

All he could see was his beloved late wife. He was dreaming –behind her was just blank white, no background at all. In all the excitement of escaping, the pain of his massive loss had dulled, pushed aside for necessity.

Now it came full force when he looked into his beloved's eyes. Tears welled up in him, streaming down his cheeks.

"I'm so sorry, Polly. I couldn't save you or Eve."

"Eve will be fine," she said, stroking away his tears. "She is her father's daughter." Her proud beautiful smile broke his heart all over again.

"And her mother's daughter," he croaked. "This is a dream right? This isn't another Matrix-style inner universe is it?"

"Something like that."

Adam groaned, "I hate this supernatural crap."

"I know, my Obi-Wan Kenobi. But I heard what you said to Hadjkai, about your destiny."

"I was just countering his statement, nothing more."

There was a sad smile on Polly's beautiful face.

"No you weren't; you meant every word. You have a great destiny ahead of you, Adam. And I'll be with you every step of the way." She stroked his cheek again, and leaned down, kissing him ever so softly on his forehead.

He blinked.

He looked around to find himself in a massive stone-built square room, surrounded by medical machinery, with alien writing carved into them. An older bespectacled human man was stood over him, adjusting holographic controls over the bed.

"He's awake," the older man announced to someone Adam couldn't see.

"*Well done, Paverson,*" the voice of Hadjkai said.

Adam turned his head, and looked into his own face.

Hadjkai chuckled at the surprise on Adam's face.

"*Welcome back to the land of the living, Adam Caine. Before you strain your brain, I have had you cloned. Your body is strong, stronger than any mortal being in this universe. Me and my brothers will use these clone bodies to rule the nineteen galaxies.*"

"Like hell you will."

Hadjkai smiled, and gestured with a long sweep of his arm. Adam saw more versions of himself. Each one was different, with different hairstyles, different tattoos, and even different coloured eyes, but they were all him, fully grown, the same age as him. Oddly enough, none of them had Adam's short hair and trimmed beard.

They all smiled in concert, none of which comforted him.

"That's strangely disconcerting," he said sarcastically. "So what now, arsehole?"

"*Arsehole?*" Hadjkai, in his new meat suit, chuckled. "*Interesting cursive. You are as defiant as ever. You have an interesting mind, Adam Caine. Full of pain and violence, yet you still hold onto the softer side of life: love and hope. A strange contradiction for a former Special Boat Service NCO, wouldn't you say?*"

Adam snorted derisively. "What the hell do you know about the SBS?"

"*I made it a point to look the term up. I was rather surprised: your name pops up two thousand years ago in relation to the unit —a unit which was disbanded at the same time as your beloved Royal Marines. The SBS, as you call it, was a black operations unit, committing acts of sabotage, murder, and mayhem in the name of your country.*"

"Murder?" Adam grumbled, though in fairness he didn't protest too much. He knew his past, and his past actions, and had made peace with his time in the SBS. He wasn't about to let some alien super-villain dredge those memories up for some kind of kick.

"*Yes, you're past is riddled with bodies. Perhaps we are more alike than I gave you credit for, Caine. Or should I say Obi-Wan?*"

Adam felt the old anger flow through him once again, and he strained against the restraints, and roared defiantly. The smiles on the faces of the identical-looking clones disappeared in an instant.

Hadjkai was chuckling mirthlessly, however.

"*In your mind, you know that you have always struggled with your anger at the world. For years you have shown the world a calm and collected appearance, yet underneath there has always been a raging psychopath desperate to get out. Your attempt to have a quiet family life ended in violence, as you knew it always would.*"

"Go fuck yourself," said Adam as emotionlessly as he could.

"*I would prefer not to. You said before it is your destiny to stop people like me. How will you do that tied to that bed?*"

Adam smiled for the first time with humour.

"You've seen my mind, my memories. You know it's never stopped me before."

Hadjkai's face —or Adam's face depending on one's viewpoint- fell, fear spreading when one of the clones came running in, a plasma rifle in one hand.

"*Hadjkai, Terran Navy vessels just arrived in orbit with two Kra Nal cruisers.*"

Hadjkai moved towards the tunnel entrance with his brothers, then turned back with a evil smile on his face to look at Caine. His smile dropped when he saw that Caine's bed was empty. Panic rose in him. Gardner held a knife in one hand, the bindings on the bed open and limp.

Caine was nowhere to be seen.

"*Noooooooo!*" he screamed, anger and wrath building inside of him. "*Damn you Caine!*"

There was a chuckle that sounded like Caine's voice coming from the entrance tunnel, echoing more and more as its owner moved away from them faster and faster.

Hadjkai shot Gardner half a dozen times in the chest with a plasma pistol, then led the way out of the tomb/prison.

The brothers, leaving behind the seven coloured dull spheres and a rather confused Dr. Paverson, charged through the tunnels, and out into the daylight. Hadjkai spat and shouted as the Kara Marazov blasted into the air, and down the valley, leaving a cloud of dust in its wake.

* * *

"We've reached orbit of Gorrh," announced Captain Crown.

"Thankyou, Captain." Sansky turned to Lieutenant Colonel Fordram, the commander of the taskforce's limited Army detachments. "Colonel, gather as many of your troops as you can for a ground assault." He then turned to Fordram's starfighter wing temporary opposite number. "Squadron Leader... Feyton, is it? I realise that in Wing Commander Salva's absence it falls on you to command his wing, but you are the senior squadron commander. Have your squadrons launch immediately."

Feyton nodded, and accompanied Fordram off the bridge.

Sansky watched them go, and noticed their unsubtle glances at each other. He wondered why they were hiding it when everybody knew they were an item. He hoped that in the next few hours, they wouldn't regret their decision to pursue the relationship.

He returned his attention to Crown, and the holographic simulation of Gorrh itself. The surface was a mishmash of hundreds of thousands of random stone structures, including some of the biggest statues he had ever seen. There were hundreds of life-signs, but the bizarre nature of the planet's surface made the readings untrustworthy.

"Admiral," the sensors operator called out. "The sensors are detecting a small ship in the planet's lower atmosphere. It is currently holding an anchored position thirteen miles above the planet's surface. I am also detecting a powered down unmanned freighter directly below it, and some bizarre energy readings."

"What kind of energy readings?"

"I am not sure, sir. Our sensors are not calibrated to analyse these kinds of energy. We would need a science vessel."

"Which we don't have," Sansky pointed out.

"Whatever it is, it is probably what we are after," Crown pointed out from beside Sansky. The ship commander was stood, arms folded, watching status reports from across the *Wolf Brother* itself, not actually watching what Sansky was looking at. The vice-admiral smiled; Crown had a habit of ignoring all else besides the needs of his own ship.

"Sir, the Kra Nal cruisers are heading into the planet's atmosphere."

"Dammit," cursed Sansky. He turned to the Army detachment's bridge liaison. "Get those troop transports in the air now."

* * *

Fordram and Feyton were stood at the entrance to her squadron's hangar.

Some of the 690th Squadron's pilots were waiting for her beside her fighter, though all had the sense not to look in the direction of the two senior officers embracing. When they had finished kissing, Fordram continued holding her in his big arms, his armour making the embrace awkward.

They let go of each other, and looked into each other's eyes.

"You still owe me that drink, Jarna," he smiled.

"Well then, you better come back in one piece then hadn't you?" She jabbed an accusing finger at the chest piece of his grey armour. "I expect a grunt like you can handle that kind of responsibility, yes?"

He put on a mock look of anger. "Well in that case, flygirl, you better hold yourself to that same responsibility."

She held her own mock look of anger for all of five seconds, until a beaming smile appeared on her face. They hugged again, and she strode off towards her waiting pilots, leaving him watching her rear wiggling around in her flight suit.

"Attention on deck!" shouted Flight Lieutenant Grace. The pilots snapped to attention as one, trying to hide their smirks.

"At ease," ordered Feyton. She took one last look behind her, and watched as Fordram snapped his helmet on, and gave her a mock salute, tapping two fingers above his glowing right eye. She returned the salute, and returned her attention to her pilots.

"Alright people, for now this is going to be a standard patrol sortie. The 690th will lead the way, coordinating overall actions." The other squadron commanders joined the group. "77th and 431st Squadrons will escort the Army transports down to the surface. 10th, 876th, and 5139th Squadrons will run patrols around the planet, with the rest of us taking up positions around the fleet." She looked at the other commanders. "Any questions?"

One hand went up, belonging to the commander of the 876th.

"Is it true we could expect Okarnagans on this mission?"

Feyton nodded. "As crazy as that sounds, it looks like the old enemy are back. There is the possibility that they could show up here, hence why most of us will have to stay in orbit with the fleet."

There were looks of concern and confusion among the pilots arrayed in front of her.

"Don't think about it, that's what you have me and the vice-admiral for. Anymore questions?" There weren't. "Good. Commanders, to your squadrons;

690th to your fighters. Let's get in the air." The group broke up, leaving Grace and Feyton alone with her fighter.

"Is this for real? The Okarnagans?" he asked.

She nodded, "Afraid so, Sam."

Grace swore loudly, making some of the nearby deck crew flinch reflexively.

"Why the hell are we here, at the tombworld of all places?"

Feyton shrugged. "Sansky believes it could be universally important. Not only that, an old friend of mine is in trouble down there." When Grace frowned, she explained. "His name is Caine; although I haven't seen him in nearly ten years, I still owe him for saving my life."

"Who is he?"

"I never really got the chance to find out, but he's one of the good guys."

Grace sighed, but nodded, and headed for his own blocky Rhino starfighter.

Feyton jumped up the ladder, and into her cockpit. Her crew chief pushed her helmet onto her head, strapping it under her chin, and pulling the visor down. She clipped the facemask on, and began her quick pre-flights, powering the craft up. The Rhino's four engines roared to life, and the fighter rocked noticeably on its launch cradle.

All around her, the rest of her squadron were doing the same.

Her crew chief gave her the thumbs up, and she returned the gesture, before sliding back the canopy, and locking it in place.

She goosed the anti-gravs, lifting the ship off the cradle, and then slammed the throttle forward. 8gs pushed her into her flight chair, and the fighter raced through the hangar's forcefield and into open space.

Her scanners showed that the rest of the squadron was right behind her. Either side of the squadron's hangar, the rest of the Wolf Brother's fighters and bombers raced into space, and towards their assigned duties. Fighters from the other ships joined them in formation.

Feyton flicked open the squadron's comm channel.

"This is 690 Leader, all pilots report in."

All of the 690ths pilots reported in random order, all green across the board.

"Form into flights, and begin the patrol."

* * *

Colonel Fordram, in full combat armour, walked out into the hangar currently occupied by the Army detachment's dropships. Normally it would have been used for heavy bombers, but none were available for the *Wolf Brother.*

Fordram was in command of over five hundred soldiers of the Fleet Protection Group, all of which had been gathered from across the taskforce to be grouped here in this hangar.

"Colonel," a soldier said, with Major's pips on his chest plate. It was Ager, Fordram's second-in-command, carrying a modified plasma carbine, same as his own. "Everybody's ready and raring to go, sir."

Fordram clapped an armoured gauntlet on his friend's shoulder.

"Let's get going then," he said as emotionlessly as possible. His mind was still on the woman he had just left behind. He flicked on the external helmet speakers. "Listen up people!" he shouted. Immediately, everybody in the hangar stopped still and looked towards him intently. "Two minutes to launch! Mount up, and prepare for takeoff!"

"Yes, sir!" the entire room shouted in reply.

Ager stood by his side.

"Have you read any of the intelligence files on Gorrh, sir?"

"None whatsoever," Fordram said a little too cheerily. Ager glared at him as best he could whilst the other watched the hundreds of armoured troops file into the camouflage-painted troop transports.

"Oh good," said Ager, "I thought it was just me. Have I ever told you how much you inspire me, colonel?"

Fordram snorted, and strode towards the small command transport.

"What?" Ager cried innocently. "What?"

* * *

"Admiral," a comms officer shouted across the bridge.

Sansky sighed at the potential for another crisis. He crossed the massive bridge to stand at the junior-grade Lieutenant's shoulder. The young officer flinched at his presence, but tried to maintain some dignity.

"What is it, Lieutenant?"

She pointed to a holographic display on her right.

"Sir, we received a transmission from the *HMS Culter Cleuch Shank.* They claim to have been attacked by a small group of black-and-red warships that appeared from the Linkway, assaulted them and simply downloaded their entire computer database."

"What's their status?"

"Disabled, sir. But they're relatively intact. Captain Keenan reports that the enemy seemed merely interested in staying in one piece and retrieving their database."

"In one piece?" asked Crown, appearing suddenly by Sansky's side. "That doesn't sound like the Okarnagans that attacked Ckeer Najoor."

Sansky nodded. "You're right. Does Keenan say anything else?"

"No, sir, but he sent detailed scans of the attacking ships." The officer brought up holographic displays of the ships in question, one at a time. Sansky looked at the ships, and realised one of them was different to the others. He touched the graphic of the ship, and enlarged it. It was like the others, but it had gigantic antennae and communications spikes all across its bow and flanks.

"Command and Control maybe?" posited Crown.

Sansky could only agree. "It must act as a forward control ship for the fleet behind. They attack the Culter Cleuch Shank, download as much of its operational guidelines, fleet command codes, etcetera as they could before skulking back to the Linkway."

"Why not destroy the Shank?" asked Crown.

"Leave survivors to tell the tale of the horror of the attack maybe? Or perhaps they simply didn't have the time to finish the Shank off?" The latter theory seemed more plausible to both officers, given that the Shank was a specialised hostile-environment warship, and was bigger and more heavily armoured than its opponents.

Sansky suddenly had a thought. He plunged his hands into the trouser pockets of his uniform, and dug out a data storage device.

"Plug this in to your console, use the codes and frequency supplied within. When it's set up, send this message: Sansky to Project Lympstone. Have a mission for your best-trained squad; the General is involved, and could possibly need assistance as well. Will send specifics after confirmation of involvement. Sansky out."

He nodded to the officer, who sent the message, and returned the device back to him.

Crown frowned at him, but Sansky smiled.

"Specialists. Better you don't know."

* * *

Evelyn –Eve- re-read the letter she had written.

She hoped it was succinct enough that her father wouldn't finish reading it halfway through from grief. She knew her father: he would be upset by the content of her letter. But there was nothing she could do about it: she had to send it.

After plotting a course to the long-range shuttle's original base, she sat back in the pilot's chair, and re-read it yet again:

Daddy.

I am so sorry for what happened. You know I could not help it. I wish so much that there could have been another way. And I wish I could have been as strong as you, and as well trained; then I would have had the strength to resist my biological mother's control.

I will never forgive myself for shooting mummy.

I do not expect you to, but I hope one day you will forgive me.

I love you so much Daddy, but please don't follow me; you won't find me, and I don't intend to let you either. I know I'm only young, and you'll undoubtedly try to find me, but as I said, you won't find me –you taught me well, daddy.

Goodbye daddy.

I love you.

* * *

The *Kara Marazov* hung above Gorrh's surface like a moon orbiting the planet. The ship was motionless, rigidly still against the high winds. If it was sentient, it would be crying, or keening. Its master was in pain, and it could do nothing to alleviate it.

Adam stood in the open doorway, a paper copy of Eve's letter limp in one hand.

He couldn't bear to look anymore and headed into the cockpit. He slumped into the pilot's chair, and leaned back, looking out at the grey landscape above and below the Kara. It was a bleak planet, and it was even worse in the cockpit with him. The lights were off, and he had no intention of turning them on just yet.

He was encompassed in grief and pain.

It surrounded him as surely as did the darkness of the room around him, like a mist hanging round a solitary solemn mountain. Tears streamed down his cheeks, and his shoulders shook as he tried desperately to control the sobs that came hand-in-hand with the tears. His head was hung low, chin against chest, his arms draped pathetically over the arms of his high-backed chair.

Dim light from outside glinted off something solid and metal in one of his limp hands.

It was a gun, a firearm in fact; a solid-round weapon in an age of lasers and force fields, it was a rare and antiquated thing to see, but a dangerous thing nonetheless —more so in Caine's hands.

The Walther P99 —the same weapon he had recovered from a trophy cabinet on the Core Lord's flagship- was fully loaded, the action cocked, and its safety flicked to the off position.

Someone was screaming his name in the distance, but he ignored it, the noises around him sounding as if he was underwater, muffled, distant, and ultimately unimportant. His mind replayed his worst nightmare over and over, and all it did was add to his utter misery. His worst nightmare had indeed happened: she had been taken from him.

She had been taken from him.

The streams of tears became rivers, and he held the gun up higher, looking at the straight lines of the barrel and the serial number scratched off.

Then he pointed the barrel at himself, and stared into its darkness.

Her little green face kept coming unbidden to his mind, and the shouting and screaming continued in the background.

He didn't care anymore.

Why should he?

His finger tightened on the trigger.

Goodbye, Adam Caine.

He squeezed the trigger. The hammer slammed forward. There was a loud crack and a boom, and the action slammed backwards. The casing ejected sideways, and the bullet jumped out of the barrel.

And then the darkness took him.

And he was still awake.

"Wha-?"

There was a hand holding his arm, the pistol in his own hand, pointed just far enough away that the bullet had missed his head, and impacted on the bulkhead behind the rear chair.

"Who?"

He looked up into the face of his beautiful wife.

"Polly?" He searched for words, and yet could not express his confusion besides a goldfish-like expression with his lips. "H-how?"

She didn't say anything at first, just smiled. There was something different about her though, as it had been on Gorrh's surface: she appeared as she had when she had first fully come into his life from the *Icarus*. She looked younger, with shorter hair, and her skin was pale from her time in the artificial environment of the *Starship Icarus*. And yet, there was something older in her eyes.

"You're just a figment of my imagination," he stated.

"If that is what you wish to believe," she replied, that same beautiful smile on her lips.

"You don't sound like her," he pointed out.

She shrugged, and moved around him, her eyes never leaving his.

"I am a projection of your will and destiny. A reminder, if you like, of the destiny you recently accepted as your own. And you *do* have a great destiny ahead of you."

"You mean stopping Hadjkai isn't it?"

"You know it is never as easy as that, my love."

He stood up, dropping the pistol from his hand. He reached out to Polly, and was shocked to discover his hand pass through her as if she wasn't there.

"This is a whole new level of weirdness."

"And yet, you are not disturbed by it."

"*That's* why it's weird. So what now? You haunt me until I fulfil this so-called destiny?" Despite his anger at being used by the universe once again, he desperately wanted to hold her, and kiss her. But he knew he couldn't, and it tore him up inside. "Why should I? I've lost my family and my home; why should I care about the universe anymore?" He retrieved the pistol once again, feeling the weight of it in his hands.

"Because the universe cares about you, *General*."

The use of that title was a slap to the face. A reminder, she had said. He stared at the gun in his hand once again, and thought about his past, and what he had set up for the future.

"Lympstone..."

"*...is* the future," she finished for him. "You know what is to come; especially now you know the Core is behind the destruction of Ckeer Najoor, and the Mertiks and Okarnagans are working for them. You unwittingly set this chain of events off with the death of Yh'reth'gar's grandfather, thus opening the door for the Patriarch to want vengeance against you. You set this in motion, and you are the only one capable of finishing it."

He couldn't deny some of what she was saying, though he didn't agree that he was the only one. He was, however, sure that he could make a difference right here and now.

He sighed; once again, he knew he would have to commit unspeakable acts in the name of defending others.

He nodded, blinked, and realised Polly was gone, taking his heart with him.

He stalked into his bunkroom, ignoring the pictures of Polly and Eve strewn about the place by Hadjkai. He opened the locker under the bed, and pulled out an old uniform. It had been repaired long ago, and had faded with age. But the *Icarus* unit patch was still emblazoned on the shoulder. Underneath it sat an SA-80 and enough magazines to take down an army.

"Let's do this."

* * *

"Admiral!" the sensors operator shouted. "The *Kara Marazov* is moving!"

Sansky was already moving towards the command pulpit, calling for the holographic display to activate. Nothing could prepare him for just how quickly the ship descended, straight towards the surface. It overtook the Army transports, and blasted past the hovering Kra Nal cruisers.

It suddenly halted to a stop, and a single life-form jumped out of its airlock at a height equivalent to three storeys, which then disappeared from the sensors.

Adam, he thought.

The ship launched off again, and returned to its vigil far above the surface.

So he's back in the fight. Sansky smiled. *Good.*

* * *

Hadjkai saw the *Kara Marazov* from a distance. He saw Caine jump from its wing, and disappear into the myriad statues and tombs.

He saw it, and he panicked.

Terran transports were descending through the atmosphere overtaking the slow Kra Nal cruisers, escorted by several squadrons of Terran Rhino starfighters.

This was going to get bad.

* * *

The Command & Control ship exited the Linkway with its escorts, its commander seething with anger at the Chieftain's slight against him. He was under orders to monitor the pending battle from afar, and relay enemy formations and communications.

He had already taken out his frustration on several subordinates, their blood still smeared against the bulkheads where he had killed them.

The ship —and its escorts- had taken up position between the planet's two moons, using the gravitic anomalies created by two lunar gravity masses close together to mask their engines. He despised skulking behind a moon, but the Chieftain was the Chieftain and could not be disobeyed.

"My lord," one of the crew shouted, "We are detecting strange energy emissions coming from directly behind us."

"Be specific," he growled.

"I am unable to, sir," the other replied, his voice quaking with fear. Alarm suddenly filled his face and vocal chords. "Unknown warship de-cloaking directly behind us, my lord! They are powering weapons and shields, and locking onto us."

"Destroy them!" he bellowed.

The ship was smaller than the Okarnagan battleships, and yet it unleashed a torrent of energy fire on the bigger ships. It was sleek and coloured in a khaki green colour that would have been at home in a forest or a grassy plain.

The deck heaved beneath the commander, throwing him to the floor in an undignified heap. The rest of his crew were similarly in disarray, only one barely managing to pull herself back to her station —the weapons officer.

"Shields are down, my lord!" she cried. "Our weapons are gone! The other ships are trying to turn and attack, but the enemy ship is too fast! Wait, a different energy reading. They're teleporting on board the-"

A white light filled the bridge, and suddenly ten black-clad figures appeared, wielding large primitive silenced firearms. They slaughtered the bridge crew almost noiselessly. Then their leader produced a silenced sidearm, and put three rounds through the commander's chest.

The commander lived long enough to realise that the squad leader was not a Terran.

* * *

Colonel Gretop Sojun looked down at the corpse of the ship's commander and smiled. It felt good to be in action again. He had spent too long training.

With a few quick gestures, he ordered the rest of his elite squad to secure the bridge. He tapped the comms device on his wrist.

"Sojun to *RMS Black Knight*. We are aboard, and have secured the enemy's bridge."

"*Acknowledged, Colonel. We've disabled the escort ships. We'll cloak, and remain on-station until you need us.*"

"Roger. Sojun out." He nodded to his communications specialist, who immediately crossed to the nearest computer terminal, and went to work. Outside, through the viewports, the *Black Knight's* visible form wavered, then disappeared from view, the distortion lasting only a second.

"I have a link, sir."

"Sojun to Sansky, come in."

"*I hear you, Colonel,*" came the Terran admiral's reply.

"We have taken control of the Okarnagan Command and Control vessel's bridge. My comms specialist is downloading their database now. After that, we'll try to disrupt their communications."

"Understood, Sojun. Good luck. We may have further need of your services, and that of your rather impressive vessel."

Sojun let out a curse frequently expressed by his beloved General.

"Crap."

* * *

Unaware of the capture of the C&C vessel, and the disabling of its escorts, the Chieftain's fleet emerged from the Linkway. Scout ships and smaller warships arrived first, spreading out on random vectors. Ugly black starfighters rushed out, wave upon wave speeding towards the Terrans and Gorrh.

Then the bigger ships appeared: seventeen large mainline battleships; twenty-three smaller battleships like those seen at Ckeer Najoor; fifty-seven heavy cruisers; twenty regular cruisers; one-hundred-twelve frigates, destroyers, and gunship-sized vessels; there was also a trio of super-heavy capital ships –two carriers, and a dreadnaught. But a ship that could barely fit through the yawning Linkway entrance dwarfed all of them. It dwarfed Gorrh's smaller moon.

A city-ship: a titan.

It thundered through slowly and surely, the other ships like gnats beside it.

Sansky saw the massive city-ship. Inwardly, he quaked with fear: his small taskforce was nothing compared to this thing and its escorting fleet. Outwardly though, for the sake of those around him, he maintained a perfect composure.

"Time to intercept?" he asked patiently.

"Fifteen minutes," answered Crown.

Silently, he knew it was going to be a long fifteen minutes.

* * *

Fordram was not aware of any danger until it reached out and smashed one of his transports apart. Sat in the cockpit of the command transport, reviewing the data coming in on the ship that had overtaken them towards the surface, he had never suspected a thing.

Then the pilot shouted a warning of a missile lock.

Confused, Fordram had craned his neck to peer round the pilot's chair, and look out of the cockpit window. Four missiles snaked up from the ground on long white contrails.

The pilot suddenly twisted the transport, and one missile went by underneath. The other three hammered against the nearest transport, obliterating it completely. The crew and troops didn't even have a chance to scream for help. A large fireball, and a hundred men died in an instant.

"Get us on the ground *now*," he growled to the pilot.

"Trying, sir."

"Where are those damn starfighters?"

684

Just as he said that, two flights of Rhinos from the 77th blasted past the command transport, spitting energy fire at the unseen missile emplacements. Explosions blossomed on the surface as it sped closer and closer towards them. The starfighters pulled away, splitting off into pairs and climbing back into the sky.

Thrusters roared as the transports slowed their descent.

"Forty seconds to landing, Colonel," the pilot announced.

He relayed the information back to his men, and braced himself for the inevitable thunderous jolt of a hard landing. It came a lot sooner than forty seconds, and he heard several complaints from his troops.

The first soldiers out of the troop bay were quick to report the firing of automated defences around the valley they had landed in, as well as the lack of life forms around them. Fordram ran out of the troop bay clutching his carbine tightly. Panic was spreading through his troops: sustained combat was not what they were trained to do, and now they were pinned by incoming fire from unseen positions.

This wasn't going to be as easy as Admiral Sansky had hoped.

* * *

Feyton rolled her Rhino over so that she could see the incoming Okarnagans.

The squadrons accompanying the Army transports had already reported they were under fire, and one of the transports was lost. She desperately prayed it wasn't the command transport, and that Fordram was alright.

Now 690th Squadron was moving past the *Wolf Brother*, along with the others of the patrol. The fighters sped past the remaining battleships of the taskforce, the sensors going crazy with the sheer amount of starfighters ahead of them.

She clicked on the comms.

"All fighters form up on me. Flying V formation by flights."

There was a chorus of acknowledgements. Her scanners showed the rest of her wing form up behind her, each flight of four craft making up a part of the wings of the giant V-shape.

"Go weapons free," she ordered. "Conserve your fuel; let them come to us. This is going to be intensely rough, ladies and gentlemen. Keep your wingman safe, and trust in them and the rest of your squadron mates. Good luck."

Her targeting computer nearly overloaded with the sheer amount of possible targets ahead. She had to compensate by only targeting the nearest squadron of enemy ships. The ugly fighters closed the gap remarkably fast, pulling away from the comfort and protection of their motherships.

Wolf Brother, *King's Herald*, and *Wisconsin* punished them for it. The three big ships unleashed a massive fusillade of energy into the oncoming waves of enemy starfighters. Hundreds of starfighters were obliterated before the three Terran capital ships were forced to stop so as not to hit their own.

On her scanners, she saw the *King's Herald* and *Wisconsin* spread out in a defensive formation both sides and forward of the *Wolf Brother*. This was indeed going to get ugly.

Multiple missile locks blared at her, and her holographic HUD was alight with hundreds of targets. Lines of smoke streaked out of the cloud of debris, missiles coming out in waves.

The missiles slammed into the Rhinos at random.

Four craft from the 91st were vaporised by multiple hits, another seven from the 444th, and three each from the 78th (Bomber) and 111th. She saw the indicator signals of two of her own squadron wink out of view.

Then they were into the enemy.

The two forces swept between each other, like fingers from opposite hands interlacing with one another.

Feyton rolled and pulled back on the flight stick to bring her craft into a loop to avoid a flight of the enemy, only to have to repeat the manoeuvre in the opposite direction to break a missile lock, taking her up over the engagement for a few precious seconds. The missile sailed past and out into deep space. She dove back into the fray, keeping her inertial dampeners at 94% to 'keep it interesting' as Grace always joked.

She pushed the fighter into a steep climb, before rolling to port, and falling in behind a pair of black enemy birds that were homing in on a pair of her squadron mates, Seven and Eight. Her wingman, Two, was still to her left, steady as ever.

She stomped on the left yaw pedal and the port target fell into her holographic target reticle, which glowed red as it got a lock. She flicked weapon control over to the plasma cannons in the pointed nose cone, and squeezed the trigger. Grouped pulses of energy flashed out and struck the rear of the enemy fighter.

The rear end disintegrated, exploded, and sent the ship tumbling away to slam helplessly into one of its compatriots.

Her wingman copied her, and blasted the other target apart, leaving behind a fireball.

"*Thanks, Lead,*" commed Seven, before he and Eight made a sharp snap-roll, and dove into a large dogfight towards the centre, where the 78th (Bomber) were being slaughtered.

Twisting her craft this way and that, her comm clicked, and Grace's voice filtered through the speakers in her helmet on their private channel.

His voice was strained, obviously flying his pants off.

"*Lead, this is Five. We're getting pounded. I just lost Six, and I've lost contact with Nine and Ten. Can't get through to the 91st anymore either.*"

"Yeah, I think I just saw the last of the 78th be wiped out."

"*We need to get out of this engagement.*"

"Agreed, but if we don't tie up these fighters, they'll be free to engage the *Wolf Brother*. Besides, Sansky won't like it."

"*I don't think we have a choice; we're going to have to disengage.*"

"Yeah." She flicked it over to the inter-squadron channel. "All fighters retreat to Point Alpha immediately. Try to lose them if you can; no heroics, that's an order. Everybody out now." She flipped her Rhino over onto its starboard wing to slip between two enemy craft that blasted past, firing wildly.

She flicked the comms channel over to secured.

"*Wolf Brother*, this is 690 Lead. We can't hold on anymore. We are retreating to Point Alpha."

There was a pause, and Sansky's voice came through the speakers.

"*Acknowledged, 690 Lead. Once you're out, we'll bracket them.*"

"Understood. Lead out."

Just as she said that, Two erupted into a ball of flame. She heard a brief scream of pain and fear over the comm before he was gone forever. Others were dancing and weaving, fighting for their lives. The blue of the Terran starfighters were becoming fewer and fewer among the black and red of the Okarnagans.

Gods, we'll be lucky if even a few of us make it out alive. She didn't express the thought, but it was foremost in her mind, as she pulled back on the stick, and pointed her craft towards the pre-arranged retreat rendezvous.

She had barely made it to the edge of the engagement zone when everything went white.

* * *

Adam stalked through the forest of tombstones and statues, his feet barely making a whisper of a noise on the stone floor. He crept forward to a position overlooking the valley, with a good vantage point of all sides. Making sure to stay behind the giant foot of a half-wrecked statue, he peered out and looked down below.

Three automated sentry guns were ideally located at one end of the valley to set up a crossfire that had effectively pinned the entire Terran Army company in the shadow of their own dropships.

The starfighters escorting the dropships had disappeared, presumably to join the large fight that had developed in space. The Army company had no air support; the dropships' weapons were designed for close-range anti-troop fire.

He smiled. He would have to change that. He tapped the comms device on his wrist.

"*Kara*. Target the three sentry guns currently firing from the north end of the valley. One missile each should do it; fire when you have a target lock."

"*Acknowledged,*" the computer's reply came. "*Targets locked. Firing.*"

Three streaks of smoke flashed down into the valley, and three fireballs blossomed out from the former positions of the guns.

Smiling, Adam slid down the slope in front of the statue, and bounded across to the nearest destroyed gun. The shadow of the *Kara* dissipated as it once again returned to a safe position.

He saw movement ahead, and gripped the rifle in his hands.

* * *

Smoke and vaporised stone wafted across the valley floor as Fordram watched the black-clad soldier disappear into the forest of tombstones. Whoever it was, it was no Terran soldier, and was an unknown element.

He couldn't believe how quickly the guns had been destroyed with a simple missile strike from above.

The guns had stopped; that was all that mattered.

He charged out of cover, expecting a hot death at any second, but none came. Ager was right behind him, and then the whole battalion was up and on the move.

C Company were already headed for the freighter still powered down on the ground, moving with best possible speed.

Two platoons from D Company stayed to guard the dropships whilst Fordram led the charge towards the destroyed auto guns, his breathing heavy as he continued to carry the weight of his full armour. The holographic display of the inside his helmet visor showed nothing ahead, just random outlines of the tombstones and the men around him.

Comms were quiet, his men professional to the core.

He felt a shadow pass over him, and he glanced up for a second.

It was the private yacht *Red Stallion*, belonging to the civilian consultant accompanying Sansky.

Fordram cursed the Kra Nal historian for his impatience.

"*My scanners show several life-signs ahead, colonel,*" the pilot's disembodied voice said.

"Then keep back next to the dropships." He hoped the civilian would follow his orders –it was a combat zone after all.

There was a sigh from the speakers, "*Alright, colonel.*"

Fordram shook his head in frustration before bounding over a small wall, and taking cover behind a black-iron mausoleum that had vicious spikes around the lips of its roof. The *Red Stallion* span on its central axis, and coasted lazily, almost reluctantly, back towards the dropships, its owner uttering nothing more than a muttered curse.

Fordram sent a comm-message to the troops guarding the dropships to keep an eye on the Kra Nal civilian and keep him in check as much as they could.

He peeked round the corner of the mausoleum, trying to determine if there were any more threats. There was a whistling sound, and the head of the man next to him suddenly exploded, throwing bits of gore and helmet shards across his squad mates. Someone threw up inside his or her helmet, though Fordram didn't see who it was, and nobody owned up to it.

Calls came from around the valley floor of more than one sniper among the tombstones higher up, though nobody could get a fix. Every one of his squads were pinned down, helpless to do anything, lest they join the growing number of dead.

Fordram prayed that whoever had been helping them so far, wasn't about to stop.

* * *

Rarkai, the youngest of the Seven, smiled as another of the Terran soldiers lost his head from his energy rifle. He was having too much fun, taking shots at random soldiers. Most shots just impacted on whatever cover they were hid behind. Every now and then, he would get lucky, and find one slow enough to get caught out, who would then literally lose their heads.

He was lying in the prone position between two tombstones that left him in dark shadows, rifle to his shoulder, scope enclosing his eye socket. He was in a prime killing position.

He, more than any of the others, was a true sociopath –taking immense pleasure only from other people's pain. Among a family of psychopaths, he had committed the most truly heinous crimes, and all for his own amusement. He wasn't interested in power as the others were, just the next victim.

And there were hundreds of potential victims down there, through his scope. Once upon a time, he would have eschewed a sniper rifle; but this was fun, and there was nothing to fear. Not that fear had ever bothered him.

He chuckled as he sighted another soldier.

There was a loud click of metal on metal.

Rarkai turned to look down the barrel of a solid-round pistol. In the last instant of his life, Rarkai was frightened, not just for himself, but also for his brothers. That instant disappeared along with the brains of his clone body, as Caine shot him through the forehead with his Walther P99.

* * *

Tirkai, the other sniper, and the next one up in the age ranking of the seven brothers, pulled away from his scope and looked over at his little brother's sniping position. There was no movement, no sign of his being aware. He turned his rifle around, and looked through the scope at the other position.

There was a shape there, and he was relieved to see that it was the clone body of his brother.

No, wait, he corrected. *He has a beard, and cropped hair; and his rifle is different.*

Tirkai realised that the rifle itself was pointing in his direction.

Panic made him hesitate for a second. It wasn't much of a hesitation, but it was enough. His heart beating faster and faster, he fumbled with the trigger.

Just as his finger tightened, the bullet entered the scope, smashed both ends to pieces, and exited through the back of Tirkai's skull.

* * *

Adam stood up from his own prone position, and slung his sniper rifle over one shoulder, taking up his prized and dependable SA80 once again. Down below in the valley, the Terran soldiers hadn't quite realised they were no longer under attack from the snipers.

Without a hint of emotion, he slipped back into the shadows.

* * *

Fordram saw light reflect off something metallic at what he presumed was one of the sniper spots as he craned his neck to see. No more energy rounds flew down at his position or anyone else's.

Apparently, the Terrans' guardian angel wasn't finished after all.

He saw a glimpse of a soldier dressed in black before it disappeared.

He knew he shouldn't be relying on outside help, but his men were only FPG troopers, not special forces, nor frontline troops. They were simply not equipped or trained for frontline combat like this.

With the immediate threat gone, at least for now, he ordered his troops to break cover, and continue their advance on the target area, albeit as reluctantly as possible.

* * *

"*What the hell was that*?" several pilots screamed.

Feyton had lost consciousness, draped over the flight controls as she was. Her helmet was cracked, and several of her instruments were dull and non-responsive. She looked around, and saw the other fighters of her group in a similar amount of disarray. None were moving, and some were even dark, the indicator dark on her instruments.

Wreckage was everywhere.

And some of it was Terran.

* * *

Crown looked flabbergasted.

"They just blew up their own starfighters with a nuke?"

Sansky was equally taken aback.

"I-" he tried to explain it rationally. "They just wanted a clean shot at us." He held back his fears as he always did, and snapped Crown out of his stupor, placing a firm hand on the shorter Terran's shoulder. "Put the planet between us and the Okarnagans, Captain."

There were bloodcurdling screams of panic from the comms speakers that were cut off suddenly by a brilliant white flash. Sansky braved the actinic flash of the light to see the *King's Herald* come apart from the inside, the suggestion of a long white line issuing from the Okarnagan city-ship.

A super-weapon.

He bellowed in Crown's face. "NOW CAPTAIN!"

* * *

The remaining ships in Sansky's taskforce turned as one, thrusters flaring, sublight engines burning brightly. But it wasn't enough.

Another beam of white light shot out of the city-ship's pointed prow. Although it missed the battleships, it took out the cruisers *Loch Na Keal* and *Vale of Taunton Deane*, the two modified destroyers, and the gunships *Arktown*, *Broadmayne*, *Albecq*, and *Shadoxhurst*, as well as severely damaging the cruiser *Wilson's Pike*, and crippling the cruiser *Barnbarroch*.

The five remaining gunships tailed the battleships.

Just as they rounded the planet, the city-ship opened fire again.

The beam slashed past the *Wolf Brother* and sliced the *Wisconsin* in half, before the ship's power core detonated from the sudden destruction.

* * *

Everybody on the *Wolf Brother*'s bridge stared in mute shock at the *Wisconsin*'s mangled skeletal corpse. The starfighter carrier was beyond the city-ship's explosive touch now, hiding behind the planet's mass along with the remaining gunships.

Sansky turned to find Crown in a heap on the floor. Tears were streaming down his face, and he was sobbing.

Sansky remembered the competitive streak Crown had had with the *Wisconsin*'s captain, his wife. Crown had just seen his wife die right in front of him. He nodded to the medics, who carted away the captain away on a floating stretcher.

"I'm sorry my friend," he said softly to the *Wolf Brother*'s commander.

Through the sobs, the younger man replied, "To hell with you. You brought this on all of us."

Sansky stumbled backwards as if he'd been slapped in the face.

Had he brought this on, by volunteering his force? Had he gotten all those brave men and women killed simply to save his friend? Adam was important, but was he THAT important that hundreds had died for him?

The answer came easily to him: yes.

Adam would die a hundred times over to save others; his family had been destroyed because of the enemies he had made saving *millions*, even billions, of lives. So many owed Adam a great deal.

As did Raymond.

As did everybody.

Right now, however, he could do nothing to help Adam. The starfighters and bombers were either destroyed, or crippled near Gorrh's moons, hopefully away from the engagement zone.

* * *

Feyton's fighter was working, its engines green, and the weapons still active. But many others were not in such good condition. Already she could see sublight engines flaring and dying around her as the other surviving pilots tried to cold-start their craft. One failed miserably and fatally, as a damaged circuit caused a feedback overload, and detonated the small fighter's engines, taking yet another pilot with it.

Feyton had maybe fifteen pilots and craft left, but only eight of them could fly and fight, the rest were stuck in powerless ships, their fighters having been too close to the nuclear explosion to not be affected by the device's EMP. They had no main life support, but their flight suit's emergency supply would keep them alive for approximately two and a half hours.

After that though, they would start dying quickly.

"All craft that can hear me; we need to start-"

There was a scream of a warning from her headset, and suddenly one of the wounded birds exploded, followed by another, and another. Some of the Okarnagan fighters had survived the fratricide their leaders had committed on their comrades. There were maybe twenty of them, firing on the powerless Terrans.

It made Feyton sick to her stomach.

She goosed the throttle, and pulled the fighter into a climb. She was joined by the other eight, who formed up as best they could.

Their ordnance was mostly gone, only a few missiles between the nine of them. It would have to do.

"Pick your targets," she said into her helmet mic, "and fly the best you've ever flown before. Our friends are counting on us beating them. Good luck, and good hunting."

The twenty enemy craft came head-on, in a large gaggle. They must have been low on missiles as well, because not one piece of solid ordnance was launched; their mistake. Those that had missiles in Feyton's adhoc squadron loosed them, taking out five of the enemy before the two sides once again intertwined.

Feyton rolled her Rhino to port, putting it on the tip of its wing, and slipped between two oncoming fighters, loosing off an energy shot that took out the third behind them. She stomped on the yaw pedal, and pulled on the flight stick, to bring her in behind the two that had passed her.

The green targeting reticle fell upon the starboard target as the two tried to weave through a large thicket of wreckage from their own ships. The reticle turned red, and Feyton tightened her finger on the trigger.

Plasma leapt from the nose of her Rhino, and disintegrated the rear of the target. The craft flipped over and on to one side, before smashing into its compatriot, turning both into one big fireball.

Feyton's squadron split into pairs, with the ninth serving as an extra wingman for her and Grace.

Grace, and a fighter from one of the other squadrons who she had now dubbed Two, stayed either side of her as she performed a barrel roll to avoid yet another wreckage. She saw the indicator for one of her other wing-pairs disappear as they mixed with a group of five enemies.

She was losing this battle fast.

Naturally, that was when fate decided to make things worse.

An enemy battleship drifted over the engagement, noticeably keeping the moon between it and the city-ship. It threw a massive shadow over the whole dogfight.

It opened fire.

Feyton squeezed her eyes shut as plasma filled the space around her. She didn't want to see the end coming. And she didn't.

She was still alive.

She couldn't believe it.

Her comms crackled, forcing her eyes open to make her realise that the Okarnagan fighters were gone, just more smouldering wreckage.

"Captured vessel to Terran Starfighters, do you copy?" a disembodied voice demanded.

"I copy," she replied. "This is Squadron Leader Feyton of 690th Squadron. Who are you?"

"In all fairness, you probably don't want to know, but right now we're here to rescue you since the Wolf Brother *is currently hiding to avoid being destroyed by that bloody super-weapon. Those of you that can fly can land in the empty fighter bay on the port side of this ship; we'll tractor the rest in."*

Although she didn't trust or know whoever had captured the enemy vessel, she was still incredibly grateful that someone had bothered to rescue her and her pilots.

"Acknowledged captured vessel. And thankyou."

"Our pleasure. Sojun out."

* * *

On the surface, things were going a bit smoother for Fordram now that there were no more interruptions, or at least none yet. His men moved up towards the parked freighter in standard loose skirmish formation, his men scanning and sweeping every nook and cranny for possible enemy combatants, or possibly even booby traps.

He led the way up the ramp and under the shadow of the freighter, stepping slowly and cautiously. He gestured for his squad to spread out, whilst the rest of the battalion searched the landing area, and inside the freighter itself for anything useful, or anything deemed potentially harmful.

When they found nothing, he contacted the unit guarding the troop transport, and ordered them, the transports, and the *Red Stallion* to move in and settle just below the freighter.

He looked back and up to see the same two Kra Nal cruisers that had appeared earlier finally starting a slow descent towards the ground.

Anger took hold of him then as he realised they had been waiting for him and his men –and their guardian angel- to clear the way so that they wouldn't be in harm's way. The cruisers thundered in over the heads of the soldiers, hovering just above the tallest of the statues, a hundred metres above them.

Drop bays opened along the keel of the dainty ships, and atmospheric fighters dropped out, and roared past, taking up patrols near and far. Next came a large shuttle that descended slowly, almost delicately, to land next to the newly arrived *Red Stallion*, and disgorged a large group of robed and uniformed Kra Nal. Many of them were armed whilst some carried bizarre equipment that Fordram had no way of knowing what their use was.

The leader strode up to Fordram.

"You are Lieutenant Colonel Fordram?" the robed Kra Nal asked.

"I am," he replied, not bothering with the courtesy of taking his helmet off.

"You may stand down now, colonel. We will finish this. It is our duty, after all."

"So why didn't you come down and help us before?" demanded Fordram. "Or were you just waiting until all the traps were sprung so that your people wouldn't be harmed?"

"Are you accusing us of something, colonel?"

"Cowardice," another voice said. Fordram recognised it as belonging to M'Der Tr'n, the so-called Famous Historian, who up until now had been faceless to him. The colonel hadn't even realised the *Stallion* had landed. "You watched as Fordram's men were slaughtered, and then only came down when you knew you would be safe."

The Kra Nal leader glared at Tr'n.

"You have no business being here. You were removed from your position as Minister of Justice over a century ago, and as such you are trespassing on Justice Ministry property. As are you, colonel."

Fordram shrugged. "I do not care for you or your rules." Dozens of his men were gathering around the Kra Nal, holding their weapons rather menacingly.

"And as for me, Deputy Director. I'm here because the owner of that ship," he said pointing to the *Kara Marazov*, "is my best friend. You really think you can just barge in here, and take over?"

There was suddenly a booming chuckle amplified from hidden speakers that echoed around the valley, and could be heard over the humming of the cruisers' anti-gravs.

A figure appeared on the top hull of the large parked freighter. It looked vaguely tattooed and muscled, though Fordram couldn't tell with the light of the system's sun directly behind it.

"You are all going to die; the planets across the universe will burn and fade away. Your people will-" His voice was cut off with a sickening squelching noise. Something bladed and metallic poked out of his throat. Blood spilled down his front, and he tried to move but he was paralysed.

The metallic object disappeared, and the victim dropped lifelessly on the hull of the freighter.

M'Der Tr'n was smiling at the figure still stood behind the body, who nodded, threw a mock salute, and disappeared again.

"Who the hell was that?" demanded Fordram.

Tr'n gave him a knowing smile. "That was Caine."

* * *

Adam jumped from the freighter to a nearby outcropping of stone, and melted into the shadows, tracking a path along the top until he came to the entrance to the Seven Stones tomb complex.

Rifle to his shoulder, he once again employed every piece of stealth training he had ever come across.

Three down, four to go.

* * *

"I wonder how the General's getting on," someone said idly.

They were still waiting for the comms specialist to finish downloading the Okarnagan ship's database and protocols. It was taking longer than expected —not because it was encrypted, but because the computer's programming was such a primitive mess.

Sojun rolled his eyes.

"Who are you people?" asked Feyton, for the sixth time since being brought aboard.

"Specialists," was all Sojun would ever say.

To Feyton's eyes they seemed extremely dangerous —they had taken control of a massive battleship with a handful of men, and rescued her survivors. The ship's former crew, were apparently stuck in escape pods in space along with the wreckage of two other ships.

The Specialists were all wearing old-style patterned camouflage, of a style she had seen once before, long ago, on the *Gold Royale*. Were they related somehow, she wondered?

Her pilots, all of them in fact, were either in the hangar attempting to repair what they could of their fighters, or in the ship's limited infirmary being patched up by the Specialists' medic. Sojun had promised that the injured would soon be transferred to their ship, though Feyton didn't understand that since they were already on a ship.

"You didn't think we walked here, did you?" inquired Sojun with a hint of mischief in his voice that she remembered from her days on the luxury liner. This wasn't Caine, but he had heavily influenced Sojun.

They were stood on the bridge, watching the Okarnagan fleet draw closer and closer towards Gorrh. They had already passed the moons, and were moving into a high orbit of the planet.

Something beeped on Sojun's wrist. He looked down at it, nodded, and then turned.

"Time to ship out, people."

"I've only got ninety percent of the computer downloaded, colonel," the comm specialist complained.

"It'll have to do. Boat's here."

"Like to see you say that to Major Dandridge's face," the specialist muttered under his breath. One or two of the other Specialists snickered as quietly as they could as they packed what gear they had into their packs.

"What was that?"

"Nothing, sir," the specialist said quickly.

"Good."

"Where are we going?" asked Feyton.

"You'll see," Sojun replied. His men gathered around him and Feyton, making her wonder just what the hell was going to happen, and were her pilots about to experience the same thing?

A tingling sensation filled her body, and she finally understood.

Not for the first time, everything went white.

* * *

As the city-ship entered orbit, several rather large craft detached from its hull, and descended through the atmosphere to a point not far from the end of the target valley, their hulls still smoking from the fiery abuse of re-entry.

Ramps extended down to the ground, and armoured troops filed out.

Thousands of troops.

* * *

The white light dissipated, and Feyton found herself standing on the slick, and somewhat advanced bridge of another ship.

"Welcome aboard the *RMS Black Knight*. You must be Squadron Leader Feyton."

Feyton could only nod as a handsome young officer wearing the same coloured camouflage fatigues approached with a somewhat mischievous demeanour, and a professional air about him.

Unlike the Specialist squad she had so far encountered, he was Terran, with a Karmanan accent.

"Major Dandridge." He stuck his hand out, and Feyton shook it gratefully.

"This is an amazing ship, Major."

Dandridge smiled. "It gets us where we want to go. Excuse me for a second." He turned to his XO. "Re-activate the cloak, and put us on a heading to the *Wolf Brother* that takes us *over* the Okarnagan main fleet."

"Aye, Major," the officer replied.

Dandridge turned his attention to Sojun. "Get what you needed, sir?"

Sojun nodded to his comm specialist who plugged in his database to a secure console. The information downloaded, and in the meantime, Feyton needed to know about her pilots.

"They've already been taken to our medical bay, though you will all be transferred to the *Wolf Brother* when we meet with them. Assuming the Okarnagans will let us of course. Having a cloaking device and an overpowered ship doesn't mean squat when going up against a vessel like that city-ship." He turned to Sojun again. "I don't suppose any more of *our* ships are going to be involved in this?"

Sojun shook his head. "MkFayden's got some big operation going on in the Fruga Sector. Those that aren't part of the operation are still either being built or are in final shakedowns."

Again, Sojun shook his head. "That's why I'm infantry, and you're a starship commander, Beck. All this talk of shakedowns and construction gets on my nerves."

"You and the Generals both."

Sojun snorted, which Feyton realised was through a ridged nose.

The ship's lights darkened as the cloaking device activated, and the triple forward viewscreens showed the stars moving, and the planet Gorrh getting larger and closer.

"What about the ships you left behind?" asked Feyton.

Sojun gave her a cruel smile. "You'll see." He nodded to the comms specialist from his Specialist squad, who pulled out a control device from one of his many pockets, and pushed a central button on it.

Feyton frowned, as nothing seemed to happen, and then noticed the readouts for the ship's sensors. The ship they had left behind was suddenly moving. As the *Black Knight* passed silently and unseen over the Okarnagan fleet, the communications and control battleship Sojun had captured finally appeared on the enemy's sensors.

Communications went berserk, the fleet commanders demanding to know what it was doing out of position.

They realised too late that the ship wasn't stopping.

Energy batteries opened up along the port side of the city-ship, and pummelled the C&C ship, stripping away its limited shields, and then began frantically pounding the hull. The outer hull was stripped away in seconds, leaving the exposed superstructure. The engines sputtered out, but there was enough momentum to keep it going for what Sojun had in mind for it.

The city-ship was too massive to completely shield it, and thus its flanks were vulnerable.

The C&C ship slammed into the port flank of the city-ship and erupted into a gigantic fireball that flashed across the bigger ship's hull, slagging it completely. The explosion of the C&C ship's power core obliterated a large portion of the giant's port side, leaving a hole big enough to fly several battleships through.

The Okarnagan fleet stopped its advance, confused at what seemed like an attack from their own people.

None of them noticed the ripple of the *Black Knight*'s cloaked passing as it sailed passed them.

Feyton, however, was unconvinced, looking around at the *Black Knight*'s bridge as if the cloak might fail at any moment. Dandridge noticed her behaviour, and smiled, sidling up to her.

"This cloaking device and this ship are well tested, Squadron Leader. We've already tested them under genuine combat conditions against far more advanced opponents. This cloak is almost impenetrable."

"It's the almost bit that worries me, Major."

* * *

"Energy spike, Admiral!" the sensors officer cried, "Directly to port!"

"What kind of energy spike? Is it a weapon?"

"No, sir." The officer looked towards the port bridge window in time to see a mottled green starship waver into view. It hung there, making no threatening view.

Sansky, however, was smiling.

"Contact the *Black Knight*'s commander."

"I have them, sir," the comms operator announced.

A human's face appeared on the nearest viewscreen to Sansky; it was a face Sansky recognised –a former Navy destroyer commander who had resigned his commission and joined Project Lympstone.

"Dandridge."

"*Hello again, Admiral Sansky. It's good to see you, despite the circumstances.*"

"What can I do for you?"

"*We have a few things that belong to you, I believe. You may want to lower what's left of your shields.*" Sansky nodded to the tactical officer, who promptly did as he was told. The tactical displays showed that the shields were down, and suddenly a bright white light filled the *Wolf Brother*'s bridge.

The light dissipated, and there stood a group of his fighter pilots.

Feyton looked haunted beyond reason: she had lost almost her entire fighter wing in one single engagement –it was enough to make someone go crazy, though Sansky knew the feeling.

Feyton and the others were led away, some sporting serious injuries that had been healed recently.

This was turning into a nightmare, and no progress had been made besides the efforts of the *Black Knight*'s crew.

"*Admiral.*" Dandridge's voice brought Sansky out of his reverie. "*We have discovered some information we retrieved from the Okarnagan computers.*" He nodded to someone off screen, and the comms operator announced the arrival of a data packet from the *Black Knight*. "*Personally, I... I think you should take it to Parliament and the Admiralty. It confirms everything the General was worried about.*"

Sansky frowned.

The comms operator came over slowly, his hand shaking as he handed a digipad to Sansky. The officer had read it, and was visibly upset by what the information contained. Sansky took the digipad, read it, and then re-read it.

"That can't be right," he said without thinking.

"I'm sorry, Admiral, but as far as we're concerned it is. The intel is solid, and the data is uncorrupted and untouched. It's genuine." Dandridge, aware of his high-ranking audience, continued, *"With the help of the Okarnagans, Terra was destroyed by the Core."*

* * *

Fadrkai, the second eldest of the seven brothers, waited with his younger brother Ranakai; both were armed with heavy rifles, guarding the entrance to the catacombs that contained their former prison.

Hadjkai and Trolkai –the most technologically minded of the brothers- were attempting to activate a weapon beneath the surface of the planet. It was a last-resort weapon left behind by the Kra Nal that had imprisoned the seven brothers so that their 'evil' would be wiped out forever if they ever escaped.

Hadjkai had other plans, however.

As the dutiful younger brothers, Fadrkai and the others would follow Hadjkai's orders, no matter what they might or might not think of the idea.

Ranakai suddenly snapped round, weapon up, pointing down the tunnel towards the entrance, the light of the outside world barely seeping around the distant corners. Behind them, the orange glow of their former prison kept their backs warm, and the entrance lit.

"I heard something," said the younger brother.

"It's just your imagination," Fadrkai scoffed. "You're not used to using that human clone body. It's somewhat more limiting than our old bodies."

"I swear I heard something," growled Ranakai. He started to step forward, passing from the light of the entrance into the darkness of the tunnel. He disappeared from Fadrkai's view, though his footsteps were still evident, however softly they might be.

Then the footsteps stopped.

He steeled himself, and was about to go in himself when a body was thrown into the light of the tomb. It was identical to Fadrkai, albeit with a single wound –a stab wound in his throat.

He bent down to look more closely at the wound to see what could have made it.

He found his answer when a muscled arm wrapped around his throat. It pinched his carotid perfectly, cutting the circulation off to his head, whilst simultaneously crushing his windpipe shut.

He could feel his life draining away just as something sharp pierced his throat.

* * *

Adam dropped the clone's lifeless body, and stepped into the main chamber. Everything was as he had left it. Almost.

Gardner's corpse was laid out on the table he himself had been tied to, his arms and legs pushed together in a strange sign of respect. That was when he noticed the cloning scientist huddled in a corner, staring at the body of the former intelligence commander, and hugging his knees to his chest.

Two of Adam's clones were stood at the centre of the monumental tomb, adjusting the controls of a gigantic holographic three-dimensional map that hung above them. It showed all nineteen galaxies.

In his ten years since coming to this century, Adam had extensively studied the political and geographical situation in explored space. The odd assembly of galaxies was a subject he and Polly had talked about over breakfasts in Rino. He had been somewhat ignorant in comparison to her, and had learned a lot.

He fought down the rising tide of grief, and concentrated on the scene before him.

The galaxies spun around a central point that looked suspiciously like the planet Gorrh.

At the outer edge of the formation sat the Milky Way, surrounded by the Small and Large Magellanic Clouds, partnered with the Andromeda and Triangulum Galaxies. Pegasus Galaxy hung nearby, with the Savage Halo, the M-561 Galaxy and the T'Kleth Halo. Surrounding Gorrh's odd place just outside explored space sat the Spider Galaxy, the Grey Swirl, the Tri-Cluster of galaxies, as well as the Raka Fron, Nightmare Storm, and the so-called 'Dark Galaxy'. Off by itself, far from the others, was the Y-40 Galaxy, the source of all Adam's problems.

"The Nineteen Galaxies, Adam," boomed his own voice, yet at the same time something else, like the pits of hell existed in his throat.

Hadjkai was looking at him, having noticed his arrival. He had his arms raised wide, like some showman presenting a fabulous piece of art. In all fairness, it was a piece of art –beautiful even. But its presence in this tomb of all places was ominous to say the least. Especially given Gorrh's astrological place on the map.

"Beautiful, isn't it?"

"Given the context, no," replied Adam.

"You wound me, Caine."

"Not as much as I've wounded your brothers."

Hadjkai's face fell, and Trolkai stopped what he was doing with the holographic controls.

"I suspected as much," said Hadjkai. Trolkai looked at his older brother with some concern. Clearly, the younger of the two had been expecting no problems. But then, Hadjkai had seen into Caine's mind –he had seen how destructive the human could be.

Adam looked at the holographic map above them.

"So what are you up to now, Hadjkai? Gonna destroy the universe?"

Trolkai snapped his round, alarm on his face.

"How did-?"

Hadjkai quieted him with a venomous glare.

Alarm filled Adam.

"Why do you want to destroy the universe? More importantly, how?"

"My dear Caine, do you really think I'd tell you how? As to why, well, why not? We can start the universe over again; or better yet, destroy this one, and go somewhere better, somewhere where we have no reputation; no responsibilities to others; somewhere that hasn't destroyed our families."

Adam thought about it, or at least gave the impression of thinking about it. It wasn't even a tempting offer, and the fact that Hadjkai had offered it in the hope of a positive answer showed that he didn't know Adam as well as he thought.

This was the kind of decision that had seen him leave the SBS: the ends justify the means and all that. It was a viewpoint Adam had never agreed with, despite all his years of violence.

In the end, it was an easy decision.

He shot Hadjkai through the chest, the P99 in his hand moving quicker than anyone could see. Before the older clone could hit the stone floor, Adam turned the pistol on the younger brother, ignoring the identical face to his own.

"What does this thing do?" he shouted.

Trolkai's eyes were wide and full of fear and grief, watching as his brother hit the ground with a thud. Adam grabbed a handful of the young clone's shirt, and pressed the gun to his forehead.

"What. Does. It. Do?"

"It... It's a singularity generator embedded within the core of the planet. The Justice Ministry put it there as a last resort if we ever got out. Only the machinery was too old when we eventually did escape."

"What kind of a last resort destroys nineteen whole galaxies?"

Adam could see the wheels turning behind Trolkai's eyes, deciding whether to help or hinder.

"It's only designed to destroy the planet and star system. Hadjkai ordered me to modify it to draw power from the system's sun and the nebulae and the surrounding spatial phenomena. With that much power it can destroy the entire universe."

"How do I destroy it?"

Trolkai didn't answer, defiance in his eyes.

"How. Do. I. Destroy it?" Adam repeated.

"You can't. You can only disable it." He pointed to the holographic controls. Adam made the mistake of looking, and felt something solid and sharp jab into his side. He looked down to see a slender knife handle protruding from between his ribs. The pain was excruciating, and he found he was already wheezing.

His finger squeezed on the trigger. The bullet splattered Trolkai's brains all over the pillar behind him.

Adam ripped the knife out, and stalked over to the controls. He slapped the big red square control marked disable, and then accidentally overloaded the power conduits so that they all destroyed themselves with a rumbling thunder from underneath his feet. The holographic controls dissipated like mist in a breeze, no longer able to sustain power.

He moved over to Hadjkai.

The criminal was still alive, a sucking bullet wound in the dead centre of his chest. He was dying.

"Why?" he asked, his voice a hoarse croak. "You could have had so much power at the tips of your fingers. The power to change the universe to your own making."

"Nobody should have that much power, not even those who would use it for good."

"You're a fool."

"Maybe, but I've come to peace with my so-called foolish decisions, including leaving the SBS." He sighed. "My grandfather once taught me two words that have stuck with me ever since, and have kept me in good stead over the years: Never surrender."

"Words to live by." And then he was gone, the life gurgling away to nothing in his chest.

Adam stood up, dropped the sniper rifle, and applied a tight bandage to his chest. It would hold for a short while. He needed to get to a medical facility of some sort.

He left the tomb behind, and walked out into the light of the miserable world outside.

* * *

Fordram was checking his wounded when his company's silent guardian angel stalked out of the tomb entrance. The Kra Nal saw him, and rushed into the tomb entrance behind him.

"Colonel," Caine said. "How are your men?" Something on his wrist beeped. He checked it, cursed, and looked back up to Fordram.

"I've lost thirty-three men, and another twenty are wounded, why? Who are you?"

"A friend, colonel." He pointed to the sky. "You're going to need as many friends as you can get."

A tangy smell of ozone filled their nostrils and their sinuses felt like they were on fire. Fordram knew the signs: orbital bombardment.

A blinding white light suddenly filled the area, and a beam of white light shafted down and swept across the top of the left side of the valley. It vaporised the rock and stone formations, throwing clouds of dust into the air that drifted down and around the Terrans.

Another sinus-burning shaft of light sizzled down from the heavens.

It seared along the opposite side of the valley.

The dust obscured everything except the small position occupied by Fordram's company, and even then it was hard to tell one man from another.

Fordram felt his sinuses burning again, and again the shaft of white light burned down. He closed his eyes, expecting this to be the end. Gone, vaporised in an instant.

He opened them again, several second after the beam should have hit. More dust was kicked up into the air, but he had and his men were still there.

Something vast came out of the dust above, and slammed into the ground, smashing through half his company like an avalanche. Chunks of metal flew in every direction, and the shockwave of the impact concussion threw armoured soldier and debris into the air alike.

A piece of metal impaled the man next to Fordram, though the 'friend' just stood there, and watched the mayhem with dispassionate ease.

"One of the Kra Nal cruisers," said Caine. "Some kind of super-weapon is my guess."

"Why didn't they just finish us off?" asked Fordram.

"They still might. But I think they're interested in this planet and what's down here considering the people they're allied with."

"And what is down here?" he demanded.

The black-clad soldier smiled. It was a sad smile.

"Me."

* * *

"They did what?"

"The city-ship fired on the surface, admiral."

Sansky looked at the holographic tactical display with some confusion. What the hell was Adam doing down there? And were the Okarnagans serious about obtaining him for their apparent masters, the Core?

"Time until *Atlantis* arrives?" he asked to no one in particular.

"Two hours, admiral."

"Have they been apprised of the data we received?"

"Yes, sir. Still two hours."

"Nark."

* * *

M'Der was happily ensconced back in the *Red Stallion*. Adam was outside, assisting with casualties, whilst M'Der was given the job of keeping in contact with the remaining Kra Nal cruiser, the *Wolf Brother*, and its remaining escort.

The news from the starfighter carrier was less than encouraging: *Atlantis* was still two hours away, and the Okarnagans had launched a large craft that had landed on the planet's surface.

Whatever it was, it was big.

Sansky's estimated guess had been to classify it as a possible troop transport; one big enough to carry several regiments' worth of troops.

He bolted out of the *Stallion*, and down the ramp, running up to Adam.

"Adam, Raymond thinks there's a troop transport parked nearby, possibly with several regiments of Okarnagans inside."

"Fuck. Well, we're gonna just have to wait for -"

"Mister Caine!" the voice belonged to the Kra Nal leader. Although the voice boomed, it also sounded terrified after having seen his ship come crashing down around his ears, so to speak. "You defiled and destroyed our property in the Seven Stones prison!"

M'Der saw the look in Adam's eyes, and looked away for a few seconds. He heard a crack, a muffled yelp of pain, and a thump. When he turned back his fellow Kra Nal was lying on the floor, nursing a broken jaw, backing away on his elbows from Adam.

"Do something useful, and bring that other cruiser down, and get these men evacuated off this planet!"

"I will do no such thing!"

"YES YOU WILL!" roared Adam. He pulled out the P99, and aimed the barrel at the other's head, clicking back the hammer. The Kra Nal whimpered and nodded enthusiastically, before talking into a comms unit on his belt.

"M'Der, get as many of the wounded onto the *Red Stallion* as you can and fly them out of here. Those Army troop transports were under the cruiser when it came down so we're relying on you and the Justice Ministry."

"Do you really think we can do it?" asked Fordram.

Adam nodded.

"Yeah, I do."

"You've got a plan, haven't you?"

Adam smiled, and looked over at the *Kara Marazov*, still hanging passively above the carnage below.

"Yeah I do."

* * *

The Okarnagan troop transport, carrying twelve thousand troops, had touched down with a thump at the end of the valley. The dust from the orbital strikes and the downed alien cruiser had by that time reached the transport's position.

The whale-like vessel's thrusters had pushed back the dust. Now the dust rushed back in as the ramps clunked down on the broken stone ground. Troops charged out in their hundreds, spilling out onto the valley floor.

The legion commander marched out of the transport, weapons at the ready. The Chieftain had given him the honour of leading this beachhead.

He lived for about five seconds after stepping off the ramp until a missile snaked out of the dust, and impacted his armour. It threw him backwards into the troop bay before it detonated. The explosion gutted the transport, killed half of the warriors, and set off the ship's aging power core. The unstable mix of concussive explosion and antimatter ruptured with the force of a nuclear bomb, annihilating the entire legion.

The *Kara Marazov* rushed out of the dust, buffeted by the shockwaves of the explosion, before it raced for the sky.

* * *

Adam checked his sensors, making sure the *Red Stallion* and the Kra Nal cruiser were safely away, skimming barely metres above the planet's surface. The plan was for them to carry on that way, and then pop up out of the atmosphere below the *HMS Wolf Brother's* orbit.

So far, so good.

The hard part belonged to him and the *Kara*.

He wished he'd installed a cloaking device long ago.

Now was not the time for such thinking; he needed to be focused on keeping up his side of the plan. He pushed the *Kara* up through the atmosphere, and out into space, directly below the Okarnagan fleet.

The sensors went bananas trying to keep up with the ship movements above him.

Weapons locks blared loudly in his ears before he cancelled them out.

He disarmed the missiles in the lower fin, although kept the shields raised.

He activated the comms unit, putting it on an all-channels broadcast.

"This is Captain Caine of the private yacht *Kara Marazov*. I am offering my unconditional surrender to the Chieftain of the Okarnagan fleet. Please respond."

No voice responded.

He noted with some concern the Core warship hanging beside the monolithic city-ship. Although the revelation that the Okarnagans, and indeed the Mertik, were working for his old enemy, he hadn't expected to see them again for quite some time.

Their presence, and the statement from Evelyn's biological mother, confirmed Adam's theories and worries about the Core. They weren't done with the Terrans.

Now he had a purpose: once he enacted his plan, and they somehow all made it out of the Gorrh system alive, then Project Lympstone would be his sole focus. Of course, that all depended on his plan working.

The city-ship filled the cockpit window, red hull everywhere. He could clearly see horrendous damage on one side of the massive vessel. *Had the Wolf Brother* been able to inflict some hurt on the huge ship?

Could he use it to his advantage?

No was the answer.

Fleet tactics were Raymond's forte not his. He was a ground forces man, always had been; always would be.

He flew the *Kara* to the coordinates, and found to his surprise that it was a hangar. He had half-expected it to be a spot directly in front of one of their undoubtedly huge cannons.

Landing, he was met by nobody. The hangar was empty, but lights were flashing in one direction, towards an open door. He picked out one of the HK assault rifles, with enough magazines to take down a regiment of troops. He slipped a couple of Rijiin disc-grenades into his leg pocket, before climbing out of the ship.

He followed the lights, somewhat taken aback by the lack of guards.

The flashing line of lights led him through a long corridor, up twenty floors in a lift, and then down yet another long corridor that led to a massive chamber. The lights led to a raised platform in the middle of the chamber.

A throne.

He dropped just as something sharp and metallic whooshed past his head.

He squeezed the trigger, and let loose a pair of bursts that elicited the gurgle of a mortal wound. The muzzle flash briefly lit the room, revealing nothing but a series of statues, and several moving figures with horns on their heads.

Something shifted off to his left, and he let loose another burst that took someone else.

There was a chuckle from within the darkness, and it was flecked with the clacks of a beak. Adam knew not to make a response beyond bringing pain to the owner. He couldn't pinpoint the source of the voice, however, and discovered there was more movement all around him.

He cursed silently, and kept his assault rifle swinging around, trying to pinpoint the enemy. In the end, he simply pulled a pair of the disc-grenades out, pushed the red circle on one side, and threw them in different directions. He covered his ears and eyes, and felt the crump of the detonations.

He swung the rifle back up, and fired at the sound of someone crying with pain.

The cry disappeared, and was replaced by silence.

He fired again in the direction he had thrown the other grenade. He heard the wet thunk of several bullets impacting on flesh. There was a gargled cry, and a curse from a different direction. Adam let loose on automatic at the source of the curse, hearing the impacts once again.

"That's enough," a rough voice demanded.

The lights came on full blast, blinding Adam for a second. When he could see again, there were a group of Beelzebub-like aliens stood around the massive chamber.

The room was bare -a grey metal colour, with not one decoration anywhere to be seen. Okarnagan bodyguards lined the walls, standing to attention, and holding ceremonial blades of varying size and shape.

"So, this is the indestructible Caine."

Adam turned to look into the face of the devil himself.

The Chieftain.

His face was split by an evil grin, filled with pointed teeth that looked more at home in a shark's mouth. Two horns sprouted from the top of his forehead, and long black hair flowed down around his armoured shoulders.

The armour he wore looked like a bastardised version of the Terran Army's, but coloured crimson with neat handwritten blessings and such on it.

In his clawed hand, the Chieftain held a straight sword; Adam hoped it was ceremonial as well. All he had were his firearms, grenades, and the combat knife on his belt. He hadn't used a sword since he was a boy, practicing with his grandfather in the grounds of his father's home.

"We have someone in common, Caine." The Chieftain nodded over Adam's shoulder. He turned.

It was a Core warrior. It wore the black and gold armour of a member of the royal family. Just as before, it looked like a bird, but walked almost like a man, its talons clicking on the metal floor.

"I am Yh'reth'narn."

Adam frowned. "Yh'reth'gar's brother?"

The creature nodded.

And Adam shot him full on, emptying the magazine.

He swung round.

The Chieftain knocked the rifle out of his hands with the sword.

Not ceremonial.

Adam threw himself backwards, rolled, and brought both hands up, the combat knife in one, point down. It wasn't going to do much, but it was better than using his bare hands.

"You'll regret that, Caine. We were just going to test you, break you down, and have you join us. But now I'm going to kill you; and then I'm going to kill all your friends and family."

Adam growled.

"Your people already destroyed my family, my entire planet." He leapt forward, and ducked under the sword that swung at his head. It whistled over his head, and he lashed out with the knife.

It rebounded with a hiss.

He was protected by a forcefield.

Hesitating for a second at this development, the Chieftain swung down, and sliced open Adam's arm. Blood flowed down his arm, and he cried out with the pain. The sword swung again, and missed Adam's throat by a millimetre.

He scurried back, and rolled away from another hard strike that struck the floor and sent sparks splashing across the deck and singing his fatigues. The backhand stroke of the sword sliced open his arm below the other wound.

He could feel his body slowing, his blood loss becoming close to intolerable. The stab wound in his chest had barely had time to heal with the help of the *Kara's* small first aid kit, and even then it had been rudimentary at best.

The Chieftain seemed to realise this, and stepped up his strong swings, barely missing Adam as he rolled and ducked out of the way. Adam tried pulling the Walther out of its holster, but a backswing sliced his hand.

The Okarnagan raised the sword for a deathblow.

"Chieftain!" someone shouted. It was Yh'reth'narn.

"WHAT?!"

"Caine is the Patriarch's prize, not yours."

The Core prince, a smoking hole in his armour, but very much alive, stepped over and placed a strong taloned hand on the Chieftain's sword, preventing that final blow.

"Why does the Patriarch want me?" asked Adam.

"Because you murdered my younger brother, and according to my father's former benefactor –the one you call Gold- my grandfather."

"The First."

"Indeed."

"That's not why you've been working with the Okarnagans and the Mertik. Not to mention the Idle Guns pirates in the Dark Galaxy." He slumped on the floor, his muscles weakening. "The invasion is really happening."

"Oh yes, Adam Caine," clacked Yh'reth'narn. He crouched down next to the stricken human. "My brother Yh'reth'gar may have been foolish for attacking the Terran Consortium with so little ships, but he had the right idea. My father wants you with him when he wipes humanity from the face of this universe." He nodded to two Core warriors, who carried some equipment with them. They moved forward.

Adam was about to protest when Yh'reth'narn shot him with a stun pistol.

The last thing he saw was the prince grinning evilly from behind his beak.

* * *

So far, nothing had followed them.

Of course, as Adam always believed, the universe had a sense of humour.

Just as the *Red Stallion* broke orbit directly beneath the *Wolf Brother,* Okarnagan starfighters –survivors of the previous fight lost in the atmosphere- came racing out of the clouds, and immediately started firing on the *Stallion.*

Even with the shields up, the furious onslaught punished the converted cargo shuttle. Incoherent plasma fire streamed from the following Kra Nal cruiser. It fired ineffectively between the fighters, who were even now splitting up to take on both the Stallion and the cruiser.

Warning lights flashed across M'Der's consoles. The shields were failing with each pass of the fighters. The engines were struggling to outrun the enemy and fight Gorrh's gravity.

There was a murmur of worry from the wounded soldiers on his ship, who were littered on the floor.

M'Der slammed the throttle forward, pushing it to full sublight. The *Stallion* began shaking under the strain. It was meant to be a luxury yacht, not a ship like the *Kara Marazov.* The warnings came thick and fast, distracting him from the controls.

A missile slammed into the Stallion's fat engines, throwing the ship forward. It kept going, spinning end-over-end, and overtaxing the inertial dampeners. M'Der felt the g-forces press down on him as the ship kept going.

He blacked out.

* * *

The Wolf Brother sent its gunships down towards the *Stallion.*

The *Baghdad* and the *Kevin J. Anderson* slashed in either side of the rolling *Stallion,* obliterating four fighters in seconds. The Farsight, National Treasure, and the Jarvis moved around and out, before coming in towards the formation of attacking fighters.

The Okarnagans were slaughtered by the specialised fighter-hunter gunships.

But the *Stallion* was still spinning out of control.

The gunships turned as one, and flew in formation around the Stallion.

They tried desperately to tractor it, but the Stallion was starting to fall back down towards Gorrh, her engines no longer keeping her up. The ship jerked around, buffeted by the atmosphere. The hull began to glow from the friction of re-entry.

M'Der woke up to see the forward cockpit window begin to crack under the pressure and heat. The cracks spread across the transparent material unnaturally quickly. He tried to back away from the window, but found he was pinned into his seat by the g-forces of the re-entry.

The ship's hull groaned under the pressure.

This is it, he thought. I'm about to die, with almost nothing to show for it. Dammit Adam, where are you when I need you?

The hull's groans became unbearably loud as the ship descended further and further down towards the planet surface. Fire poured through the cracks in the window, the heat singing M'Der's minimal eyebrows.

The heat was so intense he was struggling to breathe, the fire burning the oxygen around him and searing his lungs.

He could clearly see the clouds beneath him as the ship raced downward hideously fast.

The ship burst through the clouds, shuddering and groaning like an aging hipster. The fire dissipated as the ship began to tip in another direction by the strength of the atmosphere rushing past it.

Just as the ground rushed up to meet the *Red Stallion*, M'Der felt a tingling sensation fill his entire body.

* * *

"Got them!"

Colonel Sojun smiled as M'Der Tr'n appeared on the *Black Knight's* teleport pad, along with three-dozen wounded Terran soldiers. The Kra Nal let out a huge sigh of relief, and then fainted.

"Get them all to the med-bay," he ordered, before returning to the bridge.

"Where's the General?" asked Dandridge.

Sojun shook his head.

He didn't know.

* * *

Adam awoke two hours later, his head pounding, and his wounds aching.

He was still lying on the floor. When he looked down, he could see the repairs the Core warriors had made to him. His weapons had been removed, though he wasn't chained to a table as he had on Yh'reth'gar's flagship. In fact, he wasn't restrained at all.

"Welcome back to the land of the living, as you humans say." The voice belonged to Yh'reth'narn, who was stood over him in a menacing pose. The Chieftain was nearby, conferring with one of his men. He looked angry, or upset; Adam couldn't tell with an alien that looked like a comical depiction of Satan.

Yh'reth'narn, however, was ignoring them for the moment, intent on his brother's killer.

"Tell me, Caine. How did my brother die?"

"He tripped and hit his head on a brick."

The Core prince kicked him in the side, and Adam curled up in response.

"I threw him out of an airlock," grunted Adam. He received another kick, knocking the wind out of his lungs with a whoomph of air.

"Then I will watch as my father throws you out of an airlock," the thing cackled.

An Okarnagan warrior burst into the throne chamber, out of breath, with panic all over his satanic face.

"Chieftain! Chieftain!"

"What is it?" the Chieftain snapped impatiently. He was fingering the hilt of his sword, itching to use it on the warrior who had burst in so dramatically and disrespectfully. The warrior, not noticing the subtle movements, ran up to his Chieftain.

"My Lord Chieftain. The Terrans are here!"

"I already know that, idiot!"

"No, sir. The others are here; the ones that followed us. One of their dreadnaughts just came out of lightspeed outside our weapons range, along with a massive fleet of smaller ships. Our sensors identify her as the *Atlantis*."

"The High Admiral's flagship," the Chieftain whispered. "So, the First Star Lady herself has come out to deal with us. Alright you're forgiven warrior. Bring the fleet around to meet this new threat. Has their been any news from our beachhead on the surface?"

The warrior shook his head.

Caine was smiling.

"They're dead. Before I came here, I put a missile into their troop bay." Adam used his fingers to describe a mushroom cloud. "Destroyed in a couple of seconds."

The Chieftain, rage in his yellow eyes, advanced on Adam, and pulled out his vicious sword.

The deck suddenly tipped, overbalancing everyone, and sending them to the deck.

Adam leapt towards Yh'reth'narn, moving like lightning, and ignoring the ache of the healed wounds. He whipped the Core prince's short knife out of its scabbard, turned the alien around, and slit its throat, before charging towards the Chieftain again.

The Okarnagan reached for the control box on its belt to activate his personal shield. But the deck tipped again, and tumbled him towards Adam. Adam, not ready, went flying into the Chieftain, and the pair of them fell to the deck.

Adam swore profusely, tried to bring the knife back to him, and found he couldn't.

He looked over at the Chieftain to find the knife embedded in the Chieftain's exposed neck, a comical look of shock frozen on the alien's face, permanently stuck like that in death.

The bodyguards, shocked that this human could murder both their Chieftain and their greatest ally in the blink of an eye, hesitated. Adam snapped up the Chieftain's aging plasma sidearm, and blasted three in quick succession.

He killed another two before the others realised their predicament, and scrammed.

The deck began to rumble constantly.

He bolted for the door he had arrived through.

* * *

HMS Atlantis hammered the city-ship from afar. Its attending fleet, made up of the largest gathering of Terran Navy vessels in combat since the last Interior War, sliced towards the Okarnagans.

The Okarnagans turned to face this new threat, though the city-ship simply rolled to keep its undamaged flank pointed towards the Terrans.

The *Aurora*, a *Valkyrie*-class, took multiple hits to its mid-section. Its shields down, the city-ship's guns pounded it until it snapped in half, spilling its unlaunched starfighters into space along with its crew and pilots.

Three *Diligent*-class battleships surged around the *Aurora's* skeleton, firing for full effect. They were ahead of the rest of the fleet, laying down fire as the others followed in behind.

An Okarnagan battleship rammed the Pykestone, smashing both vessels to pieces, whilst the *Cape Law* and *Woolbist* obliterated a line of enemy frigates, paving the way for the *Atlantis* to keep shooting at the titan in the middle.

An Okarnagan heavy cruiser, damaged by fire from the Cape Law, made a suicidal run at the *Atlantis*. The cruiser *HMS Pass of Balmaha* interceded itself between the two, and used itself as a shield, the two ships exploding in an orgy of destruction. Its sacrifice was not in vain, as a pair of Knight-class battleships moved forward in its place to act as starship batmen.

The Okarnagans finally woke up properly.

Their mainline battleships moved up in one large formation, firing waves of energy at the *Terrans*. Twelve cruisers were obliterated in the blink of an eye. The *Atlantis* turned some of her less powerful guns on them, taking out three before the *Terran* battleships moved too close to the Okarnagans for the dreadnaught to hit the enemy without hitting its friends.

Starfighter engagements flashed between the big ships, like flies fighting over the corpses of elephants. They swarmed around them, forming swirling patterns in space. Every now and then a missile would fly loose of the formation to strike an enemy ship, impacting on the shields, and providing a tiny opening for the other side.

The fight descended into a massive brawl, the two sides no longer separated.

In one section of the fight, targets became so thick the *HMS Glen Orrin* accidentally fired on the battleship *Osea Island,* which was destroyed by pinpoint firing from two Okarnagan mainline battleships. *The Glen Orrin* exacted a hasty revenge on the two, firing for all it was worth, even going so far as to pump energy from its engines so that it could fire over-charged shots to defeat their shields.

In another part of the fight, the Halsinger and two fellow destroyers were destroyed when they tried to sneak around behind a trio of enemy battleships. The battleships, pushed back by Terran equivalents, reversed straight into the small ships, pulping them against their shields.

The Okarnagans weren't having it any easier: a dozen of their cruisers accidentally wandered into a beam of energy from the city-ship that was meant for the *Atlantis.* One, missing half of its structure, ploughed into the damaged shields of one of the Okarnagan mainline battleships. Instead of being destroyed, the wrecked cruiser skipped off the shields, bringing them down in the process, before spinning into the unshielded aft of another.

The first battleship was ripped apart by concentrated fire from the Terrans. The second simply span towards the edge of the engagement zone, spewing flame and debris before crashing into two more of the smaller battleships and a slew of starfighters.

And so the battle went on.

Space was filled with debris, the two fleets manoeuvring around each other, with both the *Atlantis* and the city-ship keeping just outside the horrendous killzone between them.

* * *

Scarlett watched from the massive bridge of the Atlantis, watching the multitudes of the ship's officers swarm around her. Lieutenant Commander Gorsson made sure she was left alone for the most part, occasionally telling her which ships had been lost, or which starfighter squadrons had been completely wiped out.

Her thoughts were lost in the data flowing across the holographic displays hanging around her. She could not get over just how many people she had lost in one single action. In the last two weeks, since the Okarnagans had first struck, she had lost close to a hundred thousand men and women, officers and enlisted. It beggared belief.

This was the single most costly military campaign in Terran Navy history since the Battle of Karmana a thousand years ago.

She remembered Sansky's initial debriefing after the threat of the Core had been neutralised ten years ago. He had claimed that the Core were not some small group, but a numerically superior race that had conquered an entire galaxy, and held sway over many races outside the Y-40 Galaxy. That debriefing had led to the establishment of Fort Sentinel, guarding one of the few major routes between Terran and Alliance territories, and the Core's home galaxy.

If Sansky and Caine were right, this battle was only the beginning.

Ty approached her cautiously.

"Milady, the enemy mainline battleships are beginning to weaken. They only have three left, and five of their smaller battleships. This could be a good opportunity to make a break towards the city-ship."

"Agreed," she said, without reviewing the data herself. She trusted Ty's judgment. "Coordinate with the other ship commanders to provide a break for the *Atlantis*. Have all starfighters form up behind us for a hit-and-run strike."

Ty nodded, and returned to his own command post overlooking the rest of the bridge.

The swirling combat began to break apart as the *Atlantis* suddenly surged forward towards the city-ship. The massive dreadnaught brushed aside the smaller Okarnagan ships, destroying others with its massive weapons batteries.

The starfighters formed up as best they could in the wake of the dreadnaught, gathering back into what remained of their squadrons.

The Terran battleships *Bolt's Law* and *Haytor Vale* suddenly surged forwards as well, followed by the entire Terran fleet, pummelling anything red in their way, focussing their efforts in one particular area of the enemy formation.

The Okarnagans broke under the sudden pressure. They turned to run, but found the *Atlantis* and her charges simply did not let up, firing and firing. The city-ship, side on to the resurgent Terran fleet, did not have enough weaponry to deal with the entire fleet at the same time. It was too slow and cumbersome to turn and bring its super-weapon to bear.

The Terrans suddenly split off from their flagship, and let it pass by, taking on the fleeing smaller ships.

Atlantis hammered the city-ship, its forward mega-batteries chewing through the huge shields as it closed the distance between the two. The city-ship's shields flared for a brief second, before their emitters exploded along one small section of the titan's flank.

The starfighters that had hung in *Atlantis'* wake suddenly popped out from behind the protection of the dreadnaught's mass, surging around it, and through the opening made in the shields.

The starfighters, piloted by some of the SC's most gifted pilots, raced around between the titan's hull and shields, shooting any viable target. They moved too fast for the city-ship's gunners to track them. Some even sent missiles into the gaping hole on its port flank, initiating internal cascading explosions.

* * *

The deck tipped again as Adam raced down the corridor.

The guiding lights had disappeared, with only emergency lighting to guide him. Even then, power surges made the lights flicker. In the frantic fight with the Chieftain, he had forgotten the direction he needed to go.

And yet, he was still going the way he needed to go.

Every now and then, he would see Polly beckoning him towards her. When he reached her, she would disappear, and re-appear further on.

He carried on like this until he stumbled into the hangar.

Sat in the middle was his beloved starship.

He smiled, though the ache of his healed wounds were ever a constant reminder of what he had survived. He struggled up the ladder rungs on the side of the ship, and flopped through the airlock, letting it close behind him.

The consoles lit up as he entered the cockpit, the sensors wild with data.

The *Atlantis* had arrived, and was currently pummelling the city-ship around him, whilst starfighters were playing havoc with the hull of the ship.

He had to get out; preferably before the Terran Navy brought the city-ship down around his ears.

The Kara hummed to life beneath him.

Flames licked up from around the ship, threatening to engulf it and him.

He punched the throttle to full, and the *Kara Marazov* roared out of the hangar, and into space. Debris fell all around the ship as he pushed it towards the portside opening. Weapons locks and warnings blared for his attention, but he ignored them, using the *Kara's* incredible manoeuvrability and speed to shake them off.

A mega-battery had him dead to rights when it suddenly exploded.

The *Kara* passed out of the city-ship's shadow, narrowly avoiding a dying Okarnagan battleship attempting to right itself, an into space. Something brushed past the *Kara* going the other way. There was nothing on the sensors.

A cloaked ship.

His guess was confirmed when the communications lit up.

"*Kara Marazov*, this is *RMS Black Knight*, do you read?"

"I read you loud and clear, *Black Knight*. What's your status?"

"Just paving the way for the Wolf Brother, General," Dandridge's voice said cheerily. "Sansky is right behind us; he's the reason we're here after all."

With that, the Valkyrie-class starfighter carrier thundered past the *Kara*, its weapons alight, pounding the positions that had locked onto Caine's ship. Alongside it came a flowery cruiser of another race. Adam took the *Kara* to a safe distance from the battle. As much as he wanted to be a part of it, he was exhausted and beaten, and had little strength to continue.

He felt himself slipping once again into unconsciousness, though this time it was with heartfelt relief.

Just as his eyes began to close, he saw the massive city-ship break apart, thus effectively ending the Okarnagan threat for now.

Then darkness took him once again.

* * *

Blue Falls.

Two weeks later.

The Parliament building stood like a beacon of light in the centre of New Terra's –and the Consortium's- capital city. All around, skyscrapers reached up for the morning clouds, a testament to the majesty and strength of the Terrans. The city itself was built on the edge of a cliff, between the two halves of the River Septus, at the centre of a massive delta. The city extended over and down the cliff face, with a total population of fifty million.

A nondescript military shuttle flew above the city, and landed on a shuttle pad halfway up the Parliament's towering edifice. Its escort of four Rhino starfighters set down next to it, forming a cordon around their charge.

It settled on its landing claws, hunched like an old man.

The doors opened, and out stepped five uniformed officers. Three wore the duty uniforms of Terran Navy officers, complete with peaked caps and shiny shoes. The other two were dressed in close-collared black tunics. Both had rank tapes on their shoulders: one had a Colonel's two diamond pips and a crown, the other a Major General's crossed sword and scabbard topped by a diamond pip. Both wore green berets.

The five stepped into the building proper, and were guided to the Main Hall, where the Parliament awaited them.

They were shown to a podium at the centre of the cavernous room, surrounded by hundreds of elected representatives from around the Terran Consortium. This was an emergency session of the Parliament, though the Military Council was too spread out on assignments to be at this particular meeting.

High Admiral Scarlett stepped up to the podium, and a spotlight lit her up.

The room went silent.

"You all know me. You have seen the data sent to Parliament two weeks ago. Presumably you have all reviewed the data."

The Speaker of the House replied in the affirmative.

"Then you all know why I am here."

One of the elected officials, the Roper Sector representative, stood up and used the controls on his chair to ask for permission to be heard. The Speaker gave permission.

"You are here," the representative began, "because you want to propose an invasion of the Y-40 Galaxy, as well as military action against the Mertiks, and a mop-up action to hunt down the remaining Okarnagans that escaped the Battle of Gorrh."

"Indeed I do. As you know, although I have full military control, I cannot wage an act of war on a grander scale without permission from this Parliament."

"Then you do not have it," said the Prime Minister. The tall, thinning man in an impeccably tailored suit was stood below the Speaker's pulpit, holding a digipad, presumably with the relevant data on. He stepped forward to stand before Scarlett at the podium. "You come to us with unreliable data from equally unreliable sources."

"I'm sorry Prime Minister, I do not follow."

She knew where this was going.

"The Okarnagans have been our age-old enemy; do you really think they could not forge this information? You are expecting us to believe that Ancient Terra was destroyed not by some freak asteroid event, but in fact was purposely destroyed by some unknown alien race."

"Yes, Prime Minister."

"And this information was retrieved by a squad of specialists? Specialists that are not a part of the Terran military."

"Yes, Prime Minister." She could feel her ire rising.

"You did not think to confirm or rule out this information. Nor did you have permission to be allied with an independent military force, one which was in fact brought in by one of your subordinates."

Scarlett gritted her teeth. "Yes, Prime Minister."

"This government will not sanction an invasion of another galaxy, especially given that there are plenty of other races to be threatened by this so-called Core between them and us."

"We cannot sit idly by and wait for them to invade us," she countered.

"Are you so sure that they will invade us?" he asked.

"Yes." She said it with great conviction, yet it seemed to fall on deaf ears. She felt a strong hand on her shoulder, and vacated the podium. The green bereted general stepped up, or rather limped up, his injuries still not fully healed yet.

"Who are you?" asked the Prime Minister.

"I am Major General Adam Caine, commanding officer of the independent specialists that retrieved the data. This is Colonel Sojun, the commander of my elite units."

"*The* Adam Caine? The Ghost?"

"Yes, Prime Minister."

"Am I to understand that Project Lympstone is yours then?"

Adam, dressed in the uniform of Project Lympstone's military unit, tried not to show the shock he felt. How could the Prime Minister know about it? How much did he know? Only Scarlett and a handful of Navy officers were aware of the project.

"Yes, Prime Minister."

"Why should we trust you? You are, in the eyes of Navy Intelligence, a criminal and a major threat to our society."

Adam gritted his teeth.

"I bring you a dire warning: the Core are going to invade. Their representatives have said as much to me over the last few years. It's going to happen whether you believe me or not, whether you trust me or not."

"You bring us vague warnings, and unsubstantiated rumours, *General* Caine."

"You're a fuckin' idiot."

Adam stormed off the podium, and breezed past Scarlett, who was quietly fuming at her government's ineptitude. Both Caine and Sojun stalked out of the Main Hall, and back to the landing pad. At a signal from Caine, a camouflaged shuttle appeared from seemingly nowhere.

It touched down next to the Terran craft.

Both of them stepped aboard, Caine muttering about the Terrans being damn fools.

"What destination shall I tell the *Black Knight*, General?" asked the pilot. "Back to Lympstone, sir?"

Caine shook his head, removing the prized green commando beret from his head.

"First, we go to Ckeer Najoor."

* * *

Ckeer Najoor.

He had come down alone aboard the *Kara Marazov*.

He wanted to see what was left of the planet. The Navy had buried the dead, so Raymond had informed him, and put out the fires of the burning settlements, including Rino. But his old friend had told him that they had put Polly's grave away from the rest.

He trudged away from the *Kara*, and went to kneel down in front of the metal headstone. It was inscribed with her name, date of birth, date of death, and a quote underneath: "Never surrender."

Tears streamed down his cheeks once again.

But he found he couldn't say anything appropriate except one thing.

"I love you, Polly. I always have, and I always will."

He stood, and walked back to the *Kara*.

* * *

Fullina.

The shuttle was escorted to the Alliance's main airbase some distance from the capital city to be on the safe side. The shuttle was boarded by Alliance troops, who found a green-skinned Mertik woman at the controls. She surrendered to them without a fight.

"My name is Ayanka; I'm returning this stolen shuttle, and I wish to join your NCIS."

Ayanka was escorted to a cell, never once mentioning her given name of Evelyn Caine. She would forget her old life, and make a new one.

A grizzled veteran wearing civilian clothes, and an NCIS badge on his chest approached her.

A new life, starting right here and now.

* * *

New Terra.

Raymond Sansky walked into the large home he shared with his wife and adopted children overlooking New Amsterdam. Hannah was in the kitchen making something she called pot roast, the house's holographic helper assisting her in her attempt.

He walked straight into the kitchen and swept Hannah up in his arms.

"I love you, my dear wife. I promise I'll never leave you."

She just smiled, and basked in the loving moment.

* * *

Kra Nal homeworld.

M'Der Tr'n sat down at his desk. He hadn't touched his house on the homeworld in a century, though was glad it was still here in good condition.

Sadness had filled him for the last month. He had lost both Eve and Polly, and now would probably never hear from Adam again. The human had disappeared to his fortress Lympstone, preparing for a war that would inevitably come. Sansky was apparently now on leave with his family, out of contact for a while.

He looked at his forlorn desk, and found a digipad and stylus.

He began to write:

'A Comprehensive History of the Nineteen Galaxies, Volume 1: Adam Caine...'

* * *

Lympstone.

Not so long ago, it had been home to a single member of a non-corporeal species, and an enclave of murderous mercenaries. Now it was something else. The planet served as the home base for Adam Caine's secret project. The original enclave had been expanded and updated, whilst obstacle courses, rifle ranges, armouries, classrooms, and barracks had all been built around one small area.

It was now his home, Adam realised.

All that was left was Lympstone, and its future.

The *Black Knight*'s shuttle thumped down in the middle of the central parade ground, surrounded on all sides by thickly built high armoured buildings. The thrusters cut out, and the doors opened.

Caine and Sojun were greeted by Brigadier General MkFayden, Caine's second-in-command, who showed his commanding officer to a temporary podium at the centre of the parade ground.

"Welcome back to Lympstone, General," the former Terran Army officer smiled. Although he was older than before, he had more of a spring in his step than when Adam had rescued him and his regiment from the war-wracked world of Sojun's birth. In fact, all of his surviving troops had signed up along with MkFayden. Many of which were arrayed before him.

There were two thousand troops in perfect formation, stood to attention. They all faced him with expectant looks on their faces. This was their passing out parade after all.

He stepped up to the podium, cleared his throat and spoke. As he spoke, he looked over the sea of green berets and camouflage fatigues, and gave a tiny, almost unnoticeable smile filled with nostalgia and brief happiness. But it was gone.

"Ladies and gentlemen. I am your commanding officer, Major General Caine. Many years ago, the unit you have helped revive became a byword for professionalism, duty, integrity, honour, and courage. They fought to defend their homes, their people, their way of life." He paused for effect. "Today, you have all proven yourselves worthy to wear the Green Beret. From now on, you are the best of the best. I am proud of each and every one of you."

One of the Sergeants led a quick hurrah that resounded across the massive courtyard.

"From now on, you are all Commandos."

Caine smiled; another loud hurrah.

"Welcome to the Royal Marines."

THE LEGEND HAS ONLY JUST BEGUN...

Epilogue

January 4020ad.

A small blockade of ships sat at the mouth of a red inter-universe Linkway, all surrounding a large station that hung like a knife suspended in water several thousand kilometres away from the entrance. It was bigger than the ships around it, dwarfing them in fact, with the same royal blue hull plating, and a bulbous centre.

Fort Sentinel, as it was officially called, stood guard over the Linkway entrance –Sentinel Point- that led into the Y-40 Galaxy, a zone quarantined for twenty years by the Terran Navy. The ships on duty were cycled out every few months to be replaced by fresh ships and crews, usually ones just off rest and recreation time. As a result, it was an unfavourable assignment, and an extremely dull one at that.

Nothing happened at Sentinel Point, except for the odd smuggler trying to get into the quarantine zone to find a new monetary source.

The small taskforce guarding the Point was made up of a battleship, a heavy cruiser, two cruisers, three frigates, a destroyer and a quartet of gunships. There were also enough starfighter patrols to make up nine Rhino squadrons, though not all were in space at the same time.

The Linkway entrance flashed several times and something came through.

It was a ship, as red as human blood, and covered in uneven spikes that gave it the appearance of an insane pineapple, a similar size to the heavy cruiser. It came out of the Linkway, and thundered directly towards Fort Sentinel, weapons armed, shields raised.

Any attempt at contact by the Terran crews was met by static and white noise. When the ship came within weapons range of the station, it opened up with a wave of laser fire that jumped the distance in hundredths of a second, splashing against the station's shields ineffectively.

The battleship, the *Serenity*, swung in parallel with the mysterious ship, and opened fire itself. Its pounding heavy plasma cannons ripping through the enemy's shields in a spectacular show of fireworks. The ancient heavy cruiser, *Ripper*, came in on the other side, its forward guns opening up as well.

The enemy ship's hull buckled and warped under the plasma barrage. Chunks of it broke off, and flew into space in their dozens, leaving a trail as it continued on its course. Flames poured out of the holes and cracks, flashing out of existence as the vacuum sucked the oxygen out.

The ship came apart in pieces as the *Ripper* and *Serenity* pulled away from the wreckage, leaving the station's own defences to rip it into vapour. All that was left was the command section, and a cloud of electrically charged dust. With no injuries to the crews of the ships and station, investigative teams set about trying to determine who they were and why they had attacked.

The *Serenity* moved in close to the wreckage.

And then something massive came through the Linkway. It was covered in big red spikes as well, and barely made it through the entrance it was so huge. It was fat, bulbous, and looked nothing like a starship, but more like a floating city. Weapons lock alarms blared across the small Terran fleet as the thing locked onto them with battleship-sized weapons batteries.

A volley from one of the gargantuan weapons vaporised the *Ripper*, leaving nothing but particles.

Gormogon and *Lister*, the two cruisers, tried to turn to meet this new threat, but weren't fast enough, smashing against the invisible shields of the planet-sized ship. The smaller ships scattered, though all but two of those were vaporised as well, leaving the two survivors, *Reliable* –a frigate- and *Runner* –a gunship- to scramble away from the fight, and towards the supposed safety of the space station.

The station -a single tall piece of architecture that was anchored at edge of the gravitational fields between the system's star and the Linkway entrance- was dwarfed by the thing coming towards it.

The behemoth stripped the station of shields in the blink of an eye.

Escape pods ejected from the station's sides, powering away into space; each and every one were hit by pinpoint plasma fire from the giant's smaller weaponry. *Serenity* desperately manoeuvred in between the attacker and the station. Rather than destroy it, however, the titan caught it in a net of a dozen powerful tractor beams, and dragged it into its cavernous landing bays.

It was torn apart by mining and dissection lasers, killing the crew, and exposing the computer core to the attackers. The core was kept, and the weapons scavenged, the rest thrown back into space as useless.

Reliable and *Runner* made a run from the station to the other smaller Linkway opposite the titan. Rather than target the smaller ships, the titan fired a multitude of attitude thrusters, and slipped ponderously sideways. A *flood* of red starships poured through the Linkway entrance, and trailed after the remaining Terrans, whilst the titan tractored the station into its gaping jaws, and devoured it as well.

The smaller red ships caught up with the fleeing Terrans almost instantly, hounding them, exchanging energy fire, lighting the space up between them like Christmas trees. *Runner*'s engines flared out under the barrage, and the ship twisted in space, unable to control its movement any longer.

The nose of the ship swung round, and the vessel began to spin erratically until it slammed into the side of a battleship-sized vessel. Both ships were destroyed, a fireball that engulfed three other ships nearby.

The *Reliable* kept powering forwards, no longer firing, shunting extra power to its engines and shields. It worked for a short while until a lucky torpedo from a distant battleship struck the aft end and took out its shields, and annihilated a large part of its sublight engine block. Fire spewed into space, but the ship kept going, albeit slower.

The ship managed to get within a hundred thousand kilometres before suddenly veering away. Something small darted from underneath the *Reliable* in a straight line towards the blue Linkway.

It was a standard Navy shuttlecraft —a box with wings and engines. It shot into the Linkway, though not before being hit by a stray energy round that clipped its port wing, shearing it off. Trailing sparks and debris, the shuttle disappeared into the Linkway tunnels.

The *Reliable*'s crew were determined to give the shuttle extra time to escape, turning the ship so that it sat at the mouth of the tunnel. The curious enemy ships came in closer to inspect what it was doing when it suddenly detonated via the self-destruct. The graymanium-powered energy core created a cascade of destruction that began with tearing a hole in the space/time continuum. The reaction between the hole and the Linkway entrance was astronomically bad as space was ripped asunder.

Shockwaves shattered and vaporised dozens of the red ships, erasing them from existence.

Reliable's sacrifice sealed the tunnel shut, preventing the enemy ships from using it to leave the star system, thus ensuring the shuttle's escape.

* * *

In the cavernous throne room of the titan, a single lone figure sat in the shadows, watching the visual feeds on hundreds of monitors surrounding him. He was armoured, though his stance, and body language suggested he normally wore heavy armour plating.

Like the rest of his kind, his skin was black as night, and his facial features had a hideous bird-like appearance, with a large obsidian beak, and black inner lips. But instead of a crest on top of his head, he had long shaggy white hair that draped around his powerful shoulders.

He was the Patriarch, lord and commander of the Core.

His elbows were resting on the arms of the gold-gilded throne, taloned fingers steepled in front of him as he continued to watch the floating screens. The Linkway entrance leading into the so-called Dark Galaxy proper was gone —the humans had shown great resourcefulness and willingness to sacrifice themselves for their mission. It was something to consider, a weakness to exploit.

The screens showed several of his experimental ships leaping to faster-than-light speeds, attempting to get to another star system with a working Linkway entrance so as to cut the shuttle off.

The Patriarch knew they would not succeed, but had ordered the attempt anyway.

Not that it mattered —the Core would sweep across this precious universe, and conquer every thing and every being in it, and truly become the lords of all creation.

And finally, he thought, *I shall have my revenge on the Terrans and Adam Caine...*

About the Author

This is John Scott's first published work, and hopefully not the last. Despite a lack of experience in the writing industry (or lack of sanity), he is planning several more stories featuring Adam Caine. Currently, he lives in Chard, Somerset, dating a gorgeous girl called Julz, and verbally sparring with a madman named Rowland.

Lightning Source UK Ltd.
Milton Keynes UK
04 September 2010

159395UK00001B/89/P

9 781452 063874